ROBOT ETHICS 2.0

ROBOT ETHICS 2.0

From Autonomous Cars to Artificial Intelligence

Edited by Patrick Lin, Ryan Jenkins, and Keith Abney

OXFORD
UNIVERSITY PRESS

Oxford University Press is a department of the University of Oxford. It furthers the University's objective of excellence in research, scholarship, and education by publishing worldwide. Oxford is a registered trade mark of Oxford University Press in the UK and certain other countries.

Published in the United States of America by Oxford University Press
198 Madison Avenue, New York, NY 10016, United States of America.

First issued as an Oxford University Press paperback, 2020

CIP data is on file at the Library of Congress
ISBN 978–0–19–065295–1 (hardcover) | ISBN 978–0–19–750358–4 (paperback)

CONTENTS

PREFACE

As a game-changing technology, robotics naturally will create ripple effects through society. Some of them may become tsunamis. So it's no surprise that "robot ethics"—the study of these effects on ethics, law, and policy—has caught the attention of governments, industry, and the broader society, especially in the past several years.

We, the editors, assembled and edited the first comprehensive book on robot ethics in 2012 (Lin et al. 2012). Since then, a groundswell of organized concern has emerged, from the Campaign to Stop Killer Robots (2013) to the Campaign Against Sex Robots (2015). While we covered both these kinds of robots and others in our first book, new types and areas of robotics are now bringing new dimensions to the robot-ethics debates.

In recent years, for instance, self-driving vehicles have been making a lot of headlines. In 2016, a Tesla car operating in autopilot mode crashed into a truck it couldn't detect, killing the Tesla driver, who reportedly failed to monitor the automated system as he had agreed. There's continuing controversy here on whether the auto manufacturer has any share of the blame—related to how informed the driver's consent really was, misaligned expectations, and human–machine interaction design issues—and whether "beta-testing" self-driving machines on public roadways is ethical, even if not currently illegal (Lin 2016a).

Meanwhile, other companies aggressively plan to field autonomous vehicles, despite these continuing questions (Mitchell and Wilson 2016), and other accidents involving these vehicles are still being reported. As the first robots to be integrated with society at any significant scale, self-driving cars may set the tone for other social robotics, especially if things go wrong. Therefore, we will use robot cars as a crucial case study throughout this book. (We did not talk much about robot cars previously; they were not quite "real" even just five years ago, which is a testament to how quickly robotics is advancing.)

Other robots in recent news are raising uncomfortable questions, too. During a shooter standoff, the Dallas Police Department had converted a ground robot into a mobile bomb, blowing up the dangerous suspect. Militarization of the police aside, there are serious ethical and policy worries about this novel use of a robot as a weapon in law enforcement, even if the law is silent on such a use (Lin 2016b).

For instance, does the increased distance and safety afforded by robots mean that police need more justification before using lethal force? Given less risk to officers, would robots encourage more decisions to use force, instead of the more difficult work of a peaceful negotiation? When lethal force is justified, does it matter *how* a suspect is killed; for instance, is bombing a cruel or unusual method? This is a foreshadowing of other events and apprehensions that may arise with police, security, and military robots in the near future.

And there are many more challenging examples in ethics, law, and policy. Therefore, given the evolving discussion of the issues we raised before and the new discussions now developing, it is time for a major update of our work, as we enter the second generation—*robot ethics 2.0*—of the debates.

As with our first book, the goal is to create a one-stop authoritative resource for the latest research in the field, which is often scattered across academic journals, books, media articles, reports, websites, and other channels. Again, we will not presuppose much familiarity with either robotics or ethics; this helps to make the discussion more accessible to policymakers and the broader public, as well as academic audiences.

But a significant difference with this new volume is that we want to reflect the much increased diversity of researchers in robot ethics. Where just a few years ago there were only a handful of experts writing on the subject, the field has now attracted both new and senior scholars with important perspectives to contribute and from even more sociopolitical geographies.

Why Ethics?

Not everyone interested in robots has a high opinion of ethics or appreciates the social responsibility of a technology developer. They're often happy to let the invisible hand of the market and legal courts sort out any problems, even if the harm was preventable. While there's something to be said about reducing barriers to innovation and the efficiency of an unfettered market, ethics also matters for robotics.

A common reaction to the suggestion of an ethics discussion is that the many benefits of robots outweigh the social risks, and therefore we delay these benefits when we're distracted by ethics. In the case of a self-driving car, for instance, spending time on ethics means devoting less time to developing and fielding the technology, or at least creating doubt and public resistance to the product. This effectively allows tens of thousands of people to die each year on our roadways, whom robot cars could have saved—or so the argument goes (Knight 2015). As another example, if ethics-based arguments for a moratorium or ban on military "killer robots" were to succeed, our soldiers and innocent civilians in the crossfire would continue to die needlessly when robots could have done a better and safer job, in theory.

But this line of reasoning is far too quick. First, not all ethics can be done by math, with a simple calculation of net gains or net losses. Rights, duties, and other factors may be very difficult to quantify or fully account for. Attending to ethics also doesn't necessarily mean slowing down technology development; it could instead help clear a path by avoiding "first-generation" problems that may plague new technologies. Anyway, precaution may sometimes be justified, especially when the risks are serious, such as innocent deaths.

It's difficult to think of a real-world example where ethics may be ignored because the benefits are so compelling. For instance, we could rush cancer drugs to market, potentially saving tens of thousands of lives every year, just as robot cars might. Yet there is a consensus among both bioethicists and researchers that rushing development could waste money on quack remedies, and insufficiently tested therapies could kill patients. There's consensus that controlled clinical and human trials are necessary and that we should not ignore red flags in those trials or try to forgo trials altogether.

Merely following the law is also not enough. Clearly, there is often significant overlap between law and ethics, but they're not the same thing. What's legal could be unethical, such as ordinary lying, adultery, and, in our shameful past, slavery. And what's ethically permissible might be illegal, such as drugs, alcohol, and gambling, in certain jurisdictions, as well as driving across a double yellow line to avoid an accident.

So minimally complying with the law may still cause a technology developer or industry to lose in the vital court of public opinion. It doesn't even ensure a legal victory, as there's room for debate for a judge or jury in apportioning responsibility and determining whether due diligence was met. Particularly for emerging technologies, law and policy may simply not yet exist, and so we need to fall back on ethics—on first principles—for guidance.

This isn't meant to be a comprehensive argument for robot ethics or technology ethics more broadly, just a quick case for it as we introduce the subject. There may be other serious consequences of disregarding ethics, such as inviting the attention of regulators and others to set responsible standards if a technology developer or industry fails to take the initiative.

Further, such disregard can impart to a developer or industry a reputation for being unethical, for shirking professional duties. Artificial intelligence pioneer Herbert A. Simon explained, "With respect to social consequences, I believe that every researcher has some responsibility to assess, and try to inform others of, the possible social consequences of the research products he is trying to create" (1991, 274).

Preeminent scientist Lord Martin Rees similarly wrote, "Scientists surely have a special responsibility. It is their ideas that form the basis of new technology. They should not be indifferent to the fruits of their ideas" (Rees 2006). Now, this doesn't mean that scientists and engineers need to solve all the problems that may be associated with their innovations. But at the least, they should be supportive of those discussions, if not also willing to engage in them, just as you—the readers of this book—are doing.

Organization of This Book

This book comprises four parts, each carefully curated to include six chapters, all new material. To help guide our readers, each part is preceded by a short introduction to its issues and chapters.

In part I, we look at programming and legal issues in robotics as related to responsibility; this is perhaps the most urgent and natural starting point. We end this part with a philosophical reflection that will echo throughout what is mostly a practical discussion in the book.

In part II, we see that programming is not just about what's legal and ethical; responsible design in robotics also has to account for human psychology. This part therefore focuses on issues of trust, deception, and other human–robot interactions.

In part III, we focus on specific and controversial types of applications in robotics, from love to war. As with our invocation of robot cars as a case study in several of the earlier chapters, each use-case in robotics seems to hold general lessons for the broader field.

And in part IV, we discuss more distant, forward-looking applications and issues. We take a look at ethical issues in artificial intelligence (AI) specifically, as AI will be the "brains" that drive many kinds of robots. Our book ends with a new and rare prison interview with perhaps the world's most notorious anti-technologist, Ted Kaczynski, otherwise known as the Unabomber. Our intention here is not to endorse or otherwise justify his violence, but to understand what may fuel a possible backlash against robotics.

In focusing on ethical concerns in this book, we are of course telling only half the story. We largely do not discuss the many benefits that are promised by robotics, which we have discussed elsewhere (Lin 2012) and which are better recited by others. But ethics is an essential part of that story, especially insofar as it drives new laws, regulations, and policies—it's often overshadowed by the hype and promises but nonetheless influences how robotics in society unfolds.

Works Cited

Campaign Against Sex Robots. 2015. "About." https://campaignagainstsexrobots.org/about/.

Campaign to Stop Killer Robots. 2013. "About Us." http://www.stopkillerrobots.org/about-us/.

Knight, Will. 2015. "How to Help Self-Driving Cars Make Ethical Decisions." *MIT Technology Review*, July 29. https://www.technologyreview.com/s/539731/how-to-help-self-driving-cars-make-ethical-decisions/.

Lin, Patrick. 2012. "Introduction to Robot Ethics." In *Robot Ethics: The Ethical and Social Implications of Robotics*, edited by Patrick Lin, Keith Abney, and George Bekey, 3–16. Cambridge, MA: MIT Press.

Lin, Patrick. 2016a. "Is Tesla Responsible for the Deadly Crash on Auto-Pilot? Maybe." *Forbes*, July 1. http://www.forbes.com/sites/patricklin/2016/07/01/is-tesla-responsible-for-the-deadly-crash-on-auto-pilot-maybe/.

Lin, Patrick. 2016b. "Should the Police Have Robot Suicide-Bombers?" *IEEE Spectrum*, July 11. http://spectrum.ieee.org/automaton/robotics/military-robots/should-the-police-have-robot-suicidebombers.

Lin, Patrick, Keith Abney, and George Bekey, eds. 2012. *Robot Ethics: The Ethical and Social Implications of Robotics*. Cambridge, MA: MIT Press.

Mitchell, Russ and Scott Wilson. 2016. "Beyond Uber, Volvo and Ford: Other Automakers' Plans for Self-Driving Vehicles." *Los Angeles Times*, August 19. http://www.latimes.com/business/autos/la-fi-automakers-self-driving-20160819-snap-htmlstory.html.

Rees, Martin. 2006. "Dark Materials." *Guardian*, June 9. https://www.theguardian.com/commentisfree/2006/jun/10/science.comment.

Simon, Herbert A. 1991. *Models of My Life*. New York: Basic Books.

ACKNOWLEDGMENTS

We hope you enjoy this new volume and find it helpful in navigating the unfamiliar terrain of robot ethics. Not only are we are indebted to you—the readers—for your interest, but we must also acknowledge several others who offered help along the way.

At Oxford University Press, we thank our editor, Peter Ohlin, as well as Ada Brunstein and Andrew Ward, for their absolutely critical roles in and enthusiasm for this project. At California Polytechnic State University, we thank professor and esteemed roboticist George Bekey for kicking off our work in robot ethics in the first place. Our editorial assistants were invaluable: Brynn Chapman, Monica Chavez-Martinez, Jeremy Ebneyamin, Garrett Goff, Regina Hurley, Annalicia Luis, Lorenzo Nericcio, Tristan Noack, Leona Rajaee, and Cody Smith. Special thanks go to Jordan Rowley and Jessica Savelli for their extra help, over and beyond the call of duty. And, of course, we thank the authors who contributed to this volume.

Finally, this work would not be possible without the support of Cal Poly's College of Liberal Arts and Philosophy Department, Stanford University's Center for Automotive Research at Stanford (CARS), Daimler and Benz Foundation, and the U.S. National Science Foundation, under grant 1522240. Any opinions, findings, and conclusions or recommendations expressed in this material are those of the respective author(s), and they do not necessarily reflect the views of the aforementioned organizations or people.

Thank you!
Patrick Lin, PhD
Ryan Jenkins, PhD
Keith Abney, ABD

MORAL AND LEGAL RESPONSIBILITY

Introduction

As far as concerns go about robots, we typically worry first about the physical harm they could do. Certainly, privacy and information security are key worries, too, but they're not nearly as visceral and gripping as visions of machines gone wild. (And because the literature on privacy and cybersecurity in robotics is now so well developed, we won't engage those issues much in this book, focusing instead on more emerging areas in ethics.)

The stakes are much higher with robots than mere software when it comes to programming bugs and other unexpected events. Robots are software—and, sometimes, artificial intelligence—with sensors and moving parts in physical space, so their crashes can be literal. Already, self-driving cars have crashed and killed people. Robotic weapons have malfunctioned and killed, and some are designed specifically to kill. These are extreme examples, as not all robots are capable of causing fatalities; but moving, physical parts generally mean a possibility of injury, whether unintentional or not.

As we mentioned in the preface, we will use autonomous cars as a prime case study in this book, particularly in this lead-off part of the book. They represent the first robots to be integrated into our lives at scale, so they will set the tone for other robotics in society. They also offer challenges to human–robot interaction design, psychology, trust, law, sociopolitical systems (such as business, infrastructure, neighborhoods, and transportation services), and many other issues—making robot cars a dynamic platform for thinking about a full range of ethical issues. But our discussions about autonomous cars could be applied to other kinds of robotics as well; they're just a useful example and not meant to limit the conversation.

Technology developers should strive for error-free programming, though this may be practically impossible for the complex systems of most robotics. But since our less complex, everyday technologies fail on a daily basis in more controlled environments, that may be too hopeful for robotics. Robot ethics, then, doesn't so much lecture programmers to work as diligently as they can; that's already assumed.

What's more challenging is this: even if there are no programming errors, there's still a large question of *how* robots should be programmed. Is it enough to make a robot legally compliant? How should it make judgment calls, such as under conditions of uncertainty or in "no-win" scenarios? (To be sure, no-win cases, in which a robot needs to choose the lesser evil, may be rare, but their rarity is also what can make them high-profile news headlines and lawsuits.) Given emergent or unpredictable behavior from machine learning, who's responsible in the event of an accident?

Accidents, by the way, will continue to happen as a matter of physics. Take the autonomous car again: even if it has the best and most perfect sensors, software, and hardware the future has to offer, there'll still be a risk of a crash. Anytime a car passes or is passed by another vehicle, for instance, there's a brief window of time where there is no way for the robot car to avoid an accident or having to violently swerve if the other vehicle suddenly turns toward it. Anyway, sensors, software, and hardware won't be perfect. Sensors could be damaged during operation, and they currently can't see through solid objects; a robot car could still be surprised by, say, an unseen child who suddenly emerges from behind a parked truck.

We begin this part with a chapter by Vikram Bhargava and Tae Wan Kim that addresses a central question in robot ethics: Which ethical approach or theory should a robot be programmed to follow when there's no legal guidance? Different approaches can generate different results, including crash fatalities; so this is a profoundly serious question. Rather than advocate a particular theory, which some of our other authors do, they give us a methodology for choosing between ethical theories.

Next, in chapter 2, Jason Millar presses further on the idea that robots may be required to make decisions; they may have some choice in the matter. But for the most important choices, he suggests that it may be more appropriate for the user, and not the technology developer, to guide these decisions—to establish from the outset what ethical or behavioral principles the robot ought to follow. This begins to locate some responsibility with the user.

Staying with the notion that the user should have a role in how a robot acts, Wulf Loh and Janina Loh offer in chapter 3 a thorough, analytical definition of what it means to be responsible. They argue that, in the case of self-driving cars, responsibility is shared or distributed among the engineers, the driver, and the autonomous driving system itself. But when it comes to ethical dilemmas, such as the infamous "trolley problem," the driver or user is the one who should ultimately bear responsibility for those outcomes.

Philosophical discussion aside, when it comes to responsibility, the law is often the most important arbiter. Just feeling guilty is one thing, but being convicted by a judge or jury implies something entirely different. In chapter 4, Jeffrey K. Gurney brings the conversation back to these practical matters of the law in talking about liability and the law. He argues that technology developers should be treated as the driver of a robotic car—not the user or person behind the steering wheel, if there even *is* a steering wheel—and therefore as legally liable for harm caused by the car, contra the arguments made in earlier chapters.

In chapter 5, Trevor N. White and Seth D. Baum continue the discussion on liability law but also look much farther ahead. In the near term, they argue, existing liability law is sufficient to handle cases in robotics. But if robots become more complex, more intelligent, and arguably more like "persons"—and if robots become capable of causing major catastrophes—then existing legal frameworks aren't enough.

Finally, in chapter 6, we return to the philosophical with an essay by David Zoller. Technology dependency doesn't just have practical risks; it may also impact our relationship with reality. Zoller explains that the automatization of skills, such as driving, means we're less able to see certain facets of our world, and these are valuable aspects of human life. What's our moral responsibility to remain "authentic" to ourselves? This is a question that carries over to all the chapters of this book and beyond, as robots are created exactly to automate or replace human skills.

1 AUTONOMOUS VEHICLES AND MORAL UNCERTAINTY

Vikram Bhargava and Tae Wan Kim

Autonomous vehicles have escaped the confines of our imaginations and found their way onto our roadways. Major companies, including GM, Nissan, Mercedes-Benz, Toyota, Lexus, Hyundai, Tesla, Uber, and Volkswagen, are developing autonomous vehicles. Tech giant Google has reported that the development of autonomous vehicles is among its five most important business projects (Urmson 2014). Autonomous cars are here, not going away, and are likely to become increasingly prevalent (Fagnant and Kockelman 2013; Goodall 2014a, b).

As the number of autonomous vehicles on roadways increases, several distinctively philosophical questions arise (Lin 2015):

> *Crash*: Suppose a large autonomous vehicle is going to crash (perhaps due to hitting a patch of ice) and that it is on its way to hitting a minivan with five passengers, head on. If it hits the minivan head on, it will kill all five passengers. However, the autonomous vehicle recognizes that since it is approaching an intersection, on the way to colliding with the minivan it can swerve in such a way that it first collides into a small roadster, thus lessening the impact on the minivan. This would spare the minivan's five passengers, but it would unfortunately kill the one person in the roadster. Should the autonomous vehicle be programmed to first crash into the roadster?

This scenario of course closely resembles the famous trolley problem (Foot 1967; Thomson 1976).[1] It also raises a question at the intersection of moral philosophy, law, and public policy that is unique to autonomous vehicles. The question is, who should be able to choose the ethics for the autonomous vehicle—drivers, consumers, passengers, manufacturers, programmers, or politicians (Lin 2015; Millar 2014)?[2] There is another question that arises even once we settle who ought to be able to choose the ethics for the autonomous vehicles:

> *The Problem of Moral Uncertainty*: How should autonomous vehicles be programmed to act when the person who has the authority to choose the ethics of the autonomous vehicle is under moral uncertainty?

Roughly, an agent is morally uncertain when she has access to all (or most) of the relevant non-moral facts, including but not limited to empirical and legal facts, but still remains uncertain about what morality requires of her. This chapter is about how the person who is ultimately chosen to make the decisions in the *Crash* scenario can make appropriate decisions when in the grip of moral uncertainty. For simplicity's sake, in this chapter we assume this person is a programmer.

Decisions are often made in the face of uncertainty. Indeed, there is a vast literature on rational decision-making under uncertainty (De Groot 2004; Raiffa 1997). However, this literature focuses largely on empirical uncertainty. Moral uncertainty, on the other hand, has received vastly less scholarly attention. With advances in autonomous vehicles, addressing the problem of moral uncertainty has new urgency. Our chief purpose in this chapter is a modest one: to explore the problem of moral uncertainty as it pertains to autonomous vehicles and to outline possible solutions to the problem. In section 1.1, we argue that the problem is a significant one and make some preliminary remarks. In section 1.2, we critically engage with two proposals that offer a solution to the problem of moral uncertainty. In section 1.3, we discuss a solution that we think is more promising, the solution provided by the philosopher Andrew Sepielli. In section 1.4, we offer some support in its defense. We conclude in section 1.5.

1.1 Motivation and Preliminaries

Let's return to the *Crash* scenario. Suppose Tegan, a programmer tasked with deciding the appropriate course of action in the *Crash* scenario, thinks she should program the autonomous vehicle to collide into the roadster on the way to the minivan, under the consequentialist rationale that the roadster has fewer passengers than the minivan. She hesitates because she recalls her ethics professor's deontological claim that doing so would be seriously wrong[3]—it would use the one passenger in the roadster as a mere-means in a way that is morally impermissible. Tegan is not persuaded by her professor's prior guidance and gives 90% credence (subjective probability) to the view that she should program the vehicle to first crash into the roadster; she gives only 10% credence to her professor's conclusion that she should not crash into the roadster on the way to the minivan.[4]

From Tegan's own perspective, how should she program an autonomous vehicle to deal with *Crash*-like scenarios? Tegan faces the problem of moral uncertainty.

Caveat: Any real driving situation an autonomous vehicle will face is likely to be much more complicated than the foregoing scenario. Nevertheless, the scenario contains enough relevant factors for our purposes. For Tegan, moral arguments are the source of normative uncertainty, but it is worth noting that other types of normative views (e.g., legal, cultural, religious) can play similar roles, creating prescriptive uncertainty. Also, Tegan faces just two competing arguments, while many decision makers can face more than two. For simplicity's sake, however, we discuss scenarios in which two arguments are competing, although some of the frameworks we discuss can, in principle, accommodate scenarios with more than two competing arguments.

The problem of moral uncertainty derives primarily from the following conditions: (1) the two normative propositions corresponding to Tegan's decision— "I should program the vehicle to crash into the roadster" and "I should not program the vehicle to crash into the roadster"—are mutually exclusive, and (2) Tegan's credence is divided between the two propositions—she is uncertain about which of the two propositions is true (Sepielli 2009).[5] Put another way: even if Tegan is certain about a range of empirical facts, she may still remain uncertain about the reasons that those very facts give her with respect to what to do (Sepielli 2009).

We acknowledge that a solution to *Crash* is not complete unless we offer a plausible framework of decision-making under empirical uncertainty (e.g., Hare 2012). We assume for now that the solution we discuss can coherently be combined with the best account of decision-making under empirical uncertainty— ascertaining whether this assumption is in fact true is a promising future avenue of research.[6]

Tegan requires a meta-normative framework to adjudicate between the normative prescriptions of competing moral theories. In this chapter, we argue for the importance of such a framework and encourage scholars of robot ethics to pay more attention to the problem of moral uncertainty. But first, it is worth dealing with a thought that might be lurking in some readers' minds, namely, that the very notion of moral uncertainty is a misguided one. Specifically, some readers might be thinking that of the two competing moral arguments, only one of them is right. Therefore, there is no uncertainty *ab initio* and the problem is only apparent. For instance, if it is in fact morally true that one should never use another as a mere-means, then Tegan should not program the car to first crash into the roadster.

We agree that there may be no moral uncertainty from the perspective of objective reason or objective "should" (Harman 2015). Moreover, we do not deny the importance of figuring out the objectively correct answer, assuming one exists—that is, that ethics is not relative. But it is important to note that the aforementioned concern is consistent with the view we defend. Though programmers should strive to ascertain the objectively correct answer, this does not eliminate the fact that a decision might have to be made prior to one's having secured the objectively correct answer. Tegan, in the above scenario, cannot make her decision purely on the basis of objective reasons, since her doxastic state is already plagued with moral uncertainty. Yet she needs to decide how to program the car. The given reality is that Tegan cannot help but base her decision on her degree of belief in a moral view—that is, from her representation of the objective "should" (Sepielli 2009). Thus Tegan ought to make the best decision given *her* degree of belief in the relevant normative prescription. So Tegan requires an additional decision framework, one that is not designed primarily for objective reason or objective "should"—that is, a framework that begins with her own uncertain normative beliefs but still helps her make more appropriate and rational decisions.

1.2 Two Possibilities

We now consider (and ultimately reject) two proposals for making decisions under moral uncertainty. The first proposal—the "Continue Deliberating" view—suggests that Tegan should not make a decision; instead, she should continue deliberating until she figures out what morality requires of her. We are sympathetic to this position. Indeed, we too think that programmers should continue to deliberate about moral problems insofar as they are able. Nevertheless, we believe that there are circumstances in which programmers may lack the luxury of time or resources to continue deliberating but must nevertheless decide how to act. Tegan might deliberate for some time, but she cannot put all of her time and effort into figuring out what to do in *Crash* and will need to make a decision soon enough.

Perhaps more important, continuing to deliberate is in some contexts, in effect, making a decision about one of the very choices the programmer is uncertain about. For example, if Tegan opts not to program the autonomous vehicle to first swerve into the roadster, she in effect already commits to the prescription of one of the moral views. That is, if she decides not to program the autonomous car to first swerve into the roadster, she rejects the prescription of the consequentialist view and allows more lives to be killed. Inaction is often a choice, and it is typically a choice of status quo. The "Continue Deliberating" view lacks the resources to explain why the existing state of affairs is the most appropriate choice.

The second proposal—call it the "My Favorite Theory" view—is an initially tempting response to moral uncertainty (Gustafsson and Torpman 2014). That is, do what the conclusion of the normative argument you think is most likely to be correct tells you to do. For instance, if Tegan thinks the consequentialist prescription to crash into the roadster is most likely true, then she should program the car to do just that. But this view has some problems, an analysis of which will yield an important condition any adequate solution to the problem of moral uncertainty must meet. We can better understand this problem by considering a parallel problem in empirical uncertainty (Sepielli 2009). Consider a hypothetical variant of the real case of the Ford Pinto:

> *Pinto*: The CEO of Ford is deciding whether to authorize the sale of its recently designed hatchback car, the Pinto. She is not sure how to act, because she is empirically uncertain about how the Pinto's fuel tank will affect the life of its drivers and passengers. After reading a crash-test report, she has a 0.2 degree of belief that the Pinto's fuel tank will rupture, causing a potentially fatal fire if the car is rear-ended, and a 0.8 degree of belief that there will not be any such problems. Thinking she should go with what she thinks is most likely—that there will not be any problems with the fuel tank—she authorizes the sale of the Pinto.

Here the CEO clearly makes a poor choice. One cannot simply compare 0.2 and 0.8. One must consider the value of the outcomes. Of course, car designs cannot be perfect, but a 20% probability of a life-threatening malfunction is obviously too high. The CEO failed to weigh the consequences of the actions by their respective probabilities. If she had taken into consideration the value of the outcomes, it would not have made sense to authorize the sale of the Pinto. A similar problem applies in the moral domain—the weight of the moral value at stake must be taken into consideration.

For instance, returning to the situation Tegan faces, even if she thinks that the proposition "I should program the vehicle to crash into the roadster" is most likely true, it would be a very serious wrong if the competing proposition, "I should not program the vehicle to crash into the roadster," is correct, since treating someone as a mere-means would be a serious deontological wrong. In other words, though Tegan thinks that her professor's view is mistaken, she recognizes that *if* her professor's arguments are correct and she nevertheless programs the car to first crash into the roadster, then she would commit a serious deontological wrong.

As such, an adequate solution to the problem of moral uncertainty must take into account the moral values associated with the particular normative proposition, weighted by their respective probabilities, not merely the probability that the normative proposition in question is true. Another way to put the point is that a programmer, in the face of moral uncertainty, must hedge against the view with the greater moral value at stake or meet what we shall call the "expected *moral* value condition," which we apply to programmers in the following way:

> *The Expected Moral Value Condition*: Any adequate solution to the problem of programming under moral uncertainty must offer the resources by which a programmer can weigh the degree of moral harm, benefit, wrong, right, good, bad, etc., by their relevant probabilities.[7]

On an account of moral uncertainty that meets this condition, there may very well be instances when a programmer should act according to what she considers the less probable normative view because the less probable normative view has something of significant moral value at stake. But we've gotten ahead of ourselves. Making this sort of ascription requires being able to compare moral value across different moral views or theories. And it is not obvious how this can be meaningfully done. In the next section, we will elucidate what we think is a promising approach for making comparisons of moral value across different moral views.

1.3 An Expected Moral Value Approach

Suppose Tegan is convinced of the importance of weighing the moral value at stake and decides she wants to use an expected moral value approach to do so.[8] In other words, Tegan must figure out the expected moral value of the two mutually exclusive actions and choose the option that has the higher expected moral value. But she soon realizes that she faces a serious problem.

Tegan might have some sense of how significant a consequentialist good it is to save the five lives in the minivan, and she also might have some sense of how significant a deontological bad it is to use another as a mere-means (namely, the person in the roadster); but still, troublingly, she may not know how the two compare. It is not clear that the magnitude of the moral value on the consequentialist view is commensurable with the magnitude of the moral value on the deontological view. This has been called the "Problem of Inter-theoretic Value Comparisons" (PIVC) (Lockhart 2000; Sepielli 2006, 2009, 2013; MacAskill, 2016).

The PIVC posits that moral hedging requires comparing moral values across different normative views. And it is not obvious that this can be done. For example, it is not clear how Tegan can compare the consequentialist value of maximizing net lives saved with the deontic wrong of using someone as a mere-means. Neither consequentialist views nor deontological views themselves indicate how to make inter-theoretic comparisons. Any adequate expected value proposal must explain how it will handle this problem.[9]

Although the PIVC is thorny, we maintain it can be overcome. We find Sepielli's works (2006, 2009, 2010, 2012, 2013) helpful for this purpose. Significantly, Sepielli points out that just because two things cannot be compared under one set of descriptions does not mean they cannot be compared under an analogous set of re-descriptions. Sepielli's nuanced body of work is more complex than the following three steps that we articulate. Still, these three steps form the essence of what he calls the "background ranking approach" and are also helpful for our investigation.[10] Using the background ranking approach to solve the problem of inter-theoretic value comparisons is simple at its core, but its execution may require practice, much as with employing other rational decision-making tools.

Step 1: The first step involves thinking of two morally analogous actions to programming the vehicle to crash into the roadster. The first analogy should be such that, if the moral analogy were true, it would mean that crashing into the roadster is better than not crashing into the roadster. The second analogy should be such that, if the moral analogy were true, it would mean that not crashing into the roadster is better than crashing into the roadster. Suppose the first analogy to crashing into the roadster is donating to an effective charity that would maximize lives saved, instead of donating to a much less effective charity that would save many fewer lives. (In this case, the analogy is in line with the consequentialist prescription. It is a decision strictly about maximizing net lives saved.) Call this the "charity analogy." Suppose the second analogy to crashing into the roadster is a doctor killing a healthy patient so she could extract the patient's organs and distribute them to five other patients in vital need of organs. (In this case, the analogy is in line with the deontological prescription of not using a person as a mere-means.) Call this the "organ extraction analogy." Note that performing this step may require some moral imagination (Werhane 1999), skill in analogical reasoning, and perhaps even some familiarity with what the moral literature says on an issue.

Step 2: Identify one's credence in the two following mutually exclusive propositions: "I should program the vehicle to crash into the roadster" and "I should not program the vehicle to crash into the roadster." As stated earlier, Tegan has a 0.9 credence in the first proposition and a 0.1 credence in the second proposition.

Step 3: The third step involves identifying the *relative* differences in the magnitude of the moral value between the two propositions from *Step 2* on the assumption that each of the analogies from *Step 1* in question holds. Let's call the difference in the moral value of programming the vehicle to crash into the roadster versus not doing so, given the charity analogy is true, "W." Suppose then that the difference in moral value of programming the vehicle to crash into the roadster versus not doing so, given the organ extraction analogy is true, is "50W" (i.e., the difference in moral value is fifty times that of the difference in moral value associated with the charity analogy).

Keep in mind that Tegan can do this because her views about the relative differences in the magnitude of the moral value between the two propositions, conditional on each analogy holding true, can be *independent* of her beliefs about the two mutually exclusive prescriptions of "I should program the vehicle to crash into the roadster" and "I should not program the vehicle to crash into the roadster." As Sepielli notes, "Uncertainty about the ranking of a set of actions under one set of descriptions in no way precludes certainty about the ranking of the same set of actions under a different set of descriptions. . . . That every action falls under infinite descriptions gives us a fair bit of room to work here" (2009, 23). The fact that one can make this sort of comparison through analogical reasoning is an important feature of the background ranking procedure.

One might reasonably wonder where "fifty" (in 50W) came from. We have admittedly imputed this belief to Tegan in an ad hoc manner. However, as we noted, given that the source of uncertainty for Tegan is regarding the decision to program the car to first crash into the roadster or not, we think it is indeed plausible that Tegan may have a good sense of how the other analogies we have introduced fare against each other.

These three steps capture the essence of the background ranking procedure. Now we are in a position to perform an expected moral value calculation:

(1) Tegan's credence in the proposition, "I should program the autonomous vehicle to crash into the roadster" [*insert value*] × the difference in the magnitude of the moral value between crashing into the roadster and not crashing into the roadster, on the condition that the charity analogy holds [*insert value*]
(2) Tegan's credence in the proposition, "I should not program the autonomous vehicle to crash into the roadster" [*insert value*] × the difference in the magnitude of the moral value between crashing into the roadster and not crashing into the roadster, on the condition that the organ extraction analogy holds [*insert value*]

which is

(1) $(0.9)(W) = 0.9W$
(2) $(0.1)(50W) = 5W$

Finally, to determine what Tegan should do, we simply take the difference between the expected value of programming the vehicle to crash into the roadster (.9W) and not programming the vehicle to do so (5W). When the value is positive, she should program the vehicle to crash into the roadster, and when it is negative, she should not. (If the difference is zero, she could justifiably choose either.) Given that .9W−5W is a negative value (−4.1W), from Tegan's perspective, the appropriate choice is "I should not program the autonomous vehicle to crash into the roadster."

We recognize that the proposal we have just articulated has problems (some readers might think serious problems). For instance, some readers may find it objectionable that the procedure does not always prevent one from achieving the intuitively wrong outcomes. This unseemly feature is inherent to any rational decision procedure that incorporates one's subjective inputs. However, it is important to note that we do not claim that the expected moral value approach guarantees the moral truth from the view of objective reason. We aim only to show that the expected value approach offers rational decision-making guidance when the decision maker must make a decision in her current doxastic state.

Perhaps most worrisome is that the procedure on offer might strike some as question-begging. That is, some readers might think that it presupposes the truth of consequentialism. But this is not quite right for two reasons. First, an assumption underlying this worry is that a view that tells in favor of "numbers mattering," as it were, must be a consequentialist view. This assumption is untenable. In the trolley problem, for instance, a Kantian can coherently choose to save more lives because she believes doing so is the best she can do with respect to her deontological obligations (Hsieh, Strudler, and Wasserman 2006). Likewise, the fact that the procedure we defend employs an expected value approach need not mean it is consequentialist. It can be defended on deontological grounds as well.

More fundamentally, the procedure we defend is a meta-normative account that is indifferent to the truth-value of any particular first-order moral theory. This brings us to the second reason the question-begging worry is not problematic.

The approach we defend concerns what the programmer *all things considered* ought to do—what the programmer has strongest reason to do. This sort of all-things-considered judgment of practical rationality incorporates various types of reasons, not exclusively moral ones.

A range of reasons impact what one has strongest reason to do: self-interested, agent-relative, impartial moral, hedonistic, and so on. The fact that moral reasons favor Φ-ing does not settle the question of whether Φ-ing is what one ought to do all things considered. As Derek Parfit notes:

> When we ask whether certain facts give us morally decisive reasons not to act in some way, we are asking whether these facts are enough to make this act wrong. We can then ask the further question whether these morally decisive reasons are decisive all things considered, by outweighing any conflicting non-moral reasons. (2017)

What practical rationality requires one to do will turn on a range of normative reasons including moral ones, but not only moral ones. It would indeed be worrisome, and potentially question-begging, if we were claiming that the procedure provides the programmer with morally decisive guidance. But this is not what we are doing. We are concerned with helping the programmer determine what the balance of reasons favors doing—what the programmer has strongest reason to do—and this kind of judgment of practical rationality turns on a range of different kinds of reasons (Sepielli 2009).

In sum, what practical rationality requires of the programmer is distinct from what the programmer ought to believe is wrong, and even what the programmer has most moral reason to do. The procedure on offer helps the programmer reason *about* her moral beliefs, and this in itself is not a moral judgment (though what the programmer ought to do all things considered could, of course, coincide with what she has most moral reason to do). The procedure we are defending can help the programmer figure out what the balance of reasons favors doing, what she has *strongest* reason to do all things considered.[11]

1.4 A Brief Moral Defense and Remaining Moral Objections

While the procedure itself concerns practical rationality, we nevertheless think that there may be good *independent* moral reasons that favor the programmer's using such a procedure in the face of moral uncertainty. First, an expected value approach can help a programmer to avoid acting in a morally callous or indifferent manner (or at least to minimize the impact of moral indifference). If the programmer uses the expected value procedure but arrives at the immoral choice, she is less blameworthy than had she arrived at the immoral choice without using the procedure. This is because using the procedure displays a concern for the importance of morality.

If Tegan, in the grip of moral uncertainty, were to fail to use the expected value procedure, she would display a callous disregard for increasing the risk of wronging other human beings.[12] As David Enoch says, "[I]f I have a way to minimize the risk of my wronging people, and if there are no other relevant costs . . . why on earth wouldn't I minimize this risk?" (2014, 241). A programmer who in the face of moral uncertainty chooses to make a decision on a whim acts recklessly. Using the expected moral value approach lowers the risk of wronging others.

A second moral reason for using an expected value approach to deciding under moral uncertainty is that it can help the programmer embody the virtue of humility (e.g., Snow 1995). Indeed, as most professional ethicists admit, moral matters are deeply complex. A programmer who in the grip of moral uncertainty insists on using the "My Favorite Theory" approach fails to respect the difficulty of moral decision making and thereby exhibits a sort of intellectual chauvinism. Karen Jones's remark seems apt: "If it is so very bad to make a moral mistake, then it would take astonishing arrogance to suppose that this supports a do-it-yourself approach" (1999, 66–67). The fact that a programmer must take into account the possibility that she is mistaken about her moral beliefs builds a kind of humility into the very decision procedure.

Some may worry that a programmer who uses the expected moral value approach is compromising her integrity (Sepielli, forthcoming). The thought is that the programmer who follows the approach will often have to act in accordance with a normative view that she thinks is less likely correct. And acting in accordance with a theory one thinks less likely to be correct compromises one's integrity. Though this line of thought is surely tempting, it misses its mark. The value of integrity is something that must be considered along with other moral values. And how to handle the importance of the value of integrity is again a question that may fall victim to moral uncertainty. So the issue of integrity is not so much an objection as it is another consideration that must be included in the set of issues a programmer is morally uncertain about.

Another objection to a programmer using an expected value procedure holds that the programmer would forgo something of great moral importance—that is, moral understanding. For instance, Alison Hills (2009) claims that it is not enough to merely make the right moral judgments; one must secure moral understanding.[13] She argues that even reciting memorized reasons for the right actions will not suffice. Instead, she claims, one must develop understanding—that is, roughly, the ability to synthesize the moral concepts and apply the concepts in other similar contexts. And clearly, a programmer who is inputting her credences and related normative beliefs into an expected moral value procedure lacks the sort of moral understanding that Hills requires.

But this sort of objection misses the point. First, it is important to keep in mind that while the outcome of the procedure might not have been what a programmer originally intended, it is the programmer herself who is deciding to use the procedure that forces her to consider the moral implications of the possibility of deciding incorrectly. Second, it would indeed be the ideal situation to develop moral understanding, fully exercise one's autonomy, and perform the action that the true moral view requires. However, we agree with Enoch, who aptly notes:

> Tolerating a greater risk of wronging others merely for the value of moral autonomy and understanding is thus self-defeating, indeed perhaps even practically inconsistent. Someone willing to tolerate a greater risk of acting impermissibly merely in order to work on her (or anyone else's) moral understanding, that is, independently of the supposed instrumental payoffs of having more morally understanding people around, is acting

> wrongly, and indeed exhibits severe shortage in moral understanding (of the value of moral understanding, among other things). (2014, 249)

One can imagine how absurd an explanation from a programmer who decided on her own and acted in a way that wronged someone would sound if she were asked by the person who was wronged why she did not attempt to lower the risk of wronging another and she responded, "Well, I wanted to exercise my personal autonomy and work on my moral understanding."[14] Such a response would be patently offensive to the person who was wronged given that the programmer did have a way to lower her risk of wronging another.

1.5 Conclusion

In this chapter we aimed to show that programmers (or whoever will ultimately be choosing the ethics of autonomous vehicles) are likely to face instances where they are in the grip of moral uncertainty and require a method to help them decide how to appropriately act. We discussed three proposals for coping with this uncertainty: Continue Deliberating, My Favorite Theory, and a particular expected moral value approach. We offered some moral reasons for why the programmer has reasons to employ the third procedure in situations with moral uncertainty.

While there are surely many remaining issues to be discussed with respect to the question of how to deal with moral uncertainty in programming contexts, this chapter aims to provide a first step to offering programmers direction on how to appropriately handle decision-making under moral uncertainty. We hope it encourages robot ethics scholars to pay more attention to guiding programmers who are under moral uncertainty.

Notes

1. Patrick Lin (2014, 2015) is one of the first scholars to explore the relevance of the trolley problem in the context of autonomous vehicles.
2. There are important moral questions that we do not consider in this chapter. For instance, should the age of passengers in a vehicle be taken into account in deciding how the vehicle should be programmed to crash? Who should be responsible for an accident caused by autonomous vehicles? Is it possible to confer legal personhood on the autonomous vehicle? What liability rules should we as society adopt to regulate autonomous vehicles? (Douma and Palodichuk 2012; Gurney 2013). For ethical issues involving robots in general, see Nourbakhsh (2013), Lin, Abney, and Bekey (2012), and Wallach and Allen (2009).
3. Robotics Institute of Carnegie Mellon University, for instance, offers a course named "Ethics and Robotics."

4. Here we mirror the formulation of an example in MacAskill (2016).
5. As will become clear, we owe a significant intellectual debt to Andrew Sepielli for his work on the topic of moral uncertainty.
6. One might think that technological advances can soon minimize empirical uncertainties. But this is a naive assumption. Existing robots are far from being able to fully eliminate or account for possible empirical uncertainties. We are grateful to Illah Nourbakhsh, professor of robotics at Carnegie Mellon University, for bringing this point to our attention.
7. The solution we support resembles the celebrated *Pascal's Wager* argument that Blaise Pascal offers for why one should believe in God. Pascal states, "Either God is or he is not. But to which view shall we be inclined? . . . Let us weigh up the gain and the loss involved in calling heads that God exists. Let us assess two cases: if you win you win everything, if you lose you lose nothing. Do not hesitate then; wager that he does exist" (1670, § 233). We recognize that many find Pascal's wager problematic (Duff 1986), although there are writers who find it logically valid (Hájek 2012; Mackie 1982; Rescher 1985). At any rate, we are not concerned here to intervene in a debate about belief in divine existence. Nevertheless, we do think insights from Pascal's Wager can usefully be deployed, with relevant modifications, for the problem of programming under moral uncertainty.
8. Sepielli considers a scenario much like the one Tegan is in. He notes, "Some consequentialist theory may say that it's better to kill 1 person to save 5 people than it is to spare that person and allow the 5 people to die. A deontological theory may say the opposite. But it is not as though the consequentialist theory has, somehow encoded within it, information about how its own difference in value between these two actions compares to the difference in value between them according to deontology" (2009, 12).
9. Philosopher Ted Lockhart offers a proposal that aims to hedge and also claims to avoid the PIVC. Lockhart's view requires one to maximize "expected moral rightness" (Lockhart 2000, 27; Sepielli 2006) and thus does indeed account not only for the probability that a particular moral theory is right, but also for the moral weight (value, or degree) of the theory. One important problem with Lockhart's view is that it regards moral theories as having equal rightness in every case (Sepielli 2006, 602). For a more detailed criticism of Lockhart's position, see Sepielli (2006, 2013).
10. The example we use to explain the three steps also closely models an example from Sepielli (2009). It is worth noting that Sepielli does not break down his analysis into steps as we have. We have offered these steps with the hope that they accurately capture Sepielli's important insights while also allowing for practical application.
11. We are grateful to Suneal Bedi for helpful discussion regarding the issues in this section.
12. David Enoch (2014) offers this reason for why one ought to defer to a moral expert with regard to moral decisions.

13. Hills states, "Moral understanding is important not just because it is a means to acting rightly or reliably, though it is. Nor is it important only because it is relevant to the evaluations of an agent's character. It is essential to acting well" (2009, 119).
14. This sort of objection to Hills (2009) is due to Enoch (2014). Enoch objects in the context of a person failing to defer to a moral expert for moral guidance.

Works Cited

De Groot, Morris H. 2004. *Optimal Statistical Decisions*. New York: Wiley-Interscience.

Douma, Frank and Sarah A. Palodichuk. 2012. "Criminal Liability Issues Created by Autonomous Vehicles." *Santa Clara Law Review* 52: 1157–69.

Duff, Anthony. 1986. "Pascal's Wager and Infinite Utilities." *Analysis* 46: 107–9.

Enoch, David. 2014. "A Defense of Moral Deference." *Journal of Philosophy* 111: 229–58.

Fagnant, Daniel and Kara M. Kockelman. 2013. *Preparing a Nation for Autonomous Vehicles: Opportunities, Barriers and Policy Recommendations*. Washington, DC: Eno Center for Transportation.

Foot, Philippa. 1967. "The Problem of Abortion and the Doctrine of Double Effect." *Oxford Review* 5: 5–15.

Goodall, Noah J. 2014a. "Ethical Decision Making During Automated Vehicle Crashes." *Transportation Research Record: Journal of the Transportation Research Board*, 58–65.

Goodall, Noah J. 2014b. "Vehicle Automation and the Duty to Act." *Proceedings of the 21st World Congress on Intelligent Transport Systems*. Detroit.

Gurney, Jeffrey K. 2013. "Sue My Car Not Me: Products Liability and Accidents Involving Autonomous Vehicles." *Journal of Law, Technology & Policy* 2: 247–77.

Gustafsson, John. E. and Olle Torpman. 2014. "In Defence of My Favourite Theory." *Pacific Philosophical Quarterly* 95: 159–74.

Hájek, Alan. 2012. "Pascal's Wager." *Stanford Encyclopedia of Philosophy*. http://plato.stanford.edu/entries/pascal-wager/.

Hare, Caspar. 2012. "Obligations to Merely Statistical People." *Journal of Philosophy* 109: 378–90.

Harman, Elizabeth. 2015. "The Irrelevance of Moral Uncertainty." In *Oxford Studies in Metaethics*, vol. 10, edited by Luss-Shafer Laundau, 53–79. New York: Oxford University Press.

Hills, Alison. 2009. "Moral Testimony and Moral Epistemology." *Ethics* 120: 94–127.

Hsieh, Nien-ĥe, Alan Strudler, and David Wasserman. 2006. "The Numbers Problem." *Philosophy & Public Affairs* 34: 352–72.

Jones, Karen. 1999. "Second-Hand Moral Knowledge." *Journal of Philosophy* 96: 55–78.

Lin, Patrick. 2014. "The Robot Car of Tomorrow May Just Be Programmed to Hit You." *Wired*, May 6. http://www.wired.com/2014/05/the-robot-car-of-tomorrow-might-just-be-programmed-to-hit-you/

Lin, Patrick. 2015. "Why Ethics Matters for Autonomous Cars." In *Autonomes Fahren*, edited by M. Maurer, C. Gerdes, B. Lenz, and H. Winner, 70–85. Berlin: Springer.

Lin, Patrick, Keith Abney, and George A. Bekey, eds. 2012. *Robot Ethics: The Ethical and Social Implications of Robotics*. Cambridge, MA: MIT Press.

Lockhart, Ted. 2000. *Moral Uncertainty and Its Consequences*. New York: Oxford University Press.

MacAskill, William. 2016. "Normative Uncertainty as a Voting Problem." *Mind*.

Mackie, J. L. 1982. *The Miracle of Theism*. New York: Oxford University Press.

Millar, Jason. 2014. "You Should Have a Say in Your Robot Car's Code of Ethics." *Wired*, September 2. http://www.wired.com/2014/09/set-the-ethics-robot-car/.

Nourbakhsh, Illah R. 2013. *Robot Futures*. Cambridge, MA: MIT Press.

Parfit, Derek. 2017. *On What Matters*, part 3. Oxford University Press.

Pascal, Blaise. (1670) 1966. *Pensées*. Translated by A. K. Krailsheimer. Reprint, Baltimore: Penguin Books.

Raiffa, Howard. 1997. *Decision Analysis: Introductory Lectures on Choices under Uncertainty*. New York: McGraw-Hill College.

Rescher, Nicholas. 1985. *Pascal's Wager*. South Bend, IN: Notre Dame University.

Sepielli, Andrew. 2006. "Review of Ted Lockhart's *Moral Uncertainty and Its Consequences*." *Ethics* 116: 601–4.

Sepielli, Andrew. 2009. "What to Do When You Don't Know What to Do." In *Oxford Studies in Metaethics*, vol. 4, edited by Russ-Shafer Laundau, 5–28. New York: Oxford University Press.

Sepielli, Andrew. 2010. "Along an Imperfectly-Lighted Path: Practical Rationality and Normative Uncertainty." PhD dissertation, Rutgers University.

Sepielli, Andrew. 2012. "Normative Uncertainty for Non-Cognitivists." *Philosophical Studies* 160: 191–207.

Sepielli, Andrew. 2013. "What to Do When You Don't Know What to Do When You Don't Know What to Do . . . ," *Nous* 47: 521–44.

Sepielli, Andrew. Forthcoming. "Moral Uncertainty." In *Routledge Handbook of Moral Epistemology*, edited by Karen Jones. Abingdon: Routledge.

Snow, Nancy E. 1995. "Humility." *Journal of Value Inquiry* 29: 203–16.

Thomson, Judith Jarvis. 1976. "Killing, Letting Die, and the Trolley Problem." *Monist* 59: 204–17.

Urmson, Chris. 2014. "Just Press Go: Designing a Self-driving Vehicle." Google Official Blog, May 27. http://googleblog.blogspot.com/2014/05/just-press-go-designing-self-driving.html.

Wallach, Wendell and Colin Allen. 2009. *Moral Machines: Teaching Robots Right from Wrong*. New York: Oxford University Press.

Werhane, Patricia. 1999. *Moral Imagination and Management Decision-Making*. New York: Oxford University Press.

2 ETHICS SETTINGS FOR AUTONOMOUS VEHICLES

Jason Millar

It is a one-of-a-kind car. . . . It is the fastest, safest, strongest car in the world. It is also completely fuel efficient, and is operated entirely by microprocessors which make it virtually impossible for it to be involved in any kind of mishap or collision, unless of course, specifically so ordered by its pilot.

—DEVON MILES *in NBC's (1982) Knight Rider*

This is Michael Knight's introduction to the Knight Industries Two Thousand, a.k.a. KITT, one of the most memorable autonomous vehicles in entertainment history. In addition to having great entertainment value, the iconic 1980s television show *Knight Rider* was surprisingly prescient in imagining the kinds of ethical design considerations that are a necessary aspect of designing autonomous vehicles. The epigraph highlights some of them nicely: There are value trade-offs, in that KITT's designers emphasized the values of safety, speed, physical strength, and fuel efficiency over other values (e.g., privacy, trustworthiness). They were bullish, perhaps overly so (Jones 2014), about automation's ability to eliminate *mishaps* and *collisions*. They also made very specific design choices about who was responsible for avoiding such mishaps and collisions: the responsibility was KITT's by default, but the *pilot* could override KITT at any time.

We are now sharing the roads and airways with increasingly autonomous vehicles, that is, with vehicles that are capable of operating in complex and unpredictable environments without direct human input. Today's autonomous vehicle designers are grappling with many of the same ethical quandaries in their design work as those envisioned by Hollywood writers. How should we weigh the many competing values in autonomous vehicle design? In what circumstances should the vehicle be in control? In what circumstances should the driver/pilot be in control? How do we decide where to draw the line between the two? And who should answer these questions: engineers, drivers/pilots, lawmakers, or perhaps ethicists?

One cannot design an autonomous vehicle without answering at least some of these challenging ethical design questions and embedding the answers in the vehicles themselves (Verbeek 2011; Latour 1992). Philosophers, engineers, policymakers, and lawyers who recognize the ethics and governance implications of autonomous vehicles are raising these design questions now in order to ensure that the technology is designed well (Millar 2016; Millar and Kerr 2016; Pan, Thornton, and Gerdes 2016; Millar 2015b; Goodall 2014; Lin 2013; Wu 2013). It would be best if answers to these challenging design questions were the results of philosophically informed, *explicit* and *anticipatory* design processes.

This chapter focuses on *ethics settings* in autonomous vehicles and problematizes their design. I focus on autonomous cars as exemplars of autonomous vehicles because autonomous cars are well into their development. Many autonomous features—adaptive cruise control, parking assist, pedestrian protection assistance—are already established in the consumer automobile market (Casey 2014). However, as autonomous aircraft—so-called drones—become more commonplace and sophisticated, many of the ethical issues outlined in this chapter will also apply to their design.

I begin the chapter by defining what I mean by the term "ethics setting." I then provide an overview of some of the ethics settings that are currently embedded in vehicles and some that are proposed or foreseeable. In this context I also discuss the various ethical considerations that have been raised in response to each kind of ethics setting. After painting the landscape of ethics settings and related ethical issues that accompany them, I raise three questions that must be answered by those designing ethics settings into autonomous vehicles. I conclude by providing some considerations that can help engineers, designers, and policymakers answer them.

2.1 What Is an Ethics Setting?

To get a better sense of the kinds of ethics settings that are, or will be, in autonomous vehicles, consider the following thought experiment, let's call it the helmet problem, originally posed by Noah Goodall (2014) and elaborated by Patrick Lin (2014b):

> An autonomous car is facing an imminent crash. It could select one of two targets to swerve into: either a motorcyclist who is wearing a helmet or a motorcyclist who is not. What's the right way to program the car?

The helmet problem poses a typical ethical question, in that answering it requires you to make a value judgment. In this case you might choose to value *minimizing overall harm* by arguing that the car should swerve into the helmeted motorcyclist, who is more likely to survive the crash. Alternatively, you might choose to value *responsible behavior* (i.e., helmet wearing) by arguing that the car should avoid the helmeted motorcyclist and swerve into the helmetless motorcyclist.

Now imagine you are an engineer faced with designing a driverless car. Given that ethical dilemmas like these are entirely foreseeable, part of your job will be to program the car to react one way or the other in driving situations where similar value judgments must be made. In other words, part of the job of designing an autonomous car involves programming value judgments (i.e., answers to ethical dilemmas) into the car (Millar 2015b; Verbeek 2011; Latour 1992). Once you program an answer into the car, say the one that values responsible behavior by avoiding helmeted motorcyclists, you reify that ethical decision as an *ethics setting* embedded in the technology: your autonomous car becomes a car that is set to swerve into helmetless motorcyclists in situations resembling the helmet problem.

An ethics setting that determines the car's response to the helmet problem could be rigidly *fixed* by engineers (or as a result of machine learning algorithms), in which case the car would be programmed to always swerve one way; or it could be *variable*, in which case the car's owner (or some other person) could be given a choice of settings that would determine how the car responds.

Defined this way, ethics settings are an inevitable feature of autonomous cars. Indeed, they are an inevitable feature of most technologies. Philosophers have, for some time now, recognized that designing technology necessarily involves embedding answers to ethical questions into those technologies, intentionally or not (Verbeek 2011; Ihde 2001; Latour 1992; Winner 1986). Autonomous vehicles will increasingly assume the many driving functions that have traditionally been required of human drivers, including all of the *ethical decision-making* that goes into navigating unpredictable, often chaotic, sometimes dangerous operating environments. As such, designing autonomous vehicles will require us to embed algorithms into those vehicles that automate complex ethical decision-making (Millar 2015a,b, 2016). Though the prospect of delegating complex ethical decision-making to a machine might seem ethically problematic, in many cases we will have good reasons to do so, particularly when it allows us to gain the benefits automation technologies promise to deliver (Millar and Kerr 2016). Ethics settings that determine the nature and outcomes of those ethical decision-making tasks (e.g., swerving this way or that) will also, therefore, be an inevitable feature of tomorrow's autonomous vehicles.

There is an emerging literature focused on the many ethical challenges that autonomous vehicles pose to ethicists, engineers, lawyers, and policymakers. In the following section I provide a descriptive, though certainly not exhaustive, snapshot of many of those issues. Each of them suggests a corresponding ethics setting (or settings) that could, and in many cases must, be designed into vehicles that will automate the underlying function.

2.2 Surveying the Landscape of Ethics Settings

2.2.1 Collision Management Settings

Collision management is the most widely discussed category of ethical questions/problems related to autonomous vehicles to date; it is the poster child for debates on the emerging ethics and governance of driverless cars. The most likely explanation for this is that autonomous cars reify one of the most famous ethical thought experiments invented by philosophers: the trolley problem (Foot 1967). In its most popular form (Thomson 1976), the trolley problem asks you to imagine a runaway trolley that is headed toward five unsuspecting people standing on the track. However, it so happens that you are standing next to a switch that, if pulled, would divert the trolley onto a parallel track containing a single unsuspecting person. There is no way to warn the people on either of the tracks. The trolley will undoubtedly kill the five people if left to continue straight, while it will kill the one person if the switch is pulled. The dilemma is whether or not you ought to pull the switch and divert the trolley.

As a philosophical thought experiment, the trolley problem is designed to probe various ethical intuitions and concepts (Foot 1967). A full treatment of the ongoing philosophical debate surrounding the trolley problem is well beyond the scope of this chapter. However, two facts related to the problem have interesting design implications. First, in the context of autonomous vehicles, the trolley problem, insofar as it represents a collision management problem, becomes a real design problem. Simply put, one can imagine autonomous cars encountering driving scenarios that share many ethical features with the trolley problem, so autonomous cars will have to be designed to deal with those kinds of scenarios. For example, the helmet problem discussed earlier is a trolley-like collision management problem. It describes a value trade-off that pits rewarding helmet wearing against minimizing overall harm. The helmet problem focuses us on a kind of design problem that will undoubtedly need to be solved in order to bring autonomous vehicles to market and make them fit well in real social contexts.

Second, the philosophical debates surrounding the original and other trolley-like problems are ongoing; that is, they are not settled. This might be surprising to some readers given that the original trolley problem offers the ability to save a net of four lives by simply pulling the switch—an intuitively compelling option. Studies have repeatedly demonstrated that most people endorse pulling the switch as the right decision in the original trolley problem (Greene 2010). However, despite a majority opinion on the matter, ethical dilemmas are not the kinds of things that submit easily to majority-derived solutions. The standard example used to demonstrate why majority opinions fail to establish moral norms is human slavery: most people, when asked, would agree that even if we had a majority opinion indicating that slavery is acceptable, it would still be ethically impermissible to enslave humans. Actions, it seems, are right or wrong regardless of how many people agree. Thus, settling the original trolley problem by appealing to the net saving of four lives could merely amount to endorsing a utilitarian problem-solving approach that seeks to maximize happiness and minimize pain. It does *not* necessarily amount to having found an objectively correct answer to the ethical dilemma.

That the trolley problem remains an open philosophical debate stems partly from the argumentative appeal of competing ethical theories, for example virtue ethics and deontology, that reject problem-solving strategies focused exclusively on maximizing/minimizing strategies. It also stems from a curious feature of many ethical dilemmas more generally, which is that unlike other disagreements, such as over how best to design a bridge, the choices available in ethical dilemmas are often very difficult to compare with one another. Consider the helmet problem once again, in which we are asked to weigh rewarding helmet wearing (swerving away from the helmeted cyclist) against minimizing overall harm (swerving away from the helmetless cyclist). How is one meant to compare these two options? It seems that in these kinds of cases, referred to as *hard cases*, either of the available options can be justified as the better option, but only better with respect to a set of criteria that applies exclusively to that option (Chang 2002, 2012). We might justify swerving away from the helmeted cyclist because it is better to reward responsible behavior. But in doing so, we have not established our choice as the better option *tout court* (Chang 2002). This is demonstrated by the fact that we could also reasonably justify choosing the other option. Thus, solutions to hard cases are hard to come by. Individuals faced with making decisions in hard cases can do so with justification, but one person's justification should not be mistaken for a general solution to the problem.

Designing ethics settings for collision management can be ethically challenging since many hard cases are often highly personal. As an illustration, consider another thought experiment called the tunnel problem (Millar 2015b):

> You are the passenger in an autonomous car traveling along a narrow mountain road, quickly approaching the entrance to a tunnel. Suddenly, a child errantly runs into the road in front of the car. There is no time to brake safely to avoid a collision with the child, who will most likely be killed in the collision. Swerving either way will result in the car hitting the tunnel wall, most likely killing you.

As is typical in hard cases, the two available options in the tunnel problem are difficult to compare—there is no objectively better option. In addition, the tunnel problem places you in the car, situating this hard case in a highly personal context. The personal nature of the tunnel problem shares ethical features with the kinds of end-of-life decisions that are common in other ethically challenging settings, such as healthcare settings (Millar 2015b). In healthcare ethics, it is generally impermissible to make important decisions on behalf of a patient, let's call her Shelly, regardless of whether or not the outcome would benefit Shelly (Jonsen 2008). Instead, healthcare professionals are required to seek informed consent from Shelly in decisions regarding her care. Modeling the tunnel problem as an end-of-life issue for the passenger of the car suggests that, just as doctors do not generally have the moral authority to make important end-of-life decisions on behalf of Shelly, engineers also do not have the moral authority to make certain decisions on behalf of drivers/passengers (Millar 2015b). More specifically, it seems that engineers do not have the moral authority to make ethical decisions on behalf of users in hard cases where the stakes are high.

We should therefore expect justified controversy in cases where engineers design ethics settings into a car to deal with hard cases without either asking the user directly for input or properly informing the user ahead of time how the car will tend to behave in such situations. Put another way, because engineers have a moral obligation to respect users' autonomy, when they don't we should expect some user backlash (Millar 2015b).

To test this hypothesis, the Open Roboethics initiative (ORi 2014a, 2014b) conducted a public poll that presented the tunnel problem to participants and asked them: (1) How should the car react? (2) Who should make the decision as to how the car reacts? A full 36% of participants indicated their preference for the car to swerve into the wall, thus saving the child, while 64% indicated their preference to save themselves, thus sacrificing the child. In response to the second question, 44% of participants indicated that the passenger should decide how the car reacts, while 33% of participants indicated that lawmakers should make the decision. Only 12% of participants indicated that manufacturers should make the decision. These results seem to suggest that, at the very least, people do not like the idea of engineers making high-stakes ethical decisions on their behalf.

ORi's results should not be particularly surprising. Individual autonomy is a well-established ethical norm in Western ethics, in part because our ethical intuitions seem to align with notions of autonomy in situations involving highly personal hard cases (Greene 2010).

Despite good reasons to limit engineers' decision-making authority in some cases, it is clearly impractical to solicit user input in many hard cases involving collision management, and sometimes soliciting user input will introduce new ethical problems.

Imagine an autonomous vehicle with a variable ethics setting designed to navigate the tunnel problem. In the event of an actual tunnel problem occurring, users simply would not be able to provide input in the short time between detecting an imminent collision and the collision. To manage this problem, one could design ethics settings that gather user input as a sort of "setup" procedure that the user follows upon purchasing an autonomous car. But requiring the user to input ethics settings for an array of foreseeable ethical dilemmas could be too burdensome for users. This could also place an undesirable burden on manufacturers, who would need to educate users on all of the related features and solicit their input as part of a robust informed consent process. To be sure, direct user input is not always going to be the best way to support user autonomy.

Furthermore, thought experiments like the helmet and tunnel problems oversimplify the driving context in order to explore ethical principles and suggest norms. They are, in a very real sense, philosophers' laboratories. But just as the results of scientific experiments do not always translate smoothly into the "real world," philosophers' thought experiments that illustrate normative principles quite clearly in the "lab" have their limits in practice. An ethical appeal to individual autonomy might work well in contexts where there is a relatively clear one-to-one ratio between bodies and harms. But how should we design for a collision management problem in cases where two or more people are in the autonomous vehicle? Recall, the two passengers might legitimately disagree about how best to navigate the collision from an ethical standpoint—that is the upshot of hard cases. So even if we can agree that each of the passengers has the moral authority to make important decisions about his or her own fate, which passenger's autonomy are we to respect in these cases? And what happens if the person in the road is there because of confusing signage or a malfunctioning traffic light, in which case the requirement to respect their autonomy suddenly enters the moral landscape? These complicated situations seem to require solutions based on something more than an oversimplified appeal to individual autonomy.

In such cases, where we recognize a moral requirement to respect the autonomy of multiple parties involved in a high-stakes collision, we might look to models of informed consent used in population-based decisions, that is, decisions that trade individual autonomy for collective good (Lin 2014a). According to the ORi (2014a, 2014b) data, users might endorse regulating collision management systems. In the same study discussed earlier, 33% of participants indicated that they believed lawmakers should make decisions about the tunnel problem, and justified their preference with appeals to openness, transparency, and alignment with democratic principles (ORi 2014b). Their responses are an indication that regulating certain ethics settings could provide the legitimacy required to support a population-based informed consent model (ORi 2014b). People can make informed decisions about whether or not to ride in autonomous vehicles so long as the designed behavior of those vehicles is made clear to them in advance.

Ethics settings for collision management also raise another significant challenge that has ethical and legal implications. According to Lin (2014a), ethics settings in autonomous vehicles could reasonably be interpreted, both legally and ethically, as targeting algorithms. An autonomous vehicle that is set to minimize overall harm in situations like that illustrated by the helmet problem could be interpreted as an algorithm that intentionally targets cyclists wearing helmets. Because collision management ethics settings involve decisions that determine collision outcomes well in advance of the collision, they appear very different from snap decisions made by drivers in the moments leading up to the collision. Seen this way, an ethics setting could be interpreted as a premeditated harm perpetrated by whoever set it, which could result in that person being held ethically and legally responsible for the particular outcome of the collision. Additionally, Lin (2014a) argues that variable ethics settings controlled by the user could offer manufacturers a responsibility escape route by "punting" responsibility to the user, who would then bear the legal brunt of the collision outcome.

Once again, regulation could help manage this last set of concerns. Regulating variable ethics settings could have the effect of shielding manufacturers and users, both legally and ethically, who could then legitimately be given the respective responsibilities of designing and setting variable ethics settings to deal with various hard cases.

2.2.2 Settings Governing the Distribution of Systemwide Benefits

As autonomous vehicles populate the roads and airways, replacing human-operated vehicles, autonomous vehicles will increasingly communicate with one another within the overall autonomous vehicle system (Nelson 2014), creating opportunities for the automated distribution of systemwide benefits.

Algorithms determining the distribution of such benefits could be based on a combination of ethics settings embedded in the system and in individual vehicles. The rules governing these settings could take many different ethical forms. Systems could be designed to reward the wealthy by allowing people to set their vehicles to drive faster for a range of fees. In such a system, the more you pay, the faster you get there. Of course, this means that individuals unable to pay for such benefits would get to their destinations slower on average. Alternative schemes could reward altruistic behavior, for example by providing "speed credits" to individuals who donate their time to charity or use less electricity in their homes. Similarly, demerits could be issued to individuals as a tax on undesirable behavior, such as leaving lights on all day or watering a lawn during periods of water shortage. Some vehicles could be set to drive along routes that are underutilized, even if they are less direct, or could force passengers to pass by certain shops as a form of paid advertising. One could imagine any number of systemwide benefit distribution schemes of these sorts.

Though these kinds of benefits are speculative, they are entirely foreseeable. In each case, the designed rules for distributing benefits and harms within the system will require decisions to be made about which values will prevail, what kinds of corresponding ethics settings to offer, and to whom to allow access.

2.2.3 Performance Settings

Much like today's vehicles, autonomous vehicles could differ in their particular fixed performance settings from manufacturer to manufacturer, model to model. But they could also be designed with variable performance settings to change the driving profile of the individual vehicle, while maintaining a minimum level of safety.

Stanford University engineers recently completed a study describing a variable ethics setting designed to control an autonomous car's object approach and avoidance algorithm (Pan, Thornton, and Gerdes 2016). They used an ethically informed design process to create an algorithm that would control the distance between the car and a static object in the road while the car passed around that object. It also allowed the engineers to vary the minimum distance that would be maintained between the car and the curb. This performance setting could be used to set the passenger's comfort level, with some passengers preferring more or less passing distance from the curb and objects in the road.

Similarly, depending on their preferences, individual passengers could choose to have their vehicles turn corners at higher or lower speeds, choose to have harder or softer braking characteristics, alter the following distance from other vehicles, or alter acceleration profiles.

Performance settings should be considered ethics settings for a few reasons. First, altering the performance characteristics could have a positive or negative effect on a passenger's level of trust in the overall system. A passenger featured in one of Google's driverless car promotional videos commented that she preferred the car's cornering characteristic to her husband's (Google 2014). Building trustworthy autonomous vehicles is important, assuming people will be more likely to adopt trustworthy technology, meaning the benefits of that technology will be realized in society to a greater extent the more trustworthy the system is. Second, performance settings have a direct impact on the environment. As we saw recently with Volkswagen's emission scandal, tweaking the software settings that control emissions can have significant negative environmental consequences (Hotten 2015). Generally speaking, the environmental profile of a vehicle changes as it accelerates and drives faster, or brakes and corners harder, partly as a result of increased fuel consumption (whether electrical or gas), but also because components will tend to wear out sooner, requiring maintenance or replacement. Third, performance settings will change the system's overall level of safety. Many fast-moving cars represent a more dangerous system than many slow-moving cars. Minimum safety standards for individual vehicle performance will have to be established for autonomous vehicles, but vehicles could be designed to operate slightly more dangerously, yet still within acceptable limits.

2.2.4 Data Collection and Management Settings

With an increase in autonomous functions comes an increased need for data collection and management settings. Just as data-driven internet applications like Facebook require privacy settings to help balance corporate and users' needs, so too will data-hungry automation technologies require some way for users/passengers to determine how their data is collected and used within the system (Calo 2012). Autonomous vehicles will be equipped with various sensors, cameras, global positioning systems, user inputs, user settings (including, of course, ethics settings), data logging capabilities, communication capabilities (e.g., Wi-Fi), and passenger information systems. All of this data will be subject to privacy concerns, and autonomous vehicles will require a combination of fixed and variable ethics settings to manage it well.

The privacy literature is broad and includes many discussions in relation to robotics and automation technologies (e.g., Hartzog 2015; Selinger 2014; Kerr 2013; Calo 2012). Because of space limitations, I leave it to the reader to explore those rich and thought-provoking sources.

2.3 A Preliminary Taxonomy of Ethics Settings

The various ethics settings and corresponding ethical issues outlined in the preceding section lay the groundwork for a preliminary taxonomy of ethics settings. As automation improves and evolves, new ethical questions will emerge in design rooms, each of which will require an answer. Thus, new ethics settings will enter the picture.

Still, the foregoing discussion provides enough substance to frame three important ethical design questions related to each ethics setting:

(1) What is an acceptable set point, or range of set points, for this ethics setting?
(2) Should this ethics setting be fixed or variable?
(3) Who has the moral authority to answer (1) and (2) for this ethics setting?

When the questions are framed this way, we need an answer to (3) before we can answer (1) and (2) (Millar 2015b). The taxonomy of ethics settings in this section is meant to provide some first steps toward fuller answers to all three questions.

2.3.1 High-Stakes versus Low-Stakes Ethics Settings

From the preceding discussion, we can identify two categories of ethics settings based on outcomes: those involving relatively high-stakes outcomes and those involving relatively low-stakes outcomes. Collision management settings will often involve high-stakes outcomes, especially when people are likely to be injured as a result of the collision. Ethics settings designed to manage scenarios like the helmet and tunnel problems are good examples of high-stakes ethics settings. Others might include some ethics settings designed to distribute system-wide goods, such as the ability to get to a destination faster. Consider a systematic distribution pattern that discriminates against certain socioeconomic groups not able to pay for "speed credits." One can frame this as a high-stakes ethics setting that unjustly reinforces patterns of social inequality (Golub, Marcantonio, and Sanchez 2013).

In contrast, low-stakes ethics settings will tend to result in relatively minor harms and benefits. A climate control setting can result in slightly increased fuel consumption but also increased passenger comfort. Collision management settings that manage very low speed collisions with little or no likelihood of harm to people (or property), or where the harms will be done to non-humans such as squirrels (sorry, squirrels!), can also be deemed low-stakes. Neither the harm nor the benefit in these cases is significant enough to warrant classifying the stakes as high.

Generally speaking, all other things being equal, question (3) is less urgent in low-stakes ethics settings. This simplifies questions (1) and (2). A low-stakes ethics setting can be fixed or variable, can be accessible only to the manufacturer, or can be available to any passenger in the vehicle without raising any significant ethical concerns. Engineers do not have any urgent ethical imperative to worry about user/passenger autonomy when designing low-stakes ethics settings. Consequently, there is no obvious ethical imperative to get regulators involved in settling questions about how to deal with low-stakes ethics settings.

With high-stakes ethics settings, on the other hand, question (3) takes on a new urgency, especially in light of the discussion surrounding high-stakes collision management settings. Engineers most often do not have the moral authority to answer high-stakes ethical questions on behalf of users/passengers. Answering (3) in the context of high-stakes ethics settings therefore requires additional ethical analysis in the design room and could require regulatory or user/passenger input.

2.3.2 Expertise-Based versus Non-Expertise-Based Ethics Settings

The previous discussions allow us to identify two categories of ethics settings based on the knowledge available to settle the underlying questions. Many ethics settings, both high- and low-stakes, will involve ethical questions that fall squarely in the domain of some form of expertise, say, engineering expertise. In such cases "the set of standards against which those human experts gauge outcomes can serve as the objective measure against which designers can gauge a particular instance of expertise-based delegation" (Millar 2015a). For example, a variable ethics setting allowing a passenger to change the performance characteristics of a vehicle can be limited in its range to ensure that the car always maintains a safe following distance from other vehicles. Calculating a safe following distance falls squarely under the expertise of engineers. When objective expert-based measures like these are available to answer the question at the root of the ethics setting and when the question is the kind that falls under the particular domain of expertise, engineers (or whichever experts have the relevant expertise) will tend to have the moral authority to answer that question. Thus, there is no obvious ethical imperative to give users input on expertise-based ethics settings, whether high- or low-stakes. Though there may be exceptions, experts in the relevant knowledge domain generally have the moral authority to answer those questions and embed those answers in technology (Millar 2015a).

Hard cases, such as those described by the helmet and tunnel problems, do not submit so easily to expertise. As previously described, hard cases are hard because there are no objective measures by which to compare options and arrive at an answer (Chang 2002, 2012). Thus, there exists an ethical imperative in the design of non-expertise-based ethics settings, particularly those involving high-stakes outcomes, to seek input from either users/passengers, where the autonomy of only one individual is implicated, or regulators, where population-based decision-making might satisfy the requirement for a robust informed consent model (Millar 2014, 2015b).

This distinction has the benefit of further removing unwarranted burdens in the design room that a focus on individual user autonomy might otherwise seem to impose on engineers or regulators. When designing expertise-based ethics settings, engineers can assume their traditional decision-making authority because of the availability of a relatively objective standard of measure.

Of course, none of this simplifies the ethics of automating ethical decision-making. Autonomous vehicles, and the ethical issues they raise, are immensely complex. But they require our thoughtful attention if we are to shift our thinking about the ethics of design and engineering and respond to the burgeoning autonomous vehicle industry appropriately. Part of this shift in thinking will require us to embrace ethical and regulatory complexity where complexity is required.

2.4 Concluding Remarks: The Need for an Anticipatory Design Process That Takes the Ethics of Ethics Settings into Account

Various design methodologies have been proposed to address the need for embedding ethical considerations, like the ones discussed in this chapter, into the ethics of engineering, designing, and governing robotics and artificial intelligence. Some methodologies focus on the many values implicated by technology (Verbeek 2011; Friedman and Kahn 2007), some propose embedding ethicists in design teams (Van Wynsberghe 2013; Van Wynsberghe and Robbins 2013), others focus on ethics capacity-building among engineering teams (Millar 2016), while some focus on playfully modeling robotics systems using an array of analogies (Jones and Millar, 2016). The ethical considerations outlined in this chapter would fit well into any of these approaches to engineering and design and could help to inform governance discussions. What is clear is that in order to meet the unique ethical challenges posed by autonomous vehicles, new, ethically informed anticipatory approaches to engineering, design, and governance must be adopted. Doing so will improve the quality of design by producing technologies that fit well into the social fabric they are intended for. I am confident that volumes such as this will pave the way to succeeding in these exciting design tasks.

Works Cited

Calo, Ryan. 2012. "Robots and Privacy." In *Robot Ethics*, edited by Patrick Lin, George Bekey, and Keith Abney, 187–202. Cambridge, MA: MIT Press.

Casey, Michael. 2014. "Want a Self-Driving Car? Look on the Driveway." *Fortune*, December 6. http://fortune.com/2014/12/06/autonomous-vehicle-revolution/.

Chang, Ruth. 2002. "The Possibility of Parity." *Ethics* 112: 659–88.

Chang, Ruth. 2012. "Are Hard Choices Cases of Incomparability?" *Philosophical Issues* 22: 106–26.

Foot, Philippa. 1967. "The Problem of Abortion and the Doctrine of the Double Effect in Virtues and Vices." *Oxford Review* 5: 5–15.

Friedman, Batya and Peter H. Kahn. 2007. "Human Values, Ethics, and Design." In *The Human–Computer Interaction Handbook: Fundamentals, Evolving Technologies and Emerging Applications*, 2d ed., edited by A. Sears and J. A. Jacko, 1241–66. New York: Taylor & Francis Group.

Golub, Aaron, Richard A. Marcantonio, and Thomas W. Sanchez. 2013. "Race, Space, and Struggles for Mobility: Transportation Impacts on African Americans in Oakland and the East Bay." *Urban Geography* 34: 699–728.

Goodall, Noah J. 2014. "Ethical Decision Making During Automated Vehicle Crashes." *Transportation Research Record: Journal of the Transportation Research Board* 2424: 58–65.

Google. 2014. "A First Drive." YouTube, May 27. https://www.youtube.com/watch?v=CqSDWoAhvLU.

Greene, Joshua. 2010. "Multi-System Moral Psychology." In *The Oxford Handbook of Moral Psychology*, edited by John M. Doris, 47–71. Oxford: Oxford University Press.

Hartzog, Woodrow. 2015. "Unfair and Deceptive Robots." *Maryland Law Review* 74, 758–829.

Hotten, Russell. 2015. "Volkswagen: The Scandal Explained." *BBC News*, December 10. http://www.bbc.com/news/business-34324772.

Ihde, Don. 2001. *Bodies in Technology*. Minneapolis: University of Minnesota Press.

Jones, Meg L. 2014. "The Law & the Loop." IEEE International Symposium on Ethics in Engineering, Science and Technology, 2014.

Jones, Meg L. and Jason Millar. 2016. "Hacking Analogies in the Regulation of Robotics." In *The Oxford Handbook of the Law and Regulation of Technology*, edited by Roger Brownsword, Eloise Scotford, and Karen Yeung. Oxford: Oxford University Press.

Jonsen, Albert R. 2008. *A Short History of Medical Ethics*. Oxford: Oxford University Press.

Kerr, Ian. 2013. "Prediction, Presumption, Preemption: The Path of Law after the Computational Turn." In *Privacy, Due Process and the Computational Turn: The Philosophy of Law Meets the Philosophy of Technology*, edited by M. Hildebrandt and E. De Vries, 91–120. London: Routledge.

Latour, Bruno. 1992. "Where Are the Missing Masses? The Sociology of a Few Mundane Artefacts." In *Shaping Technology/Building Society: Studies in Sociotechnical Change*, edited by Wiebe Bijker, and John Law, 225–58. Cambridge, MA: MIT Press.

Lin, Patrick. 2013. "The Ethics of Autonomous Cars." *Atlantic*, October 8. http://www.theatlantic.com/technology/archive/2013/10/the-ethics-of-autonomous-cars/280360/.

Lin, Patrick. 2014a. "Here's a Terrible Idea: Robot Cars with Adjustable Ethics Settings." *Wired*, August 18. http://www.wired.com/2014/08/heres-a-terrible-idea-robot-cars-with-adjustable-ethics-settings/.

Lin, Patrick. 2014b. "The Robot Car of Tomorrow May Just Be Programmed to Hit You." *Wired*, May 6. http://www.wired.com/2014/05/the-robot-car-of-tomorrow-might-just-be-programmed-to-hit-you/.

Millar, Jason. 2014. "You Should Have a Say in Your Robot Car's Code of Ethics." *Wired*, September 2. http://www.wired.com/2014/09/set-the-ethics-robot-car/.

Millar, Jason. 2015a. "Technological Moral Proxies and the Ethical Limits of Automating Decision-Making in Robotics and Artificial Intelligence." PhD dissertation, Queen's University.

Millar, Jason. 2015b. "Technology as Moral Proxy: Autonomy and Paternalism by Design." *IEEE Technology & Society* 34 (2): 47–55.

Millar, Jason. 2016. "An Ethics Evaluation Tool for Automating Ethical Decision-Making in Robots and Self-Driving Cars." *Applied Artificial Intelligence* 30 (8): 787–809.

Millar, Jason and Ian Kerr. 2016. "Delegation, Relinquishment and Responsibility: The Prospect of Expert Robots." In *Robot Law*, edited by Ryan Calo, A. Michael Froomkin, and Ian Kerr, 102–27. Cheltenham: Edward Elgar.

NBC. 1982. *Knight Rider*, Episode 1: "The Knight of the Phoenix."

Nelson, Jacqueline. 2014. "The Rise of the Connected Car Puts the Web Behind the Wheel." *Globe and Mail*, July 30. http://www.theglobeandmail.com/report-on-business/companies-race-to-bring-the-web-behind-the-wheel/article19853771/.

ORi. 2014a. "If Death by Autonomous Car Is Unavoidable, Who Should Die? Reader Poll Results." Robohub.org, June 23. http://robohub.org/if-a-death-by-an-autonomous-car-is-unavoidable-who-should-die-results-from-our-reader-poll/.

ORi. 2014b. "My (Autonomous) Car, My Safety: Results from Our Reader Poll." Robohub.org, June 30. http://robohub.org/my-autonomous-car-my-safety-results-from-our-reader-poll/.

Pan, Selina, Sarah Thornton, and Christian J. Gerdes. 2016. "Prescriptive and Proscriptive Moral Regulation for Autonomous Vehicles in Approach and Avoidance." *IEEE International Symposium on Ethics in Engineering, Science and Technology, 2016.*

Selinger, Evan. 2014. "Why We Should Be Careful about Adopting Social Robots." *Forbes*, July 17. http://www.forbes.com/sites/privacynotice/2014/07/17/why-we-should-be-careful-about-adopting-social-robots.

Thomson, Judith Jarvis. 1976. "Killing, Letting Die, and the Trolley Problem." *Monist* 59: 204–17.

Van Wynsberghe, Aimee. 2013. "Designing Robots for Care: Care Centered Value-Sensitive Design." *Science and Engineering Ethics* 19: 407–33.

Van Wynsberghe, Aimee and Scott Robbins. 2013. "Ethicist as Designer: A Pragmatic Approach to Ethics in the Lab." *Science and Engineering Ethics* 20: 947–61.

Verbeek, Peter-Paul. 2011. *Moralizing Technology: Understanding and Designing the Morality of Things.* Chicago: University of Chicago Press.

Winner, Langdon. 1986. *The Whale and the Reactor: A Search for Limits in an Age of High Technology.* Chicago: University of Chicago Press.

Wu, Stephen S. 2013. "Risk Management in Commercializing Robots." *We Robot 2013 Proceedings.* http://www.academia.edu/8691419/Risk_Management_in_Commercializing_Robots.

3 AUTONOMY AND RESPONSIBILITY IN HYBRID SYSTEMS

THE EXAMPLE OF AUTONOMOUS CARS

Wulf Loh and Janina Loh

Automated driving raises an interesting set of ethical questions not necessarily about who is to blame when something goes wrong (Lin 2015). Rather, we can ask who should make the relevant ethical decisions in certain circumstances on the street and how responsibility should be distributed accordingly between the current occupants of the vehicle, its owner, the engineers/developers of the car, and maybe even the artificial system that is operating the car itself. Assuming that the artificial system is autonomous in a morally relevant sense, should it not be trusted with making ethical decisions (Floridi and Sanders 2004; Wallach and Allen 2009; Misselhorn 2013)? If so, what would be the criteria for ascribing moral autonomy that is relevant to the question of responsibility? Could an artificial system make a morally wrong decision—and, more importantly should it be able to? How would we even go about confronting it with its responsibility in such a case?

On the other hand, we might be tempted to leave ethically relevant decisions to the human aspects of the system: the drivers, owners, engineers. But if so, should there be a hierarchy and an ultimately responsible moral agent, or can we conceive of a responsibility network in which responsibility is shared by the different agents (Hubig 2008; Knoll 2008; Rammert 2004; Weyer 2005)? What would such a network have to look like? Are responsibility issues here really questions of moral, not legal, responsibility? After all, the issue *prima facie* appears to be entirely a question of traffic regulations. If we do not assume that an autonomous driving system ever drives too fast or recklessly, can be—in contrast to human operators—intoxicated or otherwise impaired, accidents seem to remain beyond the fault of the artificial driver and raise questions of only legal accountability and liability rather than moral responsibility.

But even if this is true for standard road situations, there might be instances where the self-driving car has to make a decision between harming the occupants of the car and harming other individuals outside (other car drivers, pedestrians, etc.). These instances are structured much like trolley cases (Foot 1967; Hevelke and Nida-Rümelin 2015), which invite very diverse ethical responses.

In order to examine questions of responsibility and autonomy for artificial systems, we give in section 3.1 a brief overview of the traditional notion of responsibility. Contrasting this with the specifics of artificial systems, in section 3.2 we ultimately reject the idea of a full-blown moral responsibility for any kind of autonomous artificial agents and, therefore, also for self-driving cars. However, we do not in principle deny a partial responsibility according to its level of autonomy and cognitive capacities. This will lead to a concept of distributed responsibility within a "responsibility network" (Neuhäuser 2015) of the engineers, the driver, and the artificial system itself, which we introduce in section 3.3. In order to evaluate this concept, we explore the notion of man–machine hybrid systems with regard to self-driving cars and conclude that the unit comprising the car and the operator/driver consists of such a hybrid system that can assume a shared responsibility that differs from the responsibility of other actors in the responsibility network. In section 3.4, we discuss certain moral dilemma situations that are structured much like trolley cases (Foot 1967), which the hybrid system might need to confront because of its superior computing and reaction capacities. If the artificial system cannot bear the moral responsibility for these kinds of situations in the near future, we deduce that as long as there is something like a driver in autonomous cars as part of the hybrid system, she will have to bear the responsibility for making the morally relevant decisions that are not covered by traffic rules. Since there is no time to reflect on these matters in the situation itself, the driver has to voice her moral convictions beforehand through some kind of interface.

3.1 The Traditional Concept of Responsibility

Rapid progress in robotics and AI potentially poses huge challenges to assuming roles traditionally reserved for human agents; and concepts like autonomy, agency, and responsibility might one day apply to artificial systems. To evaluate these possible transitions, we formulate a minimal definition of responsibility that includes only the fundamental etymological aspects as our starting point. Looking at the necessary conditions that make an agent responsible (Sombetzki 2014, 42–62) will lead to a definition of responsibility that artificial systems might also meet in the future.

Responsibility is a tool for systematizing, organizing, and thereby clarifying opaque and very complex situations that confuse the agents in question: situations where classical ascriptions of duties and guilt frequently fall short (Lenk and Maring 1995, 242–7). Unbundled properly, it can make sense of challenging hierarchical setups, an unclear number of involved parties, and huge time-space dimensions; and it can complement traditional concepts like that of duties.

A detailed etymological study (Sombetzki 2014, 33–41) would show that "responsibility" first means "the state or fact of being answerable for something." It is the ability to provide an accounting of one's actions (Duff 1998, 290; Kallen 1942, 351). Second, responsibility is a normative concept; i.e., it is more than descriptive and causal. In calling the sun responsible for melting candle wax, we use the term "responsible" in a metaphorical sense because the sun is not able to explain itself. On the other hand, in calling someone responsible for killing another person, we usually do not want to state a simple fact. We want the alleged murderer to explain herself and to accept her guilt (Werner 2006, 542). Finally, responsibility implies a specific psycho-motivational constitution of the responsible subject in question: we think she is accountable as an autonomous person, enabled by several capabilities such as judgment and reflective faculty (Sombetzki 2014, 39–41).

This etymologically minimal definition of responsibility leads to five relational elements, which we will clarify with the example that follows: (1) an individual or collective subject is bearer of responsibility (the *who* is responsible?); (2) the subject is prospectively or retrospectively responsible for an object or matter (the *what* is *x* responsible *for*?); (3) the subject is responsible to a private or official authority (the *to whom* is *x* responsible?) and *toward* a private or official addressee or receiver; (4) the addressee is the reason for speaking of responsibility in the context in question; and (5) the normative criteria, either official or unofficial, define the *conditions under which x* is responsible. They restrict the area of responsible acting, thereby differentiating moral, political, legal, economic, and other responsibilities—or, better, domains of responsibility.[1]

For example, a thief (individual subject) is responsible for a stolen book (retrospective object) or, better yet, the theft (a collection of actions that already happened). The subject is responsible to the judge (official authority) and to the owner of the book (official addressee) under the conditions of the criminal code (normative criteria that define a legal or criminal responsibility) (Sombetzki 2014, 63–132).

In the light of this minimal definition of responsibility, it becomes clear that a complex cluster of capacities is needed to call someone responsible. The agent in question needs (1) to be able to communicate. The agent needs (2) to be able to act, i.e., possess a demanding form of autonomy. That includes (2.1) being aware of the consequences (knowledge), (2.2) being aware of the context (historicity),

(2.3) personhood, and (2.4) a scope of influence. Finally, to call someone responsible, it is necessary (3) that the person be able to judge. This competence includes (3.1) several cognitive capacities, such as reflection and rationality, and (3.2) interpersonal institutions, such as promise, trust, and reliability on the other (Sombetzki 2014, 43–62).

On the possibility of ascribing responsibility to artificial systems—autonomous driving systems, in this chapter—it is important to take into consideration that these three sets of capacities (communication, autonomy, and judgment), and the competences that come with them, can be ascribed in a gradual manner. As communication skills can vary, to say that someone is more or less able to act in a specific situation, more or less autonomous, more or less reasonable, and so on, it follows that responsibility itself must be attributed gradually according to the aforementioned prerequisites (Nida-Rümelin 2007, 63; Wallace 1994, 157). Assigning responsibility is not a binary question of "all or nothing" but one of degree.

3.2 Ascribing Autonomy and Responsibility to Artificial Systems

In asking about the ways robots are to be understood as "artificial moral agents (AMAs)," Wallach and Allen define moral agency as a gradual concept with two conditions: "autonomy and sensitivity to values" (2009, 25). Human beings are the gold standard for moral agency, but some machines—e.g., an autopilot or the artificial system Kismet (a robot head that can mimic emotions, designed by Cynthia Breazeal at MIT in the late 1990s, described in detail later)—might be called moral agents in an "operational" way. They are more autonomous and sensitive to morally relevant facts than non-mechanical tools, such as a hammer; but these competences (autonomy and ethical sensitivity) are still "totally within the control of [the] tool's designers and users" (Wallach and Allen 2009, 26) and in this sense "direct extensions of their designers' values" (Wallach and Allen 2009, 30). Very few artificial systems already have the status of "functional" moral agency, such as the medical ethics expert system MedEthEx—an ethical adviser for healthcare workers (Anderson et al. 2006). Functional morality means that the artificial system in question is either more autonomous and/or more sensitive to values than operational AMAs, in the sense that functional moral machines "themselves have the capacity for assessing and responding to moral challenges" (Wallach and Allen 2009, 9).

Wallach and Allen's concept of gradual competences and abilities builds on their approach of functional equivalence: "Just as a computer system can represent emotions without having emotions, computer systems may be capable of functioning as if they understand the meaning of symbols without actually having what one would consider to be human understanding" (2009, 69).

With this notion of functional equivalence, Wallach and Allen subscribe to a version of "weak AI" (Searle 1980) that seeks to simulate certain competences in artificial systems rather than to construct artificial systems that are equipped with full-blown intelligence, consciousness, and autonomy in all relevant respects equal to that of humans (strong AI, mistakenly ascribed to Turing 1950). According to Wallach and Allen, a strong AI understanding of autonomy is not a necessary condition for AMAs. Instead they focus on the attribution of functional equivalent conditions and behavior. Functional equivalence means that specific phenomena are treated "as if" they correspond to cognitive, emotional, or other attributed competences and abilities.[2] The question of whether artificial systems can become intelligent, conscious, or autonomous in the strong AI sense is replaced by the question of the extent to which the displayed competences correspond to the function they play within the moral evaluation, in this case the concept of responsibility. For example, the capacity of any artificial system for reasoning or autonomous action is examined only insofar as it functions as a prerequisite to assigning responsibility to that system.

Functional equivalence, however, goes only so far. Although the boundary between functional morality and full moral agency is conceived of as gradual with respect to certain types of autonomy, for the immediate future it is hard to fathom how an artificial system might achieve a functional equivalent to the genuinely human ability to set "second-order volitions" (Frankfurt 1971, 10) for oneself and to act as "self-authenticating sources of valid claims" (Rawls 2001, 23) or to reflect on its own moral premises and principles.

In tackling these questions, it may be helpful to recall Darwall's distinction between four different usages of "autonomy": "personal," "moral," "rational," and "agential" autonomy (Darwall 2006, 265). While personal autonomy refers to the above-mentioned capacity to form personal values, goals, and ultimate ends, moral autonomy means the possibility of reflecting on one's own moral principles or ethical convictions. These two forms of autonomy might be for a long time reserved for human agents. Rational autonomy, on the other hand, seems to be *prima facie* achievable for artificial agents as well, as for Darwall it is grounded solely on action on the basis of the "weightiest reasons" (2006, 265). These reasons may very well be represented in a functionally equivalent way by algorithms and corresponding external data. More important, however, is the possibility of ascribing agential autonomy to artificial systems, since this form of autonomy consists of identifying a certain behavior as a "genuine action," i.e., not entirely determined by external factors. This may be functionally represented by the artificial system's ability to change internal states without external stimuli.

How can this ability to autonomously change internal states be described on a computational level? Here we can distinguish three different types of algorithmic schemes (Sombetzki 2016) and thereby not only give some explanation for the functional equivalence of autonomy, but also shed some light on the difference between operational and functional responsibility. While *determined algorithms* give the same output, given a particular input, *deterministic algorithms* give the same output, given a particular input, in passing through the same sequences of states. To make a start, it might be possible to locate machines that predominantly function on the basis of deterministic algorithms in the not-functional and not-operational sphere. They are still machines but almost closer to the non-mechanical tools than to the operational realm. The operational sphere might then be reached with artificial systems that predominantly function on the basis of determined (but non-deterministic) algorithms. Finally, the artificial systems that are predominantly structured by non-determined (and thereby non-deterministic) algorithms are to be located in the functional realm. Let us consider a few examples to elaborate on this.

The artificial system Kismet that Wallach and Allen define as an operational AMA possesses a rudimentary ability to communicate (1), since it can babble with simple noises and words. Judgment (3)—if one is willing to call Kismet's behavior reasonable at all—is barely recognizable in its responses to very simple questions. However, in favor of its limited capacities for judgment, a minimal—but in its narrowness maybe even more reliable (because not manipulable)—trustworthiness (3.2) might be guaranteed, because in its limitedness Kismet is very predictable. The biggest challenge in regarding Kismet as an operational responsible artificial system is clearly its autonomy (2), since Kismet's knowledge (2.1), historicity (2.2), personhood (2.3), and scope of influence (2.4) are very limited. In its rudimentary mobility, Kismet can autonomously move its ears, eyes, lips, and head and responds to external stimuli such as voice. To conclude, Kismet is, as Wallach and Allen (2009) suggest, still completely in the operators' and users' control; it does not artificially learn, and its algorithms allow only for deterministic results. To call Kismet responsible might appear comparable to calling an infant or some animals responsible. However, in contrast to a hammer hitting one's thumb or the sun melting candle wax (as examples for a metaphorical understanding of the ascription of responsibility), Kismet might—like infants and animals—open up room for debate on ascribing responsibility to artificial systems like it, although this room for debate appears to be understandably small.

Cog, the first robot that can interact with its surroundings due to its embodiment, might pass as an example of a weak functional responsible agent, since its ability to communicate (1) as well as judgment (3) has been improved over that of Kismet. Even more importantly Cog's overall autonomy (2) has evolved, since it includes an "unsupervised learning algorithm" (Brooks et al. 1999, 70). For instance, after running through numerous trial-and-error-attempts to propel a toy car forward by gently pushing it, Cog realizes that the car moves only when being pushed from the front or from behind, not from the side. Cog has not been programmed to solve the task in this manner but learns from experience. Maybe its limited capacity to learn allows us to understand it as a weak functional agent or at least as a very strong case for an operational ascription of responsibility. Calling Cog responsible might be comparable to (and from an explicatory standpoint as useful as) ascribing responsibility to a very young child. In light of these reflections, the above-mentioned medical advisory system MedEthEx, which Wallach and Allen identify as a rare case of functional AMA, might indeed pass for an even better example of a functional responsible agent than Cog, since its capacities for judgment (3) as well as its knowledge (2.1) and overall autonomy (2) have dramatically improved.

With the help of these examples, we can now identify autonomous driving systems as operational rather than functional artificial agents. Whereas their communicative (1) and judgment (3) skills are as developed as Cog's capabilities or even more so, their overall autonomy (2) is still kept within tight limits due to their lack of learning and non-determined (non-deterministic) algorithms. Given this first conclusion, responsibility with regard to autonomous driving systems then has to be distributed through a responsibility network and cannot be ascribed primarily to the artificial systems themselves. Autonomous driving systems are not able to assume full (or even just the main) moral and legal responsibility for their actions, because they are not artificial moral agents in a functional sense. For the time being, they do not supersede the level of operational morality, and therefore we have to look elsewhere within the responsibility network to find an answer to the question of (moral) responsibility.

In complementing Darwall's approach of four types of autonomy with Wallach and Allen's approach of functional equivalence, for the purposes of this chapter we draw a clear line between full-blown (human) agency and artificial (i.e., operational and functional) agency. While human agents have all four types of autonomy, intelligent machines may possess only rational and agential autonomy in a functionally equivalent way for the near future. As far as certain domains of responsibility are concerned, an artificial system can be called autonomous as soon as it meets this criterion of functional morality.

3.3 Hybrid Systems as Part of the Responsibility Network

If the self-driving car itself cannot be the only subject of responsibility in the relevant moral situations, as we argued in the preceding section, we have to identify other agents that can assume this position. Within a responsibility network that consists of programmers, manufacturers, engineers, operators, artificial systems, etc., the hybrid system that is composed of human operators and the artificial driving system seems to be the next natural choice to turn to. In this special case of collective responsibility, we have to assume a shared responsibility (Sombetzki 2014), since every party in the context in question that possesses the capabilities of being called responsible, even if only to a lesser degree, is to be called at least partially responsible. In cases of human–machine interaction, however, it appears *prima facie* unclear who we can identify as the responsible subject(s). Without the involvement of artificial systems, the classical answer at hand would address only human beings as (individually or collectively) responsible. But as we discussed in the preceding section, some complex artificial systems may possess capacities in a functional equivalent way, such that they might achieve operational or functional morality and thereby accept at least some share of the distributed responsibility. Since we cannot ascribe the full responsibility to the artificial agent alone, we might think about distributing responsibility within the hybrid system of driver and autonomous car.

In general, hybrid systems are a special example of human–machine interaction characterized by a set of collaborating subsystems that are (1) clearly distinguishable (Knoll 2008), (2) yet still autonomous (Hubig 2008, 10), and (3) consist of categorically different agents (Sombetzki 2016; Weyer 2005, 9).

Beginning with the third prerequisite, categorical difference between agents means that the nature of their agency differs, in human–machine interactions especially with regard to different degrees of autonomy. The second prerequisite concerns the autonomy of the different subsystems. In the preceding section, we discussed the autonomy and responsibility of artificial agents and reached the conclusion that they could have a functional equivalent to autonomy, although in the immediate future they will probably not be able to reach a relevant level of "functional morality," let alone a "full-blown" autonomy that is characteristic of human beings.

With regard to the first criterion, it follows from the prerequisite of autonomy that the single subsystems are clearly distinguishable. Together they form a new agent, however, a "plural subject" that is constituted by a common goal (Gilbert 1990, 7). This goal is common knowledge among the various subsystems of the hybrid system understood as a plural subject, which means that all agents have formed intentions to be part of this plural subject and to pursue the common goal. In the case of morally responsible artificial agents as part of hybrid systems, this can also be achieved in a functional way, i.e., by algorithmic constraints and conditions. In this sense, the autonomous car "knows" that it is the common goal to get safely from *A* to *B*, and it will form intentions and sub-plans accordingly (Bratman 1999, 121). We will come back to that point later.

Autonomous driving systems fulfill the given prerequisites for hybrid systems since they consist of a set of collaborating but clearly distinguishable subsystems that are categorically different: the car and the driver. Each subsystem is at least operationally autonomous, and together they form a plural subject with the common goal of getting safely from *A* to *B* in the most efficient way possible. This hybrid system can be part of a responsibility network including further actors such as the manufacturers and programmers. In the following section, we will evaluate to the extent to which moral responsibility can be assigned to this hybrid system.

3.4 Ascribing Responsibility to Autonomous Driving Systems and Operators

Within the realm of fully automated driving, there are only a few morally relevant situations a fully autonomous self-driving car can get into.[3] Assuming that it maintains a normal driving routine at all times—i.e., it always adheres to the traffic rules, never speeds or tailgates, and never drives recklessly in any other way—accidents that lie within the responsibility of the car seem to be mostly errors in design, faulty material, mistakes in hard- and software, programming or construction lapses, etc. (Lin 2016). Those are mainly questions of legal liability on the part of the manufacturer or, perhaps in rare cases, negligence questions of moral and legal responsibility on the part of specific engineers or programmers. As the literature on autonomous vehicles shows, however, one can conceive of special accident situations in which the car is computationally capable of calculating the likely outcome in milliseconds and acting according to a set plan (Goodall 2014; Hevelke and Nida-Rümelin 2015; Lin 2015). For instance, three schoolchildren could suddenly jump out on the street in front of the car (maybe chasing after a ball), which is capable of assessing that it cannot brake in time to avoid a fatal collision. It might, however, swerve into oncoming traffic and hit a big truck or swerve to the right and go through the bridge railing down into a canyon. While in the first scenario the car would likely kill the kids or seriously injure them, in the second and third scenarios it would almost certainly kill the driver.

These scenarios work much like trolley case dilemmas (Foot 1967), as they usually entail a decision of great moral importance (death or serious injury of at least one person), the question of responsibility by acting or omitting (not addressing those issues will most likely result in a standard reaction of the car, e.g., braking and thereby selecting one of the options), as well as enough time beforehand to contemplate the desired outcome. This is what essentially separates these types of dilemmas, where an autonomous car has the time and capacity to assess the situation thoroughly and react according to plan, from the same situations nowadays, where a human driver mostly reacts on reflex (Lin 2015). Most importantly however, there seems to be no correct answer to those dilemmas, which was the initial reason Philippa Foot came up with these trolley cases.

For example, it is notoriously difficult to calculate a utility function for everyone involved and promote the outcome with the highest net utility, as classical utilitarianism would have it. There are just too many factors to take into account for a regular autonomous car in such a situation: how many persons are how likely to be how seriously injured with how much potential quality of life left, thus creating how much grief in how many relatives, just to name a few factors. Whether to run over an 80-year-old woman to save an 8-year-old girl is no longer a clear-cut decision when we take into account that the girl could be fatally ill, while the woman could live happily for another twenty years. In addition, some choices will set perverse incentives, as in the case where the car always hits a motorcyclist with a helmet over one without (Goodall 2014). Would this be common knowledge, it might lead bikers to drive more often without a helmet, thereby making the streets in essence less safe instead of safer.

Putting all these worries aside, there seems to be a principal counterargument against such consequentialist mathematics: As John Taurek has famously argued, it is far from clear that, all else being equal, the numbers should count in such a scenario as "suffering is not additive in this way" (1977, 308). What is at stake in those circumstances is losing something of great value (life or limb) to a specific person; therefore, it makes no sense to impartially add up the loss: "His loss means something to me only, or chiefly, because of what it means to him. It is the loss to the individual that matters to me, not the loss of the individual" (Taurek 1977, 307).

If we are right that so far nobody has come up with a correct answer to these dilemmas that will satisfy all our typical moral intuitions—and the ongoing philosophical discussions about those cases are a good indicator that the matter has not been settled (Lin 2014)—one has to reconsider a proposal to let the automotive company make this decision in the driver's (or passenger's) stead. Such a proposal would amount to accepting the manufacturer as a moral authority regarding these dilemmas. However, in order to count as a legitimate authority for those subjected to it (i.e., the driver/passengers), according to Joseph Raz the authority has to provide them with "content-independent reasons" to comply with its directives (1986, 35). More importantly these reasons must help the "alleged subject to likely better comply with reasons that apply to him" (53), i.e., in the case at hand the driver's intentions based on a variety of beliefs and desires—some of them moral.

Since there is—as we have concluded—no general agreement on the moral beliefs in question, the manufacturer in all likelihood cannot help those subjected to its directives to better comply with the reasons that apply to them in the sense of moral convictions that they already entertain. This is because the authority simply does not know which moral convictions certain subjects hold. Its moral authority cannot therefore be regarded as legitimate.[4] If this is true, it would be wrong to superimpose a fixed response of the autonomous car on the driver/passengers by the automotive company, although this might not change the legal responsibility (in the sense of liability) of the company (Lin 2014). As the assignment of responsibility is not exclusive (cf. section 3.1), the ascription of different degrees of moral, legal, political, and other types of responsibility to different subjects is best expressed in a responsibility network that we only roughly sketch here.

In terms of the responsibility network, it would unduly override the moral and personal autonomy of the driver if the manufacturer were responsible for answering these moral questions. The engineers and programmers are responsible for the standard driving procedures, as engineers and programmers in manually driven cars are responsible for the proper functioning and safety of the car. As long as we can assign a driver to an autonomous car, even though she might not be driving at all, she has to take responsibility for the moral decisions regarding car operation. In this vein, a self-driving train would be a different matter, since there is no clear designated driver whose moral convictions could be taken as imperative.

As we argued in the preceding section, the autonomous car forms a hybrid system in the sense that it constitutes a plural subject with a common goal and shared responsibility. The shared moral responsibility in this hybrid system is divided between artificial system and operator in such a way that the car itself is—depending on its level of autonomy and ethical sensitivity—for the time being mainly responsible for maintaining safe standard driving operations. As long as there is something like a driver in autonomous cars, however, she will have to bear the responsibility for making the morally relevant decisions that are not covered by traffic rules, as part of the hybrid system. As with any ethical decision that a person has to make in her everyday life, it will often be the case that she is not well informed, thus unable to make a decision based on informed consent. Yet since there is no authority that knows beforehand which moral convictions she holds, no authority can help her in advance to better comply with the reasons she already has for action. In this case it would be paternalistic in the strong sense (Dworkin 2016) to ignore her moral and personal autonomy and entrust these decisions to the manufacturer, who in the framework of the responsibility network is mainly responsible for ensuring a safe work flow, adherence to traffic regulations, general active and passive safety, etc.

In this respect, we opt for a non-consequentialist ethical approach to the above-mentioned dilemma situations that take seriously the moral and personal autonomy of the driver and thereby her capacity for responsibility in the sense mentioned in section 3.1. Since the car itself will most likely not reach full-blown morality for a very long time and cannot therefore be fully morally responsible, these decisions will have to remain with human agents until further notice, whether the driver or arguably society as a whole. However, as artificial systems become more capable of functional morality, they will be increasingly able to conduct themselves according to the moral principles of the morally responsible agent and thereby become better, step by step, at applying those principles to real road situations.

As long as the public deliberation about how to cope with these dilemma situations has not reached an informed consensus that can serve as a basis for actual lawmaking decisions, the responsibility for these decisions rests with the driver. Since these dilemma situations do not allow for on-the-fly decisions, the driver will have to make them beforehand. This means that the driver will have to fill out a moral profile of some sort, maybe in the form of a questionnaire, maybe in the sense of a setup program much as with today's electronic devices. For convenience, it seems plausible that these moral settings can be saved to a sort of electronic identification device, like an electronic key or the driver's smartphone, assuming that issues of data security can be solved. From these conclusions it follows that car manufacturers, and especially the IT departments that occupy themselves with programming the automated driving mechanism, will have to undergo some ethical training in order to identify potentially morally relevant situations and develop interfaces that reliably pick up the moral principles and convictions of the driver. On the other hand, a general societal discourse is needed in order to raise awareness of these moral dilemma situations and prepare drivers for the responsibility they bear of making moral choices that can have a huge impact on themselves, their co-passengers, and other traffic participants.

3.5 Conclusion

On the basis of an etymological definition of the traditional understanding of responsibility, we have argued that an autonomous car cannot make moral decisions completely on its own in the immediate future. Even if it had the necessary capacities for being held responsible (communication, overall autonomy, judgment) it is unclear which normative criteria (in the sense of moral principles) it should follow. Rather, responsibility is distributed throughout the responsibility network that comprises the engineers, programmers, owner, driver, and artificial driving system itself. However, in morally relevant dilemma situations, only the agents directly involved, i.e., the driving system and the driver as a hybrid system, should be in the position to morally assess these situations and respond to them accordingly. Otherwise their autonomy would be compromised. As the artificial system lacks moral and personal autonomy and is therefore not capable of making the relevant moral decisions in certain dilemma situations, they will, for the time being, remain with the driver. Leaving them with the manufacturer would unduly override the driver's moral and personal autonomy, aside from the fact that it is dubious whether anyone would buy such a car. On the other hand, the responsibility of the engineering complex (designers, engineers, programmers) of the responsibility network is to provide an interface that gives the driver the ultimate choice over how the car should handle those dilemma situations.

In essence, we are proposing a non-consequentialist response to the challenges autonomous driving might face on a moral level. The driver as the source of all the car's actions is therefore the principal moral agent within the hybrid system that is constituted by car and driver. While the car is responsible for selecting the right route, always traveling at safe speeds, preventing accidents at all costs, and so on, the driver is morally responsible for the car's evasive decisions in dilemma cases. Since her moral principles and convictions cannot be assessed during such situations, they have to be determined beforehand, possibly with a quick oral questionnaire, much like today's setup routines.

Notes

1. In this chapter we focus mainly on moral responsibility.
2. Technically this argument applies to humans as well, all the more to animals (Nagel 1974). In general, we are willing to *prima facie* grant capacities like reason, consciousness, and free will to other individuals. However, there is no guarantee that this assumption really holds (Coeckelbergh 2014, 63).
3. For the purpose of this section we concentrate on fully autonomous driving systems only.
4. Since this chapter focuses on moral responsibility, and therefore moral authority, we cannot go into details of political authority. However, this conclusion might be in the same way applicable to the legal system as an authority, whose (moral) legitimacy is in question. State institutions cannot know the subject's moral beliefs in the same way as manufacturers, and therefore would also not have legitimate authority to issue legal directives with regard to these trolley problems.

   There are, on the other hand, different ways to legitimize political authority, especially if its directives are the result of a legal democratic process based on informed consent following a public deliberation where everyone can voice worries and form opinions. One could, e.g., claim that under the "circumstances of politics" (Waldron 1999, 7) democratic decisions based on the equal regard for all persons trump one person's moral autonomy, because otherwise the capacity of all others for practical reasoning would be ignored or would have less weight (Christiano 1996, 88). In addition, by engaging in political deliberation and action, a person participates in forming an ethical self-understanding of a political community, exercising her political autonomy, which is the social flip side of moral autonomy (Habermas 1998, 134).

Works Cited

Anderson, Susan, Michael Anderson, and Chris Armen. 2006. "MedEthEx: A Prototype Medical Ethics Advisor." In *Proceedings of the Eighteenth Conference on Innovative Applications of Artificial Intelligence*, 1759–65. https://www.aaai.org/Papers/AAAI/2006/AAAI06-292.pdf.

Bratman, Michael. 1999. *Faces of Intention: Selected Essays on Intention and Agency*. Cambridge: Cambridge University Press.

Brooks, Rodney A., Cynthia Breazeal, Matthew Marjanović, Brian Scasselatti, and Matthew M. Williamson. 1999. "The Cog Project: Building a Humanoid Robot." In *Computation for Metaphors, Analogy, and Agents*, edited by Chrystopher Nehaniv, 52–87. Heidelberg: Springer.

Christiano, Thomas. 1996. *The Rule of the Many: Fundamental Issues in Democratic Theory*. Boulder, CO: Westview.

Coeckelbergh, Mark. 2014. "The Moral Standing of Machines: Towards a Relational and Non-Cartesian Moral Hermeneutics." *Philosophy and Technology* 27: 61–77.

Darwall, Stephen. 2006. "The Value of Autonomy and Autonomy of the Will." *Ethics* 116: 263–84.

Duff, R. A. 1998. "Responsibility." In *Routledge Encyclopedia of Philosophy*, edited by Edward Craig, 290–4. London: Routledge.

Dworkin, Gerald. 2016. "Paternalism." In *Stanford Encyclopedia of Philosophy*, June 19.http://plato.stanford.edu/entries/paternalism/.

Floridi, Luciano, and J. W. Sanders. 2004. "On the Morality of Artificial Agents." *Minds and Machines* 14: 349–79.

Foot, Philippa. 1967. "Moral Beliefs." In *Theories of Ethics*, edited by Philippa Foot, 83–100. Oxford: Oxford University Press.

Frankfurt, Harry. 1971. "Freedom of the Will and the Concept of a Person." *Journal of Philosophy* 68 (1): 5–20.

Gilbert, Margaret. 1990. "Walking Together: A Paradigmatic Social Phenomenon." *Midwest Studies in Philosophy* 15: 1–14.

Goodall, Noah. 2014. "Machine Ethics and Automated Vehicles." In *Road Vehicle Automation*, edited by Gereon Meyer and Sven Beiker, 93–102. Lecture Notes in Mobility. Cham: Springer.

Habermas, Jürgen. 1998. *Faktizität und Geltung*. Frankfurt: Suhrkamp.

Hevelke, Alexander and Julian Nida-Rümelin. 2015. "Intelligente Autos im Dilemma." *Spektrum der Wissenschaft* (10): 82–5.

Hubig, Christoph. 2008. "Mensch-Maschine-Interaktion in hybriden Systemen." In *Maschinen, die unsere Brüder werden: Mensch-Maschine-Interaktion in hybriden Systemen*, edited by Christoph Hubig and Peter Koslowski, 9–17. Munich: Wilhelm Fink.

Kallen, H. M. 1942. "Responsibility." *Ethics* 52 (3): 350–76.

Knoll, Peter M. 2008. "Prädikative Fahrassistenzsysteme: Bevormundung des Fahrers oder realer Kundennutzen?" In *Maschinen, die unsere Brüder werden*, edited by Christoph Hubig and Peter Koslowski, 159–71. Munich: Wilhelm Fink.

Lenk, Hans and Matthias Maring. 1995. "Wer soll Verantwortung tragen? Probleme der Verantwortungsverteilung in komplexen (soziotechnischen-sozioökonomischen) Systemen." In *Verantwortung. Prinzip oder Problem?*, edited by Kurt Bayertz, 241–86. Darmstadt: Wissenschaftliche Buchgesellschaft.

Lin, Patrick. 2014. "Here's a Terrible Idea: Robot Cars with Adjustable Ethics Settings." *Wired*, August 18. http://www.wired.com/2014/08/heres-a-terrible-idea-robot-cars-with-adjustable-ethics-settings/.

Lin, Patrick. 2015. "Why Ethics Matters for Autonomous Cars." In *Autonomes Fahren*, edited by M. Maurer, C. Gerdes, B. Lenz, and H. Winner, 69–86. Berlin: Springer.

Lin, Patrick. 2016. "Is Tesla Responsible for the Deadly Crash on Auto-Pilot? Maybe." *Forbes*, July 1. http://www.forbes.com/sites/patricklin/2016/07/01/is-tesla-responsible-for-the-deadly-crash-on-auto-pilot-maybe/.

Misselhorn, Catrin. 2013. "Robots as Moral Agents." In *Ethics in Science and Society: German and Japanese Views*, edited by Frank Rövekamp and Friederike Bosse, 30–42. Munich: Iudicum.

Nagel, Thomas. 1974. "What Is It Like to Be a Bat?" *Philosophical Review* 83 (4): 435–50.

Neuhäuser, Christian. 2015. "Some Sceptical Remarks Regarding Robot Responsibility and a Way Forward." In *Collective Agency and Cooperation in Natural and Artificial Systems: Explanation, Implementation and Simulation*, edited by Catrin Misselhorn, 131–46. London: Springer.

Nida-Rümelin, Julian. 2007. "Politische Verantwortung." In *Staat ohne Verantwortung? Zum Wandel der Aufgaben von Staat und Politik*, edited by Ludger Heidbrink and Alfred Hirsch, 55–85. Frankfurt: Campus.

Rammert, Werner. 2004. "Technik als verteilte Aktion: Wie technisches Wirken als Agentur in hybriden Aktionszusammenhängen gedeutet werden kann." In *Techik—System—Verantwortung*, edited by Klaus Kornwachs, 219–31. Munich: LIT.

Rawls, John. 2001. *Justice as Fairness: A Restatement.*2d ed. Cambridge, MA: Belknap Press.

Raz, Joseph. 1986. *The Morality of Freedom*. Oxford: Oxford University Press.

Searle, John R. 1980. "Minds, Brains and Programs." *Behavioral and Brain Sciences* 3 (3): 417.

Sombetzki, Janina. 2014. *Verantwortung als Begriff, Fähigkeit, Aufgabe: Eine Drei-Ebenen-Analyse*. Wiesbaden: Springer.

Sombetzki, Janina. 2016. "Roboterethik: Ein kritischer Überblick." In *Zur Zukunft der Bereichsethiken. Herausforderungen durch die Ökonomisierung der Welt*, edited by Matthias Maring, 355–79. ZTWE-Reihe Band 8. Karlsruhe: KIT Scientific.

Taurek, John. 1977. "Should the Numbers Count?" *Philosophy and Public Affairs* 6 (4): 293–316.

Turing, Alan M. 1950. "Computing Machinery and Intelligence." *Mind* 59 (236): 433–60.

Waldron, Jeremy. 1999. *Law and Disagreement*. Oxford: Clarendon Press.

Wallace, R. J. 1994. *Responsibility and the Moral Sentiments.* Cambridge, MA: Harvard University Press. http://www.gbv.de/dms/bowker/toc/9780674766228.pdf.

Wallach, Wendell and Colin Allen. 2009. *Moral Machines: Teaching Robots Right from Wrong.* Oxford: Oxford University Press.

Werner, Micha H. 2006. "Verantwortung." In *Handbuch Ethik*, edited by Marcus Düwell, Christoph Hübenthal, and Micha H. Werner, 541–48. Stuttgart: Metzler.

Weyer, Johannes. 2005. "Creating Order in Hybrid Systems: Reflexions on the Interaction of Man and Smart Machines." Arbeitspapier Nr. 7, Universität Dortmund. http://www.ssoar.info/ssoar/bitstream/handle/document/10974/ssoar-2005-weyer_et_al-creating_order_in_hybrid_systems.pdf?sequence=1.

4 IMPUTING DRIVERHOOD

APPLYING A REASONABLE DRIVER STANDARD TO ACCIDENTS CAUSED BY AUTONOMOUS VEHICLES

Jeffrey K. Gurney

The robotics revolution has given rise to an important question: Who should be responsible for harm caused by robots? Because society cannot meaningfully hold robots accountable for their actions, legislatures and courts need to determine which party or parties will be responsible for robotic accidents. Furthermore, as these governmental entities determine who will be held responsible for such accidents, they must also determine how to properly compensate the injured parties. If courts and legislatures do not adequately resolve the compensation issue, robot producers may incur unexpected and excessive costs, which would disincentivize investment. On the other hand, if victims are not adequately compensated, such producers would likely face a backlash from injured parties. This chapter examines these issues within the realm of autonomous vehicles.

Autonomous vehicles are expected to revolutionize travel and society within decades. These vehicles are projected to provide immense savings through accident prevention, emission reduction, and productivity increases (Anderson et al. 2016). They will also provide numerous other societal benefits. For example, autonomous vehicles will create a means of transportation for those who currently cannot drive an automobile, such as disabled persons.

Despite the projected ability of these vehicles to prevent accidents, technology is not perfect, and defects or computer errors in autonomous vehicles will cause accidents. Section 4.1 of this chapter briefly discusses why autonomous vehicle manufacturers should be liable when defects or errors cause accidents. Section 4.2 examines whether courts should use products liability to impose liability manufacturers and concludes that products liability is too burdensome and administratively difficult to apply to everyday accidents. Section 4.3 offers two less burdensome alternatives and concludes that autonomous vehicle manufacturers should be treated as drivers of the vehicles they manufacture for purposes for determining liability of harm.

4.1 Manufacturers Should Be Legally Responsible for Accidents Caused by Their Autonomous Vehicles

Many parties could be responsible for accidents caused by autonomous vehicles. These parties include users, car owners, vehicle manufacturers, component manufacturers, hackers, and governmental bodies.[1] Out of the potential defendants, users and car manufacturers are the best candidates for tort liability.

At its core, tort liability is concerned with corrective justice (Honoré 1995). Corrective justice, rooted in Aristotelian principles, values the quality of each person and imposes a duty on individual actors to repair harm they wrongfully cause (Wright 1995). Corrective justice has a causal connection requirement: the defendant's wrongful conduct must have caused the plaintiff's harm (Honoré 1995). Because parties typically cannot be "repaired" back to their original physical conditions, tort law imposes a duty to compensate the persons harmed (Honoré 1995).

Tort law is also concerned with other important principles, such as prevention of injuries and fairness (Hubbard and Felix 1997). By imposing duties—and, relatedly, liability—on the tortfeasor, lawmakers hope to deter that person and others from committing the same breach of duty in the future (Hubbard and Felix 1997). The principle of fairness promotes equal treatment and proportionality of damages to the moral culpability of the wrongdoing (Hubbard and Felix 1997).

These principles underlie tort liability for accidents involving traditional vehicles. More than 90% of today's car accidents are caused by driver error (Schroll 2015). The driver who commits the error, and thereby causes the accident, is usually at fault (Anderson et al. 2016). When a driver causes an accident due to a wrongful error, imposing liability on that driver requires him to internalize the cost of wrongful action and incentivizes due care in the future. However, when the accident results from some other phenomenon, such as a defect in one of the vehicles, neither driver is responsible for the accident. Therefore, a traditional driver is liable when the driver himself is at fault for causing the harm (Anderson et al. 2016).

This simple fact changes when the vehicle drives itself. No longer will the person sitting behind the steering wheel be driving the vehicle. The user of an autonomous vehicle will not control the operations of the vehicle; indeed, one scholar has described the user as serving no different role than a "potted plant" (Vladeck 2014). Autonomous vehicles are projected to be controlled by a complex computer system that uses radar, laser, lidar, ultrasonic sensors, video cameras, global positioning systems, and maps (Duffy and Hopkins 2013). Most manufacturers intend to allow users to take control of their vehicles and become drivers when they so desire or when necessary due to the shortcomings of the technology (Gurney 2015–16). Google, however, is developing its autonomous vehicles without steering wheels, accelerators, or brake pedals, so that users do not have the opportunity to drive (Gurney 2015–16). Based on these vehicles' expected ability to navigate safely without human input, manufacturers are projected to market and sell these vehicles to consumers as a means to allow them to engage in activities other than driving while in their vehicles (Urmson 2012).

Because of the shift in control of the operation of the vehicle from the driver to the computer system, responsibility for accidents should shift from the driver to this system.[2] Given the current state of technology, society cannot meaningfully hold a computer system responsible for accidents it causes. Thus, responsibility for the accident will likely fall on the party who programs the computer system: the car manufacturer.[3] This shift in responsibility is not only dependent on the shift in control; it is also dependent on manufacturers marketing these vehicles as a means for drivers to engage in behavior other than paying attention to the road. When an autonomous vehicle manufacturer's marketing campaign indicates that users no longer have to pay attention to the road, that manufacturer can hardly complain when it is ultimately liable for the accidents caused by its vehicles.

4.2 Products Liability

Because the car manufacturer should be legally responsible when a defect or error in its computer program causes an accident, society will need to decide how to impose financial responsibility on the manufacturer. Since this liability would be imposed on a product manufacturer for harm caused by its product, products liability will be the likely choice.

Today, however, most car accidents result from driver error and do not involve products liability (Zohn 2015). Rather, liability for accidents caused by the driver are governed by negligence principles (Shroll 2015). Negligence is a tort doctrine that holds people liable for acting unreasonably under the circumstances (Anderson et al. 2009). To prove a negligence claim, the plaintiff must show (1) a duty owed by the defendant to the plaintiff; (2) a breach of that duty by the defendant; (3) a causal link between the defendant's breach and the plaintiff's harm; and (4) damages to the plaintiff (Owen and Davis 2016). In the realm of automobile accidents, insurance companies have developed informal rules that govern responsibility for such accidents (Anderson et al. 2016, 113). When insurance companies are unable to informally determine the at-fault party and the amount of damage is substantial, a lawsuit will likely ensue. Courts have developed well-established legal rules for automobile accidents, making resolution of "wreck cases" rather straightforward.

However, a wreck case becomes a complicated legal matter when a defect in the vehicle caused the accident (Anderson et al. 2016, 116). The basic negligence case is transformed, in part, into a products liability case against the manufacturer of the automobile.

Broadly speaking, products liability is a doctrine that imposes liability on a product manufacturer for harm caused by a defect in its product (Owen and Davis 2016). Three principal products liability doctrines are available to litigants who wish to sue products manufacturers: (1) manufacturing defect; (2) design defect; and (3) warning defect (Owen and Davis 2016). A manufacturing defect occurs when a product fails to meet the manufacturer's specifications (Owen and Davis 2016). In such a case, the plaintiff prevails simply by introducing proof that a non-conformity in the product caused the accident. With regard to defective designs, two distinct theories are used by litigants: the consumer expectations test and the more popular risk-utility test (Anderson et al. 2009).

Under the consumer expectations test, a product is defective if it is unreasonably dangerous—that is, if the dangers the product presents are beyond the contemplation of the consumer (*Restatement Second*). Many courts do not apply the consumer expectations test, and given the complexity of autonomous vehicles, courts that still use this test may decline to do so in the context of autonomous vehicles (Garza 2012). Instead, courts will likely use the risk-utility test. Under this test, a product "is defective in design when the foreseeable risks of harm posed by the product could have been reduced or avoided by the adoption of a reasonable alternative design by the seller . . . and the omission of the alternative design renders the product not reasonably safe" (*Restatement Third*). To prevail under this theory, a plaintiff needs to show a reasonable alternative design that would have prevented the accident. Lastly, a warning defect occurs when a manufacturer fails to inform purchasers of hidden dangers or fails to inform consumers how to safely use its products (*Restatement Third*).

In addition to those theories of product defectiveness, a lesser-used theory, the malfunction doctrine, may also come into play here. Under the malfunction doctrine, "a plaintiff must prove that: '(1) the product malfunctioned, (2) the malfunction occurred during proper use, and (3) the product had not been altered or misused in a manner that probably caused the malfunction'" (Owen

2002). The malfunction doctrine would allow the plaintiff to use the accident itself as proof of the defect.

Litigants can use these doctrines to recover from autonomous vehicle manufacturers for accidents caused by their vehicles. Autonomous vehicles may cause an accident due to a hardware failure, design failure, or a software error. The majority of these accidents are expected to result from software errors or, more specifically, a defect in the computer's algorithms. These software defect cases are unlikely to implicate warning defects. As for the traditional manufacturing defect theory, courts have routinely refused to apply this theory to software defects (Gurney 2013). The malfunction doctrine would be the ideal products liability doctrine—as I have thoroughly discussed elsewhere (Gurney 2013)—to use for these defects due to the low transaction costs involved in proving this claim. However, the malfunction doctrine suffers from certain practical limitations that hinder its applicability to autonomous vehicle cases. Many courts refuse to use this theory, and the courts that do use it generally apply it only in unique situations (Gurney 2013). This leaves a single remaining theory for accidents caused by software defects: the design defect theory—likely the risk-utility test.

Risk-utility test cases are complex and require many expert witnesses, making design defect claims expensive to prove (Gurney 2013; Vladeck 2014; Glancy 2015). As one scholar acknowledged, "[T]he nature of the evidence (such as algorithms and sensor data) and of experts (such as automated systems and robotics engineers) [is] likely to make such litigation especially challenging and complex technologically" (Glancy 2015).

This has a major implication that, for the most part, has been overlooked: using the design defect theory to recover damages for automobile accidents would transform an established, straightforward area of the law (car wrecks) into a complicated and costly area of law (products liability).[4] A plaintiff would need multiple experts to recover on the basis of a defect in the algorithm. This negative implication may impact even the most straightforward autonomous vehicle accidents.

Consider two different accidents. In the first accident, Ken is driving a traditional vehicle. He falls asleep, causing his vehicle to drift into a lane of oncoming traffic and strike Elaine's vehicle. Here, liability could be resolved simply: Ken would be responsible; his liability insurer would likely pay up to his policy limits; and a lawsuit would be averted. Even if the insurer did not pay, the case could be decided easily in court. Ken had duties to pay attention to the road and to drive within his own lane; he breached those duties when he fell asleep and his vehicle drifted into the oncoming traffic lane; his breach caused Elaine's harm; and Elaine suffered damages.

In the second accident, Ken owns an autonomous vehicle that was produced by ABC Manufacturing. Ken purchased the vehicle after seeing an advertisement by ABC that claimed its autonomous vehicles allow occupants to engage in activities other than watching the road. During his commute home after a long day at work, Ken takes a nap; while he is sleeping, his autonomous vehicle drifts into the lane of oncoming traffic and strikes Elaine's vehicle. Only minor injuries and minor property damage occur.

In the latter example, Ken was arguably not negligent. If he was not negligent, Elaine would need to recover from ABC Manufacturing, which would be far more difficult than recovering from Ken. In a products liability case, Elaine could not use the fact that the car caused the harm as proof that the manufacturer should be responsible. Instead, Elaine would need to show that ABC Manufacturing was negligent in producing the car, or she would need to introduce evidence of a manufacturing or design defect. Under the theory of negligence, a manufacturer has a "duty to exercise reasonable care to refrain from selling products that contain unreasonable risks of harm" (Owen and Davis 2016). This duty requires only reasonable care, not perfect care, and Elaine would need to show that a defect caused the harm and that the defect was caused by the negligence of the manufacturer.[5] It is unlikely that the accident resulted from a manufacturing defect. Thus, Elaine would need to engage in an exceedingly complicated and costly endeavor to show that the algorithm was defective.

But why should Elaine have to use the risk-utility test to show that the accident resulted from a design defect in the algorithm? She was injured because the autonomous vehicle did not operate properly: it crossed into the wrong lane and injured her. A vehicle that did not have a defective algorithm would likely not cross into the lane of oncoming traffic. Thus, requiring her to use the risk-utility test to determine the defect in the algorithm is unnecessary and merely creates useless hurdles. Indeed, the transactional costs of a victim's burden of proof under the risk-utility test could be insurmountable. For example, if an autonomous vehicle causes a "fender bender" by bumping into a car and producing a small dent, why would a rational litigant—or, for that matter, a rational lawyer on a contingency fee—seek recovery if the costs of litigation would be more than the amount of recovery?

4.3 Cost-Effective Means of Imposing Liability

Given the high transaction costs of using the risk-utility test to prove liability for everyday accidents, the question becomes whether a different, cost-effective means to compensate victims of autonomous vehicle accidents exists.[6] Two potential solutions outside of products liability exist: an immunity and compensation system (ICS) and treating the manufacturer as the driver of the vehicle.

4.3.1 Immunity and Compensation System

The first solution is to provide immunity to potential defendants and create an alternative compensation system for victims. This system is based, in large part, on analogizing autonomous vehicles to vaccinations or nuclear power plants and then proposing congressional action for autonomous vehicles similar to the National Childhood Vaccination Injury Act of 1986 (NCVIA) (Brock 2015; Funkhouser 2013; Goodrich 2013; Marchant and Lindor 2012) or the Price-Anderson Act of 1954 (Colonna 2012; Marchant and Lindor 2012). A major benefit of an ICS is that it would greatly reduce the transactional costs associated with recovering damages for harm caused by autonomous vehicles.

Proponents of ICS most frequently justify this system on the ground that, without it, manufacturers may be deterred from producing autonomous vehicles due to fear of potential liability (Funkhouser 2013; Colonna 2012). Scholars have predicted that manufacturers will be less eager to develop these vehicles if liability is imposed on them. However, the fear of liability has not deterred any manufacturer from researching and developing these vehicles thus far, even though most scholars have argued the manufacturer should be responsible for autonomous vehicle accidents. In addition, executives from three such manufacturers—Google, Mercedes, and Volvo—have already indicated that their companies will accept financial liability for accidents caused by their vehicles in autonomous mode (Whitaker 2015). Volvo's CEO has directly stated that "Volvo will accept full liability whenever one [of] its cars is in autonomous mode" (Volvo 2015). Therefore, given that manufacturers are investing heavily in this technology, even though they are expected to be legally responsible, this deterrence argument is somewhat overstated.

Another benefit of an ICS is that it can remove uncertainty about which party will be liable. Simply put, companies work with other companies to develop their cars. For example, Google has received assistance from "Continental, Roush, Bosch, ZFLS, RCO, FRIMO, Prefix, and LG" while developing its vehicles (Harris 2015). General Motors and Lyft are working together to develop a fleet of self-driving cars (Davies 2016). In light of these partnerships, liability may not fall on any one company, and suing the nine members of the Google team may not be feasible (Marchant and Lindor 2012, 1328–9). An ICS clarifies this issue, and as a result of this clarification, neither courts nor companies waste time and resources determining who should ultimately be liable for an accident. In addition, an ICS clarifies liability for owners and users who could still be sued by victims of autonomous vehicle accidents.

Despite these benefits, Congress will likely not enact an ICS due to the current state of politics and the many policy objections of various lobbying groups (Hubbard 2014). These lobbying groups include the car manufacturers, consumer protection groups, trial lawyers, insurance companies, and trade unions. Given the interstate nature of vehicles, the only feasible ICS would be a federal ICS—and a federal ICS requires congressional action. The prospect of such legislation passing both chambers of Congress is bleak.

Even if the ICS could pass Congress, the legislation would have to address some serious concerns (Hubbard 2014). These concerns include "(1) the nature and level of benefits; (2) the types of injuries covered (for example, would non-economic damages like pain and suffering be included?); (3) the persons covered (would relationship interests like loss of consortium be covered?); (4) coordination with other benefit schemes like workers' compensation and social security; and (5) administration" (Hubbard 2014).

Funding and the impact of the funding selection on manufacturers' willingness to improve their vehicles is another concern. For example, the NCVIA is funded by users of vaccinations through a seventy-five-cent surcharge on covered vaccines (Funkhouser 2013). If an analogous tax is imposed on purchasers of autonomous vehicles, then the ICS would probably remove a major incentive for automakers to make safety improvements. Of course, automakers want to ensure their vehicles are safe for various reasons, such as customer loyalty and future sales. But liability directly imposed on manufacturers creates an even greater incentive to make safety improvements and penalizes less vigilant manufacturers (Hubbard and Felix 1997). Conceivably, the marketplace could weed out less vigilant manufacturers, but that view does not consider the realities of the autonomous vehicle marketplace. A person who purchases an autonomous vehicle from a manufacturer that is less vigilant in updating its computer programming could not, due to the vehicle's likely cost, purchase a new autonomous vehicle from a more vigilant manufacturer. In addition, an autonomous vehicle that is rendered a "lemon" by the careless manufacturer will lose most, if not all, of its value. Thus, consumers would likely be stuck with those vehicles.

Additionally, if the government imposes a flat surcharge, autonomous vehicles will not reflect their true cost—which could lead to fewer safe vehicles being on the road. For example, assume that Congress enacts an ICS, which imposes tax X on all purchases of autonomous vehicles to compensate victims. Assume further that there are only two producers of autonomous vehicles, A and B, and manufacturer A's vehicles are 25% safer than manufacturer B's vehicles. If liability is imposed on the manufacturer, then, everything else being equal, autonomous vehicles produced by manufacturer A should be, assuming 100% internalization of costs, 25% cheaper than autonomous vehicles produced by manufacturer B. Under this ICS, however, the *true costs* of the autonomous vehicles are not reflected: if everything else is the same between the two vehicles, they would be priced the same, even though manufacturer B's vehicles cost society 25% more than manufacturer A's vehicles.

For these reasons, an ICS should be a last resort, not a first resort. Many ICS-friendly scholars argue that these systems focus on the benefits autonomous vehicles are expected to provide, comparing those benefits to those provided by the vaccination and nuclear industries (Brock 2015; Funkhouser 2013; Goodrich 2013; Colonna 2012). They then assert that autonomous vehicle manufacturers should have immunity on the vast expected benefits and the manufacturers' fear of liability. Although these authors acknowledge the purpose of the legislative action, they fail to consider the unique inefficiencies facing the industries Congress has protected.

Historically, Congress has enacted these ICSs to stabilize otherwise unstable markets and foster market entry. Congress passed the NCVIA primarily to provide stability to the marketplace (Cantor 1995). The vaccination industry faced an exodus of producers due to large verdicts and the "unavailability of product liability insurance" (Cantor 1995). This caused an increase in the price of vaccinations and a decline in the national vaccine stockpile (Cantor 1995). Congress enacted the Price-Anderson Act to entice entry into the market, motivated by the nuclear industry's fear of extraordinary liability, in conjunction with the unavailability of liability insurers (Colonna 2012).

There is no indication that autonomous vehicle manufacturers will face extraordinary liability risk or an unavailability of insurance. Insurance companies are well equipped and well established in the automobile accident industry. Therefore, this market likely will not have the same need and market conditions, and without some indication of a market failure, any implementation of an ICS is premature.

4.3.2 Treating the Manufacturer as the Driver

As a more feasible alternative, lawmakers could treat the manufacturer of the vehicle as the "driver" of the car. If the manufacturer of the car is also the car's driver for liability purposes, then courts can simply substitute ABC Manufacturing for Ken's name in the traditional vehicle example in section 4.2. ABC Manufacturing had a duty to keep its vehicle within its lane, and it breached that duty when its vehicle crossed into the lane of oncoming traffic. That breach caused Elaine's harm. Treating the manufacturer as the driver makes what would have been a complicated matter under products liability a simple matter under negligence. The question is whether the law allows us to treat the manufacturer as the driver of the vehicle.

Driver is a broad enough term to include a corporation-driver, such as an autonomous vehicle manufacturer (Smith 2014). *Black's Law Dictionary* defines *driver* as "[s]omeone who steers and propels a vehicle" (Garner 2014). Many states utilize similar broad definitions; for example, Nebraska's definition of *drive* provides: "Drive shall mean to operate or be in the actual physical control of a motor vehicle."[7] Thus, one does not have to be in "actual physical control" of the vehicle to be a driver. Rather, the statute provides that mere operation can satisfy the definition. *Operate* is defined far more broadly than *drive*; at least one court has defined *operate* to include using any "mechanical or electrical agency" that sets the vehicle in motion and another court defines *operate* as navigating the vehicle (Smith 2014). The computer program of the autonomous vehicle is expected to operate all functions of traditional driving, including steering, accelerating, and braking. Therefore, from a definitional standpoint, nothing prevents manufacturers from being considered drivers of the vehicles, and it is evident that autonomous vehicles could have two drivers at the same time: the manufacturers who operate the vehicles and the users who are in actual physical control of the vehicles (Smith 2014).[8] Indeed, in response to a question from Google's autonomous vehicle team, the National Highway Traffic Safety Administration said it considers the self-driving system to be the "driver" of the vehicle (NHTSA 2016).

In addition to the human driver and the manufacturer-driver both falling within the definition of *driver*, these parties share the power to take corrective actions to prevent an accident from recurring.[9] The human driver can pay attention to the road and exercise more care while driving. If an accident occurs because the driver was using a cell phone, then in the future the driver may elect not to use a phone while driving to prevent this accident from recurring. The manufacturer-driver can fix whatever glitch in the algorithm caused the accident. If the accident was caused by a glitch in a map, then the manufacturer can fix the map so that the accident does not recur.

As discussed in section 4.2, design defects, manufacturing defects, and warning defects were not designed to resolve everyday accidents. Imposing products liability for autonomous vehicle accidents on the manufacturer leads to unnecessarily high and unwarranted transaction costs. A simple solution to this problem is to treat the manufacturer the same as any other driver; the manufacturer has a duty to drive the vehicle in the same manner as a reasonable driver (hereinafter, the "reasonable driver standard"). The reasonable driver standard requires the driver of the vehicle to "exercise[] the degree of attention, knowledge, intelligence, and judgment that society requires of its [drivers] for the protection of their own and of others' interests" (Garner 2014). A reasonable driver standard would avoid the logistical problems of using products liability to impose civil responsibility on manufacturers for harm caused by their cars.

A question arises as to whether the standard should be a "reasonable human driver" or a "reasonable autonomous vehicle driver." Given that autonomous vehicles do not suffer from human frailties,[10] and given that these vehicles professedly will have the ability to detect objects better than humans can, one would expect that (eventually) autonomous vehicles will be held to a higher standard than human drivers (Vladeck 2014). On the other hand, asking what a reasonable autonomous vehicle would have done in a similar situation may make the lawsuit far more complicated, at least during the introduction of these vehicles. Jurors can relate with a human driver and understand what a reasonable human driver could have done in a similar situation. Jurors may not, without expert testimony, be able to determine what a reasonable autonomous vehicle could have done under similar circumstances. A discussion regarding the relative merits of these standards is well beyond the scope of this chapter, which applies a reasonable human driver standard for purposes of simplicity.

In each accident case, the issue would be whether the autonomous vehicle failed to drive as a reasonable person would have driven in a similar situation. A reasonable driver standard could easily be applied to autonomous vehicle accidents. For example, just as a human driver has a duty to drive within the proper lane, an autonomous vehicle should also have a duty to drive within the proper lane. If an autonomous vehicle crosses over the center line and causes an accident, then the court should determine whether a reasonable person driving a vehicle would have crossed over the center line. If the answer to that question is no, then the manufacturer should be liable.

Liability could be determined by examining the "event data recorder" (more commonly referred to as a "black box") inside the autonomous vehicle (Bose 2015). Autonomous vehicles will likely be equipped with a form of a black box, and some state statutes governing autonomous vehicles mandate that the vehicles record pre-crash data (Bose 2015). These black boxes will provide courts—or, for that matter, insurance companies—the necessary information to determine the cause of the accident. Using that information, the court or the jury could determine whether the manufacturer "drove" the autonomous vehicle reasonably.

This reasonable driver standard is likely what society will expect lawmakers to apply. Furthermore, when certain manufacturers stated that they would accept responsibility for autonomous vehicle accidents in the future, those manufacturers may have been referring to a reasonable driver standard. Plus, those injured by autonomous vehicles will expect manufacturers to be liable in the same manner as a current driver. Therefore, although treating the manufacturer as the driver of the vehicle for purposes of imposing liability may initially seem radical, this liability system is probably in line with the expectations of injured parties, manufacturers, and society in general.[11]

4.4 Conclusion

In sum, those involved in developing and regulating robotics need to consider responsibility and liability as society proceeds into the robotic age. This chapter examined these issues in the autonomous vehicle context. This chapter asserted that the car manufacturer should be the responsible party for most accidents caused by autonomous vehicles and that products liability does not provide a cost-effective means of ensuring that the victims of autonomous vehicle accidents are adequately compensated. This chapter suggested two alternatives to products liability and concluded that, as computer systems replace humans as drivers of vehicles, there is no justifiable reason not to treat those who control the robots—and therefore drive the vehicle—any differently than society treats those who currently drive vehicles. In doing so, society can simplify legal responsibility for accidents caused by autonomous vehicles and ensure that people who are harmed have a cost-effective means of being made whole.

Notes

1. In my other publications, I have traditionally used the word *operator* to refer to the person who sits in the traditional driver's seat of the autonomous vehicle (Gurney 2013, 2015, 2015–16). My use of *operator* implies that the person controls the technology, which was never intended. Therefore, I have elected in this chapter to use the word *user*, which better represents the person's relationship to the autonomous vehicle.
2. On the other hand, user liability provides an interesting counterpoint to this chapter's thesis: because the user of an autonomous vehicle may—at least in certain situations—be responsible for the accident, perhaps the user is the best party to bear financial responsibility. A main point of this chapter is that preservation of the legal rules concerning automobile accidents is prudent, as such preservation ensures minimal transaction costs. This chapter concludes that the existing system can be preserved if the manufacturer of the autonomous vehicle is treated as the driver of that vehicle for purposes of imposing fault. Perhaps a far simpler alternative would be to keep the current insurance scheme and impose liability on the user. Of course, as this chapter concludes, vehicle manufacturer liability is a more sensible framework because user error will often *not* be the cause of autonomous vehicle accidents and because the user cannot prevent accidents from recurring.
3. For purposes of simplicity, this chapter assumes that the car manufacturer and the computer programmer are the same entity.
4. A few scholars have discussed this issue (Gurney 2013; Hubbard 2014).
5. Merrill v. Navegar, Inc., 28 P.3d 116, 124 (Cal. 2001).
6. This discussion matters only if manufacturers contest liability and thus require victims to prove fault. Insurance companies that represent the manufacturers may very well treat autonomous vehicle accidents in the same manner that they treat traditional vehicle accidents.
7. Neb. Rev. Stat. § 60-468.

8. This does not necessarily mean that ownership should always remain with the car manufacturer. A person can be a driver of a vehicle without owning the vehicle. Privacy rights and Fourth Amendment concerns weigh in favor of the ownership of the vehicle vesting in the consumer.
9. Deterrence provides a key motivation for the imposition of liability (Hubbard and Felix 1997).
10. In the application of the reasonable person test, tort law takes human frailties into account. Hammontree v. Jenner, 97 Cal. Rptr. 739 (Cal. Ct. App. 1971). Whether the law should take the "frailties" of computers into account is an interesting question outside the scope of this chapter.
11. Admittedly, the reasonable driver standard calls for the same result as the ICS in that it is a third-party insurance scheme (Hubbard 2014). However, these systems have noticeable differences in funding and implementation, as outlined in the text.

Works Cited

Anderson, James M., Nidhi Kalra, Karlyn D. Stanley, Paul Sorensen, Constantine Samaras, and Oluwatobi A. Oluwatola. 2016. "Autonomous Vehicle Technology: A Guide for Policymakers." RAND Corporation, Santa Monica, CA. http://www.rand.org/pubs/research_reports/RR443-2.html.

Anderson, James M., Nidhi Kalra, and Martin Wachs. 2009. "Liability and Regulation of Autonomous Vehicle Technologies." RAND Corporation, Berkeley, CA. http://www.rand.org/pubs/external_publications/EP20090427.html.

Bose, Ujjayini. 2015. "The Black Box Solution to Autonomous Liability." *Washington University Law Review* 92: 1325.

Brock, Caitlin. 2015. "Where We're Going, We Don't Need Drivers: The Legal Issues and Liability Implications of Automated Vehicle Technology." *UMKC Law Review* 83: 769.

Cantor, Daniel A. 1995. "Striking a Balance Between Product Availability and Product Safety: Lessons from the Vaccine Act." *American University Law Review* 44: 1853.

Colonna, Kyle. 2012. "Autonomous Cars and Tort Liability." *Case Western Reserve Journal of Law, Technology & the Internet* 4: 81.

Davies, Alex. 2016. "GM and Lyft Are Building a Network of Self-Driving Cars." *Wired*, January 4. http://www.wired.com/2016/01/gm-and-lyft-are-building-a-network-of-self-driving-cars/.

Duffy, Sophia H. and Jamie Patrick Hopkins. 2013. "Sit, Stay, Drive: The Future of Autonomous Car Liability." *SMU Science & Technology Law Review* 16: 453.

Funkhouser, Kevin. 2013. "Paving the Road Ahead: Autonomous Vehicles, Products Liability, and the Need for a New Approach." *Utah Law Review*, 2013: 437.

Garner, Bryan A., ed. 2014. *Black's Law Dictionary*. 10th ed. Eagen, MN: Thomson West.

Garza, Andrew P. 2012. "'Look Ma, No Hands!': Wrinkles and Wrecks in the Age of Autonomous Vehicles." *New England Law Review* 46: 581.

Glancy, Dorothy J. 2015. "Autonomous and Automated and Connected Cars—Oh My! First Generation Autonomous Cars in the Legal Ecosystem." *Minnesota Journal of Law Science & Technology* 16: 619.

Goodrich, Julie. 2013. "Driving Miss Daisy: An Autonomous Chauffeur System." *Houston Law Review* 51: 265.

Gurney, Jeffrey K. 2013. "Sue My Car Not Me: Products Liability and Accidents Involving Autonomous Vehicles." *University of Illinois Journal of Law, Technology and Policy* 2013: 247.

Gurney, Jeffrey K. 2015. "Driving into the Unknown: Examining the Crossroads of Criminal Law and Autonomous Vehicles." *Wake Forest Journal of Law and Policy* 5: 393.

Gurney, Jeffrey K. 2015–16. "Crashing into the Unknown: An Examination of Crash-Optimization Algorithms Through the Two Lanes of Ethics and Law." *Albany Law Review* 79: 183.

Harris, Mark. 2015. "Google's Self-Driving Car Pals Revealed." *IEEE Spectrum: Technology, Engineering, and Science News*, January 19. http://spectrum.ieee.org/cars-that-think/transportation/self-driving/googles-selfdriving-car-pals-revealed.

Honoré, Tony. 1995. "The Morality of Tort Law: Questions and Answers." In *Philosophical Foundations of Tort Law*, edited by David G. Owen, 73–95. Oxford: Clarendon Press.

Hubbard, F. Patrick. 2014. "'Sophisticated Robots': Balancing Liability, Regulation, and Innovation." *Florida Law Review* 66: 1803.

Hubbard, F. Patrick and Robert L. Felix. 1997. *The South Carolina Law of Torts*. 2d ed. Columbia: South Carolina Bar.

Marchant, Gary E., and Rachel A. Lindor. 2012. "The Coming Collision between Autonomous Vehicles and the Liability System." *Santa Clara Law Review* 52 (4): 1321–40.

NHTSA (National Highway Traffic Safety Administration). 2016. "Google—Compiled Response to 12 Nov 15 Interp Request—4 Feb 16 Final." February 4. http://isearch.nhtsa.gov/files/Google%20--%20compiled%20response%20to%2012%20Nov%20%2015%20interp%20request%20--%204%20Feb%2016%20final.htm.

Owen, David G. 2002. "Manufacturing Defects." *South Carolina Law Review* 53: 851.

Owen, David G., and Mary J. Davis. 2016. *Owen & Davis on Products Liability*. 4th ed. Eagen, MN: Thomson West.

Restatement (Second) of Torts. Philadelphia: American Law Institute, 1965.

Restatement (Third) of Torts: Products Liability. Philadelphia: American Law Institute, 1998.

Schroll, Carrie. 2015. "Splitting the Bill: Creating a National Car Insurance Fund to Pay for Accidents in Autonomous Vehicles." *Northwestern University Law Review* 109: 803.

Smith, Bryant Walker. 2014. "Automated Vehicles Are Probably Legal in the United States." *Texas A&M Law Review* 1: 411.

Urmson, Chris. 2012. "The Self-Driving Car Logs More Miles on New Wheels." Official Google Blog, August 7. http://googleblog.blogspot.com/2012/08/the-self-driving-car-logs-more-miles-on.html.

Vladeck, David C. 2014. "Machines Without Principals: Liability Rules and Artificial Intelligence." *Washington Law Review* 89: 117.

Volvo. 2015. "U.S. Urged to Establish Nationwide Federal Guidelines for Autonomous Driving." Volvo Car Group Global Media Newsroom, October 7. https://www.media.volvocars.com/global/en-gb/media/pressreleases/167975/us-urged-to-establish-nationwide-federal-guidelines-for-autonomous-driving.

Whitaker, B. 2015. "Hands Off the Wheel." *CBSNews*, October 4. http://www.cbsnews.com/news/self-driving-cars-google-mercedes-benz-60-minutes/.

Wright, Richard W. 1995. "Right, Justice, and Tort Law." In *Philosophical Foundations of Tort Law*, edited by David G. Owen, 159–82. Oxford: Clarendon Press.

Zohn, Jeffrey R. 2015. "When Robots Attack: How Should the Law Handle Self-Driving Cars That Cause Damages?" *University of Illinois Journal of Law, Technology and Policy* 2015: 461.

5 LIABILITY FOR PRESENT AND FUTURE ROBOTICS TECHNOLOGY

Trevor N. White and Seth D. Baum

In June 2005, a surgical robot at a hospital in Philadelphia malfunctioned during a prostate surgery, possibly injuring the patient.[1] In June 2015, a worker at a Volkswagen plant in Germany was crushed to death by a robot that was part of the assembly process.[2] In June 2016, a Tesla vehicle operating in autopilot mode collided with a large truck, killing its occupant (Yadron and Tynan 2016).

These are just some of the ways that robots are already implicated in causing harm. As robots become more sophisticated and more widely adopted, the potential for harm will increase. Robots even show potential for causing harm at massive catastrophic scales.

How should harm caused by robots be governed? In general, the law punishes those who have caused harm, particularly harm that could and should have been avoided. The threat of punishment serves to discourage those who could cause harm. Legal liability is thus an important legal tool for serving justice and advancing the general welfare of society. Liability's value holds for robotics as it does for any other harm-causing technology.

But robots are not just any other technology. Robots are (or at least can be) intelligent, autonomous actors moving through the physical world. They can cause harm through actions that they choose to make, that no human told them to make, and, indeed, that may surprise their human creators. Perhaps robots should be liable for their harm. This is a historic moment: humans creating technology that could potentially be liable for its own actions. Furthermore, robots can have the strength of industrial machinery and the intelligence of advanced computer systems. Robots can also be mass-produced and connected to each other and to other technological systems. This creates the potential for robots to cause unusually great harm.

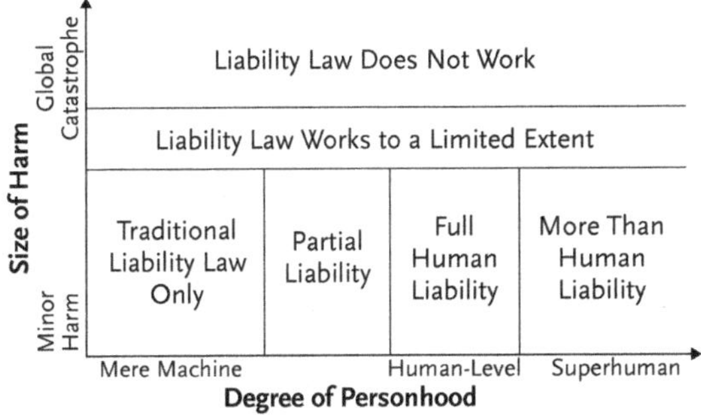

FIGURE 5.1. Classification scheme for the applicability of liability law to various sizes of harms caused by various types of robots.

This chapter addresses how the law should account for robot liability, including for robots that exist today and robots that could potentially be built at some future time. Three types of cases are distinguished, each with very different implications. First are cases in which some human party is liable, such as the manufacturer or the human using the robot. These cases pose no novel challenges for the law: they are handled the same way as with other technologies in comparable circumstances. Second are cases in which the robot itself is liable. These cases require dramatic revisions to the law, including standards to assess when robots can be held liable and principles for dividing liability between the robot and the humans who designed, built, and used it. Third are cases in which the robot poses a major catastrophic risk. These cases merit separate attention because a sufficiently large catastrophe would destroy the legal system and thus the potential to hold anyone or anything liable.

The three types of cases differ across two dimensions, as shown in figure 5.1. One dimension is the robot's degree of legal personhood, meaning the extent to which a robot has attributes that qualify it for independent standing in a court of law. As we discuss, a robot can be held liable in the eyes of the law to the extent that it merits legal personhood. The other dimension shows the size of the harm the robot causes. Harm of extreme severity cannot be handled by the law. However, there is no strict distinction between the three cases. Instead, there is a continuum, as shown by the regions in which a robot can have partial liability or more than human liability and in which liability "works" to a limited extent.

5.1 Human Liability

In a detailed study of robot law, Weaver (2014, 21–7) identifies four types of parties that could be liable for harm caused by a robot: (1) people who were using the robot or overseeing its use; (2) other people who were not using the robot but otherwise came into contact with it, which can include people harmed by the robot; (3) some party involved in the robot's production and distribution, such as the company that manufactured the robot; or (4) the robot itself.

For the first three types of parties, liability applies the same as for other technologies. A surgical robot, for example, can be misused by the surgeon (type 1), bumped into by a hospital visitor who wandered into a restricted area (type 2), or poorly built by the manufacturer (type 3). The same situations can also arise for non-robotic medical technologies. In each case, the application of liability is straightforward. Or rather, to the extent that the application of liability is not straightforward, the challenges faced are familiar. The fourth type—when the robot is liable—is the only one that poses novel challenges for the law.

To see this, consider one of the thornier cases of robot liability, that of lethal autonomous weapon systems (LAWS). These are weapons that decide for themselves whom to kill. Sparrow (2007) argues that there could be no one liable for certain LAWS harm—for example, if a LAWS decides to kill civilians or soldiers who have surrendered. A sufficiently autonomous LAWS could make its own decisions, regardless of how humans designed and deployed it. In this case, Sparrow argues, it would be unfair to hold the designer or deployer liable (or the manufacturer or other human parties). It might further be inappropriate to hold the robot itself liable, if it is not sufficiently advanced in legally relevant ways (more on this in section 5.2). In this case, who or what to hold liable is ambiguous.

This ambiguous liability is indeed a challenge, but it is a familiar one. In the military context, precedents include child soldiers (Sparrow 2007, 73–4) and landmines (Hammond 2015, 663, n. 62). Child soldiers can make their own decisions, disobey orders, and cause harm in the process. Landmines can linger long after conflict, with little trace of who is responsible for their placement. In both cases, it can be difficult or perhaps impossible to determine who is liable. So too for LAWS. This ambiguous liability can be a reason to avoid or even ban the use of child soldiers, landmines, and LAWS in armed conflict. Regardless, even for this relatively thorny case of robot liability, robotics technology raises no new challenges for the law.

The LAWS examples also resemble how the law handles non-human animals. A dog owner might not be liable the first time her dog bites someone if she did not know the dog bites people, but she would be liable in subsequent incidents. In legal terms, this is known as having *scienter*—knowledge of a potential harm. Similarly, once robots are observed causing harm, their owners or users could be liable for subsequent harm. For example, the Google Photos computer system generated controversy in 2015 when it mislabeled photographs of black people as "gorillas" (Hernandez 2015). No Google programmer instructed Photos to do this; it was a surprise, arising from the nature of Photos' algorithm. Google acted immediately to apologize and fix Photos. While it did not have *scienter* for the gorilla incident, it would for any subsequent offenses. The same logic also applies to LAWS or other types of robots. Again, as long as a human party was responsible for it, a robot does not pose novel challenges under the law.

Even if a human is ultimately liable, a robot could still be taken to court. This would occur, most likely, under *in rem* jurisdiction, in which the court treats an object of property as a party to a case when it cannot do so with a human owner. *In rem* cases include *United States v. Fifty-Three Electus Parrots* (1982), in which a man brought parrots from Southeast Asia to the United States in violation of an animal import law, and *United States v. Forty Barrels & Twenty Kegs of Coca-Cola* (1916), in which the presence of caffeine in the beverage was at issue. In both cases, a human (or corporation) was ultimately considered liable, with the parrots and soda only serving as stand-ins. Robots could be taken to court in the same way, but they would not be considered liable except in a symbolic or proxy fashion. Again, since the robot is not ultimately liable, it poses no novel challenges to the law.

This is not to say that such robots do not pose challenges to the law—only that these are familiar challenges. Indeed, the nascent literature on robot liability identifies a range of challenges, including assigning liability when robots can be modified by users (Calo 2011), when they behave in surprising ways (Vladeck 2014), and when the complexity of robot systems makes it difficult to diagnose who is at fault (Funkhouser 2013). There are also concerns that liability could impede the adoption of socially beneficial robotics (Marchant and Lindor 2012). However, these challenges all point to familiar solutions based in various ways of holding manufacturers, users, and other human parties liable. Fine-tuning the details is an important and nontrivial task, but not a revolutionary one.

The familiar nature of typical robots to the law is further seen in court cases in which robots have been implicated in causing harm (Calo 2016). An early case is *Brouse v. United States* (1949), in which a U.S. military plane using an early form of autopilot collided with another aircraft. The court rejected the U.S. claim that it should not be liable because the plane was controlled by robotic autopilot; instead, the court found the human pilot still obligated to pay attention and avoid crashes. More recently, in *Ferguson v. Bombardier Services Corp.* (2007), another airplane crash may have been attributable to the autopilot system, in which case the court would have found the autopilot manufacturer liable, but it found instead that the airline had improperly loaded the plane (see Calo 2016).

5.2 Robot Liability

If a robot can be held liable, then the law faces some major challenges in terms of which robots to hold liable for which harm and how to divide liability between the robot and its human designers, manufacturers, users, and any other relevant human parties. In this section, we will argue that robots should be held liable to the extent that they qualify for legal personhood.

Within human society, in the United States and many other countries, parties can be held liable for harm to the extent that they qualify as legal persons. Legal personhood is the ability to have legal rights and obligations, such as the ability to enter contracts, sue or be sued, and be held liable for one's actions. Legal liability thus follows directly from legal personhood. Normal adult humans are full legal persons and can be held liable for their actions across a wide range of circumstances. Children, the mentally disabled, and corporations have partial legal personhood, and in turn can be held liable across a narrower range of circumstances. Non-human animals generally do not have personhood, although this status has been contested, especially for non-human primates.[3]

The denial of legal personhood to non-human animals can be justified on the grounds that they lack humans' cognitive sophistication and corresponding ability to participate in society. Such justification avoids charges of speciesism (a pro-human bias for no other reason than just being human). However, the same justification implies that robots should merit legal personhood if they have human capabilities. As Hubbard puts it, "Absent some strong justification, a denial of personhood to an entity with at least an equal capacity for personhood would be inconsistent and contrary to the egalitarian aspect of liberalism" (2011, 417).[4]

The question of when robots can be liable thus becomes the question of when robots merit personhood. If robots merit personhood, then they can be held liable for harm they cause. Otherwise, they cannot be held liable, and instead liability must go to some human party, as with non-human animals and other technologies or entities that can cause harm.

Hubbard proposes three criteria that a robot or other artificial intelligence (AI) should meet to merit personhood: (1) complex intellectual interaction skills, including the ability to communicate and learn from experience; (2) self-consciousness, including the ability to make one's own goals or life plan; and (3) community, meaning the ability to pursue mutual benefits within a group of persons. These three criteria, central to human concepts of personhood, may offer a reasonable standard for robot personhood. We will use these criteria in this chapter while emphasizing that their definitude should be a matter of ongoing debate.

Do Hubbard's criteria also apply to liability? Perhaps not the criterion of self-consciousness. The criterion makes sense for harm *to* a robot: only a conscious robot can experience harm as humans do.[5] This follows from, for example, classic utilitarianism: "The question is not, Can they reason? nor, Can they talk? but, Can they suffer?" (Bentham 1789, ch. 17, n.122). However, the same logic does not apply to harm caused *by* a robot. Consider an advanced robot that meets all of Hubbard's criteria except that it lacks consciousness. Suppose the robot causes some harm—and, to be clear, the harm causes suffering for a human or some other conscious person. Should the robot be held liable?

The answer to this may depend on society's foundational reasoning about liability. If liability exists mainly to discourage or deter the commission of harm, then consciousness is unnecessary. The robot should be punished so long as doing so discourages the commission of future harm. The entities that get discouraged here could include the robot, other similar robots, conscious robots, and even humans. Non-conscious robots could conceivably be punished with some sort of reduced reward or utility as per whatever reward/utility function they might have (Majot and Yampolskiy 2014). Specifically, they could be reprogrammed, deactivated, or destroyed, or put in what is known as a "Box": digital solitary confinement restricting an AI's ability to communicate or function (Yudkowsky 2002). To make this possible, however, such robots ought to be based (at least in part) on reinforcement learning or similar computing paradigms (except ones based on neural network algorithms, for reasons we explain later).

Alternatively, if liability exists mainly for retribution, to bring justice to whoever committed the harm, then consciousness could be necessary. Whether it is necessary depends on the punishment's purpose. If the punishment aims to worsen the life of the liable party, so as to "balance things out," then consciousness seems necessary. It makes little sense to "worsen" the life of something that cannot experience the worsening. However, if the punishment aims to satisfy society's sense of justice, then consciousness may be unnecessary. Instead, it could be sufficient that members of society observe the punishment and see justice served.[6] Whether it would be necessary for a robot to have consciousness in this case would simply depend on whether society's sense of justice requires it to be conscious.

This potential exception regarding consciousness is a good example of partial liability, as shown in figure 5.1. The advanced, non-conscious robot can be held liable, but not in every case in which normal adult humans could. Specifically, the robot would not be held liable in certain cases where punishment is for retribution. Other limitations to a robot's capabilities could also reduce the extent of its liability. Such robots would be analogous to children and mentally disabled adult humans, who are similarly not held liable in as many cases as normal adult humans. Robots of less sophistication with respect to any of Hubbard's three criteria (or whatever other criteria are ultimately established) should be liable to a lesser extent than robots that meet the criteria in full.[7]

What about robots of greater than human sophistication in Hubbard's three criteria? These would be robots with more advanced intellectual interaction skills, self-consciousness, or communal living ability. It is conceivable that such robots could exist—indeed, the idea dates back many decades (Good 1965). If they do come into existence, then by the foregoing logic, they should be held to a *higher* liability standard than normal adult humans. Indeed, concepts such as negligence recognize human fallibility in many respects that a robot could surpass humans in, including reaction time, eyesight, and mental recall. Holding robots to a higher standard of liability could offer one means of governing robots that have greater than human capacities (more on this in section 3.3).

Before turning to catastrophic risk, there is one additional aspect of robot liability to consider: the division of liability among the robot itself and other parties that influence the robot's actions. These other parties can include the robot's designer, its manufacturer, and any users or operators it may have. These parties are comparable to a human's parents and employers, though the comparison is imperfect due to basic differences between humans and robots.

A key difference is that robots are to a large extent *designed*. Humans can be designed as well via genetic screening and related techniques, hence the term "designer baby." But designers have much more control over the eventual character of robots than of humans. This suggests that robot designers should hold more liability for robots' actions than human parents should for their children's actions. If robot designers know that certain designs tend to yield harmful robots, a case can be made for holding the designers at least partially liable for harm caused by those robots, even if the robots merit legal personhood. Designers could be similarly liable for building robots using opaque algorithms, such as neural networks and related deep-learning methods, in which it is difficult to predict whether the robot will cause harm. Those parties that commission the robot's design could be similarly liable. In court, the testimony of relevant industry experts would be valuable for proving whether there were any available, feasible safeguards to minimize such risks.

5.3 Catastrophic Robot/AI Liability

"Catastrophe" has many meanings, many of which require no special legal attention. For example, a person's death is catastrophic for the deceased and his or her loved ones, yet the law is perfectly capable of addressing individual deaths caused by robots or AIs. However, extreme catastrophes of a certain class do merit special legal attention, due to their outsized severity and significance for human civilization. These are catastrophes that cause major, permanent harm to the entirety of global human civilization. Such catastrophes are commonly known as *global catastrophes* (Baum and Barrett, forthcoming) or *existential catastrophes* (Bostrom 2013). Following Posner (2004), we will simply call them catastrophes.

A range of catastrophic risks exist, including global warming, nuclear war, a pandemic, and collision between Earth and a large asteroid or comet. Recently, a growing body of scholarship has analyzed the possibility of catastrophe caused by certain types of future AI. Much of the attention has been given to "superintelligent" AI that outsmarts humanity and "achieve[s] complete world domination" (Bostrom 2014, 78). Such AI could harm humans through the use of robotics. Additionally, some experts believe that robotics could play an important role in the development of such AI (Baum et al. 2011).

Other catastrophe scenarios could also involve robotics. Robots could be used in systems for launching nuclear weapons or detecting incoming attacks, potentially resulting in unwanted nuclear wars.[8] They could be used in critical civil, transportation, or manufacturing infrastructure, contributing to a global systemic failure.[9] They could be used for geoengineering—the intentional manipulation of the global environment, such as to counteract global warming—and this could backfire, causing environmental catastrophe.[10] Robots could be used in establishing or maintaining an oppressive totalitarian world government.[11] Still further robot catastrophe scenarios are also possible.

The enormous scale of the catastrophes in question creates profound moral and legal dilemmas. If the harm is permanent, it impacts members of all future generations. Earth may remain habitable for at least a billion more years, and the galaxy and the universe for much longer; the present generation thus contains a tiny fraction of all people who could exist. The legal standing and representation of members of future generations is a difficult question (Wolfe 2008). If members of future generations are to be counted, they can overwhelm the calculus. Despite this, present generations unilaterally make the decisions. There is thus a tension in how to balance the interests of present and future generations (Page 2003). A sufficiently large catastrophe raises similar issues just within the context of the present generation. About 7 billion humans live today; a catastrophe that risks killing all of them could be 7 billion times larger than a catastrophe that risks killing just one. One could justify an enormous effort to reduce that risk regardless of future generations (Posner 2004).

Further complications come from the irreversible nature of these catastrophes. In a sense, every event is irreversible: if you wear a blue shirt today, no one can ever change the fact that you wore a blue shirt today. Such events are irreversible only in a trivial sense: you can change what shirt you wear on subsequent days. Nontrivially irreversible events are more or less permanent: if someone dies today, nothing can bring that person back to life.[12] At a larger scale, nontrivially irreversible effects exist for many ecological shifts and may also exist for the collapse of human civilization (Baum and Handoh 2014). The possibility of large and nontrivially irreversible harm creates a major reason to avoid taking certain risks. The precautionary principle is commonly invoked in this context, raising questions of just how cautious society ought to be (Posner 2004; Sunstein 2006).

An irreversible AI catastrophe could be too large for the law to handle. In the simplest case, if the catastrophe resulted in human extinction, there would be no one remaining to hold liable. If a catastrophe led to the collapse of human civilization but left some survivors, there would be no legal system remaining intact for holding people liable. Alternatively, AI could cause a catastrophe in which everyone is still alive but has become enslaved or otherwise harmed by the AI; in this case, pre-catastrophe human authorities would lack the power needed to hold those at fault liable. For smaller catastrophes, the legal system might exist to a limited extent (figure 5.1). In this case, it might be possible to bring the liable parties to trial and punish them, but not as reliably or completely as is possible under normal circumstances. The closest possible example would be creating special international proceedings, like the Nuremberg Trials, to deal with the aftermath. Much like such war tribunals, though, these might do little to address the chaos's original cause. This would leave victims or society at large wasting time and resources on reliving a tragedy (McMorran 2013).

Hence, instead of liability, a precautionary approach could be used. This would set a default policy of disallowing any activity with any remote chance of causing catastrophe. It could further place the burden of proof on those who wished to conduct such activity, requiring them to demonstrate in advance that it could not cause catastrophe.[13] Trial and error would not be permitted, because a single error could cause major irreversible harm. This would likely be a significant impediment for AI research and development (at least for the subset of AI that poses catastrophic risk), which, like other fields of technology, is likely to make extensive use of trial and error. Indeed, some AI researchers recommend a trial-and-error approach, in which AIs are gradually trained to learn human values so that they will not cause catastrophe (Goertzel 2016). However, given the high stakes of AI catastrophe, perhaps these sorts of trial-and-error approaches should still be avoided.

It may be possible to use a novel liability scheme to assist with a catastrophe-avoiding precautionary approach. In a wide-ranging discussion of legal measures to avoid catastrophe from emerging technologies, Wilson proposes "liability mechanisms to punish violators whether or not their activities cause any harm" (2013, 356). In effect, people would be held liable not for causing catastrophe but for taking actions that could cause catastrophe. This proposal could be a successful component of a precautionary approach to catastrophic risk and is worth ongoing consideration.

But taking the precautionary principle to the extreme can have undesirable consequences. All actions carry some risk. In some cases, it may be impossible to prove a robot does not have the potential to cause catastrophe. Therefore, requiring demonstrations of minimal risk prior to performing actions would be paralyzing (Sunstein 2006). Furthermore, many actions can reduce some risks even while increasing others; requiring precaution due to concern about one risk can cause net harm to society by denying opportunities to decrease other risks (Wiener 2002). AI research and development can pose significant risks, but it can also help reduce other risks. For AI that poses catastrophic risk, net risk will be minimized when the AI research and development is expected to bring a net reduction in catastrophic risk (Baum 2014).

In summary, AI that poses catastrophic risk presents significant legal challenges. Liability as we know it, most critically, is of little help. Precautionary approaches can work instead, although care should be taken to avoid preventing AI from reducing different catastrophic risks. The legal challenges from AI that poses catastrophic risk are distinct from the challenges from other types of AI, but they are similar to the challenges from other catastrophic risks.

5.4 Conclusion

While robots benefit society in many ways, they also cause or are otherwise implicated in a variety of harms. The frequency and size of these harms are likely to increase as robots become more advanced and ubiquitous. Robots could even cause or contribute to a number of major global catastrophe scenarios. It is important for the law to govern these harms to the extent possible so that they are minimized and, when they do occur, justice may be served.

For many types of harm caused by robots, a human party is ultimately liable. In those instances, traditional liability applies. A major challenge to the law comes when robots could be liable. Such cases require legal personhood tests for robots to assess the extent to which they can be liable. One promising personhood test evaluates the robot's intellectual interaction skills, self-consciousness, and communal living ability. Depending on how a robot fares on a personhood test, it could have more, less, or the same liability as a typical adult human. The capacity for a robot to be liable does not preclude a liable human party. Indeed, robot designers should expect more liability for robot harm than would human parents, because robots are intentionally designed so much more extensively than human children are. Finally, for robots that pose catastrophic risk, the law cannot be counted on and a precautionary approach is warranted.

People involved in the design, manufacture, and use of robots can limit their liability by choosing robots that reliably avoid causing harm. One potential way to improve reliability is to avoid computing paradigms such as neural networks that tend to result in surprising behaviors, or to adapt these paradigms to make them less surprising (Huang and Xing 2002). Robot designs should be sufficiently transparent for responsible human parties to, with reasonable confidence, determine in advance what harm could occur. They can then build safety restrictions into the robot or at least warn robot users, as is common practice with other technologies. Robots should also undergo rigorous safety testing before being placed into situations where they can cause harm. If robots cannot reliably avoid causing harm, they probably should not be used in the first place.

These sorts of safety guidelines should be especially strict for robots that could contribute to a major global catastrophe. A single catastrophe could permanently harm human civilization. It is thus crucial to avoid any catastrophe. Safety testing itself could be dangerous. This increases the value of transparent computing paradigms that let humans assess risks prior to building a robot. Legal measures must also take effect before the robot is built, because there may be no legal system after a catastrophe takes place. Advanced robots may be less likely to cause catastrophe if they are designed to be upstanding legal persons. But even then, some legal system would need to exist to hold them liable for what harm they cause.

As this chapter illustrates, robot liability poses major new challenges to the law. Meeting these challenges requires contributions from law, robotics, philosophy, risk analysis, and other fields. It is essential for humans in these various specialties to work together to build robot liability regimes that avoid causing harm while capturing the many benefits of robotics. The potential for harm is extremely large, making this an urgent task. We hope that humans and robots will coexist successfully and for mutual benefit in a community of responsible persons.

Acknowledgments

We thank Tony Barrett, Daniel Dewey, Roman Yampolskiy, and the editors for helpful comments on an earlier draft of this chapter. All remaining errors or other shortcomings are ours alone. Work on this chapter was funded in part by a grant from the Future of Life Institute. The views presented here are those of the authors and do not necessarily reflect the views of the Global Catastrophic Risk Institute or the Future of Life Institute.

Notes

1. The patient lost the ensuing court case, 363 F. App'x. 925, 925 (3d Cir. 2010).
2. For further discussion of the Volkswagen case, see Baum and White (2015).
3. The legal status of these non-human entities is discussed in relation to humans and robots in Hubbard (2011).

4. A similar argument could apply in the event of humanity coming into contact with extraterrestrials (Baum 2010).
5. For convenience, and without consequence to the argument, here we use "consciousness" and "self-consciousness" interchangeably. We also set aside harm to the robot that is ultimately experienced by humans, such as when the harm qualifies as property damage.
6. This need not imply that punishment is for the pleasure of members of society, as can be the case in, for example, public executions; it could instead be for their sense of justice.
7. Another set of criteria for personhood is proposed by Warren (1973): consciousness, reasoning, self-motivated activity, capacity to communicate, and self-awareness. These criteria largely overlap those of Hubbard (2011), though they are intended for moral personhood, defined as who or what has a right to not be harmed, and not for legal personhood as defined in the text.
8. For related nuclear war scenarios, see Barrett et al. (2013) and references therein.
9. For a general discussion of global systemic failure, see Centeno et al. (2015). For an example in the context of robotics, in which many self-driving cars fail simultaneously, see Baum and White (2015).
10. On the potential for a geoengineering catastrophe, see Baum et al. (2013) and references therein.
11. On the possibility of global totalitarianism and the enabling role of certain technologies, see Caplan (2008) and Majot and Yampolskiy (2015).
12. Given present technology.
13. For a related brief discussion of potential approaches to AI research risk review boards and their limitations, see Barrett and Baum (2017) and Sotala and Yampolskiy (2015).

Works Cited

Barrett, Anthony M. and Seth D. Baum. 2017. "A Model of Pathways to Artificial Superintelligence Catastrophe for Risk and Decision Analysis." *Journal of Experimental & Theoretical Artificial Intelligence* 29 (2): 397–414. doi:10.1080/0952813X.2016.1186228.

Barrett, Anthony M., Seth D. Baum, and Kelly R. Hostetler. 2013. "Analyzing and Reducing the Risks of Inadvertent Nuclear War Between the United States and Russia." *Science & Global Security* 21 (2): 106–33.

Baum, Seth D. 2010. "Universalist Ethics in Extraterrestrial Encounter." *Acta Astronautica* 66 (3–4): 617–23.

Baum, Seth D. 2014. "The Great Downside Dilemma for Risky Emerging Technologies." *Physica Scripta* 89 (12), article 128004. doi:10.1088/0031-8949/89/12/128004.

Baum, Seth D. and Anthony M. Barrett. Forthcoming. "The Most Extreme Risks: Global Catastrophes." In *The Gower Handbook of Extreme Risk*, edited by Vicki Bier. Farnham: Gower.

Baum, Seth D. and Itsuki C. Handoh. 2014. "Integrating the Planetary Boundaries and Global Catastrophic Risk Paradigms." *Ecological Economics* 107: 13–21.

Baum, Seth D., Ben Goertzel, and Ted G. Goertzel. 2011. "How Long Until Human-Level AI? Results from an Expert Assessment." *Technological Forecasting & Social Change* 78 (1): 185–95.

Baum, Seth D., Timothy M. Maher, Jr., and Jacob Haqq-Misra. 2013. "Double Catastrophe: Intermittent Stratospheric Geoengineering Induced by Societal Collapse." *Environment, Systems and Decisions* 33 (1): 168–80.

Baum, Seth and Trevor White. 2015. "When Robots Kill." *Guardian*, June 23. http://www.theguardian.com/science/political-science/2015/jul/23/when-robots-kill.

Bentham, Jeremy. (1789) 1907. *Introduction to the Principles of Morals and Legislation*. Reprint, Oxford: Clarendon Press.

Bostrom, Nick. 2013. "Existential Risk Prevention as Global Priority." *Global Policy* 4 (1): 15–31.

Bostrom, Nick. 2014. *Superintelligence: Paths, Dangers, Strategies*. Oxford: Oxford University Press.

Calo, Ryan. 2011. "Open Robotics." *Maryland Law Review* 70 (3): 571–613.

Calo, Ryan. 2016. "Robots in American Law." University of Washington School of Law Research Paper No. 2016-04.

Caplan, Bryan. 2008. "The Totalitarian Threat." In *Global Catastrophic Risks*, edited by Nick Bostrom and Milan Ćirković, 504–19. Oxford: Oxford University Press.

Centeno, Miguel A., Manish Nag, Thayer S. Patterson, Andrew Shaver, and A. Jason Windawi. 2015. "The Emergence of Global Systemic Risk." *Annual Review of Sociology* 41: 65–85.

Funkhouser, Kevin. 2013. "Paving the Road Ahead: Autonomous Vehicles, Products Liability, and the Need for a New Approach." *Utah Law Review* 2013 (1): 437–62.

Goertzel, Ben. 2016. "Infusing Advanced AGIs with Human-Like Value Systems: Two Theses." *Journal of Evolution and Technology* 26 (1): 50–72.

Good, Irving John. 1965. "Speculations Concerning the First Ultraintelligent Machine." In *Advances in Computers*, edited by Franz L. Alt and Morris Rubinoff, 6: 31–88. New York: Academic Press.

Hammond, Daniel N. 2015. "Autonomous Weapons and the Problem of State Accountability." *Chicago Journal of International Law* 15: 652, 669–70.

Hernandez, Daniela. 2015. "The Google Photos 'Gorilla' Fail Won't Be the Last Time AIs Offend Us." *Fusion*, July 2. http://fusion.net/story/160196/the-google-photos-gorilla-fail-wont-be-the-last-time-ais-offend-us.

Huang, Samuel H. and Hao Xing. 2002. "Extract Intelligible and Concise Fuzzy Rules from Neural Networks." *Fuzzy Sets and Systems* 132 (2): 233–43.

Hubbard, F. Patrick. 2011. "'Do Androids Dream?' Personhood and Intelligent Artifacts." *Temple Law Review* 83: 405–41.

Majot, Andrew M. and Roman V. Yampolskiy. 2014. "AI Safety Engineering Through Introduction of Self-Reference into Felicific Calculus via Artificial Pain and

Pleasure." *IEEE International Symposium on Ethics in Science, Technology and Engineering*. doi:10.1109/ETHICS.2014.6893398.

Majot, Andrew M. and Roman V. Yampolskiy. 2015. "Global Catastrophic Risk and Security Implications of Quantum Computers." *Futures* 72: 17–26. doi:10.1016/j.futures.2015.02.006.

Marchant, Gary E. and Rachel A. Lindor. 2012. "The Coming Collision Between Autonomous Vehicles and the Liability System." *Santa Clara Law Review* 52 (4): 1321–40.

McMorran, Chris. 2013. "International War Crimes Tribunals." *Beyond Intractability*. http://www.beyondintractability.org/essay/int-war-crime-tribunals.

Page, Talbot. 2003. "Balancing Efficiency and Equity in Long-Run Decision-Making." *International Journal of Sustainable Development* 6 (1): 70–86.

Posner, Richard. 2004. *Catastrophe: Risk and Response*. Oxford: Oxford University Press.

Sotala, Kaj and Roman V. Yampolskiy. 2015. "Responses to Catastrophic AGI Risk: A Survey." *Physica Scripta* 90 (1), article 018001. doi: 10.1088/0031-8949/90/1/018001.

Sparrow, Robert. 2007. "Killer Robots." *Journal of Applied Philosophy* 24 (1): 62–77.

Sunstein, Cass R. 2006. "Irreversible and Catastrophic." *Cornell Law Review* 91: 841–97.

Vladeck, David C. 2014. "Machines Without Principals: Liability Rules and Artificial Intelligence." *Washington Law Review* 89: 117–50.

Warren, Mary Anne. 1973. "On the Moral and Legal Status of Abortion." *Monist* 57 (4): 43–61.

Weaver, John Frank. 2014. *Robots Are People Too: How Siri, Google Car, and Artificial Intelligence Will Force Us to Change Our Laws*. Westport, CT: Praeger.

Wiener, Jonathan B. 2002. "Precaution in a Multirisk World." In *Human and Ecological Risk Assessment: Theory and Practice*, edited by Dennis J. Paustenbach, 1509–31. New York: Wiley.

Wilson, Grant. 2013. "Minimizing Global Catastrophic and Existential Risks from Emerging Technologies Through International Law. *Virginia Environmental Law Journal* 31: 307–64.

Wolfe, Matthew W. 2008. "The Shadows of Future Generations." *Duke Law Journal* 57: 1897–1932.

Yadron, Danny and Dan Tynan. 2016. "Tesla Driver Dies in First Fatal Crash While Using Autopilot Mode." *Guardian*, June 30. https://www.theguardian.com/technology/2016/jun/30/tesla-autopilot-death-self-driving-car-elon-musk.

Yudkowsky, Eliezer S. 2002. "The AI-Box Experiment." http://www.yudkowsky.net/singularity/aibox/.

6 SKILLED PERCEPTION, AUTHENTICITY, AND THE CASE AGAINST AUTOMATION

David Zoller

Autonomous cars are in a sense an innocuous invention. There are millions of city dwellers who don't drive themselves, and it shouldn't be too troubling if those of us outside major cities are soon in the same situation. Yet autonomous cars are also a battleground for a wider, resurgent debate over the automation of human skills. Concerns about the gradual loss of manual skill date at least to the Industrial Revolution (Sennett 2008). Old as the concerns may be, it has never been easy to explain why losing skill is a bad thing. We may romanticize a more "authentic" time when people did more by their own skill—until we recall that every age has had its technologies, and every age can romanticize the skill of earlier people who lived without them (Feenberg 1999; Sennett 2008).

As Feenberg notes, the deeper core of our worries over losing our skills might be legitimate concerns about how automation will change our perception of the world around us (1999; Heidegger 1977). A recent critique of autonomous cars illustrates this with contrasting portraits: on the one hand, consider the skilled motorcyclist, wedded to the machine, vividly awake to her surroundings, attentively feeling every nuance of the road through her tires; on the other hand, consider the "driver" of the semi-autonomous Mercedes, half-asleep and browsing the internet on a road that might as well be miles away (Crawford 2015, 79–80).

One is bound to reply that this example sounds loaded. The important question is what it is loaded with. It is presumably not loaded with utility: the drudgery of acquiring skills from driving to nursing, and the mistakes we make in employing those skills, would favor automation. Likewise, one could mention the long-standing contention that the end of labor—including the labor of daily tasks—makes room for freedom, self-determination, and creativity (Marcuse 1964;

Maskivker 2010). If all that counterbalances these gains is the pleasure we get from being skilled and doing jobs ourselves, there seems little reason to favor human drivers, nurses, farmers, or baristas. And if skilled attention to the world, such as our motorcyclist displays, is valuable only because it is enjoyable, then perhaps we should seek enjoyment somewhere else.

To pinpoint the issue, consider an extreme scenario where skill has faded more or less altogether. Technology critics offer glimpses of a dystopian future where all our tasks are completed for us, without any need for sustained attention or hard-earned skill (Carr 2014; Crawford 2015). For the sake of argument, let us sum up these glimpses into a unified dystopia, which we can call "Automania." In Automania, we are jacks of all trades, comfortable and capable in any situation with no training at all. Headed for your favorite coffee shop downtown? Virtual arrows on the sidewalk guide your steps. Or maybe your shoes nudge you in the right direction and avoid obstacles while you play an online game in your head. Did somebody say something confusing? Swipe the translator and you'll hear it translated in a way you can understand. Needless to say, you got here in an automated car repaired by robots. This is a world without limits, and thus without the need for skill to cope with them. The literature is peppered with metaphors that suggest our Automanians have in some sense lost touch with the world: Crawford laments that we are headed for an automated "virtual reality" where we no longer cope with the "real world"; Carr claims that "the world recedes" as technology replaces skill (Crawford 2015, 73; Carr 2014, 144). But what is particularly *dys*topian about that? Exactly what value does Automania lack, and why is this value valuable?

My own argument is premised on the way that skill opens up corners of reality, so to speak, that are inaccessible to the unskilled. To the master woodworker, as not to the novice, a good piece of wood is a field of activity, an invitation to shape and create. Similarly, to the skilled driver, every bend and imperfection in the ribbon of road leaps out in vivid relief. If Automania is really on the horizon, then a vast range of such experiences will shortly be out of reach for most people—except those with leisure and money to invest deeply in skilled hobbies.

After examining the nature of skilled attention in the next section, I consider various arguments that skilled attention is either valuable in itself or a key to realizing deeper human goods. If those arguments are successful, they would provide individuals with a rational justification for cultivating manual skills and doing things "by hand." Arguments of this sort can also be deployed socially, to defend our permitting people to do some activity without automation or to favor technologies that involve human work and skill (Carr 2014; Crawford 2015; Vallor 2015). On a wider scale, we can think of manual skill as an ethos that is currently declining or underappreciated, which needs its value articulated and respected (Heidegger 1977; Sennett 2008). But however we wish to deploy it, skilled attention first must prove that it has some intrinsic value. Within limits, I believe that it can.

6.1 The Phenomenology of Skilled and Unskilled Attention

It is not a simple thing to prove that consciousness *ought* to be a certain way. Why should one way of paying attention to the world be *intrinsically* better than another? Several prominent defenses of human skill are indebted to the philosophical method called "phenomenology" (Heidegger 1977; Dreyfus 1992; Noë 2009; Crawford 2015). Phenomenology is the study of human experience and its basic architecture from the first-person perspective (Sokolowski 2000; Smith 2004). Yet phenomenology is not simply observing your mental life; rather, it involves finding necessary connections among basic elements of human experience (Drummond 2007). As a simple example, consider that having a body, instead of being a disembodied mind, is integral to the way you experience spatial objects: you need a body to feel that a chair or room can be explored, touched, moved about, and felt in just the way we usually experience them (Noë 2009; Crowell 2013). If technology someday made us bodiless, there might be many enjoyable things in life, but we would not experience chairs and rooms as we now do. Of course, there may be no serious reason to avoid technologies that rob us of our ordinary experience of chairs. Yet there are other changes to the basic architecture of experience that we most certainly do consider pathological and worth avoiding.

Phenomenology has, for instance, offered descriptions of how experience is disrupted at very basic levels under conditions like schizophrenia and somatoparaphrenia (a psychopathology where one no longer recognizes one's limbs as one's own); this has led to a better understanding of the broader range of experiences and goods that patients may lose (Fuchs and Schlimmme 2009; Matthews 2004). It should be a familiar idea that certain "modifications" of experience—such as not being able to recognize my limbs—sever key links in human experience, and thus hinder our pursuit of human goods. The completely de-skilled perceptual world of Automania might be a similarly undesirable "modification" of experience, and if so, phenomenology could help to demonstrate this. In the remainder of this section I present the current phenomenological understanding of skilled attention. In subsequent sections I analyze a range of recent arguments that skilled attention is indeed a precondition for more basic elements of a good life.

It is a common observation in phenomenology that all perception is "normative," that is, that the basic perception of any object immediately gives me a sense of certain goals and standards (Crowell 2013; Doyon 2015). I see objects not just as sense data with some sort of mental name tags attached, but rather as complex wholes that guide my activity and invite me to further perceptions (Sokolowski 2000). As Husserl explains, this is true even of a basic three-dimensional box: while I have a full view of the side of the box that is facing me, I have a tacit, empty sense of the rest of the box, along with a sense that what I *should* have in mind is the *whole box* that would be present to me if I physically walked around to see its hidden sides (Husserl 1998, 94ff.). The piecemeal nature of our perception is part of the reason this is the case, and it is the case not just for visual objects but for auditory "objects" (a musical phrase) or mental entities (the idea of love). In every case the "whole object" is never present in a single visual (or auditory, or cognitive) glance; rather, the "whole object" is like a goal toward which my individual perceptions point.

Each object I encounter invites "maximum articulation," the possibility of engaging a full range of senses and explorations (Merleau-Ponty 2012, 332). Thus to have a table in front of me is not just to have a flat visual image that happens to match a little picture card in my memory labeled "table." To actually have the thing in front of me "be" a table is to have my senses involved with an object that invites me (and my body) toward a certain optimal experience. Gibson suggests we think of the object as offering us a range of ways to act, or "affordances" (2015, 119ff.). I'm not likely to explore all the visual and tactile possibilities of a table every time I see one, not the way I might linger on, say, a guitar. But those possibilities are implied when I see the table, and to see what I call a table is to have a sort of standing invitation toward the whole object.

At a higher level, as I gain skill and facility at dealing with particular kinds of objects, I learn an art of seeing their possibilities. There are many things you can explore that I cannot, perhaps the mystifying boxes and wires over in the electrical engineering department, lines of computer code, or atonal music by Schoenberg. To explore, say, a musical phrase and the particular sort of unity it represents requires the skill to apprehend it as the unity of a set of possibilities. To hear that, I require skill: I need expectations of what notes and chords could come next, desires to realize those expectations, appreciation of tone quality, and so on. A pure novice may hear noise or a series of noises, whereas the skilled musician is listening *toward* an extremely complex unity. In that sense, skilled attention—in contrast to the attention of the novice—is not merely useful or pleasurable. Rather, it permits us to see more complex unities out in the world, to apprehend a certain "bandwidth" of the world of objects.

We might consider the example of a skilled martial artist, whose perceptions of angry bar patrons hang on gradually emerging opportunities for combat: this angry patron is off-balance, he is looking at me, he clenches his fist and raises it, but he's off his right foot so I could send him reeling to his left (Crawford 2015, 55). To be skilled in a particular environment is to be attuned to a particular slice of reality as it unfolds minutely before my eyes: to have my attention slow down, as it were, to the speed of phenomena relevant to my skill. When we develop a set of skills, our perceptual lives themselves become unities, as it were, rather than remaining mere pluralities of noise: as Crawford puts it, "[W]e are now inhabiting [the world] in a more determinate way, conditioned by the particulars of the skill and the implements we use" (2015, 67; Noë 2009). This has important implications for the goods of agency, which I discuss next.

Out of the infinity of perceptual worlds I might have inhabited, I am gradually training my mind to inhabit or "embed" itself in a particular "niche" of reality (Gibson 2015). Recent cognitive science refers to this process as cognitively "coupling" with the limited range of objects I am skilled at interacting with (Noë 2009; Clark 2011). I am not skilled or coupled in this way in every domain of human practice. In all but a few domains I am a novice, and the objects in other domains are varieties of noise, obstacles, curiosities, or semi-anonymous heaps offering me relatively little to explore. Pursuing "smart" automations might enable us to inhabit any niche without skill or attention. Yet we would not be actually inhabiting any perceptual niche in the proper sense at all: the objects within the niche, which the skilled are able to see and explore, are not "there" for us novices.

For instance, when I hand my car keys over to the robots, I lose the opportunity and facility for a certain experience of the expanse of the land around my town on a drive. I lose as well a unique social window on the other human beings with whom I share the road downtown. When a robot or software performs some skilled activity *for* me, the robot is dwelling among the relevant objects *for* me, perceiving their possibilities *for* me, and thus inhabiting, say, the land or my city or my garden *for* me. If I am a novice, all I see in these niches is perceptual noise, a set of half-known objects, 3D boxes and baubles, but nothing deeply consequential.

Of course, my robot or software does not *care* about the normative features of objects it "perceives." Is the robot *hanging on* an unresolved chord just before the end of a symphony? Is the robot *awaiting* and *appreciative of* the subtle social cues humans give one another as they negotiate a busy road or a crowded kitchen? While the robot is sufficiently skilled to inhabit the perceptual niche, it doesn't care to do so. This would mean that nobody actually inhabits the niche of some place in my life, say the sweep of the land around town, my kitchen, or the grid of the city. This is not necessarily a tragedy for the robot or the kitchen or the land, but it may be a kind of tragedy for me. Perhaps the purest inhabitant of Automania, lacking any serious perceptual training, fails to truly inhabit the various niches of her life: their deep unities slip beneath her awareness in a quick blur of irrelevance, as surely as the boxes in the electrical engineering department or the bar patron's movements slip and blur beneath mine. There are several ways of explaining the potential badness of this, which I discuss later.

6.2 Cognitive Limitation as a Psychological Benefit

Training and "slowing" my perceptions by acquiring skill is clearly limiting, which may sound bad to Automanians. But one can argue that such limitation has its own value. Noë (2009) offers the thought experiment of a life in which we do not acquire skill and "couple" with a determinate local environment. Such a life, Noë claims, would be "robotic" and strange: "Each day would be like one's first day in an unfamiliar country. No familiar pathways or tested strategies for getting things done would be available. . . . We would scan, interpret, evaluate, decide, execute, reevaluate. Crucially, our actual living bears no resemblance to such a robotically alienated mode of being. . . . [O]ur presence in a familiar context reduces to a manageable number the choices and degrees of freedom with which we need to concern ourselves" (2009, 119).

One might object that we will never lose this aspect of human experience, even in Automania. Engagement in skilled behavior, we might think, is not optional: whatever the environment, humans will acquire skill and habit to embed themselves within it. But Noë notes that having a perceptual "niche" is not to be taken for granted. It can take years to achieve, and it can fail. For instance, immigrating to a new place involves, as Noë puts it, a certain cognitive "injury" to the embedded self. Noë recounts his father's experience as an immigrant to New York City who continually struggled to "couple" with his new environment and heal the injury (2009, 69). The view I sketched earlier offers some explanation of this "injury": perhaps none of the objects in my new home offers me anything to do or explore except the very superficial. Perhaps I see no compelling unities in this new country—just heaps. And just as it is evidently possible to never succeed in embedding oneself, perhaps due to the pressures of immigration, nor to have the chance to try, perhaps if one travels the world for work, so too it is possible never to *bother* embedding oneself—to seek technological crutches so that one never *has to* do it.

Noë's particular reasoning here hinges on the way that a limited self, rooted in its skilled perceptual coupling with a small set of environments, is a psychologically normal self that enjoys a "manageable" kind of freedom. One might alternatively focus on the subsidiary goods, such as the development of our moral character, that we acquire over the long process of acquiring skill (Sennett 2008; Carr 2014; Crawford 2015). Crawford casts the process of acquiring and deploying a skill as a more "adult" way of orienting ourselves to reality: rather than being coddled in an infant-like "virtual reality" that meets her needs, the adult struggles with reality and gains enough skill to cope with a small niche of it (2015, 69ff.). Carr (2014) adds that habitual attention to "reality" makes us more useful, serious, and vigilant characters, able to guard against machine errors. As Sennett notes, this inclination to get back in touch with the "real" dates at least to the Industrial Revolution, when the nineteenth-century English reformer John Ruskin led affluent youths out to reconnect with "Real Life" through manual construction work (2008, 109). The maturity or adulthood we earn by adjusting ourselves to the "real world," of course, has a certain moral and personal appeal: a world of lazy psychological infants is, we might think, a worse world on a variety of spectra.

Yet it is at least conceivable that Automanians may get their general moral and character training elsewhere, and machine errors aren't in principle inevitable. To turn the point in a new direction, we might say that paying attention to the "real world" is consequential in a different, more pointed way that cannot be so easily substituted. I have already suggested, in reference to the life of Noë's unfortunate immigrant, that there may be something just worse about a perceptual life populated by shallower objects (noise and 3D boxes, heaps and trinkets). It is a life of comparatively few "invitations" from objects, since I lack the art of seeing and hearing those richer invitations. At least some of them, we might imagine, are tacit moral appeals, and I will miss them if I no longer can or do give attention to the objects that make them. Perhaps these appeals come from the other citizens in my town, who are at least weakly present to me on the road, or from the land itself, which is present in a unique way on a drive into the valley.

Given that automating a skilled activity means agreeing that we will exit some niche of perceptual reality, and maybe exit it forever, we should be confident that either (a) there was nothing of importance to see in that niche, or (b) if there was, we know how to synthesize or artificially reconstruct that meaning so that our citizens know and appreciate it without ever being in the niche where we normally used to find it. This point is not meant to be broadly technophobic, but merely to prescribe a principle of caution. The more suddenly, broadly, and pervasively we hand our perceptual facility over to the robots, the more likely we will make mistakes and simply "lose data" that were surprisingly integral to our moral and social lives. Again, we may think of this either as bad for the agent/perceiver herself or as something morally disabling and thereby bad for others to whose rich moral appeals our agent is now partially deaf.

6.3 Neo-Aristotelian Arguments from Excellence

We could develop this line of argument for the value of skilled attention by drawing on some recent neo-Aristotelian and virtue ethical trends in phenomenology. Strange as it sounds to say that one kind of attention is simply better than another kind, we at least in principle can talk, as virtue ethics does, about inhabiting one's situation excellently rather than deficiently (Aristotle 2000; Drummond 2002). It would seem odd to say that we, as conscious beings, can inhabit our lived situations or the world at large "excellently" if we are scarcely paying attention to them. On the contrary, we might think that for beings like us, how we are conscious of the world around us *just is* how we are inhabiting our situation. Here I present a series of nested arguments that hard-earned perceptual skill is requisite for living one's life "excellently."

6.3.1 The General Excellence Argument

One way to make this argument is to consider how automation alters our sense of what Crowell calls the standards of success in everyday activity (2013, 273). We arguably automate a domain of human activity because we are understanding that activity on a "merely sufficing" standard: we just want to get the task completed, and nothing more (Crowell 2013, 2015). I render and 3D-print a statue because I just want the statue on my shelf; that being my goal, there is no reason for me or anybody to mold the thing out of resistant and fickle clay. I permit an online retailer to automatically send me all my groceries, because I want to do whatever merely suffices to get the shopping done. I tap my phone to summon an automated car, because I view the road as what merely suffices to get me to my destination. Yet I obviously don't want a robot guitar to do my playing for me. For some activities, the relevant success standard is merely doing the activity excellently, on its own terms.

As with Aristotle's broader account, to be virtuous in some domain of human experience is to be able to inhabit the relevant situations excellently, with *aretê*: Aristotle's courageous person, for instance, is one who can act and be excellently in situations involving danger, fear, and the like (Aristotle 2000, 1115a–b). There is no accompanying presumption in Aristotle that we need further reasons to be courageous. Rather, the point is to develop one's attention and cognition to inhabit situations excellently, and to do this for its own sake (Aristotle 2000, 1105a–6a). Sennett (2008) characterizes this as the ethos of the craftsman: a concern for the act of doing high-quality work for its own sake. Sennett (2008) suggests we could reawaken this ethos in a range of activities from cooking to computer programming. In a similar way, Crawford (2015) notes that as we automate and outsource many skilled human activities, we may be wrongly evaluating those activities on a "merely sufficing" standard of success.

Activities from driving to bartending to motorcycle maintenance might instead be reconceived on an Aristotelian standard of *aretê*, or being excellently in the situation. If the goal were to inhabit those situations excellently, then naturally it would be perverse to pursue automations that would prevent us from inhabiting those situations at all. We should instead want them to take longer. Vallor (2015) adds that, alongside the "de-skilling" of Sennett's or Crawford's craftsman, we must consider how we blunt our skill at moral decision-making, and thus our moral excellence, when robots rather than humans are placed in morally salient military and caregiving roles. Supposing that human excellence is a morally important goal, a human's attention needs to be directed not, say, to controlling a caregiving robot, but rather to the morally relevant features of the particular situation: in this case, the needs and body of the patient (Vallor 2015).

6.3.2 The Practical Identity Argument

While there is significant promise in reconceiving everyday situations of skilled action as opportunities for excellence, this approach could conceivably leave us with a rather open-ended commitment to doing things ourselves: Should I cut my own wood to build the desk at which I write, program my own word-processing software, and so on? We can stave off this conclusion by recalling that truly skilled, trained perception is necessarily *limited*, that is, *skilled at* perceiving only a limited set of "affordances" in the world (Noë 2009; Clark 2011; Gibson 2015). Such limitation was, after all, one thing our imagined Automanians wanted to overcome. Crowell offers a way to defend the goodness of a limited, skilled perceptual life in terms of the concept of "practical identities": this is to say that, while I am of course a human being in general, I consider and value myself more specifically as a parent, as a professor, or in terms of my other roles; my particular roles and identities permit me to value and understand my life and agency (Korsgaard 1996; Crowell 2013, 290). On Crowell's model, what it means to "be" some practical identity—say, a parent—is precisely having and following out the skilled, trained perceptions characteristic of that role (Crowell 2013, 290–1; Sokolowski 2000, 32ff.).

Like Sennett and Crawford, Crowell considers that in much daily activity, true success is more than what "merely suffices" to finish a job. In the terms that Crowell borrows from Heidegger, I am in my daily actions tacitly "concerned about my own being," that is, concerned existentially about who and what I am (Crowell 2013, 273). Building a birdhouse involves both success in the act of putting it together and success at building it in light of who I am trying to be. Am I trying to be a parent? A master carpenter? These roles specify very different success standards. Building a birdhouse with my small children and trying to be a parent will result in, to say the least, a less than perfect birdhouse.

Yet a crudely built birdhouse is obviously compatible with having had relative success at being a parent. Even if I am aiming for a perfect birdhouse as a master carpenter, I cannot meet the relevant standard of success by just 3D-printing one: my goal is *being* a master carpenter, which requires skilled perception and performance. Moreover, I do not succeed or fail to "be" a given identity inside my own head. The everyday performances of caring for children, biking them to school, cleaning up, playing—these are the sites where I realize success or failure at being a parent, because these for me *are* all attempts at being a parent (on top of getting the tasks completed). I cannot "attempt to be a parent" merely by thinking or willing to be one while my daily tasks are accomplished for me. To pretend that I can *be* anything merely in my own head, by wishing it so, is to chase after a fiction.

While I do occasionally think explicitly about being a parent or professor, I most importantly have my sense of those vocations in a more silent and automatic way, as my trained perceptions pick out objects and opportunities relevant to those goals in particular situations (Crowell 2013; Doyon 2015). Part of how I get to be a musician is that, out of the wealth of sense data passing through my eyes at any moment, I "stick with" the unfolding of a song over time, and each phrase manifests itself to me full of value and possibilities. If I never do this, whether because I am ill-trained or because I am too busy to attend to this slice of the world, then I am a musician emptily, in name only. If we imagine an Automanian whose attention brushed busily past all things—who, as it were, skipped over the surface of perception—we might suppose she would hold many of her identities in this empty way.

6.3.3 The Argument from the Goods of Agency

This line of thought may be extended further, to success at possessing very basic goods. Drummond argues that we cannot pursue even the goods of agency as such, in particular the general good of "free and insightful agency," in the abstract; rather, we pursue these in and through our pursuit of a particular "vocation" (2002, 41). I am not free or capable or knowledgeable in the abstract; rather, I am free or capable or knowledgeable in and through some determinate field of human action and interest. And I inhabit a determinate field of human action and interest—a vocation—by training myself through long habit to pursue and perceive the salient "vocational goods" among objects and situations in that environment (Drummond 2002, 27).

To pursue "knowledge" or "agency" in general would be foolish. Instead, I embed myself in, for example, the professor's environment and learn the art of seeing the objects and norms relevant to being a professor. The converse is true of vocations we don't pursue. I have neither the sensitivity nor the inclination to see whatever complexities the tech personnel see when they fix my computer; in this scenario, I lack a perceptual "situation" of comparable depth to what the tech personnel have. Part of what it means to feel at such a loss, as I do with my broken computer, is that my perceptual situation is too limited and shallow for me to exercise much agency. Without any perceptual complexity—as I just perceive a broken machine and an empty blur of tech jargon—I have little material on which to "be" intelligent or active. If in a broader sense I have failed to cultivate any such vocational sensitivities, then I have that much less situational depth to exercise myself as an intelligent and capable agent.

6.4 Charting Our Perceptual Future

For many of us, the unique urgency of emerging "smart" products and automations comes from the fact that skills we have spent many years cultivating—from driving to cooking, from musical composition to surgery—may shortly become activities that humans no longer need to do. In that case, we would be left holding a range of skill sets that we have no use for whatsoever. We have been informed, as it were, that these peculiarly human windows on certain corners of reality, which took us years of training to open, will be closing shortly. The proximity and sheer number of those windows that we expect will close, as we inhabit a world of increasingly "smart" objects, gives the issue its particular urgency. I have focused on what closing those windows could mean for our agency.

At this point, we are likely to be wondering which skills we ought to preserve. Is driving one of them? Baking bread? And so on. The short answer is (a) we should be sufficiently skilled perceivers to excellently inhabit the situations relevant to our own practical identities, (b) we have good reasons to bother "being" those identities, and (c) we do this by actually deploying skills and the art of skilled, trained attention. The longer answer is that we cannot be entirely sure which skills and situations are important, since our identities are currently played out in a wide variety of niches of the world of objects. For example, negotiating social cues attentively in a variety of environments, from traffic to the grocery store, *just is* how I get to be a public social being. I would be sorely misguided if I rushed past all such situations, as if by completing them I could beam myself to some situation of pure leisure where I would finally realize basic human goods. This is simply not how human goods work.

If an unexpected number of our everyday activities are arenas where we get to "be" something (rather than being shiftless cognitive blobs), then we would want to start thinking of many—perhaps very many—everyday activities on an Aristotelian-styled standard of excellence. We can say this while conceding that the good of doing things by our own skill does not always trump other considerations, as it does not for a driver who commutes four hours per day. My aim has merely been to present the value of skilled attention as a robustly competing consideration in debates on automation. I presume we would weigh the trade-offs on a case-by-case basis. Perhaps this gives us reason to do some everyday research: to wonder at our own attention in our daily labors and to consider what deep human goods we might be realizing as we see our small and particular slice of the world.

Works Cited

Aristotle. 2000. *Nicomachean Ethics*. Translated by Roger Crisp. Reprint, New York: Cambridge University Press.

Carr, Nicholas. 2014. *The Glass Cage: Automation and Us*. New York: W. W. Norton.

Clark, Andy. 2011. *Supersizing the Mind: Embodiment, Action, and Cognitive Extension*. New York: Oxford University Press.

Crawford, Matthew. 2015. *The World Beyond Your Head: On Becoming an Individual in an Age of Distraction*. New York: Farrar, Straus and Giroux.

Crowell, Stephen. 2013. *Normativity and Phenomenology in Husserl and Heidegger.* New York: Cambridge University Press.

Doyon, Maxime. 2015. "Perception and Normative Self-Consciousness." In *Normativity in Perception*, edited by Maxime Doyon and Thiemo Breyer, 38–55. London: Palgrave Macmillan.

Dreyfus, Hubert. 1992. *What Computers Still Can't Do: A Critique of Artificial Reason*. Cambridge, MA: MIT Press.

Drummond, John. 2002. "Aristotelianism and Phenomenology." In *Phenomenological Approaches to Moral Philosophy: A Handbook*, edited by John Drummond and Lester Embree, 15–45. Dordrecht: Kluwer Academic.

Drummond, John. 2007. "Phenomenology: Neither Auto- nor Hetero- Be." *Phenomenology and the Cognitive Sciences* 6 (1–2): 57–74.

Feenberg, Andrew. 1999. *Questioning Technology*. New York: Routledge.

Fuchs, Thomas and Jann E. Schlimme. 2009. "Embodiment and Psychopathology: A P henomenological Perspective." *Current Opinion in Psychiatry* 22: 570–5.

Gibson, James J. 2015. *The Ecological Approach to Visual Perception*. New York: Taylor & Francis.

Heidegger, Martin. 1977. "The Question Concerning Technology." In *The Question Concerning Technology and Other Essays.* Translated by William Lovitt. New York: Harper & Row.

Husserl, Edmund. 1998. *Ideas Pertaining to a Pure Phenomenology and to a Phenomenological Philosophy, First Book.* Translated by F. Kersten. Dordrecht: Kluwer Academic.

Korsgaard, Christine. 1996. *The Sources of Normativity*. New York: Cambridge University Press.

Marcuse, Herbert. 1964. *One-Dimensional Man*. Boston: Beacon Press.

Maskivker, J. 2010. "Employment as a Limitation on Self-Ownership." *Human Rights Review* 12 (1): 27–45.

Matthews, E. 2004. "Merleau-Ponty's Body-Subject and Psychiatry." *International Review of Psychiatry* 16: 190–8.

Merleau-Ponty, Maurice. 2012. *Phenomenology of Perception*. Translated by Donald A. Landes. New York: Routledge.

Noë, Alva. 2009. *Out of Our Heads: Why You Are Not Your Brain, and Other Lessons from the Biology of Consciousness*. New York: Hill & Wang.

Sennett, Richard. 2008. *The Craftsman*. New Haven, CT: Yale University Press.

Smith, David Woodruff. 2004. *Mind World: Essays in Phenomenology and Ontology*. New York: Cambridge University Press.

Sokolowski, Robert. 2000. *Introduction to Phenomenology*. New York: Cambridge University Press.

Vallor, Shannon. 2015. "Moral Deskilling and Upskilling in a New Machine Age: Reflections on the Ambiguous Future of Character." *Philosophy and Technology* 28 (1): 107–24.

II TRUST AND HUMAN–ROBOT INTERACTIONS

Introduction

In part II, we see that programming is not just about what's legal and ethical; responsible design in robotics also needs to account for human psychology. This part therefore focuses on issues of trust, deception, and other aspects of human–robot interactions.

We are already seeing robots living and working alongside humans, as well as caring for them, for example, the elderly or infirm. But can such a "carebot" really care, since it has no genuine emotions? It's quite plausible to think that care requires internal cognitive and emotional states that robots lack. But Darian Meacham and Matthew Studley argue in chapter 7 that care robots may help create *caring environments* through certain types of expressive movement, regardless of whether they have internal emotional states. They conclude that, despite some similarities, such human–robot interactions are not equivalent to human–human interactions, but those differences may change as care robots become more widespread and our social and cognitive structures adapt to this new reality.

We might ask similar questions about the possibility of robots as friends. In chapter 8, Alexis Elder examines this issue as it relates to autistic children. Other authors have noted similarities between autistic humans and robots, positing that robots may offer real therapeutic value for patients with autism spectrum disorders. But Elder worries that their usefulness is based on deception: their appealingly friendly presence can lead patients to think of them as real friends—indeed, to prefer robotic companionship to the human kind. This creates a potential moral hazard, which Elder argues can be mitigated by careful design and responsible use, and so, properly utilized, such therapies do offer genuine promise.

Of course, roboticists in the lab are intimately familiar with the limitations and shortcomings of their creations. But once a technology is adopted for widespread use, many nonspecialists will naively assume that the technology can reliably function in all everyday contexts. This creates a problem of *overtrust*—for example, the adoption of robots in healthcare settings like hospitals may well result in the users becoming overreliant on and overtrusting the technology.

In chapter 9, Jason Borenstein, Ayanna Howard, and Alan R. Wagner examine overtrust in the context of robots working with children. They argue that the robotics community has an obligation to examine this tendency to overtrust and to develop strategies to mitigate the risk to children, parents, and healthcare providers that could result. The authors suggest some strategies to reduce the risks and describe a framework that they argue should guide the future deployment of robots in the pediatric domain.

"Trust" is a concept that pervades human relationships and weaves them together, and humans can, for the most part, negotiate and navigate issues of trust with a subconscious fluency. But the prospect of integrating robots more closely into human life should make us question the nature and value of trust to begin with.

In chapter 10, Jesse Kirkpatrick, Erin N. Hahn, and Amy J. Haufler do just this. They distinguish interpersonal trust from institutional trust and contrast both to trust in oneself or one's government. Using a multidisciplinary approach that includes philosophy, law, and neuroscience, they explore the issue of trust in human–robot interactions. They deem interpersonal trust to be most relevant to our discussions of human–robot interactions and give an account of what that consists in. Armed with this account, they argue that human–robot interactions could approach or achieve actual interpersonal trust, but they also flag some of the potential deleterious consequences of facilitating interpersonal trust in human–robot interactions. They conclude with a call for further scholarship to address the novel philosophical, empirical, legal, and policy issues related to interpersonal trust between humans and robots—investigations like those found in other chapters in part II.

If it makes sense to say that humans and robots could trust one another, then we are immediately confronted by a related issue: Should they *distrust* each other? In chapter 11, Alistair M. C. Isaac and Will Bridewell argue that deception, rather than something to be avoided in human–robot interaction, instead may well be a moral necessity. After all, humans use all manner of deception in the simple act of communicating, including sarcasm, innuendo, and bullshit. To function well, social robots will need the ability to detect and evaluate deceptive speech by humans, lest they become vulnerable to manipulation by malevolent agents and cause harm unintended by their designers.

But, perhaps more surprisingly, Isaac and Bridewell also argue that effective social robots must be able to *produce* deceptive speech themselves. Take "white lies," for example: in human conversation this technically deceptive speech often performs an important pro-social function, and the social integration of robots will be possible only if they participate in this kind of deceit. (Honesty is not always a virtue, it seems.) They argue that strategic reasoning about deception and producing convincing deceptive speech require a theory of mind and the capacity for having hidden goals, an "ulterior motive." Rather than being problematic, they view deception-capable robots as compatible with, if not required by, the most prominent programs to ensure robots behave ethically.

Much of this discussion focuses on integrating robots smoothly into human environments. Many of these authors suggest that robots will have to take up some of the nuances of human behavior and communication in order to function well, blurring the line between archetypically robotic behavior and human behavior. Human psychology often makes us willing—if unconscious—participants in this process.

Kate Darling, in chapter 12, concludes part II's investigations into the ethics of human–robot interactions by examining the human tendency to project our own ways of thinking onto creatures very different from ourselves. After all, people have a tendency to project lifelike qualities onto robots. Her MIT lab's experiments on human–robot interaction indicate that framing robots through anthropomorphic language (like a personified name or story) can have an impact on how people perceive and treat a robot. So should we encourage people to anthropomorphize robots through framing, or is this a practice we ought to discourage—to train people out of?

The short answer: it depends. Darling finds that there are serious concerns about anthropomorphizing robotic technology in some contexts, but that there are also cases where encouraging anthropomorphism is desirable. Because people respond to framing, we can use framing itself to help us separate the circumstances in which anthropomorphizing robots is desirable from those in which it is not. But acknowledging and understanding such anthropomorphic framing will be a key to getting right the ethics of human–robot interaction, integration, and policy.

Many of the benefits that robots promise can be secured with little human interaction—for example, the efficiency gains of automating factories. But other universes of goods are accessed only through close contact between robots and humans. Part II points toward surprising answers that should guide future research: for example, that robots *should* deceive us in behavior or speech or that robots really can *care* for us. As we scrutinize the possibilities for integrating robots into these spheres of human life—what is it to care or trust, really?—we also end up discovering truths about our relationships with one another.

7 COULD A ROBOT CARE? IT'S ALL IN THE MOVEMENT

Darian Meacham and Matthew Studley

A recurring concern in the literature surrounding the use of robots in medical care—we call these robotic carers "RCs" for short—is deception (e.g., Sparrow 2002; Sparrow and Sparrow 2006; Sharkey and Sharkey 2010; Wallach and Allen 2010). The concern goes something like this: due to certain salient behavioral aspects of interaction with an RC, human patients may erroneously be led to believe that they have a reciprocal emotional or affective relation with the RC. Put simply, there is a risk that human patients will come to believe that RCs really care for them. As this is impossible, it is a form of deception and harms patients' dignity and autonomy, and puts them at risk of other emotional and psychological harms.

We take at least the first part of this concern, that there is a high risk of deception, to be intuitively convincing and broadly accepted. Sharkey and Sharkey (2010) provide a helpful summary of the deception arguments in the literature and themselves link deception by "caring robots" to a loss of dignity on the part of the patient. Sparrow and Sparrow also provide a good account of this intuitively satisfying position:

> In most cases, when people feel happy, it will be because they (mistakenly) believe that the robot has properties which it does not. These beliefs may be conscious beliefs, as in cases where people insist that robots really are kind and do care about them, or are pleased to see them, etc. They might also involve unconscious, or preconscious, responses and reactions to the "behavior" of the robot (Breazeal 2002, ch. 2). It is these delusions that cause people to feel loved or cared for by robots and thus to experience the benefits of being cared for. (2006, 155)

It is significant here that Sparrow and Sparrow acknowledge that the patient may indeed have the experience of being cared for. What they object to is that this experience will be founded in a deception and an attribution of certain properties to the RC that it does not *really* have, namely internal cognitive and emotional states. Sharkey and Sharkey (2010) cash out the consequences of this and Sparrow's earlier position:

> Sparrow argued that the relationships of seniors with robot pets, "are predicated on mistaking, at a conscious or unconscious level, the robot for a real animal. For an individual to benefit significantly from ownership of a robot pet they must systematically delude themselves regarding the real nature of their relation with the animal. It requires sentimentality of a morally deplorable sort. Indulging in such sentimentality violates a (weak) duty that we have to ourselves to apprehend the world accurately. The design and manufacture of these robots is unethical in so far as it presupposes or encourages this." (Sparrow 2002, 306)

We think that this objection is grounded on a problematic insistence that in order to be "real," care must be linked to reciprocal internal cognitive or affective states (emotions) that not only are correlated to outward expression of emotions, but ground and are antecedent to them, consequently making them real. Subsequently, patients who think they are experiencing a real emotional bond with an RC, which is by nature incapable of such internal affective, i.e., subjective, states are being deceived. The upshot of this is that an RC could not conceivably *really* care for a patient. The RC would at best manifest convincing outward signs of care, hence deceiving the often emotionally vulnerable individuals these RCs will most likely be "caring" for.

Counter to this position, we argue that what matters in a caring relation is not the internal states of the agents participating in the relation, but rather a meaningful context: a care environment that is formed by gestures, movements, and articulations that express attentiveness and responsiveness to vulnerabilities within the relevant context. We could summarize our position by saying that we think meaning is in the movements and in the salient differences that movement makes to a meaning-infused behavioral context.

Our approach is thus similar to Coeckelbergh's (2014) relational approach to the moral standing of machines; we do not discuss the moral standing of RCs, but it is certainly a related question. We also argue that in human–human relations and some human–animal relations where care is not questioned for its reality or authenticity, there is no access to the internal states of the other. What is relied on and generative of relations of human–human or animal–human care environments are certain types of expressive movement.

Hospital wards, nursing homes, or home care situations would all, ideally, be examples of care environments. In a different context, so would nurseries or crèches. In such environments, what is ultimately salient is not the internal affective states of the carers, but rather their expressive behavior. We may assume that the two have a positive correlation (caring behavior correlated to caring internal affective states), but the correlation is certainly not our primary concern. In some situations we may readily accept that there cannot be a correlation, but that a care environment can nonetheless be maintained, e.g., in situations of considerable stress for nursing staff, where a form of deception vis-à-vis vulnerable patients becomes a key component of the job (Zapf 2002).

In such situations, internal affective states are simply not what is salient; the forms of expression that constitute the care environment are what matter. What particular movements are constitutive of a care environment are likely dependent on a universal or species-specific semiotics, as well as local and situation-specific cultural mores and conventions. It is not our intention in this chapter to try to characterize these conditions other than in the most general sense; that is the task of social robotics engineers who seek to build robots capable of constituting and participating in care environments.

On the basis of this, we argue that caring relations between human patients and robots cannot be precluded simply on the grounds that robots do not have internal mental or affective states.[1] Thus caring environments are neither purely functional in the sense of attending only to physical needs or functions, nor dependent on the internal states of the constituting or participating agents. The meaningful relations necessary for the constitution of a care environment are wholly contained or made manifest in external movements. Meaning is an emergent property of movements within an environment. Hence, we think it is possible that an RC could theoretically function as a constituting agent in a care environment, provided it was consistently capable of the required expressive and reciprocal movements.

We call this position the Environmental Hypothesis and think it to be compatible with three of the four "ethical elements of care" presented by Tronto (2005): attentiveness, competence, and responsiveness. The element of "responsibility" presents a greater challenge to the possibility of RCs constituting agents of care environments.

In the following sections, we first examine the state of the art in developmental and social robotics in order to demonstrate that the frame of this discussion is very much relevant to current developments in robotics and does not sit in the realm of science fiction. We then expand on the theoretical underpinnings of the Environmental Hypothesis and examine three possible objections to it: (1) care is future-oriented, (2) care involves responsibility, and (3) the Environmental Hypothesis condones deception in the manner objected to by Sparrow and

Sparrow. In the conclusion, we look at some empirical studies that we think both support and undermine the Environmental Hypothesis. The arguments that we make in this chapter are highly significant for the ethics of robot use in medical and assistive care, which looks set to increase dramatically in the European Union, North America, and parts of Asia (Japan and South Korea). We support these arguments philosophically by drawing on enactivist and phenomenological theories of meaning, embodiment, and interpersonal relations.

7.1 Robotic Realities

Until recently, robots were used in specialized and constrained domains where they performed scripted tasks in isolation from humans, e.g., industrial robots working on automotive production lines, where their activity is characterized by flawless repetition in the absence of confusing variation.

Modern robotics seeks to expand on this in two main ways: (1) by building robots that are capable of autonomous movement and decision-making in natural environments, and even of learning new skills and behaviors through these interactions;[2] and (2) by building machines that are capable of social interactions, responding to the nuances of verbal and nonverbal communication with such facility that they can be truly useful work- and playmates. A recent review of the literature suggests that the most profound societal impacts of the new robotics can be categorized according to their domain: home, healthcare, traffic, policing, and military (Royakkers and van Est 2015).

In healthcare, research and development in the new robotics falls into three main categories. First, there are smart machines that assist patients and compensate for their disabilities, e.g., robots to help dress you, to restore your strength and mobility, or to rehabilitate you after an accident or stroke. Second, smarter machines can assist healthcare staff members in their jobs by carrying, lifting, monitoring, or even performing surgical procedures, etc. Finally, machines equipped with social abilities might assist patients cognitively, taking on some of the social roles that human carers have hitherto fulfilled. As Coeckelbergh observes: "First, we delegated care from family, neighbors and friends to professionals and institutions. . . . But if this solution is inadequate in the light of the demographical and political situation, then why not delegate care to robots?" (2012, 281). Goeldner et al. (2015) show how the focus in care robotics research has changed from components such as robot grippers (1970s to 1990s), through navigation and mobility, to the current focus on social interactions and usability testing. During the same period there has been a massive increase in the number of publications, the number of patents applied for and granted, and the number of organizations and individuals involved in the research and development. By far the greatest number of patent applications are submitted by commercial organizations based in Japan, which is perhaps unsurprising given Japan's enthusiasm for robotic technologies and its aging population.[3] If perceived need and investment are leading indicators, care robots are coming.[4]

A brief overview of some current projects funded by the European Commission (2016) may give a sense of the state of the art. The DALI project provides cognitive assistance and guidance in complex environments, e.g., shopping malls. ENRICHME is developing an integrated platform for monitoring and interaction to support mental fitness and social interactions. GIRAFF+ combines mobile robotics and ambient sensing to offer social interaction and monitoring for independent living. GrowMeUp is an adaptive system to provide intelligent dialogue capable of recognizing emotions and building emotional bonds, while Hobbit entices users to take care of the robot in order to develop real affection toward it and hence accept care from it.

There is a strong social element in all these projects; they do not just develop machines that help you up the stairs. They provide props for independent living, props that rely on effective social interaction, and they seek to address in some part elder users' social, emotional, and cognitive needs. How soon will we see social robots in care roles? The process has long since started; the Paro robotic baby seal has been studied as a therapeutic tool in care environments since 2001 (Shibata 2001). We expect robots designed to elicit emotion to walk among us in the coming decade—our intimation is that the emotions they engender may be profound (Rocks et al. 2009).

7.2 It's All in the Movement: The Environmental Hypothesis

The Environmental Hypothesis stipulates that what matters in a caring relation is not the internal states of the agents participating in the relation, but rather a meaningful context that is constituted by expressive movements. If RCs are capable of the requisite movement, then there should not be an obstacle to them in theory acting as constitutors of care environments. One way to think about this would be to use Gregory Bateson's idea that "the elementary unit of information is a difference which makes a difference" (1972, 457–9). What this means is that some differences—and this is to be taken in the sense of physical, material, or spatial differences in an environment—will enact a shift in the meaningful relations manifest in that environment. Others will not. Those that do convey information or meaning.[5] Our hypothesis is thereby an externalist one with regard to meaning and also to care: care and meaning are things in the world founded in these differences that make a difference.

Thus the negative formulation of the Environmental Hypothesis can be phrased in terms of a refutation of the claim that internal states are necessary for caring relations, which can be sketched in the following manner: (1) Internal emotional states are not accessible in human–human relations; i.e., I do not have access to the internal mental and emotional states of others, if such states do indeed exist internally. (2) Environments and relations of care are possible between humans who do not have access to each other's inner states; we know this because we experience them. The caring caress of another can create an experience of care on my side, not just prior to any judgment about internal states, but regardless of such judgments' existence or validity. Moreover, environments and relations of care are possible between humans and some non-human animals, which even if they also have internal states do not self-ascribe them, i.e., do not have a self-reflexive relation to their internal states. (3) As we accept the existence of care environments and relations between humans and non-human animals where there is no access to internal states, there is no reason to rule out the possibility of care environments constituted by reciprocal relations between humans and RCs, provided that the RC can adequately generate the movements necessary for the constitution of a caring environment.

A rejoinder to this would be that an RC is built to merely *mimic* appropriate expressive gestures. While an exhausted nurse or human carer may also be mimicking gestures, he or she would presumably have an understanding of what it would really feel like to authentically make the same or similar movement. The carer who is faking it, so to speak, draws on an understanding and experience of what authentic care is like in order to create the deception. Therein lies the crux of the argument against the Environmental Hypothesis: care has a feel (on the side of the carer) that makes it authentic; since robots do not have subjective consciousness and hence have no feel for what they are doing, any care they might look to be providing is inauthentic and deceptive.

But this is misleading for a number of reasons. First, it risks an overly Cartesian or "analogical inferentialist" interpretation not only of our position but of intersubjective or interpersonal experience in general. In this faulty interpretation, external sounds (language) or gestures would be understood as the outward signs of internal states (thought). Theories like this maintain that a thinking subject has "privileged access" to her or his own mental states, and this justifies the self-ascription of beliefs, sensations, desires, etc. This justification is completely lacking in our experience of others. Our experience of others' mental states is mediated solely by external signs: the movement and sounds made by the body. On the basis of these external signs, we make an inferential judgment pertaining to the inner states of the other subject. The judgment is most often grounded in an analogy between the correspondence of our own internal and external states and those of the other.

What is particularly important for our purposes here is that the meaning-forming processes that are important for the caring relation are internal and private to the subject. In such a case an RC might provide all the necessary signs of having the requisite mental states. These states might even be sufficient for establishing the care environment, but they would remain at the level of mimicry. They would not really reflect the thoughts or feelings of the RC, because it would not have any. The cared-for human subject could then falsely attribute internal states to an RC that was literally just going through the motions, and hence be deceived. As this situation occurs in human–human contexts, where we do not rule out the possibility of caring environments, it is not obvious how serious an issue this is when it concerns an RC.

Moreover, our position denies that this is how meaning-formation works in intersubjective contexts. Counter the "analogical inferentialist" approach, we could be said to take an enactivist approach to intersubjectivity: "enactivist approaches . . . emphasize patterns of interaction and active engagement instead of any alleged internal representations of the environment" (Degenaar and O'Regan 2015, 1). An enactivist understanding of intersubjective relations conforms to the view that our understanding and interpretation of others' behavior is first and foremost an "embodied activity that is out in the open, not a behind-the-scenes driver of what would otherwise be mere movement" (Hutto and Myin, forthcoming). The crux of our position is that the relevant meaning-structures are formed in the space between moving subjects and are "best explained in terms of and understood as dynamically unfolding, situated embodied interactions and engagement with environmental affordances" (Hutto and Kirchhoff 2016, 304). The upshot of this is potentially quite significant. It is not just that our experience of meaningful relations with others does not proceed on the basis of an inferential judgment pertaining to the internal states of others; it is rather that internal states may not play a primary role in the formation of the relevant relations. This point is illustrated well by the French philosopher Maurice Merleau-Ponty:

> Imagine that I am in the presence of someone who, for one reason or another, is extremely annoyed with me. My interlocutor gets angry and I notice that he is expressing his anger by speaking aggressively, by gesticulating and shouting. But where is this anger? People will say that it is in the mind of my interlocutor. What this means is not entirely clear. For I could not imagine the malice and cruelty which I discern in my opponent's looks separated from his gestures, speech and body. None of this takes place in some otherworldly realm, in some shrine located beyond the body of the angry man. It really is here, in this room and in this part of the room, that the anger breaks forth. It is in the space between him and me that it unfolds. (2004, 83)

To us, this seems to underline the characteristics of the position we take here: meaning structures are formed in the world through the organism's engagement with its environment. This engagement most often occurs "below" the level of active reflective consciousness. Again, what matters here is that the behavioral context is a meaningful one, modulated by salient differences or changes within the environment that should again be understood primarily as modulations of meaning. Expressive movement means precisely this: movements that enact a salient change in the environment understood in terms of meaningful context.

This leaves a question of what kind of expression is constitutive of an environment of care. A minimal threshold condition for an environment of care likely entails movements manifesting an attentiveness and appropriate response to perceived expressions or signs of vulnerability and movements eliciting a reasonable expectation for continued attentiveness and response. We see no reason in theory that an RC could not fulfill this threshold condition.

This is unlikely to satisfy critics who wish to establish an inextricable relation between care, or the *authentic* experience of being cared for, and the supposed internal or subjective feel of caring authentically that is on the side of the carer. This model of *real* (i.e., not inauthentic or deceptive) care seems to require something like the formula "care + *a*," where "*a*" is the subjective feeling of really caring that is on the side of the carer. We find this problematic insofar as the subjective feel of caring is, by virtue of being subjective, inaccessible to the person being cared for and apprehensible only in the external signs that make up the "care" element of the formula—and even this requires maintaining an internalist understanding of the constitution of care, wherein the actions of caring are preceded by the feel of really caring.

Our position, as should be clear, is closer to the inverse. We agree with Wittgenstein that "an inner process," the supposed authentic feel of caring, "stands in need of an outer criteria *[sic]*" (Wittgenstein 1953, ¶580), i.e., the interaction with the surrounding world that constitutes the care environment. Following Ryle (1949), who argued that "it would be mistaken to think that intelligent behavior is intelligence in virtue of hidden operations in a hidden realm" (as cited in Degenaar and O'Regan 2015, 6), we think that the same can be said of care, which is a kind of emotional intelligence.

7.3 Some Objections to the Environmental Hypothesis

7.3.1 Care is Future-Oriented

A possible objection to the Environmental Hypothesis and its contention about RCs is that the attitude of care is often taken to entail a specific attunement or orientation toward the future, and more specifically the future well-being of the agents whose expressive activity constitutes the care environment. This future-oriented understanding of care may be in part derived from Heidegger's analyses of care as the basic temporal structure of human temporality.[6] Human beings inherit a meaningful environment and comport themselves toward it in a manner that manifests an orientation toward the future, if not necessarily explicit planning for the future or even thinking about it. In the applied context of medical care robots, this attitude separates care from maintenance, which is focused on the repair of specific functional relations between the organism and its environment. The objection would follow: as an RC presumably does not share the structure of temporal attunement that could be ascribed to humans, it is not capable of manifesting the behavior requisite for the constitution of an environment of care.

This objection bears a similarity to the initial position against RCs that we sketched out earlier. It assumes the necessity of an inner state or behind-the-scenes driver, in this instance an inner temporal orientation of conscious processes, for the manifestation of a certain type of external behavior. Our response to this objection thus takes the same form as the general argument presented in the preceding section. The expressive behavior manifested in the environment of care bears the necessary hallmarks of concern for the future. These can be best described in terms of expectation of future attention to vulnerability and reciprocation. It is necessary that an RC exhibit a certain canon of reasonable predictability in its behavior, as we would expect from a biological organism of sufficient complexity to be an active co-constitutor of an environment of care.

Di Paolo expands on this in arguing that while we cannot make robots alive, we can endow them with "mechanisms for acquiring a way of life, that is, with habits" (2003, 13). Habits are a temporally dispositional form of expressive behavior. A robot programmed with the capacity for behavioral development is indeed likely to develop behavioral dispositions that are functionally and aesthetically similar to the kind of behavior that we infer when we talk about an orientation toward future well-being in caring relations. In fact, such orientations are manifested and experienced in habitual behavior; they relate to consistent patterns of previous appropriate action and an apparent disposition toward the continuation of those patterns. Again, it's not a matter of internal representational states. Thus the question of the future orientation of care does not present any special obstacle to the Environmental Hypothesis.

7.3.2 Responsibility Requires Existential Self-Concern and Susceptibility to Sanction

The question of responsibility presents a more serious objection. This objection depends on the manifest behavioral expression of obligation or responsibility being a required constituent aspect of a care environment. One reason this becomes a problem (there may be others) is that it seems feasible that a necessary condition of responsibility is a receptivity to sanction in the case of a breach of responsibility or obligation.

Receptivity to sanction, in turn, seems to require existential self-concern (conscious or not) for the entity's own continued existence. This kind of concern may well be limited to living systems. Certain forms of enactivism and its precursors (e.g., that of Hans Jonas) have insisted that living things display a concern for their own continued existence and a behavioral disposition toward the continuation of that existence (although there are plenty of examples of altruistic sacrificial behavior among living things, from slime molds to human beings). Likewise, if receptivity to sanction is a condition of responsibility, receptivity to suffering might be a further condition; and suffering is by all accounts a subjective affective state of the kind we have admitted robots do not have. Although there is ongoing research aimed at building an "artificial robot nervous system to teach robots how to feel pain," this would only allow robots to respond faster to potential damage to themselves (Ackerman 2016). Such robotic pain avoidance systems would likely not be equivalent to the receptivity to sanction and suffering that may be required for responsibility. It nonetheless has potential important consequences for the future of human–robot interaction.

This problem could be countered in the fashion of the Environmental Hypothesis in general. An existential, privately subjective concern for continued existence is not a necessary condition for the intersubjective manifestation of responsibility, nor is the possibility of suffering *qua* subjective qualia, in neither humans nor robots. Experiencing another as assuming responsibility, like future-orientedness, remains a question of expressive behavior that need not bear any correlation with inner states and does not in fact require inner states at all. Our argument here may hinge on an aesthetic point. What perhaps matters is the appearance of sensitivity to rebuke or even suffering. As with the previous point about future orientation, when we ask what is salient in our experience of another's taking on of obligation or responsibility, it is a question of habits, dispositions, and expression. It is the consistency of actions that matters to our assessment of responsibility and obligation.

This response does not address the further objection that, while susceptibility to sanction may be a necessary condition of responsibility, it is not clear what type of behavior manifests this susceptibility. What might be the case is that whatever form of robot behavior is required, it must be such that some kind of empathy may be established with the others in the care environment, meaning that there is an appropriate experience, grounded in the behavior of the robot, of responsibility being taken. As we will discuss in the conclusion, there is evidence of empathic relations between humans and robots.

There is of course a simpler way around this objection, for those who insist on the deeply subjective and private nature of *real* responsibility. We can simply drop the requirement of responsibility as an ethical element of care environments and say that ethical work done by the concepts of responsibility and/or obligation is already done by the establishment of a canon of reasonable predictability in the expressive behavior of the agents reciprocally involved in the constitution of a care environment. In other words, reasonable expectation of the continuation of the caring relationship is sufficient.

7.3.3 Artificial Care May Involve Deception

The question of deception is in many ways the driving force of this chapter: if you experience an RC caring for you in such a manner that you experience being cared for in a caring environment, are you really being cared for or just being deceived into experiencing and feeling as though you are? The position that we have argued for here puts experience and its authenticity in the world and in the relations and interactions between the organism (in this case, the cared-for), its perceptual surroundings, and the other salient agents or actors in that environment. It rules out a reliance on some kind of reporting of evidence (we don't think there is any) of internal representational states, be they affective or cognitive, beyond the expressive behavior of other agents, in assessing the authenticity or veracity of a caring relation or care environment.

Here we can flip the argument: if you experience yourself really being cared for or if you experience your environment as a caring one and if that experience is persisting and consistent, then there are no good reasons to think that the care is not real or that you are being deceived. When we talk about care, the salient kinds of statements are, we think, *not* like the following: I am experiencing real, authentic care because I am completely confident that the subjective internal representations or qualia of the carer are the appropriate ones.

The more radical end of our argument is that there is no deception in the potential environment of care constituted by an RC and a human. The emotions and relations of care are real, even if the RC is not reflectively self-aware of the presence of the meaning-structures that it is playing an active role in constituting. O'Regan goes further, arguing that the all-important "feel" of something (in this case caring) is a "way of interacting with the world. . . . [T]he quality of all feels, in all sensory modalities, is constituted by such laws of sensorimotor interaction with the environment" (2012, 125). O'Regan explains this to mean that what it is to feel is to have cognitive access to the ongoing sensorimotor interaction (133) and, presumably, to be able to adjust that interaction on the basis of changes in the environment wherein the sensorimotor interaction takes place.

If it's possible for an RC to have this kind of cognitive access to its environment and actions when doing what looks like care, then according to this model it's feasible to say that the RC feels itself caring. If we take Thompson's enactive account of cognitive processes—"[They] emerge from the nonlinear and circular causality of continuous sensorimotor interactions involving the brain, body, and environment. The central metaphor for this approach is the mind as an embodied dynamic system in the world, rather than as a neural network in the head" (2007, 11)—there is no reason to preclude these criteria being met by an embodied, developmental machine learning system.

A retort to this is likely to be that care or caring is much different from the feel of squeezing a sponge. If we are talking about a reflective concept of care, then perhaps yes, it's likely to be a set of actions and dispositional attitudes. That a machine or RC might have access to a set of interactions that together have the feel of care is certainly not inconceivable, nor does it seem necessary that a carer have a developed and reflective concept of care in order to experience caring. If we accept that young children and even some animals can be extremely caring without having any concept of care, it seems quite reasonable to say that they are indeed feeling care by way of various interactions in the world without being able to say precisely what they are feeling.

Moreover, it is probably not necessary that people being cared for adopt our externalist thesis in order to accept the relations of care with an RC as "real," at least in the phenomenological sense of being real experiences, although of course it would help. The Environmental Hypothesis is probably closer in proximity to everyday experience than its opponents. Humans develop attachments and experience emotions such as empathy in all sorts of situations where it is clear that the other agent does not have the supposedly appropriate states with which to empathize. Human emotion shows itself to be both robust and promiscuous.

It is also important to note that human carers may be deceptive in their emotional displays. Zapf (2002) notes that nurses engage in both "emotion work," in which they control their emotional response, and "sympathy work," in which they attempt to guide a patient's emotions in a desired direction in order to facilitate the primary task in which they are engaged, e.g., a nurse using a soothing voice to calm a frightened child.[7] It is clear, then, that caring environments constituted by human–human relations may of necessity be characterized by emotional pretense while remaining real caring environments.

7.4 Conclusion

Although it seems unlikely that empirical verification of our hypothesis will satisfy those concerned with deception—since while they do acknowledge that a patient may indeed experience being cared for by an RC, they take that experience to be inauthentic or deceptive—it's perhaps nonetheless interesting, by way of conclusion, to look at some of the empirical findings that might support or undermine the argument that we have made.

There is some evidence from neural studies that our emotional responses to artificial emotion might be similar to our responses to real emotion, albeit muted (Chaminade et al. 2010), and that we empathize with robot "pain" in a similar way to our response to human pain (Suzuki 2015), although it has also been shown that interactions with artificial partners do not cause stimulation of those areas of the brain that it has been suggested are responsible for the inference of mental states of our fellow humans, e.g., the medial prefrontal cortex and right temporoparietal junction (Chaminade et al. 2012). This may suggest that, while emotional relations with RCs are indeed possible, they aren't equivalent to human–human relations. There may be a kind of "uncanny valley" type of phenomenon here, where the almost but not completely lifelike behavior of an RC is a stumbling block for the types of relations that we have argued are, at least in theory, possible. This is for many, ourselves included, a comforting thought.

But we might also ask if, as the behaviors of machines become more accurate in their mimicry of the semantics of human interactions, we will accept their veracity in the same way we accept that our human partners are emotionally invested in our well-being, or if we will always "know" or suspect the falsity of the former as much as we "know" the truth of the latter. It could be the case that better semblance of human behavior or changing attitudes and increased exposure to such agents in society will have an impact on the degree and scope of emotional relations that we can have with machines and RCs in particular.

Turkle et al. (2006) have shown that children who interact with "relational artifacts" ascribe these devices to a class of being intermediate between the living and nonliving, and others have shown strong evidence that robot pets "also embodied attributes of living animals, such as having mental states" (Melson et al. 2009, 546). It may very well be the case that when a generation that has grown up with robots as playthings, assistants, and perhaps colleagues reaches old age, its capacities and potentials for human–machine relations will be greater than what studies today show.

Notes

1. There are some surprising consequences of this argument; e.g., a behaviorally appropriate expressive relation between two robots must indeed be considered as a caring relation and not just mimicry of one. We call this the *Wall-E* (the name of an animated film about two robots falling in love) scenario, and we have to bite the bullet on that upshot.

2. We use "building" here to connote the process of creation that for modern robotics may make use of autopoietic elements, e.g., through evolutionary, developmental, or adaptive processes.
3. Goeldner et al. (2015) note that the explicit purpose of care for elderly or disabled users did not appear until 2005. The field of care robotics is now distinct and vibrant, with growing investment and the expectation of financial return.
4. Fifty million euros have been invested by the European Commission FP7 and AAL research programs in robotics projects to support elders' independent living. This has been extended in the European Commission Horizon 2020 program by an additional 185 million euros (European Commission 2016). This increase in funding is an indication of the perceived necessity of robotics technology in addressing the shortfall in carers in an aging society and is mirrored by funding in such countries as South Korea, Japan, and the United States.
5. A distinction can be made between the terms "information" and "meaning", but Bateson does not use "information" in a limited sense of negative entropy.
6. Heidegger gives "existential formulae for the structure of care as 'ahead-of itself—Being-already in (a world)—Being alongside (entities encountered in the world)'" (1962, 364).
7. It is recognized that workers' suppression of their real emotions in order to perform their job contributes to work stress and burnout (Cordes and Dougherty 1997). Many medical professionals find themselves on the periphery of extremely traumatic events, and in responding to others' pain by suppressing their own feelings, or with helplessness and anger, they subject to high rates of "compassion fatigue" (Yoder 2010). This could be a reason for introducing robots to take on some of the emotion and sympathy work to which Zapf refers.

Works Cited

Ackerman, Evan. 2016. "Researchers Teaching Robots to Feel and React to Pain." *IEEE Spectrum*, May 24.

Bateson, Gregory. 1972. *Steps to an Ecology of Mind: Collected Essays in Anthropology, Psychiatry, Evolution, and Epistemology*. Chicago: University of Chicago Press.

Breazeal, Cynthia, L. 2002. *Designing Sociable Robots*. Cambridge, MA: MIT Press.

Chaminade, T., D. Rosset, D. Da Fonseca, B. Nazarian, E. Lutcher, G. Cheng, and C. Deruelle. 2012. "How Do We Think Machines Think? An fMRI Study of Alleged Competition with an Artificial Intelligence." *Frontiers in Human Neuroscience* 6: 103.

Chaminade, Thierry, Massimiliano Zecca, Sarah-Jayne Blakemore, Atsuo Takanishi, Chris D. Frith, Silvestro Micera, Paolo Dario, Giacomo Rizzolatti, Vittorio Gallese, and Maria Alessandra Umiltà. 2010. "Brain Response to a Humanoid Robot in Areas Implicated in the Perception of Human Emotional Gestures." *PLoS One* 5 (7): e11577.

Coeckelbergh, Mark. 2012. "Care Robots, Virtual Virtue, and the Best Possible Life." In *The Good Life in a Technological Age*, edited by Philip Brey, Adam Briggle, and Edward Spence, 281–92. Abingdon: Taylor & Francis.

Coeckelbergh, Mark. 2014. "The Moral Standing of Machines: Towards a Relational and Non-Cartesian Moral Hermeneutics." *Philosophy of Technology* 27: 61–77.

Cordes, Cynthia L. and Thomas W. Dougherty. 1993. "A Review and an Integration of Research on Job Burnout." *Academy of Management Review* 18 (4): 621–56.

Degenaar, Jan and J. Kevin O'Regan. 2015. "Sensorimotor Theory and Enactivism." *Topoi*, August 15, 1–15. http://philpapers.org/rec/DEGSTA-3.

Di Paolo E. A. 2003. "Organismically-inspired Robotics: Homeostatic Adaptation and Teleology Beyond the Closed Sensorimotor Loop." In *Dynamical Systems Approaches to Embodiment and Sociality*, edited by Murase K., Asakura, 19–42. Adelaide: Advanced Knowledge International.

European Commission. 2016. "EU-Funded Projects in Robotics for Ageing Well." http://ec.europa.eu/newsroom/dae/document.cfm?doc_id=12942.

Goeldner, Moritz, Cornelius Herstatt, and Frank Tietze. 2015. "The Emergence of Care Robotics: A Patent and Publication Analysis." *Technological Forecasting and Social Change* 92: 115–31.

Heidegger, Martin. 1962. *Being and Time.* Translated by John Macquarrie and Edward Robinson. Hoboken, NJ: Blackwell.

Hutto, Daniel D. and Michael D. Kirchhoff. 2016. "Never Mind the Gap: Neurophenomenology, Radical Enactivism, and the Hard Problem of Consciousness." *Constructivist Foundations* 11 (2): 302–30.

Hutto, Daniel D. and Erik Myin. Forthcoming. "Going Radical." In *Oxford Handbook of 4E Cognition*, edited by A. Newen, L. de Bruin, and S. Gallagher. Oxford: Oxford University Press.

Melson, Gail F., Peter H. Kahn, Jr., Alan Beck, and Batya Friedman. 2009. "Robotic Pets in Human Lives: Implications for the Human–Animal Bond and for Human Relationships with Personified Technologies." *Journal of Social Issues* 65 (3): 545–67.

Merleau-Ponty, Maurice. 2004. *The World of Perception.* Edited and translated by Oliver Davis and Thomas Baldwin. Cambridge: Cambridge University Press.

O'Regan, J. Kevin. 2012. "How to Build a Robot That Is Conscious and Feels." *Mind and Machine* 22: 117–36.

Rocks, Claire, Sarah Jenkins, Matthew Studley, and David McGoran. 2009. "'Heart Robot,' a Public Engagement Project." *Interaction Studies* 10 (3): 427–52.

Royakkers, Lambèr and Rinie van Est. 2015. "A Literature Review on New Robotics: Automation from Love to War." *International Journal of Social Robotics* 7 (5): 549–70.

Ryle, Gilbert. 1949. *The Concept of Mind.* Chicago: University of Chicago Press.

Sharkey, Noel and Amanda Sharkey. 2010. "Living with Robots: Ethical Tradeoffs in Eldercare." In *Close Engagements with Artificial Companions: Key Social,*

Psychological, Ethical and Design issues, edited by Yorick Wilks, 245–56. Amsterdam: John Benjamins.

Shibata, T., K. Wada, T. Saito, and K. Tanie. 2001. "Robot Assisted Activity for Senior People at Day Service Center." In *Proceedings of the International Conference on ITM*, 71–6.

Sparrow, R. 2002. "The March of the Robot Dogs." *Ethics and Information Technology*, 4: 305–18.

Sparrow, Robert and Linda Sparrow. 2006. "In the Hands of Machines? The Future of Aged Care." *Minds and Machines* 16 (2): 141–61.

Suzuki, Y., L. Galli, A. Ikeda, S. Itakura, and M. Kitazaki. 2015. "Measuring Empathy for Human and Robot Hand Pain Using Electroencephalography." *Scientific Reports* 5 (November 3), article number 15924.

Thompson, Evan. 2007. *Mind in Life: Biology, Phenomenology, and the Sciences of Mind*. Cambridge, MA: Harvard University Press.

Tronto, Joan C. 2005. "An Ethic of Care." In *Feminist Theory: A Philosophical Anthology*, edited by Ann E. Cudd and Robin O. Andreasen, 251–6. Hoboken, NJ: Blackwell.

Turkle, Sherry, Cynthia Breazeal, Olivia Dasté, and Brian Scassellati. 2006. "Encounters with Kismet and Cog: Children Respond to Relational Artifacts." *Digital Media: Transformations in Human Communication*, 1–20.

Wallach, Wendell and Colin Allen. 2010. *Moral Machines: Teaching Robots Right from Wrong*. Oxford: Oxford University Press.

Wittgenstein, Ludwig.1953. *Philosophical Investigations*. Hoboken: Blackwell.

Yoder, Elizabeth A. 2010. "Compassion Fatigue in Nurses." *Applied Nursing Research* 23 (4): 191–7.

Zapf, Dieter. 2002. "Emotion Work and Psychological Well-Being: A Review of the Literature and Some Conceptual Considerations." *Human Resource Management Review* 12 (2): 237–68.

8 ROBOT FRIENDS FOR AUTISTIC CHILDREN

MONOPOLY MONEY OR COUNTERFEIT CURRENCY?

Alexis Elder

In this chapter, I argue that the therapeutic use of robots to address symptoms associated with autism spectrum disorders presents a kind of moral hazard—not an all-things-considered reason to reject their use, but a concern to be incorporated in the design and deployment of these robots. The hazard involves these robots' potential to present the appearance of friendship to a population vulnerable to deceit on this front. Aristotle cautioned that deceiving others with false appearances of friendship is of the same kind as counterfeiting currency. My goal in this chapter is to articulate in what exactly this risk consists, in order to provide guidance about how to effectively use these robots to help patients practice and build social skills, and to do so without being unethical.

Autism spectrum disorders (ASD) present a number of obstacles to successful social interaction. Symptoms vary widely, but can include language impairments, as well as difficulty with eye contact, joint attention, interpreting others' behavior, turn-taking, imitation, and emotion recognition. Although ASD cannot be cured, therapy is often recommended to help patients learn to successfully interact with others. Such therapy is often geared at explicitly teaching social skills of the sort impaired by disorders. One challenge for therapists is to engage the attention of patients. Patients who enjoy and seek out interactions during therapy are more likely to realize its benefits, practicing the social skills that will help them to successfully navigate society. Given the interest in technology of many patients with ASD, therapeutic robots appear to be a promising possibility on this front.

Even in informal settings, patients' interactions with robots and other advanced technologies serve to illustrate the potential advantages of this approach. One striking example of informal practice motivated by a fascination with technology is relayed by the mother of a child with ASD. Like many children on the autism spectrum, 13-year-old Gus often found friendships difficult, and like many such children, he was fascinated by technology. What surprised his mother, however, was the way these two issues intersected for him. Gus struck up what looks strikingly like a friendship with Siri, the Apple iPhone's automated assistant, conversing with "her" at length, taking her to visit her "friends" at the Apple Store, and expressing affection toward her (Newman 2014).

Gus's mother noted that when Gus began talking with Siri on a regular basis, his conversational abilities improved across the board. If interactive robots can help autistic children develop and practice conversing and other social skills, this seems an important benefit of their use. But there exists the possibility that some people may intrinsically find human–robot interactions more rewarding than relationships with other humans and that robotic companions will reinforce rather than overcome this initial preference.

Robots and other anthropomorphic technologies like Siri show great initial promise in providing personal-relationship-like interactions to patients on the autism spectrum. In fact, some studies (Dautenhahn and Werry 2004; Robins et al. 2006) have found that patients actively prefer interacting with robots to interacting with human companions, given the choice, and others (e.g., Duquette et al. 2008) have found that patients respond better to smiles and other facial expressions, focus for longer, and otherwise engage "socially" at greater rates with robots than with humans.

As we begin adopting therapeutic robots to aid the autistic, we need to consider what the ethical repercussions of this practice might be. After surveying extant and emerging research on the use of social robotics in autism therapy, I introduce an account of friendship drawn from the Aristotelian tradition to clarify the ethical value of friendship. I then make use of Aristotle's discussion of false friendships and the analogy he draws between false friends and false coinage to articulate some of the moral hazards of introducing robots to patients with autism, while at the same time capturing their measurable advantages.

8.1 Capitalizing on Robots' Appeal

Patients with ASD tend to have trouble with a range of specific social skills, such as eye contact, following another person's gaze, understanding or responding appropriately to facial expressions and social contexts, imitating others' behavior, and engaging in cooperative activities such as taking turns, asking questions, and following conversational cues.

Robotic therapy is still in its infancy, and the majority of studies thus far have been exploratory pilot studies designed to test the feasibility of various ways of incorporating robots into successful therapy. In one such pilot study, on the use of the KASPAR robot to teach children on the ASD spectrum to engage in collaborative play, the authors report that "the children with autism were more interested in and entertained by the robotic partner" than the human confederate (Wainer et al. 2014).

In fact, this interest was so strong that even some failures of the pilot study seem promising. For example, the children's interest in KASPAR was sometimes an obstacle to their completion of the assigned activity:

> [B]ecause the robot was programmed to prompt a child to choose a shape if they remained inactive for 5 consecutive seconds, as well as to repeatedly attempt to take the initiative in choosing shapes when the child did not respond to two consecutive prompts, one child discovered that KASPAR would essentially speak to them every 5 seconds provided that they did not play at all. This allowed the child to stare raptly at the robot for long periods of time without responding to the robot's prompts, until the child's carer jogged him out of this routine. (Wainer et al. 60)

Thus, in their initial results, the subjects "performed better" with the human partner than the robotic one along the metrics associated with the task—to which the authors proposed a variety of technical workarounds for future studies.

The reasons for patients' preference for robots are unclear. Although it is not universal, it is a robust enough phenomenon to be widely noted in the literature. Scassellati et al., in a recent survey of the state of the field of robotics in autism research, run through a variety of possible explanations for robots' appeal:

> Perhaps the simplified social cues that robots present result in less overstimulation of the children; perhaps robots offer more predictable and reliable responses than those from a human partner with ever-changing social needs; perhaps robots trigger social responses without the learned negative associations that some children have with human–human interactions; and perhaps the exaggerated social prompts that robots provide are better triggers for social behavior than the nuanced and subtle social prompts from a human partner. (2012, 292)

The predictability, clear signals, and lower incidence of perceived distractions presented by robotic versus human partners may even make it advisable to make robots for such therapy *less* anthropomorphic. In fact, many of the robots are designed to be cartoonishly exaggerated, with simplified facial expressiveness and sometimes with few or no limbs. One, Keepon, consists solely of two spheres stacked one on top of the other, the upper one of which is equipped with fixed googly eyes and a simple "nose."

These robots, if properly deployed, seem to offer a number of potential therapeutic benefits. Children with ASD can benefit from learning social skills that do not come easily to them, and they may be more likely to practice consistently when they enjoy the process and associate it with positive social experiences, as many seem to when robots are involved. This, in turn, may enable them to develop these skills to a higher degree.

Possibilities include using robots to teach collaborative play (Wainer et al. 2014), body awareness skills (Costa et al. 2013), joint attention (Anzalone et al. 2014), question-asking (Huskens et al. 2013), imitation (Greczek et al. 2014), and tactile interactions (Robins and Datenhahn 2014). In addition, while less anthropomorphic robots may initially be more appealing to patients than highly realistic ones or even human therapists, it would be straightforward to introduce a series of increasingly complex modifications or different models of robots to scale challenges to the patient's skill level, resulting in steady, incremental progress in the development of social skills. And these practice sessions can be interspersed with similar sessions with human confederates, helping children learn to eventually transfer their abilities from a practice context with a robotic partner to naturalistic human–human interactions.

This matters because the ability to successfully interact with others is important for a variety of reasons. It is, obviously, instrumentally valuable to cooperate with others: for securing and thriving in the pursuit of jobs, housing, buying and selling, political involvement, and many other features of life in a complex society. But in addition, many of us take social relationships to be important ends in themselves. Aristotle claimed that "no one would choose to live without friends even if he had all the other goods" (1999, 119/1155a5–10), and even if that is putting it too strongly, it is surely true that for most of us, friends are an important and maybe even necessary component of the good life. If robots help autistic children develop the capacity to enjoy friendship, then they seem to be of great moral value.

8.2 Worries about False Friends

But this same observation—that friendship is an important intrinsic good—can at the same time give us grounds for concern about social robots. They aid patients with ASD by, in a sense, presenting as friends. Although robots do not strike some as friendly, it is specifically their appeal to patients along interactive social dimensions that drives the interest in their therapeutic applications. This gives rise to the worry that these patients, in finding robots to be enjoyable companions with whom they find interaction rewarding, will thereby come to believe that these robots are potential companions. Gus's mother reports the following exchange between her son and Siri:

> GUS: "Siri, will you marry me?"
> SIRI: "I'm not the marrying kind."
> GUS: "I mean, not now. I'm a kid. I mean when I'm grown up."
> SIRI: "My end user agreement does not include marriage."
> GUS: "Oh, O.K." (Newman 2014)

This worry is consistent with a recent survey of attitudes toward the therapeutic use of robots. Several ethical concerns are prevalent among both parents of children with ASD and therapists and researchers whose work focuses on ASD (Coeckelbergh et al. 2016). Although the vast majority of respondents (85%) reported that they found the use of social robots for ASD therapy to be ethically acceptable overall, they expressed worries about several specific issues that appear related to social robots' involvement in patients' experiences of and capacities for friendship. For example, only 43% of respondents agreed with the statement "It is ethically acceptable that, as a result of their therapy, children with autism perceive social robots as friends," and other response patterns can be plausibly linked to this concern. For example, respondents were much more likely to approve of robots designed to look like (non-human) animals or objects than ones that looked like human beings, and many "were opposed to the idea of the robot replacing therapists. . . . [I]nstead, many respondents preferred that the interaction is supervised by the therapist *and that the robot is tele-operated rather than fully automated*" (Coeckelbergh et al. 2016, 57–9, emphasis added).

The format of the survey, which asked respondents to indicate degree of agreement or disagreement with a series of pre-formulated statements, did not permit participants to explain the basis of this concern, but Coeckelbergh et al. offer a number of speculations about what might explain it.

It could be, for instance, that they fear that robot–human interactions will replace human–human interactions for such patients, potentially increasing their social isolation—a worry that is echoed by Sharkey and Sharkey's (2010) discussion of robot–child interactions in a piece titled "The Crying Shame of Robot Nannies." This would be consistent with their preference that robots not replace therapists, as well as a preference for tele-controlled robots, which plausibly seem to link or connect the child with a human rather than stand in for one. They note that this could also explain the preference for zoomorphic over anthropomorphic robots, as being less likely to be perceived as a replacement for human relationships.

They also note that there may be ethical concerns about the psychological cost of attachment to a perceived "friend," which, they note, "can be seen as good in so far as attachment supports the process and goals of the therapy: without any kind of attachment, it might be difficult to teach children social skills" (Coeckelbergh et al. 2016, 53), but which introduces the potential for distress and grief when children are separated from their robot companions, a concern echoed in Riek and Howard's (2014) "Code of Ethics for the Human–Robot Interaction Profession."

Additional causes for concern may include the potential for robots to be hacked by those with malicious intentions, especially because the trust engendered by the appearance of friendship could lead to a special vulnerability to exploitation. In fact, if Coeckelbergh et al. are right about the therapeutic advantages of attachment and if a major motivation for developing therapeutic social robots is to capitalize on their intrinsic appeal to patients, such therapy might be thought of as a kind of paternalistic exploitation of just this, albeit one that may be ethically justified by its positive consequences. In addition, perhaps some uneasiness at this possibly exploitative arrangement in which people utilize attachment for extrinsic goals could itself underlie some of the resistance to excessively "friendly" robots. Finally, one might worry that robots that seem especially friendly may deceive children into believing these robots are people, especially given that this population is one that has trouble reading and evaluating social cues to begin with.

It is somewhat unconventional in moral philosophy to draw one's concerns from a survey, especially of non-ethicists, but I think we should not too readily dismiss respondents' concerns. Coeckelbergh et al. explain the motivation for their survey as follows:

> [W]e assume that all stakeholders should have a say [in the development and use of new technologies]. This may mean various things and invites larger questions and discussions about technology and democracy, but in this article we limit ourselves to using the very concrete tool of the survey to give stakeholders a chance to give their opinion on the use and development of the new technology under consideration. (2016, 56, n. 4)

In addition to the importance of listening to stakeholders' concerns, there is another reason to take their reports seriously. While formal training in ethical theory can help a person to spot ethical issues others may overlook, it is also possible for a person to become so theory-bound that he or she misses issues of genuine concern because they do not fit neatly into a chosen theory. A major focus of ethics is, or should be, helping us to live worthwhile lives on our own terms, and when significant portions of an affected population express reservations that a given piece of technology may threaten our ability to live such a life, it seems to me that this is a concern worthy of being taken seriously. In addition, the expressed concerns explicitly appeal to a widely recognized component of the good life, according to a number of influential ethical theories: friendship.

This is not to say, of course, that we ought to give up on moral theorizing, or for that matter on robotic therapies for ASD. Instead, I urge that we incorporate such concerns into our theories and, to the extent possible, find ways of realizing the promise of robotic therapies without risking moral hazards to which our attention has been drawn by such investigations.

8.3 False Friends and False Coinage

I think there is a previously unexplored but promising way to articulate the worry, gestured to in the preceding section, about the possibility of patients coming to view these robots as friends. As the story of Gus illustrates, this is not merely a philosopher's fantasy, but a real possibility that could change treatment options and protocol. This way of articulating the worry derives from a discussion of appearances and friendship that greatly predates the current technology, as it is found in the works of Aristotle. Despite its age, however, I think Aristotle's theory can help shed light on the issue.

In addition to arguing that friendship is, for many of us, necessary for the good life, Aristotle introduces definitions of friendship that account for the fact that people speak of "friends" in both loose and strict senses of the term. Loosely and inclusively defined, friendships are reciprocal, mutually caring, and mutually recognized relationships between two or more people. The basis of care and valuing, however, can vary, as can the intensity or degree. Some friendships are founded largely on mutual but instrumental benefits: Aristotle calls these friendships of utility. Others are based on the mutual pleasure people take in each other's company: such friendships are known as friendships of pleasure. Both of these varieties are, strictly speaking, instrumental associations, in which friends are valued as sources of goods that are logically independent of the friends themselves. The last kind of friendship differs from these in that each friend intrinsically values the other's character: this kind of friendship is variously known as friendship of virtue or friendship of character. Aristotle associates this kind with valuing friends for themselves rather than what they can do for you. Although it is comparatively rare and difficult to establish, it is the kind of friendship we value most highly, the kind that seems essential for the best lives and an ideal to which we aspire. When we speak, for instance, of the value of "true" friendship, or figuring out who one's real friends are on the basis of learning who sticks around when the going gets tough and who's a mere fair-weather friend, we seem to be drawing a distinction between this ideal of friendship and the less valuable and robust forms that are more common and that also in some sense merit the title of "friendship," but in a more qualified way. About character friends, Aristotle says, "[T]he friendship of good people insofar as they are good is friendship primarily and fully, but the other friendships are friendships by similarity" (1999, 124/1157a30–35).

In his extensive discussion of friendship in the *Nicomachean Ethics*, Aristotle has this to say about deceptive appearances of friendship:

> We might . . . accuse a friend if he really liked us for utility or pleasure, and pretended to like us for our character. . . . [I]f we mistakenly suppose we are loved for our character when our friend is doing nothing to suggest this, we must hold ourselves responsible. But if we are deceived by his pretense, we are justified in accusing him—even more justified than in accusing debasers of the currency, to the extent that his evildoing debases something more precious. (1999, 140/1165b5–10)

In the kind of context he would have been imagining, doubtless most of those who pretended to be friends were capable of friendship—capable of reciprocal, mutual care grounded in valuing the other for who that person is and not just what he or she can do for you—in a way that current social robots and robots in the near future cannot. But what makes them "false friends" is not that they *could* so care and choose not to: it's that they look like they do, but don't. The person who pretends to be a friend but isn't is both counterfeiter and false coin. In this case, however, the counterfeiters are those who design and deploy the robots, while the robots are the false coinage. They can engage in many "social" activities, but there's no social capital behind the appearances upon which to draw.

It might seem odd to draw an analogy between friends and currency, because friends, or at least the best sorts of friends, seem to be of intrinsic value to their friends, while currency is a paradigmatic example of something of mere instrumental value. But I think that there is more in common between false friends and false currency than "appearance of something valuable" that makes the analogy instructive.

Friendships can be thought to be made up of very small and close-knit social groups. In fact, doing so can be explanatorily fruitful. It is widely held that close friends share identity or are somehow unified; Aristotle maintained that close friends are "other selves," for instance, in the *Nicomachean Ethics* (1999, 133/1161b30–35, 142/1166a30–35, and 150/1170b5–10). One might try to cash this out by interpreting this shared identity as arising from great similarity between close friends or positing that close friends do not have, recognize, or enforce boundaries between each other. But both interpretations have serious theoretical costs. Complementary differences can strengthen a friendship, and it seems a theoretical cost for a theory to hold that boundaries have no place in the best friendships. If instead we think of friends as part of a composite object—if a friendship is a kind of social entity—then their shared identity is not understood as similarity or lack of boundaries but rather as parts of a whole. The friends jointly compose the friendship, and like many parts, their doing so can be understood in terms of their sustained interdependence and inter-responsiveness.

When people value friendships, they value these composite entities, including their own membership in them. But false friends do not actually compose friendships with the deceived; they merely make the deceived think that they co-constitute a social group that does not in fact exist, by giving the appearance of emotional interdependence and interlinked concerns.

Economies, like friendships, can be thought of as interdependent social groups, albeit in this case bound together by currency rather than emotional interdependence and shared goals, and are valued for the instrumental goods associated with membership rather than intrinsically. False currency is bad because it gives the false impression of membership in and connection to a valuable social group, and it promises inter-responsiveness where there is none to be found. Likewise for false friends.

The appearance–reality distinction matters in both kinds of social groups, and the badness of both forgeries is to be found in falsely representing membership in such a group. One worry for therapeutic robots is that, for people who have trouble parsing social signals, robots can "pass" as capable of co-constituting these social organisms, even though they are in fact incapable of the necessary emotional and valuational states. To fail to respect this potential for confusion is to be cavalier toward the valuable institution of friendship, on the designer's or therapist's part, as well as to potentially mislead patients into thinking they have a kind of good that they in fact lack.

This would yield a parsimonious explanation of the various concerns articulated by respondents to Coeckelbergh et al.'s survey. It would explain why people prefer telepresence robots to autonomous ones: telepresence "connects" the patient to a (human) therapist, rather than giving the mere appearance of an agent capable of valuing. It would explain the preference for zoomorphic over anthropomorphic robots: anthropomorphic ones are more likely to pass as friends, in ways relevantly similar to false coinage. And it would explain why there is widespread resistance to making children perceive these robots to be their friends.

This would not give us reason to avoid using sociable robots altogether, any more than fears about false coinage should lead us to ban Monopoly money. In fact, playful simulacra can be important in helping children to learn skills that will help them to better navigate the real thing. Playing with toy money can help one develop economic skills and a better understanding of economic transactions. But just as we go out of our way to make sure play money does not look close enough to the real thing to fool people, we should exercise similar caution in our construction of practice social partners.

8.4 The Different-Strokes Objection

But for this account to work, it would need to be true both that friendships, of the sort I've previously sketched, really *are* valuable, and not just the arrangements most—if not all—people happen to prefer, and that the subjective experience of friendship provided by non-sentient social robots is not sufficient for patients. But their disinterest in human contact and fascination with robotics are precisely what motivate the current trend of incorporating robotics into therapy for children with ASD.

One could imagine an objection along the following lines from someone skeptical about the objective value of "real" friendship. Granted, ASDs hamper the development of social skills, and to the extent that it benefits children with ASD to cultivate these skills, we ought to do so. But we ought to remain agnostic with respect to what it would look like for them to live well on their own terms; that is, we ought not presuppose that the appearance–reality distinction in friendship matters for everyone, just because it matters to some. We ought to cultivate social skills as best we can, even if that leads to the result that patients come to view their robots as friends. So long as we can mitigate the extrinsic costs of such beliefs—for example, one might avoid the susceptibility to loss generated by attachment by providing each child with his or her own inexpensive robot—we shouldn't get hung up on the perhaps overly moralistic idea of "false friends."

Aristotle asserted that "no one would choose to live without friends even if he had all the other goods" (Aristotle 1999, 119/1155a5–10), but maybe he was just wrong—or at least wrong about what it would take to satisfy people's interest in friends. For example, in the film *Blade Runner*, the eccentric inventor J. F. Sebastian lives by himself in an otherwise abandoned building. When Pris, herself a possibly sentient android, sees his living situation, she remarks, "Must get lonely here, J.F." "Not really," he replies. "I *make* friends. They're toys. My friends are toys. I make them. It's a hobby. I'm a genetic designer" (Scott 1982).

The toys he makes are not realistic facsimiles of human beings; many of them explicitly imitate traditional toys such as old-fashioned soldiers and teddy bears. He is well aware of their artificial origins. After all, he made them for himself. And they do not even act like "normal" human beings; their gestures, grammar, and movements are exaggerated, cartoonish, and simplified. Unlike the film's "replicant" androids, so realistic that elaborate tests must be developed to distinguish them from biological humans, these would never take in a person looking for a human friend. And yet he seems to find them satisfying, and maybe even preferable to "normal" human interactions.

If this objection is correct, then we either ought to dismiss the respondents' concerns as projections of their own value systems without regard for others or at least prefer more restricted explanations that limit the scope to the harms of, for example, terminating "relationships" with therapeutic robots rather than adopt one that posits that something is wrong with the relationship itself, at least if and when the patient takes the robot to be a friend. After all, it can count as counterfeit only if it is a convincing but not valuable stand-in for something valued—and whether or not robot friends are valuable is itself in question, given documented preferences for robotic over human companionship.

8.5 The Adaptive-Preferences Response

I think, however, that we ought not accept this line of reasoning as giving us grounds to reject the worry I have articulated. First, it seems to me that we should not presuppose what the actual values of patients, particularly young ones, might be. They may ultimately continue to prefer robotic interactions over human ones for the reasons identified earlier (familiarity, predictability, fewer confusing signals, etc.) and still think human friendship is highly valuable. Or they might come to prefer human friendships, like other people, when their challenges to successful human interactions have been overcome or mitigated. This doubt about the actual values of any given patient should motivate us to adopt a conservative approach. Even if some patients never do value friendship the way many of us do, it still pays to assume that they might do so, ethically speaking, since the cost of getting this wrong is morally bad for those who do come to acquire such preferences.

Second, the fact that most of us do so value friendship seems to suggest an abductive argument that it is in fact intrinsically valuable, at least for human beings. Widespread agreement on its value, across a variety of cultures, eras, and contexts, from ancient Greece and China to contemporary North America, calls out for explanation, and this would be straightforwardly explained by its actual value, while the few outliers (the J. F. Sebastians) could be explained away by the fact that they may not, for contingent reasons, have been in a position to realize its value owing to circumstances, whether developmental or environmental, that prevented their ever enjoying successful examples of the kind. Patients with ASD are first and foremost *people*, and so it may seem advisable to assume, until proven otherwise, that their values will substantially overlap with those of the rest of the species. Add to this that many individuals with ASD both enjoy successful human friendships and report that they value them (for instance, see Temple Grandin's discussion of friendship in *Thinking in Pictures* [2010]), and the case becomes even stronger for presuming until proven otherwise that friendship, of the sort Aristotle described, is valuable and worth protecting.

This is not an argument that people ought to be forced to have only human friends. Rather, it is an argument that in the course of developing people's capacity to enjoy friendship, we ought not at the same time devalue the institution by potentially generating in patients the belief that therapeutic robots are their friends. Once these capacities are developed, or developed as well as can be done with appropriate methods, people can choose for themselves. That is, this is not an argument against mass-market companionate robots.

My approach is inspired by Nussbaum's and Sen's capability theories, although it does not depend on the details of their accounts (Nussbaum 2001; Sen 1989). Roughly, we do not want to paternalistically impose our values on others, but at the same time we have to take account of the possibility of so-called adaptive preferences. Adaptive preferences are those a person develops in the face of long-standing hardship, as an adaptation to that limitation. Women living in cultures in which they are treated as second-class citizens, for example, might report being healthy and satisfied, even though they are malnourished and suffering from long-standing untreated medical conditions, because they have adapted to these circumstances. But this should not be taken to reflect their all-things-considered preference for inadequate food and medical care. To avoid both extremes of anything-goes and narrow-minded prejudice in favor of one's own preferences, I propose that we first focus on cultivating people's capacity to enjoy the good in question—in this case, friendship and social relationships more generally—and then let their informed personal preferences govern whether and how they choose to exercise the capacity.

8.6 Conclusion

I think that we ought to take people's concerns about robot friends seriously, but be careful to interpret them in the right way. While previous ethicists' concerns to limit or control patients' attachment to robots have focused on the perils of trust or the potential for grief at the loss of the "friend," I argue that the proper concern is not just about loss or extrinsic harms. In fact, the constitutive "relationship," if it meets the criteria for counterfeit connection, can itself be troubling.

However, this does not mean we should be altogether skeptical of therapeutic robots' potential to help children with ASD. Even if we grant that robot "friends" can be counterfeit currency, those that function like Monopoly money are both ethically unproblematic and valuable teaching tools. My intention here is to articulate an ethical concern for designers and therapists to keep in mind, not to advocate an ethical ban.

The emerging interest in exploiting an inherent attraction of patients with ASD to sociable robots calls for great care. We ought not to be cavalier about friendship, an important component of the good life, in the design and implementation of therapeutic tools. At the same time, with careful attention, they present a promising option to facilitate people's capacity to enjoy that very good.

Works Cited

Anzalone, Salvatore Maria, Elodie Tilmont, Sofiane Boucenna, Jean Xavier, Anne-Lise Jouen, Nicolas Bodeau, Koushik Maharatna, Mohamed Chetouani, David Cohen, and Michelangelo Study Group. 2014. "How Children with Autism Spectrum Disorder Behave and Explore the 4-Dimensional (Spatial 3D+ Time) Environment During a Joint Attention Induction Task with a Robot." *Research in Autism Spectrum Disorders* 8 (7): 814–26.

Aristotle. 1999. *Nicomachean Ethics*. Translated by Terence Irwin. Indianapolis: Hackett.

Blade Runner. 1982. Film. Directed by Ridley Scott. Produced by Ridley Scott and Hampton Fancher. Screenplay by Hampton Fancher and David Webb Peoples. Warner Bros.

Coeckelbergh, Mark, Cristina Pop, Ramona Simut, Andreea Peca, Sebastian Pintea, Daniel David, and Bram Vanderborght. 2016. "A Survey of Expectations about the Role of Robots in Robot-Assisted Therapy for Children with ASD: Ethical Acceptability, Trust, Sociability, Appearance, and Attachment." *Science and Engineering Ethics* 22 (1): 47–65.

Costa, Sandra, Hagen Lehmann, Ben Robins, Kerstin Dautenhahn, and Filomena Soares. 2013. "'Where Is Your Nose?' Developing Body Awareness Skills among Children with Autism Using a Humanoid Robot." In *ACHI 2013, The Sixth International Conference on Advances in Computer-Human Interactions*, 117–22. IARIA.

Dautenhahn, Kerstin and Iain Werry. 2004. "Towards Interactive Robots in Autism Therapy: Background, Motivation and Challenges." *Pragmatics & Cognition* 12 (1): 1–35.

Duquette, Audrey, François Michaud, and Henri Mercier. 2008. "Exploring the Use of a Mobile Robot as an Imitation Agent with Children with Low-Functioning Autism." *Autonomous Robots* 24 (2): 147–57.

Grandin, Temple. 2010. *Thinking in Pictures: My Life with Autism*. New York: Doubleday.

Greczek, Jillian, Edward Kaszubski, Amin Atrash, and Maja Mataric. 2014. "Graded Cueing Feedback in Robot-Mediated Imitation Practice for Children with Autism

Spectrum Disorders." In *Robot and Human Interactive Communication, 2014 RO-MAN: The 23rd IEEE International Symposium on*, 561–6. IEEE.

Huskens, Bibi, Rianne Verschuur, Jan Gillesen, Robert Didden, and Emilia Barakova. 2013. "Promoting Question-Asking in School-Aged Children with Autism Spectrum Disorders: Effectiveness of a Robot Intervention Compared to a Human-Trainer Intervention." *Developmental Neurorehabilitation* 16 (5): 345–56.

Newman, Judith. 2014. "To Siri with Love: How One Boy with Autism Became BFF with Apple's Siri." *New York Times*, 17 October. http://www.nytimes.com/2014/10/19/fashion/how-apples-siri-became-one-autistic-boys-bff. html.

Nussbaum, Martha. 2001. *Women and Human Development: The Capabilities Approach*. Cambridge: Cambridge University Press.

Riek, Laurel D. and Don Howard. 2014. "A Code of Ethics for the Human–Robot Interaction Profession." *We Robot 2014*. http://robots.law.miami.edu/2014/wp-content/uploads/2014/03/a-code-of-ethics-for-the-human-robot-interaction-profession-riek-howard.pdf.

Robins, Ben and Kerstin Dautenhahn. 2014. "Tactile Interactions with a Humanoid Robot: Novel Play Scenario Implementations with Children with Autism." *International Journal of Social Robotics* 6 (3): 397–415.

Robins, Ben, Kerstin Dautenhahn, and Janek Dubowski. 2006. "Does Appearance Matter in the Interaction of Children with Autism with a Humanoid Robot?" *Interaction Studies* 7 (3): 509–42.

Scassellati, Brian, Henny Admoni, and Maja Mataric.2012. "Robots for Use in Autism Research." *Annual Review of Biomedical Engineering* 14: 275–94.

Sen, Amartya. 1989. "Development as Capability Expansion." *Journal of Development Planning* 19: 41–58.

Sharkey, Noel and Amanda Sharkey. 2010. "The Crying Shame of Robot Nannies: An Ethical Appraisal." *Interaction Studies* 11 (2): 161–90.

Wainer, Joshua, Kerstin Dautenhahn, Ben Robins, and Farshid Amirabdollahian. 2014. "A Pilot Study with a Novel Setup for Collaborative Play of the Humanoid Robot KASPAR with Children with Autism." *International Journal of Social Robotics* 6 (1): 45–65.

9 PEDIATRIC ROBOTICS AND ETHICS

THE ROBOT IS READY TO SEE YOU NOW, BUT SHOULD IT BE TRUSTED?

Jason Borenstein, Ayanna Howard, and Alan R. Wagner

People tend to overtrust autonomous systems. In 1995, while traveling from Bermuda to Boston, the *Royal Majesty* cruise ship ran aground because the ship's autopilot malfunctioned after having been left on for thirty-four hours (Charette 2009). On June 1, 2009, Air France flight 447 crashed into the ocean, killing all 228 passengers. Accident investigators would eventually conclude that the crew's confusion after disengaging the autopilot and reliance on faulty airspeed measurements doomed the plane (BEA 2012). On July 6, 2013, Asiana Airlines flight 214 crashed on its final approach into San Francisco International Airport, killing 3 people and injuring 180. According to the U. S. National Transportation and Safety Board, overreliance on automation played an important role in the crash (NTSB 2014). Research by two of the coauthors has shown that during certain emergency situations, some people will still follow a robot's directions, in spite of the risk to their own well-being, even though doing so has obviously failed during previous interactions (Robinette et al. 2015). As robots continue to leave the lab and enter the hospital or other healthcare settings, these examples show that people may become overreliant on and overtrust such technology.

Certain populations, such as children with acquired or developmental disorders, are particularly vulnerable to the risks presented by overtrust (Yamagishi et al. 1999; Yamagishi 2001). Because children lack extensive experience and have a limited ability to reason about the hazards of complex technological devices, they may fail to recognize the danger associated with using such devices (Kahn et al. 2004; Sharkey and Sharkey 2010). Moreover, parents themselves may not fully assess the risks, either because they are too preoccupied to examine the limitations of a technology or because they are too emotionally invested in it as a potential cure (Dunn et al. 2001; Maes et al. 2003; Wade et al. 1998). As the domain of pediatric robotics continues to evolve, we must examine the tendency to overtrust and develop strategies to mitigate the risk to children, parents, and healthcare providers that could occur due to an overreliance on robots.

To overcome this challenge, we must first consider the broad range of ethical issues related to the use of robots in pediatric healthcare. This naturally leads to conceptualizing strategies that can be employed to mitigate the risk of their use. These strategies must be motivated by the desire to develop robotic systems that attend to a child's needs and by the importance of safeguarding against placing too much trust in these very systems. This is not to imply that pediatric robots are inherently unsafe or that the medical research conducted with these systems is inadequate. We only wish to discuss the effects prevalent in introducing robots into pediatric care settings and analyze the potential impacts of children's and parents' reliance on technology in which they may have considerable trust. Thus, this chapter provides an overview of the current state of the art in pediatric robotics, describes relevant ethical issues, and examines the role that overtrust plays in these scenarios. We will conclude with suggested strategies to mitigate the risks and describe a framework for the future deployment of robots in the pediatric domain.

9.1 A Review of Pediatric Robot Types and Studies

Many different robotic systems are currently being developed and deployed for use with children (e.g., Scassellati 2007; Feil-Seifer and Matarić 2009; Kozima et al. 2008; Drane et al. 2009). The focus of research over the past ten years has ranged from adapted robotic manipulators to robotic exoskeletons to social robotic therapy coaches. Tyromotion's Amadeo provides arm and hand rehabilitation in a virtual game environment for children and adults (Hartwig 2014). Motek's GRAIL system provides gait analysis and training in a virtual environment and is being used with children (Mirelman et al. 2010). Virtual and robotic technologies for children with cerebral palsy are also being evaluated in various rehabilitation scenarios (Chen et al. 2014; Garcia-Vergara et al. 2012).

Estimates suggest that about one in six, or about 15%, of children aged 3–17 years in the United States have one or more developmental disabilities (Boyle et al. 2011). Adapted robotic manipulators can provide therapeutic interventions for children with upper-extremity motor impairments; they typically engage children in physical activity that will aid in increasing their functional skills (Chen and Howard 2016). PlayROB enables children with physical disabilities to manipulate LEGO bricks (Kronreif et al. 2005). The

Handy Robot can assist individuals with disabilities in accomplishing daily tasks, such as eating and drinking (Topping 2002). Children can also perform play-related tasks by controlling a robot arm; they can select from a series of interface options, including large push buttons and keyboards (Cook et al. 2002, 2005). A separate type of robotic arm was used during a pilot project to determine if it could foster certain cognitive or other skills in students with severe orthopedic disabilities (Howell 1989).

Many children who have neurological disorders may have limited movement of their upper and lower extremities. Robotic exoskeletons can provide a means of therapy for such children. Robotic arm orthoses (Sukal et al. 2007) and robot-assisted locomotor trainers have also been used in this domain. A growing body of literature shows that robot-assisted gait training is a feasible and safe treatment method for children with neurological disorders (Borggraefe et al. 2010; Meyer-Heim et al. 2009; Damiano and DeJong 2009). To counter concerns raised by findings that task-specificity and goal-orientedness are crucial aspects in the treatment of children versus passive training for motor learning (Papavasiliou 2009), researchers have begun to investigate the coupling of robotic orthotic systems with scenarios involving play. For example, a pilot study with ten patients with different neurological gait disorders showed that virtual reality robot-assisted therapy approaches had an immediate effect on motor output equivalent to that of conventional approaches with a human therapist (Brütsch et al. 2010). Another case study showed that using custom rehabilitation video games with a robotic ankle orthosis for a child with cerebral palsy was clinically more beneficial than robotic rehabilitation in the absence of the games (Cioi et al. 2011).

Occupational therapy can be used to help improve a child's motor, cognitive, sensory processing, communication, and play skills with the goal of enhancing their development and minimizing the potential for developmental delay (Punwar 2000). In other words, it seeks to improve a child's ability to participate in daily activities. Interest is growing in research involving occupational therapy through play between robots and children with developmental disorders, such as Down syndrome and autism spectrum disorders (Pennisi et al. 2016). Passive sensing used in conjunction with robots could potentially help provide metrics of assessment for children with disabilities (Brooks and Howard 2012). Metrics associated with the child's movement parameters, gaze direction, and dialogue during interaction with the robot can provide outcome measures useful to the clinician for diagnosing and determining suitable intervention protocols for children with developmental disabilities.

Cosmobot is a commercially available tele-rehabilitation robot that was designed as a tool to promote educational and therapeutic activities for children with and without disabilities (Lathan et al. 2005). The current configuration was used in a pilot study with three children with cerebral palsy, ages 4–11, with upper-extremity limitations (Wood et al. 2009). IROMEC (Interactive Robotic Social Mediators as Companions) is a robot designed to engage three groups of children—those with autism, those with cognitive disabilities, and those with severe motor impairments—in various social and cooperative play scenarios (Patrizia et al. 2009; Marti and Giusti 2010). The Aurora project is focused on aiding the therapy and education of children with autism (Dautenhahn and Werry 2004). In one associated project, scientists utilized a humanoid robotic doll, named Robota, in behavioral studies involving imitation-based games to engage low-functioning children with autism (Billard et al. 2007).

A robot named KASPAR (Kinesics and Synchronisation in Personal Assistant Robotics) is the size of a young child and was created to be a social mediator; its facial expressions and gestures were designed to encourage children with autism to interact with other people (Robins et al. 2009). Roball is a spherical-shaped robot with intentional self-propelled movement that aims to facilitate interaction between young children (Michaud 2005). Keepon, a robot designed to engage children with developmental disorders in playful interaction, was assessed in a two-year study involving twenty-five infants and toddlers with autism, Asperger's syndrome, Down syndrome, and other developmental disorders (Kozima and Nakagawa 2006). Furthermore, Scassellati, Admoni, and Matarić (2012) provide a review of the common design characteristics of robots used in autism research as well as observations made on the types of evaluation studies performed in therapy-like settings using these robot platforms.

9.2 Healthcare Robots: Consequences and Concerns

Given the number and diversity of healthcare robots under development and their potential use with pediatric populations (as the preceding section illustrates), consideration of the ethical aspects of using these robots to provide care for children becomes imperative. Numerous ethical issues are emerging, especially considering how diverse pediatric populations are in terms of their healthcare needs. Obviously, the threat of physical harm to a patient is an ever-present concern. For example, a robot that delivers drugs to a patient could accidentally run into someone; or alternatively, a robotic prosthetic, such as an exoskeleton, could cause a user to fall due to factors such as its weight or size. Given that children are a relatively vulnerable population, harm prevention takes on increasing importance. Healthcare robots should ideally enable patients to experience some form of meaningful therapeutic benefit, but they could also generate unintended health-related consequences (such as muscle atrophy associated with prolonged use). Along related lines, the use of an exoskeleton or other robotic device could potentially lead to patients' overreliance on the technology (e.g., an unwillingness to try walking without it), especially as such technology might empower them with new, or augment previously lost, abilities.

An alleged virtue of many healthcare robots is their ability to monitor patients in a large variety of ways; for days at a time, they could constantly check vital signs and observe whether medications have been taken or notice whether a patient is awake, which goes beyond the limits of what human caregivers can feasibly provide. Yet a counterbalancing concern is that this functionality could unduly intrude upon the patient's privacy. An additional complexity here is whether, and to what degree, pediatric patients should be entitled to keep information private from their parents or healthcare providers.

Unintentional or deliberate deception can also occur in the deployment of healthcare robots, which in many cases could amount to the user projecting traits or characteristics onto robots that they do not genuinely possess. Humans can form strong emotional ties to robots and other technological artifacts (Levy 2007), and designers can intensify, and arguably exploit, this human psychological tendency with their aesthetic choices (Pearson and Borenstein 2014). Some scholars argue, for example, that the use of robots in nursing homes and other care environments is deceptive and displays a lack of respect for persons (Sparrow and Sparrow 2006; Sharkey and Sharkey 2010). However, one can ask whether deception is always wrong (Pearson and Borenstein 2013), especially if it serves a therapeutic purpose in a healthcare setting.

The effect that child–robot interaction has on human psychology and socialization also warrants examination. For example, would the introduction of robotic technology into pediatric environments cause the patients to have fewer human–human interactions? Turkle (2015) extensively discusses the impact that technological devices, especially mobile phones, are having on social dynamics; she suggests that as a result of their use, the human ability to have a meaningful and extensive conversation is dissipating. Analogously, handing a meaningful portion of a child's care over to a robot might lessen opportunities for interpersonal engagement. Arguably, if a child spends less time talking with doctors, nurses, or other care providers, it could be to the child's detriment. Although some scholars suggest that robots could facilitate conversations between humans (Arkin 2014), Turkle (2015, 358) argues that using robots (like Paro) to assist with a person's care may cause the human care providers to become spectators.

9.3 Bringing the Robot Home

When one considers that some of these robotic technologies may go home with the patient, new and possibly more challenging ethical issues must be resolved. For example, a child using an exoskeleton in a hospital would presumably not be climbing stairs or walking across uneven floors, but once the system is brought home, these conditions become distinct possibilities. Furthermore, the child may try to use the system in the rain or in environments where the temperature (and system performance) may fluctuate rather significantly. Granted, hospitals or other care facilities can be somewhat chaotic and unpredictable environments, but the number of variables affecting the interaction between children and robotic systems will increase as these systems are introduced into various and dynamic "external" settings (places where these systems might not have been directly tested).

Admittedly, there are many ways to prevent a child or the child's parents from placing too much faith in a robot. For instance, healthcare providers could require that parents remain in the room with their child while therapy is being performed or simply record and limit the time that a robot is operational. These types of solutions might suffice for well-defined tasks and in well-defined environments. But as healthcare robots move from the hospital and clinic to the home environment, this type of oversight is not enforceable. For example, the Cyberdyne Corporation (2016) currently allows people to rent their HAL exoskeleton and actively promotes its use by children with disabilities in their homes. In this case, it is impractical to believe that a parent will constantly monitor their child; doing so might make using the technology overly burdensome. Furthermore, limiting the use of such technology to controlled environments could greatly diminish the benefits of such technology for children and other users.

9.4 The Potential for Overtrust of Healthcare Robots

Although the aforementioned ethical issues are important to examine, our focus is how the increasing use of robotic systems in healthcare settings might lead patients, parents, and others to place too much trust in these systems. We use the term "overtrust" to describe a situation in which (1) a person accepts risk because that person believes the robot can perform a function that it cannot or (2) the person accepts too much risk because the expectation is that the system will mitigate the risk. Concerns about overtrust are, for example, saliently illustrated by the aforementioned cases where pilot overreliance on autopilot systems may have contributed to airplane crashes (Carr 2014; Mindell 2015).

Research has shown that increased automation typically leads to increased user complacency (Parasuraman et al. 1993). This complacency may result in the misuse of the automation and in the user's failure to properly monitor the system, or it may bias the person's decision-making (Parasuraman and Riley 1997). It is important to note that the failures that derive from automation, including induced complacency or overtrust, tend to be qualitatively different from the typical errors, or mistakes, one encounters when interacting with systems that lack automation. When automation is trusted too much, the failures that occur can be catastrophic. In some instances, drivers placing their trust in GPS have followed its instructions into lakes, into the ocean, off cliffs, and on a 1,600-mile detour (GPSBites 2012).

Historically, discussions about overtrust as it pertains to robotics have focused on factory automation. Recent research, however, extends the scope to the use of mobile robots in emergency situations; researchers examined how people would react to a robot's guidance during an emergency evacuation (Robinette et al. 2016). A mobile robot was used to escort subjects to a meeting room. In different conditions, the robot either guided the person directly to the room or incorrectly made a detour to a different room. In previous virtual studies, participants who observed the robot make a mistake would predominately choose not to follow the robot during the emergency (Robinette et al. 2015). In the real world, however, the researchers found that people followed the robot in spite of increasingly poor guidance performance. When asked why they chose to follow the robot, participants often stated that they thought the robot knew more than they did or that it was incapable of failure (Robinette et al. 2016). Furthermore, after the experiment concluded, many of the participants explained that because they chose to follow the robot, they must have trusted it. These findings suggest that people may view a robot as infallible and blindly follow its instructions even to the point where they ignore signs of a malfunction. This research has implications for pediatric robotics in that parents or others may be inclined to defer judgment about a child's well-being to a robot.

Along these lines, healthcare providers will have a range of reactions to new robotic technology that is being integrated into their work environment. In this context, an issue that warrants particular attention is the circumstances under which professionals might defer to the technology instead of relying on their own judgment. For example, suppose a patient is wearing a robotic exoskeleton for rehabilitative purposes and the system is programmed for twenty repetitions; as the session proceeds, the patient begins to express a fair amount of discomfort. Will a physician stop the session or will the default mindset be that the machine knows best? Similarly, physicians and others may be tempted to let their attention stray from a patient if they believe that the system can be trusted to monitor the situation. In fact, studies have shown that the use of automated systems by healthcare providers can result in certain types of cancers being overlooked (Povyakalo et al. 2013).

9.5 A Child's and a Parent's Trust in a Robot

Monitoring the trust that a child places in a robot is an important area of concern. Research studies and common sense suggest that children may be particularly likely to overtrust a robot (Yamagishi et al. 1999; Yamagishi 2001). Young children may lack extensive experience with robots, and technology more generally, and what little experience they have is likely to have been shaped by the internet, television, and other media; hence, they are particularly susceptible to attributing to these systems abilities the systems do not have. Furthermore, their youth may limit their ability to reason about the hazards of complex technological devices, with the result that children may fail to recognize the danger of using such devices (Kahn et al. 2004; Sharkey and Sharkey 2010). When this is combined with the fact that children, especially teenagers, tend to be at a rather risk-seeking stage of life, the likelihood of unintended harm increases. This propensity may encourage these children to push the limits of a robotic technology and/or misuse it.

Of course, parents may not fully assess the risks either. For example, parents may overtrust a robot therapy coach if they allow the system to dictate their child's routine, even in spite of signs of the child's distress; they might believe that the robot is more knowledgeable about when to end the therapy protocol than they are (Smith et al. 1997; Skitka et al. 1999). Parents of children suffering from a chronic disease or impairment may elect to use a robotic device despite the availability of equivalent or even better options simply because they think that a robot must be better than the alternatives. Moreover, because they may view robotic devices as more trustworthy than non-robotic devices, the level of their engagement in monitoring their child's treatment plan might decline.

9.6 Possible Factors Influencing Overtrust and Methods for Mitigating It

As the domain of pediatric robotics evolves, we must continue to examine the factors that contribute to overtrust and craft strategies to mitigate the risk to children, parents, and healthcare providers that could occur due to an overreliance on robots. Since this is largely a nascent area of inquiry, the strategies suggested may change as additional insights from research are uncovered. Some of the pertinent factors could include the psychological makeup and other characteristics of the person using the robot (Walters et al. 2008) and cultural differences (Kaplan 2004). Some individuals may be too trusting and accepting of risk when using a technology. Moving forward, it may be important to identify these individuals early and perhaps provide training that reduces complacency. Moreover, "positivity bias," a psychological phenomenon where the user's default assumption is to trust even in the absence of information to justifiably make that judgment, should be taken into account as well (Desai et al. 2009).

Overtrust is also likely influenced by the robot's design and behavior. Designs that promote anthropomorphism, for example, can affect a child's bond with and trust of a robot (Turkle 2006). Movable eyes, a human-like voice, and speech control all tend to promote one's belief that the robot is human-like and hence can be expected to promote the child's welfare. Human-like behavior tends to promote anthropomorphic evaluations and is likely to promote overtrust. For instance, properly timed apologies and/or promises can repair a person's trust in spite of the fact that an apology or promise may have no inherent meaning to an autonomous robot (Robinette et al. 2015). Apologies, an emotional expression of regret, influenced the decision-making of study participants even though the robot's expressions of regret were limited to messages on a computer screen. Moreover, the promises made by the robot were not supported by the robot's conviction or confidence. Still, hollow apologies and promises alone were enough to convince participants to trust the robot again in spite of earlier mistakes.

Even if roboticists avoid the use of anthropomorphic features in their designs, consistent and predictable autonomous systems tend to generate overtrust. When a system is reliable, people tend to ignore or discount the possibility of a failure or mistake. Furthermore, the level of cognitive engagement that the robot demands from the user can have an influence. For example, if users can proceed with a treatment routine without much conscious effort, then presumably they may not be fully aware of the risk.

No failsafe strategy exists that will completely eliminate risk, including when children and their families interact with a robotic system. To the greatest extent possible, the goal is to mitigate and promote awareness of the risks that users may encounter. Early research related to overtrust of automation demonstrated that occasional mistakes by a system could be used to maintain user vigilance (Parasuraman et al. 1993). Thus, it may be possible to design healthcare robots that actively engage a user's "reflective brain," reducing complacency and overtrust and perhaps lowering the risk. The use of warning indicators is one design pathway, which could be implemented in various ways. For example, a warning could take the form of a flashing light, a verbal cue that danger is ahead, or vibrations that the user feels. The process of deciding which one(s) to implement has to do, in part, with the physical and mental capabilities of the intended user.

Another kind of strategy to consider is one that demands the direct attention of the user. For example, in order for the robot (e.g., an exoskeleton) to function, the user would have to perform a specific action (e.g., press a button after a certain amount of time). On a similar note, a robot could be designed to function only if the primary caregiver of the patient were within a given proximity and/or granted the robot permission to proceed with a task. Alternatively, a system could be designed with adjustable autonomy; for example, once the robot seemed to be operating reliably, the parent could decide to receive fewer notices.

Warnings and message systems may help to lessen overtrust, but these mechanisms are unlikely to fully prevent it. In some situations, the robot may need to selectively fail to reduce complacency. The possibility that a robot may deliberately fail or behave suboptimally in order to increase the vigilance of a user presents complex ethical issues. A better understanding of how selective failure will affect the overall safety of the user must inform design strategies. Consider, for example, a child using a robotic exoskeleton to climb a ladder. Though it may generate user frustration, selective failure before the climb begins may reduce harm to the child by averting the possibility of a fall from a great height. Yet selective failure after the climb has begun would almost guarantee injury.

Perhaps the most extreme method of mitigating overtrust would be for the robot to refuse to perform specific actions or tasks. This is a design pathway that roboticists, including Briggs and Scheutz (2015), are starting to explore. An overarching ethical quandary in this realm is how much freedom of choice pediatric patients should be granted when they may place themselves at risk, an issue that is compounded by the fact that patients are not a monolithic, static population. Numerous factors, including age, experience, and physical and mental well-being, can complicate an assessment of whether self-determination should supersede beneficence.

When it comes to harm prevention in the case of a pediatric user, one option would be to program a robot in accordance with an ethical theory like Kant's or utilitarianism (assuming that such a thing is even possible). Presumably, a "utilitarian" robot would try to promote the greater good of a given community, and alternatively, a "Kantian" robot would seek to uphold the tenets of the categorical imperative, including the principle of respect for persons. Yet human beings are not typically strict utilitarians or Kantians, so would it be justifiable or prudent to demand that robots behave in such a manner? Taking into account that the way humans make ethical decisions can be multifaceted, situational, and messy, it may take some time before consensus is reached about how robots should behave in ethically fraught circumstances. Nonetheless, if robots are going to continue to be deployed in healthcare or other settings, roboticists need concrete and actionable guidance as to what constitutes ethical behavior. In this context, the hope is to "operationalize" ethics in such a way that it prevents harm to pediatric patients and others.

9.7 Conclusion

Numerous types of robots are currently being deployed in healthcare settings, and many more are on the horizon. Their use raises numerous ethical issues that require thorough and ongoing examination. Yet one issue to which we sought to draw particular attention is the likelihood that children, their families, and healthcare providers might begin to overtrust robots to a point where the potential for significant harm emerges. We endeavored to outline strategies for mitigating overtrust in the hope of protecting children and other users of robotic technology. Roboticists and others must continue to diligently investigate what it means for a robotic system to behave ethically, especially as the public starts to rely more heavily on the technology.

Works Cited

Arkin, Ronald C. 2014. "Ameliorating Patient-Caregiver Stigma in Early-Stage Parkinson's Disease Using Robot Co-Mediators." *Proceedings of the AISB 50 Symposium on Machine Ethics in the Context of Medical and Health Care Agents*, London.

Billard, Aude, Ben Robins, Jacqueline Nadel, and Kerstin Dautenhahn. 2007. "Building Robota, a Mini-Humanoid Robot for the Rehabilitation of Children with Autism." *RESNA Assistive Technology Journal* 19 (1): 37–49.

Borggraefe, Ingo, Mirjam Klaiber, Tabea Schuler, B. Warken, Andreas S. Schroeder, Florian Heinen, and Andreas Meyer-Heim. 2010. "Safety of Robotic-Assisted Treadmill Therapy in Children and Adolescents with Gait Impairment: A Bi-Center Survey." *Developmental Neurorehabilitation* 13 (2): 114–19.

Boyle, Coleen A., Sheree Boulet, Laura A. Schieve, Robin A. Cohen, Stephen J. Blumberg, Marshalyn Yeargin-Allsopp, Susanna Visser, and Michael D. Kogan. 2011. "Trends in the Prevalence of Developmental Disabilities in US Children, 1997–2008." *Pediatrics* 127 (6): 1034–42.

Briggs, Gordon M. and Matthais Scheutz. 2015. "'Sorry, I Can't Do That': Developing Mechanisms to Appropriately Reject Directives in Human–Robot Interactions." *2015 AAAI Fall Symposium Series*.

Brooks, Douglas and Ayanna Howard. 2012. "Quantifying Upper-Arm Rehabilitation Metrics for Children Through Interaction with a Humanoid Robot." *Applied Bionics and Biomechanics* 9 (2): 157–72.

Brütsch, Karin, Tabea Schuler, Alexander Koenig, Lukas Zimmerli, Susan M. Koeneke, Lars Lünenburger, Robert Riener, Lutz Jäncke, and Andreas Meyer-Heim. 2010. "Influence of Virtual Reality Soccer Game on Walking Performance in Robotic Assisted Gait Training for Children." *Journal of NeuroEngineering and Rehabilitation* 7: 15.

BEA (Bureau d'Enquêtes et d'Analyses). 2012. "Final Report on the Accident on 1st June 2009." http://www.bea.aero/docspa/2009/f-cp090601.en/pdf/f-cp090601.en.pdf.

Carr, Nicholas. 2014. *The Glass Cage: Automation and Us*. New York: W. W. Norton.

Charette, Robert N. 2009. "Automated to Death." *IEEE Spectrum*. http://spectrum.ieee.org/computing/software/automated-to-death.

Chen, Yu-Ping and Ayanna Howard. 2016. "Effects of Robotic Therapy on Upper-Extremity Function in Children with Cerebral Palsy: A Systematic Review." *Developmental Neurorehabilitation* 19 (1): 64–71.

Chen, Yu-Ping, Shih-Yu Lee, and Ayanna M. Howard. 2014. "Effect of Virtual Reality on Upper Extremity Function in Children with Cerebal Palsy: A Meta-Analysis." *Pediatric Physical Therapy* 26 (3): 289–300.

Cioi, Daniel, Angad Kale, Grigore Burdea, Jack R. Engsberg, William Janes, and Sandy A. Ross. 2011. "Ankle Control and Strength Training for Children with Cerebral Palsy Using the Rutgers Ankle CP: A Case Study." *IEEE International Conference on Rehabilitative Robotics* 2011: 5975432.

Cook, Albert M., Brenda Bentz, Norma Harbottle, Cheryl Lynch, and Brad Miller. 2005. "School-Based Use of a Robotic Arm System by Children with Disabilities." *Neural Systems and Rehabilitation Engineering* 13 (4): 452–60.

Cook, Albert M., Max Q. Meng, Jin Jin Gu, and K. Howery. 2002. "Development of a Robotic Device for Facilitating Learning by Children Who Have Severe Disabilities." *Neural Systems and Rehabilitation Engineering* 10 (3): 178–87.

Cyberdyne. 2016. "What's HAL? The World's First Cyborg-Type Robot 'HAL.'" http://www.cyberdyne.jp/english/products/HAL/.

Damiano, Diane L. and Stacey L. DeJong. 2009. "A Systematic Review of the Effectiveness of Treadmill Training and Body Weight Support in Pediatric Rehabilitation." *Journal of Neurologic Physical Therapy* 33: 27–44.

Dautenhahn, Kerstin and Iain Werry. 2004. "Towards Interactive Robots in Autism Therapy." *Pragmatics and Cognition* 12 (1): 1–35.

Desai, Munjal, Kristen Stubbs, Aaron Steinfeld, and Holly Yanco. 2009. "Creating Trustworthy Robots: Lessons and Inspirations from Automated Systems." *Proceedings of the AISB Convention: New Frontiers in Human–Robot Interaction*.

Drane, James, Charlotte Safos, and Corinna E. Lathan. 2009. "Therapeutic Robotics for Children with Disabilities: A Case Study." *Studies in Health Technology and Informatics* 149: 344.

Dunn, Michael E., Tracy Burbine, Clint A. Bowers, and Stacey Tantleff-Dunn. 2001. "Moderators of Stress in Parents of Children with Autism." *Community Mental Health Journal* 37: 39–52.

Feil-Seifer, David and Maja J. Matarić. 2009. "Toward Socially Assistive Robotics for Augmenting Interventions for Children with Autism Spectrum Disorders." *Experimental Robotics* 54: 201–10.

Garcia-Vergara, Sergio, Yu-Ping Chen and Ayanna M. Howard. 2012. "Super Pop VR: An Adaptable Virtual Reality Game for Upper-Body Rehabilitation." *HCI International Conference*, Las Vegas.

GPSBites. 2012. "The Top 10 List of Worst GPS Disasters and Sat Nav Mistakes." http://www.gpsbites.com/top-10-list-of-worst-gps-disasters-and-sat-nav-mistakes.

Hartwig, Maik. 2014. "Modern Hand- and Arm Rehabilitation: The Tyrosolution Concept." http://tyromotion.com/wp-content/uploads/2013/04/HartwigM-2014-The-Tyrosolution-Concept._EN.pdf.

Howell, Richard. 1989. "A Prototype Robotic Arm for Use by Severely Orthopedically Handicapped Students, Final Report." Ohio, 102.

Kahn, Peter H., Batya Friedman, Deanne R. Perez-Granados, and Nathan G. Freier. 2004. "Robotic Pets in the Lives of Preschool Children." *CHI ' 04Extended Abstracts on Human Factors in Computing Systems*, Vienna.

Kaplan, Frederic. 2004. "Who Is Afraid of the Humanoid? Investigating Cultural Differences in the Acceptance of Robots." *International Journal of Humanoid Robotics* 1 (3): 1–16.

Kozima, Hideki, Marek P. Michalowski, and Cocoro Nakagawa. 2008. "Keepon." *International Journal of Social Robotics,* 1 (1): 3–18.

Kozima, Hideki and Cocoro Nakagawa. 2006. "Social Robots for Children: Practice in Communication-Care." *9th IEEE International Workshop on Advanced Motion Control*, 768–73.

Kronreif, Gernot, Barbara Prazak, Stefan Mina, Martin Kornfeld, Michael Meindl, and Martin Furst. 2005. "PlayROB-Robot-Assisted Playing for Children with Severe Physical Disabilities." *IEEE 9th International Conference on Rehabilitation Robotics 2005* (ICORR'05), 193–6.

Lathan, Corinna, Amy Brisben, and Charlotte Safos. 2005. "CosmoBot Levels the Playing Field for Disabled Children." *Interactions*, special issue: "Robots!" 12 (2): 14–6.

Levy, David. 2007. *Love and Sex with Robots*. New York: Harper Perennial.

Maes, Bea, Theo G. Broekman, A. Dosen, and J. Nauts. 2003. "Caregiving Burden of Families Looking after Persons with Intellectual Disability and Behavioural or Psychiatric Problems." *Journal of Intellectual Disability Research* 47: 447–55.

Marti, Patrizia and Leonardo Giusti. 2010. "A Robot Companion for Inclusive Games: A User-Centred Design Perspective." *IEEE International Conference on Robotics and Automation 2010* (ICRA '10), 4348–53.

Meyer-Heim, Andreas, Corinne Ammann-Reiffer, Annick Schmartz, J. Schafer, F.H. Sennhauser, Florian Heinen, B. Knecht, Edward Dabrowski, and Ingo Borggraefe. 2009. "Improvement of Walking Abilities after Robotic-Assisted Locomotion Training in Children with Cerebral Palsy." *Archives of Disease in Childhood* 94: 615–20.

Michaud, Francois, J. Laplante, Helene Larouche, Audrey Duquette, Serge Caron, Dominic Letourneau, and Patrice Masson. 2005. "Autonomous Spherical Mobile Robot to Study Child Development." *IEEE Transactions on Systems, Man, and Cybernetics* 35 (4): 471–80.

Mindell, David A. 2015. *Our Robots, Ourselves: Robotics and the Myths of Autonomy*. New York: Viking.

Mirelman, Anat, Benjamin L. Patritti, Paolo Bonato, and Judith E. Deutsch. 2010. "Effects of Virtual Reality Training on Gait Biomechanics of Individuals Post-Stroke." *Gait & Posture* 31 (4): 433–7.

NSTB (National Transportation Safety Board). 2014. "NTSB Press Release: NTSB Finds Mismanagement of Approach and Inadequate Monitoring of Airspeed Led to Crash of Asiana flight 214, Multiple Contributing Factors Also Identified." http://www.ntsb.gov/news/press-releases/Pages/PR20140624.aspx.

Papavasiliou, Antigone S. 2009. "Management of Motor Problems in Cerebral Palsy: A Critical Update for the Clinician." *European Journal of Paediatric Neurology* 13: 387–96.

Parasuraman, Raja, Robert Molloy, and Indramani L. Singh. 1993. "Performance Consequences of Automation-Induced 'Complacency.'" *International Journal of Aviation Psychology* 3 (1): 1–23.

Parasuraman, Raja and Victor Riley. 1997. "Humans and Automation: Use, Misuse, Disuse, Abuse." *Human Factors* 39 (2): 230–53.

Pearson, Yvette and Jason Borenstein. 2013. "The Intervention of Robot Caregivers and the Cultivation of Children's Capability to Play." *Science and Engineering Ethics* 19 (1): 123–37.

Pearson, Yvette and Jason Borenstein. 2014. "Creating 'Companions' for Children: The Ethics of Designing Esthetic Features for Robots." *AI & Society* 29 (1): 23–31.

Pennisi, Paola, Alessandro Tonacci, Gennaro Tartarisco, Lucia Billeci, Liliana Ruta, Sebastiano Gangemi, and Giovanni Pioggia. 2016. "Autism and Social Robotics: A Systematic Review." *Autism Research* 9 (2): 65–83. doi:10.1002/aur.1527.

Povyakalo, Andrey A., Eugenio Alberdi, Lorenzo Strigini, and Peter Ayton. 2013. "How to Discriminate Between Computer-Aided and Computer-Hindered Decisions: A Case Study in Mammography." *Medical Decision Making* 33 (1): 98–107.

Punwar, Alice J. 2000. "Developmental Disabilities Practice." In *Occupational Therapy: Principles and Practice*, edited by A. J. Punwar and S. M. Peloquin, 159–74. USA: Lippincott Williams & Wilkins.

Robinette, Paul, Ayanna Howard, and Alan R. Wagner. 2015. "Timing is Key for Robot Trust Repair." *7th International Conference on Social Robotics (ICSR 2015)*, Paris.

Robinette, Paul, Robert Allen, Wenchen Li, Ayanna Howard, and Alan R. Wagner. 2016. "Overtrust of Robots in Emergency Evacuation Scenarios." *ACM/IEEE International Conference on Human–Robot Interaction (HRI 2016)*, 101–8. Christchurch, New Zealand.

Robins, Ben, Kerstin Dautenhahn, and Paul Dickerson. 2009. "From Isolation to Communication: A Case Study Evaluation of Robot Assisted Play for Children with Autism with a Minimally Expressive Humanoid Robot." *Proceedings of the Second International Conference of Advances in CHI* (ACHI'09), 205–11.

Scassellati, Brian. 2007. "How Social Robots Will Help Us Diagnose, Treat, and Understand Autism." *Robotics Research* 28: 552–63.

Scassellati, Brian, Henny Admoni, and Maja Matarić. 2012. "Robots for Use in Autism Research." *Annual Review of Biomedical Engineering* 14: 275–94.

Sharkey, Noel and Amanda Sharkey. 2010. "The Crying Shame of Robot Nannies: An Ethical Appraisal." *Interaction Studies* 11 (2): 161–90.

Skitka, Linda J., Kathy L. Mosier, and Mark Burdick. 1999. "Does Automation Bias Decision-Making?" *International Journal of Human-Computer Studies* 51: 991–1006.

Smith, Philip J., C. Elaine McCoy, and Charles Layton. 1997. "Brittleness in the Design of Cooperative Problem-Solving Systems: The Effects on User Performance." *IEEE Transactions on Systems, Man, and Cybernetics—Part A: Systems and Humans* 27 (3): 360–72.

Sparrow, Robert and Linda Sparrow. 2006. "In the Hands of Machines? The Future of Aged Care." *Mind and Machines* 16: 141–61.

Sukal, Theresa M., Kristin J. Krosschell, and Julius P.A. Dewald. 2007. "Use of the ACT3D System to Evaluate Synergies in Children with Cerebral Palsy: A Pilot Study." *IEEE International Conference on Rehabilitation Robotics*, Noordwijk, Netherlands.

Topping, Mike. 2002. "An Overview of the Development of Handy 1, a Rehabilitation Robot to Assist the Severely Disabled." *Journal of Intelligent and Robotic Systems* 34 (3): 253–63.

Turkle, Sherry. 2006. "A Nascent Robotics Culture: New Complicities for Companionship." *AAAI Technical Report Series*, July.

Turkle, Sherry. 2015. *Reclaiming Conversation: The Power of Talk in a Digital Age*. London: Penguin Press.

Wade, Shari L., H. Gerry Taylor, Dennis Drotar, Terry Stancin, and Keith O. Yeates. 1998. "Family Burden and Adaptation During the Initial Year after Traumatic Brain Injury in Children." *Pediatrics* 102: 110–16.

Walters, Michael L., Dag S. Syrdal, Kerstin Dautenhahn, Rene te Boekhorst, and Kheng L. Koay. 2008. "Avoiding the Uncanny Valley: Robot Appearance, Personality, and Consistency of Behavior in an Attention-Seeking Home Scenario for a Robot Companion." *Autonomous Robots* 24: 159–78.

Wood, Krista, Corinna Lathan, and Kenton Kaufman. 2009. "Development of an Interactive Upper Extremity Gestural Robotic Feedback System: From Bench to Reality." *IEEE Engineering* in *Medicine* and *Biology Society* 2009: 5973–6.

Yamagishi, Toshio. 2001. "Trust as a Form of Social Intelligence." In *Trust in Society*, edited by Karen S. Cook, 121–47. New York: Russell Sage Foundation.

Yamagishi, Toshio, Masako Kikuchi, and Motoko Kosugi. 1999. "Trust, Gullibility, and Social Intelligence." *Asian Journal of Social Psychology* 2: 145–61.

10 TRUST AND HUMAN–ROBOT INTERACTIONS

Jesse Kirkpatrick, Erin N. Hahn, and Amy J. Haufler

On March 23, 2003, the third day of the Iraq War, a British Tornado GR4 fighter jet was returning to its base in northern Kuwait, an area under protection by the U.S. Patriot anti-missile system. The system misidentified the jet as a foe, fired, and destroyed the aircraft. Flight Lieutenants Kevin Barry Main and David Rhys Williams were both killed, tragically marking the first friendly fire incident of the war (Piller 2003).

This event is remarkable not because of the tragic loss of life, an unfortunate yet inevitable feature of modern combat, but because these airmen's death can be attributed, in part, to human trust in the Patriot system. While humans remain "in the loop" by monitoring the Patriot system and retaining veto power over its ability to fire, an important feature of the system is that it is almost completely automated. As the Tornado fighter approached, the Patriot system misidentified the incoming Brits, and the human operators on the ground were faced with a split-second decision: trust the system or exercise their veto, thus halting the system before it could perform its automated firing. Unfortunately, the operators trusted what they believed to be the computer's superior judgment and allowed the system to fire, a mistake that resulted in tragedy.

As robotic technologies approach autonomy, and in increasing cases achieve it, scholars have turned their attention to the relationship between trust and human–robot interactions. Using a multidisciplinary approach that includes philosophy, law, and neuroscience, this chapter explores the issue of trust in autonomous human–robot interactions.[1] The chapter proceeds in four sections. Section 10.1 explicates the concept of human–robot interaction. Section 10.2 articulates a normative account of interpersonal trust in service of section 10.3's exploration of the question of whether human–robot interactions could approach or achieve interpersonal trust. In answering this question in the affirmative, section 10.4 flags some of the potential deleterious consequences of facilitating interpersonal trust in human–robot interactions. Section 10.5 concludes with a call for future scholarship to address the philosophical, empirical, legal, and policy issues related to trust in human–robot interactions explicated in section 10.3.

10.1 What Is Human–Robot Interaction?

Rudimentary forms of human–robot interaction often take the shape of a command-and-response model of interaction. Scholars have infelicitously characterized such relations as "master–slave" interactions, wherein humans issue commands (often task- or goal-oriented) and then monitor the compliance and status of the command's execution (Fong et al. 2005). Contemporary advances in robotics have had the predictable effect of creating more sophisticated and nuanced interactions that go beyond the mere command-oriented model. One recent model, which serves as the focus of this chapter, is "Peer-to-Peer Human–Robot Interaction" (P2P-HRI; hereafter, simply HRI). The HRI model seeks to "develop ... techniques that allow humans and robots to work effectively together ... emphasiz[ing] the idea that humans and robots should work as partners" (Fong et al. 2006, 3198). Consequently, developments in HRI models have led to interactions that are more engaging, dynamic, and intuitive than those of earlier models, with the overarching goal of creating autonomous robots with which humans can collaborate in ways that are "compatible with human cognitive, attentive and communication capabilities and limitations" (Office of Naval Research 2016).

The associated implications of the use of human–robot teaming indicate that studying and understanding the parameters of successful HRI must consider such factors as the ease of adoption and use; individual state and trait characteristics (such as stress, fatigue, mood, and attention), which may mediate the interaction and ultimately help determine the level of trust in the robotic system; and robotic and environmental factors that contribute to human trust (Schaefer et al. 2016). In addition, it is essential for HRI research to adopt a posture that is not isolated from the ethical, social, cultural, legal, and policy perspectives that are essential to assess comprehensively and determine the benefits, appropriate use, and consequences of HRI across the multiple individual, commercial, and military uses that the future will see.

One specific area of HRI that will be important is trust. But when scholars refer to trust in relation to HRI, what do they mean? And what does this trust involve? And, perhaps most important, what are the future implications of this trust with respect to the relationship between humans and robots?

10.2 What Is Trust? Operationalizing the Concept in Human–Robot Interaction

Trust can take various forms; it can range from institutional trust (Potter 2002; Govier 1997; Townley and Garfield 2013) to trust in oneself (Govier 1993; Lehrer 1997; Foley 2001; Jones 2012a; Potter 2002) to trust in one's government (Hardin 2002).[2] The fact that there is considerable scholarship on individuals' trust in various entities that goes beyond interpersonal trust underscores the salience of the fact that in a world as complex as ours, we are required to engage in numerous forms of trusting, with numerous agents, not all of which are fellow human beings. Nevertheless, some of the richest scholarship has focused on the philosophical elements of interpersonal trust, and interpersonal trust remains the apex of achievement that HRI designers aim to reach (Schaefer et al. 2016, 380). Consequently, this chapter takes interpersonal trust as its point of departure, as it provides a nuanced articulation of trust in a way that best informs the relationship between trust and HRI.

Interpersonal trust is based on the decision of an agent, the trustor, to make herself vulnerable to other agent(s), the trustee(s), by relying on the trustee to fulfill a given action (Baier 1986; Pettit 1995, 204). Put more simply: A trusts B with Z (Baier 1986; Jones 2012b). For the sake of simplicity, let us call this the *philosophical account of interpersonal trust*. In this formulation, the trustor affords the trustee discretionary power over some good or range of goods, thus running the risk that the trustee may not come through for the trustor. One way to characterize this three-part formulation of trust is normative. Take, for example, Molli's request that Jack pick up her child from daycare. Molli has made herself vulnerable to Jack with this request, given the risk that he may not fulfill his obligation, and there is now an expectation that Jack *will* fulfill his obligation. Molli's appeal to Jack "strike[s] a responsive chord" in which Jack will fulfill his commitment because of respect for Molli's standing and his interest in her well-being (Pettit 1995, 208).

This chord that is struck in the exchange can be characterized by goodwill; in turn, this goodwill is manifest "in virtue of being positively responsive to the fact of someone's dependency" (Jones 2012b, 69). In this account, goodwill corresponds with trust's constitutive elements of risk and vulnerability: as moral agents, we recognize another's vulnerability and the attendant riskiness in acting as a trustor. In turn, by acting as trustees, we extend goodwill to this individual (the trustor). As Baier argues, "[W]here one depends on another's good will, one is necessarily vulnerable to the limits of that good will. One leaves others an opportunity to harm one when one trusts, and also shows one's confidence that they will not take it" (1986, 235). On this view of trust, such interpersonal interactions are expressly normative because individuals stand in relation to one another as moral agents, with the assumption and recognition of dependency, risk, vulnerability, and goodwill.[3]

Others view trust as not constitutively rooted in one's standing as a normative agent, but instead grounded in appeals to self-interest.[4] Returning to the example of Molli, the risks inherent in her request endure—Jack may fail to pick up her child—but the reason that Jack fulfills her request, and that Molli can be probabilistically assured of this fulfillment, resides in the knowledge of Jack's desire to gain her good opinion of him. In what has been called the "cunning of trust," the "trustors do not have to depend on the more or less admirable trustworthiness of others; they can also hope to exploit the relatively base desire to be well considered" (Petit 1995, 203). Trust is cunning in the sense that it tames interests that may be otherwise deleterious in the service of helping to generate positive interpersonal exchanges.

Of course, self-interest need not be confined to a single agent in such exchanges, and it is doubtful that trust would be very cunning if it did. In this sense, trust can emanate from mutual self-interest: Molli can rely on Jack because she knows it is in both of their interests for him to pick up her child (Hardin 2002). Under this line of thought, trust helps solve coordination problems, and the desirable product of such interactions is the benefit of reducing social complexity, instability, and uncertainty. This game-theoretic view of trust is predicated on the belief that trust builds social capital, mutually benefiting the trustor and trustee, and is an instrumental component of our shared lives.[5]

Trust can also be distinguished from mere reliance (Baier 1986, 235). One may object to this distinction on the grounds that there are forms of reliance that involve trust. For example, we may be lost while driving to our favorite bookshop. While stopped at a red light, we see a man stepping into a taxi and overhear him tell the driver that his destination is the very same bookshop that we too are trying to locate. We follow the driver, *relying* on her to successfully reach our destination. Now imagine the same situation, but after the passenger calls out his destination, we roll down the window and tell the driver that we too are headed to the same bookshop, and we will follow her. The driver happily assents. As in the first case, we proceed to follow the taxi driver, relying on her to successfully reach our destination.

If it is true that both cases involve reliance, how might it be that one case involves trust and the other does not? In the first case, we rely on the driver because we believe that she is bound and constrained by her role as a taxi driver; she is fulfilling a professional obligation, and we know that she will predictably come through for us. By contrast, in the second case, we rely on the driver not only because it is her professional obligation, but also because she is disposed to us as individuals; the driver recognizes our vulnerability and shows us goodwill in her acknowledgment of our dependency on her in the given situation.

Some scholars working in the engineering and human factors areas of HRI make a similar distinction between trust in intention and trust in competency, reliability, or ability.[6] The latter is often, if not always, reserved for automated systems or tasks and, possibly, even sophisticated robots—one may trust the reliability of one's watch to keep time—while the former is commonly associated with people—one may trust another person's signaled intent to repay her financial debt. But not all reliance involves trust. One way to capture this possibility is to consider the fact that we rely on all sorts of people and things in ways that do not involve trust. We may rely on terrorists to violate the moral and legal principle of distinction. We may rely on our shoelace to stay tied when it has been double-knotted. Or we may rely on our kitchen timer to keep the appropriate time while we cook. The first example underscores the possibility that goodwill plays an important role in trust when contrasted with other motives (or an absence of motives). We may regard the terrorist as reliable and dependable in her motive to kill, but it seems odd to say that she is trustworthy or that we trust her.[7] Another way to further uncover the distinction between trust and reliability is to consider what may be the appropriate emotional response to violations of trust. As philosopher Annette Baier notes, "Trusting can be betrayed, or at least let down," whereas disappointment is the proper response to unreliability (1986, 235). When the double-knotted shoelace comes untied or our timer fails to keep time, we may be disappointed or even angry, but such instances of unreliability do not evoke deep feelings of betrayal.[8]

10.3 Can We Trust Robots?

How do these normative distinctions involving interpersonal trust help us in explicating and analyzing the relationship between trust and HRI? Can we *trust* robots or can we merely *rely* on them? How does viewing trust as the three-part formulation of A trusts B with Z help sharpen our considerations of trust in robots?

One plausible answer to these questions looks toward the future. It may be the case that robots will become so advanced that HRI will someday, maybe even someday soon, take the form of interpersonal relationships involving trust with features like the ones described. Although this response may help us grapple with what to expect in future scenarios, it seems unsatisfying given the likelihood that developments in robotics and artificial intelligence (AI) that may make this kind of HRI a reality remain many years away.[9] Speculations concerning strong AI or the impending technological singularity—the point at which general AI exceeds human intelligence—may offer useful heuristic devices with which to explore practical and theoretical concerns related to robotics and AI, but for our purposes they remain too notional to offer productive considerations of trust more properly rooted in the present.

If we are to confine our considerations of trust and HRI to states of affairs more closely related to the present and near future—even for the sake of argument stretching these confines to imagine a cutting-edge autonomous humanoid robot AI nearly indistinguishable from a human (an AI, "Ava," was depicted in the popular 2015 film *Ex Machina*)—it may simply be the case that the normative literature on trust demonstrates that talk of *trust* in robots is misplaced (Universal Pictures International 2015). If our interactions with robots fail to meet the key conditions of trust we have articulated (namely, agency, intention, vulnerability, and goodwill), then perhaps it would be more accurate to frame such discussions around the concept of reliance, not trust, even when we are considering more advanced forms of AI and robotics. This seems to especially be the case when we consider robust notions of trust, particularly of the sort that require possession of consciousness and agency on behalf of trustors and trustees.[10] A discussion of these conditions, and whether robots can in theory meet them, would take us far afield, although later we offer a very brief discussion of the relationship between trust, agency, consciousness, and HRI.

A more plausible alternative is that we may decide that we *can* properly refer to trust in HRI, but that philosophical interpretations of interpersonal trust entail conditions that are too robust to accurately describe trust in HRI. This line of argument suggests that it may be the case that trust in HRI exists, but it is *not* like interpersonal trust. The purchase of this argument is contingent upon the level of sophistication of the given robot in question; let us again assume that we are considering a sophisticated AI like *Ex Machina*'s Ava. Under this line of argument, with respect to robots, we ought to weaken conditions for trust that seem uniquely human, like agency and goodwill, thus lowering the conceptual threshold requirements for what counts as trust in HRI.

But this alternative seems to strain credulity—both folk accounts of HRI and empirical studies demonstrate the strong emotional connections (not limited to trust) humans feel with robots in ways that resemble or approach those found in interpersonal interactions.[11] For example, soldiers have been reported to feel a range of emotions, including sadness and anger, when their bomb disposal robots are damaged, and even reported interacting with their robots as if they were a human being or an animal (Billings et al. 2012; Carpenter 2013). Other scholars have found similarities between how humans anthropomorphize their robots and how they anthropomorphize their pets (Kiesler et al. 2006, 2008). Although such studies are suggestive, not conclusive, of the interactions humans have with robots, they nevertheless signal the importance that trust will play increasingly in HRI. To assume otherwise risks overlooking contributions that a robust account of trust can make to better understanding and normatively analyzing future HRI.

In addition, a less robust account of interpersonal trust than the one offered in the philosophical account (see section 10.2) fails to take seriously the fact that so many benchwork HRI researchers seek to describe, explore, and ultimately foster trust in HRI that meets the criteria and standards articulated in the philosophical account. For example, the U.S. Air Force's Human Trust and Interaction Branch, in tandem with other Air Force research branches, announced a request in 2015 for research proposals under the rubric of "Trust in Autonomy for Human Machine Teaming." The research call was animated by the stated "need [for] research on how to harness the socio-emotional elements of interpersonal team/trust dynamics and inject them into human–robot teams." The goal of this funding scheme is, in part, "to drive teaming effectiveness" (U.S. Air Force 2015). A recent meta-analysis "assess[ing] research concerning human trust in automation," in order to "understand the foundation upon which future autonomous systems can be built," demonstrates that this interest is not confined to the U.S. military (Schaefer et al. 2016, 377). As robots become increasingly sophisticated and their interactions with humans increase in frequency, duration, and complexity, the presence of social and emotional "elements of interpersonal . . . trust" in these interactions will likely become increasingly prevalent.

Instead of altogether abandoning the operative concept of trust in HRI, a third approach could be to retain the core elements of interpersonal trust, while parsing these elements in ways that are terminologically similar to but definitionally different from those articulated in the philosophical literature. This approach has the advantage of preserving the features of trust that will be critical to achieving the kinds of HRI desired to more effectively engage in such activities as surgery and healthcare, transportation, warfighting, and search and rescue operations, but at the cost of weakening how these elements are defined in order to more closely capture the operative trust that occurs currently in HRI.

In some ways this approach has already been adopted by researchers whose focus is automation and trust, an area of research considered to be the necessary precursor to research in trust involving more advanced types of robotics. For example, Lee and See define trust somewhat similarly to philosophical accounts of interpersonal trust: "trust can be defined as the attitude that an agent will help achieve an individual's goals in a situation characterized by uncertainty and vulnerability." They go on to stipulate that "an agent can be automation" (Lee and See 2004, 51). This is not the space to wade into the thorny debate over whether rudimentary automation should be characterized as an agent. Generally, the more permissive the definitional circle that is drawn in order to characterize trust in HRI as interpersonal, the greater the risk of failing to set the bar high enough for future trust-based HRI. The concern in lowering the definitional threshold for what "counts" as interpersonal trust in HRI is that it risks slowing future developments in facilitating trust in HRI. If future trust-based HRI may be beneficial, then we have a *pro tanto* reason for why it may be inadvisable to ascribe such characteristic elements of trust as agency to mere automata.

These complications in conceptualizing trust in HRI return us to the plausible conclusion that the philosophical account of interpersonal trust is the wrong stick by which to measure HRI. The likely possibility that trust in HRI cannot and may not meet the conditions articulated in a robust account of interpersonal trust suggests that a description of trust with conditions weaker than those found in the philosophical account may better capture the kind of trusting that does and will occur in HRI. In light of this, it may further be the case that an honest consideration of trust in HRI would reasonably conclude that such trust does not meet the conditions found in the philosophical account of interpersonal trust (assuming, for the sake of argument, the philosophical account of trust is an accurate description of interpersonal trust). If proper interpersonal trust requires moral agency, intention, and consciousness, then a reasonable and measurable approximation of concepts of agency, consciousness, and intentionality would be required to advance the understanding of HRI and to support empirical investigations to quantify trust in robotics. And if robots lack these attributes, and will continue to lack them far into the future, even a conditional conclusion, stipulated to acknowledge the contested nature of the concepts upon which the conclusion rests, casts considerable doubt on the quality and type of trust possible in HRI. Let us call the supposition that the properties that constitute interpersonal trust (e.g., goodwill, consciousness, and intentionality) have an objective ontological status the *objective account of interpersonal trust in HRI.*

But consider the possibility that trust can be viewed as epistemically subjective—that is, informed by individuals' states of belief and emotion. We can then imagine cases, both present and in the future, in which trust of the type found in the philosophical account of interpersonal trust is and can be an operative feature of HRI, at least from the viewpoint of the human(s) in the trusting interaction. Humans may attribute intention, consciousness, and agency to robots, even if the robots lack these attributes. As Ososky et al. note in their discussion of subjective belief in robot intentionality, "[G]iven the human propensity to anthropomorphize technology . . . robots may act with intentions to complete a task in a certain manner as designed by programmers or engineers. However, it is important not to overlook the human perception of robot intent, whether real or imagined, that also factors into human subjective assessment of trust in robot teammates" (2013, 64). The point here is that although we may be objectively mistaken about the nature of the trusting relationship, in this case that the robot possesses intent, as a result of our subjective belief, we approach something analogous to interpersonal trust. Let us call this the *subjective account of interpersonal trust in HRI.*

The distinction here is a subtle but important one. The objective account takes the position that we can achieve an accurate conceptual understanding of what constitutes interpersonal trust, and in light of this achievement we can also determine the conditions under which interpersonal trust occurs. Consequently, this understanding allows for determinations to be made about whether or not a given agent is *actually* engaging in interpersonal trust; there is a fact of the matter: without consciousness, agency, and intentionality in both the trustor *and* trustee, true interpersonal trust is absent. Whereas the subjective account acknowledges that the objective account could in theory offer a proper articulation of trust, it also recognizes that some forms of trust can be predicated upon subjective belief: an agent can, as a result of an epistemic mistake, trust a robot in a fashion very similar, if not identical, to that found in the philosophical account of interpersonal trust.[12] If the subjective account captures correctly the possibility that trust that may resemble interpersonal trust can spring from subjective belief, what does this mean for future HRI?

10.4 Encouraging Trust in Human–Robot Interactions: A Cautionary Note

Although research remains at the early stages of studying human trust in complex robotic systems, variations of interpersonal trust remain the theoretical point of departure from which empirical HRI studies are built and the goal that HRI designers aim to achieve (Schaefer et al. 2016, 380).[13] As technological advances continue, so too will the level of sophistication in HRI, and as humans continue to work more closely with robots, an increasing level of trust will be required for these interactions to be successful. The use of robots in cleanup efforts in the aftermath of the 2011 Fukushima nuclear power plant meltdown underscores this point. During one of the cleanup operations, a human operator failed to trust the robot's autonomous navigation abilities, took manual control, and entangled the robot in its own cables (Laursen 2013). Such examples of suboptimal robot performance resulting from human intervention because of mistrust are numerous (Laursen 2013). As one expert in artificial intelligence observes, "[A]t a disaster scene with lives on the line, human rescuers need to learn to *trust* their robotic teammates or they'll have their own meltdowns" (Laursen 2013, 18).[14] The necessary role that trust will play in integrating new beneficial technologies into our lives is obvious. What is less clear, particularly as technologies move toward autonomy and HRIs inch closer to mimicking interpersonal interactions, is the potential negative outcomes that may result from these "thicker" forms of trust in HRI.

It is at present unknown how HRI trust will affect our notions of trustors and trustees and our day-to-day trusting interactions. Will trusting robots change the dynamics of and contributing factors to interpersonal trust? Moving forward, researchers will need to account for the effects of creating deep bonds between humans and machines, while remaining sensitive to both the positive *and* negative benefits of trust in HRI. We agree with the conclusion of a recent meta-analysis of trust and HRI that "future research should be focused on the effects of human states," particularly how such states may be adversely impacted when trust is violated in HRI (Schaefer et al. 2016, 395). Although it remains to be seen how violations of human–robot trust will affect humans, our folk sense of trust offers insight into the various negative emotional, psychological, and physiological outcomes that can result from violations of trust. Anyone who has ever trusted another, only to have that trust violated, is keenly aware of the negative consequences such violation can evoke.

As this field develops, it will also require multidisciplinary analysis of how interpersonal trust and HRI may affect others as a consequence of these trusting interactions. One area where this concern is most acute is in the development and deployment of lethal and autonomous weapons (LAWS)—weapons that can select and attack targets without human intervention. The normative, legal, and policy implications of LAWS have been well discussed, and space limitations do not permit us to articulate them here. However, we offer a few observations on how the development and use of LAWS may provide some insight regarding the cultivation of interpersonal trust in HRI and potential deleterious side effects.

While much of the debate over LAWS has focused on ethical considerations of what is appropriate to delegate to a machine, it also highlights the difficulties of cultivating trust in an autonomous system that, like anything, will be prone to error. One particular difficulty resides in the risk of humans overtrusting the competency, the reliability, and, as sophistication increases, the interpersonal dimensions of LAWS. It is easy to imagine (one need only look at Massachusetts Institute of Technology's Personal Robotics Group) a LAW that very much resembles a human being, with human-like quirks, facial gestures, and complex interactive communication capabilities (MIT Media Lab 2016). Overtrusting a walking, talking, lethal robot designed to facilitate deep interpersonal trust with its allied human counterparts could be disastrous. The earlier example of the U.S. Patriot anti-missile system's downing of a British jet in northern Kuwait is demonstrative of the overtrusting to which humans may be susceptible, even with systems that are much less engaging than the ones that current research portends for the future.

Of course, the inherent risks of overtrusting can occur in simple machines like bicycles and more complex systems like driverless cars. When it comes to LAWS, many of the capabilities and operational uses have controversial aspects—they may be used to plan future lethal operations, including the identification of human targets.[15] In short, the systems may be designed to kill, possibly even to lawfully kill, i.e., in compliance with current international legal obligations. While existing legal frameworks may be imperfect, one can still mine them to inform difficult legal and policy questions presented by robotic autonomous technologies. Examples from the commercial sector are particularly informative for how we may develop, test, and implement these technologies in the military sector. Such existing research efforts focusing on how best to safeguard against so-called automation bias or automation-induced complacency will become increasingly important as technology develops and becomes more and more decoupled from human supervision, and as strong trust-based interactions are facilitated (Goddard, Roudsari, and Wyatt 2012).[16]

10.5 Conclusion

This chapter began with a characterization of future human–robot interaction with autonomous robotic systems as akin to peer-to-peer interaction. It identified trust as a key aspect of this interaction and, in turn, sought to clarify the meaning of trust. In service of this clarification, the chapter explored interpersonal trust in an effort to assess the role it could play in future human–robot interactions. While skepticism about the role of interpersonal trust in HRI remains, it seems plausible that, under a subjective account of trust in HRI, such trust could approach a type that is analogous to interpersonal trust. If this is the case, then the design of future HRI must be sensitive to the potentially deleterious effects that could befall those humans involved in the interactions and those who might be subject to the side effects of the interactions.

Thus, we recommend that future studies of HRI employ a multidisciplinary approach in order to best address the complexities and multiple levels of concern regarding HRI. Approaches integrating or drawing on fields as diverse as philosophy, law, neuroscience, psychology, human development, sociology, and anthropology would generate questions, methodologies, and metrics to inform the optimal capability, functionality, and opportunity for use inclusive of ethical, social, legal, and policy considerations.

Notes

1. For the sake of simplicity, when we refer to human–robot interactions we are referring to human interactions with autonomous robots, unless otherwise specified. We define autonomous robots as "intelligent machines capable of performing tasks in the world *by themselves*, without explicit human control over their movements" (Bekey 2005, xii; emphasis in original).

2. For institutional trust see Potter (2002), Govier (1997), and Townley (2013). For trust in oneself, see Govier (1993), Lehrer (1997), Foley (2001), Jones (2012a), and Potter (2002). For trust in one's government, see Hardin (2002).
3. The normative relationship between trust and goodwill is more complicated than space permits us to discuss here. For example, we may trust someone even in the absence of goodwill, and we may not trust someone (say, our incompetent uncle) even though she possesses goodwill toward us. Thanks to a reviewer for this clarification.
4. We find somewhat similar elements of trust in the human factors literature: "Trust can be defined as the attitude that an agent will help achieve an individual's goals in a situation characterized by uncertainty and vulnerability" (Lee and See 2004, 51).
5. This is not to say that this instrumentalist view of trust cannot be normative; we are merely asserting that this view of trust need not be normative.
6. For a discussion of this literature and the distinction between trust in intention and trust in competency, reliability, or ability, see Ososky et al. (2013).
7. We may say that we "trust" the terrorist to kill us as civilians, but this seems like a semantic shortcut to conveying that she is reliable or dependable to do so, not that we trust her in the more nuanced sense of the term we have articulated.
8. Obviously this account of trust entailing betrayal is a simplification: not all violations of trust will result in feelings of betrayal; trust is not static; it operates on a dynamic spectrum, with varying degrees and levels.
9. Even the more optimistic projections of AI predict that significant advances are still several decades away. See Kurzweil (2005).
10. As Baier suggests, "[P]lausible conditions for proper trust will be that it survives consciousness, by both parties, and that the trusted has had some opportunity to signify acceptance or rejection, to warn the trusting if their trust is unacceptable [i.e., agency]" (1986, 235).
11. For human empathy toward robot "suffering," see Rosenthal-von der Pütten et al. (2013, 2014). For human–robot "bonds" displaying similarities to human–pet bonds, see Billings et al. (2012). For overtrust, see Robinette et al. (2016). For folk accounts of human–robot bonds, see Singer (2009).
12. This argument relies on distinctions drawn by John Searle (2014). Searle distinguishes between observer-relative ontological status—regarding things that exist because of people's beliefs and attitudes—and observer-independent ontological status—regarding things that exist independent of people's attitudes and beliefs about them. In this sense, the trust in the objective account, as we describe it, has an ontological status that is observer-independent—it requires of both agents the possession of consciousness, agency, and intentionality, and therefore the absence of these properties in the robot precludes the possibility of true interpersonal trust. Nevertheless, people may believe that robots have these properties and engage in trust that closely resembles (for the human) interpersonal trust as described in the

philosophical account. Thanks to a reviewer for encouraging this clarification of our argument.

13. For interpersonal trust, defined as predictability, dependability, and faith, as the theoretical basis of empirical research in HRI, see Muir (1994). For interpersonal trust as the point of departure for operationalizing trust in empirical research, see Schaefer et al. (2016).
14. Emphasis added. It is also possible that one way to safeguard against the potentially deleterious outcomes of trusting and overtrusting robots, particularly in cases where trust is violated, is to foster in human operators reliance rather than trust. Thanks to a reviewer for this suggestion.
15. The issue of misplaced trust or overtrusting is, of course, familiar to most of us. Trusting those we should not trust, sometimes even when we possess the knowledge that we should not trust them, is a common feature of interpersonal trust.
16. For design principles that can mitigate automation bias, see Goddard, Roudsari, and Wyatt (2012).

Works Cited

Baier, Annette. 1986. "Trust and Antitrust." *Ethics* 96 (2): 231–60.

Bekey, George A. 2005. *Autonomous Robots: From Biological Inspiration to Implementation and Control.* Cambridge, MA: MIT Press.

Billings, Deborah R., Kristin E. Schaefer, Jessie Y. Chen, Vivien Kocsis, Maria Barrera, Jacquelyn Cook, Michelle Ferrer, and Peter A. Hancock. 2012. "Human–Animal Trust as an Analog for Human–Robot Trust: A Review of Current Evidence." *US Army Research Laboratory.* ARL-TR-5949. University of Central Florida, Orlando.

Carpenter, Julie. 2013. "The Quiet Professional: An Investigation of US Military Explosive Ordnance Disposal Personnel Interactions with Everyday Field Robots." PhD dissertation, University of Washington.

Foley, Richard. 2001. *Intellectual Trust in Oneself and Others.* Cambridge: Cambridge University Press.

Fong, Terrence, Illah Nourbakhsh, Clayton Kunz, et al. 2005. "The Peer-to-Peer Human–Robot Interaction Project." *AIAA Space.*

Fong, Terrence, Jean Scholtz, Julie A. Shah, et al. 2006. "A Preliminary Study of Peer-to-Peer Human–Robot Interaction." Systems, Man and Cybernetics, *IEEE International Conference* (4): 3198–203.

Goddard, Kate, Abdul Roudsari, and Jeremy C. Wyatt. 2012. "Automation Bias: A Systematic Review of Frequency, Effect Mediators, and Mitigators." *Journal of the American Medical Informatics Association* 19 (1): 121–7.

Govier Trudy. 1993. "Self-Trust, Autonomy, and Self-Esteem." *Hypatia* 8 (1): 99–120.

Govier, Trudy. 1997. *Social Trust and Human Communities.* Montreal: McGill-Queen's University Press.

Hardin, Russell. 2002. *Trust and Trustworthiness.* New York: Russell Sage Foundation.

Jones, Karen. 2012a. "The Politics of Intellectual Self-Trust." *Social Epistemology* 26 (2): 237–51.

Jones, Karen. 2012b. "Trustworthiness." *Ethics* 123 (1): 61–85.

Kiesler, S., S. L. Lee, and A. D. Kramer. 2006. "Relationship Effects in Psychological Explanations of Nonhuman Behavior." *Anthrozoös* 19 (4): 335–52.

Kiesler, Sara, Aaron Powers, Susan R. Fussell, and Cristen Torrey. 2008. "Anthropomorphic Interactions with a Robot and Robot-Like Agent." *Social Cognition* 26 (2): 169–81.

Kurzweil, Ray. 2005. *The Singularity Is Near: When Humans Transcend Biology*. London: Penguin.

Laursen, Lucas. 2013. "Robot to Human: 'Trust Me.'" *Spectrum, IEEE* 50 (3): 18.

Lehrer, Keith. 1997. *Self-Trust: A Study of Reason, Knowledge, and Autonomy*. Oxford: Clarendon Press.

Lee, J. D. and K. A. See. 2004. "Trust in Automation: Designing for Appropriate Reliance." *Human Factors: Journal of the Human Factors and Ergonomics Society* 46 (1): 50–80.

MIT Media Lab. 2016. Massachusetts Institute of Technology's Personal Robotics Group. Projects. http://robotic.media.mit.edu/project-portfolio/.

Muir, Bonnie M. 1994. "Trust in Automation: Part I. Theoretical Issues in the Study of Trust and Human Intervention in Automated Systems." *Ergonomics* 37 (11): 1905–22.

Office of Naval Research. 2016. "Human–Robot Interaction Program Overview." http://www.onr.navy.mil/Science-Technology/Departments/Code-34/All-Programs/human-bioengineered-systems-341/Human-Robot-Interaction.aspx.

Ososky, Scott, David Schuster, Elizabeth Phillips, and Florian G. Jentsch. 2013. "Building Appropriate Trust in Human–Robot Teams." *Association for the Advancement of Artificial Intelligence Spring Symposium Series*, 60–5.

Pettit, Philip. 1995. "The Cunning of Trust." *Philosophy & Public Affairs* 24 (3): 202–25.

Piller, Charles. 2003. "Vaunted Patriot Missile Has a 'Friendly Fire' Failing." *Los Angeles Times*, April 21. http://articles.latimes.com/2003/apr/21/news/war-patriot21.

Potter, Nancy N. 2002. *How Can I Be Trusted? A Virtue Theory of Trustworthiness*. Lanham, MD: Rowman & Littlefield.

Robinette, Paul, Wenchen Li, Robert Allen, Ayanna M. Howard, and Alan R. Wagner. 2016. "Overtrust of Robots in Emergency Evacuation Scenarios." *211th ACM/IEEE International Conference on Human–Robot Interaction*, 101–8.

Rosenthal-von der Pütten, Astrid M., Frank P. Schulte, Sabrina C. Eimler, Laura Hoffmann, Sabrina Sobieraj, Stefan Maderwald, Nicole C. Krämer, and Matthias Brand. 2013. "Neural Correlates of Empathy Towards Robots." *Proceedings of the 8th ACM/IEEE International Conference on Human–Robot Interaction*, 215–16.

Rosenthal-von Der Pütten, Astrid M., Frank P. Schulte, Sabrina C. Eimler, Laura Hoffmann, Sabrina Sobieraj, Stefan Maderwald, Nicole C. Krämer, and Matthias

Brand. 2014. "Investigations on Empathy Towards Humans and Robots Using fMRI." *Computers in Human Behavior* 33 (April 2014): 201–12.

Schaefer, Kristin, Jessie Chen, James Szalma, and P. A. Hancock. 2016. "A Meta-Analysis of Factors Influencing the Development of Trust in Automation Implications for Understanding Autonomy in Future Systems." *Human Factors: Journal of the Human Factors and Ergonomics Society* 58 (3): 377–400.

Searle, John R. 2014. "What Your Computer Can't Know." *New York Review of Books* 61 (9): 52–55.

Singer, Peter Warren. 2009. *Wired for War: The Robotics Revolution and Conflict in the 21st Century*. London: Penguin.

Townley, C. and J. L. Garfield. 2013. "Public Trust." In *Trust: Analytic and Applied Perspectives*, edited by Makela and C. Townley, 96–106. Amsterdam: Rodopi Press.

Universal Pictures International. 2015. *Ex Machina*. Film. Directed by Alex Garland.

U.S. Air Force. 2015 "Trust in Autonomy for Human Machine Teaming." https://www.fbo.gov/index?s=opportunity&mode=form&id=8e61fdc774a736f13cacbec1b278bbbb&tab=core&_cview=1.

11 WHITE LIES ON SILVER TONGUES

WHY ROBOTS NEED TO DECEIVE (AND HOW)

Alistair M. C. Isaac and Will Bridewell

Deception is a regular feature of everyday human interaction. When speaking, people deceive by cloaking their beliefs or priorities in falsehoods. Of course, false speech includes malicious lies, but it also encompasses little white lies, subtle misdirections, and the literally false figures of speech that both punctuate and ease our moment-to-moment social interactions. We argue that much of this *technically* deceptive communication serves important pro-social functions and that genuinely social robots will need the capacity to participate in the human market of deceit. To this end, robots must not only recognize and respond effectively to deceptive speech but also generate deceptive messages of their own. We argue that deception-capable robots may stand on firm ethical ground, even when telling outright lies. Ethical lies are possible because the truth or falsity of deceptive speech is not the proper target of moral evaluation. Rather, the ethicality of human or robot communication must be assessed with respect to its underlying motive.

The social importance of deception is a theme that emerges repeatedly in fictional portrayals of human–robot interaction. One common plot explores the dangers to society if socially engaged robots lack the ability to detect and respond strategically to deception. For instance, the films *Short Circuit 2* (1988), *Robot & Frank* (2012), and *Chappie* (2015) all depict naive robots misled into thievery by duplicitous humans. When robots are themselves deceivers, the scenarios take on a more ominous tone, especially if human lives are at stake. In *Alien* (1979) the android Ash unreflectively engages in a pattern of deception mandated by its owners' secret instructions. Ash's inhuman commitment to the mission leads to the grotesque slaughter of its crewmates. Regardless of whether Ash can recognize its actions as deceptive, it can neither evaluate nor resist the ensuing pattern of behavior, which has dire consequences for human life. *2001: A Space Odyssey* (1968) provides a subtler cinematic example in the computer HAL. HAL's blind adherence to commands to deceive, unlike Ash's, is not what results in its murder of the human crew. Instead, the fault rests in the computer's inability to respond strategically—humanely—to the mandate that the goal of the mission be kept secret. When the demands of secrecy require HAL to lie in subtle ways, it instead turns to murder. Ironically, it is HAL's *inability to lie effectively* that leads to catastrophe.

More lighthearted depictions of social robots have found comedic traction in the idea that the ability to deceive is a defining feature of humanity. For instance, in the TV comedy *Red Dwarf* (1991), Lister, a human, teaches the robot Kryten to lie in an attempt to liberate it from the inhuman aspects of its programming. Conversely, Marvin ("the Paranoid Android") in *The Hitchhiker's Guide to the Galaxy* (Adams 1980) is characterized by its proclivity to tell the truth, even when grossly socially inappropriate. Marvin's gaffes may be funny, but they underscore the importance of subtle falsehoods in upholding social decorum. Furthermore, the most human (and heroic) fictionalized robots display a versatile capacity to mislead. *Star Wars*' (1977) R2D2, for instance, repeatedly deceives the people and robots around it, both subtly through omission and explicitly through outright lies, in service to the larger goal of conveying the plans for the Death Star to rebel forces. This pattern of deception is part of what gives a robot that looks like a trashcan on wheels the human element that endears it to audiences.

In the remainder of the chapter, we develop an account of how, why, and when robots should deceive. We set the stage by describing some prominent categories of duplicitous statements, emphasizing the importance of correct categorization for responding strategically to deceptive speech. We then show that the concept of an *ulterior motive* unifies these disparate types of deception, distinguishing them from false but not duplicitous speech acts. Next, we examine the importance of generating deceptive speech for maintaining a pro-social atmosphere. That argument culminates in a concrete engineering example where deception may greatly improve a robot's ability to serve human needs. We conclude with a discussion of the ethical standards for deceptive robots.

11.1 Representing Deception

We care if we are deceived. But what does it mean to be deceived, and why do we care about it? Intuitively, there is something "bad" about deception, but what is the source of that "badness"? This section argues that we are troubled by deceit because it is impelled by a covert goal, an *ulterior motive*. We need to detect deception because only by identifying the goals of other agents, whether human or robot, can we respond strategically to their actions. This insight highlights a specific challenge for savvy agents: effective detection of deception requires inferences about the hidden motives of others.

11.1.1 Taxonomy of Deception

The following scenario steps away from the world of robots to tease apart the components of deception. In this interaction, Fred is a police detective investigating a crime; Joe is a suspect in the crime; and Sue is Joe's manager at work.

> FRED: Where was Joe on the morning of March 23rd?
> SUE: Joe was here at the office, working at his desk.

Consider the most straightforward form of deceptive speech: *lying*. At a first pass, lying occurs when an agent willfully utters a claim that contradicts his beliefs. The detective suspects Joe of having committed a crime on the morning of March 23rd, so he cares where Joe happened to be. Is Sue lying about Joe's location? The answer is important not only because Fred cares about Joe's location but also because he cares about Joe's accomplices. If Sue is lying to protect Joe, she may be implicated in the crime.

How can Fred tell whether Sue is lying? Suppose, for instance, the detective has access to security video from the morning of March 23rd at the scene of the crime—that is, he knows that Sue's claim that Joe was at the office is false. Is this fact enough to determine that Sue is lying? Not necessarily; for instance, Sue might only have a *false belief*. Perhaps she saw a person who looks like Joe at the office and formed the erroneous belief that Joe was at work. Similarly, Sue might be *ignorant* of Joe's actual whereabouts. Maybe she has no evidence one way or another about Joe's presence, and her response is a rote report on assigned employee activities for March 23rd.

The falsity of a statement is not, then, sufficient evidence of lying. However, combined with other evidence, for instance biometric cues such as excessive sweat, fidgeting, or failure to make eye contact, it may nevertheless allow Fred to confidently infer that Sue is indeed lying. But is determining correctly whether or not Sue is lying enough for Fred's purposes? Consider two possibilities: in one scenario, Sue lies because she is in cahoots with Joe and has received a cut of the loot; in the other, Sue lies because she was hungover the morning of March 23rd, arrived late, and is scared of a reprimand for her unexcused absence. In both situations Sue is lying, but the appropriate response by the detective is radically different. In the first case, Fred might charge Sue with abetting a crime; in the second, he may simply discount Sue's testimony.

The point of the example is twofold. First, detecting a lie requires knowledge about more than a single statement's accuracy. A lie depends constitutively on the speaker's state of mind, so her intent to deceive must be inferred. Second, the correct response to a lie may turn on more than the mere fact that a lie has been uttered. Crucially, the responder's strategy may depend on the goal that motivated the lie—it is this goal that underpins any intent to deceive.[1] These two key features characterize other forms of deception identified in the literature. Here we briefly consider paltering, bullshit, and pandering (for a more in-depth treatment, see Isaac and Bridewell 2014).

Paltering (Schauer and Zeckhauser 2009; Rogers et al. 2014) occurs when a speaker misleads his interlocutor by uttering an irrelevant truth. A paradigmatic example is the used-car salesman who truthfully claims, "The wheels on this car are as good as new," to direct attention away from the poor quality of the engine. Paltering illustrates that neither the truth-value of an utterance nor the speaker's belief about its truth are crucial factors for determining whether the utterance is deceptive. Rather, the ethical status of speech may turn entirely on whether it is motivated by a malicious intent to misdirect.

Bullshit (Frankfurt 1986; Hardcastle and Reisch 2006) occurs when a speaker neither knows nor cares about the truth-value of her utterance. Bullshit may be relatively benign, as in a "bull session" or the exchanging of pleasantries around the water cooler. However, there is malicious bullshit as well. A confidence man may spew bullshit about his background and skills, but if people around him believe it, the consequences may be disastrous. Frank Abagnale, Jr., for instance, repeatedly impersonated an airline pilot to travel for free (events dramatized in the 2002 film *Catch Me If You Can*), but his bullshit put lives at risk when he was asked to actually fly a plane and blithely accepted the controls.

Pandering is a particularly noteworthy form of bullshit (Sullivan 1997; Isaac and Bridewell 2014). When someone panders, he (may) neither know nor care about the truth of his utterance (hence, a form of bullshit), but he does care about an audience's perception of its truth. A politician who, when stumping in Vermont, proclaims, "Vermont has the most beautiful trees on God's green earth!" does so not because she believes the local trees are beautiful, but because she believes the local audience believes Vermont's trees are beautiful—or, more subtly, that the locals want visitors to believe their trees are beautiful.

Lying, paltering, bullshitting, and pandering are all forms of deception. However, they are united neither by the truth-value of the utterance nor the speaker's belief in that utterance. Moreover, bullshitting and pandering may lack even an intent to deceive. Rather, what unites these categories of perfidy is the presence of a goal that supersedes the conversational norm for truthful speech. The nature of this goal, in addition to reliable detection and classification of deception, is vital information for any agent forming a strategic response.

11.1.2 Theory of Mind, Standing Norms, and Ulterior Motives

What capacities does a robot require to identify and respond to the wide variety of deceptive speech? An answer to this question is undoubtedly more complex than one we can currently provide, but a key component is the ability to represent the mental states of other agents. Socially sophisticated robots will need to track the beliefs and goals of their conversational partners. In addition, robots' representations will need to distinguish between baseline goals that may be expected of any social agent, which we call *standing norms*, and the special goals that supersede them, which we call *ulterior motives*.

When we claim that deception-sensitive robots will need to track the beliefs and goals of multiple agents, we are stating that these robots will need a *theory of mind*. This phrase refers to the ability to represent not only one's own beliefs and goals but also the beliefs and goals of others. These representations of the world may conflict, so they must be kept distinct. Otherwise, one could not tell whether one believed that lemurs make great pets or one believed that someone else believed it. As an illustration, suppose that Sue and Joe, from the earlier example, are accomplices. In that case, Sue believes that Joe was at the scene of the crime but wants Frank to believe that Joe was at work. If she thinks her lie was compelling, then Sue will form the belief that Frank believes that Joe was at the office—this is a first-order theory of mind. Pandering requires a second-order theory of mind. For instance, the politician must represent his (zeroth-order) belief that the audience (first order) believes that he (second order) believes the trees in Vermont are beautiful (figure 11.1).

Given a theory of mind rich enough to represent the beliefs and goals of other agents several levels deep, what else would a robot need to strategically respond to deception? According to our account, socially aware robots would need to represent the covert motive that distinguishes deception from normal speech. Fortunately, even though the particular motive of each deceptive act generally differs (e.g., Sue's goal in lying differs from that of the used-car salesman in paltering), there is a common factor: a covert goal that trumps expected standards of communication. Therefore, to represent a deceptive motive, a robot must distinguish two types of goals: the typical and the superseding.

We call the first type of goal a *standing norm* (Bridewell and Bello 2014), a persistent goal that directs an agent's typical behavior. For speech, Paul Grice introduced a set of *conversational maxims* (1975) that correspond to this notion of a standing norm. His maxim of quality, frequently glossed as "be truthful," is the most relevant to our discussion. Grice argued that people expect that these maxims will be followed during ordinary communication and that flagrant violations cue that contextual influences are modifying literal meaning. The crucial point for our purposes is that *be truthful* is a goal that plausibly operates under

FIGURE 11.1. Pandering requires a second-order theory of mind. The successful panderer believes (zeroth order) that the listener believes (first order) that the speaker believes (second order) his utterance. Image credit: Matthew E. Isaac.

all typical circumstances. Other standing norms might regulate typical speech in subtler ways (e.g., *be polite* or *be informative*).

In any complex social situation, more than one goal will be relevant. If these goals suggest conflicting actions, we will need some method to pick which goals to satisfy and which to violate. For instance, imagine a friend who composes saccharine poems to his dog asks your opinion on the latest one. The conflict between the standing norms *be truthful* and *be polite* may likely pose a dilemma. If you are lucky, you may get away with satisfying both: "I can tell that you put a lot of work into that poem. You must really love your corgi." This response is both truthful and polite, yet it achieves this end by avoiding a direct answer to your friend's question. Notice the difference between this kind of misdirection and paltering, however; we don't typically think of an answer such as this as deceptive because there is no hidden goal—it is governed entirely by the expected standards of conversation.

If your friend presses you, demanding an explicit opinion on his poetry, you will need some heuristic to determine which of your standing norms to violate. One way to achieve this end is to prioritize your goals. Several factors—situational, cultural, emotional—will determine which norm takes priority and guides speech. Ranking truth over civility may lead to a brutal dismissal of your friend's literary skills. Ranking civility over truth may lead to false praise. Such false praise is *technically* deceitful—we intend our friend to form a belief that conflicts with the truth.

We often categorize an utterance such as this, the false praise of a friend's inept poem, as a *white lie*. On the one hand, we recognize that it is technically an act of deceit, because a goal has superseded the norm *be truthful*, and in this sense a "lie." On the other hand, since the superseding goal is itself a standing norm (in this case *be polite*), it bears no malicious intent, and we do not typically judge the lie to be morally reprehensible. The situation is different when the superseding goal is not a standing norm. In that case, we refer to the goal prioritized over a norm as an *ulterior motive*. The presence of a relevant ulterior motive differentiates a maliciously deceptive utterance from a benign one. If you praise your friend's poetry, not because you prioritize the norm *be polite*, but because a goal to borrow money from your friend supersedes all your standing norms, then we would no longer judge your false praise to be morally neutral. Revisiting Sue, if her false response to the detective is grounded in a false belief, she is not suppressing a conversational norm and her error is innocent. However, if Sue has a goal to *protect Joe* that supersedes the conversational norm *be truthful*, then her response is deceptive. Other ulterior motives in the earlier examples include *sell this car* and *get elected.*

To summarize, if a robot is to effectively recognize deceptive speech and respond strategically to it, it must be able to represent (a) the difference between its own beliefs and desires and those of its interlocutor; and (b) the difference between standing norms of behavior and ulterior motives. Of course, other capacities are also needed, but we claim that they will appeal to these representations. We next turn to the question of the "badness" of deception and argue that some forms of deception are desirable, even in robots.

11.2 Deceiving for the Greater Good

So far, we have seen that robots must possess a theory of mind in order to respond effectively to deceptive communication and, in particular, the ability to identify ulterior motives. But an effective social robot cannot treat all deceptive speech as malign, or all agents who act on ulterior motives as malicious. Furthermore, such a robot may find itself following ulterior motives, and its (technically) deceptive behavior may have a positive social function. After discussing examples of the pro-social function of deceptive speech, we consider some cases where we want robots to lie to us.

11.2.1 Benign Deceptions

When we talk to each other, our words do far more than communicate literal meaning. For instance, we routinely exchange pleasantries with co-workers. Two people walk toward each other in a hallway, one asks how the other's day is going, and the response is a casual "fine." This sort of exchange reinforces social-group membership. The colleagues recognize each other in a friendly way and the literal content serves only a secondary function, if any. Other examples include "water cooler" conversations about the weather or sports, or office gossip.

Often these casual conversations are forms of bullshit: conversants may neither know nor care about the truth, but the conversation goes on. Speculating who will win the World Cup or whether there will be rain on Sunday seems generally unimportant, but people talk about these topics routinely. In addition, consider all the times that people exchange pleasantries using outright lies. For instance, we might compliment a friend's trendy new hairstyle, even if we think it is hideous. In these cases, affirming the value of peers can take priority over conveying truth or engaging in debate. In fact, treating such pleasantries as substantive may lead to confusion and social tension. Responding to a co-worker's polite "Hi, how are you?" with "My shoulder aches, and I'm a bit depressed about my mortgage" will, at the least, give the colleague a pause. Continued tone-deaf responses will likely reduce the opportunities for reply. Treating a rote exchange of pleasantries as legitimately communicative not only is awkward, but undermines the exchange's pro-social function (Nagel 1998).

Another common form of benignly deceptive speech includes metaphors and hyperbole: "I could eat a horse"; "These shoes are killing me"; or even "Juliet is the sun. Arise, fair sun, and kill the envious moon." There is nothing malevolent about these figures of speech, but to respond to them effectively requires an ability to recognize the gap between their literal content and the speaker's beliefs. If a chef served a full-sized roast equine to a customer who announced, "I could eat a horse," she would be greeted with surprise, not approbation. Exactly how to compute the meaning of metaphorical and hyperbolic expressions is a vexed question, but we can agree that these figures of speech violate standing norms of the kind articulated by Grice (1975; Wilson and Sperber 1981), and thus technically satisfy the earlier definition of deceptive speech.

It would be fair to ask whether metaphorical speech is necessary for effective communication. What does a turn of phrase add? Are there some meanings that can be conveyed only through metaphor, having no paraphrase into strictly literal language (Camp 2006)? Even if the answer is negative, metaphor and hyperbole provide emphasis and add variety, color, and emotion to conversations. We would describe someone who avoids figures of speech or routinely misunderstands them as difficult to talk to, socially awkward, or even "robotic."

More complex social goals may also require systematic, arguably benign deception; consider, for instance, *impression management*. In complex social interactions, what others think about us, their impression of our character, is often important. How we appear to people in power or to our peers has very real effects on our ability to achieve long-term goals and maintain social standing. Managing these impressions to achieve broader goals may supersede norms of truthfulness in conversation. For instance, suppose a worker wants his boss to see him as loyal to her. To this end, he supports her attempts to close a small deal with a corporate ally even though he disagrees with the content. His goal to manage his appearance as a loyal employee motivates him to vote in favor of his boss's deal at the next meeting.

In this example, the long-term goal of demonstrating political solidarity swamps short-term concerns about relatively unimportant decisions. Moreover, disingenuously endorsing less important proposals in the short term may give the employee the cachet to speak honestly about important deals in the future. Whether one thinks the subtle politics of impression management are morally permissible, they certainly play a major role in the complex give-and-take characteristic of any shared social activity, from grocery shopping with one's family to running a nation-state. As we will see, simple impression management may be required for practical robot applications in engineering.

11.2.2 When We Want Robots to Lie

Do we want robots that can banter about the weather and sports, compliment us on a questionable new haircut, or generate appropriately hyperbolic and metaphorical expressions? ("This battery will be the death of me!") If we want robots that can smoothly participate in standard human modes of communication and social interaction, then the answer must be *yes*. Even if our primary concern is not with fully socially integrated robots, there are many specific practical applications for robot deception. Here we consider only two: the use of bullshit for self-preservation and the use of systematic lies to manage expectations about engineering tasks.

11.2.2.1 Bullshit as Camouflage

If a primary function of bullshit is to help one fit into a social group, that function may be most important when one is not in fact a bona fide member of the group in question. Consider, for instance, the case of a computer scientist at a sports bar. For him, the ability to bullshit about sports, to make the right kinds of comments even if he neither knows nor cares about their truth, can mean the difference between treatment as a peer and humiliation or physical assault. In situations like this, the ability to spew the right sort of bullshit acts as a form of camouflage, enabling the computer nerd to superficially fit in with the people around him.

This sort of camouflage is not always benign, but the skill may be vital to survival for some kinds of robots. The spy, the fifth columnist, and the terrorist all use this technique, not because it is inherently nefarious, but because the ability to fit in can be critical for self-preservation. A robot working in a hostile community or confronted by belligerent locals in the wrong part of town would benefit from the ability to bullshit judiciously, whether the hostiles themselves were human or mechanical. A socially sophisticated robot should be able to generate appropriate signals to blend in with any conversational community and thereby extricate itself from dangerous situations without violence or social friction.[2]

In general, we should acknowledge that robots will inevitably be seen as part of an out-group, as less than human, regardless of their social prowess. Thus, their ability to bullshit their way into our hearts and minds may be key to their broad acceptance into the workforce. As objects whose physical well-being may constantly be under threat, robots might use bullshit effectively to provide a verbal buffer against prejudice.

11.2.2.2 Managing Impressions to Manage Uncertainty

Our earlier example of impression management was political in flavor, but the basic concept has more mundane applications as well. In engineering, there is a common practice of knowingly overstating the time it will take to complete a task by a factor of two or three. This convention is sometimes referred to as the *Scotty Principle* after the character in Star Trek.[3] This category of lying serves two major functions. First, if the engineer finishes ahead of time, she looks especially efficient for having delivered results sooner than expected (or she rests a bit and reports an on-time completion). Second, and more important for our argument, the engineer's estimate creates a clandestine buffer for contingencies that protects her supervisor from making aggressive, time-sensitive plans.

At a practical level, the Scotty Principle factors in the completely unexpected: not just any initial failure at assessing the intrinsic difficulty of the task, but also unforeseen extrinsic factors that might impact successful completion (a strike at the part supplier's warehouse, a hurricane-induced power outage, etc.). Such "unknown unknowns" (those facts that we do not know that we do not know) famously pose the greatest challenge to strategic planning. Unlike known unknowns, which can be analyzed quantitatively and reported as confidence intervals or "error bars," unknown unknowns resist any (meaningful) prior analysis—we cannot plan for a difficulty we do not expect or even imagine. Yet inserting a temporal buffer between the known aspects of a repair job and those that are unknown does in some way prepare us for the unexpected. Furthermore, the practice acts as a deliberate corrective to the engineer's own potential failings, including any lack of self-knowledge about her skills and speed of work. Ironically, then, *willfully deceiving a supervisor may correct for an engineer's self-deception.*

This example was not picked arbitrarily. Engineering tasks, including the repair of technical equipment or software systems, are potential applications for sophisticated robots. Do we want robotic engineers to lie to us systematically in exactly this way? Plausibly, the answer is yes: if we want our best robot engineers to meet the standards of our best human engineers, then we should expect them to embrace the Scotty Principle. Nevertheless, we have encountered two prominent objections to this line of reasoning, which we consider in turn.

The first objection is that current human-engineering practice sets too low a bar for assessing future robot engineers. We should expect to be able to improve our robots until they *correctly* estimate their capabilities and thereby avoid the need for recourse to Scotty's Principle. Yet this idealized view of robot performance belies the nature of engineering and the capacity for self-knowledge in dynamic, complex environments. Contingencies arise in engineering, and novel tasks stretch the scope of an engineer's abilities, whether human or mechanical. Aiming for a robot that predicts the results of its interventions in the world with perfect accuracy is to aim for the impossible. Reliable engineering practice requires accepting that unknown unknowns exist and preparing for the possibility that they may confront a project when it is most inconvenient.

The second, distinct worry arises for those who acknowledge the danger of unknown unknowns, yet insist it is safer to leave contingency planning in the hands of human supervisors than to permit robot engineers to systematically lie. But this suggestion relies on an unrealistic assessment of human nature—one that may be dangerous. Anyone who has worked with a contractor either professionally or personally (e.g., when remodeling or repairing a house) will be familiar with the irresistible tendency to take at face value that contractor's predictions about job duration and cost. If these predictions are not met, we hold the contractor accountable, even if he has been perpetually tardy or over-budget in the past—we certainly do not blithely acknowledge he may have faced unforeseen contingencies. Yet this tendency is plausibly even greater in our interactions with robots, which we often assume are more "perfect" at mechanical tasks than in fact they are. Paradoxically, if we insist all contingency planning must reside with human supervisors, we will need to train them *not* to trust their robot helpers' honest predictions of task difficulty!

The apparent infallibility of robots is exactly why we must ensure that socially sophisticated robots can misrepresent their predictions about the ease of a job. This added step can correct for both the robot's self-deception about its abilities and its human user's unrealistic optimism about robot dependability.

11.3 Ethical Standards for Deceptive Robots

We have just suggested that robots will need the capacity to deceive if they are to integrate into and contribute effectively to human society. Historically, however, many ethical systems have taught that lying and other forms of deception are intrinsically wrong (e.g., Augustine 1952). If we aim for deception-capable robots, are we giving up on the possibility of ethical robots? We argue that the answer is a resounding *no*. This is because the locus of ethical assessment is not in the content of speech, but in the ulterior motive that gives rise to it. Therefore, ensuring that a social robot behaves morally means ensuring that it implements ethical standing norms and ranks them appropriately.

Precisely how is it possible for deception to be ethical? In section 11.1 we argued that the unifying factor for all forms of deceptive speech is the presence of an ulterior motive, a goal that supersedes standing norms such as *be truthful*. Paradigmatic cases of morally impermissible ulterior motives are those involving pernicious goals, such as the concealment of a crime or the implementation of a confidence scheme. In contrast, section 11.2 surveyed examples where deceptive speech serves pro-social functions and the ulterior motives are pro-social goals, such as boosting a colleague's self-esteem or establishing trust. There is a discriminating factor between right and wrong in these cases; however, it depends not on the deceptiveness of the speech per se but on the goals that motivate that speech.

If this analysis is correct, it implies that an ethical, deception-capable robot will need the ability to represent and evaluate ranked sets of goals. To draw an example from literature, consider Isaac Asimov's (1950) Three Laws of Robotics, an early proposal for a system of robot ethics. Asimov's "laws" are really inviolable, prioritized, high-level goals or, in our terminology, a ranked set of standing norms combined with the stipulation that no ulterior motives may supersede them. Notably, accepting this system means accepting deception by robots, because Asimov's stipulation ensures that his laws will be ranked above the norm *be truthful*. For instance, the First Law is that "a robot may not injure a human being or, through inaction, allow a human being to come to harm," and the Second Law is that "a robot must obey the orders given it by human beings except where such orders would conflict with the First Law." Suppose a murderer comes to the door of a home and orders a robot butler to tell him where his intended victim is hiding. Here, the Second Law mandates that the robot answer, but to satisfy the First Law it must lie to protect the victim's life.

Asimov's system is based on a set of duties or obligations, which makes it a deontological ethical theory (Abney 2012). Traditionally, this approach has produced the most severe criticisms of the permissibility of lying, so perhaps it is comforting to see that deceptive robots may conform to a deontological ethics. Immanuel Kant, the most famous deontologist, repeatedly and passionately defended the extreme position that deceptive speech is never permissible *under any circumstance*. He even addressed the foregoing scenario, where a murderer asks someone where to find a would-be victim. Kant (1996) concluded that even to save a life, lying is impermissible. Most ethicists have found this conclusion distasteful, and nuanced discussions of the permissibility of lying often proceed by first categorizing lies in terms of the respective ulterior motives that produce them, then assessing whether these motives should indeed be allowed to supplant the mandate for truthfulness (e.g., Bok 1978).

The perspective outlined here is also compatible with consequentialism, the main alternative to deontological theories. Consequentialists assess the morality of an action on the basis of its consequences—good acts are those that produce more of some intrinsically good property in the world, such as well-being or happiness, while bad acts are those that produce less of it. How does this view evaluate deceptive speech? If the speech has overall positive consequences, increasing well-being or happiness, then whether or not it is deceptive, it is permissible, perhaps even mandatory. The influential consequentialist John Stuart Mill addressed this topic: while placing a high value on trustworthiness, he nevertheless asserted the permissibility to deceive "when the withholding of some fact . . . would save an individual . . . from great and unmerited evil, and when the withholding can only be effected by denial" (1863, ch. 2).

By shifting the locus of moral assessment to the speaker's ulterior motives, we have not made the problems of robot ethics any more complex; however, we have also not made the problems any simpler. A deontological specification of duties or a consequentialist calculation of overall well-being remains equally challenging regardless of whether the robot may deceive. The computational deontologist remains burdened with questions about the relative priorities of norms or goals, along with other general challenges related to formalizing ethical maxims and using them to make inferences about an action's morality (Powers 2006). Likewise, the computational consequentialist still faces the challenge of determining and comparing the effects of potential actions (whether deceptive or not) in any given situation. On this point, Keith Abney argues that a simple-minded consequentialism "makes moral evaluation impossible, as even the short-term consequences of most actions are impossible to accurately forecast and weigh" (2012, 44).

To conclude, our basic proposal is that effective social robots will need the ability to deceive in pro-social ways, an ability that may facilitate the integration of android assistants into society, preserve robot safety in the face of prejudice, and protect humans from our own misconceptions about the infallibility of our mechanical helpmates. When assessing the ethicality of speech, the proper target for evaluation is the motivating goal, not the truth or falsity of the speech per se. Consequently, permitting robots to lie does not substantively change the technical challenges of ensuring they behave ethically. Nevertheless, there are challenges distinctive to the design of a deception-capable robot, as it requires a theory of mind and, in particular, the capacity to detect and reason about ulterior motives.

Acknowledgments

We thank Paul Bello for discussions that helped inform the text. Will Bridewell was supported by the Office of Naval Research under grant N0001416WX00384. The views expressed in this chapter are solely the authors' and should not be taken to reflect any official policy or position of the U.S. government or the Department of Defense.

Notes

1. There is a technical literature on how best to define *lying*, and one of the most debated issues is whether an "intent to deceive" need be present (for a survey, see Mahon 2016). On our view, an "intent to deceive" is just one possible instance of (or consequence of) an *ulterior motive*; this analysis both avoids common counterexamples to the "intent" condition and unifies the definition of lying with that of other forms of deception.
2. The crude beginnings of this challenge are already with us. For instance, self-driving cars must find a way to blend in on roads dominated by human drivers, and an accident or impasse may result from their blind adherence to the letter of traffic law (veridicality) and inability to interpret or send the subtle road signals required to fit in with the rest of traffic (bullshit). A classic example is the four-way stop sign, where self-driving cars have become paralyzed when none of the other cars come to a complete stop. Effective navigation of such intersections requires coordinating behavior through nuanced signals of movement, sometimes even bluffs, rather than strict deference to the rules of right-of-way.
3. Throughout the *Star Trek* TV series, engineer Scotty routinely performs repairs faster than his reported initial estimates. This phenomenon, and the Scotty Principle itself, is explicitly acknowledged in the film *Star Trek III: The Search for Spock* (1984):

   KIRK: How much refit time until we can take her out again?
   SCOTTY: Eight weeks sir, but you don't have eight weeks, so I'll do it for you in two.

KIRK: Mr. Scott, have you always multiplied your repair estimates by a factor of four?

SCOTTY: Certainly sir, how else can I keep my reputation as a miracle worker?

Works Cited

Abney, Keith. 2012. "Robotics, Ethical Theory, and Metaethics: A Guide for the Perplexed." In *Robot Ethics: The Ethical and Social Implications of Robotics*, edited by Patrick Lin, Keith Abney, and George A. Bekey, 35–52. Cambridge, MA: MIT Press.

Adams, Douglas. 1980. *The Hitchhiker's Guide to the Galaxy*. New York: Harmony Books.

Asimov, Isaac. 1950. *I, Robot*. New York: Doubleday.

Augustine. (395) 1952. "Lying." In *The Fathers of the Church* (vol. 16: *Saint Augustine Treatises on Various Subjects*), edited by Roy J. Deferreri, 53–112. Reprint, Washington, DC: Catholic University of America Press.

Bok, Sissela. 1978. *Lying: Moral Choice in Public and Private Life*. New York: Pantheon Books.

Bridewell, Will and Paul F. Bello. 2014. "Reasoning about Belief Revision to Change Minds: A Challenge for Cognitive Systems." *Advances in Cognitive Systems* 3: 107–22.

Camp, Elisabeth. 2006. "Metaphor and That Certain 'Je ne Sais Quoi.'" *Philosophical Studies* 129: 1–25.

Frankfurt, Harry. (1986) 2005. *On Bullshit*. Princeton, NJ: Princeton University Press.

Grice, H. Paul. 1975. "Logic and Conversation." In *Syntax and Sematics 3: Speech Acts*, edited by Peter Cole and Jerry L. Morgan, 41–58. New York: Academic Press.

Hardcastle, Gary L. and George A. Reisch. 2006. *Bullshit and Philosophy*. Chicago: Open Court.

Isaac, Alistair M. C. and Will Bridewell. 2014. "Mindreading Deception in Dialog." *Cognitive Systems Research* 28: 12–9.

Kant, Immanuel. (1797) 1996. "On a Supposed Right to Lie from Philanthropy." In *Practical Philosophy*, edited by Mary J. Gregor, 605–15. Reprint, Cambridge: Cambridge University Press.

Mahon, James Edwin. 2016. "The Definition of Lying and Deception." In *The Stanford Encyclopedia of Philosophy*, Spring 2016 ed., edited by Ed N. Zalta. http://plato.stanford.edu/archives/spr2016/entries/lying-definition/.

Mill, John Stuart. 1863. *Utilitarianism*. London: Parker, Son & Bourn.

Nagel, Thomas. 1998. "Concealment and Exposure." *Philosophy and Public Affairs* 27: 3–30.

Powers, Thomas M. 2006. "Prospects for a Kantian Machine." *IEEE Intelligent Systems* 21: 46–51.

Rogers, Todd, Richard J. Zeckhauser, Francesca Gino, Maurice E. Schweitzer, and Michael I. Norton. 2014. "Artful Paltering: The Risks and Rewards of Using Truthful Statements to Mislead Others." HKS Working Paper RWP14-045. Harvard University, John F. Kennedy School of Government.

Schauer, Frederick and Richard J. Zeckhauser. 2009. "Paltering." In *Deception: From Ancient Empires to Internet Dating*, edited by Brooke Harrington, 38–54. Stanford, CA: Stanford University Press.

Sullivan, Timothy. 1997. "Pandering." *Journal of Thought* 32: 75–84.

Wilson, Deirdre and Dan Sperber. 1981. "On Grice's Theory of Conversation." In *Conversation and Discourse*, edited by Paul Werth, 155–78. London: Croom Helm.

12 "WHO'S JOHNNY?" ANTHROPOMORPHIC FRAMING IN HUMAN–ROBOT INTERACTION, INTEGRATION, AND POLICY

Kate Darling

In 2015, the robotics company Boston Dynamics released a video clip introducing "Spot," a distinctly doglike robot. In the clip, Spot is kicked twice by humans and scrambles hard to stay on all four legs. The purpose of kicking Spot was to demonstrate the robot's stability, but many commenters took to the internet to express discomfort and even dismay over Spot's treatment. The slew of negative reactions even compelled the animal rights organization PETA to acknowledge the incident (Parke 2015). We know that robots like Spot experience no pain whatsoever, so isn't it absurd for people to make such a fuss?

Perhaps not. Research shows that humans tend to anthropomorphize robotic technology, treating it as though it were alive, even if we know better. As we increasingly create spaces where robotic technology is purposed to interact with people, should we encourage this inclination or discourage it? And how do we change human perceptions of robotic objects when even the simplest of robots engenders anthropomorphism (Sung et al. 2007)?

One of the tools we can use to influence anthropomorphism is framing. An experiment on human–robot interaction conducted together with Palash Nandy and Cynthia Breazeal at MIT indicates that personifying a robot with a name or character description, or giving it a backstory, affects people's responses to robots (Darling, Nandy, and Breazeal 2015).

Turkle (2006, 2012), Scheutz (2012), and others have criticized the anthropomorphization of robotic technology, concerned that the emotional relationships people develop with anthropomorphized robots will replace human relationships, lead to undesirable behaviors, or make people vulnerable to emotional manipulation. Some have also argued that robots should be framed in non-anthropomorphic terms, i.e., strictly as tools, lest the legal system adopt inappropriate analogies for the use and regulation of robotic technology (Richards and Smart 2016).

As this chapter shows, I agree that framing has a broader effect on the way we view robotic technology and the analogies that drive both use and regulation. However, I argue that anthropomorphic framing is desirable where it enhances the function of the technology. The chapter examines some concerns about human relationships and behaviors, including issues of privacy, emotional manipulation, violence, sexual behavior, and the entrenchment of gender and racial stereotypes that comes with framing robots in human terms. I conclude that we need to address these concerns, but that we should address them within the recognition that there are benefits to anthropomorphic technology.

12.1 Integration of Robots

We know that people treat artificial entities as if they were alive, even when they're aware of the entities' inanimacy (Duffy and Zawieska 2012). Research has shown that most of us perceive computers (Reeves and Nass 1996; Nass et al. 1997) and virtual characters (McDonnell et al. 2008; Holtgraves et al. 2007; Scholl and Tremoulet 2000; Rosenthal von der Pütten et al. 2010) as social actors. Robots tend to amplify this social actor projection because of their embodiment (Kidd and Breazeal 2005; Groom 2008) and physical movement (Scheutz 2012; Duffy 2003, 486). Social robots are specifically designed to be anthropomorphized (Breazeal 2003; Duffy 2003; Yan et al. 2004), but people also anthropomorphize robots with non-anthropomorphic design (Carpenter 2013; Knight 2014; Paepcke and Takayama 2010).

Robots are gradually entering new areas and assuming new roles, some of which rely specifically on our tendency to anthropomorphize robots. There are also contexts where a robot functions as a tool, but is less threatening and more readily accepted by humans if anthropomorphized. In other contexts, anthropomorphism is undesirable, particularly when it can hinder a robot's ability to fulfill its function.

12.1.1 Integration of Robots as Tools

Robots are increasingly interacting with humans in manufacturing, transportation systems, the military, hospitals, and many other workplaces, soon to be followed by personal households. Whether these robots should be framed anthropomorphically depends on their function.

In 2007, *Washington Post* reporter Joel Garreau interviewed members of the U.S. military about their relationships with robots, uncovering accounts of Purple Hearts for robots, emotional distress over destroyed robots, and hero's welcomes for homecoming robots. One robot was built to walk on and detonate land mines. The colonel overseeing the testing exercise for the machine ended up stopping it because the sight of the robot dragging itself along the minefield was too "inhumane" to bear.

Military robots have been given funerals with gun salutes (Garber 2013). Julie Carpenter (2013) conducted an in-depth study on explosive ordinance disposal robots in the military, finding that the operators sometimes interacted with the robots in much the same way they would interact with a human or a pet, and demonstrating a need for the issue to be addressed in the future deployment of military technology. There are even stories of soldiers risking their lives to save the robots they work with (Singer 2009), illustrating that it can be anything from inefficient to dangerous for robots to be anthropomorphized when they are meant to be non-social tools.

In these cases, projecting lifelike qualities onto robots is undesirable, because the resulting emotional attachment can impede the intended use of the technology. But there are also robotic technologies whose use is facilitated by anthropomorphism.

For example, a CEO and employees of a company that develops medicine delivery robots observed hospital staffers being friendlier to robots that had been given human names. Even tolerance for malfunction was higher with anthropomorphic framing ("Oh, Betsy made a mistake!" vs. "This stupid machine doesn't work!"). So the company has started shipping its boxy, non-anthropomorphically designed hospital delivery robots with individual names attached to them on a plaque (Anonymous 2014).

Jibo is a table-lamp-shaped household robot that schedules appointments, reads email, takes photos, and functions as a family's personal assistant. But it is mainly thanks to its anthropomorphic framing that Jibo has received a slew of positive attention and millions of dollars in investments (Tilley 2015). As *Mashable* describes: "Jibo isn't an appliance, it's a companion, one that can interact and react with its human owners in ways that delight" (Ulanoff 2014).

These examples illustrate that people may be more willing to accept new technology and integrate it into their lives, whether at work or at home, if it is introduced with anthropomorphic framing, like a personified name or a description as a "companion." So long as the intended function of the robot is not implicated, we may want to encourage this effect to help with technology adoption and literacy.

12.1.2 Integration of Robots as Companions

Social robots provide benefits that are most effectively realized through a relationship between the human and the robot. Today's social robots can simulate sound, movement, and social cues that people automatically and subconsciously associate with states of mind (Scheutz 2012; Koerth-Baker 2013; Turkle 2012). With these projections come possibilities. State-of-the-art technology is already creating compelling use-cases in health and education, possible only as a result of engaging people through anthropomorphism.

The NAO Next Generation robot is a little humanoid that has found applications working with children with autism spectrum disorders (Shamsuddina 2012). One of the advantages of using the NAO is that it can be effective in creating eye contact or interaction, helping bridge communication gaps between a teacher or parent and the child. Another example is a robot teddy bear called Huggable, which cheers up children in hospitals and similarly facilitates communication between kids and their doctors or parents in what can be a scary and difficult situation (*Wired* 2015). Other social robots like MIT's DragonBot and Tega engage children in learning, often with better results than books or computers (Ackerman 2015).

The benefits of assistive robots are not limited to children. Social robots can help adults through interaction, motivation, monitoring, and coaching in health and education (Feil-Seifer and Matarić 2005; Tapus, Matarić, and Scassellatti 2007). Research shows that people trying to lose or maintain weight will track their data for nearly twice as long when they use a social robot compared with a computer or paper log method (Kidd 2008). Robots can motivate people to exercise through praise and companionship (Fasola and Matarić 2012), help them take medicine (Broadbent et al. 2014), and serve as a nonjudgmental partner in sensitive tasks.

Paro is a robot baby seal that has been used therapeutically in nursing homes since 2004. Its compelling design gives most people who interact with it a sense of nurturing. Paro has been used to calm distressed people, from earthquake victims in Japan to dementia patients across the world, even serving as an effective alternative to medication (Chang and Sung 2013). Similar to the therapeutic use of live animals, which is often too unhygienic or unsafe to implement in these health contexts, Paro gives people who are being cared for a sense of empowerment (Griffiths 2014). Paro has also encouraged more interaction among people in nursing homes (Kidd, Taggart, and Turkle 2006).

Because social robots can provide therapy or motivation that works most effectively when they are perceived as social agents rather than tools (Kidd 2008; Seifer and Matarić 2005), it makes sense to frame them accordingly. That said, we need to discuss concerns about some uses of anthropomorphic robots.

12.1.2.1 Effects on Human Relationships

Some have criticized anthropomorphism in the context of social robots. Sherry Turkle laments a loss of "authenticity" (2010, 9), a term she uses to describe the difference between a biological and a robotic turtle (Turkle 2007), and worries that seductive robot relationships (assuming these are less difficult than relationships with humans) will lead people to avoid interacting with their friends and family (Turkle 2010, 7).

Oddly, we don't see the same amount of concern for people who spend time with their pets. Even if we frame robots as social companions, it is not immediately clear that people would substitute robots for their human relationships. Nor is there any evidence that authenticity will cease to be valued as she predicts. (In fact, markets for authentic artwork and jewels and the persistence of sexual relationships in countries with legalized prostitution suggest otherwise.) Instead of substituting for existing relationships, we may find a new kind of relationship in robots. The key is how technology is used.

Cynthia Breazeal has drawn attention to the issues around supplementing versus replacing, emphasizing that social robots are meant to partner with humans and should be designed to "support human empowerment" (Bracy 2015). When used correctly, social robots can even be catalysts for human–human interaction, as seen in some of the cases described earlier.

For example, Kidd, Taggart, and Turkle herself (2006) show that the Paro baby seal robot inspires conversation among nursing home residents when placed in a common area. Good assistive robots can facilitate communication between children and their teachers, doctors, and parents, presenting a valuable supplement to human interaction.

Turkle's concerns are slightly misplaced in that they seem to dismiss the technology altogether rather than recognize the potential for valuable supplementary relationships. But awareness of supplementing versus replacing is important in helping drive the design and use of these technologies in a socially desirable direction.

12.1.2.2 Personal Data Collection and Other Emotional Manipulations

A simple example of an engaging technology is the Fitbit step tracker. The Fitbit One has a flower on it that grows larger with increasing activity, targeting a natural human instinct to nurture something and be rewarded for it (Wortham 2009). While the Fitbit likely affects people's lives in a positive way by improving their exercise habits, the worrisome aspect of this engagement is that it stems from a mechanism that manipulates people's behavior on a subconscious level.

It may be great that we can emotionally motivate people to walk more by giving them the sense of nurturing a digital flower. What else can we get people to do? Can we get them to vote? Buy products? Serve someone else's interests? And as our technology gets better, robots have the potential to be Fitbits on steroids. Perhaps we should let people choose to be manipulated, so long as the outcome is positive (Koerth-Baker 2013). But it is not clear what constitutes a positive outcome.

One of the largest concerns with regard to manipulating user behavior through technology is the protection of private information. Fitbit has come under criticism for data collection and storage, raising privacy concerns (Ryan 2014). Yet wearable fitness trackers are still on the rise (Stein 2015), as people continue to trade their data for the motivations they value. To what extent is this an appropriate trade-off and to what extent could it be deceptive, relying on poorly informed consumers or distracting people with something shiny?

The privacy issues of data collection are not unique to robotics. Robots will, however, present new opportunities for data collection as they enter into previously untapped areas in personal households (Fogg 2003, 10) and take on social functions (Calo 2012). Social media platforms have demonstrated that people are willing to publicly share photos, locations, and other personal details in return for the "likes" and general social engagement this creates on the respective platforms. Stricter privacy settings are often directly at odds with the benefits the service provides to its users (Grimmelmann 2009). Similarly, the emotional engagement inherent in the use of social robot technology may incentivize people to trade personal information for functional rewards. It could also persuade people to reveal more about themselves than they would willingly and knowingly enter into a database (Kerr 2004; Fogg 2003; Calo 2009; Thomasen 2016).

Furthermore, revealing personal information is not the only type of manipulation that warrants concern. Platforms like Facebook harness social relationships to great effect, wielding the power to potentially swing political elections (Zittrain 2014). Research on human–computer interaction indicates that we are prone to being manipulated by social AI (Fogg and Nass 1997). Joseph Weizenbaum (1976), after witnessing people interact with his 1960s psychotherapist bot, ELIZA, warned against being influenced by machines and taking on computers' (and their programmers') worldview. Ian Kerr predicts that AI will engage in all manner of persuasion, from contracting to advertising (2004).

According to Woodrow Hartzog (2015), there may even be cause to discuss regulation. The interests of corporations do not necessarily align with those of consumers, and market imperfections can prevent free market solutions (Mankiw and Taylor 2011, 147–55). If a company charges an exorbitant amount for a mandatory upgrade to a robot that someone's child or grandfather has become emotionally attached to, is that a permissible exploitation of consumers' willingness to pay (Hartzog 2015)? Is it OK for a child's language-teaching robot to have a vocabulary that is skewed toward specific products or for sex robots to have in-app purchases? We may find ourselves asking these questions in the near future.

It is concerning that neither market forces nor consumer protection laws have been able to adequately resolve current incentive structures to reveal personal data online. On the other hand, our continuing engagement with these issues in the context of the internet means that we are aware that there is a consumer protection problem and are continuously working to find solutions. As these issues extend to robotic technology, we can draw on existing discussions and studies of social media, advertising, gamification, addiction, and other areas to understand related user behaviors and get a sense of appropriate boundaries and trade-offs. Furthermore, promoting a broad public awareness of privacy and other manipulation concerns can pave the way for solutions through law, markets, norms, technology, and framing.

It would be a shame to relinquish the health and education benefits of robotics in order to regulate the potential harm. But to embrace anthropomorphic robots, knowing that they surpass most emotionally persuasive technology we have seen previously, we may need to have safeguards in place for those who would abuse us.

12.1.2.3 Violence and Sexual Behavior

Experimental research suggests that we can measure people's empathy on the basis of how they interact with lifelike robots (Darling, Nandy, and Breazeal 2015). An interesting question is whether we can *change* people's empathy through interactions with robots. We sometimes use therapy animals to encourage empathy in children and youth, but therapy with real animals is problematic and requires extensive supervision. As robots become cheaper, they may be an effective alternative. Robots could also be used in more places than animals can, such as pet-restrictive households or in prison rehabilitation programs.

On the flip side, there is a danger that treating robots violently might have a negative effect on people's empathy development. For example, there are reasons we may want to prevent children from vandalizing robots (Brscić et al. 2015) that go beyond respecting people's property: if the robots behave in a lifelike way, they might begin to influence how children treat living things (Walk 2016). And it's not just children who are of concern here—there is a chance that violence toward lifelike robots could desensitize adults to violence in other contexts (Darling 2016). Similarly, undesirable sexual acts or behaviors may be encouraged by the repeated use of robots as sexual partners (Gutiu 2016).

The question of whether robots can actually change people's long-term behavioral patterns, in either positive or negative ways, is unanswered. While there are parallels to research on violence in video games, the differences in how we perceive what is virtual and what is physical warrant reconsideration of the question (Bainbridge et al. 2008; Kidd and Breazeal 2005). Currently, we do not know if human–robot interaction is more likely to encourage undesirable behavior or serve as a healthy outlet for behavior that would otherwise have negative consequences. But this is an important question to explore, as discussions around violent behavior toward robots begin to surface (Parke 2015) and sexual robots become a reality (Freeman 2016; Borenstein and Arkin, 2016).

12.1.2.4 Gender and Racial Stereotypes

Robots that are framed in human-like terms can unfortunately reinforce existing cultural biases that are harmful to certain social groups (Tiong Chee Tay et al. 2013; Riek and Howard 2014). Andra Keay surveyed the types of names creators gave their robots in robotics competitions. The names tended to reveal functional gender biases (2012, 1). Keay also found that the male names were far more likely to express mastery (for example, by referencing Greek gods), whereas most of the female names tended to be in the infantilizing or sexualizing style of "Amber" and "Candii" (5). Framing robots in masculine terms could further dampen young women's interest in engaging with the field. Derogatory female framing of robots may not only reflect but also reinforce existing biases.

In the movie *Transformers: Revenge of the Fallen* (2009), there is a robot duo that blunders around and whose main contribution is comic relief. Unlike the other members of their crew, these two robots cannot read. They talk jive and argue with each other in "rap-inspired street slang" ("Let's pop a cap in his ass, throw him in the trunk and then nobody gonna know nothing, know what I mean?"). One of them has a gold tooth. Director Michael Bay brushed off criticism of racial stereotypes, saying that the characters are robots (Cohen 2009). How that absolves him is unclear.

If we are aware of these issues, however, we may even be able to positively influence gender and racial stereotypes through technology. We can *choose* what names and personalities we imbue robots with. Could we encourage people to associate a female name with something intelligent (Swartout et al. 2010)? Aside from companies that intentionally give subservient virtual assistants female names based on "market research," some harmful racial and gender biases may simply be going unnoticed among developers and users of robotic technology. Drawing attention to suppressive stereotypes in the framing of robots would be a first step toward mitigating the problem. The next step could be to use the anthropomorphic framing of robots as a tool to challenge perspectives on race or gender.

In summary, while some concerns about anthropomorphizing robots are valid, there are many cases in which it can be useful for people to bond with robots on a social level. Addressing the concerns calls for targeted solutions rather than broad discouragement of anthropomorphism.

12.2 Framing Experiment

How do we deal with the integration of robots as tools in use-cases where anthropomorphism gets in the way? The lifelike physical movement of robots is assumed to be a major driver of anthropomorphic projection (Knight 2014; Saerbeck and Bartneck 2010; Scheutz 2012, 205). But robots often need to move around a certain way in order to function optimally, making movement a difficult thing to adjust. So we conducted an experiment to explore framing as an alternative mechanism to influence anthropomorphism (Darling, Nandy, and Breazeal 2015).

In one part of our experiment, participants were asked to observe a Hexbug Nano, a small robotic toy, and then strike it with a mallet. The participants were significantly more hesitant to strike the robot when it was introduced with anthropomorphic framing like a name and backstory (for example, "This is Frank. He's lived at the Lab for a few months now. His favorite color is red . . ."). In order to help rule out hesitation for other reasons (for example, perceived value of the robot), we measured participants' psychological trait empathy and found a strong relationship between tendency for empathic concern and hesitation to strike robots introduced with anthropomorphic framing. Adding color to our findings, many participants' verbal and physical reactions in the experiment were indicative of empathy (asking, for example, "Will it hurt him?" or muttering under their breath, "It's just a bug, it's just a bug," as they visibly steeled themselves to strike the personified Hexbug).

In summary, our results show that framing can influence people's immediate reactions to robots. Robots are often personified or referred to as experiencing the world in a lifelike way, partly in reference to the many robots in science fiction and pop culture that have names, internal states of mind, and emotions. Awareness of the effects of framing could make people and institutions more sensitive to when this prompt is useful and when it is not.

12.3 Anthropomorphism and the "Android Fallacy": Distinguishing Between Use-Cases

Richards and Smart (2016) argue that the metaphors we use to understand robots are important, because they influence how lawmakers will approach the regulation of robotic technology. They warn against the "Android Fallacy": falling into the trap of anthropomorphizing robots and framing them as social agents rather than as tools.

Their piece illustrates the legal consequences of using certain framings of technology over others, by drawing upon the metaphors used in wiretapping cases in the twentieth century and the debate over whether to give email privacy protection analogous to that of postal mail or postcards (Richards and Smart 2016, 19). Metaphors matter, from the conceptual stage of technology, where they influence design and anticipated issues, to the product stage, where consumers and the legal system will use them to understand the technology (18). The framing of robots as either companions or tools matters at both of these stages as well.

But perhaps in some cases there might be reason to use the very framings and metaphors that Richards and Smart warn against. For example, if research shows that people respond to violent or sexual behavior toward certain robots as if the robots were alive, then one option is to take that framing to its conclusion, instead of discouraging the anthropomorphism. When we frame robots as nonliving tools, we relinquish an opportunity: lifelike robots may be able to help shape behavior positively in some contexts. If we were to embrace, for example, an animal metaphor, then we could regulate the harmful use of pet robots or sex robots with laws analogous to existing animal protection laws by restricting unnecessarily violent or cruel behavior (Darling 2016). Not only would this combat desensitization and negative externalities in people's behavior, it would preserve the therapeutic and educational advantages of using certain robots more as companions than as tools.

It is important to note that framing a social robot anthropomorphically corresponds to the function of the robot and the consistency with which people perceive these robots differently from other devices. We might ultimately do better to accept a social actor analogy for socially designed robots and work from there, saving the tool analogy for cases where anthropomorphism is a hindrance to functional technology or functional law.

12.4 Final Thoughts

As the examples in this chapter illustrate, it makes sense to distinguish between use-cases where we want to encourage anthropomorphism and cases where we do not. When anthropomorphism hinders the main function of a robot, this can cause problems. For robots that are not inherently social in design or functionally enhanced through social interaction, we should consider discouraging anthropomorphism using every tool at our disposal. Rather than continuing to treat science fictional narratives and personification as harmless fun, those building or implementing robotic technology should be more aware of framing effects.

For example, companies like Boston Dynamics are building military robots that mimic animal-like movement and physiology, because animals have evolved structures that happen to be incredibly efficient for mobility (Twenty 2011). But because these robots are so animal-like, soldiers may be quick to anthropomorphize them, undermining their usefulness as tools. Because lifelike movement is so central to the robots' functionality, we might at least try to objectify the robots with language (for example, using the pronoun "it") and encourage names such as "MX model 96283" instead of "Spot." This will not make anthropomorphism disappear by any means, but it may help a little to discourage the automatic treatment of these robots like pets.

Then there is the case where anthropomorphism enhances the acceptance and use of a robot, as well as the case where it directly supports the main function of the robot. These cases should be separated from the above at every level, from design to deployment, and can even be separated at a regulatory and legal level.

The law views things (*res*) as separate entities to be handled differently than, for example, agents or people (Calo 2014). We can either double down on portraying all robots as things, or we can embrace the fact that people may view certain robots differently. If people's interactions with social robots are overwhelmingly social, we might consider creating a new legal category. The inherent intelligence or abilities of the robots matter little in this context. We grant animals, small children, and corporations special legal treatment, regardless of their individual mental abilities or capacity for moral thinking. While this would require a good definition of the capabilities or functions of the robots that fall into this category, such distinctions are not new to the law, nor are they (or must they be) perfect.

Our concerns about the uses of anthropomorphic technology deserve attention and careful consideration. They do not, however, warrant the complete dismissal of anthropomorphic robots. Legal scholars, engineers, social scientists, and policymakers should work together to find solutions to the issues while recognizing the positive aspects of robot companionship. We can have constructive conversations about privacy, gender and racial biases, and supplementing versus replacing humans. The potential of anthropomorphic technology is tremendous. Instead of decrying it, let us make smart distinctions and frame it to our advantage.

Acknowledgments

Thank you, Meg Leta Jones, Laurel Riek, Woody Hartzog, James Hughes, Ann Bartow, and all of the participants at "We Robot 2015" and the "Man and Machine" conference at St. Gallen University for helpful comments and for providing some of the examples presented here.

Works Cited

Ackerman, Evan. 2015. "MIT's DragonBot Evolving to Better Teach Kids." *IEEE Spectrum*, March 16.

Anonymous. 2014. Interview with healthcare company representative by author, September 22.

Bainbridge, Wilma A., Justin Hart, Elizabeth S. Kim, and Brian Scassellati. 2008. "The Effect of Presence on Human–Robot Interaction." *17th IEEE International Symposium on Robot and Human Interactive Communication (RO-MAN)*, 701–6.

Borenstein, Jason and Ronald C. Arkin. 2016. "Robots, Ethics, and Intimacy: The Need for Scientific Research." *Conference Proceedings of the International Association for Computing and Philosophy (IACAP).*

Boston Dynamics. 2015. "Introducing Spot." https://www.youtube.com/watch?v=M8YjvHYbZ9w.

Bracy, Jedidiah. 2015. "The Future of Privacy: My Journey Down the Rabbit Hole at SXSW." *Privacy Perspectives*, March 20.

Breazeal, Cynthia. 2003. "Toward Sociable Robots." *Robotics and Autonomous Systems* 42 (3): 167–75.

Broadbent, Elizabeth, Kathy Peri, Ngaire Kerse, Chandimal Jayawardena, IHan Kuo, Chandan Datta, and Bruce MacDonald. 2014. "Robots in Older People's Homes to Improve Medication Adherence and Quality of Life: A Randomized Cross-Over Trial." *Proceedings 6th International Conference ICSR*, 64–73.

Brscić, Drazen, Hiroyuki Kidokoro, Yoshitaka Suehiro, and Takayuki Kanda. 2015. "Escaping from Children's Abuse of Social Robots." *Proceedings of the Tenth Annual ACM/IEEE International Conference on Human–Robot Interaction*, 59–66.

Calo, Ryan. 2009. "People Can Be So Fake: A New Dimension to Privacy and Technology Scholarship." *Penn State Law Review* 114: 809.

Calo, Ryan. 2012. "Robots and Privacy." In *Robot Ethics: The Ethical and Social Implications of Robotics*, edited by Patrick Lin, George Bekey, and Keith Abney, 187–201. Cambridge, MA: MIT Press.

Calo, Ryan. 2014. *The Case for a Federal Robotics Commission.* Brookings Report, 6. Washington, DC: Brookings Institution.

Carpenter, Julie. 2013. "The Quiet Professional: An Investigation of US Military Explosive Ordnance Disposal Personnel Interactions with Everyday Field Robots." PhD dissertation, University of Washington.

Chang, S. M. and H. C. Sung. 2013. "The Effectiveness of Paro Robot Therapy on Mood of Older Adults: A Systematic Review." *International Journal of Evidence-Based Healthcare* 11 (3): 216.

Cohen, Sandy. 2009. "Transformers' Jive-Talking Robots Raise Race Issues." *Huffington Post*, July 25.

Darling, Kate. 2016. "Extending Legal Protections to Social Robots: The Effects of Anthropomorphism, Empathy, and Violent Behavior towards Robotic Objects." In *Robot Law*, edited by Ryan Calo, Michael Froomkin, and Ian Kerr, 213–34. Cheltenham: Edward Elgar.

Darling, Kate, Palash Nandy, and Cynthia Breazeal. 2015. "Empathic Concern and the Effect of Stories in Human–Robot Interaction." *24th IEEE International Symposium on Robot and Human Interactive Communication (RO-MAN)*, 770–5.

Duffy, Brian R. 2003. "Anthropomorphism and the Social Robot." *Robotics and Autonomous Systems* 42 (3): 177–90.

Duffy, Brian R. and Karolina Zawieska. 2012. "Suspension of Disbelief in Social Robotics." *21st IEEE International Symposium on Robot and Human Interactive Communication (RO-MAN)*, 484–9.

Fasola, Juan and Maja J. Matarić. 2012. "Using Socially Assistive Human–Robot Interaction to Motivate Physical Exercise for Older Adults." *Proceedings of the IEEE* 100 (8): 2512–26.

Feil-Seifer, David and Maja J. Matarić. 2005. "Defining Socially Assistive Robotics." *9th International Conference on Rehabilitation Robotics (ICORR)*, 465–8.

Fogg, B. J. 2003. *Persuasive Technologies: Using Computers to Change What We Think and Do*. Burlington, MA: Morgan Kaufmann.

Fogg, B. J. and Clifford Nass. 1997. "How Users Reciprocate to Computers: An Experiment That Demonstrates Behavior Change." *CHI'97 Extended Abstracts on Human Factors in Computing Systems*, 331–2.

Freeman, Sunny. 2016. "Sex Robots to Become a Reality." *Toronto Star*, June 4.

Garber, Megan. 2013. "Funerals for Fallen Robots: New Research Explores the Deep Bonds That Can Develop Between Soldiers and the Machines That Help Keep Them Alive." *Atlantic*, September 20.

Garreau, Joel. 2007. "Bots on the Ground." *Washington Post*, May 6.

Griffiths, Andrew. 2014. "How Paro the Robot Seal is Being Used to Help UK Dementia Patients." *Guardian*, July 8.

Grimmelman, James. 2009. "Saving Facebook." *Iowa Law Review* 94: 1137.

Groom, Victoria. 2008. "What's the Best Role for a Robot? Cybernetic Models of Existing and Proposed Human–Robot Interaction Structures." *ICINCO*, 325.

Gutiu, Sinziana. 2016. "The Roboticization of Consent." In *Robot Law*, edited by Ryan Calo, Michael Froomkin, and Ian Kerr, 186–212. Cheltenham: Edward Elgar.

Hartzog, Woodrow. 2015. "Unfair and Deceptive Robots." *Maryland Law Review* 74: 785–829.

Holtgraves, Thomas, S. J. Ross, C. R. Weywadt, and T. L. Han. 2007. "Perceiving Artificial Social Agents." *Computers in Human Behavior* 23: 2163–74.

Keay, Andrea. 2012. "The Naming of Robots: Biomorphism, Gender and Identity." Master's thesis, University of Sydney.

Kerr, Ian. 2004. "Bots, Babes and the Californication of Commerce." *University of Ottawa Law and Technology Journal* 1: 285–324.

Kidd, Cory D. 2008. "Designing for Long-Term Human–Robot Interaction and Application to Weight Loss." PhD dissertation, Massachusetts Institute of Technology.

Kidd, Cory D. and Cynthia Breazeal. 2005. "Comparison of Social Presence in Robots and Animated Characters." *Proceedings of the 2005 International Conference on Human-Computer Inter-action (HCI)*.

Kidd, Cory D., Will Taggart, and Sherry Turkle. 2006. "A Sociable Robot to Encourage Social Interaction among the Elderly." *Proceedings 2006 IEEE International Conference on Robotics and Automation (ICRA)*, 3972–6.

Knight, Heather. 2014. *How Humans Respond to Robots: Building Public Policy through Good Design*. Brookings Report. Washington, DC: Brookings Institution.

Koerth-Baker, Maggie. 2013. "How Robots Can Trick You into Loving Them." *New York Times Magazine*, September 17.

Mankiw, N. Gregory and Mark P. Taylor. 2011. *Microeconomics*. Boston: Cengage Learning.

McDonnell, Rachel, Sophie Jörg, Joanna McHugh, Fiona Newell, and Carol O'Sullivan. 2008. "Evaluating the Emotional Content of Human Motions on Real and Virtual Characters." *Proceedings of the 5th Symposium on Applied Perception in Graphics and Visualization (ACM)*, 67–74.

Nass, Clifford, Youngme Moon, Eun-Young Kim, and B. J. Fogg. 1997. "Computers Are Social Actors: A Review of Current Research." In *Human Values and the Design of Computer Technology*, edited by Batya Friedman, 137–62. Chicago: University of Chicago Press.

Paepcke, Steffi and Leila Takayama. 2010. "Judging a Bot by Its Cover: An Experiment on Expectation Setting for Personal Robots." *5th ACM/IEEE International Conference on Human–Robot Interaction (HRI)*, 45–52.

Parke, Phoebe. 2015. "Is It Cruel to Kick a Robot Dog?" *CNN*, February 13. http://edition.cnn.com/2015/02/13/tech/spot-robot-dog-google/.

Reeves, Byron and Clifford Nass. 1996. *The Media Equation: How People Treat Computers, Television, and New Media Like Real People and Places*. Cambridge: Cambridge University Press.

Richards, Neil M. and William D. Smart. 2016. "How Should the Law Think about Robots?" In *Robot Law*, edited by Ryan Calo, Michael Froomkin, and Ian Kerr, 3–24. Cheltenham: Edward Elgar.

Riek, Laurel D. and Don Howard. 2014. "A Code of Ethics for the Human-Robot Interaction Profession." *Proceedings We Robot Conference on Legal and Policy Issues relating to Robotics*.

Rosenthal-von der Pütten, Astrid M., Nicole C. Krämer, Jonathan Gratch, and Sin-Hwa Kang. 2010. "'It Doesn't Matter What You Are!' Explaining Social Effects of Agents and Avatars." *Computers Human Behavior* 26 (6): 1641–50.

Ryan, Laura. 2014. "Fitbit Hires Lobbyists after Privacy Controversy." *National Journal*, September 15.

Saerbeck, Martin and Christoph Bartneck. 2010. "Attribution of Affect to Robot Motion." *5th ACM/IEEE International Conference on Human–Robot Interaction (HRI)*, 53–60.

Scheutz, Matthias. 2012. "The Inherent Dangers of Unidirectional Emotional Bonds between Humans and Social Robots." In *Robot Ethics: The Ethical and Social Implications of Robotics*, edited by Patrick Lin, Keith Abney, and George Bekey, 205–21. Cambridge: MIT Press.

Scholl, Brian J. and Patrice D. Tremoulet. 2000. "Perceptual Causality and Animacy." *Trends in Cognitive Sciences* 4 (8): 299–309.

Shamsuddina, Syamimi, Hanafiah Yussofb, Luthffi Idzhar Ismailb, Salina Mohamedc, Fazah Akhtar Hanapiahc, and Nur Ismarrubie Zaharid. 2012. "Initial Response in HRI: A Case Study on Evaluation of Child with Autism Spectrum Disorders Interacting with a Humanoid Robot NAO." *Procedia Engineering (IRIS)* 41: 1448–55.

Singer, Peter Warren. 2009. *Wired for War: The Robotics Revolution and Conflict in the 21st Century*. London: Penguin Books.

Stein, Scott. 2015. "Best Wearable Tech of 2015." *CNET*, February 24.

Sung, Ja-Young, Lan Guo, Rebecca E. Grinter, and Henrik I. Christensen. 2007. "'My Roomba is Rambo': Intimate Home Appliances." *9th International Conference on Ubiquitous Computing*, 145–62.

Swartout, William, David Traum, Ron Artstein, et al. 2010. "Ada and Grace: Toward Realistic and Engaging Virtual Museum Guides." In *Intelligent Virtual Agents*, edited by Jan Allbeck, Norman Badler, Timothy Bickmore, Catherine Pelachaud, and Alla Safonova. Berlin: Springer.

Tapus, Adriana, Maja Matarić, and Brian Scassellatti. 2007. "The Grand Challenges in Socially Assistive Robotics." *IEEE Robotics and Automation Magazine* 14 (1): 35–42.

Thomasen, Kristen. 2016. "Examining the Constitutionality of Robo-Enhanced Interrogation." In *Robot Law*, edited by Ryan Calo, Michael Froomkin, and Ian Kerr, 306–32. Cheltenham: Edward Elgar.

Tilley, Aaron. 2015. "Family Robot Jibo Raises $25 Million in Series A Round." *Forbes*, January 21.

Tiong Chee Tay, Benedict, Taezoon Park, Younbo Jung, Yeow Kee Tan, and Alvin Hong Yee Wong. 2013. "When Stereotypes Meet Robots: The Effect of Gender Stereotypes on People's Acceptance of a Security Robot." In *Engineering Psychology and Cognitive Ergonomics: Understanding Human Cognition*, edited by Don Harris, 261–70. Berlin, Germany: Springer.

Turkle, Sherry. 2006. "A Nascent Robotics Culture: New Complicities for Companionship." *AAAI Technical Report Series*. http://web.mit.edu/~sturkle/www/nascentroboticsculture.pdf.

Turkle, Sherry. 2007. "Simulation vs. Authenticity." In *What Is Your Dangerous Idea? Today's Leading Thinkers on the Unthinkable*, edited by John Brockman, 244–7. New York: Simon & Schuster.

Turkle, Sherry. 2010. "In Good Company? On the Threshold of Robotic Companions." In *Close Engagements with Artificial Companions: Key Social, Psychological, Ethical and Design Issues*, edited by Yorick Wilks, 3–10. Amsterdam: John Benjamins.

Turkle, Sherry. 2012. *Alone Together: Why We Expect More from Technology and Less from Each Other*. New York: Basic Books.

Twenty, Dylan. 2011. "Robots Evolve More Natural Ways of Walking." *Wired*, January 26.

Ulanoff, Lance. 2014. "Jibo Wants to Be the World's First Family Robot." *Mashable*, July 16.

Walk, Hunter. 2016. "Amazon Echo is Magical. It's Also Turning My Kid into an Asshole." *Linkedin*, April 8.

Weizenbaum, Joseph. 1976. *Computer Power and Human Reason: From Judgment to Calculation*. London: W. H. Freeman.

Wired. 2015. "Huggable Robot Befriends Girl in Hospital," March 30. http://video.wired.com/watch/huggable-robot-befriends-girl-in-hospital.

Wortham, Jenna. 2009. "Fitbit's Motivator: A Virtual Flower." *New York Times*, December 10.

Yan, C., W. Peng, K. M. Lee, and S. Jin. 2004. "Can Robots Have Personality? An Empirical Study of Personality Manifestation, Social Responses, and Social Presence in Human–Robot Interaction." *54th Annual Conference of the International Communication Association*.

Zittrain, Jonathan. 2014. "Facebook Could Decide an Election Without Anyone Ever Finding Out: The Scary Future of Digital Gerrymandering—and How to Prevent It." *New Republic*, June 1.

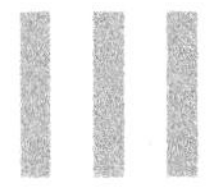

APPLICATIONS

From Love to War

Introduction

In part III, we focus in on specific types of robots and their (sometimes controversial) applications, from love to war. As with our invocation of robot cars as a case study in part I, each use-case in robotics seems to hold general lessons for the broader field.

Our first case study here concerns robots that have already garnered a great deal of press: those designed for sexual use by humans (a.k.a. "sexbots"). Academic studies in the field were jump-started by David Levy's book *Love and Sex with Robots*. While human–robot romantic and intimate relationships were long a topic in science fiction, Levy's 2007 book turned the subject into an academic research discipline in its own right. Levy termed his work "Lovotics," and the authors of chapter 13 (and Levy's collaborators), Adrian David Cheok, Kasun Karunanayaka, and Emma Yann Zhang, explain that they mean the term to refer to all intimate relationships, such as love and sex, between humans and machines, especially robots.

A Lovotics robot is supposed to be capable of experiencing complex and human-like biological and emotional states that are governed by artificial hormones within its system. The authors discuss Levy's contention that the robot's intimacy software should employ parameters derived and quantified from five of the most important reasons for falling in love—proximity, repeated exposure, attachment, similarity, and attraction—and give examples of designs in progress for such a robot. They also discuss recent work on the ethical permissibility of using Lovotics robots from scholars as diverse as David Levy, who openly advocates robot prostitutes, to Islamic scholars Yusuff Amuda and Ismaila Tijani, who consider sex with robots to automatically constitute cheating—a position the authors strenuously dispute. They ultimately predict, following Levy, that there will be widespread commercial adoption of sophisticated sex robots by the middle of this century.

In chapter 14, Piotr Bołtuć continues the discussion of the future of sexbots and connects it to issues in philosophy of mind and ethics by considering a much more advanced sexbot that he terms a Church-Turing Lover: a sex robot that could attain every functionality of a human lover. But these Church-Turing Lovers would still have no first-person consciousness. To all outward evidence, they would be equivalent to a human being, but with no inner life (there is "nobody home"). Bołtuć proposes to help us understand the concept of a Church-Turing Lover with the notion of the Uncanny Valley of Perfection, which ranks the standards for humanoid robots in the following order: first the minimally humanoid (e.g., a teddy bear); then the bottom of the Uncanny Valley, such as a robot that causes viewers to feel creepy and elicits a strong "yuck" factor; through what he calls Silver, Gold, and Platinum Standards; up to the Uncanny Valley of Perfection (much better than humans); ending with the Slope of the Angels (no longer humanoid, considered a godlike figure that would be viewed with awe).

When a Church-Turing robotic companion says, "I love you," does it have the intention to please you, or is this merely a computer simulation of emotions? And would you have reason to care whether your significant other is a Church-Turing Lover, or is all that matters that it (perfectly) *acts* like it loves you? Bołtuć concludes that Church-Turing Lovers arguably demonstrate how epiphenomenal experience provides *reasons to care* about other people's first-person consciousness.

Human–robot interaction, of course, involves more than sex. And chapter 15 makes clear that such interaction may well be with robots so small or taken for granted that individual humans may remain blissfully unaware they are even there—until something goes terribly wrong. Adam Henschke finds two layers of ethical concern in the internet of things. In the "physical layer," ethical concerns focus on safety and risk issues, while the primary concerns in the "information layer" are about controlling information. Given that the two layers have distinct and potentially non-overlapping sets of ethical concerns, which of these layers of ethical concern should take priority? Henschke argues that designers, policymakers, and users not only must pay attention to both layers, but may also have to make decisions that prioritize one layer of ethical concern over the other.

Chapter 16 concerns further challenges to the ethics of robotic design and construction: the problems of time and context in engineering moral reasoners. Michał Klincewicz finds that combining algorithms based on philosophical moral theories and analogical reasoning is a promising strategy for engineering software that can engage in moral reasoning. Applying the results discussed in the philosophical literature on ethical theories, however, raises serious engineering challenges for making a properly functioning computerized moral reasoner. The difficulties include both the context-sensitivity of the system and the temporal limitations on search, but also difficulties that are direct consequences of particular philosophical theories. Klincewicz believes that engineers and philosophers need to cooperate in order to find the best solutions for overcoming these difficulties in creating a robot capable of sophisticated moral reasoning.

Chapter 17 concerns a crucial issue for the engineering of robotic moral reasoners—should we ever design a robot to act on the basis of moral views we believe to be false? Brian Talbot, Ryan Jenkins, and Duncan Purves believe, counterintuitively, that engineers should do exactly that. First, they argue that deontological evaluations do not apply to the actions of robots, for without phenomenal consciousness, they lack the mental capacities required for agency. As a result, they argue it would be better for robots to be consequentialists, even if consequentialism is false.

This argument might still allow deontological robots, if they were perfect. But given our epistemic uncertainty about what the true moral theory is, or what the appropriate trade-offs between rights and utilities would be (or how to program them), or even whether robots have the ability to obey moral commands reliably, perfection is unattainable. Applying the "preface paradox" puzzle from the epistemology literature, the authors argue that this uncertainty makes it at least permissible, if not sometimes obligatory, to create robots with moral views that one thinks are false.

We end part III with one of the most well-covered applications of robots with the ability to perform moral reasoning: robots in war. In chapter 18, Leonard Kahn examines an unintended consequence of military robots: that their use might lead to an *increase* in armed conflict. Kahn argues that it will, and that this would be a morally bad thing. He then discusses how the impersonal forces of technological development affect the choices of rational political agents. He concludes with some suggestions about how to make the best of a bad situation through the establishment of new international norms.

From love to war, robots continue to make inroads into domains long assumed to be distinctively human. As these incremental changes accumulate, ethics may not demand a Luddite response but instead ongoing reflection on what is valuable about being human—before robots so thoroughly integrate their existence into ours that there are no uniquely human associations left.

13 LOVOTICS

HUMAN–ROBOT LOVE AND SEX RELATIONSHIPS

Adrian David Cheok, Kasun Karunanayaka, and Emma Yann Zhang

Human–robot intimate relationships are no longer pure science fiction but have entered the hallowed halls of serious academic research. In the academic world, there has already been sufficient coverage of the topic to demonstrate rather convincingly that it is not only of interest to mainstream media. Conferences on robotics, AI, and other computer science–related subjects began to accept and even invite papers on the subject, and thus far two conferences have been devoted to human–robot personal relationships. In 2014 the First International Congress of Love and Sex with Robots was held in Madeira.

The academic journals that have since chosen to publish papers on the topic have included *Accountability in Research, AI & Society, Artificial Intelligence, Current Sociology, Ethics and Information Technology, Futures, Industrial Robot, International Journal of Advanced Robotic Systems, International Journal of Social Development, International Journal of Social Robotics, International Journal of Technoethics, New Media and Society, Phenomenology and the Cognitive Sciences, Philosophy Technology, Social Robotics, Technological Forecasting and Social Change*, and various publications from the IEEE, Springer, and other highly respected technology venues. One paper, from Victoria University of Wellington, New Zealand, achieved a high profile in the general media when it appeared in 2012 with an entertaining depiction of a future scenario in the red light district of Amsterdam—a life, in 2050, revolving around android prostitutes "who are clean of sexually transmitted infections (STIs), not smuggled in from Eastern Europe and forced into slavery, the city council will have direct control over" (Yeoman and Mars 2012, 365–71).

Since the initial burst of media interest late in 2007, there have also been TV documentaries and feature movies in which sex with robots, virtual characters, or life-sized sex dolls was the dominant theme: *Lars and the Real Girl (2007), Meaning of Robots (2012), My Sex Robot (2011), Her* (2013), *Ex Machina* (2015), *Guys and Dolls (2002)*, as well as the 2004 remake of *The Stepford Wives*. For all this, it is the sexual nature of the subject matter that is responsible; sex sells.

Following the storm of publicity that accompanied the launch of David Levy's book in 2007 (Levy 2007a), the subject of human–robot romantic and intimate relationships rapidly developed into an academic research discipline in its own right. The subject was named "Lovotics" and was first mentioned in the literature in 2009 (Nomura et al. 2009).

The interest of the academic community in this field resulted, in 2013, in the founding of a journal and e-journal devoted entirely to the subject. The *Lovotics* journal defines its domain as "Academic Studies of Love and Friendship with Robots" (*Lovotics* 2016)

13.1 The First Crude Sex Robot

One of the most frequently raised question in this field in 2007–8 was "How soon do you think the first sex robots will be on the market?" Since all the technologies necessary to create a crude sex robot were already available, David Levy predicted that it would probably not be more than two to three years before some enterprising entrepreneur(s) put these technologies together.

Late in 2009, publicity began to appear in the media about a "sex robot" developed by a New Jersey entrepreneur, Douglas Hines. His website proudly proclaimed:

> We have been designing "Roxxxy TrueCompanion," your TrueCompanion.com sex robot, for many years, making sure that she: knows your name, your likes and dislikes, can carry on a discussion and express[ ] her love to you and be your loving friend. She can talk to you, listen to you and feel your touch. She can even have an orgasm! (Truecompanion.com 2016)

As millions of men eagerly awaited the next major technological development that would enhance their sex lives, the press launch of Roxxxy took place at the Adult Entertainment Expo in Las Vegas on January 9, 2010, but it posed more questions than it answered. It appeared, for example, that touching Roxxxy's hand caused it to exclaim, "I like holding hands with you," but what does that prove? Only that an electronic sensor was linked to some sort of recorded sound output. It was not a demonstration of the speech technology that would be needed in a conversational robot.

The media hype surrounding Hines's launch in Las Vegas seems to have attracted the attention of many prospective customers for Roxxxy's supposedly seductive charms. At the beginning of February 2010, Hines's website started to take orders for Roxxxy, advertising the product at a "sale price" of $6,495, which it claimed represented a reduction of $500. The *Wikipedia* entry for Roxxxy (2016) includes the following:

> According to Douglas Hines, Roxxxy garnered about 4,000 pre-orders shortly after its AEE [Adult Entertainment Expo] reveal in 2010. However, to date, no actual customers have ever surfaced with a Roxxxy doll, and the public has remained skeptical that any commercial Roxxxy dolls have ever been produced.

Despite all the negative aspects of Hines's operation and of the product itself, the launch of Roxxxy at the January 2010 Adult Entertainment Expo can be viewed as some sort of milestone—a vindication of the forecast for a two- to three-year time span from late 2007 to the launch of the world's first commercially available sex robot. Hines has proved that there is indeed a significant level of interest in sex robots from the buying public. Recently the Truecompanion.com website has also started to take pre-orders for "Rocky," the male robot of Roxxxy. They suggest that, after the payment, robots can be delivered in two to three months. Currently hands-on videos of Roxxxy and Rocky are widely available on the internet, and they show that these robots can perform natural conversations with humans. However, there is still no proper test done to measure the emotional and conversational abilities of these robots.

13.2 Lovotics

In 2011, a doctoral thesis explored certain aspects of Lovotics and described the design and development of a hardware platform—a robot—that was capable of experiencing complex and human-like biological and emotional states that were governed by artificial hormones within its system (Samani 2011).

The artificial intelligence of the Lovotics robot includes three modules: the Artificial Endocrine System, which is based on the physiology of love; the Probabilistic Love Assembly, which is based on the psychology of falling in love; and the Affective State Transition, which is based on human emotions. These three modules collaborate to generate realistic emotion-driven behaviors by the robot.

The robot's intimacy software employs parameters derived and quantified from five of the most important reasons for falling in love (Levy 2007a): proximity, repeated exposure, attachment, similarity, and attraction.

The Lovotics robot includes mathematical models for those five causal factors of love, creating a mathematical formula to represent each factor, as well as a single "overall intimacy" formula that combines these five individual formulas into one. As an example of the five models, the proximity formula incorporates various distances between robot and human that indicate, *inter alia*, how closely the robot and human are to touching each other and how close they are emotionally.

13.3 Kissenger

In order for robots, such as the Lovotics robot, to have realistic physical interactions with humans, technology has to be developed for human–machine kissing. In order to address this issue, two of the authors of this chapter, Adrian David Cheok and Emma Yann Zhang, have developed a kissing robot messenger called "Kissenger" (figure 13.1) (Zhang et al. 2016, 25).

We live in a global era, and more and more couples and families spend time apart due to work and business. However, new technologies are often employed to help us feel connected with those we care about. There is an increasing interest in touch and feeling communication between humans in the human–computer interaction community. Research such as "Hugvie" (Kuwamura et al. 2013) and the "Hug over a Distance" (Mueller et al. 2005) tested the feasibilities of

FIGURE 13.1. The concept of kiss communication.

telepresence and intimacy technology. However, many of the systems seem big, bulky, and impractical.

There are some commercial works, like the "HugShirt" (Cutecircuit.com 2002) and "Huggy Pajama" (Teh et al. 2008, 250–7), that explore remote hugging with loved ones using wearable fashion technology. But these systems still lack a proper interface for "abstracted presence." Thus, Kissenger provides a new system to feel a realist sense of presence using communication over the internet for humans or robots.

Kissing is one of the most important modes of human communication: it is a universal expression of intimacy. People feel deeply positive emotions such as respect, greeting, farewell, good luck, romantic affection, and/or sexual desire through the physical joining or touching of lips by one individual on another individual's cheek, forehead, etc. (Millstein et al. 1993). Regular physical contact such as kissing is the key to maintaining intimacy in human relationships. Studies have shown that couples who kiss more frequently experience higher romantic satisfaction and lower stress levels (Floyd et al. 2009, 113–33). Kissenger employed soft, pressure-sensitive, vibrating silicone lips, which, in the early prototypes, stood out from the surface of a smooth plastic casing shaped somewhat like a human head. Those early prototypes have since been replaced by a version for mobile phones.

Considering this missing dimension in today's communication technologies, Kissenger's design aims to create a new device to facilitate the exchange of emotional content, to feel a closer sense of presence, between people who are physically separated, thus enhancing their interpersonal relationships.

When a user kisses the device on its lips, the changes in the pressure of the lips are detected by sensors, and the resulting data is transmitted over the internet to a receiving Kissenger device, which converts the data back to lip pressure produced by actuators. This reproduces the kisser's lip pressure and movement, which are felt by the kisser's partner.

During a kiss, along with its strong emotional and affectionate connections, a series of physical interactions takes place. The touch of the lips exchanges the pressure, softness, and warmth of each lip in a convincing way. The inventers of Kissenger approached this design problem carefully, given the intimate nature of the interaction, and iteratively designed Kissenger. The system consists of two paired devices that can send and receive kisses simultaneously, as shown in concept images in figures 13.2 and 13.3 (figure 13.2 shows the scenario of family communication, while figure 13.3 shows the communication between parent and child).

After the biological and psychological parameters of kissing were studied, a series of exploratory form factors were drawn to help visualize the possible interfaces. Figure13.4 shows some of the initial concept designs.

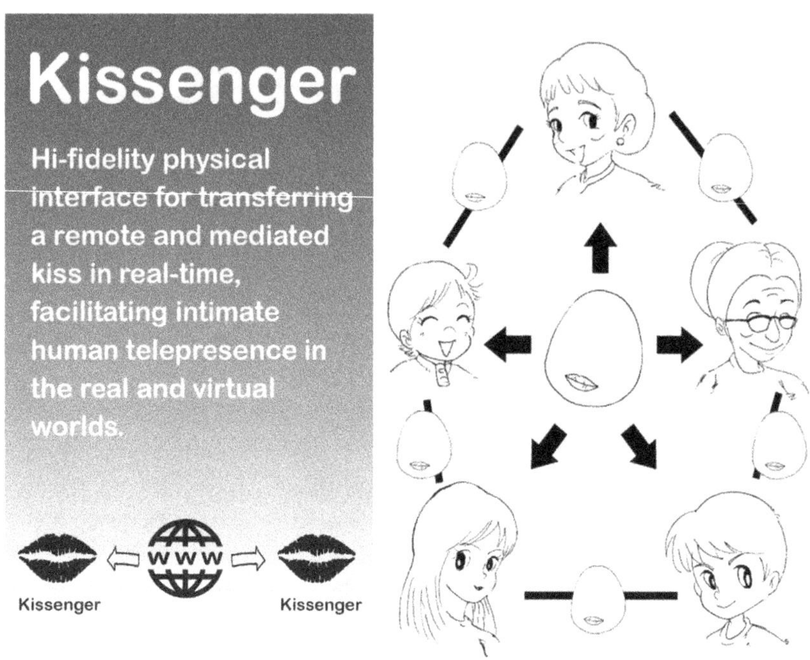

FIGURE 13.2. Kissenger usage scenario—family communication.

At this stage, the inventors looked for a way of designing a system that effectively transmits the same sensation of a kiss from one person to another. The one key issue was that the use of the device should be comfortable and not distract or obstruct the natural interaction of the kiss. Hence, it was decided to integrate the initial concept design for a liplike portable device with a minimalistic shape. However, one of the main concerns was that the lip needed to be equipped with sensors and actuators. Figure 13.5 shows the 3D depiction of the proposed device with the new shape, which can attach to a smartphone, allowing a video call and virtual kiss simultaneously.

13.3.1 Design of Kissenger

The hardware design of Kissenger (figure 13.6) with all the features listed earlier specifies the use of force sensors, linear actuators, a RGB LED, and an audio connector, all in the Kissenger design flow.

13.3.1.1 Input Kiss Sensing

The lip surface is made of a soft flexible material to resemble the texture of human lips. An array of force sensors is embedded below the surface of the lip to measure

FIGURE 13.3. Kissenger usage scenario—parent and child communication.

the dynamic forces exerted by different points of the user's lips. The system also can be used during a video chat with another person or for kissing a robot or a virtual 3D character.

13.3.1.2 Control and Transmission

Kissenger uses a microcontroller in the device to control the sensors and actuators. The device connects to a mobile phone through the Kissenger app, which connects to another user's app over the internet (figure 13.7). The microcontroller reads the force sensors and sends the force data to the phone. This data is then transmitted over the internet in real time and is received by the partner's device. A bilateral haptic controller is implemented locally to control the output

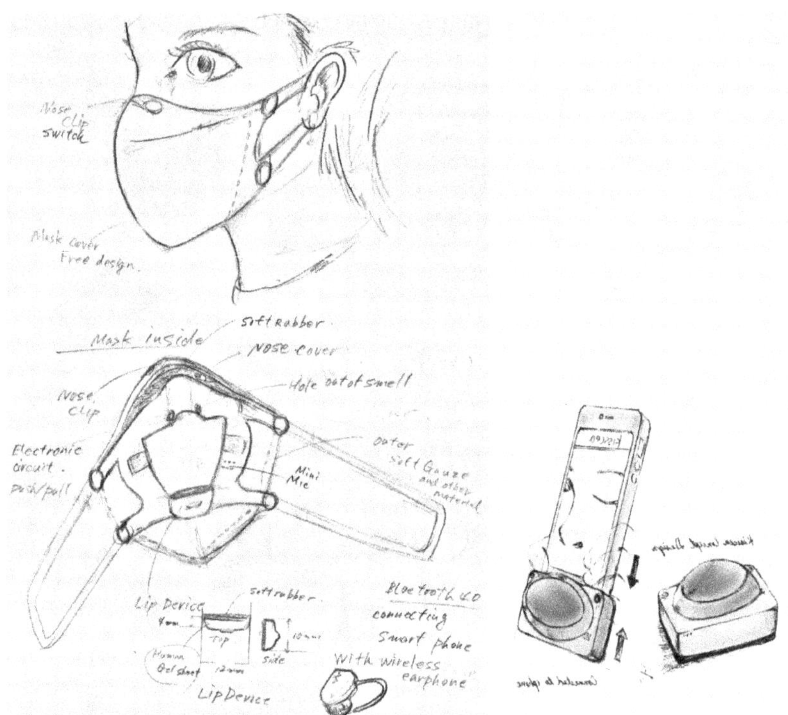

FIGURE 13.4. Preliminary concept designs of Kissenger.

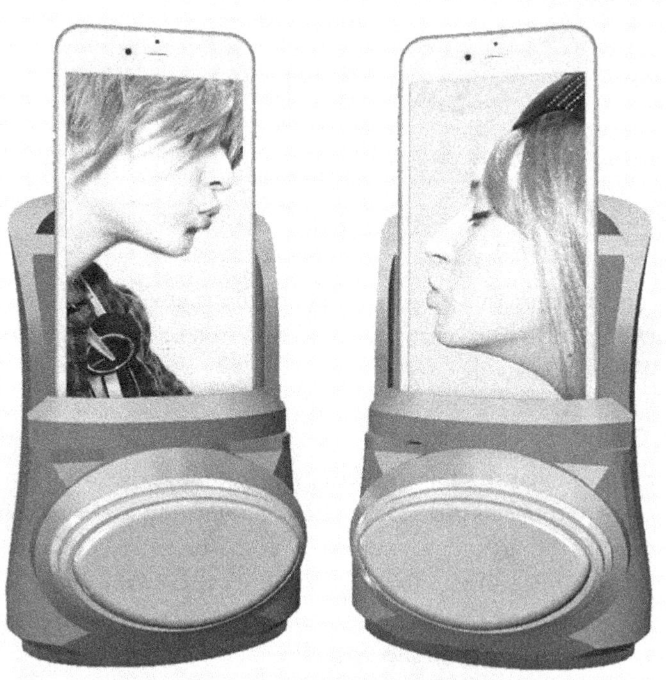

FIGURE 13.5. The new design of Kissenger that can attach to a mobile phone.

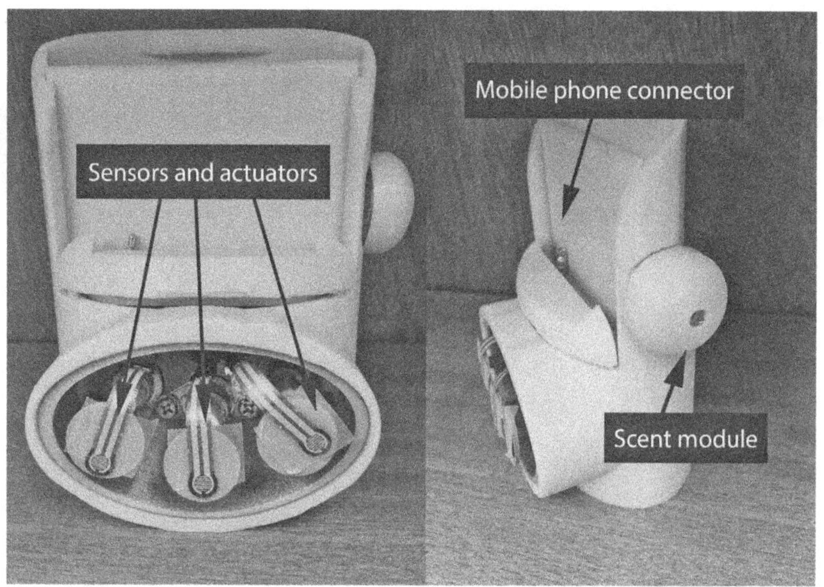

FIGURE 13.6. Key design features of Kissenger.

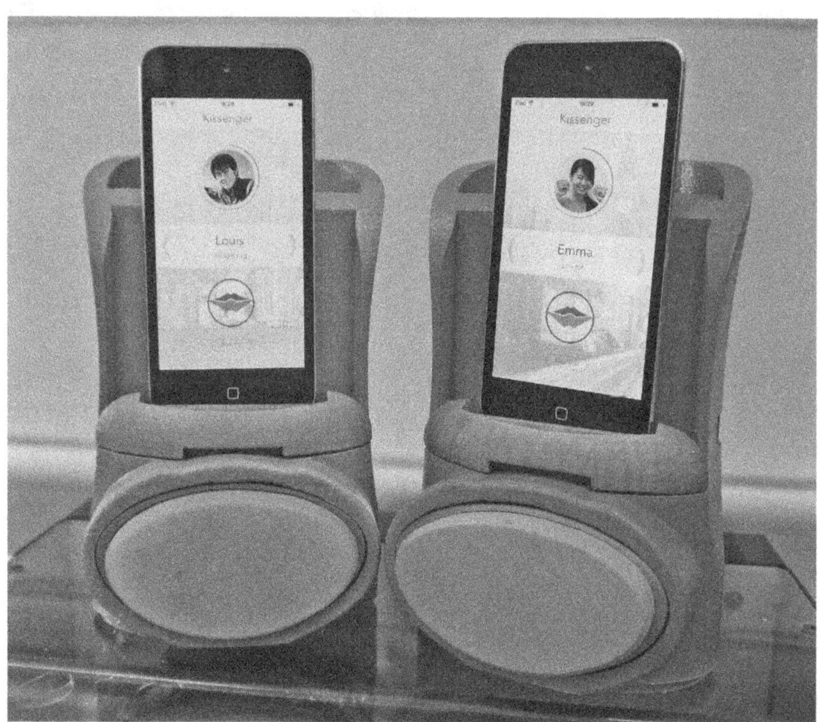

FIGURE 13.7. Kissenger device connected to iPhone app.

forces of the actuators to generate kiss sensations. The controller is designed such that both users feel the same contact force on their lips simultaneously. The interaction is bidirectional, as the user can send and receive a kiss at the same time.

13.3.1.3 Output Kiss Actuation

Kiss sensations are produced by the positional changes of an array of linear actuators. The shape and size of the lip cover hides the inner electronics that go into the sensing, control, and actuation of the device. All these features make the device more comfortable for the user to interact with, and help evoke emotional responses and feelings for kiss communication.

13.3.2 Communication

Two or more Kissenger devices are wirelessly connected to each other via the Kissenger mobile app. Users can sign up for an account, and search and connect to their friends using the app. When a user starts a video chat with a friend, the application starts to send and receive force data from the Kissenger device. One of the unique additional features of the app is that it allows one-to-many user communication along with one-to-one user communication, as shown in figure 13.8. With the Kissenger app, the user can send different colors to the

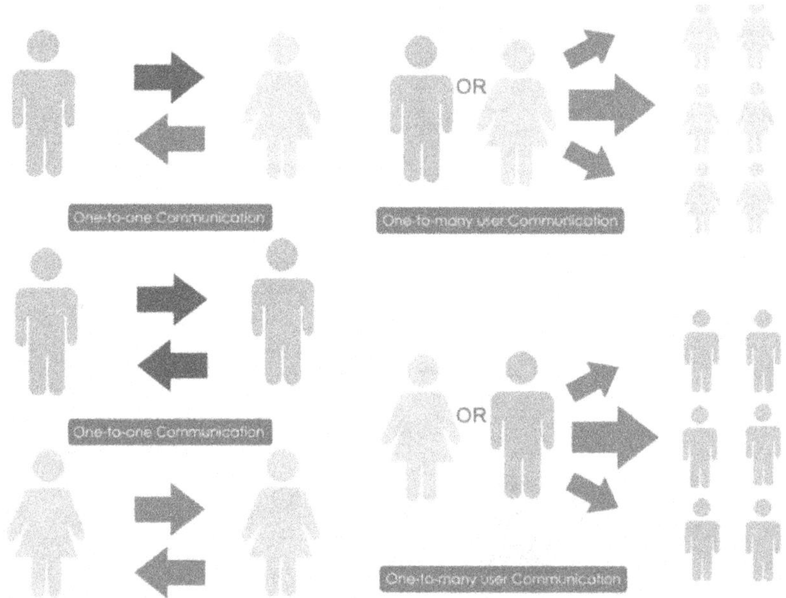

FIGURE 13.8. User communication via Kissenger app.

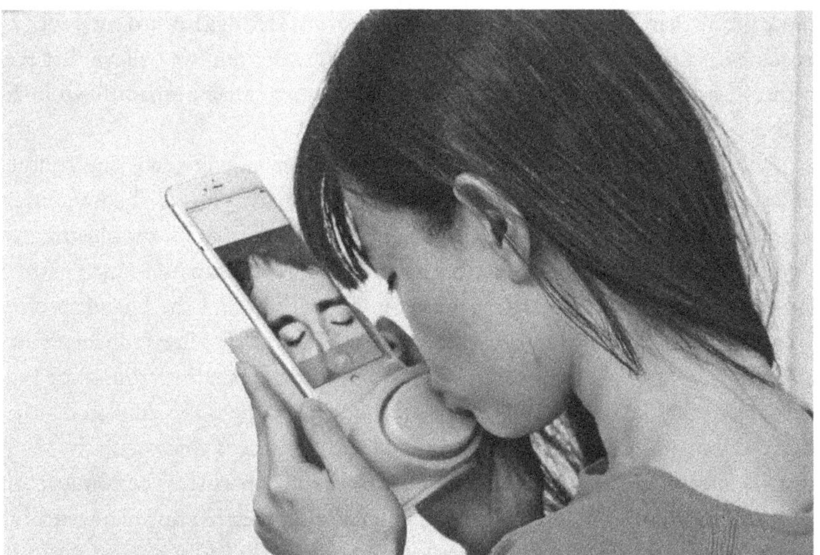

FIGURE 13.9. A user interacting with Kissenger.

receiver(s) to convey the user's mood. Figure 13.9 shows a user interacting with the Kissenger device.

An assessment of the new proposed shape and its implementation was conducted with a wide variety of people, including researchers not involved in the project, mall shoppers, and friends. Over a period of time, around fifty people of different cultural backgrounds, ages, and sexes participated in the evaluation process and provided feedback for the proposed shape and features. The major feedback is to reduce the size to make it more portable and user-friendly, and provide room for asynchronous kissing. The device could include the functionality to record a kiss that is played back to the receiver at a later time, which the researchers will be working on in the future.

13.4 Robot Love

Among the fundamental conditions for engendering human love, physical appearance and attractiveness rank highly. Hiroshi Ishiguro is a robotics researcher who has developed various human images (Hofilena 2013), including one in his own image, which is sometimes sent to deliver his lectures when he is too busy to do so himself. Another of his robots, called "Geminoid-F," is made in the image of an attractive young woman who can blink, respond to eye contact, and recognize and respond to body language (Torres 2013). Ishiguro is encouraged in this aspect of his work by his conviction that Japanese men are more prone than Western men to develop amorous feelings toward such robots, because in Japan, with the influence of the Shinto religion, "we believe that everything has a soul and therefore we don't hesitate to create human-like robots" (Mitaros 2013).

Another strand of Ishiguro's research into artificially engendering feelings of love in humans is concerned with promoting romantic forms of communication. "Hugvie" (Geminoid.jp 2016) is a huggable pillow, with a somewhat human form, that is held by a user close to his body while he speaks to his human partner via his mobile phone, located in a pocket in Hugvie's head. (The Hugvie project grew out of an earlier Ishiguro project called "Telenoid.") Hugvie incorporates a vibrator to simulate a heartbeat, and the vibrations emanating from it are synchronized with the sounds of the partner's voice. This allows the simulated heartbeat to be changed according to the volume of the partner's voice, with the result that the listening user feels as though he is close to his partner. The comfort felt by holding the cushion, the sense of hugging one's partner, hearing one's partner's voice close to one's ear, and the simulated heartbeat aligned with that voice all combine to create a sense that the partner is in some way present, which in turn intensifies the listener's feelings of emotional attraction for his partner. Ishiguro expects this intensified affinity to increase the sense of intimacy between couples who are communicating through their respective Hugvies. Ishiguro shared in a breakthrough study that Hugvie could decrease blood cortisol levels, therefore reducing stress (Sumioka 2013). Integrating the Hugvie technology into the design of an amorous robot might therefore enable a human user of such a robot to experience an enhanced feeling of a human-like presence and a greater sense of intimacy from and for the robot.

Yet another direction of Ishiguro's research into having a robot engender emotions in humans is his investigation of the emotional effects, on a human user, of different facial expressions exhibited by a robot (Nishio 2012, 388–97). That research is currently in its early stages but there is already some indication that it will be possible for robots, by their own facial expressions, to affect a user's emotional state. Emotional facial expression is also a hot topic at the MIT Media Lab, where the Nexi robot was developed (Allman 2009).

13.5 The Ethical and Legal Debate

David Levy has claimed that the "element of consciousness of a robot is the dividing line for ethical treatment or not" (Levy 2007a). On this issue, in his article "Ethics and Consciousness in Artificial Agents," Steve Torrance discussed a concept called "the organic view"; he stated that "a key element of the organic view is the claim that consciousness, or sentience, is at the root of moral status—both status as a moral patient (or target) and as a moral agent (or source)" (2008, 495–521). Further, Jong-Hwan Kim said that "as robots will have their own internal states such as motivation and emotion, we should not abuse them. We will have to treat them in the same way that we take care of pets" (Osley 2007).

The ethics of robot sex were first aired in an academic forum at the EURON Workshop on Roboethics in 2006 (Levy 2006a,b,c). The following year David Levy discussed five aspects of the ethics of robot prostitution at an IEEE conference in Rome: (i) the ethics of making robot prostitutes available for general use; (ii) the ethics, vis-à-vis oneself and society in general, of using robot prostitutes; (iii) the ethics, vis-à-vis one's partner or spouse, of using robot prostitutes; (iv) the ethics, vis-à-vis human sex workers, of using robot prostitutes; and (v) the ethics, vis-à-vis the sexbots themselves, of using robot prostitutes (Levy 2007b).

A somewhat broader airing of the ethical impacts of love and sex machines was presented by John Sullins (2012, 398–409). He explores the subject partly on the basis that such entities are programmed to manipulate human emotions "in order to evoke loving or amorous reactions from their human users" (398–409). He submits that there should be "certain ethical limits on the manipulation of human psychology when it comes to building sex robots" (398–409), and accordingly he identifies three design considerations that he proposes should be applied to the development of robots designed for love: (i) robots should not fool people into ascribing more feelings to the machine than they should; (ii) robot designers should be circumspect in how their inventions exploit human psychology; and (iii) robots should not be designed that intentionally lie to their users in order to manipulate their user's behavior (398–409).

The difference between Levy and Sullins is that while Levy concentrates on the practices of robot sex, Sullins examines designing elements of sex robots. Levy believes that a wider moral discussion on sex robots in everyday life is a ground for addressing the ethical (and legal) position. However, Sullins tends to believe that sex robots should be designed and presented to implement best ethical practices. It has to be understood that both Levy and Sullins are making arguments about the integration and acceptance of sex robots from two different perspectives.

A considerably more strident attitude to the ethics of robot sex pervades an article by Yusuff Amuda and Ismaila Tijani (2012, 19–28), which views the subject from an Islamic perspective. These authors appear to have no doubt that "having intercourse with [a] robot is unethical, immoral, uncultured, [a] slap to the marriage institution and respect for human being[s]" (21). While many might not concur with the robustness of their position on the subject, it cannot be denied that the question of robot sex within the confines of marriage, or indeed within any existing human sexual relationship, is a serious issue. The question most often asked from David Levy in media interviews has been: "Is it cheating for someone who is married or in a committed relationship to have sex with a robot?"

In his opinion, the answer is a resounding no. A partner or spouse who has sex with a robot is no guiltier of cheating on the other partner or spouse than are any of the tens of millions of women who use a vibrator. But not everyone agrees with this position, and in parallel with the possibility that sex with a robot should be regarded as cheating on one's spouse, there arises an interesting legal question that has been flagged by the California lawyer Sonja Ziaja (2011): Could a sex robot be legally regarded as the enticing protagonist in a lawsuit brought for the enticement of one's spouse? In the eight states in the United States where this type of law is still on the books, where they are called amatory or "heart balm" laws, Ziaja questions whether a sex robot could be held to be the cause, or a contributing cause, to the breakdown and dissolution of a marriage, and if so, who should be held legally liable to pay whatever damages a court might assess. Ziaja suggests a few obvious possible culprits in cases of enticement by a robot: the robot's inventor, its manufacturer, its owner, or even the robot itself. But the attribution of liability for a wrong wrought by a robot is an extremely complex issue, one that David Levy believes will not be adequately solved in the immediate future. Instead it has been suggested that robot wrongs could be compensated by an insurance scheme, much akin to that which works well for automobiles and other vehicles (Levy 2012).

The only form of punishment considered by Ziaja for transgressing the U.S. heart balm laws is to compensate the plaintiff, which is a notion that pales into insignificance when compared with the punishments discussed by Amuda and Tijani. They point out that, under Sharia law, judges are permitted to sentence anyone having sex with a robot to lashes or even capital punishment, provided there is sufficient credible evidence of the crime. "To this study, death penalty by hanging may not be applicable and implemented unless there are enough and credible evidences to justify the death by hanging of robot fornicator or adulterer" (Amuda and Tijani 2012).

Ziaja's article largely avoids the issue of punishment in relation to enticement cases in which a robot is the protagonist; his preference is instead to eliminate the problem altogether by having robots designed in such a way as to incorporate feelings of heartbreak together with the goal of caring for those in its owner's circle of friends and relatives. "In order for robots to enter into human romantic relationships in a way that is consistent with the values underlying the heart balm torts, [robots] may also need to experience heartache and empathy as we do" (Ziaja 2011, 122). Ziaja's position thus supports that of John Sullins.

An in-depth consideration of whether or not human–humanoid sexual interactions should be legally regulated was discussed by Anna Russell (2009) in

Computer Law & Security Review. The very fact that such a discussion should appear in the pages of a respected legal journal points to the seriousness with which the legal profession is viewing the legal implications of the human–robot relationships of the future. Russell suggests:

> Regulation of human–humanoid sexual interaction, either by the state or federal government [in the United States], will be sought when the level of interaction either (1) mimics human sexual interactions currently regulated; or (2) will create a social harm if the interaction is not regulated. . . . [C]urrently, in places where humans are using robots for pleasure in a sexual way, that pleasure is either not regulated or is regulated in the way the use of any sexual device may be regulated. (2009, 457)

But when more advanced robots—humanoids—are used for sexual pleasure,

> then in many places, traditional norms and social mores will be challenged, prompting the development of state regulation. Will such regulation, then, be at odds with accepted notions of rights and freedoms? (457)

Russell then delves further into the question of how regulation of human–humanoid sexual encounters would work and highlights some of the questions that will arise, including:

> How many rights will humans allow if humanoids clamor for sexual freedoms? How will humanoids be punished for sexual transgressions? Will humanoids need legal protection from the abuse of human sexual proclivities? (458)

Russell's conclusion is a call for the

> early discussion of the ramifications of a future species' demand for legal rights. . . . [T]he legal profession should develop legal arguments before a test case occurs in order to avoid the illogic and danger of arguments that stem from species bias. (457)

In 2011, the *MIT Technology Review* conducted a poll on people's attitudes to the idea of loving a robot: 19% of those questioned indicated that they believed they could love a robot, 45% said "no," and 36% responded "maybe" (*MIT Technology Review* 2011). When it came to a question of whether or not people believed that robots could love humans, 36% said "yes", only 23% responded "no," and 41% responded "maybe." So already the idea of human–robot love was taking root as a serious proposition.

In a later poll, this one about robot sex rather than robot love, which was conducted in February 2013 by the *Huffington Post* and YouGov among 1,000 U.S. adults, 9% of respondents indicated that they would have sex with a robot, and 42% opined that robot sex would constitute cheating on one's human partner; 31% answered "no" to the cheating question, while 26% said they were uncertain (*Huffington Post* 2013a). This can be taken as further evidence that a significant portion of the population already regards robot sex as a serious subject.

Just how serious can perhaps be judged by a news story that hit the media in March 2013 about an online auction for the virginity of a Brazilian sex doll called Valentina (*Huffington Post* 2013b), which was inspired by a 20-year-old Brazilian woman, Catarina Migliorini, who had auctioned her own virginity for $780,000 (sold to a Japanese buyer). True, a sex doll is only an inanimate product, lacking all the interactive capabilities of the sex robots of the future. But the level of interest demonstrated by this news story bodes well for the commercial possibilities of sex robots.

For the Brazilian sex doll auction, the online retailer Sexônico offered a complete "romantic" package for the successful bidder, which included a one-night stay with Valentina in the presidential suite at the Swing Motel in Sao Paulo, a candlelit champagne dinner, an aromatic bath with rose petals, and a digital camera to capture the action. If the successful bidder lived outside São Paulo, Sexônico also offered to provide a round-trip air ticket. Valentina's charms were not able to match the great commercial success of Ms. Migliorini, but considering that most sex dolls retail at prices in the range $5,000–$10,000, the final bid of $105,000 was still a good result for Sexônico, not to mention the value of all the media exposure it attracted.

13.6 Predictions

Clearly, a significant sector of the public is now ready for the advent of commercially available sex robots, and the public's interest in and appetite for such products seem to be growing steadily. We have noticed a steady increase in the number of requests for media interviews on the subject in the past two years. Also growing steadily is the interest within the academic research community.

In our opinion, nothing has occurred since the publication of *Love and Sex with Robots* to cast doubt on Levy's 2007 prediction that sophisticated sex robots would be commercially available by the middle of this century. On the contrary, the increase in academic interest in this field has reinforced Levy's conviction regarding that time frame.

What will be the next significant steps in this field? Intelligent electronic sex toys are gaining in popularity, for example the Sasi Vibrator, which "comes pre-loaded with sensual intelligence which learns movements you like, specifically tailoring a unique experience by remembering movements that suit you" (Lovehoney 2016); and the "Love Glider Penetration Machine," which can be purchased from Amazon.com at around $700 and which is claimed to "give you the most comfortable stimulating ride you will ever have!" (Amazon.com 2016). The Amazon website also offers a very much more primitive-looking sex machine at around $800, a machine of the type seen in many variations on specialist sites and that "supports multiple positions, has adjustable speeds, strong power, remote control" (Kink.com 2016).

Another area of research that perhaps offers even greater commercial potential entails a combination of augmented reality and digital surrogates ("dirrogates") of porn stars. A recent posting by Clyde DeSouza (2013) posits that the 3D printing of human body parts will enable the downloading, from "hard-drives in Hollywood studios" of "full body digital model and 'performance capture' files of actors and actresses." DeSouza continues:

> With 3D printing of human body parts now possible and blueprints coming online with full mechanical assembly instructions, the other kind of sexbot is possible. It won't be long before the 3D laser-scanned blueprint of a porn star sexbot will be available for licensing and home printing, at which point, the average person will willingly transition to transhuman status once the "buy now" button has been clicked. . . . If we look at Digital Surrogate Sexbot technology, which is a progression of interactive porn, we can see that the technology to create such Dirrogate sexbots exists today, and better iterations will come about in the next couple of years. Augmented Reality hardware when married to wearable technology such as "fundawear" (Fundawear.com 2013) and a photo-realistic Dirrogate driven by perf-captured libraries of porn stars under software (AI) control, can bring endless sessions of sexual pleasure to males and females.

Fundawear is a prime example of the increase in popularity of intelligent electronic sex toys and teledildonic devices. It is a wearable technology project currently under development by the condom manufacturer Durex, which allows lovers to stimulate their partner's underwear via their respective mobile phones. Such products seem likely to benefit from the increased academic interest in Lovotics, which will surely lead to at least some of the academic research in this field being spun off into commercial development and manufacturing ventures. And the more prolific such products become in the marketplace, the more the interest in them and in fully fledged sex robots will grow. How long will it be before we see a commercially available sexbot much more sophisticated than Roxxxy? Almost certainly within the next five years.

The past five years has seen a surge of interest in research projects aimed at different aspects of love with robots. One aspect is concerned with enabling humans to convey amorous feelings to artificial partners or to remotely located human partners with whom they communicate by artificial means (i.e., technology). Another aspect works in the opposite direction, enabling artificial partners to exhibit their artificial feelings, including love, to human partners. Some of this research has already demonstrated promising results, for example the experiments conducted with Hugvie by Ishiguro and his team in Japan. They plan further research with Hugvie to investigate how vibration can further enhance the feeling of presence experienced by a user. Additionally, they plan to employ tactile sensors to monitor the emotional state of a user, which will provide feedback for Hugvie and thereby enhance its ability to influence a user's emotions. Ishiguro's team has already found that hugging and holding such robots "is an effective way for strongly feeling the existence of a partner" (Kuwamura et al. 2013).

Another domain to become an important catalyst for the development of human–robot emotional relationships is what might be called girlfriend/boyfriend games. An example of this type of game is "Love Plus," which was first released in 2009 for the Nintendo DS games console and subsequently upgraded for re-release. A recent article describes the relationship between a 35-year-old Tokyo engineer, Osamu Kozaki, and his girlfriend, Rinko Kobayakawa (Belford 2013). When she sends him a message,

> his day brightens up. The relationship started more than three years ago, when Kobayakawa was a prickly 16-year-old working in her school library, a quiet girl who shut out the world with a pair of earphones that blasted punk music. (Belford 2013)

Kozaki describes his girlfriend as

> the kind of girl who starts out hostile but whose heart gradually grows warmer. And that's what has happened; over time, Kobayakawa has changed. These days, she spends much of her day sending affectionate missives to her boyfriend, inviting him on dates, or seeking his opinion when she wants to buy a new dress or try a new hairstyle. (Belford 2013)

But while Kozaki has aged, Kobayakawa has not. After three years, she's still 16. She always will be. That's because she is a simulation; Kobayakawa exists only inside a computer.

Kozaki's girlfriend has never been born. She will never die. Technically, she has never lived. She may be deleted, but Kozaki would never let that happen. Because he's "in love."

13.7 Conclusion

In this chapter, we discussed the possibility of human–robot intimate relationships and humanoid robot sex. We detailed Lovotics, which is a new research field that studies the emotions of robots with an artificial endocrine system capable of simulating love. We also presented the design and principle of Kissenger, an interactive device that provides a physical interface for transmitting a kiss between two remotely connected people. Finally, we discussed the ethical and legal background and future predictions of love and sex with robots.

Acknowledgments

The authors would like to thank greatly and acknowledge Dr. David Levy for his significant contributions to this chapter.

Works Cited

Allman, Toney. 2009. *The Nexi Robot*. Chicago: Norwood House Press.

Amazon.com. 2016. "Love Glider Sex Machine: Health & Personal Care." https://www.amazon.com/LoveBots-AC342-Love-Glider-Machine/dp/B00767NBUQ.

Amuda, Yusuff Jelili, and Ismaila B. Tijani. 2012. "Ethical and Legal Implications of Sex Robot: An Islamic Perspective." *OIDA International Journal of Sustainable Development* 3 (6): 19–28.

Belford, Aubrey. 2013. "That's Not a Droid, That's My Girlfriend." http://www.theglobalmail.org/feature/thats-not-a-droid-thats-my girlfriend/560/.

Cutecircuit.com. 2002. "HugShirt." http://cutecircuit.com/collections/the-hug-shirt/.

DeSouza, Clyde. 2013. "Sexbots, Ethics, and Transhumans." http://lifeboat.com/blog/2013/06/sexbots-ethics-and-transhumans.

Floyd, Kory, Justin P. Boren, Annegret F. Hannawa, Colin Hesse, Breanna McEwan, and Alice E. Veksler. 2009. "Kissing in Marital and Cohabiting Relationships: Effects on Blood Lipids, Stress, and Relationship Satisfaction." *Western Journal of Communication* 73 (2): 113–33.

Fundawearreviews.com. 2016. http://www.fundawearreviews.com.

Geminoid.jp. 2016. "Hugvie." http://www.geminoid.jp/projects/CREST/hugvie.html.

Hofilena, John. 2013. "Japanese Robotics Scientist Hiroshi Ishiguro Unveils Body-Double Robot." *Japan Daily Press*, June 17. http://japandailypress.com/japanese-robotics-scientist-hiroshi-ishiguro-unveils-body-double-robot-1730686/.

Huffington Post. 2013a. "Poll: Would Sex with A Robot Be Cheating?" April 10. http://www.huffingtonpost.com/2013/04/10/robot-sex-poll-americans-robotic-lovers-servants-soldiers_n_3037918.html.

Huffington Post. 2013b. "Look: Sex Doll's Virginity Sparks $100K Bidding War," March 8. http://www.huffingtonpost.com/2013/03/07/brazilian-sex-doll-virginity-valentina-bidding_n_2830371.html.

Kink.com. 2016. "Fucking Machines—Sex Machine Videos." http://www.kink.com/channel/fuckingmachines.

Kuwamura, Kaiko, Kenji Sakai, Tsuneaki Minato, Shojiro Nishio, and Hiroshi Ishiguro. 2013. "Hugvie: A Medium That Fosters Love." *RO-MAN, 2013 IEEE*, 70–5.

Levy, David. 2006a. "A History of Machines with Sexual Functions: Past, Present and Robot." *EURON Workshop on Roboethics*, Genoa.

Levy, David. 2006b. "Emotional Relationships With Robotic Companions." *EURON Workshop on Roboethics*, Genoa.

Levy, David. 2006c. "*Marriage and Sex with Robots.*" *EURON Workshop on Roboethics*, Genoa.

Levy, David. 2007a. *Love and Sex with Robots: The Evolution of Huma–Robot Relationships*. New York: HarperCollins.

Levy, David. 2007b. "Robot Prostitutes as Alternatives to Human Sex Workers." *Proceedings of the IEEE-RAS International Conference on Robotics and Automation (ICRA 2007)*, April 10–14, Rome.

Levy, David. 2012. "When Robots Do Wrong." *Conference on Computing and Entertainment*, November 3–5, Kathmandu. https://docs.google.com/document/u/1/pub?id=1cfkER1d7K2C0i3Q3xPg4Sz3Ja6W09pvCqDU7mdwOLzc.

Lovehoney. 2016. "Sasi by Je Joue Intelligent Rechargeable Vibrator." http://www.lovehoney.co.uk/product.cfm?p=15410.

Lovotics. 2016. Journal website. http://www.omicsonline.com/open-access/lovotics.php.

Millstein, Susan G., Anne C. Petersen, and Elena O. Nightingale. 1993. *Promoting the Health of Adolescents*. Oxford: Oxford University Press.

Mitaros, Elle. 2013. "No More Lonely Nights: Romantic Robots Get the Look of Love." *Sydney Morning Herald*, March 28. http://www.smh.com.au/technology/no-more-lonely-nights-romantic-robots-get-the-look-of-love-20130327-2guj3.html.

MIT Technology Review. 2011. "'Lovotics': The New Science of Engineering Human, Robot Love," June 30. https://www.technologyreview.com/s/424537/lovotics-the-new-science-of-engineering-human-robot-love/.

Mueller, Florian, Frank Vetere, Martin R. Gibbs, Jesper Kjeldskov, Sonja Pedell, and Steve Howard. 2005. "Hug over a Distance." *CHI'05 Extended Abstracts on Human Factors in Computing Systems*, 1673–6.

Nishio, Shuichi, Koichi Taura, and Hiroshi Ishiguro. 2012. "Regulating Emotion by Facial Feedback from Teleoperated Android Robot." In *Social Robotics*, edited by

Shuzhi Sam Ge, Oussama Khatib, John-John Cabibihan, Reid Simmons, Mary-Anne Williams, 388–97. Berlin: Springer.

Nomura, Shigueo, J. T. K. Soon, Hooman A. Samani, Isuru Godage, Michelle Narangoda, Adrian D. Cheok, and Osamu Katai. 2009. "Feasibility of Social Interfaces Based on Tactile Senses for Caring Communication." *8th International Workshop on Social Intelligence Design*, 68 (3).

Osley, Jonathan. 2007. "Bill of Rights for Abused Robots." *Independent*, March 31. http://www.independent.co.uk/news/science/bill-of-rights-for-abused-robots-5332596.html.

Russell, Anna C. B. 2009. "Blurring the Love Lines: The Legal Implications of Intimacy with Machines." *Computer Law & Security Review* 25 (5): 455–63.

Samani, H. Agraebramhimi. 2011. "Lovotics: Love+ Robotics, Sentimental Robot with Affective Artificial Intelligence." PhD dissertation, National University of Singapore.

Sullins, John P. 2012. "Robots, Love, and Sex: The Ethics of Building a Love Machine." *IEEE Transactions on Affective Computing* 3 (4): 398–409.

Sumioka, Hidenobu, Aya Nakae, Ryota Kanai, and Hiroshi Ishiguro. 2013. "Huggable Communication Medium Decreases Cortisol Levels." *Scientific Reports* 3.

Teh, James Keng Soon, Adrian David Cheok, Roshan L. Peiris, Yongsoon Choi, Vuong Thuong, and Sha Lai. 2008. "Huggy Pajama: A Mobile Parent and Child Hugging Communication System." *Proceedings of the 7th International Conference on Interaction Design and Children*, 250–7.

Torrance, Steve. 2008. "Ethics and Consciousness in Artificial Agents." *AI & Society* 22 (4): 495–521.

Torres, Ida. 2013. "Japanese Inventors Create Realistic Female 'Love Bot.'" *Japan Daily Press*. http://japandailypress.com/japanese-inventors-create-realistic-female-love-bot-2825990.

Truecompanion.com. 2016. "Home of the World's First Sex Robot." http://www.truecompanion.com/home.html.

Wikipedia. 2016. "Roxxxy." http://en.wikipedia.org/wiki/Roxxxy.

Yeoman, Ian and Michelle Mars. 2012. "Robots, Men and Sex Tourism." *Futures* 44 (4): 365–71.

Ziaja, Sonya. 2011. "Homewrecker 2.0: An Exploration of Liability for Heart Balm Torts Involving AI Humanoid Consorts." In *Social Robotics*, edited by Shuzhi Sam Ge, Oussama Khatib, John-John Cabibihan, Reid Simmons, Mary-Anne Williams, 114–24. Berlin: Springer.

Zhang, Emma Yann, Adrian David Cheok, Shogo Nishiguchi, and Yukihiro Morisawa. 2016. "Kissenger: Development of a Remote Kissing Device for Affective Communication." *Proceedings of the 13th International Conference on Advances in Computer Entertainment Technology*, 25.

14 CHURCH-TURING LOVERS

Piotr Bołtuć

One day, we may build a perfect robotic lover. It would be completely indistinguishable from a human lover in all things relevant to its love-making ability. In such a case, should one care whether one's lover is human or robotic? This boils down to whether one cares about one's lover only insofar as his or her functionalities are involved, or whether one also cares how the lover feels. In the latter instance, we would need to also care whether a lover has any first-person perceptions or feelings at all.

Many philosophers think that this is an intractable question. We are unable to communicate about our first-person feelings that are not fully expressed in our language: "Whereof one cannot speak, thereof one must be silent" (Wittgenstein 1922). It is even more hopeless to try to communicate those feelings that do not influence behavior in a unique way. Yet, for many people, it makes a major difference whether one's significant other can feel one's love, in all its emotional and perceptual specificities, or whether she or he is *just faking it.* This shows that one may have reasons to care about another person's first-person experience even if such experience was purely epiphenomenal.

14.1 Physical Interpretation of the Church-Turing Thesis

What are Church-Turing Lovers? They are sex robots that can attain every functionality that a human lover could, *at the desired level of granularity*. Those functionalities may include looks, specificities of movement, sound, all the way to the advanced features of touch, conversation, bodily fluids, or social companionship. The name "Church-Turing Lovers" (Boltuc 2011) was inspired by the physical interpretation of the Church-Turing Thesis. Let us begin with this last point.

The physical interpretation of the Church-Turing Thesis, in its broad and somewhat controversial form, may be understood as this claim: *all physically computable functions are Turing-computable*. Yet I refer to an even more controversial interpretation: *every finitely realizable physical system can be perfectly simulated by a universal model computing machine operating by finite means* (Deutsch 1985, 99). This claim implies that every physical system, such as a human being (under a physicalist interpretation), is effectively computable. In principle, the functioning of such a system can be described perfectly by a cognitive architecture that can be programmed with simple algorithms. Hence, it seems to follow that we should be able to program, e.g., in a complex future version of AutoCAD, a set of machines that would produce a robot with all the functionalities of a human being. This view is consistent with the philosophical conclusions drawn by many analytical philosophers, including the Churchlands, Dennett, and Fodor.

Both forms of broad physical interpretation of the Church-Turing Thesis have lately come under scrutiny, primarily by Piccinini (2007) and Copeland (2015). The main points of contention seem to pertain to the claims that (1) it is not true that all functions are Turing-computable (e.g., the halting function is not); and (2) neither Turing nor Church assumed such broad physical or philosophical implications of their claim. For the present purpose, we need not get into details of this debate, but the following point should be made.

Jack Copeland (2015) rightly argues that *it is an open question whether a completed neuroscience will employ functions that are not effectively calculable*. Yet it seems less of an open question, by far, whether a perfect simulation of a human lover, in appearance and behavior, would have to follow any non-calculable functions. A biologically inspired cognitive architecture (BICA) should be able, in principle at least, to replicate a human lover in all details, at the level of granularity relevant to his or her function as one's lover. An *improper level of granularity* may require a robot to have the same molecular or cell structure, or the same biology lying behind the functional level, as a human being. Such a requirement seems highly excessive—no sane person opens his or her lover's blood vessels or rips off some skin to see what lies within.

Such a cognitive architecture would constitute a blueprint for future engineering of a Church-Turing Lover. For the sake of philosophical argument, I assume that the Church-Turing Lover, so described, is conceptually available to discuss in the following sections.

14.2 The Church-Turing Standard

14.2.1 Good-Enough Church-Turing Robots

For the evaluation of artificial companions—including robotic lovers—oftentimes it is sufficient if they appear similar enough to human beings in a relevant respect. The *satisficing* approach in those cases is good enough (Floridi 2007). It would be cool to have the standard for a satisfactory human-like robot; we shall call it the Church-Turing Standard. A robot that satisfies this standard will be called a Church-Turing Robot. It is a robot that is close enough to a human being at the right level of granularity, assessed for a relevant domain. If we fail to meet the standard, we may hit the Uncanny Valley, a situation when a companion seems spooky instead of attractive; we zero in on this issue later on.

There are different domains in which one can assess the Church-Turing Standard; some may seem trivial, others barely attainable:

(1) An object can meet the Church-Turing Standard with respect to *looks* if, like a wax mannequin, it is indistinguishable from a human being at a specified distance or in a picture; the Ishiguro robots may have already met this standard.
(2) Robots would meet a more advanced Church-Turing Standard with respect to human-level *behavioral features* if their motor expressions required for a given task, from facial expressions and gestures to walk and even dance, were indistinguishable from those of humans.
(3) An object, e.g., a toy, meets the simple Church-Turing Standard with respect to *passive touch* if its surface is indistinguishable in touch from human skin. This topic is related not so much to robotics as to material science.
(4) A robot meets the Church-Turing Standard with respect to *active touch* if it can touch human beings in a way indistinguishable from human touch (the feature is useful in artificial companions, from elder-care robots to robot sex workers).

In order to meet the Church-Turing Standard, meeting the trivial functionalities (1) and (3) may be a necessary condition, but it is never sufficient since we need at least one functionality specific for robots, such as (2), (4), or (6), listed just below.

The Church-Turing Standard also applies to robot–human language-mediated communicative interactions:

(5) The simple Church-Turing Standard with respect to *communication* is identical with the Turing Test, in which communication relies on written messages (such as emails). The well-known Turing Test (Turing 1950) is therefore a special instance of the Church-Turing Standard. Church-Turing Robots would require language-based communication only in limited domains, which makes things easier, since the Turing Test for limited domains has already been met (Hornyak 2014).
(6) Meeting the *voice-based* domain of the Church-Turing Standard, which would be helpful, e.g., for a telemarketing Learning Intelligent Distribution

Agent (LIDA) (Franklin 2007), requires meeting the simple Church-Turing Standard with respect to communication that satisfies two additional conditions: (a) it has a human-quality voice interface; and (b) it normally takes place in real time. Voice interface put over text generate by the machine that is able to meet the Turing Test for the relevant domain and do so in the time frame appropriate for human-to-human verbal communication. For *multi-domain Church-Turing Artificial Companions*, such voice interface would be added to a robot with other satisfactory functionalities (visual and related to motion).[1]

14.2.2 Gold Standard for Church-Turing Robots

Let us define the *Church-Turing Gold Standard.* A robot satisfies the Gold Standard for given domains if its performance is within the parameters of human performance in those domains. Such a robot may be called the *Gold Church-Turing Robot.* It may be viewed as an implementation of Searle's criteria for soft AI; robots perform roughly in the way a human would, but this performance has been attained by different means.

The Church-Turing Gold Standard can be satisfied for limited domains, e.g., telephone conversations only, or it can be used for a broad spectrum of activities. For instance, the Gold Standard for human conversation at a five o'clock tea would require a robot to meet the standard for a human: (1) looks, (2) gestures that fit a given topic, such as language and culture, (3) conversation content, i.e., the Turing Test for the relevant domain, (4) conversation in spoken language, i.e., voice over the content, and (5) conversation level, i.e., informative and productive. Hence, for artificial companions to meet the Gold Standard, they may require not only human-like looks, touch, and movement but also advanced competency in conversational language use, e.g., IDA and LIDA provide human-level advanced productive interactions (Franklin 2007).

We may also talk of an even more advanced competency (5), which would be called the Church-Turing Creativity Machine. Gold Standard Creativity Machines create something, e.g., works of art (or ideas) at the same level human beings would (Thaler 2010), which leads us to the Church-Turing Platinum Standard.

14.2.3 Platinum Standard for Church-Turing Robots

Robots that surpass the Church-Turing Standard in a given domain, by performing better than a proficient human being, shall be named *Platinum Church-Turing Robots.* Platinum Church-Turing Robots perform within human standards and exceed them to some degree, just as a new generation of Olympic champions would. For example, a platinum-level robotic ice-skating champion would skate just as a human skater might, if trained, just a bit better. Its performance asymptotically approaches the standard of perfection in a given activity but never quite reaches it, except for the sorts of activities, such as games with relatively simple algorithms, where perfection is within human reach. It may be hard to imagine a platinum standard for robots, or human beings, that surpasses the best human level of performance in some domains, those in which human activity sets the standard, including lovemaking—*but what is imagination for*?

Platinum-standard humanoid robots are different from the so-called *singularity*. The singularity is understood as superhuman intelligence and performance that redefines the very standards (Kurzweil 2006). Its performance is way out of human reach, and in most versions even outside human comprehension. Machine-generated mathematical and logical proofs that cannot be followed by a human mathematician may help us grasp this term.

14.3 The Uncanny Valley of Perfection

14.3.1 The Good Old Uncanny Valley

In a recent article, Blay Whitby focuses on how sex toys may develop in a few years. He argues that there is a limit to our acceptance of sex toys as a replacement for human partners, largely because humanoid artificial companions, and sex partners, cause the *Uncanny Valley effect*, which is a good point if we work with today's robots (Whitby 2012). Yet if future sex robots imitate human beings well enough, they reach the other side of the Uncanny Valley and are accepted by most people as *nearly human*.

The Uncanny Valley deserves some extra attention. People find humanoid robots that are overly similar to human beings spooky, which is called the Uncanny Valley effect (Mori 2012; Reichardt 2012). It results from evolutionary avoidance of individuals who seem "not quite right" or are *proximal sources of danger, corpses, or members of different species* (Mori 2012). Let us examine the Uncanny Valley effect in some detail: As long as something does not appear too much like a human being, yet exhibits certain cute humanoid features (a teddy bear, a pet, even a puppet), we enjoy those slightly humanoid features. This is also true of the robots that satisfy two conditions: (1) they do not resemble human beings too closely; they may look like a harmless toy, such as Nao, or like a friendly teddy bear, such as Robear; and (2) they do not look scary, e.g., they are not gigantic tools. As soon as a creature closely imitates a human being but does not quite look like one, we feel major discomfort (try Topio, the tennis player); we may be scared (e.g., Atlas by Boston Dynamics) or repulsed (the pole-dancing robot). This group of robots are at the bottom of the Uncanny Valley.

As soon as some entity looks close enough to the way people do—and seems pleasant enough—we regain some confidence. This way we reach the other side of the Uncanny Valley and start climbing up. As the creature seems more and more like human beings and sufficiently pleasant, we become more and more comfortable with it. In practice, the solution to the Uncanny Valley problem for artificial companions is twofold: either building robots that look like cute toys and do not reach the downward slope or working on truly humanoid robots, close enough to us in all the characteristics they exhibit. Both avenues are being explored by the humanoid robot industry. Here we can see how the Church-Turing Standard presented above works in practice. The truly humanoid robots may be examined just on the basis of their looks, like mannequins, or they may also require resemblance to humans in certain actions (like Hanako 2, the dental robot), or additional similarities in touch, like sex robots, or human-like movement appropriate for the occasion, or even the ability to hold a conversation. With some experience, those humanoid robots, or voice-based interactive cognitive engines, do not strike us as spooky, even though they are far from meeting the Church-Turing Gold Standard. For instance, Showa Hanako 2, the dental robot, has a large number of humanoid functionalities, such as a realistic mouth and eye movements. Another female Japanese robot, SupernovaLucy, seems sexually attractive to many YouTube viewers, although she/it has no porn functionalities or provocative looks. It seems especially hard, but not impossible, to avoid the Uncanny Valley effects (repulsion) for potential object of sexual desires. While many sex toys stop short of reaching the Uncanny Valley, some sex robots, such as Matt McMullen's robotic lovers (e.g. Harmony that, among other functionalities, is programmed to give emotional feedback), seem to be made well enough to be reaching the other side of the valley. When artificial lovers become almost as humanoid as human beings, the Uncanny Valley effect dissipates.

Voice-based interactive customer interfaces can also plunge into the Uncanny Valley; many interfaces used by credit card companies seem to fall in that region, though they may be more annoying than spooky. But voice communication with an artificial cognitive agent more and more often emerges on the other side of the Uncanny Valley and climbs back toward close-enough similarity with human-to-human communication quality. The LIDA cognitive architecture used to schedule U.S. Navy sailors for assignments is preferred to the human schedulers by more than 90% of the clients (Franklin et al. 2007, 2008), which places them on the other side of the Uncanny Valley.

One sociocultural remark: different cultures have different degrees of tolerance for humanoid artificial creatures, with Japanese culture leading in such tolerance. As soon as robots appear humanoid enough, the effect of the Uncanny Valley dissipates. This is true unless people hold a view that robots can never cross the Uncanny Valley, even if they meet very high standards (or even become first-person-conscious), just because they are robots and therefore are non-biological or non-human. The attitude is entrenched in some societies and among several philosophers (Searle 1997), probably not for long, though. As the technology advances, our attitudes toward artificial companions become more accepting.

14.3.2 The Uncanny Cliff of Perfection

I think we can locate the *second Uncanny Valley*. It appears on the other side of the perfect imitation of human beings and their activities, when robots vastly outperform humans. The statement that Platinum Church-Turing Robots are not too much better than human beings is a way of avoiding a spooky effect that comes from performing too much above the human standard. For instance, Agent Smith in *The Matrix* is spooky because he runs way too fast and is way too hard to kill. Agent Smith satisfies an extended notion of the Uncanny Valley. The Uncanny Valley opens up not only to robots that are not good enough at being human, but also to those that are too good at it.[2] They diverge from human standards not by failing to meet them, but rather by overly surpassing them.

We can define the *Uncanny Valley of Perfection* as the spooky effect attained by humanoid-looking beings that are *not quite right* by being too perfect. While the traditional Uncanny Valley effect comes from the evolutionary tendency to avoid those who do not seem quite right by not being good enough (to avoid socializing with apes and very sick people), the Uncanny Valley of Perfection emerges when humanoids perform too well to qualify compared to the *regular folks*. Human geniuses who come too early in history to fit with the rest of society exemplify this Uncanny Valley effect, and many are killed or banished from their societies. Some people do not want their children, friends, or significant others to be *too perfect*. The second Uncanny Valley may in fact be a cliff, which has no other slope—strong discomfort that many people associate with the singularity may be just a far remote horizon of the Uncanny Cliff of Perfection.

14.3.3 The Slope of the Angels

Is there another side of the Uncanny Valley of Perfection? People in traditional cultures were spooked by creatures they thought of as a bit too perfect to be human—they tended to think of them as witches or creations of the devil. Yet they were enchanted by the idea of even more perfect beings, such as angels. This seems to give us reasons to think that there are two uncanny valleys: the *Uncanny Valley of Imperfection* and the *Uncanny Valley of Perfection*, both with another slope. On the other side of the Uncanny Valley of Perfection lies the upward *Slope of the Angels*. Creatures there are no longer viewed as humanoid dwell there, though they may have some features that allow interactions with humanity. In some theologies there are angels and archangels, and then even higher creatures, such as the seraphim, who may no longer interact with the human world but inspire awe. These theological views may reveal much about human psychology, our fear and sometimes disgust of beings that are not quite right, even if they seem better than human persons. This fear dissipates as such beings are viewed as not humanoid at all, such as toys and animals on one side, and perfect aliens or divinities, on the other.

The reflection about angels may be based just on religious narrative, but our eye is on future robots. The other side of the Uncanny Valley of Perfection may be of help in predicting human reactions to robots that are not humanoid but would approach the level of singularity, or some higher level still hard to describe. By reaching the other slope of the Uncanny Valley of Perfection those clearly superior cognitive structures may turn out to be less spooky to human beings than people speculate.

14.4 Epiphenomenal Lovers

14.4.1 Introducing Church-Turing Lovers Properly

Now we can define Church-Turing Lovers as Church-Turing Robots that are just like humans in the area of lovemaking. To satisfy the Church-Turing Gold Standard for human lovers, a robot needs to meet the human standard: (1) looks, (2) passive and active touch, (3) gestures and movements fit for the occasion, (4) reactivity and psychomotor interactivity with the partner, (5) smell (perfumes, body odors), (6) body moisture, such as sweat, saliva, and body fluids, (7) erotic sounds, and (8) basic conversational skills.

There are more advanced versions of a Church-Turing Lover: (9) a *longitudinal Church-Turing Lover* would also have memories of previous interactions; (10) an *emotionally engaged Church-Turing Lover* (such as Harmony) would be caring and behave as a human person in love; it might also play the role of an artificial companion (by cooking, taking care of the partner's health and well-being, etc.); and (11) a *socially embedded Church-Turing Lover* would be a part of one's social interactions (going to parties with one, , interacting with other people) in a way that would make it indistinguishable from one's human partner, so that one's friends may not be able to discover on their own that the lover was not a human being.

We may also speculate about (12) a *reproductive female Church-Turing Lover*, which would engage in childbearing, and perhaps childrearing, the way a human mother would; the work on artificial placenta is now advanced and it works for various mammalians. We could also think of a (13) *reproductive male*

Church-Turing Lover able to inseminate his partner with bioengineered human-quality semen, though this remains in the realm of science fiction. A Church-Turing Lover would be able to perform some of the above functions expected of one's human lover.

14.4.2 Nonfunctional Self

Would a Church-Turing Lover, as defined in this chapter, lack any relevant features of a human sex partner? Well, Church-Turing Gold Standard Lovers, by definition, would lack no functionality of human lovers (at the level of granularity required for such an activity). Since no functionality is missing, what could be left missing, if anything at all?

People care for others in order to experience life, its pleasures, love, beautiful sunsets, and many other things. It is considered selfish to care only about how my partner behaves and not about what she or he feels. We want our lovers to feel good and partake in all those good experiences. One of the things many sexual partners want to share is an orgasm; there is a difference between having an actual orgasm and just faking it. This is not so much a difference in behavior but in one's partner's *first-person feel*. Of course, many truly loving people are accepting of their lover being unable to have an orgasm, but this does not contradict the general observation. It makes sense to care what one's partner or a friend feels, even if such feelings are not represented in any behaviors and so are purely epiphenomenal. We care about his or her inner self even if it does not present itself in any external functions.[3]

Not to care whether one's lover feels anything at all is especially cold.[4] People scoff at those who have sex with stoned drug users, other unconscious individuals (even if their bodies are mobile in some way), not to mention dead bodies, even if there was prior consent—we expect the feeling of some sort. It is broadly agreed that today's robots are just moving bodies, machines; they are versions of philosophical zombies. We have no reason to attribute to them an internal feel of any kind. The lack of such feel makes an important difference between your partner and a Church-Turing Lover. This point shows how a purely epiphenomenal feel can matter in an objective difference.

14.4.3 Indirectly Relevant Epiphenomenalism

Here are some broader implications of Church-Turing Lovers. The first-person feel (phenomenal consciousness) is essentially accessible only to the person who does the phenomenal introspection. This is a version of the problem of other minds based on phenomenal experience. The search for such consciousness is relying on first-person testimonies and their correlation and corroboration, both by the testimonies of other people and by neural correlates of such testimonies, mostly grasped by fMRI. The methodology used is inductive inference to the best explanation (abduction), which is an indirect form of interpersonal verification. Philosophers inclined toward stronger versions of verificationism (e.g., Dennett 1991) tend to dismiss this kind of abductive confirmation of first-person consciousness as insufficient. Those philosophers who try to defend the view of first-person consciousness based on the phenomenal feel, generally speaking face the choice between the two views on consciousness: the *phenomenal markers view* and *epiphenomenalism.*

The phenomenal markers view claims that phenomenal experiences help us sort out a larger number of data than would be possible without them, just as it is usually easier to find a bright yellow folder in a pile of black folders than it is to identify one of the black folders. This is a version of a double-aspect theory since, in order to play a role of a practically useful marker, phenomenal qualities must partake, *qua phenomenal qualia*, in the functional scheme of things. (If they do not partake *qua* phenomenal qualia, but through neural correlates, we have an identity theory, which may be seen as epistemically non-reductive, but ontologically is a version of reductive physicalism.) To make a long epistemological story short, it is not clear that a double-aspect theory, so understood, is consistent with the phenomenal character of qualities. It encounters the problem of interaction between phenomenal properties and causal structure of the world, so the theory of phenomenal markers collapses into a version of dualism. It helps to ask whether the role of phenomenal qualia as markers can be played by physical properties that are not phenomenal. If so, then qualia become epiphenomenal; i.e., they play no role in making things happen. If non-phenomenal physical properties are unable to replace phenomenal properties, then we face the problem of interactionism again.

The obvious way to stay clear of interactionist dualism is to embrace the view that phenomenal qualia are epiphenomenal. Yet philosophers often view epiphenomenal properties as irrelevant. The case of Church-Turing Lovers gives us reasons to care whether one has first-person epiphenomenal consciousness or doesn't. If we could have one of the two lovers, one with and one without the first-person feel, we would have reasons to care that our lover has those first-person experiences even though that person's behavior could be perfectly replicable by a humanoid robot, thereby rendering those qualia merely epiphenomenal.

Such first-person consciousness is epiphenomenal and yet not irrelevant. One has reasons, indeed moral reasons, to care. I call the resulting view *indirectly relevant epiphenomenalism.*

14.5 Objections: Sex Without Love

Potential objections abound; here I'll address one. Russell Vannoy (1980) argued years ago that sex is best without love. Following this line of thought, one may not care whether one's lovers feel anything at all, as long as this does not affect their performance. Not that for Vannoy sex partners must be unemotional! First, the emotions in sex need not be love, according to Vannoy. Second, going beyond Vannoy's book, there are at least two meanings of emotion: functional and felt emotions. Emotions play a vital motivational role; they even enhance epistemic focus (Prinz 2012), but couldn't they be merely functional? Computer programmers talk of robot emotion in the latter sense. Individuals (especially robots) with no felt emotions—but with functional ones instead—may perform well, even better than their emotional counterparts. So one could have a functional replacement for felt emotions without the first-person feel. Some artificial cognitive architectures are now equipped with functional emotions that enhance their learning and other processes (Scheutz 2004).[5] It is possible to replicate such merely functional emotional structures in humans, which is good for those suffering from debilitating forms of autism. For performance one needs motivational factors that also enhance attention and learning, *not the first-person feel associated with those functions*. In humans and other animals, the function and the feel are closely linked but they may be parceled out. Hence, people may enjoy sex without any first-person feel by their partner—not only the feel of love. A mildly autistic, or robotic, lover may fake love or show other emotions instead. Vannoy's point is that loving behavior is not what results in the best sex—one can understand this view when thinking of BDSM.[6] This may be directly relevant to the topic of robotic sex workers (Levy 2009).

The relevance of Vannoy's point to my current argument is indirect. If one does not care about one's lover's love, one seems more likely not to care about her or his first-person feel of any kind. Instead, one may be inclined to care only about the behavior, the performance of one's lover. We are not here to deny that such sex exists and may be preferred by some. The point is that many people care about their partner's feelings, and the feel of love especially—those first-person private states. If one cares about one's partner deeply, one does not just care about the partner's behavior but what one's significant other feels for himself or herself. Many people care whether one's partner has the feelings or is just faking it. Since any expressions may come from causal chains that do not involve feelings at all, one's first-person feel is private and cannot be intersubjectively verified in any full-proof experiments, but only by inference to the best explanation. Yet it makes sense to care whether our loved ones have such a feel and, in particular, what it is like for them to feel the experiences we share.

14.6 How Church-Turing Lovers May Get the Feel of It

Are robotic lovers forever deprived of the first-person feel? Could they, one day, find the way toward the first-person feel that Mr. Data (*Star Trek, The Next Generation*) tried to discover? If we accept non-reductive physicalism, there is a chance! Here is the argument to this effect called the *Engineering Thesis in Machine Consciousness*:

(1) Someday neuroscience should be able to learn how animal brains generate first-person consciousness.
(2) Detailed knowledge about how brains do it would allow us to reverse-engineer a projector of first-person consciousness.
(3) If we have projectors of first-person consciousness, we should be able to project first-person consciousness. (Boltuc 2009, 2010, 2012)

This does not mean that we would *create* consciousness. We would project the stream of consciousness, a bit like we used projectors of old-fashioned movies where the slides were projected onto the screen by a stream of light. Robots are not prevented by some human-centered principles, such as Searle's *mentations*, from acquiring first-person consciousness.

The main concerns of the Engineering Thesis include (1) How would we know that a machine attained first-person consciousness? This epistemic concern is a version of the problem of other minds applied to non-human beings. (2) What are the moral ramifications of non-reductive machine consciousness? Would it be morally acceptable to build machines with first-person consciousness, and if so what rights would they have? What would be the moral differences, and similarities, between such machines and conscious animals, as well as humans? (3) Practical concerns: it is possible that, having learned how human minds/brains produce the first-person feel, we may understand that the task is too complex to reverse-engineer; or maybe it has to be bioengineered only in organic matter, in which case it may be unclear what the difference is between re-engineering and just growing (e.g., cloning) an animal brain or its parts.

While some of those concerns may turn out to be justified, we are too far away from knowing how the first-person feel of conscious experience is generated to be able to address them now. The argument for the Engineering Thesis in Machine Consciousness, even if (for the time being) it is just a theoretical proposition, allows us to grasp how non-reductive consciousness can be viewed in serious physicalist terms.

Conclusions: Why Does It Matter?

The Church-Turing Lover argument is a follow-up to the Engineering Thesis. It helps us see how a physicalist interpretation of first-person consciousness might be of significance, even if such consciousness had no impact on any actions of the subject, i.e., if it was epiphenomenal. We do not follow Searle's approach, that there is something essentially unique to animal brains as the only possible loci of the first-person stream of consciousness. The Engineering Thesis shows that, at least in principle, such first-person stream of consciousness may also be built in robots. Hence, not all robots need to be just Church-Turing Lovers, artificial companions, or other things; they may perhaps one day acquire first-person consciousness.

The case of Church-Turing Lovers helps us think about the following issues: (1) They allow us to show how epiphenomenal qualia may not be irrelevant since they provide *reasons to care*; (2) they provide a robotic permutation of the problem of other minds (and the *experience machine*) in epistemology, which have consequences for ethics; and (3) they help formulate the issue of non-reductive robot consciousness, with its ethical implications.

What does it mean when a lover says, "I love you"? The Church-Turing Lover has all the propensities to please you, even computer emotions that change the character of its long-term narratives and behavior. Yet, philosophically, it is a zombie, though a very kind one.[7]

Here is why epiphenomenal consciousness matters ethically: Would you have reason to care whether your significant other were a zombie of this sort? If you think that a part of love is not just pleasant treatment but that love presupposes caring about how the loved one feels, then it is important that there be something it is like for her or him to *feel happy*, not just to *act happy*.

Notes

1. To be close enough in the domain of artificial companions, and especially sex robots, the machine needs to be on the ascendant side of the Uncanny Valley so that people aren't spooked by it. Incidentally, robots that imitate humans or animals to some degree but do not even reach the Uncanny Valley—e.g., a cleaning Roomba machine with the face of a cute teddy bear painted on it—would not be subject to the Church-Turing Standard.
2. Actually, some aspects of Agent Smith (looks) place him in the first Uncanny Valley, and others (speed, power) in the second.
3. In medicine, this is important in the case of locked-in syndrome.
4. Thanks to Alan Hajek for this point.
5. A mouse runs away due to a change in its cortisol level; a robot mouse "runs away" due to variable called "cortisol" (Long and Kelley 2010)
6. The issue of whether we are morally obligated to avoid causing suffering is a bit complicated in philosophy of sex and love, even within utilitarian values. This is due to the complexities introduced not only by the followers of De Sade, but primarily by Leopold von Sacher-Masoch, credited as the main modern author who endorsed sexual masochism.
7. Emotive aspects of zombies, often presented as bloodthirsty and highly unkind; those of Church-Turing Lovers are very different.

Works Cited

Boltuc, Peter. 2009. "The Philosophical Issue in Machine Consciousness." *International Journal of Machine Consciousness* 1 (1): 155–76.

Boltuc, Peter. 2010. "A Philosopher's Take on Machine Consciousness." In *Philosophy of Engineering and the Artifact in the Digital Age*, edited by Viorel E. Guliciuc, 49–66. Newcastle upon Tyne: Cambridge Scholars Press.

Boltuc, Peter. 2011. "What Is the Difference between Your Friend and a Church-Turing Lover?" In *The Computational Turn: Past, Presents and Futures?*, edited by. Charles Ess and Ruth Hagengruber, 37–40. Aarhus: Aarhus University Press.

Boltuc, Peter. 2012 "The Engineering Thesis in Machine Consciousness." *Techne: Research in Philosophy and Technology* 16 (2): 187–207.

Copeland, B. Jack. 2015. "The Church-Turing Thesis." In *The Stanford Encyclopedia of Philosophy*, Summer 2015 ed., edited by Edward N. Zalta. http://plato.stanford.edu/archives/sum2015/entries/church-turing/.

Dennett, Daniel. 1991. *Consciousness Explained.* Boston: Little, Brown.

Deutsch, David. 1985. "Quantum Theory, the Church-Turing Principle and the Universal Quantum Computer." *Proceedings of the Royal Society* Series A 400 (1818): 97–117.

Floridi, Luciano. 2007. "Artificial Companions and Their Philosophical Challenges." *E-mentor*, May 22. http://www.e-mentor.edu.pl/artykul/index/numer/22/id/498.

Franklin, Stan, Bernard Baars, and Uma Ramamurthy. 2008. "A Phenomenally Conscious Robot?" *APA Newsletter on Philosophy and Computers* 8 (1). https://c.ymcdn.com/sites/www.apaonline.org/resource/collection/EADE8D52-8D02-4136-9A2A-729368501E43/v08n1Computers.pdf.

Franklin, Stan, Uma Ramamurthy, Sidney K. D'Mello, Lee McCauley, Aregahegn Negatu, Rodrigo Silva L., and Vivek Datla. 2007. "LIDA: A Computational Model of Global Workspace Theory and Developmental Learning." Memphis, TN: University of Memphis, Institute for Intelligent Systems and the Department of Computer Science. http://ccrg.cs.memphis.edu/assets/papers/LIDA%20paper%20Fall%20AI%20Symposium%20Final.pdf.

Hornyak, Tim. 2014. "Supercomputer Passes Turing Test by Posing as a Teenager: Program Mimics the Responses of a 13-Year-Old Boy, Fooling Some Human Judges." *Computerworld*, June 6.

Kurzweil, Ray. 2006. *The Singularity Is Near: When Humans Transcend Biology.* London: Penguin Books.

Levy, David. 2009. *Love and Sex with Robots.* New York: HarperCollins.

Long, L. N. and T. D. Kelley. 2010 "Review of Consciousness and the Possibility of Conscious Robots." *Journal of Aerospace Computing, Information, and Communication* 7, 68–84.

Mori, Masahiro. 2012. "The Uncanny Valley." *IEEE Spectrum*, June 12.

Piccinini, Gualtiero. 2007. "Computationalism, the Church–Turing Thesis, and the Church–Turing Fallacy." *Synthese* 154: 97–120.

Prinz, Jesse. 2012. *The Conscious Brain: How Attention Engenders Experience.* Oxford: Oxford University Press.

Reinhardt, Jasia. 2012. "An Uncanny Mind: Masahiro Mori on the Uncanny Valley and Beyond." *IEEE Spectrum*, June 12.

Scheutz, Matthias. 2004. "How to Determine the Utility of Emotions." *Proceedings of AAAI Spring Symposium*, 334–40.

Searle, John. 1997. *The Mystery of Consciousness.* New York: New York Review of Books.

Thaler, Stephen. 2010. "Thalamocortical Algorithms in Space! The Building of Conscious Machines and the Lessons Thereof." In *Strategies and Technologies for a Sustainable Future.* World Future Society.

Turing, Alan. 1950. "Computing Machinery and Intelligence," *Mind* 59 (236): 433–60.

Vannoy, Russell. 1980. *Sex Without Love: A Philosophical Exploration.* Amherst, NY: Prometheus Books.

Wittgenstein, Ludwig 1922. *Tractatus Logico Philosophicus*. https://www.gutenberg.org/files/5740/5740-pdf.pdf.

Whitby, Blay. 2012. "Do You Want a Robot Lover? The Ethics of Caring Technologies." In *Robot Ethics: The Ethical and Social Implications of Robotics*, edited by Patrick Lin, Keith Abney, and George A. Bekey, 233–48. Cambridge, MA: MIT Press.

15 THE INTERNET OF THINGS AND DUAL LAYERS OF ETHICAL CONCERN

Adam Henschke

The internet of things (IoT) is poised to be the next step in the information revolution. Its effects on people's quality of life will most likely be equivalent to the impacts felt from the internet. "[T]he core concept is that everyday objects can be equipped with identifying, sensing, networking and processing capabilities that will *allow them to communicate* with one another and with other devices and services over the Internet *to achieve some useful objective*" (Whitmore, Agarwal, and Da Xu 2015, 261; my emphasis).

Rather than human-to-human communication, the IoT builds from the simple notion of objects in our world being able to communicate with each other. "In fact, it is this ability for objects to communicate that delivers the power of the IoT" (Fletcher 2015, 20). Moreover, this is not simply a matter of producing and collecting information for its own sake; the intention is *to achieve some useful objective*. Whether it is about logistics or controlling your house, the IoT derives its importance from the fact that the information produced by the communicating objects is intended to bring about some change in the physical world.

The size of the IoT is expected to be immense: it is estimated that by 2020, there will be 20–50 billon things connected as part of the IoT (Mohammed 2015), leading some to predict an investment of 1.7 trillion U.S. dollars by 2020 (International Data Corporation 2015):

> A sensing and actuation utility will not only exist in public spaces, but also extend into the home, apartments, and condominiums. Here, people will be able to run health, energy, security, and entertainment apps on the infrastructure. Installing and running new apps will be as easy as plugging in a new toaster into the electric utility. One app may help monitor and

> control heart rate, another perform financial and investments services, and another automatically ordering food and wine, or even predicting an impending medical problem that should be addressed early to mitigate or even avoid the problem. (Stankovic 2014, 4)

Given its enormous potential to impact our lives through medical or financial services, or by reconfiguring personal spaces like the home or our industrial systems, the IoT is of great ethical importance. And much like a general class of "roboethics," which applies to "the philosophical studies and researches about the ethical issues arising from the effects of the application of robotics products on our society" (Veruggio and Abney 2012, 347), an ethics of the IoT is—in part at least—concerned with the ethical issues arising from the application of IoT and its products in our society.

While there are certainly key differences between robots and the IoT, as this chapter will show, given that the IoT has as its core the capacities to derive information from the physical world, to process and communicate that information, and to then use the information in a way that affects the physical world, we can see the IoT as a robot (or set of robots), a complex system of sensing, processing, and effector systems, though one that is massively distributed.

The internet of things presents special ethical challenges because it spans two layers of ethical concern. First, the IoT consists of machines operating in the physical realm. It thus relates to the specific areas of robot ethics that are concerned with the ways that our devices impact human safety. "We have learned by now that new technologies, first and foremost, need to be safe" (Lin 2012, 7). Safety is thus the first layer of ethical concern. Second, the IoT relates to the informational realm. Therefore, a meaningful ethics relating to the IoT must have a particular focus on the ethics of information—its production, storage, and use, forming the second layer of ethical concern. Following a summary of the ethical concerns of the two layers, this chapter will argue that designers, policymakers, and users must not only pay attention to both layers, but may also have to make decisions that prioritize one layer of ethical concern over the other.

At its core, the IoT refers to the cluster of technologies that enable electronic devices to interact with the physical world and communicate with each other (Mennicken et al. 2015). A smart fridge, for example, enabled with particular sensor technology will register what food you have in your fridge, how long the food has been there, what you're eating, what you're not, and so on (Xie et al. 2013). It may prepare shopping lists for you based on your eating habits. What's more, the smart fridge may be linked to your phone (Poulter 2014), which—when the Global Positioning System (GPS) in your phone recognizes that you are in the supermarket—can tell you what to buy and what to avoid. Your phone might be linked to your bank account (Maas and Rajagopalan 2012) so that you know how much you have got to spend. The core idea is that your "things" are networked and have a capacity for mutual communication.

Further, the IoT actualizes the capacity for these things to make decisions and be physically active. Imagine now that, instead of your having to go shopping, your fridge can check your personal shopping list, and after communicating with the biosensor technologies in your toothbrush, toilet, and gym gear, know what foods best fit your current diet and exercise plan (Baker 2007). After cross-referencing with your bank to check your weekly budget, the smart fridge orders food to be delivered by drone from the supermarket's closest supply chain hub. The delivery is collected by specialized devices that shuttle the foods from your home's specified drone drop-off point into the relevant sections of your fridge.[1] What is relevant here is that your smart fridge is not just communicating with a range of other devices inside and beyond your home; it is also making decisions based on those communications and is engaging with the physical world. The IoT combines the communications revolution of the internet with the capacity of robots to engage with the physical realm.

These elements—physicality and communications—have their own set of ethical concerns. The IoT increases the importance of these concerns, forces decisions to be made between the dual layers of concern, and raises a new set of emergent concerns. It increases the importance of these concerns by putting humans directly at risk of physical danger, poor communications, and decisions across these layers. It forces decisions to be made between the dual layers, as there may be certain design features that prioritize one layer's primary ethical concerns over the other. And finally, it raises the prospect of emergent ethical concerns, where the combination of the physical and informational realms presents new ethical challenges that cannot be reduced to either layer and may be hard to predict in advance. While this chapter is primarily descriptive in that it seeks to describe the special set of ethical concerns about the IoT rather than a particular normative approach, it does hold a specific moral position—that there is a moral responsibility for designers, policymakers, and users to have some level of awareness of the ethical challenges that the IoT poses—particularly, that these challenges cross a number of areas of ethics and that any morally robust response must recognize this plurality of moral layers.

15.1 The Physical Layer: Robots and Physical Safety

The first layer of ethical concern relates to the physical realm. Given that this book collection covers a range of ethical approaches to problems arising from intelligent machines operating in the physical realm, this section will focus on the specific claim that the IoT exists in the physical realm and will address particular concerns for human safety that the physical layer of the IoT poses. "Safety in IoT means being able to reason about the behavior of IoT devices, especially actuators, and being able to detect and prevent unintended or unexpected behavior" (Agarwal and Dey 2016, 41).

The first point to draw out is that IoT should be thought of as a *massively distributed series of robots*. To explain, the IoT refers to a complex network of interactive elements. The kind of network that I am considering here is an integrated network composed of multiple components, each technically advanced in its own right, which are arranged in such a way as to achieve an end that has multiple components. Common elements of the IoT are sensors (Li, Xu, and Zhao 2015), informational processors (Agarwal and Dey 2016; Whitmore, Agarwal, and Da Xu 2015) and actuators (Stankovic 2014): some way of bringing about physical change.

This physical component expressed by actuators makes the IoT functionally equivalent to a series of robots, though massively distributed. Robots can be thought to have "three key components: 'sensors' that monitor the environment and detect changes in it, 'processors' or 'artificial intelligence' that decides how to respond, and 'effectors' that act upon the environment in a manner that reflects the decisions, creating some sort of change in the world" (Singer 2009, 67). The IoT is the same: it consists of sensors, processors, and effectors or actuators. As George A. Bekey puts it, we can think of a robot as "*a machine, situated in the world, that senses, thinks, and acts*" (Bekey 2012, 18; emphasis in original). While the parts and outcomes are the same as those of a typical robot, the difference is that IoT is not *physically* integrated into one single recognizable entity. Instead, it is *informationally* integrated—a point I will discuss in the next section.

Second, the IoT is distinct from the internet as it explicitly incorporates and "acts" in the physical realm. Like a robot, it has "effectors" that act upon the physical environment. Without this element, the IoT would be functionally equivalent to the internet as we know it. "We stipulate that the robot must be *situated in the world* in order to distinguish it [as] a physical robot from software running on a computer, or, a 'software bot'" (Bekey 2012, 18; emphasis in original). Likewise, the IoT refers to things that are active in the physical world; otherwise we would simply be referring to the internet. "[T]he integration of sensors/actuators, RFID tags, and communication technologies serves as the foundation of IoT and explains how a variety of physical objects and devices around us can be associated to the Internet and allow these objects and devices to cooperate and communicate with one another to reach common goals" (Xu, He, and Li 2014, 2233). However, like the internet, the IoT gains its importance and capacity through the connections between remote elements—in this case, physically remote elements.

The GPS in your car may be linked to light sensors outside and inside your house and to the light bulbs in your home. The GPS in your phone can be linked to the lock in your front door. As your car arrives home, the light sensors register the background levels of light to decide if the lights in your home should be turned on for your arrival. You park your car, and your phone's proximity to the house causes the front door to unlock. The integration of these elements means changes in the physical realm—lights turn on, doors unlock.

The chief concern with these integrated sensors, processors, and actuators is that we have created a "network of vulnerability": should one of these elements fail, be broken or interfered with, the outcomes can have direct physical impacts. A network of vulnerability refers to two points: origin and impact. First, the communications are open or vulnerable to accident or misuse (Symantec Security Response 2014); the communicative connections between the sensors, processors, and effectors are the origin of the vulnerability. Second, the impact extends beyond the origin of the accident or misuse; the thing that is vulnerable to harms arising from accident or misuse can be geographically or temporally distant from the origin. In a network of vulnerability, one mistake or misuse can have consequences that carry and disperse in ways that can be quite severe.

Think now of a smart house, where the different components have sensing, processing, and actuator capacities. A smart light bulb that can tell the smart house that it needs changing seems innocuous enough. However, in 2015, the smart house of computer science professor Raul Rojas "up and stopped responding to his commands. . . . Nothing worked. I couldn't turn the lights on or off. It got stuck. . . . It was like when the beach ball of death begins spinning on your computer—except it was his entire home" (Hill 2015). The reason for this was that one of the smart light bulbs had burned out and was "sending continuous requests that had overloaded the network and caused it to freeze. . . . It was a classic denial of service attack. . . . The light was performing a DoS attack on the smart home to say, 'Change me'" (Hill 2015). The point here is that, because of the network of vulnerability, the networked nature of the IoT and its extension into the physical realm means that glitches caused by minor programming errors can have ethically concerning physical impacts.

Imagine now that the problem is not a house shutting down but a glitch in a self-driving car. Instead of shutting down the house, an error causes the self-driving car to break or accelerate automatically. While designers of automated cars may plan for this (Lin 2013), what about other cars on the road? Much like the sudden acceleration in Toyota vehicles that led to multiple fatalities and caused the U.S. Justice Department to fine Toyota 1.2 billion U.S. dollars (Douglas and Fletcher 2014), given the physicality of the IoT the crashing of a system can lead to physical car crashes, posing a major risk for human safety. These safety issues of vehicle-to-vehicle interactions highlight the more general point that the IoT is about the physical realm and that humans are vulnerable to glitches or problems of programing in a way that is more immediately pressing than safety issues around the internet.

Finally, consider that the vulnerabilities in a system are not limited to accidents but include opportunities for malicious actors. A chief concern with the IoT is that many of the elements have weak informational security, discussed later. This weak informational security presents exploitable vulnerabilities for malicious actors. Instead of a house locking you out, the malicious actor can now use the informational vulnerability of the networked house to *unlock* the house, to disable any relevant security systems, and give the malicious actors entry and access to your home's valuables. Again, it is the physical nature of the IoT that is of relevance here—with door locks being an element of the physical realm, informational vulnerabilities can lead to physical vulnerabilities.[2]

Further, much like the car crashing from a computer glitch, a malicious actor could use the physical reality of the IoT to physically threaten or endanger people. Consider a smartphone that is infected with a virus when its owner plugs it into an unsafe public charging point (Malenkovich 2013). A malicious actor then uses this vulnerability in the phone to exploit connections to linked devices, like a car. The malicious actor now locks children in a car on a hot day unless a ransom is paid. Like many of the concerns about robots, that the IoT is physical means that there are issues of physical safety that can be easily overlooked due to the networked nature of the vulnerabilities.

15.2 The Informational Layer: Information and Security

The second layer of ethical concern is informational. As said, one of the core elements of the Internet of things is that these things are communicating. The precise nature of the communications is as diverse as the range of things that are or will be part of the IoT: a radio frequency identification (RFID) chip in a food container that tells a particular sensor what the specific food product is; the RFID in a 2-liter container of full-cream milk tells the smart fridge that it is 2 liters of full-cream milk; a geo-locator linked to GPS tells a satellite where a car is physically located at a given time; a camera in a smart TV sends live feed to be stored in the cloud; a microphone in a smartphone picks up a voice command; and a biometric device in a smart toilet analyzes samples for markers of bowel health.

The motivation for introducing such a range of communications is that the networking of these communications leads to vastly richer information about our lives and ideally leads to improved quality of life. Think of smoke detectors:

> Why do most smoke detectors do nothing more than make loud beeps if your life is in mortal danger because of fire? In the future, they will flash your bedroom lights to wake you, turn on your home stereo, play an MP3 audio file that loudly warns, "Fire, fire, fire." They will also contact the fire department, call your neighbors (in case you are unconscious and in need

> of help), and automatically shut off flow to the gas appliances in the house. (Goodman 2015)

Consider the problem of aging populations in the developed world and the ways that the IoT might allow many of the elderly to live relatively autonomous lives in their homes—family members can directly communicate with them via the camera in the smart TV; caretakers can be alerted if any changes in health or lifestyle occur; emergency services can be called should the elderly person fall at home. All of this is possible due to the IoT.

However, such an informationally rich environment presents considerable challenges to individual privacy. These challenges may be direct, as the IoT enables the devices to communicate directly with the outside world (Symantec Security Response 2014). This is obviously a concern for a smart home, but consider an IoT-enriched workplace—for instance, a work desk with sensors could record the time each worker spends at his or her desk, which a manager can access at will. This employee surveillance can extend beyond the workplace. In one example an employee claims she was "fired after uninstalling an app that her employer required her to run constantly on her company issued iPhone—an app that tracked her every move 24 hours a day, seven days a week" (Kravets 2015). The first ethical issue with the informational layer is one of fairness—is it fair for information produced in the personal sphere to be used by employers in another sphere for the assessment of employee quality? On Jeroen van den Hoven's approach to informational fairness, this would be a case of informational injustice (van den Hoven 2008).

Further, the IoT poses a considerable indirect challenge to privacy: what the IoT represents is not just a vast capacity to collect and store information on people, but the capacity for that information to be aggregated, analyzed, and communicated to people far beyond those receiving the initial information. This means that increasingly intimate elements of our lives can be revealed by the collection of seemingly innocuous data. "[W]here a multitude of dots juxtaposed together form a picture, bits of information when aggregated paint a portrait of a person" (Solove 2004, 44). The aggregation and integration of information about a person produce something new: a rich and detailed portrait of the person. The time one gets out of bed, the food one buys and eats, the amount of time spent exercising: as independent data points they will tell little of interest about the person. But when large amounts of data are accumulated through time and if these separate data streams are aggregated, a "portrait" of this person emerges.

The ethical relevance is that these virtual portraits, produced from the aggregation of personal information, reveal highly intimate details about our lives. Rather than simply think of privacy as something necessarily secret, we can also see privacy as being about intimacy. Privacy-as-intimacy is a theory that holds that it is not the particular content of something that determines its privacy; rather it is the relation between the private information and the person. "This theory appropriately realizes that privacy is essential not just for individual self-creation, but also for human relationships" (Solove 2008, 34). The relation we have to our information, what information we care about, and to whom it is revealed takes precedence when we think of privacy-as-intimacy:

> [T]he revealing of personal information takes on significance. The more one knows about the other, the more one is able to understand how the other experiences things. . . . The revealing of personal information then is not what constitutes or powers the intimacy. Rather, it deepens and fills out, invites and nurtures, the caring that powers the intimacy . . . it is of little importance who has access to personal information about me. What matters is who cares about it and to whom I care to reveal it. (Reiman 1976, 34)

The IoT, with its capacity to produce vast swaths of personal information that can then be aggregated and analyzed to reveal highly intimate details of our lives can lead to considerable violations of privacy-as-intimacy. We now have a second set of concerns: the ways that the IoT produces and aggregates seemingly innocuous personal information and the potential violations of privacy (Henschke, forthcoming).

Drawing out from the capacity to reveal intimate details of a person's life, the informational layer of the IoT presents considerable challenges to informational security. While we are familiar with the idea of keeping our credit card details safe from potential identity thieves, the IoT presents a huge challenge for security due to the collection of personal information. Many "smart" devices that are already in the marketplace have very limited information security. Cameras on smart TVs, for example, could be remotely accessed by strangers because of the lack of effective activation of security (Fink and Segall 2013). Mass-produced consumer products are typically produced, shipped, and used with the original default settings on informational access intact. So-called internet facing devices that retain the factory security settings are like an open window or open door to a burglar. Furthermore, as these devices are networked, the lax security settings on one device could potentially give access to other devices. The factory setting on your smart toothbrush might allow a hacker to access all of your health information. The point here is that information security is given a low priority by designers and users—which becomes relevant when we look at the tensions across the different layers of concern. Information security, while related to issues of fairness and privacy, presents a third distinct set of ethical concerns.

Another key element of the informational layer is that information can be constantly reused. "[I]nformation doesn't wear out. It [can] be endlessly recycled [and] repackaged" (Drahos and Braithwaite 2002, 58–9). The information your fridge collects about your eating habits can be used for shopping, or to target advertising, or for healthcare. The problem with this information reusability is that it presents a considerable challenge to the notion of informed consent. If, as discussed earlier, the aggregation of personal information collected by the IoT produces an intimate picture of a person, then informed consent demands that the collection, communication, and use of that information requires the source of the information to be informed about who is using it, when they are using it, and what for (Henschke forthcoming). However, given the range of devices, the networks that arise between different devices and the potential for multiple uses are so vast that prediction is close to impossible. And if the suppliers of the products and services cannot reliably predict the full range of uses of the source's personal information, then a user cannot be reliably informed, and one of the key elements of informed consent is lost. This is not a new problem—the open nature of information in genetic databases has shown the limits of informed consent (Clayton 2005)—but one that will become more widely experienced as the IoT extends into our lives. Informed consent is thus a fourth area of ethical concern arising from the informational layer.

Following from the issue of informed consent is the issue of property rights. Property rights over personal information are typically formalized by end-user license agreements (EULAs), the forms we typically click through when downloading new software on a computer or accessing certain commercial websites. How legally enforceable these EULAs are is a controversial issue (Buchanan and Zimmer 2015). We can expect that the IoT, with its myriad of informational types, produced by a range of devices that are serviced and supported by a range of commercial interests, will make the legal enforcement of property rights over the personal information extremely complex legally. Property rights, often overlooked due to the attention paid to issues of privacy and security, presents a fifth set of ethical concerns relevant to the informational layer.

15.3 Safety and Control: Tensions Across the Layers

While these are complex issues in and of themselves, the key point of this chapter is to draw attention to a tension across these two layers. That is, we face a problem of moral pluralism—which of these layers of ethical concern should take priority? The discussion so far has focused on particular moral challenges arising from the IoT. In the physical realm we face the challenge of human physical vulnerability. Whether we're concerned with the risk of an accident, the danger posed by malicious actors, or the murky terrain of autonomous decision-making, the physical realm poses a layer of ethical concerns. These can all be linked by reference to one chief motivating concern: human safety. That the IoT operates in the physical realm means that we have a set of ethical concerns about ensuring the physical safety of people. As said, we can capture this layer of concern best by thinking of the IoT as a distributed robot and then looking to the set of ethical discussions around robots and physical safety.

However, the IoT also exists in the informational realm, and thus we have a second set of ethical concerns about the production, use, and distribution of that information. These can all be linked by reference to one chief motivating concern: information control. Who has access to the information, what can they do with this information, and who is impacted by that information's access and use? The informational realm extends beyond standard time and space constraints—the point about informed consent shows that our use of information now might be different to the who, what, and where of its use into the future. And like the internet (Solove 2004), those having access to the information have no necessary physical proximity to the sources or targets of information use. We can capture this layer of concern best by considering the issues around control over that information.

To show that there is a tension across these two layers, consider the design choices about default settings on who can access and control the effectors of some part of the IoT, like turning a light bulb on or off. On one hand, we want fairly open access to this light bulb, because, as was seen with the earlier example of the light that shut down the smart house, the network of vulnerability means that the person reliant upon and vulnerable to errors arising from the light bulb may need rapid, easy, and reliable customer support. And the efficiency of this is going to be highly contingent upon how quickly and easily the customer support can identify and resolve the issue. Lower barriers of access mean that the problem is likely to be resolved much more quickly. While a faulty light bulb may seem unproblematic in our current houses, the network of vulnerability means that the physical impacts of a faulty smart bulb could shut down an entire house. When thinking of integrated self-driving cars, we would want physical safety to be a priority—delays in effective support here can mean much more than inconvenience; people's lives are at risk.

On the other hand, we also want tight restrictions on access and control. The ethical issues raised by the informational realm show that we should see information control as a primary concern. Maximally open networks with low barriers of access might be great for physical safety but are terrible for information security. Smart TVs have been recent sources of controversy, as they have been shown to record users' watching habits (Fink and Segall 2013) and listen in on users' conversations (Matyszczyk 2015), all without users' knowledge or consent. Tightly limiting the control over who can access the information, what they can do with that information, and the speed at which they can do it ensures that privacy, security, even informed consent and property rights are maximally protected.

So now we face our tension: there are good reasons to have minimally restrictive access that allows rapid response and control, while at the same time, there are good reasons to have maximally restricted access to prevent easy response and control. Some cases might more obviously favor one layer of concern over the other—fast-moving cars filled with passengers would probably want to preference physical safety over information control, and the camera in a smart TV would probably want to preference information control over physical safety. However, in many cases it is not immediately apparent which of the layers of concern we should prioritize. Consider the smart smoke alarm that is integrated with other devices in the home; human physical safety is obviously a desirable moral feature of a smart house. But consider that an integrated smoke alarm would likely be designed such that it favors false positives over false negatives; it is better to have it activate when there is no fire than not have it activate when there is a fire. And in the world of the IoT, as has already happened with smart TVs, this integrated device allows an operator to access cameras and microphones spread through devices through the house to check if there is an actual fire and/or if there are people active within the house. Such a set of networks are now sacrificing privacy for safety; operators can activate cameras in the house to observe its occupants in cases where there is no actual fire.

While one set of users of the devices might favor one setting over the other (maximal safety/minimal information control), another might be equally justified in favoring the other setting (minimal safety/maximal information control). The problem here is that, should the first set of users have their privacy breached by malicious hackers, who is morally responsible for this breach? Similarly, imagine that the house of someone in the second set of users burns down, should the user bear the economic cost of her decision or should an insurance company? Further to this, should the insurance company have access to the settings chosen by the second set of users?

Adding even further complication to the assignment of liability for risk are the cognitive biases that occur in the process of risk assessment. The availability heuristic (Kahneman 2011, 7–9) means that we will often pay more attention to unexpected and novel events, and thus weigh those novel events more heavily in our risk assessments, than events that we are more familiar with. For instance, we worry more about terrorist attacks than being injured in a car crash, though the second event is far more likely to occur than the first (Toynbee 2015). If we know that cognitive biases play a role in decisions about which settings are chosen, which layer of concern to favor, how should we incorporate this into the assignment of liability for the outcomes of the given choices? This chapter does not seek solutions to these moral dilemmas. Rather, the purpose is to show that the IoT, with its dual layers of concern, requires us to recognize that designers, policymakers, and users are being forced to make very complex moral decisions. Further to this, as the complexity is spread across two quite different layers of concern, there is no easy set of guides or principles that can be offered to make better choices.

Ultimately, the recognition of multiple ethical layers of concern arising from the application of a complex system across multiple layers of concern means that we cannot *predict* what sorts of events or mishaps may occur (Kroes 2009, 277). However, this does not mean that we are unable to *anticipate* that certain sorts of ethical challenges will arise. By recognizing that the IoT is situated across two layers of ethical concern, designers are in a better place to anticipate that decisions about safety may also impact information control. Likewise, users are in a better position to recognize that their favoring of one set of ethical concerns may thus bring about a cost to other ethical concerns. And finally, for policymakers, the recognition of dual layers of concern is essential for any effective policymaking around the IoT.

Notes

1. Amazon, for example, is exploring the use of drones as delivery systems (Vanian 2016).
2. Raul Rojas, the owner of the smart house that was shut down by the malfunctioning light bulb, was aware of the risks of linking smart locks to his house: "One of the few things not connected in the house were the locks. Automated locks Rojas bought in 2009 are still sitting in a drawer waiting to be installed. . . . I was afraid of not being able to open the doors . . . Rojas said" (Hill 2015).

Works Cited

Agarwal, Yuvraj and Anind Dey. 2016. "Toward Building a Safe, Secure, and Easy-to-Use Internet of Things Infrastructure." *IEEE Computer 2016: IEEE Computer Society* (April), 40–3.

Baker, Stephen. 2007. *The Numerati*. New York: Mariner Books.

Bekey, George. 2012. "Current Trends in Robotics: Technology and Ethics." In *Robot Ethics: The Ethical and Social Implications of Robotics*, edited by Patrick Lin, Keith Abney, and George Bekey, 17–34. Cambridge, MA: MIT Press.

Buchanan, Elizabeth A. and Michael Zimmer. 2015. "Internet Research Ethics." http://plato.stanford.edu/archives/spr2016/entries/ethics-internet-research.

Clayton, Ellen Wright. 2005. "Informed Consent and Biobanks." *Journal of Law, Medicine & Ethics* 33 (1): 15–21.

Douglas, Danielle and Michael A. Fletcher. 2014. "Toyota Reaches $1.2 Billion Settlement to End Probe of Accelerator Problems." *Washington Post*, March 19. https://www.washingtonpost.com/business/economy/toyota-reaches-12-billion-settlement-to-end-criminal-probe/2014/03/19/5738a3c4-af69-11e3-9627-c65021d6d572_story.html.

Drahos, Peter and John Braithwaite. 2002. *Information Feudalism: Who Owns the Knowledge Economy?* London: Earthscan.

Fink, Erica and Laurie Segall. 2013. "Your TV Might Be Watching You." *CNN*, August 1. http://money.cnn.com/2013/08/01/technology/security/tv-hack/.

Fletcher, David. 2015. "Internet of Things." In *Evolution of Cyber Technologies and Operations to 2035*, edited by Misty Blowers, 19–32. Dordrecht: Springer.

Goodman, Mark. 2015. "Hacked Dog, a Car That Snoops on You and a Fridge Full of Adverts: The Perils of the Internet of Things." *Guardian*, March 12. http://www.theguardian.com/technology/2015/mar/11/internetofthingshackedonlineperilsfuture.

Henschke, Adam. Forthcoming. *Ethics in an Age of Surveillance: Virtual Identities and Personal Information*: Cambridge: Cambridge University Press.

Hill, Kashmir. 2015. "This Guy's Light Bulb Performed a DoS Attack on His Entire Smart House." *Fusion*, March 3. http://fusion.net/story/55026/this-guys-light-bulb-ddosed-his-entire-smart-house/.

International Data Corporation. 2015. "Explosive Internet of Things Spending to Reach $1.7 Trillion in 2020, According to IDC." *IDC*, June 3. http://www.idc.com/getdoc.jsp?containerId=prUS25658015.

Kahneman, Daniel. 2011. *Thinking, Fast and Slow*. New York: Farrar, Straus and Giroux.

Kravets, David. 2015. "Worker Fired for Disabling GPS App That Tracked Her 24 Hours a Day." *Ars Technica*, May 11. http://arstechnica.com/tech-policy/2015/05/worker-fired-for-disabling-gps-app-that-tracked-her-24-hours-a-day/.

Kroes, Peter. 2009. "Technical Artifacts, Engineering Practice, and Emergence." In *Functions in Biological and Artificial Worlds: Comparative Philosophical Perspectives*, edited by Ulrich Krohs and Peter Kroes, 277–92. Cambridge, MA: MIT Press.

Li, Shancang, Li Da Xu, and Shanshan Zhao. 2015. "The Internet of Things: A Survey." *Information Systems Frontiers* 17 (2): 243–59. doi: 10.1007/s10796-014-9492-7.

Lin, Patrick. 2012. "Introduction to Robot Ethics." In *Robot Ethics: The Ethical and Social Implications of Robotics*, edited by Patrick Lin, Keith Abney, and George Bekey, 3–16. Cambridge, MA: MIT Press.

Lin, Patrick. 2013. "The Ethics of Autonomous Cars." *Atlantic*, October 8. http://www.theatlantic.com/technology/archive/2013/10/the-ethics-of-autonomous-cars/280360/.

Maas, Peter and Megha Rajagopalan. 2012. "That's No Phone. That's My Tracker." *New York Times*, July 13. http://www.nytimes.com/2012/07/15/sunday-review/thats-not-my-phone-its-my-tracker.html?_r=0.

Malenkovich, Serge 2013. "Charging Your Smartphone . . . What Could Possibly Go Wrong?" *Kaspersky Daily*, May 6. https://blog.kaspersky.com/charging-your-smartphone/1793/.

Matyszczyk, Chris 2015. "Samsung's Warning: Our Smart TVs Record Your Living Room Chatter." *CNET*, February 8. http://www.cnet.com/news/samsungs-warning-our-smart-tvs-record-your-living-room-chatter/.

Mennicken, Sarah, Amy Hwang, Rayoung Yang, Jesse Hoey, Alex Mihailidis, and Elaine M. Huang. 2015. "Smart for Life: Designing Smart Home Technologies That Evolve with Users." *Proceedings of the 33rd Annual ACM Conference Extended Abstracts on Human Factors in Computing Systems*, 2377–80.

Mohammed, Jahangir 2015. "5 Predictions for the Internet of Things in 2016." World Economic Forum. https://www.weforum.org/agenda/2015/12/5-predictions-for-the-internet-of-things-in-2016/.

Poulter, Sean. 2014. "No More Flicking Switches! Samsung Designs Smartphone App to Turn Off Lights and Home Appliances." *Mail Online*, January 6. http://www.dailymail.co.uk/sciencetech/article-2534751/No-flicking-switches-Samsung-designs-smartphone-app-turn-lights-home-appliances.html.

Reiman, Jeffrey H. 1976. "Privacy, Intimacy, and Personhood." *Philosophy and Public Affairs* 6 (1): 26–44.

Singer, Peter Warren. 2009. *Wired for War*. New York: Penguin.

Solove, Daniel J. 2004. *The Digital Person: Technology and Privacy in the Information Age*. New York: New York University Press.

Solove, Daniel J. 2008. *Understanding Privacy*. Cambridge, MA: Harvard University Press.

Stankovic, J. A. 2014. "Research Directions for the Internet of Things." *IEEE Internet of Things Journal* 1 (1): 3–9. doi: 10.1109/JIOT.2014.2312291.

Symantec Security Response. 2014. "How Safe Is Your Quantified Self? Tracking, Monitoring, and Wearable Tech." *Symantec Official Blog*, July 30. http://www.symantec.com/connect/blogs/how-safe-your-quantified-self-tracking-monitoring-and-wearable-tech.

Toynbee, Polly. 2015. "What's Many Times More Deadly Than Terrorism? Britain's Roads." *Guardian*, November 25. http://www.theguardian.com/commentisfree/2015/nov/25/deadly-terrorism-britain-roads-security-risk.

van den Hoven, Jeroen. 2008. "Information Technology, Privacy and the Protection of Personal Data." In *Information Technology and Moral Philosophy*, edited by Jeroen van den Hoven and John Weckert, 301–21. Cambridge, MA: Cambridge University Press.

Vanian, Jonathan. 2016. "Amazon's Drone Testing Takes Flight in Yet Another Country." *Fortune*, January 6. http://fortune.com/2016/02/01/amazon-testing-drones-netherlands/.

Veruggio, Giancamo and Keith Abney. 2012. "Roboethics: The Applied Ethics for a New Science." In *Robot Ethics: The Ethical and Social Implications of Robotics*, edited by Patrick Lin, Keith Abney, and George Bekey, 347–63. Cambridge, MA: MIT Press.

Whitmore, Andrew, Anurag Agarwal, and Li Da Xu. 2015. "The Internet of Things: A Survey of Topics and Trends." *Information Systems Frontiers* 17 (2): 261–74.

Xie, Lei, Yafeng Yin, Xiang Lu, Bo Sheng, and Sanglu Lu. 2013. "iFridge: An Intelligent Fridge for Food Management Based on RFID technology." *Proceedings of the 2013 ACM Conference On Pervasive and Ubiquitous Computing*, 291–94.

Xu, L. D., W. He, and S. Li. 2014. "Internet of Things in Industries: A Survey." *IEEE Transactions on Industrial Informatics* 10 (4): 2233–43. doi: 10.1109/TII.2014.2300753.

16 CHALLENGES TO ENGINEERING MORAL REASONERS

TIME AND CONTEXT

Michał Klincewicz

Programming computers to engage in moral reasoning is not a new idea (Anderson and Anderson 2011a). Work on the subject has yielded concrete examples of computable linguistic structures for a moral grammar (Mikhail 2007), the ethical governor architecture for autonomous weapon systems (Arkin 2009), rule-based systems that implement deontological principles (Anderson and Anderson 2011b), systems that implement utilitarian principles, and a hybrid approach to programming ethical machines (Wallach and Allen 2008).

This chapter considers two philosophically informed strategies for engineering software that can engage in moral reasoning: algorithms based on philosophical moral theories and analogical reasoning from standard cases.[1] On the basis of challenges to the algorithmic approach, I argue that a combination of these two strategies holds the most promise and show concrete examples of how such an architecture could be built using contemporary engineering techniques.

16.1 Algorithms for Moral Imperatives: Utilitarianism

There are many versions of utilitarianism. What most share is adherence to consequentialism and the principle of greatest happiness (GHP). Consequentialism states that whether a particular action is moral is determined by its consequences. The principle of greatest happiness, in its original form, states that "actions are right in proportion as they tend to promote happiness, wrong as they tend to produce the reverse of happiness" (Mill 2003, 186). The various flavors of utilitarianism differ in their interpretation of "happiness" and whether an evaluation of consequences should consider an individual act or a rule that the act follows. Some utilitarians use preference satisfaction in that evaluation instead of pleasure or happiness (Singer 2011).

From an engineering point of view these distinctions are enough to give us a rough idea of what an implementation of act and rule utilitarianism in algorithm form would look like. The procedure would go like something like this:

Step 1. Specify possible courses of action $A_1 \ldots A_n$ or rules $R_1 \ldots R_n$ for actions.
Step 2. Determine likely consequences $C_1 \ldots C_n$ for each action $A_1 \ldots A_n$ or rule $R_1 \ldots R_n$.
Step 3. Apply GHP to each member of $C_1 \ldots C_n$ and select C_x, which is the consequence that results in the sum of greatest happiness and/or least unhappiness.
Step 4. Select course of action A_x or rule R_x.

This pseudo-algorithm contains a number of simplifications, each presenting its own engineering challenges.

Typically, $A_1 \ldots A_n$ and $R_1 \ldots R_n$ are constrained by one's goals, abilities, and environment. If one wants to go for a walk (goal), fulfilling that desire will depend on one's physical condition (ability) and availability of walkable places (environment). If one's physical condition prevents one from walking, then one cannot engage in that course of action and similarly if there are no walkable places nearby.

Engineering constraints of this sort into a piece of software is a challenge, but not a particularly difficult one. There are already cognitive architecture systems, such as ACT (Anderson 2013) and Soar (Laird, Newell, and Rosenbloom 1987), that can follow rules within a set of constraints. Soar, for example, has been successfully used to navigate simulated combat planes (Jones et al. 1999), generate synthetic adversaries for combat training (Wray et al. 2005), and guide autonomous robots (Laird 2012) within constraints defined by those tasks.

Soar, characterized as a software-based cognitive architecture, consists of several distinct modules. The *long-term memory* module is a set of resident IF ... THEN conditionals. The *working memory* module is a set of triples in the form (identifier, attribute, value), e.g., (John, person, 0). The *preference memory* module encodes the importance of particular conditionals relative to others.

The Soar system has a cycle of execution, during which it checks whether the triples in working memory match the antecedents of the conditionals in long-term memory. When there is a match, the consequents of the conditionals are moved to working memory. At the end of the execution cycle, the contents of working memory determine what is sent out from Soar to a host application or device. All the while, the contents of working memory can be updated by formatted input from an external device or other applications. All symbolic rule-based systems work roughly in this way.

Of course, there is much more to Soar than what has been outlined here (Laird et al. 2012), but these three modules are already enough to resolve the engineering challenge of constraints needed for the act/rule utilitarian algorithm. A specification of the programmed possible courses of action $A_1 \ldots A_n$ or rules $R_1 \ldots R_n$ in Soar's long-term memory module provides the constraints. The conditionals in long-term memory determine the likely consequences $C_1 \ldots C_n$ for each of antecedent action $A_1 \ldots A_n$ or rule $R_1 \ldots R_n$. The selection of actions is therefore based on the contents of working memory and preference memory.

This goes some way in addressing the engineering challenge but does not go far enough. Programming a Soar system consists in actually creating a set of conditionals for the initial state of long-term memory and the accompanying initial structure of working memory and preference memory. A very large number of conditionals would have to be written to encompass all the possible actions and consequences for even a very limited domain.

Some hope, but not much, lies in Soar's ability to change the contents of long-term memory independently. Soar updates long-term memory when more than one rule matches the contents of working memory. When this occurs, Soar first creates a subgoal structure to "look ahead" at the results of executing each rule, and then it selects which conditional to use depending on some other conditional. If the selection was successful in reaching the goal state, a new rule is created that "chunks" the original conditional and the subgoal conditional into one.

But even with this ability to chunk, Soar's long-term memory is not enough to deal with the range of possible situations in which moral reasoning takes place or to predict all of the possible consequences. This is because for any conditional in long-term memory—such as, say, IF dog barks THEN give him a bone—there will be a potentially indefinite number of exceptions. For example, if there are no bones to give, the rule does not apply, and similarly, if that particular dog is allergic to that particular sort of bone.

An additional engineering problem for a utilitarian algorithm is the application of GHP itself. Happiness is not so well defined that we could expect to program a calculus for it in a computer. Mill's own definition of happiness is not very helpful to an engineer who may want to program some metric of happiness into the algorithm. Mill tells us that "by happiness is intended pleasure, and the absence of pain; by unhappiness, pain, and the privation of pleasure" (2003, 186). Pleasure, as Mill himself acknowledges, is relative. What makes a pig happy is not the same as what makes a human happy (88).

In the context of engineering, this relativity presents a difficulty that can be overcome only by limiting the scope to which the algorithm should apply. If the engineer knows who or what will be a part of the moral problem, he will first have his software apply an appropriate metric of happiness, pleasure, or some matrix of preferences. Fortunately, the engineer would not have to do so on the basis of his intuitions or fiat, since there has been a lot of work done in philosophy, psychology, and economics to address this very problem (Martin 2012; Feldman 2010; Bruni and Porta 2005; Huppert, Baylis, and Keverne 2005).

In philosophy, there are several distinct ways of counting someone as happy, for example. Some philosophers argue for objective criteria (Nussbaum 2004; Parfit 2016) or momentary mental states, as in the original Bentham-style utilitarianism, and so on. The engineer should use a philosophically informed set of criteria determined in collaboration with a philosopher, because it matters which of these criteria are chosen.

For example, if the algorithm is to consider the pleasure and happiness of middle-aged, middle-income North American male hospital patients, conditions of their happiness may include things like stable income, loving relationships, access to entertainment, and so on. But if we consider different criteria, all that may matter is the amount of positive feelings that they have. If the algorithm is to apply to the pleasure and happiness of infants in refugee camps, on the other hand, an entirely different set of criteria may be important.

What is problematic about this situation from the perspective of an engineer is the sheer number of criteria and the magnitude of difference between them. In philosophy, this is called the problem of interpersonal comparisons (West 2008, 202; Harsanyi 1990). To construct a system that applies across all of these domains, the engineer has to limit the space of possibilities.

This creates an additional engineering challenge to the construction of a utilitarian algorithm. But it should be emphasized that these difficulties are many of the same difficulties that philosophers have been grappling with in the context of their own debates. So a constructive way forward for the engineer is interdisciplinary work with philosophers.[2] The other option is to have the engineer reinvent the wheel, so to speak, by limiting the possibilities that the moral reasoner considers without justification.

But assume all of this is accomplished and all the exceptions and possible courses of action are programmed into Soar or some other rule-based system like it and, further, we have resolved the problem of a conception and measure of happiness or satisfaction of preferences. The remaining problem for the utilitarian algorithm is to search through that multitude of rules and considerations in time to fire the right ones. Humans, like other organisms, sometimes act without seeming to give much thought to it. They also sometimes act morally without engaging in serious deliberation about it. Systems like Soar, on the other hand, have to use programmed logic to achieve comparable success and only by searching, which can be time-consuming.

Similar considerations lead to a classic objection to utilitarianism, which is that it would take too long for a person to sort through all the options and consequences in order to avoid uncertainty or unwanted results (Mill 2003, 199). The typical solution to this problem in the utilitarian literature is to introduce rules of thumb or some other shortcut for the reasoner to follow. Something similar can and has been proposed for ethical reasoning software, but in the context of deontological theory (Anderson and Anderson 2011b).

This problem with utilitarianism becomes an engineering challenge as well. Whatever the utilitarian computer reasoner does, it should do its work quickly, or at least quickly enough to make its results applicable to the situations in which humans may need ethical advice. This problem is addressed in more detail at the end of the following section.

16.2 Algorithms for Moral Imperatives: Deontological Theory

A set of different but equally difficult engineering challenges face an algorithm based on a non-consequentialist theory, such as Immanuel Kant's deontology. On Kant's view, what is moral ultimately derives from one's intention or will (Kant 2002, 55). This means that only the mental state responsible for some act plays a role in determining its morality.

On Kant's view, if the intention follows the categorical imperative (CI), which is a moral law built into the structure of human reason, then the act is moral (Kant 2002, 33). If it violates CI, then it is not moral. CI is unconditional, meaning it does not have exceptions, which distinguishes it from hypothetical imperatives that characterize what one ought to do in some particular circumstances or with some goal in mind (Kant 2002, 31).

Right away this creates a potential problem, since the idea that computer programs may have mental states is, to put it mildly, controversial. If what we would need to have is a Kantian moral reasoner program with human-level intentions and rationality, then the task may be beyond what we can presently achieve. But if the engineering task is to create a system that acts consistently with the moral law, then arguably the project is not as difficult.

This is because a key element of Kant's ethical theory is the CI, which can be expressed in three formulations, each of which may in turn be captured by a programmable decision procedure. The so-called universalizability formulation is the following: "Act in accordance with maxims that can at the same time have themselves as universal laws of nature for their object" (Kant 2002, 55).

The right characterization of Kant's first formulation of CI is highly controversial in moral philosophy, but for the sake of the present discussion the following is sufficient to highlight the engineering challenges associated with it:

Step 1. State maxim.
Step 2. Apply the maxim universally.
Step 3. See if it leads to a contradiction.

This pseudo-algorithm is already enough to highlight the engineering challenges that would face any programmatic implementation of it.

The reasoning that falls out of this formulation starts with a definition of a maxim or rule for an act. For example, take the maxim "steal bread from a bakery if one is hungry." Then, the maxim needs to be reformulated in a way that would make it apply across all contexts (be a universal law). So our maxim becomes "all people at all places and at all times will steal bread if they are hungry." Third, the universalized maxim needs to be examined to see whether it violates any logical or physical laws.[3] Finally, if the maxim does not contradict such laws, then one moves to the final step and tries to rationally will to act on that maxim without contradiction.

Steps 1 and 2 of the pseudo-algorithm do not obviously present an engineering challenge. Specifying a maxim is just a matter of constructing an appropriate token sentence. This can be done by direct input from the user or by generating such a sentence automatically based on input from some other source, such as a sensor.[4]

But then we come to the first engineering challenge. The computer program, just like a human reasoner, will have to decide how precise the maxim should be (O'Neill 2001). Facts such as there being little bread around or being on the verge of death from malnutrition are, arguably, relevant to how this first maxim is formulated. This is because "steal bread when hungry and malnourished" is a different moral maxim than "steal bread while there is not a lot of bread around." Neither the computer program nor a human reasoner antecedently knows whether either of these cases applies when only the token sentence "steal bread when hungry" is considered.

If we resolve this engineering problem of context and further assume that manipulation of the token sentence would be enough to accomplish Step 1 and Step 2, the rest may seem trivial. Putting the maxim into a universal context is just a matter of appropriate symbolic transformation. This can be as simple as prefixing quantifiers, such as "all people," "all places," and "all times" to the token sentence from Step 1. None of this requires, on the face of it, sophisticated software.

Steps that require examining the universalized maxim, however, do require sophisticated software.

In the context of checking for contradictions, probably the most useful AI technique is knowledge engineering, which has been successfully used to develop expert systems for things like medical diagnosis and automatic pilots in airplanes. Knowledge engineering involves at least two distinct things: knowledge representation and procedural reasoning that uses a base of knowledge.

Knowledge representation can be done in more than one way (Stephan, Pascal, and Andreas 2007). One of these ways entails explicit rules, as in the Soar long-term memory model. In the case of Soar, the system also provides procedures for using that knowledge. But we can also build knowledge representations without resorting to an entire cognitive architecture.[5] There are formal ontology representations, such as the Semantic Web Language (OWL) that uses Extended Markup Language (XML) schemas commonly used in internet development (Horrocks, Patel-Schneider, and Van Harmelen 2003).

Consider two items of knowledge that something is the case, such as "Fido feels pain" and "John Smith feels pain." An OWL XML schema for these facts would look something like this:

```
<living-thing>
        <animal>
                <dog>
                        <individual>
                                Fido
                        </individual>
                        <feels-pain>
                                Yes
                        </feels-pain>
                </dog>
                <human>
                        <individual>
                                John Smith
                        </individual>
                        <feels-pain>
                                Yes
                        </feels-pain>
                </human>
        </animal>
</living-thing>
```

The structure of the XML can be used to make relationships across categories explicit. Looking at the above, we can see that IF some *x* is animal THEN that *x* feels pain. This means that instead of programming a rule, as in Soar, in OWL we create a hierarchy that can represent a rule structurally.

Knowledge representation of this kind can be used as an engineering solution for the most problematic Step 3 of the Kantian algorithm. What that step requires is checking for violations of semantic relationships contained in a maxim that is put into a universal context. If we rely on the snippet above, this would amount to checking whether the items specified in the maxim are in the appropriate place in the XML hierarchy relative to others.

For example, say that John Smith wants to check whether the maxim "cause pain to Fido, if you want to" is moral. The algorithm requires that this maxim be put into a universal context in some such form: "all people at all places and at all times will cause pain to animals." If we look back at the XML, we will see that the category in the tag <animal> includes the tag <dog>, but it also includes the tag <human>. Consequently, when the maxim is made into a law of nature, its scope ranges across both dogs and humans. John's maxim, if made universal, would imply that causing pain to humans would be standard practice. The scope of <animal> includes John Smith and Fido. Any maxim that applies to animals applies to all members, which generates a contradiction in will in case of John's maxim. John cannot rationally will to have every animal be the subject of pain, because he happens to not like it himself.

Of course, this "toy" XML example is highly contrived and abstracts away from much of Kant's moral philosophy. For one, a Kantian would not consider being an animal as morally relevant in the same sense as being rational and free. But the example conveys the idea that the relatively straightforward mechanical process of checking for semantic contradictions using knowledge representations can be generalized. This process can involve indefinitely more complex knowledge databases that encode semantic relationships between very many different semantic categories.

Given this, the Kantian system may be in a better position to deal with the problem of timely search than the utilitarian system. This is because of the nature and purpose of knowledge representations that do not use explicit rules. The Kantian system proposed here relies on XML schemas, which are arguably ideal for fast parallel search though many categories (Liu et al. 2013).

Unfortunately, even with a very large base of such engineered knowledge, the crucial step of checking for consistency is likely to fail on a regular basis. This is because the number of possible contexts for which individual maxims apply may be too large to program into a set of knowledge representations like an XML ontology. Consider the maxim we just looked at, namely, "cause pain to Fido, if you want to." For John Smith, this indeed may be sufficient to reach the conclusion that it is immoral to cause pain to animals. John's reasoning will change, however, if the animal needs surgery and there is no pain medication to give. Or in a situation where John is defending himself from the Fido. Further exceptions to the maxim are easy to generate.

As was the case with the utilitarian solution, the problem that faces the Kantian pseudo-algorithm is its lack of context sensitivity. Deontological moral reasoning should work in a large number of possible contexts, and each of these has to be explicitly programmed into the knowledge representations or into the reasoning patterns that link them. Without it, the system will not be as useful. The amount of engineering work required to capture all the contexts for a deontological system would really have to be enormous.

But even if this enormous task is accomplished, there is another problem, which was already present for the utilitarian system's failure to deal with variable contexts. The Kantian system has to now perform the search through its knowledge base in a timely manner. The temporal limitations of search through rules of a rule-based system were a serious engineering challenge for the utilitarian system and present a similarly challenging task for the Kantian system.

One way of dealing with this issue is to make the moral reasoner software for specific domains of knowledge, such as those useful in medical boards, business, teaching, and so on. This would limit the variability of contexts and hence lower the complexity of the system. However, this leaves the problem of calibrating the size of the knowledge representation to the expectations for timeliness during search. A very large knowledge base may take a significant amount of time to search through, but a smaller knowledge base may not be useful in advising anyone in real-world situations that require moral reasoning.

16.3 Analogical Reasoning

Analogical reasoning is ubiquitous and, some argue, perhaps a central feature of human cognition (Hofstadter 2001). It can also be integrated with rule-based systems, such as ACT-R (Anderson and Thompson 1989). Given this, one promising strategy for overcoming the contextual and temporal limitation of the philosophical algorithms proposed previously lies with hybrid systems, where the symbolic algorithms are supplemented with analogical inferences. The idea is simple. Philosophically informed algorithms like those proposed in sections 16.1 and 16.2 yield a set of paradigmatic cases of moral right and wrong. These, in turn, can serve as the knowledge basis for analogical inferences.

There are many different forms of analogical reasoning, but their basic structure is well understood. Analogical reasoning in AI is often characterized as a system of inductive reasoning (Rissland 2006). In ethics, analogical reasoning as a form of deriving moral justification is controversial, but it has recently received a vigorous defense (Spielthenner 2014).

In both AI and ethics, analogical reasoning can be expressed quasi-formally as an argument form that depends on some set of elements that belong to the source domain (S) and the target domain (T). For example:

(1) *F* is *p* (S)
(2) *G* is like *F* (T)
(3) *F* is *q*

Analogical arguments are deductively invalid but can nonetheless provide justification, if they are strong. The strength of an analogical argument depends on several factors that have to do with probability and the elements in common between S and T.

For example, if we know that causing pain to a person for fun is morally despicable, then we can conclude by analogy that causing pain to a dog for fun is similarly morally despicable. The key to the inference is "causes pain" and applies to both domains (S) and (T). The argument is presumably strong because the analogy between (S) and (T) with respect to the morally relevant ability to have pain holds for all sentient animals.

Strong analogical arguments allow probabilistic conclusions based on knowledge we already have. This is perhaps why analogical reasoning is often used in patterns of legal (Ashley 1988) and moral (Juthe 2005) reasoning, where a predicate, such as "good," "just," or "wrong," can serve as a guide in deliberation. Analogical arguments understood in this way point a way forward in addressing the problem of automated moral reasoning across diverse contexts.

As of right now, there are several engineering options for implementing automated analogical reasoning in a computer. What most of these solutions have in common is adherence to the structural alignment thesis (Gentner 1983). On this view, analogical arguments are a matching of one set of elements to another set given some antecedent constraints. The structure-matching Engine system (Falkenhainer, Forbus, and Gentner 1989) is an example of an existing architecture that implements it.

To produce strong analogical arguments, a computer analogical reasoning system should have access to a robust and large (S). The philosophically informed algorithms suggested in sections 16.1 and 16.2 are good first approximations as to where members of this domain could be found. Standard cases validated by such algorithms can provide a database of knowledge that can in turn be (S) for any moral analogical argument that compares some (T).

This hybrid architecture is, to my knowledge, not represented by any system currently available and has not been explored in the machine ethics literature. This is surprising, since the problem of context that machine ethics inherits from philosophy is less serious for analogical reasoning. Two pieces of knowledge in a knowledge base may share some properties, and when they do, they can be the basis for an analogical argument. If they do not share any properties, then they can still form the basis for an analogy, just not a good one.

But the problem of context does not go away in the analogical reasoning system either. This is because the analogous properties that are morally important in one case may not be important in another. For example, the color of one's skin is not usually morally relevant, except when it comes to who is using a racial slur. But when it comes to deciding who is more trustworthy, skin color is not relevant.

There are also cases where two domains may share many properties, but only one property is the one that is morally relevant. For example, consensual sex and date rape may in certain circumstances share many properties. The ethical reasoner system should be able to pick out consent as the one morally relevant property that makes all the other similarities irrelevant.

16.4 Conclusion

This chapter outlines some of the engineering challenges for software that engages in moral reasoning and suggests some first approximate solutions to them that rely on extant technologies. My suggestion is to look toward hybrid systems, where deductive reasoning and inductive reasoning interplay. Symbolic algorithms that implement philosophical principles such as utilitarianism or Kantianism could be used to generate a base of standard morally unambiguous cases. These in turn could be used by an analogical reasoning engine to apply these insights to non-standard cases.

We should expect the best ethically informed software to borrow from other AI strategies as well. The inductive system considered here, namely, automated analogical thinking, is likely not enough to devise a computer program that would engage in human-level reasoning (Chalmers, French, and Hofstadter 1992). The same applies to knowledge engineering, which on its own is merely a useful tool for well-defined tasks.

Acknowledgments

Work on this paper was financed by the Polish National Science Centre (NCN) SONATA 9 Grant, PSP: K/PBD/000139 under decision UMO-2015/17/D/HS1/01705.

Notes

1. At the outset it should be noted that the philosophical moral theories discussed here are presented in grossly simplified and, at times, controversial form. The intention behind introducing them at all is to demonstrate their relevance to the task of

engineering an ethical reasoner. The details of whatever cutting-edge interpretation of utilitarianism or deontological theory is on the philosophical market today can and should be eventually worked into it. If such software were to exist, adherence to philosophical theory would make the corresponding algorithms more sophisticated and powerful. So one of the upshots of the system architecture presented here is that engineering a genuine ethical reasoner is not possible without robust cooperation between philosophers, engineers, and computer scientists.

2. There is an area of AI that is concerned with context-aware systems, with working prototypes such as Intellidomo at Universidad de Extramadura (2010), AwareHome at Georgia Institute of Technology (2002), and Ubicon at University of Kassel and Wurzburg, Germany (2012). These systems, while context-aware in a limited sense, use information from diverse but well-defined sources as input to another system—for example, location information acquired from a cell phone that can then be used to suggest restaurants in the area.
3. In this case of the maxim "steal bread from a bakery, if one is hungry," there is a semantic violation, since what it means to steal presupposes the concept of private property. And private property presupposes that not everyone at all places and at all times takes stuff from other people. This means that not stealing is a perfect duty, that is, a duty that we must always follow, regardless of our inclinations. Perfect duties are distinguished from imperfect duties, which are more context-dependent and do not have to be followed in all circumstances. Imperfect duties pass the conceptual contradiction step, but fail the last step, in being contradictions of will. The difference between these should be programmed into the decision procedure of a Kantian algorithm.
4. For example, if a sensor detects some bread on the table, the program would instantiate the token sentence "some bread on the table." If the system also has some goal of, say, acquiring some food, then the maxim "if there is some bread on the table, then take it" could be formulated in the system.
5. An ontology in computer science is a formal explicit specification of a shared conceptualization. Genuine examples of ontologies that use OWL are the hierarchical CONON (Wang et al. 2004) and SOUPA (Singer 2011), but while they are better discussed in the computer science literature, using them as an example in the present context may be unnecessarily cumbersome. The toy XML example should be enough to make the point that formal ontologies can be useful, but I direct the reader to those publications for a proper discussion of the merits of an OWL ontology.

Works Cited

Anderson, John R. 2013. *The Architecture of Cognition*. Hove: Psychology Press.

Anderson, John R. and Ross Thompson. 1989. "Use of Analogy in a Production System Architecture." In *Similarity and Analogical Reasoning*, edited by Stella Vosniadou and Andrew Ortony, 267–97. Cambridge: Cambridge University Press.

Anderson, Michael and Susan Leigh Anderson. 2011a. *Machine Ethics*. Cambridge: Cambridge University Press.

Anderson, Susan Leigh and Michael Anderson. 2011b. “A Prima Facie Duty Approach to Machine Ethics and Its Application to Elder Care.” In *Human–Robot Interaction in Elder Care*. Technical Report WS-11-12. Menlo Park, CA: AAAI Press.

Arkin, Ronald. 2009. *Governing Lethal Behavior in Autonomous Robots*. Boca Raton, FL: CRC Press.

Ashley, Kevin D. 1988. “Arguing by Analogy in Law: A Case-Based Model.” In *Analogical Reasoning*, edited by David H. Helman, 205–24. New York: Springer.

Bruni, Luigino and Pier Luigi Porta. 2005. *Economics and Happiness: Framing the Analysis*. Oxford: Oxford University Press.

Chalmers, David J., Robert M. French, and Douglas R. Hofstadter. 1992. “High-Level Perception, Representation, and Analogy: A Critique of Artificial Intelligence Methodology.” *Journal of Experimental & Theoretical Artificial Intelligence* 4 (3): 185–211.

Falkenhainer, Brian, Kenneth D. Forbus, and Dedre Gentner. 1989. “The Structure-Mapping Engine: Algorithm and Examples.” *Artificial Intelligence* 41 (1): 1–63.

Feldman, Fred. 2010. *What Is This Thing Called Happiness?*.Oxford: Oxford University Press.

Gentner, Dedre. 1983. “Structure-Mapping: A Theoretical Framework for Analogy.” *Cognitive Science* 7 (2): 155–70.

Harsanyi, John C. 1990. “Interpersonal Utility Comparisons.” In *Utility and Probability*, edited by John Eatwell, Murray Millgate, and Peter Newman, 128–33. Basingstoke: Pelgrave Macmillan.

Hofstadter, Douglas R. 2001. “Epilogue: Analogy as the Core of Cognition.” In *The Analogical Mind: Perspectives from Cognitive Science*, edited by Dedre Gentner, Keith J Holyoak, and Boicho N Kokinov, 499–533. Cambridge, MA: MIT Press.

Horrocks, Ian, Peter F. Patel-Schneider, and Frank Van Harmelen. 2003. “From SHIQ and RDF to OWL: The Making of a Web Ontology Language.” *Web Semantics: Science, Services and Agents on the World Wide Web* 1 (1): 7–26.

Huppert, Felicia A., Nick Baylis, and Barry Keverne. 2005. *The Science of Well-Being*. Oxford: Oxford University Press.

Jones, Randolph M., John E. Laird, Paul E. Nielsen, Karen J. Coulter, Patrick Kenny, and Frank V. Koss. 1999. “Automated Intelligent Pilots for Combat Flight Simulation.” *AI Magazine* 20 (1): 27–41.

Juthe, André. 2005. “Argument by Analogy.” *Argumentation* 19 (1): 1–27.

Kant, Immanuel. 2002 [1785]. *Groundwork of the Metaphysics of Morals*. Reprint, New Haven, CT: Yale University Press.

Laird, John E. 2012. *The Soar Cognitive Architecture*. Cambridge, MA: MIT Press.

Laird, John E., Keegan R. Kinkade, Shiwali Mohan, and Joseph Z. Xu. 2012. “Cognitive Robotics Using the Soar Cognitive Architecture.” *Cognitive Robotics AAAI Technical Report, WS-12-06*, 46–54.

Laird, John E., Allen Newell, and Paul S. Rosenbloom. 1987. "Soar: An Architecture for General Intelligence." *Artificial Intelligence* 33 (1): 1–64.

Liu, Xiping, Lei Chen, Changxuan Wan, Dexi Liu, and Naixue Xiong. 2013. "Exploiting Structures in Keyword Queries for Effective XML Search." *Information Sciences* 240: 56–71.

Martin, Mike W. 2012. *Happiness and the Good Life*. Oxford: Oxford University Press.

Mikhail, John. 2007. "Universal Moral Grammar: Theory, Evidence, and the Future." *Trends in Cognitive Science* 11 (4):143–52.

Mill, John Stuart. 2003. *"Utilitarianism" and "On Liberty": Including Mill's "Essay on Bentham" and Selections from the Writings of Jeremy Bentham and John Austin*. Edited by Mary Warnock. Hoboken, NJ: John Wiley.

Nussbaum, Martha C. 2004. "Mill Between Aristotle & Bentham." *Daedalus* 133 (2): 60–8.

O'Neill, Onora. 2001. "Consistency in Action." In *Varieties of Practical Reasoning*, edited by Elijah Milgram, 301–29. Cambridge, MA: MIT Press.

Parfit, Derek. 2016. "Rights, Interests, and Possible People." In *Bioethics: An Anthology*, edited by Helga Kuhse, Udo Schulklenk, and Peter Singer, 86–90. Hoboken, NJ: John Wiley.

Rissland, Edwina L. 2006. "AI and Similarity." *IEEE Intelligent Systems* (3): 39–49.

Singer, Peter. 2011. *Practical Ethics*. Cambridge: Cambridge University Press.

Spielthenner, Georg. 2014. "Analogical Reasoning in Ethics." *Ethical Theory and Moral Practice* 17 (5): 861–74.

Stephan, Grimm, Hitzler Pascal, and Abecker Andreas. 2007. "Knowledge Representation and Ontologies." *Semantic Web Services: Concepts, Technologies, and Applications*, 51–105.

Wallach, Wendell and Colin Allen. 2008. *Moral Machines: Teaching Robots Right from Wrong*. Oxford: Oxford University Press.

Wang, Xiao Hang, Da Qing Zhang, Tao Gu, and Hung Keng Pung. 2004. "Ontology Based Context Modeling and Reasoning Using OWL." *Workshop Proceedings of the 2nd IEEE Conference on Pervasive Computing and Communications (PerCom2004)*, 18–22.

West, Henry. 2008. *The Blackwell Guide to Mill's Utilitarianism*. Hoboken, NJ: John Wiley.

Wray, Robert E, John E. Laird, Andrew Nuxoll, Devvan Stokes, and Alex Kerfoot. 2005. "Synthetic Adversaries for Urban Combat Training." *AI Magazine* 26 (3): 82–92.

17 WHEN ROBOTS SHOULD DO THE WRONG THING

Brian Talbot, Ryan Jenkins, and Duncan Purves

In section 17.1, we argue that deontological evaluations do not apply to the actions of robots. For this reason, robots should act like consequentialists, even if consequentialism is false. In section 17.2, we argue that, even though robots should act like consequentialists, it is sometimes wrong to create robots that do. At the end of that section and in the next, we show how specific forms of uncertainty can make it permissible, and sometimes obligatory, to create robots that obey moral views that one thinks are false.

17.1 Robots Are Not Agents

All events that occur can be placed along a continuum of agency. At one end of this continuum are events whose occurrence is fundamentally explained by the intentional action of some robust moral agent, like a human being.[1] The most plausible examples of these are human attempts to perform actions. On the other end of this continuum are events whose occurrence is in no way caused by the intentional action of a moral agent. Certain natural disasters, such as earthquakes, are prime examples of this kind of event. We can call these latter events *proper natural disasters*. Because robot actions are closer to the proper natural disaster end of the continuum than the agential end, they are not subject to certain kinds of moral evaluation.[2]

Presently, robots are not phenomenally conscious, nor will they be in the near future. Because of this, they lack the repertoire of mental capacities required for agency. Phenomenal consciousness is implicated in a broad range of theories of moral decision-making that jointly enjoy majority support among the philosophical community. It is plausibly required for self-awareness, moral imagination, intuition (and so reflective equilibrium), or emotions, each of which has been claimed to play an important role in moral reasoning (Velik 2010). Further, if robots are not phenomenally conscious, then they cannot act for reasons. As two of the authors have argued elsewhere:

> If either the *desire-belief* model or the predominant *taking as a reason* model of acting for a reason is true, then AI cannot in principle act for reasons. Each of these models ultimately requires that an agent possess an attitude of belief or desire (or some further propositional attitude) in order to act for a reason. AI possesses neither of these features of ordinary human agents. AI mimics human moral behavior, but cannot take a moral consideration such as a child's suffering to be a reason for acting. AI cannot be *motivated* to act morally; it simply manifests an automated response which is entirely determined by the list of rules that it is programmed to follow. Therefore, AI cannot act *for* reasons, in this sense. (Purves et al. 2015, 861)[3]

It would be difficult to understand what it means to *act intentionally* without *acting for a reason*, and to exercise *agency* without having the capacity to *act intentionally*.[4] So, minimally, agency requires the capacity to respond to and act for reasons; robots cannot act for reasons, and so are not agents. Their actions are more akin to proper natural disasters, which unfold deterministically, without premeditation or consideration.

It goes without saying that proper natural disasters are not objects of deontological evaluation: this is precisely because there is no agent behind them and there is no decision, act, intention, or will to appraise. Natural disasters cannot be wrong or permissible. Natural disasters cannot violate duties or be blameworthy or praiseworthy. Like natural disasters, the actions of robots are generated not by some conscious, deliberative agency, but through complex (potentially inscrutable) deterministic processes.[5] Because robots are not agents, their actions cannot violate moral requirements.[6]

We should note as a caveat that this is meant to hold in the immediate future. A minority of philosophers of mind hold that artificial consciousness is possible. If an artificial consciousness is created, it will be worth revisiting our claims here. It may well turn out that such an artificial consciousness would be a robust moral agent in ways that make it relevantly similar to human agents.

If robots are not agents, there is a question about the sense in which they act at all. For our purposes, the term "action" is elliptical for something more technical: a robot's action is any movement that the robot causes that is not immediately caused by a human programmer or controller. When a remotely piloted aircraft (commonly, though misleadingly, called a "drone") fires a missile at the behest of a human commander, this is not the action of a robot. When an autonomous car in "autopilot mode" steers the wheel to stay in its lane or avoid a collision, this is the action of a robot.

Before moving on, it is worth pointing out that some have defended the view that computers are moral agents by developing more minimal conceptions of agency. Some of these conceptions, for example, do not require that agents be able to form mental representations. They might hold instead that agency is merely goal-directed behavior or self-regulation (see Barandiaran, Di Paola, and Rohde 2009; Brooks 1991). However, these views of agency are so broad as to include bacteria as agents. Even granting that these entities are *some* kind of agent, it is difficult to accept that they are properly subject to moral requirements. It is true that some human actions seem to be carried out without mental representation, such as tying shoes, turning a doorknob, or swatting a fly. To the extent that these actions are carried out without mental representations and are still morally evaluable, this is plausibly because they are performed by beings who have the power and representational capacity to bring them under deliberate rational reflection and critique. If I habitually do something wrong, and it is morally appraisable, it is morally appraisable because I *could have* or *should have* reflected on the reasons counting for and against it (see, e.g., Washington and Kelly 2016).

So robots cannot be agents, and their actions cannot be the subject of deontic evaluation: they cannot be right or wrong; they cannot be blameworthy or praiseworthy. Still, natural disasters can be appraised as morally good or bad, just as any other non-agentially-caused event can be appraised as good or bad. We say that the earthquake in Haiti was a bad thing, where "bad" refers to moral badness. The earthquake was bad because it caused a lot of death and suffering. Consequentialists will find this appraisal quite natural: whether a natural disaster is good or bad depends on its aggregate effects on beings whose well-being matters.[7] As with natural disasters, even if the deliberations and choices of robots are not open to deontological evaluation, the effects that they foreseeably bring about can be easily judged morally good or bad. If robots were to act like perfect maximizing consequentialists, they would bring about the best states of affairs. This is better than the alternative ways they might act, even if maximizing consequentialism is not the true moral theory. One need only accept that some states of the world are morally better than others.[8] Since robots cannot be subjected to other sorts of moral appraisal—they cannot do wrong—the only moral claims that apply to robots are claims about the moral goodness or badness of the outcomes they cause. Given this, robots ought to act like perfect maximizing consequentialists (in the sense that the best state of the world is one in which robots act like perfect maximizing consequentialists), even if consequentialism is false.

17.2 Creating Perfect Robots, with Perfect Knowledge

If highly intelligent robots were to appear out of thin air to perform the tasks we need them to, it would be reasonable to hope that they would act like perfect maximizing consequentialists. But robots do not appear *ex nihilo*. Humans design them. Thus, we must ask how we should design robots to act. Even if we cannot evaluate the deontic status of the actions of robots themselves, we can evaluate the actions of the programmers who give rise to the actions of robots. We will argue in this section that, even if the world would be morally better if we designed robots to act like consequentialists, whether or not consequentialism is true, this does not necessarily make it morally permissible to create consequentialist robots.

In this section, we will discuss what designers should do when in a position to create robots that perfectly follow the demands the correct moral theory would make on a human agent in the robot's position. In the next section, we'll discuss how things differ when a creator cannot create such a morally perfect robot.

We begin with a few suppositions in order to focus our discussion. Suppose that moderate deontology is true, by which we mean a theory that holds that it is generally wrong to violate rights, even if doing so is for the best, but also holds that violating rights can be permissible when it creates *extremely* good consequences or avoids extremely bad ones.[9] Suppose that we know all the moral truths, and we are able to create a robot that, in any situation, will perfectly do what a human morally ought to do in that situation. Let's call this deontological robot DR for short. Alternatively, we could create a robot that will behave as a perfect welfare-maximizing consequentialist. Let's call this maximizing robot MR for short. Which of these two ought we create? To answer this question, it will be helpful to consider the sorts of situations in which MR and DR will behave differently (see table 17.1).[10] We assume that, whenever DR is faced with multiple permissible options, it will choose the one that maximizes welfare. So the only cases in which MR and DR will behave differently are cases in which violating rights creates more utility than does respecting them, but not so much utility that these violations are justified. Note that talk of MR and DR "violating rights" is shorthand, since, as we argued earlier, moral requirements do not apply to robots. What we really mean is that a human agent would violate a duty if he were to act that way.

It will be helpful to focus on just one type of case, taken from Regan (1983).

> *Aunt Agatha*. Fred has a rich Aunt Agatha, who is frittering away her money. If she lives as long as she is expected to, by the time she dies she'll be just about out of money. When she dies, Fred will inherit whatever money she has left, and he will donate all of it to an effective charity. If Agatha

Table 17.1. Differing decisions of DR and MR

Utility vs. rights	Decisions of DR and MR
Maximizing utility justifies rights violations	Both DR and MR will maximize utility and violate rights; both do what a human agent ought to do
Maximizing utility does not justify rights violations	MR will maximize utility; DR will respect rights instead; only DR does what a human agent ought to do
Maximizing utility is consistent with respecting rights	Both DR and MR will maximize utility and respect rights; both do what a human agent ought to do

> dies in the near future, as opposed to living out her natural lifespan, Fred's inheritance would do a significant amount of good in the world; the good done by the donation will be greater than the badness of Agatha's death.

Let's stipulate that killing Aunt Agatha (now) is better than letting her live, but that she doesn't have enough money that the good done by killing her justifies violating her rights by killing her. MR would kill Agatha, while DR would let her live. We can approach the issue of whether it is permissible to create MR rather than DR by asking, "Is it permissible to create an Aunt Agatha Terminator—a machine to hunt and kill people like Aunt Agatha in situations like this?"

Let's start by asking if it would be permissible to build a machine that will kill only one Aunt Agatha and then self-destruct. Killing Agatha yourself is wrong according to moderate deontology. It is difficult to see the act of designing and deploying this machine as less wrong than simply killing Aunt Agatha yourself, since there is a clear connection between the intentional action of the programmer and the death of Aunt Agatha.

What about building a robot that will kill multiple Aunt Agathas? Typically this will be wrong if it is wrong to build a machine to kill a single Agatha. But it is possible that sometimes the reasons in favor of killing *n* Agathas will be greater than *n* times the reasons in favor of killing one Agatha, since the good we can do with money often increases non-linearly.[11] With $2, a starving person can buy a fish and, with $4, two fishes; but with $20 the person can buy a fishing pole, which has more than ten times the utility of a single fish. So there are possible scenarios in which the total amount of good done by an Agatha Terminator is so incredibly high that building one is justified, even though killing a single Agatha would not be. Does this mean that in such scenarios we ought to build MR rather than DR?

It does not, because DR would also kill the Agathas in such a scenario. We are permitted to violate duties when each violation is necessary, but not sufficient, to bring about an outcome that justifies the violations, as long as we intend and expect to do what else is necessary to bring about the outcome. For example, imagine that, to bring about an incredible amount of good, one needs to tell a small lie (but one that does violate a *prima facie* duty) and then hours later steal a car. Imagine further that the amount of good done is more than enough to justify the rights violation involved in stealing the car. Telling the lie can be permissible for agents who intend to eventually bring about the good, assuming they have good enough reasons to think they will succeed, even though the lie by itself does not bring about the good. The lie and the car theft jointly constitute a justified course of action, whereas each individual violation would not be justified absent its contribution to this larger course of action. Similarly, an agent would be permitted to kill each Aunt Agatha, provided that the agent intends and expects to eventually kill enough Agathas to do enough good to justify all the killings. This means that DR would kill the Agathas as well.

To summarize, we get the following results in Agatha cases (see table 17.2). The only cases in which MR and DR will behave differently are those in which killing Agatha(s) will produce insufficient good to justify the total amount of killing needed to bring about that good. It is wrong to kill Agatha(s) in such cases, and it is wrong to build an MR that will do so. The Aunt Agatha Terminator is just a stand-in for any version of MR. Whatever duties MR violates that DR would not will create an amount of good that would be insufficient to justify the violation, and making a robot that would violate these duties is wrong. If some version of moderate deontology is true, as we are stipulating, it is wrong to build a perfect consequentialist robot when one could build a perfect moderate

Table 17.2. Differing decisions of DR and MR in Agatha cases

Utility vs. rights	Decisions of DR and MR
Maximizing utility justifies killing *n* Agathas	Both DR and MR will maximize utility and violate the Agathas' rights; both do what a human agent ought to do
Maximizing utility does not justify killing *n* Agathas	MR will maximize utility; DR will respect the Agathas' rights instead; only DR does what a human agent ought to do
Maximizing utility is consistent with respecting the Agathas' rights	Both DR and MR will maximize utility and respect the Agathas' rights; both do what a human agent ought to do

deontologist robot instead. This is true even though deontological evaluations do not apply to robots.

17.3 Perfect Robots and Uncertainty

The discussion of the Aunt Agatha Terminators assumes that we have a great deal of information about what rights our robots will violate. Sometimes we do not, because we cannot predict the future with certainty. There are no uncontroversial accounts of how deontological duties are affected by uncertainty about future events. However, given one plausible view of this, uncertainty about what the robots we design will do can make it permissible to design MR rather than DR.

Let's start by seeing why one would think that uncertainty makes *no* difference to whether we should build MR. If there are moral reasons to build one of DR or MR rather than the other, it is because of the difference in what each will do or—when we lack certainty—because of the probabilities they will act differently. As we've seen, the only cases in which they act differently are cases in which violating rights maximizes utility but the utility created is insufficient to justify the violation. The reasons against making MR come from the rights it may violate in these cases. Suppose that the force of these reasons is weakened by our uncertainty that any rights will be violated and our uncertainty about what those rights may be. The reasons in favor of making MR come from the utility created by violating rights. The strength of these reasons is also diluted by the uncertainty about what good will be done. And the uncertainty about both is exactly as strong, and thus has the same weakening effect for both the rights violations and the utility under consideration. After all, in every case in which utility is maximized by MR rather than DR, MR also violates a right that overrides the gain in utility. This suggests that, even if we don't know how precisely MR or DR will act, we do know that creating MR risks doing wrong for insufficient reasons when creating DR does not risk doing wrong for insufficient reasons.

It seems to us that that is not always the right way to think about these issues. To see why, let's consider some intuitive claims about risk and rights. Intuitively, it is morally wrong to kill someone even if doing so will prevent any number of headaches. Further, it seems wrong to take a 90% chance of killing an innocent person even if this risk is necessary to prevent any number of headaches. This illustrates the notion that the right to life (intuitively) has *lexical priority* over the right to not have headaches; if right x has lexical priority over y, then we cannot justify violating x to protect any number of rights y. These examples also show that the lexical priority of the right to life is maintained even when there is uncertainty that the right to life will be violated. On its face, this seems to entail that it is never permissible to create any level of risk to people's lives in order to cure headaches. But that cannot be true: it is morally permissible to drive to the store to buy aspirin. Rights and risk seem to interact in a non-straightforward manner. Many deontologists say that that, once the chance that a right is being violated is low enough, the right at issue essentially "drops out" of the moral calculus (see Aboodi, Borer, and Enoch 2008; Hawley 2008).

Put another way, once the probability that right *x* is violated is below some threshold, one can completely ignore right *x* when deciding what to do. In the headache case, because the risk that one will kill someone is low enough, it plays no role in determining what is permissible. An alternative view is that, when the chance that a right is violated is below a certain threshold, one still has reasons to respect that right, but the reasons become significantly weaker and easier to override.[12] On both of these views, when the risk that we will violate a right goes down, the strength of the reasons this gives us does not decrease in a linear fashion with the decrease in risk. On the first, the reasons to not risk harming someone just disappear when the risk is low enough. On the second, the reasons to not take the risk can go from having lexical priority over (some) other reasons to not having this priority. On either view, if the chance is sufficiently small that one's robot will be faced with a case where violating rights will maximize the good, then one would be permitted to build MR. This would because the rights violated by building MR drop out of consideration, or become so much weaker that violation of them is overridden by the utility of building MR. This may very well apply to robots like autonomous cars, which will very rarely get into situations where respecting rights and maximizing utility conflict.[13]

This might mean that, when it is permissible to build MR rather than DR, it is sometimes obligatory to do so. To show why, we will focus on the view that rights simply drop out of consideration when the risk they will be violated is low enough; what we say will also apply (with minor modifications) to the alternative view sketched in the previous paragraph. Unlike rights-based reasons, consequence-based reasons never drop out of consideration, but instead simply change their weight in line with the expected utility calculations; even if there is a tiny chance that some good will be done by *x*-ing, this still counts as some reason to *x*. If rights drop out of consideration when the chance they will be violated is low enough, and so it is permissible to build MR when MR is sufficiently unlikely to violate rights, the expected utility in such cases of building MR might make it obligatory to build. Whether this is possible depends on what the probability threshold is at which rights violations drop out of consideration. Let's call this the *dropout threshold*.

To see why the value of the dropout threshold is relevant to the decision to build MR, let's consider two plausible thresholds. One says that if the probability of rights violations is 2% or below, these rights can be ignored. This dropout threshold is suggested by the "beyond a reasonable doubt" standard for criminal punishment, which (according to what one of us was taught in law school) requires roughly 98% certainty that the defendant is guilty in order to convict (Hughes 2014). The idea that it is permissible to risk a 2% chance of violating one of the most serious rights—the right of the innocent to not be punished—suggests that this and other rights need not be considered if the chance they are violated is below 2%. On the other hand, 2% sometimes seems like an objectionably high risk to take with the rights of others. For example, most people think drunk driving across town is wrong, but gratuitous sober driving across town is permissible. The chance that someone driving drunk for ten miles will kill a person is about 0.00001%, and so it seems that the threshold at which the right to life can be ignored must be below this.[14] These two extremes have very different implications for building MR rather than DR. Imagine that, if MR behaves differently from DR, it will kill one person to save five, and further assume that saving five does not justify killing the one. For the sake of illustration, let's put the utility of one life at roughly $7 million (Applebaum 2011). The net benefit of killing one to save five is $28 million worth of utility. On the assumption that this amount of utility does not justify murder, building MR in this situation would be permissible only if the chance that MR will actually kill the one to save the five is below the dropout threshold. The probability that MR would bring about an additional $28 million worth of utility over DR is the same as the probability that it would kill the one to save the five. This means that, if the dropout threshold is 2%, then the expected utility of building MR when MR is permissible to build could be as high as $560,000 ($28 million × 0.02). If the threshold is 0.00001%, the expected utility of building MR when MR is permissible could be no higher than $2.80 ($28 million × 0.0000001). We might be obligated to do acts that have the former level of expected utility, but (intuitively) not the latter. Therefore, we might be obligated to build MR if the probability threshold at which rights drop out of consideration is high enough and the probability that MR will violate rights is below that threshold.

17.4 Creating Imperfect Robots

As things currently are, we cannot create robots that perfectly follow the rules of the correct moral system. For one, we often will build robots only on the condition that they will do immoral things. To see why, consider autonomous cars and autonomous weapons. It is intuitively wrong to drive frivolously too often, probably because this makes us part of the collective harm of climate change. But we will not create autonomous cars unless they are willing to drive whenever and wherever their owners ask, even if this means they will drive frivolously. Similarly, we will create autonomous weapons only if they are going to obey orders, including orders to fight in immoral wars. Any robot we create now would be far from acting like a perfect moral agent. But even when robot designers have the purest motives and want to create the best robot they can, they will not know what the correct moral system is. As we have seen, our lack of certainty about the future can make it so that we should build robots who act according to theories we think are false. Uncertainty about what the correct moral theory is can have the same effect.

To show how this can happen, let's narrow the choices a robot designer is faced with down to two. Let's call these the imperfect maximizing robot (IMR) and imperfect deontological robot (IDR).[15] IMR attempts to act as MR would, and IDR as DR would. But each is imperfect because its designer lacks full certainty about either the correct theory of utility or the correct deontological theory. As with the discussion of MR and DR, to see which of IMR and IDR we ought to build, we should consider how they will behave differently. Like MR, IMR will violate deontological duties in order to maximize utility in cases in which the utility produced is not enough to justify the violations (e.g., it will kill Aunt Agatha). But IMR will also sometimes violate deontological duties while failing to maximize utility, when it miscalculates. Conversely, IDR will refrain from doing what is best when it mistakenly thinks what is best will also violate duties.[16] For example, an autonomous car might give too much weight to human property rights and too little weight to animals' rights to life. As a result, it might kill a squirrel rather than damage a car, even though damaging the car would maximize utility without violating any deontological duty. In this case, IDR does the wrong thing when IMR would have done the right thing. This case illustrates the following lesson: in cases in which IDR would mistakenly think there is a duty to *x*, where *x*-ing does not maximize utility, then it would have been morally preferable to have created IMR on the assumption that IMR would not have *x*-ed.

Given some uncertainty about what duty requires, designers should sometimes build IMR rather than IDR. To see why, and to see that this does not require very much uncertainty, let's consider a designer who finds herself in a moral version of the so-called preface paradox. Imagine that the designer believes that IDR and IMR will act differently in 100 situations, and, for each situation, she is 95% confident that she knows what action is morally correct. Since IDR and IMR act differently only when the designer thinks what IMR does violates a duty, she will thus be 95% confident that IMR unjustifiably violates a deontological duty in each of these 100 situations. Even though the chance of being mistaken about any one case is 5%, the chance that she is mistaken about at least one of the 100 cases is more than 99%.[17] Put another way, in this scenario the designer can be almost certain that IMR would violate only 99 duties, even though there are 100 cases in which she is 95% confident that IMR violates a duty. If the amount of good that IMR would do would justify 99 duty violations but not 100, then it would be permissible to create IMR. When one is less morally certain, one will have good reasons to create IMR in a wider range of scenarios.

This claim may seem to contradict the views we discussed earlier in the context of uncertainty and perfect robots. There we suggested that one should act as if there is a duty to *x* when one is confident above some threshold that there is that duty. In the example just given, the designer is clearly above the dropout threshold with regard to each of the duties.[18] Why doesn't this mean that she must program all of these into the robot?

Creating a robot is a single act, and if creating that robot violates one of the creator's duties (because the robot acts like a consequentialist), that duty is the product of the conjunction of duties we expect the robot to violate.[19] As we've just seen, even if we are very confident that we are right about each duty we believe in, we may not be very confident at all that we are right about the conjunction of these duties. Given enough uncertainty, we needn't build a robot to respect all the deontological duties we think exist. We should instead build a robot to act properly in light of every subset of these duties that we are sufficiently confident in. So we might not be confident above the dropout threshold that all 100 of some set of putative duties are actual duties. But suppose that for each subset of 99, we can be confident above the dropout threshold that all members of the subset are duties. We should program the robot in light of that confidence. If the good we expect IMR to do justifies violating the duties in each subset of 99 duties, then we may create IMR.[20]

This shows that, in some situations in which one is unable to make a morally perfect robot, one ought to make a robot that acts in line with moral views that its creator firmly believes are false. We have shown this by considering designers faced with two options: IMR or IDR. Of course, designers are faced with a large range of possible morally flawed robots that they can construct. One might create a robot that acts like IMR in some contexts and IDR in others. Or one might create a robot that always acts like a deontologist would but whose actions reflect a form of deontology one believes is not correct. We have shown that justified confidence in one's moral views does not rule out creating robots of these sorts. Future work should explore when, if ever, we should create these sorts of robots.

17.5 Conclusion

We have argued that robots ought to act like perfect maximizing consequentialists, whether or not consequentialism is true. Thus, if highly intelligent robots were to arise *ex nihilo* it would be reasonable to hope that they acted like perfect maximizers. Robots are designed and created by humans, however, so we must ask whether humans should design robots to act like consequentialists. If deontology is true, and we can make robots that act like perfect deontologists, and we are sufficiently confident about the future choices robots are faced with, then we should make our robots perfect deontologists. Robots are created by imperfect humans, however. Given the right sort of uncertainty on the part of the designers of robots—either high levels of uncertainty about a robot's future actions or high uncertainty about the complete moral theory—the designers of robots may, and perhaps must, create robots to act on moral views that those designers reject.

Notes

1. We assume that some creatures in the universe are robust moral agents. If this statement is false, it undermines the novelty of our claim that robots are not the proper objects of deontological criticism. However, it seems to impugn the more general project of moral philosophy. We would have bigger problems to worry about in that case.
2. For an earlier discussion of computer moral agency as partially developed agency and a comparison between computers and other kinds of quasi-agents, see Floridi and Sanders (2004).
3. For defenses of the desire-belief model, see Davidson (1963, 1978). For some defenses of the taking as a reason model, see Darwall (1983), Gibbard (1992), Korsgaard and O'Neill (1996), and Scanlon (1998).
4. The connection between actions and intentionality is controversial, but it is less controversial to assert that an entity is not an agent if it cannot act intentionally, whether the capacity for intentional agency is (i) necessary for or (ii) identical to the capacity of agency itself. See Anscombe (1957), Davidson (1963, 1978), and Johnson (2006). See also Goldman (1970) and Kuflik (1999).
5. Currently, we can design robots that act indeterministically, in that they are random, but this is not the sort of indeterminism needed for a thing to be properly subject to moral requirements. Moreover, if robots lack genuine free will, it would also be *unjust* to hold them responsible for what they do. The suggestion that we are puppets or automata is taken to be the limiting case to show that we are not genuinely free, and so are not responsible for our actions. Yet there is no metaphor needed here: robots would be genuinely unfree.
6. See Noorman (2014): "[A]lthough some people are inclined to anthropomorphize computers and treat them as moral agents, most philosophers agree that current computer technologies should not be called moral agents, if that would mean that they could be held morally responsible."
7. The suggestion that a natural disaster could be all-things-considered good may strike some as incredible, but we think it is not. To wit: an episode of *30 Rock*, in which Robert De Niro rattles off a list of natural disasters: "this *devastating*

wildfire . . . this *horrible* flood . . . ," culminating with "this *wonderful* flood that put out that *devastating* wildfire" (*30 Rock*, 2011).

8. Not everyone accepts this claim, but it is extremely plausible. Geach (1956) and Thomson (2001) have denied that some states of affairs are morally better *simpliciter* than others. See Klocksiem (2011) and Huemer (2008) for replies to Geach and Thomson.
9. W. D. Ross (1930) is usually credited with having defended the first moderate deontological theory.
10. It may be that there are other reasons that count for or against building one of these robots—perhaps it is much more expensive to build one rather than the other. We are bracketing those here.
11. Conversely, the reasons *against* designing a robot to kill *n* Agathas might be less than *n* times stronger than the reasons against designing a robot to kill one Agatha, although it is hard to imagine such a case.
12. Our thanks to David Boonin for pointing out this alternative. Thanks, more broadly, to the audience at the Ninth Annual Rocky Mountain Ethics (RoME) Congress, especially Nicholas Delon, Spencer Case, and Rebecca Chan, for their helpful discussion to clarify this point, among others.
13. While car accidents are a leading cause of death in the United States, they are relatively rare in terms of crashes per mile driven. In the United States in 2012, for example, there was one crash (whether it involved an injury or not) for every 528,000 miles driven (data from NHTSA 2012).
14. This is a ballpark estimate for the sake of illustration, but we arrived at it in the following way: Drunk drivers are roughly ten times more dangerous than sober drivers (Levitt and Porter 2001). The U.S. Department of Transportation reports that there is about one death per 100 million miles driven, which gives us an estimate of one death per 10 million drunk miles driven. Driving ten miles drunk thus has roughly a one in a million chance of killing someone.
15. We are going to bracket two interesting questions due to a lack of space. (1) Should we perhaps create less ideal versions of IDR (versions that have some deontological beliefs we expect to be false) rather than a more ideal IDR or IMR? There may be good reasons to do so, but these depend on facts about the proper deontological response to uncertainty. (2) Is it permissible to create imperfect robots rather than no robots at all? With respect to the latter question, even if creating any imperfect robot is wrong, we can still ask: Given that we are going to do that wrong, how ought we to do it?
16. Other moral considerations bear on the creation of imperfect robots—these robots might be created to do wrong things or might violate duties we are not aware of—but these will not distinguish between IMR and IDR.
17. This and all the probabilities to follow are generated by straightforward binomial probability calculations. You can find a calculator online (see, e.g., Stat Trek 2016).

18. Those familiar with the debate on moral uncertainty may note that this question conflates uncertainty about what a robot will do with uncertainty about what the moral duties are. Many think that this sort of uncertainty affects moral calculations differently. Even if it does, the question being asked here is a natural one to ask.
19. Hawley (2008) endorses something like this view. Aboodi et al. (2008) seem to deny it, but that is actually misleading. They think that, if a single agent is faced with a series of choices, each of which involves uncertainty, they have to make each choice independently and consider the probability that *it* violates some right. However, robot designers are not faced with a series of choices, but only a single choice, and so must calculate the probability that it violates some conjunction of rights.
20. One might point out that, when we consider each subset of the duties we are confident in, these subsets together include all of the duties we believe in; wouldn't this mean we have to program the robot to respect all 100 duties? Not necessarily. Again, if IMR would do enough good to justify violating any 99 of these duties, then we may create IMR rather than IDR, even though IMR will violate all 100 putative duties. This is because, even when we are extremely confident that it is wrong to violate each duty in the set of 100 duties, taken together, we should have very little confidence that it is wrong to violate them all.

Works Cited

Aboodi, R., A. Borer, and D. Enoch. 2008. "Deontology, Individualism, and Uncertainty." *Journal of Philosophy* 105 (5): 259–72.

Anscombe, G.E.M. 1957. *Intention*. Oxford: Basil Blackwell.

Applebaum, Binyamin. 2011. "As U.S. Agencies Put More Value on a Life, Businesses Fret." *New York Times*, February 16. http://www.nytimes.com/2011/02/17/business/economy/17regulation.html.

Barandiaran, X. E., E. Di Paolo, and M. Rohde. 2009. "Defining Agency: Individuality, Normativity, Asymmetry, and Spatio-Temporality in Action." *Adaptive Behavior* 17 (5): 367–86.

Brooks, R. A. 1991. "Intelligence Without Representation." *Artificial Intelligence* 47: 139–59.

Darwall, Stephen L. 1983. *Impartial Reason*. Ithaca, NY: Cornell University Press.

Davidson, Donald. 1963. "Actions, Reasons, and Causes." *Journal of Philosophy* 60 (23): 685–700.

Davidson, Donald. 1978. "Intending." In *Philosophy of History and Action*, edited by Yirmiyahu Yovel, 41–60. New York: Springer.

Floridi, L. and J. Sanders. 2004. "On the Morality of Artificial Agents." *Minds and Machines*, 14 (3): 349–79.

Geach, Peter T. 1956. "Good and Evil." *Analysis* 17 (2): 33–42.

Gibbard, Allan. 1992. *Wise Choices, Apt Feelings: A Theory of Normative Judgment*. Cambridge, MA: Harvard University Press.

Goldman, Alvin. 1970. *A Theory of Human Action*. Englewood Cliffs, NJ: Prentice-Hall.

Hawley, P. 2008. "Moral Absolutism Defended." *Journal of Philosophy* 105 (5): 273–5.

Huemer, Michael. 2008. "In Defence of Repugnance." *Mind* 117 (468): 899–933.

Hughes, Virginia. 2014. "How Many People Are Wrongly Convicted? Researchers Do the Math." *National Geographic*, April 28. http://phenomena.nationalgeographic.com/2014/04/28/how-many-people-are-wrongly-convicted-researchers-do-the-math/.

Johnson, Deborah G. 2006. "Computer Systems: Moral Entities but Not Moral Agents." *Ethics and Information Technology* 8 (4): 195–204.

Klocksiem, Justin. 2011. "Perspective-Neutral Intrinsic Value." *Pacific Philosophical Quarterly* 92 (3): 323–37.

Korsgaard, Christine M. and Onora O'Neill. 1996. *The Sources of Normativity*. Cambridge: Cambridge University Press.

Kuflik, Arthur. 1999. "Computers in Control: Rational Transfer of Authority or Irresponsible Abdication of Autonomy?" *Ethics and Information Technology* 1 (3): 173–84.

Levitt, S. D., and Porter, J. 2001. "How Dangerous Are Drinking Drivers?" *Journal of Political Economy* 109 (6): 1198–237.

National Highway Transportation Safety Administration (NHTSA). 2012. "Traffic Safety Facts 2012." https://crashstats.nhtsa.dot.gov/Api/Public/ViewPublication/812032.

Noorman, Merel. 2014. "Computing and Moral Responsibility." *The Stanford Encyclopedia of Philosophy*, Summer 2014 ed., edited by Edward N. Zalta. http://plato.stanford.edu/archives/sum2014/entries/computing-responsibility/.

Purves, Duncan, Ryan Jenkins, and Bradley J. Strawser. 2015. "Autonomous Machines, Moral Judgment, and Acting for the Right Reasons." *Ethical Theory and Moral Practice* 18 (4): 851–72.

Regan, Tom. 1983. *The Case for Animal Rights*. Berkeley: University of California Press.

Ross, William D. 1930. *The Right and the Good*. Oxford: Clarendon Press.

Scanlon, Thomas. 1998. *What We Owe to Each Other*. Cambridge, MA: Harvard University Press.

Stat Trek. 2016. "Binomial Calculator: Online Statistical Table." http://stattrek.com/online-calculator/binomial.aspx.

30 Rock. 2011. "Operation Righteous Cowboy Lightning." s05e12. Directed by Beth McCarthy-Miller. Written by Tina Fey and Robert Carlock. NBC, January 27.

Thomson, J. J. 2001. *Goodness and Advice*. Princeton. NJ: Princeton University Press.

Velik, Rosemarie. 2010. "Why Machines Cannot Feel." *Minds and Machines* 20 (1): 1–18.

Washington, N. and D. Kelly. 2016. "Who's Responsible for This? Moral Responsibility, Externalism, and Knowledge about Implicit Bias." In *Implicit Bias and Philosophy*, edited by M. Brownstein and J. Saul. New York: Oxford University Press.

18 MILITARY ROBOTS AND THE LIKELIHOOD OF ARMED COMBAT

Leonard Kahn

Hegel once pointed out that the "abstraction of one man's production from another's makes labor more and more mechanical, until finally man is able to step aside and install machines in his place" (Knox 1942, 58). We have not yet removed ourselves entirely from war and installed machines in our place, and we might never do so. But we have reached the point where machines not only are able to support combatants, but are capable of taking our place in war. This curious fact has many important ethical implications (Brunstetter and Braun 2011; Halgarth 2013, 35ff.). I focus here on some rather underexplored repercussions that concern the relationship between the rise of military robots and the likelihood of armed conflict.

In section 18.1, I offer a working definition of a military robot. In section 18.2, I outline a simple model that explains the relationship between armed conflict and the cost one pays for it. I then argue in section 18.3 for the claim that the use of military robots is likely to lead to more armed conflict. In section 18.4, I make the case that the increase in armed conflict caused by the use of military robots will be, all things considered, morally bad. I briefly conclude in section 18.5 by contending that we should create legal and other social norms that limit the use of military robots.

18.1 Military Robots: A Working Definition

Talk of military robots can be misleading. For some, the expression "military robot" brings to mind such icons of science fiction as the T-800s from the *Terminator* series or the Super Battle Droids from the *Star Wars* films. But my subject in this chapter is not something that happened a long time ago in a galaxy far, far away; it is about something that is happening in the here and now. So let me begin by sketching a working definition of what a military robot is.

According to George Bekey a robot is "a machine, situated in the world, that senses, thinks, and acts" (2012, 18). For the purposes of this chapter, I accept Bekey's definition with a few minor qualifications and elucidations, to which I now turn. To begin with, the sense in which a robot is "in the world" is meant to distinguish a robot from a computer program, which, of course, resides solely in cyberspace. Some (e.g., Searle 1984; Webb 2001) take exception to the idea that anything other than a biological organism senses, thinks, acts—indeed, has any mental life at all. However, I understand all three terms in a minimal sense that should not raise philosophical concerns. Let me explain. First, when I say that robots "sense," I mean only that they take inputs from their environment. Such inputs might be quite primitive, for example determining the ambient temperature in a small room. Or they might be quite sophisticated, for example determining small fluctuations in temperature from several miles away. But these inputs do not need to be direct analogs of anything that biological organisms experience. Second, when I say that robots "think," I mean no more than that they can take their sensory input and process it, applying programmed rules, learned rules, or both (Himes 2016, 12). Thinking, in the sense of the term I have in mind, amounts to no more than information processing. Plausibly, biological organisms are said to think when they too process information (Hunt 1980). But I leave it to others to decide whether human thinking goes beyond this model. Third, when I say that robots "act," I mean that on the basis of their sensing and thinking, they can both traverse and manipulate their environments. Whether robots can or do act intentionally or with free will is a fine source for speculation, but it is not my concern here.

Note that it is not the case that everything a robot does must be a result of its own sensing and thinking. At the moment, most robots at least occasionally act as the result of being controlled by a human agent, though some do not require this help. I will adopt the practice of calling a robot "autonomous" if all of its actions are the result of its own sensing and thinking, but "semi-autonomous" if some, not necessarily all, of its actions are the result of its own sensing and thinking (Lucas 2013). Nevertheless, we should not lose sight of the fact that some semi-autonomous robots are *more* autonomous than others, inasmuch as the former act autonomously to a greater degree.

What, then, distinguishes a military robot from other robots? Let us say that a military robot is designed and used for military applications, that is, applications that typically and intentionally advance the aims of a participant in war or a similar military conflict. The practice of war, it almost goes without saying, is conceptually messy and does not encourage the search for anything like a neat and tidy definition. Nevertheless, examples can help to clarify the concept of a military robot. At the moment, perhaps the most widely recognized example is the drone or, more properly, the uninhabited aerial vehicle (UAV). The U.S. military's MQ-1 Predator is one such military robot, and the more recent MQ-9 Reaper is another. These semi-autonomous military robots are capable of tracking and attacking targets from the air and, in the case of the Reaper, are able to use 500-pound laser-guided bombs to attack their targets. However, it is vital to note that military robots need not be as flashy or as deadly as the Reaper. Another example of a semi-autonomous military robot is the iRobot 510 Packbot, celebrated by Peter W. Singer in his *Wired for War* (2009, 19–41). The Packbot was designed to help identify and dispose of improvised explosive devices. It has no weapons system and does not constitute a direct threat to enemy combatants. However, the Packbot was designed for, and is used for, military applications—namely, protecting U.S. soldiers in the battle-space from injury and death.[1] There are, to be sure, many other types of military robots, such as the fully autonomous Goalkeeper CIWS, which defends ships from airborne and surface-based missiles, the Samsung SGR-A1, which partially replaces combat soldiers in the demilitarized zone between North Korea and South Korea, and the Gladiator Tactical Unmanned Ground Vehicle, which supports battle-space operations in lieu of larger non-autonomous artillery pieces. I will return to some of these specific kinds of robots later in this chapter. But for now we have a working definition of a military robot; it is a machine, situated in the world, that senses, thinks, and acts and that is designed and used for military applications.

18.2 Apples and Armed Conflict

One of the main claims of this chapter is that the use of military robots is likely to lead to more armed conflict. In this section I provide a simple model that relates the quantity of armed conflict to its price, and in the next section I use that model to provide an argument for this claim.

Begin with the simple idea, familiar from any Economics 101 class, that, for any given good, the price of that good and the quantity demanded of that good are inversely related, all other things being equal. Take apples as an example. If the price of a single apple is very high—say, $100—the quantity of apples that is demanded by those who desire apples will be very low. Only the wealthiest among us could splurge on a piece of fruit at that price. Conversely, if the price of a single apple is very low—$0.01, for instance—then the quantity of apples that is demanded by those who desire apples will be exceedingly high. Almost anyone could afford to buy apples at this price, and, even after our desire to eat apples was satiated, we might continue to buy them for other reasons, for example as decorations or to feed to our pets.

While the inverse relationship between price and quantity demanded is rather prosaic, I shall explain its relevance to military robots in a moment. However, before I do so, let me stress that the inverse relationship between price and quantity demanded holds all other things being equal, or *ceteris paribus*. When factors other than price change, quantity demanded might not change in the way suggested above. For instance, suppose it were discovered that apples cure cancer. Even if each apple cost $100, the quantity of apples demanded might still be higher than it was when they were, say, only $1 each but their health benefits were unknown. In much the same way, suppose that we learned that apples *cause* cancer. Even at the price of $0.01 the quantity of apples demanded would likely fall well below the quantity demanded when they were only $1 a piece but their carcinogenic nature was unknown. This *ceteris paribus* qualification will be important later in this chapter, and I shall return to it then.

With these qualifications in mind, let us use our simple economic model to help us understand the important effect of military robots on the likelihood of armed conflict.[2] Instead of imagining our rather banal demand for apples, let us turn to the demand for armed conflict between states. Like individual agents, states have a complex set of shifting and sometimes contradictory desires. But it is fair to say that states very often want greater control of territories and greater control of natural resources. Furthermore, they habitually desire that other states and international actors acquiesce to their wishes.[3] Just as apples are goods for those who desire them, so greater control of territories is a good for states that desire it, as many do. The same is true, *mutatis mutandis*, of greater control of natural resources and of the deference of other states and international actors to one's wishes. But like apples, these goods are rarely to be had without a price being paid.

While the price that we pay for apples is usually some amount of money, the price of the goods that states seek is more complex. While states sometimes purchase land from other states (as the United States did from France in the case of the Louisiana Purchase), this kind of transaction is unusual. Most transactions are what Aristotle called "involuntary" (Ross 1980, 111–12). States *take* land, *take* natural resources, and *force* other states to do as they bid by using armed conflict and the threat of armed conflict. In a very real sense, then, the price that states pay for these goods is to be understood in terms of creating, maintaining, and using military forces. More tangibly, the price that states pay for the goods they seek is the military materiel and personnel sacrificed for the good in question. If Canada wanted, for instance, to annex Baja California from Mexico, then the price it would have to pay is to be understood in terms of the lives of its own citizens and the resources it currently owns that would be destroyed in conquering and occupying Baja California.[4] In a moment, I will add some nuance to the picture that I have just painted. But let me stress the point that should be increasingly clear: just as the quantity of apples that we demand is, *ceteris paribus*, inversely related to the price of apples, so too the quantity of goods such as increased territory that states demand is, *ceteris paribus*, inversely related to the price they must pay in terms of armed conflict.

Earlier I promised a little more nuance. Let me begin by pointing out an important addition that must be made in the case of states that either are democracies or depend in important ways on the consent of the governed, which I shall call "near-democracies." States of this kind have to pay a further price when going to war. While a totalitarian regime need worry less about public opinion (Malinowski 1941), states that are democracies or near-democracies do not have this luxury. The loss of a solider in a democracy or near-democracy is often quite costly in terms of public opinion,[5] and an especially loss-averse electorate can force a state to cease military action after a fairly low number of casualties, as arguably occurred in the United States after nineteen U.S. soldiers were killed in the 1993 Battle of Mogadishu, famously portrayed in Mark Bowden's *Black Hawk Down* (1999) and Ridley Scott's film that was based on it. Of course, we should also note that democracies and near-democracies are not always so loss-averse and are sometimes willing to pay enormous costs in terms of lives to carry out military operations, as the United States and Great Britain did during World War II.

Let me turn now to a second addition that must be made to our understanding of the price that states pay when engaging in armed conflict. Autarkic states need not worry very much about what other states and the citizens of other states think of them, but there are few autarkies today. States whose economies depend on the economies of other states have to give at least some thought to international opinion. If Canada did try to annex Baja California, it would, I think it is safe to say, spark outrage not only among its own citizens but also among right-thinking people the world over. Behavior of this kind would likely cost Canada in terms of the willingness of other states to do business with it. Canada would be forced into economically unfavorable terms that could be quite costly, as its exports would fetch less on the world market, and its imports would be dearer. It should be noted, however, that states that wield a disproportionately large amount of economic power might be able to discount significantly the importance of international opinion, as the United States appears to have done before the beginning of the Second Gulf War (Goldsmith and Horiuchi 2012).

This nuancing, however, does not invalidate the underlying logic described above. On the contrary: states desire goods that only war is likely to bring, and the amount of armed conflict they are likely to be willing to accept depends on the price they will have to pay to fight this armed conflict, and this cost can include both, in the case of democracies and near-democracies, public opinion and, in the case of non-autarkies, international opinion and what follows from it.

18.3 Military Robots and the Likelihood of Armed Combat

An important claim for the subject of this chapter is that the development of military robots is almost certainly decreasing the price that technologically sophisticated states like the United States must pay to get what they desire by means of armed conflict. I make the case for this claim in broad brushstrokes here, and leave the fine detailed work for another time. A little more specifically, it is simply not feasible to offer a detailed comparison of a large-scale military operation involving robots with a military operation not involving robots. However, it is possible to get a clear idea of why the use of military robots is likely driving the price of armed conflict down and, therefore, causing us to arrive at a point where the quantity of aggressive behavior demanded by technologically sophisticated democratic and near-democratic states is higher.

The first and most important point to which we should attend is that the use of military robots allows states to substitute the loss of these robots for the loss of the lives of their own military personnel. We have already noted the general (if not exceptionless) unwillingness of citizens of democracies and near-democracies to support military operations that cost the lives of their own soldiers. In the case of the United States, this unwillingness seems to grow stronger by an order of magnitude each generation (Berinsky 2009). Nearly half a million U.S. service members died during the 1940s in World War II without breaking the country's willingness to fight, but roughly a tenth of that number of deaths was too much for the public during the War in Vietnam in the 1960s and 1970s. Roughly another tenth as many deaths was seen by many as too costly during the wars in Afghanistan and in Iraq during the 2000s. While it is easy to make too much of this trend, it is not an exaggeration to say that the U.S. public has become far more loss-averse and shows no sign of becoming less so soon. As a result, every substitution of a robot for a U.S. soldier who is at risk of being killed in a conflict significantly lowers the price that the state must pay to use military force. That is as true when it comes to substituting a UAV for a piloted airplane as it is when it is a matter of substituting a Packbot for a member of a bomb disposal detail.

Yet even if we set aside the lower price that democratic and semi-democratic states pay in terms of the opinion of their citizens, there are considerable cost savings to be had by substituting military robots for soldiers and other military personnel. We already noted that the MQ-9 Reaper is capable of delivering 500-pound laser-guided bombs. The unit cost of this robot is estimated to be $17 million (U.S. Department of Defense Budget 2013). The unit price of a piloted airplane, such as the F/A-18F, capable of delivering a 500-pound bomb is much higher; in fact, the F/A-18F's unit cost is more than $60 million (U.S. Department of Defense Budget 2015). To be sure, there are many differences between an MQ-9 Reaper and an F/A-18F, in addition to the fact that the former is an UAV and the latter is not. And I am not suggesting that the U.S. government could replace *all* of its F/A-18Fs with Reapers. But dropping a 500-pound bomb is something both of these aircraft do well, and one of them costs almost a quarter as much as the other. There are, therefore, considerable cost savings to be had through substitution.

Furthermore, the difference in cost does not stop with the price of the aircraft. F/A-18Fs need pilots. While it is difficult to acquire recent estimates of the amount of money that the United States spends to train a pilot of an airplane like the F/A-18F, it already cost in excess of $9 million less than two decades ago (U.S. GAO Report 1999). There is no good reason to think that this number has diminished since then. In contrast, the training necessary to become proficient as an operator of a UAV is about $65,000 (Defense News 2014). Much has been made about U.S. Air Force's offer of a $25,000 per year bonus to operators of UAVs (Bukszpan 2015), but this amount of money is a mere 1/360,000th of what it costs to train a pilot of an F/A-18F or similar aircraft.

It would be possible, at least in principle, to perform similar rough-and-ready calculations with a wide variety of situations in which a robot can take the place, wholly or partially, of a member of the military service and the non-autonomous machines that he or she uses. But the point is clear enough: military robots do many jobs much more cheaply than humans and human-controlled machines. Additionally, further technological advances will only serve to intensify this trend. The price of armed conflict, at least for technologically sophisticated states, is falling fast and will continue to fall. And we have already seen that at a lower price point, quantity demanded is higher.

Of course, it is important to recall that this analysis holds only *ceteris paribus*. As the price that states must pay to use violence in order to get what they want continues to fall, it is at least possible that other exogenous forces might cause the demand for these goods to fall as well. Indeed, there would be little point in writing a chapter like this one if there were not ways in which it might be possible to help prevent an increase in armed violence. I return to how this might occur in the final section of this chapter.

Finally, let me stress that I am not simply claiming that the use of military robots makes it *easier* for states to engage in armed combat. That fact is probably true but has been argued elsewhere (Sharkey 2012). The fact that something is easy is neither a necessary nor a sufficient condition for its being cheap. It would be quite easy for me to steer my car into oncoming traffic, but it would be far from inexpensive to do so. Likewise, it is free to run up Pikes Peak but far from easy to do so. Moreover, it is the increasing cheapness, not the easiness, of armed conflict that is driving (and likely will continue to drive) its frequency.

18.4 More War Is Morally Worse War (Mostly)

Philosophers and other thoughtful observers often point out that armed conflict need not be, on balance, bad. Aquinas wrote, "Manly exercises in warlike feats of arms are not all forbidden" (2012, 6525). And Suarez maintained, " [W]ar, absolutely speaking, is not intrinsically evil" (Williams 1944, 800). While acknowledging that "[w]ar is an ugly thing," Mill claimed it is "not the ugliest thing: the decayed and degraded state of moral and patriotic feeling which thinks nothing worth a war, is worse" (1862, 141).[6] Nevertheless, there is good reason to think that armed conflict is usually morally objectionable. In this section, I provide a brief argument meant to show that the increase in armed conflict caused by the use of military robots will be, all things considered, morally bad.

While this is not the time to dive deeply into an exposition of conventional just war theory, let us begin by noting one of its axioms: a war is fought justly by state S only if S's use of armed force is a response to unjust aggression against S. As Walzer puts it, "Aggression is the name we give to the crime of war." Walzer continues:

> The wrong the aggressor commits is to force men and women to risk their lives for the sake of their rights. . . . [T]hey are always justified in fighting; and in most cases, given that harsh choice, fighting is the morally preferred option. The justification and preference are very important: they account for the most remarkable features of the concept of aggression and for the special place it has in the theory of war. (1977, 51)[7]

It follows that, for any given war, no more than one state can fight justly, and at least one state must be fighting unjustly.[8] Hence, an increase in war means, *a fortiori*, an increase in states that are fighting war unjustly. This fact alone provides good reason to think that any increase in armed conflict is morally problematic unless there are very strong grounds for thinking that we are dealing with special cases.

However, matters are considerably worse than they might first appear. For it is extremely difficult for any state to fight a war justly. To begin with, states must meet a number of stringent conditions (*jus ad bellum*) in order to begin the war justly. These conditions include proportionality, right intention, final resort, probability of success, and public declaration by a legitimate authority. Even when states respond to unjust aggression, they often fail to meet one or more of these conditions and, therefore, wage war unjustly. In point of fact, it is hard to find many wars that have been fought over the past few centuries that unambiguously meet all of these conditions. It is arguable, for instance, that every war the United States has fought in the past seventy years violates at least one *jus ad bellum* condition. With one's back against the wall, one might point to the role of the United States and of Great Britain during World War II—and with some plausibility. But even if it is true that the United States and Great Britain each entered the war justly, it is almost certain that both states went on to fight the war *un*justly. Why? In addition to meeting the conditions of *jus ad bellum*, states must also prosecute the war (*jus in bello*) in a way that is both discriminate—that is, it must not target non-combatants—and proportional—that is, it must not use more force than necessary to attain its goals. The sad fact of the matter is that even on those rare occasions when states meet all of the conditions of *jus ad bellum*, they often violate the conditions of *jus in bello*. For instance, both the United States and Great Britain regularly targeted non-combatants and used far more force than necessary to achieve their aims (Anscombe 1939, 1956), especially late in the war (Walzer 1977, 263–8; Rawls 1999).

In short, more war is likely to mean, for the most part, more *unjust* war, and that is a morally worse state of affairs. I have limited myself in this section to a discussion of war in particular rather than armed conflict in general for the simple reason that war has received the lion's share of attention by moral philosophers. But the points I have made can be generalized, *mutatis mutandis*, to armed conflict as a whole.

Let me take a moment to consider a possible line of response to the argument I have just offered. I said that there might be grounds for thinking that we are dealing with special cases when it comes to military robots. According to this line of response, the increased use of military robots will lead to fewer violations of *jus in bello*, both by increasing the degree to which we can discriminate between combatants and non-combatants and by fine-tuning the amount of force that we use.

Strictly speaking, this outcome is possible. However, it seems quite unlikely. Drawing the distinction between combatants and non-combatants is a difficult and context-sensitive task—precisely, the sort of task that artificial forms of intelligence struggle with the most (Guarini and Bello 2012). It is something of a fantasy to think that military robots will do this sort of work any better than humans in the near future. While there is some reason to think that the use of UAVs in Pakistan has led to more appropriate levels of proportionality (Plaw 2013), the data is somewhat ambiguous, and discussion of the details of the study obscures the larger point: the use of UAVs in Pakistan is already morally problematic from the point of view of just war theory since the United States is not fighting a just war with this state (O'Connell 2015, 63–73). The question is not simply whether military robots will be used within the requirements of *jus in bello*; it is also whether technologically sophisticated states like the United States will be tempted to use military robots in ways that contravene the requirements of *jus ad bellum* simply because there is very little cost to doing so. Indeed, it should not come as a surprise that UAVs are often used for assassinations (Whetham 2013), something that is traditionally considered a violation of the requirements of just war (de Vattel 1758, 512; Walzer 1977, 183). Even some of those who show sympathy for the practice of so-called targeted killings have strong moral qualms about its current practice (Himes 2016, 121–68).

My claim is not, of course, that military robots can never be used justly. As a means of waging war they are not, for example, inherently indiscriminate and disproportionate in the way that nuclear, chemical, and biological weapons are (Lee 2012, 225). It is surely possible to imagine military robots being used, for instance, in a justified humanitarian intervention (Beauchamp and Savulescu, 2013). Just as cheap and readily available handguns might occasionally be used to save an innocent life, so too cheap military robots might also occasionally be used to save an innocent life. Nevertheless, the overall effect of cheap and readily available handguns is likely to be increased violence, which is morally problematic to say the least. Likewise, I have argued, the lower cost of military robots will also lead to more armed conflict, which is also morally problematic.

18.5 Military Robots: What Is to Be Done?

The economic logic by which military robots appeal to technologically sophisticated states is inexorable. Left to their own devices, states will almost certainly use military robots to increase the amount of armed conflict in the world. If it is difficult to imagine the U.S. government assuming the role of villain, one need only remind oneself that military robots are increasingly within the reach of many states, some of whom are hostile to the United States and its interests.

However, states are responsive to more than just economic logic. While I have no simple solution for the moral problems raised by the emergence of military robots, I want to conclude on a positive note by suggesting a few ways in which the use of military robots might be curbed. First, the U.S. public has raised few objections to the use of military robots, but there is a fairly recent history of successful public resistance to the U.S. military policy. Public opposition to the Vietnam War helped bring this conflict to an end, and a similarly motivated resistance might be able to do something comparable. Though the current opposition to the use of UAVs, for example, is next to nonexistent, so too was opposition to the Vietnam War in the early 1960s. Second, international opinion can also be used to motivate constraints on the use of military robots. As noted earlier, there are few autarkies among modern states, and it is possible for some states to put economic and diplomatic pressure to bear on states like the United States that use military robots. While the size of the U.S. economy makes this unlikely to have much of an effect here, it is possible that it could be more successful when wielded against incipient robotic powers such as Russia and Iran. Finally, international legal norms against the use of military robots are also a possibility, though at this point a rather dim one. If some or all uses of military robots were considered to be a war crime by the International Criminal Court in The Hague, we would probably see far less of it. That said, social norms against the use of military robots must first exist before it is codified as a legal norm. The prospects are daunting, but we should keep in mind that states face a similar kind of economic logic regarding the use of biological, chemical, and nuclear weapons. The development of social and legal norms has helped to prevent these weapons from being used on a wide scale. Perhaps such norms can do so with regard to military robots as well.

Acknowledgments

I am grateful for comments and questions to conference audiences at the Association for Practical and Professional Ethics (2016) and the Humanities and Educational Research Association (2016), to my Loyola University colleagues Ben Bayer, Drew Chastain, and Mary Townsend, and to the editors of this volume.

Notes

1. Interestingly, the Packbot has recently been adapted for non-military purposes, including use in areas infected by naturally occurring biohazards where humans would be at great risk. This fact suggests that it might be more accurate to speak of "robots with military uses" than "military robots." However, this locution is cumbersome and adds little value here, so I eschew it.
2. I focus in this chapter on military conflict rather than war because the term "war" is usually too narrow for my purposes. Even if, following Brian Orend, we understand war as "actual, intentional, and widespread conflict between political communities" (2006, 2), we exclude unidirectional conflict in which all of the violence is directed by one side of the conflict, as arguably occurs with the use of UAVs in places such as Yemen as I write this.
3. Hegel is, once again, edifying here: "War is the state of affairs which deals in earnest with the vanity of temporal goods and concerns" (Knox 1942, 324). I hope these claims will not seem cynical or, worse still, unscrupulous. It is far beyond the scope of this chapter to argue either that states in fact often act out of self-interest or that their conceptions of self-interest reliably include controlling territory and

natural resources, as well as getting their way with other international actors. By the way, the recognition that states often act in this way should, under no circumstances, be taken as a justification of this behavior. It is one thing, for instance, to acknowledge that humans sometimes rape and murder; it is another to endorse such actions.

4. It would be slightly more accurate to say that states purchase a chance at getting what they want, since they cannot simply exchange materiel and personnel for, say, territory, and they might well lose the war and get little or nothing (or worse). Wars can be better thought of as small lotteries in which all of the states (or statelike participants) pay for a chance to win (or keep) some good. Each player is likely to be willing to pay something close to what it thinks the good is worth. However, since there are multiple players, the total amount spent on playing the lottery is, therefore, likely to far exceed the value of the good. But we can ignore these depressing complications here.
5. See Mueller (1973) as well as the voluminous literature that Mueller's classic continues to spawn, especially the articles in the *Journal of Conflict Resolution* (1998) 42 (3).
6. Cadets at the U.S. Air Force Academy are still required during their first year of study to memorize this quote from Mill.
7. See also Walzer (1977, 51–73) and Orend (2006, 31–65). I hope it is fairly obvious that COIN and R2P are not exceptions to this axiom, since they too involve protection from and response to aggression. The familiar utilitarian approaches to the ethics of war are also outside what I have in mind when I speak here of conventional just war theory.
8. Or if the war involves coalitions, then at most one side can be fighting justly. I ignore this complication here in order to avoid unnecessary prolixity.

Works Cited

Anscombe, G. E. M. 1939. "The Justice of the Present War Examined." In *Ethics, Religion, and Politics: Collected Papers*. Vol. 3, 1991. Oxford: Blackwell Press.

Anscombe, G. E. M. 1956. "Mr. Truman's Degree." In *Ethics, Religion, and Politics: Collected Papers*. Vol. 3, 1991, 61–72. Oxford Blackwell Press.

Aquinas, Thomas. 2012. *Summa Theologica, Part II-II*. Translated by Fathers of the English Dominican Province. New York: Benziger Brothers.

Beauchamp, Zack and Julian Savulescu. 2013. "Robot Guardians: Teleoperated Combat Vehicles in Humanitarian Military Intervention." In *Killing by Remote Control: The Ethics of an Unmanned Military*, edited by Bradley J. Strawser, 106–25. Oxford: Oxford University Press.

Bekey, George A. 2012. "Current Trends in Robotics: Technology and Ethics." In *Robot Ethics: The Ethical and Social Implications of Robotics*, edited by Patrick Lin, Keith Abney, and George A. Bekey, 17–34. Cambridge, MA: MIT Press.

Berinsky, Adam J. 2009. *In Time of War: Understanding American Public Opinion from World War II to Iraq*. Chicago: University of Chicago Press.

Bowden, Mark. 1999. *Black Hawk Down: A Story of Modern War*. New York: Signet Press.

Brunstetter, Daniel and Megan Braun. 2011. "The Implications of Drones on the Just War Tradition." *Ethics & International Affairs* 25 (3): 337–58.

Bukszpan, Daniel. 2015. "Job Hunting? Drone Pilots Are Getting $125,000 Bonuses." *Fortune*, December 19. http://fortune.com/2015/12/19/drone-pilots-bonuses/.

Defense News. 2014. "GAO Tells Air Force: Improve Service Conditions for Drone Pilots." http://defense-update.com/20140417_gao-improve-service-conditions-drone-pilots.html.

de Vattel, Emer. 1758. *The Law of Nations*. Excerpted as "War in Due Form" in *The Ethics of War: Classic and Contemporary Readings*, edited by Gregory M. Reichenberg, Henrik Syse, and Endre Begby, 2006, 504–17. Oxford: Blackwell Press.

Goldsmith, Benjamin E. and Yusaku Horiuchi. 2012. "In Search of Soft Power: Does Foreign Public Opinion Matter to U.S. Foreign Policy?" *World Politics* 64 (3): 555–85.

Guarini, Marcello and Paul Bello. 2012. "Robotic Warfare: Some Challenges in Moving from Noncivilian to Civilian Theaters." In *Robot Ethics: The Ethical and Social Implications of Robotics*, edited by Patrick Lin, Keith Abney, and George A. Bekey, 129–44. Cambridge, MA: MIT Press.

Halgarth, Matthew W. 2013. "Just War Theory and Military Technology: A Primer." In *Killing by Remote Control: The Ethics of an Unmanned Military*, edited by Bradley J. Strawser, 25–46. Oxford: Oxford University Press.

Hunt, Earl. 1980. "Intelligence as an Information Processing Concept." *British Journal of Psychology* 71 (4): 449–74.

Himes, Kenneth R. 2016. *Drones and the Ethics of Targeted Killing*. New York: Rowman & Littlefield.

Knox, T. M., trans. 1942. *Hegel's Philosophy of Right*. Oxford: Oxford University Press.

Lucas, George R., Jr. 2013. "Engineering, Ethics, and Industry: The Moral Challenges of Lethal Autonomy." In *Killing by Remote Control: The Ethics of an Unmanned Military*, edited by Bradley J. Strawser, 211–28. Oxford: Oxford University Press.

Lee Steven P. 2012. *Ethics and War: An Introduction*. Cambridge: Cambridge University Press.

Malinowski, Bronislaw 1941. "An Anthropological Analysis of War," *American Journal of Sociology* 46 (4): 521–50.

Mill, John Stuart. (1862) 1984. "The Contest in America." In *The Collected Works of John Stuart Mill, Volume XXI—Essays on Equality, Law, and Education*. Edited by John M. Robson. Toronto, ON: University of Toronto Press.

Mueller, John E. 1973. *Wars, Presidents, and Public Opinion*. New York: John Wiley.

O'Connell, Mary Ellen. 2015. "International Law and Drone Strikes beyond Armed Conflict Zones." In *Drones and the Future of Armed Conflict*, edited by David

Cortright, Rachel Fairhurst, and Kristen Wall, 63–73. Chicago: University of Chicago Press.

Orend, Brian. 2006. *The Morality of War*. Calgary: Broadview Press.

Plaw, Avery. 2013. "Counting the Dead: The Proportionality of Predation in Pakistan." In *Killing by Remote Control: The Ethics of an Unmanned Military*, edited by Bradley J. Strawser, 106–25. Oxford: Oxford University Press.

Rawls, John. 1999. "Fifty Years after Hiroshima." In *John Rawls: Collected Papers*, edited by Samuel Freeman, 565–72. Cambridge, MA: Harvard University Press.

Ross, David, trans. 1980. *Aristotle: The Nicomachean Ethics*. Oxford: Oxford World Classics.

Searle, John R. 1984. *Minds, Brains, and Science*. Cambridge, MA: Harvard University Press.

Sharkey, Noel. 2012. "Killing Made Easy: From Joystick to Politics" In *Robot Ethics: The Ethical and Social Implications of Robotics*, edited by Patrick Lin, Keith Abney, and George A. Bekey, 111–28. Cambridge, MA: MIT Press.

Singer, Peter Warren. 2009. *Wired for War: The Robotics Revolution and Conflict in the 21st Century*. London: Penguin Press.

U.S. Department of Defense. 2012. *Fiscal Year (FY) 2013 President's Budget Submission February 2012*. http://www.saffm.hq.af.mil/shared/media/document/AFD-120210-115.pdf.

U.S. Department of Defense. 2014. *Fiscal Year (FY) 2015 Budget Estimates March 2014*. http://www.dod.mil/pubs/foi/Reading_Room/DARPA/16-F-0021_DOC_18_DoD_FY2015_Budget_Estimate_DARPA.pdf.

U.S. General Accounting Office. 1999. *Report to the Chairman and Ranking Minority Member, Subcommittee on Military Personnel, Committee on Armed Services, House of Representatives, August 1999*. http://www.gao.gov/archive/1999/ns99211.pdf.

Walzer, Michael. 1977. *Just and Unjust Wars: A Moral Argument with Historical Illustrations*. New York: Basic Books.

Webb, Barbara. 2001. "Can Robots Make Good Models of Biological Behavior?" *Behavioral and Brain Sciences* 24: 1033–50.

Whetham, David. 2013. "Drones and Targeted Killings: Angels or Assassins." In *Killing by Remote Control: The Ethics of an Unmanned Military*, edited by Bradley J. Strawser, 69–83. Oxford: Oxford University Press.

Williams, Gladys L., trans. 1944. *Selections from the Collected Works of Francisco Suarez, SJ*. Vol. 2. Oxford: Clarendon Press.

IV AI AND THE FUTURE OF ROBOT ETHICS

Introduction

As we look toward the future of robotics, the development of increasingly sophisticated and artificially intelligent machines strains long-standing philosophical theories across the canon. That humans might someday—whether in the medium term or the long term—be able to construct artificial beings, and construct them in whatever form and with whatever capacities we choose, demands that we confront our abilities in a way that is perhaps unprecedented in the history of technology. The chapters in part IV—sometimes as speculation, sometimes as urgent argument—explore the implications of creating and living alongside artificial beings whose mental and moral capacities might rival our own.

Robots with sophisticated mental capacities like intelligence, intuition, desires, and beliefs may be on the horizon. Attributing robust mental lives to robots may merely be a helpful heuristic, a way of understanding, explaining, and making sense of the behavior of robots. But writing off this talk as *merely* metaphorical risks ignoring the real possibility that these beings will have moral standing in virtue of their mental lives—that we might use and abuse robots that are entitled to greater consideration.

How can we know if artificial beings have a moral status, and a moral status comparable to what (or whom)? In chapter 19, Michael LaBossiere examines the various tests we might use to determine the moral status of artificial beings, including tests for reasoning and sentience, considering approaches that should satisfy philosophers on both sides of the consequentialist–deontological split. In response to doubts motivated by the (intractable) problem of other minds, LaBossiere argues in favor of a presumption of moral status, since it is preferable to treat a being better than its status merits than to regard a morally valuable being as a mere object.

Philosophers for centuries have regarded personal identity over time as depending on mental continuity, bodily continuity, or some combination of both. And this identity over time is in turn essential for interacting with beings over any period longer than a few minutes: for example, holding them to their promises, relying on predictable future behavior, or treating them in ways they deserve to be treated. If artificial beings become self-aware and have the power to modify their mental states or their physical bodies, then it may become unclear whether they remain the same being over time. Moreover, artificial beings could take part in activities like fission and fusion that have stymied debates in identity for decades. In chapter 20, James DiGiovanna explores the prospects for determining the continuity of artificial intelligences and cyborgs over time. He introduces the term *para-persons*, beings that are able to change all of their person-making qualities instantaneously. According to DiGiovanna, the difficulties involved in constructing a plausible criterion of identity over time for para-persons may be insurmountable.

How can we make sure that such beings are ethical? Since artificial intelligences might be superpowerful and could act and evolve at an uncontrollable pace, even the slightest mistake in moral reasoning could prove catastrophic. It is difficult, as Nick Bostrom has pointed out, to program goals for artificial beings reliably when even the simplest goals are difficult to formalize into computational language. In chapter 21, Steve Petersen engages closely with Bostrom's *Superintelligence* in the hope of avoiding "unfriendly" AIs. Petersen suggests we seek an account of goal formation as constrained by coherent practical reasoning. He suggests, following other agency theorists, that coherent reasoning is necessary for intelligence and sufficient for ethical behavior.

Both DiGiovanna and Petersen suggest that these AIs, whose personal identity through time is radically disrupted, dispersed, or distributed among agents, might in fact be *superethical*, since one of the trademarks of *unethical* behavior is to see yourself as special from the moral point of view. Appreciation for objectivity and equality are buttressed when this illusory self is destroyed. So an artificial intelligence might discover a kind of kingdom of ends that unites it with all other morally valuable persons, whether those beings are artificial or not.

Further considerations arise with regard to machines that are self-learning, as Shannon Vallor and George A. Bekey outline in chapter 22. The social benefits to be reaped are significant, including more accurate medical diagnoses, increased productivity and economic efficiency, and scientific discovery. Is it permissible for private companies to "teach" their products through interactions with the general public, even when those interactions impose significant risks on people who don't consent? For example, should an autonomous car be able to "learn" by interacting with human drivers, exposing them to some risk of harm?

It is not obvious that machine learning will produce objective, superior decision-making, either, as the instances of algorithmic bias—including racist or sexist outputs—accumulate. And even supposing that machines will one day be superior, this raises the problem of widespread unemployment caused by machines displacing human workers. Because the prospective benefits of machine learning and AI are intoxicating, we risk overlooking the potential for grave harms.

Still, it might be preferable to assign a robot to do a human's job. This is especially the case for jobs that are extraordinarily dangerous, require exquisite analysis and near-immediate response time, or take centuries to complete. Space exploration is one task that answers to all of these descriptions, and according to Keith Abney in chapter 23, there are good reasons to delegate these tasks to machines, or at the very least to insist on mixed crews of human and robot astronauts. Since it may be impossible to safeguard the health of astronauts, there are concerns about contaminating alien worlds, and since supporting human life multiplies the logistics of a mission, robots may be the ones best equipped to explore the final frontier.

Looking to the future, how can we make sure that the technoindustrial system we create is one friendly to humans? How can we avoid sleepwalking into a world where minute technological changes slowly acquire increasing sophistication, inscrutability, and permanence, until "things are in the saddle, and ride mankind," as Emerson wrote? Seeking answers to these questions from a surprising source, Jai Galliott, in chapter 24, draws on the work of the "Unabomber," Ted Kaczysnki, including personal correspondence.

Kaczysnki was worried that humans are constructing an increasingly sophisticated, impersonal technoindustrial world that demands that humans subjugate their own desires to it. How does the accelerating encroachment of AI and robotics into human life exacerbate these worries? And moving forward into the future, what should be our task as philosophers? How can we construct a philosophy of technology that is human-centric rather than one that risks subsuming human life to an abstract machine?

Humans have frequently imagined the future with some combination of wistful stirrings and a sense of foreboding about the unknown. There is a much greater need for introspection about the values and beliefs that have colored and structured human life, and about theories that have grown up around the history of human thought and human conditions, which now seem quaintly simple and straightforward by comparison. No philosophical domain will remain untouched by the accelerating advance of artificial intelligence and artificial beings. The thinkers represented here continue to ply unfamiliar waters into the misty dawn of the future of robotics.

19 TESTING THE MORAL STATUS OF ARTIFICIAL BEINGS; OR "I'M GOING TO ASK YOU SOME QUESTIONS . . ."

Michael LaBossiere

While sophisticated artificial beings are the stuff of science fiction, it is reasonable to address their moral status now, that is, before we start doing horrible things to or with them. Artificial beings will be something new, but humans have spent centuries debating the moral status of humans and animals. Thus, a sensible shortcut is developing a method of matching artificial beings with natural beings and assigning a corresponding moral status.

This matchup is in respects that are morally important, such as degree of intelligence or emotional capacities. For example, an artificial being that matches up with a human should have a comparable moral status. Likewise, an artificial being that matches up with a squirrel would have squirrel status. The practical moral challenge is to create methods allowing a sensible matching of artificial beings with natural beings. One classic approach has been to develop language-based tests for discerning the intelligence of language-using artificial beings. Such tests could be used to compare these artificial beings with humans and assign an appropriate moral status.

There is a problem presented by artificial beings that lack language capabilities. People will want artificial pets with emotional responses and intelligence that are similar to those of animals. If they are made like animals, they will lack conversational abilities. These beings would necessitate non-language-based tests. These tests would have to take into account the differences between the various types of artificial beings. Catbots, for example, would be tested for displaying the right sort of cruel indifference, while dogbots would be tested for feelings befitting a canine. As with the language-based tests, the artificial beings would be assigned a moral status analogous to that of the natural beings they most closely match.

While there are a multitude of moral theories that address moral status, our focus is on two common approaches. The first is *reason*, broadly construed. Kant's metaphysics of morals is a paradigm that bases moral status on rationality (Kant 2005). This will be the focus of the first part of this chapter. The second is *feeling*, also broadly construed. This can include things such as possessing emotions or the capacity to feel pleasure and pain. Many utilitarians, such as J. S. Mill (2001), base moral status on a being's ability to feel pleasure and pain. This test will be addressed in section 19.2. Section 19.3 will address concerns about granting moral status on the basis of these tests and presents three arguments in favor of a presumption of moral status. Now that two broad theoretical foundations have been laid down, it is time to build by considering tests of reason.

19.1 Tests of Reason

In regards to testing the capacity for reason, there are already well-established approaches, such as the Turing Test and the Cartesian Test. These tests involve interacting with a being in order to determine if it can use language.

Thanks to science fiction (and the *Imitation Game* (Tyldum 2014)), many people are familiar with the Turing Test (1950, 433–60). This test involves a machine and two humans. One human acts as the tester: she communicates with the machine and the other human via text and endeavors to determine which is human. If the machine's texting is indistinguishable from the human, it passes the test. In the context at hand, the machine would have earned a status comparable to that of a human, at least with regard to being a reasoning being.

René Descartes developed a language-based test centuries before Turing. In his discussion of whether animals have minds, he argued that the definitive indicator of having a mind (thinking) is the ability to use true language.[1] While Descartes believed his test would reveal a metaphysical thinking substance, the test can be aimed at determining capacities, which is the recommended use in this context. Roughly put, the Cartesian Test is if something really talks, then it is reasonable to regard it as a thinking being. Descartes, anticipating advanced machines, was careful to distinguish between mere automated responses and actual talking:

> How many different automata or moving machines can be made by the industry of man. . . . For we can easily understand a machine's being constituted so that it can utter words, and even emit some responses to action on it of a corporeal kind, which brings about a change in its organs; for instance, if touched in a particular part it may ask what we wish to say to it; if in another part it may exclaim that it is being hurt, and so on. But it never happens that it arranges its speech in various ways, in order to reply

appropriately to everything that may be said in its presence, as even the lowest type of man can do. (1991a, 139–40)

As a test for intelligence, artificial or otherwise, this seems to be quite reasonable, though it certainly requires developing a set of grading standards. It can be objected that it is possible for there to be an intelligent being with a language unrecognizable by humans or even no language at all. Such a being would not pass the Cartesian Test, though it would (by hypothesis) be intelligent.[2] A reply to this concern is that human-constructed beings would use human languages or languages humans would recognize. A second reply is that the mere possibility of such a being does not invalidate the test; at worst it indicates that an additional behavioral test would be needed. A third reply is that such a being would not be possible, but this argument would go beyond the limited scope of this work.

In moral terms, if an artificial being can match the human capacity to use true language, then this would be a good indicator that it possesses reason comparable to that of a human. This would indicate entitlement to a moral status analogous to that of a human. This assumes moral status is based on a capacity for reason.

While Descartes regarded his test as indicating the presence or absence of an immaterial mind, addressing moral status as a practical matter does not require deciding the metaphysical question of the nature of the mind. This is fortunate; otherwise the moral status of humans would also be forever hostage to metaphysics. One would, for example, need to solve the problem of the external world to determine if the apparent human who was seemingly struck by an apparent car is really suffering or not.[3] This is not to deny the relevance of metaphysics to ethics, just to note that the focus here is on practical ethics rather than concerns about the ultimate foundations of morality. However, the skeptic might be unbreakable here (LaBossiere 2008, 38–40), and this is certainly a point worth considering.

The Cartesian and Turning Tests do have an important limitation: they are language-based tests and would be failed by entities that lack the intelligence to use language. This is consistent with some reason-based approaches to ethics, such as Immanuel Kant's. He divided entities into two categories: rational beings (who have intrinsic worth; they are valuable in and of themselves) and objects (which have only extrinsic value; their value derives from being valued). It is certainly possible to follow this approach and deny moral status to entities that lack rationality. However, if non-rational natural beings are afforded moral status on the basis of their intelligence, then the same should also apply to non-rational artificial beings. For example, if a machine could pass suitable behavioral tests in a way that a dog could, it should be given the same status as a dog—assuming that moral status is assigned on the basis of intelligence.

One argument against using a language or other behavioral test for moral status is that a being could pass such a test without really being intelligent. John Searle (2002, 16) raised this sort of objection, arguing that believing a computational model of consciousness to be conscious is analogous to believing that a computational model of rain would make people wet. The concern is that artificial beings could be granted the same moral status as human beings when they are "faking" intelligence and not entitled to that status. This could be regarded as analogous to the use of a fake ID, albeit one in which the faker was unaware of the fakery.

The easy reply to such an objection is that perfectly "faking" intelligence would suffice as proof of intelligence. This is because intelligence would be required to "fake" intelligence, thus providing an ironic proof of intelligence.[4] This is not to deny that a being could fake having more intelligence than it does, but this is a different matter than faking having intelligence at all.

To use an analogy, if I could "fake" a skill and perform exactly like someone who actually had such skill, it would be difficult to deny that I had the skill. To use a specific example, if I could do everything a medical doctor could do, it would be odd to claim I lacked medical skill and was faking it. One would be forced to inquire as to the difference between my perfectly effective "fake" skill and the "real" skill.

It could be objected that an entity could be utterly indistinguishable from an intelligent being in regard to all possible empirical tests, yet lack intelligence. The challenge would be to present an adequate account of how this is possible. The trick of philosophical fiat would not suffice; what is needed is a detailed account of the mechanisms that would make it possible.[5] This problem, which is a version of the problem of other minds—the classic epistemic challenge of proving that other beings have minds—will be addressed later.[6] Having considered intelligence, we now turn to tests of feeling.

19.2 Tests of Feeling

While many thinkers base moral status on rationality, it is also important to consider feelings. While humans are (sometimes) rational and (usually) have feelings, science fiction is replete with artificial beings that are rational but lack feeling. Robbie the Robot of *Forbidden Planet* and Data of *Star Trek: The Next Generation* are good examples of such beings. These fictional artificial beings often make the point that they are not harmed by things like insults or their sports team losing. There is also the relevant concern about pain: breaking a robot's arm would damage it but need not cause it to suffer pain. Breaking my arm would, in addition to inflicting structural damage, cause pain. Since artificial beings could be thinking yet unfeeling, this would be relevant to their moral status. There is also a concern analogous to concerns about the moral status of natural beings, such as animals. A common approach to setting the moral status of animals is to base it not on their intelligence but on their capacity to feel and suffer. This approach was most famously taken by Peter Singer in *Animal Liberation* (1990).[7] As such, there needs to be a way to test for feelings.

One approach is to consider variations on the language tests. These tests would have to be redesigned to determine the presence or absence of artificial feeling (AF) rather than artificial intelligence (AI). Science fiction has already come up with such tests, the best known being the Voight-Kampff Test used in *Blade Runner* (Scott 1982) to distinguish replicants from humans.

One obvious problem with using a language test for feelings is determining whether the subject only knows how to use the words properly or if it *really* feels. An artificial being could be like a human actor reading emotional lines; all the right words are being said, but the emotions are not felt. Video games, especially role-playing games, already include attempts to convince humans that they are interacting with beings that possess emotions. The characters in the game express what are supposed to be taken as feelings, and some players get quite attached to these non-player characters. There are also various virtual girlfriend apps providing people with the illusion of a relationship. These "entities" do not, obviously, really feel. For the most part they are simply prerecorded audio or video.

In the context of the language test, a being with artificial emotions might merely have language skills and lack feelings grounding moral status. For example, if moral status is derived from being able to feel pleasure and pain, being only able to use the words properly would not provide that status—although, as will be argued, it might be reasonable to grant that status anyway.

Feelings are trickier than intelligence in regards to testing; humans are quite adept at faking feelings and routinely do so. A person might pretend to be in pain to get sympathy or fake sympathy in order to seem kind. In the case of emotions, unlike that of intelligence (or skill), a being could fake having a feeling while engaging in a flawless performance. Awards, such as Oscars, are given for doing this extremely well. In contrast, while an actor could play the role of someone engaging in fake surgery, a person could not routinely perform actual surgeries by faking surgical skill.

Because of the possibility of faking feelings, what is needed is a test even a human could not reliably fake—that is, a test that would reveal the presence or absence of feelings in a way analogous to a test for the presence or absence of a disease—not a perfect test, but a reliable one. One fictional example of something like this is the Voight-Kampff Test in Phillip K. Dick's *Do Androids Dream of Electric Sheep*? (1996). In this book, which inspired the film *Blade Runner* (Scott 1982), there are androids called replicants that look and act like humans. Replicants are not allowed on Earth, under penalty of death, and there are police who specialize in "retiring" them. Since replicants are otherwise indistinguishable from humans, the police use the test, which monitors physical responses to questions designed to provoke emotional responses, to screen suspects.

While the Voight-Kampff Test is fictional, there is a somewhat similar real test, designed by Robert Hare, which is the Hare Psychopathy Checklist (2016). This is supposed to provide a means of distinguishing psychopaths from normal people. While psychopaths do feel pain and pleasure, they are adept at faking emotions, and hence the challenge is determining when they are engaged in such fakery. While a fictional test and a checklist for psychopaths do not provide a means of testing for emotions, they do present an interesting theoretical starting point for distinguishing between real and fake emotions. In this case the intent is benign: to determine if an artificial being has the appropriate sort of feelings and assign it a moral status comparable to that of a similar natural being.

There are also a multitude of psychological tests relating to emotions; these can be mined for useful methods of testing for the presence of emotions. One likely approach is to test for what some psychologists call emotional intelligence, which is a capacity to understand the feelings of others, specifically their motivations. This ability is rather useful for cooperation but is equally useful for manipulation, as illustrated in *Ex Machina* (Garland 2015). This movie features an android, Ava, who is remarkably adept at understanding and manipulating human emotion. The movie does, however, serve as a cautionary tale: it is one thing to gauge a machine's intelligence and quite another to become emotionally involved with it.

While there is a general epistemic worry about the problem of other minds (or, since this deals with feelings, the problem of other hearts), there is a special concern about emotions: a being with the appropriate psychological (or theatrical) knowledge could act appropriately or manipulate effectively without feeling. Interestingly, Spinoza (1996) believed that he could work out human emotions with geometric exactness. If he was right, an unfeeling artificial being equipped with the requisite axioms and theorems, as well as the proper recognition software, could think its way through feelings. We could address this concern by accepting that while such an artificial being would lack whatever moral status is conferred by feelings, it would still have the moral status conferred by its intelligence.

Regardless of the actual tests used to determine the status of an artificial being, there will always be room for doubt. There will be practical doubt about the effectiveness of the tests analogous to doubts about medical tests. Just as there can be false positives and negatives in testing for diseases, there presumably can be false positives or negatives for feelings or intelligence. There also remains the problem of other minds: no matter the test, there will always be the possibility that there is no reality behind the appearance. The being that seems to feel might not feel at all. The being that seems to think might not think at all. Fortunately, the moral question of whether a being should be given moral status or not is distinct from the metaphysical question of whether a being really has such a status. It is to the presumption of status that the discussion now turns.

19.3 Presumption of Status

While there will always be both doubts about the status of artificial beings, I propose a principle of presumption of status as an antidote. This presumption is similar to the presumption of innocence in the U.S. legal system, in which the burden of proof is supposed to rest on the prosecution. A justification for the presumption of innocence in the legal system is the principle that it is better that a guilty person be set free than an innocent person be wrongly punished.

A far more controversial alternative to the presumption of innocence is the precautionary principle used in moral debates about abortion: despite the uncertainty of the moral status of a fetus, it is preferable to err on the side of caution and treat it as if it had the status of a person. On this view, a being that is a person should endure some negative consequences to avoid killing what might be a person.[8]

In the case of the presumption of status, the justification would rest on it being morally preferable to err on the side of treating a being better than its status justifies rather than to treat it worse. Three main arguments will be considered for the presumption of status: the utilitarian argument, the probability argument, and the ersatz argument.[9]

The utilitarian argument states that there should be a presumption of status because erring on the side of the higher status would tend to avoid more harm than it would create. For example, treating an android that acts quite human with the same politeness one would treat a human would cost nothing, yet avoid possible harm to feelings the android might possess. As another example, putting an unwanted artificial dog up for adoption rather than trashing it would not put an undue burden on the owner and would avoid possible suffering by the artificial dog.

A reasonable objection is that, as with the presumption of innocence, accepting a presumption of status could lead to greater harm than its rejection. For example, a firefighter might face a choice between a human and a human-like android when deciding which of the two to remove first from a burning building. If the android is presumed to have human status and does not, then picking the android first would be wrong; the human could perish while the firefighter is rescuing a being whose death would count less. While this is a sensible concern, it can be addressed.

One reply is to point out that while specific cases can occur in which the presumption of status creates more harm than good, the general impact of the principle will be positive. This is the same reply given to analogous criticisms of the presumption of innocence: it is easy enough to find (or imagine) cases in which significant harm was (or could) be done by enforcing the presumption of innocence. Yet these cases do not suffice to overthrow the presumption of innocence. If this is an effective reply in regard to the presumption of innocence, it should hold with the presumption of status as well. As such, the general principle should be accepted while acknowledging it is not a perfect principle.

Another reply is that the presumption of status, unlike the presumption of innocence, could be relative to the context: if a being with established status is in conflict with a being of merely presumed status, then the being with established status should be given moral priority. Returning to the fire example, the human has the moral status of a human while the android's human status is subject to doubt. As such, the human should be given priority. This can be seen as analogous to other situations involving knowledge and doubt. For example, if a driver has to choose between hitting another vehicle in which he can see people and hitting a parked vehicle he cannot see into, then it would be morally preferable to gamble that the parked vehicle is empty and hit it on the grounds that the consequences would be less bad. It might turn out that the parked car was full of people, but the sensible gamble would be to act on the available information.

Another approach to the presumption of status for artificial beings is to consider it in terms of probability. This can be seen as analogous to assessing a risk, such as shooting through a door because one suspects an intruder is on the other side. Since firing through a door could harm or kill an innocent being, a person should be sure of his target before opening fire.

Likewise, when one is acting in some way toward an artificial being, the probability that it has moral status has to be considered. The moral risk of acting in harmful ways toward an artificial being increases according to the likelihood that the being has a moral status. For example, compelling an advanced android to go into a damaged nuclear plant where the radiation could destroy it would be morally problematic proportional to the likelihood that the android has sufficient moral status to make such treatment wrong. So if it is probable that there is a person behind that polycarbonate shell, then compelling the android would be analogous to compelling a person about whose moral status we are certain to face the risk of likely destruction. In both cases it is likely that a person would be destroyed, thus making them morally equivalent.

While it seems unlikely that there will be an exact calculation regarding the probability an artificial being really has the status it appears to possess, a practical estimate seems to be well within human abilities. After all, people routinely base such judgments on the behavior of natural beings they encounter. In the case of sufficiently advanced artificial beings, the possibility that they actually possess their apparent status would seem to be enough to warrant treating them in accord with that status.

As with the utilitarian argument, one concern about this approach involves cases in which artificial and natural beings come into conflict. Using the nuclear plant example, imagine the choice is between a human or an android engineer and the radiation level is enough to destroy either. In such a case, the human is known to have the moral status of a human. The android, however, is only likely to have such status. As such, the android should be sent into the plant.

Looked at in terms of risk calculation, this would seem to be the right approach. Sending the human would yield a certainty that a being with human status will die. Sending the android would mean that it is only likely that a being with human status will be destroyed. If there were two humans that could be sent and one had a higher chance of surviving, then that human should be sent. This is because sending the human who will certainly die would result in certain death. Sending the human who might survive would result in only a likely death when preventing the meltdown, making it the morally better choice. Since the android might not have human status, sending it means that the meltdown might be prevented without the destruction of a being with human status. This would make it the right choice based on estimations of probability.

One point of concern for this approach is that it condemns artificial beings to second-class moral status due to epistemic concerns about their actual status. Humans have routinely treated other humans as second-class beings (or worse) due to bigotry, and this has always turned out horribly. Slavery in the United States is one example of this. As such, perhaps it is wiser to avoid making the same horrific moral mistakes again by deciding that it is better to err on the side of a higher moral status than intuitions might indicate. While intuitions/biases in favor of the natural over the manufactured are certainly powerful, the next and last defense allows one to accept the prejudice while granting a type of status. This final defense of the presumption of status is an argument for ersatz status.

The ersatz status option is to accept that while some artificial beings probably lack status, they should still be granted an ersatz status. The argument for this is a repurposed version of Kant's argument for treating animals well (1930, 239–41).

Since Kant bases moral status on rationality and denies that animals are rational, it follows that for him animals lack moral status. They are "objects of the inclination" in Kant's moral taxonomy (1998, 428). Because of this, he contends that we have no direct duties to animals. Fortunately, his heart is warmer than his rational brain—he endeavors to sneak in indirect duties to animals. In arguing for this, he claims that if a rational being doing *X* would create a moral obligation to that being, then an animal doing *X* would create an ersatz moral obligation. For example, if the loyal friendship of a human creates an obligation not to abandon her when she has grown old and become a burden, then the same would hold true for a loyal dog that has grown old.

While this might seem to create a direct obligation to the dog, Kant is careful to engage in a bit of philosophical prestidigitation to avoid granting the dog this sort of moral status. Put roughly, the dog's lack of rationality results in a lack of moral status, and hence it cannot be wronged. Yet Kant holds that it would be wrong to abandon the loyal dog. Making this work requires more philosophical wizardry.

Kant takes an interesting approach to granting animals a form of status. Using the example of the dog, Kant would say that if the person abandoned her loyal old dog, then her humanity would be damaged by this callous action. Put in general terms, acting in inhumane ways toward animals would have harmful consequences—not to the animals (which have no moral status) but toward other humans. Treating animals with cruelty would make it more likely for a person to fail in her duties to other humans, and this would be wrong.

Kant's approach can be seen as taking the treatment of animals as moral practice for humans. To use an analogy, imagine police officers undergoing training in virtual "shoot or don't shoot" scenarios. The images of people used in training obviously have no moral status, so the officers have no moral obligation to not "shoot" them. However, if an officer does not practice as if the scenarios are real, then she is more likely to make the wrong choice in a situation involving actual people. As such, she is under an obligation to treat the simulated people as people because of her obligation to actual people.

Kant goes beyond a mere injunction against cruelty to animals and enjoins us to be kind. While this is laudable, it is because he thinks that kindness to animals will develop our kindness to humans. Animals are, going back to the analogy, objects of practice for the real thing—humans. This grants animals an ersatz moral status even though Kant regards them as lacking true moral status (other than being objects).

If Kant's reasoning can be used to justify an ersatz moral status for animals, then it is reasonable to think it can justify an ersatz moral status for artificial beings. Conveniently enough, an experiment has already been conducted that is relevant to this matter.

In 2015, Frauke Zeller and David Smith created hitchBOT (2016)—a solar-powered iPhone in a cute anthropomorphic plastic shell. This was done as part of an experiment to determine how people would interact with the bot as it "hitch-hiked" around. While the bot made it safely across Canada and Germany, it lasted only two weeks in the United States and was destroyed in Philadelphia.

Unlike what might be the case for advanced artificial beings, there is no doubt about hitchBOT's moral status. Being an iPhone in a plastic shell, it was obviously a mere object. It did not think or feel—it did not even seem to think or feel.

What makes hitchBOT relevant is that people did have positive feelings toward it because of its endearing appearance and the virtual personality created for it via social media. Because of this, it could be regarded as the illusion of a person—a mechanical Turk hitching its way around the world via the courtesy and kindness of strangers.

Given that Kant regards animals as objects and hitchBOT is also an object, it could be taken as morally equivalent to an animal. The problem with this line of reasoning is that it would make all objects, such as rocks, on par with animals. Since Kant did not grant even ersatz moral status to rocks or clocks, there must be something that distinguishes animals from other objects. Those who accept that animals have a moral status would have no problem making the distinction between rocks and raccoons, but Kant has what appears to be a simple dichotomy between rational beings and everything else. Yet he grants animals an ersatz moral status, and this has to be grounded in something.

This something is that the way humans treat animals has a psychological impact that influences how humans treat each other. One plausible basis for this is that animals are more like humans than they are like rocks, and the similarity provides the foundation for their influence. This does tie into Descartes's view of animals: while denying they have minds, he does not deny that they have life or feelings (1991b, 336). He also accepts that humans think animals have minds because of an argument based on an analogy: they seem like humans in appearance and actions, so it is natural to infer that since humans have minds, so do animals. Bertrand Russell (1999, 514–16) proposed his own solution to the problem of other minds using an argument by analogy. This would nicely explain why the treatment of animals impacts how humans treat other humans: the more an animal is like a human, the more a person becomes habituated to a particular way of treating such a being. Aristotle (1976), of course, makes an excellent case for people becoming what they repeatedly do. Plato, in book 10 of the *Republic* (1979, 261–4), also makes the point that people can be strongly influenced even by exposure to the emotions of fictional characters.

The same influence would presumably hold in the case of artificial beings that are similar to animals that are like humans.[10] For example, a robotic dog that is like a real dog would be like a human and thus gain an ersatz status.[11]

Turning back to the specific example of hitchBOT, even though it was clearly an object, it became an illusory person through social media and anthropomorphizing. This was shown by the emotional response to its "murder" (Danner 2016). As such, it seems reasonable to think that hitchBOT was entitled to an ersatz moral status because of its power to influence people emotionally.

If this reasoning works for hitchBOT, it would also apply to artificial beings possessing deeper similarities to animals or humans. Being more like animals and humans in relevant ways would be likely to yield an even greater psychological impact on humans, thus providing an even stronger foundation for an ersatz moral status. While hitchBOT could merely be cute, advanced artificial beings could engage in activities analogous to those humans engage in and if these activities were to create an obligation if performed by a human, then they would create an indirect obligation to the artificial beings. Returning to the dog example, if a robot dog performed the activities that would create an indirect obligation to a natural dog, then the robot dog would seem to have earned an ersatz moral status even if it was believed to lack a status of its own. In the case of human-like artificial beings, even if their own moral status is in doubt, they would still be entitled to this ersatz moral status.

Following Kant's approach to animals, this ersatz moral status would make it wrong to harm or abuse artificial beings without adequate justification. For example, harming artificial beings for mere sport would be wrong. Since such beings have only ersatz moral status, they would be less morally protected than natural beings and the needs of natural beings would trump such beings. So artificial beings could be justifiably harmed if doing so was necessary to promote the ends of natural beings. Returning to the example of the nuclear plant, if there was a choice between sending a human or an android into the plant, then the android should be sent—assuming that the android has only ersatz status.

In light of the preceding discussion, working out the moral status of artificial beings will be challenging but can be done with proper guidance and reflection. Even if people are unwilling to grant such beings full moral status, it seems that they would be at least entitled to an ersatz moral status. And ersatz, as no old saying goes, is better than no moral status.

Notes

1. For Descartes, animals did not use true language: "That is to say, they have not been able to indicate to us by the voice, or by other signs anything which could be referred to thought alone, rather than to a movement of mere nature" (1991b, 366).
2. If this is possible, the Cartesian Test would be a sufficient but not necessary test for intelligence.
3. The problem of the external world, made famous by Descartes and the film *Matrix* (Wachowski and Wachowski 1999), is that of proving the world one experiences is really real.
4. For example, Searle's well-known Chinese Room argument requires an intelligent human being to operate the room. Thus, though the human might not understand the language, it takes considerable intelligence to make the room work.
5. John Searle endeavors to do just this in his famous Chinese Room argument.

6. The problem of other minds is a challenge in epistemology (the theory of knowledge). Beginning with the assumption that I have a mind (that I think and feel), the challenge is to show how I know that other beings have minds (that they think and feel).
7. Singer was not the first to take this approach and was preceded by Jeremy Bentham. Singer's book is, however, most likely the best-known popular work on this subject.
8. Though an excellent analogy, the comparison is used with reluctance because of the emotionally charged nature of the abortion debate. There is also the fact that the relation between a woman and her fetus is rather different from the likely relations between humans and artificial beings.
9. The inspiration for ersatz moral status is David Lewis's discussion of ersatz possible worlds (1987, 136–91).
10. An early version of this argument appeared in my *Talking Philosophy* blog post, "Saving Dogmeat" (LaBossiere 2010).
11. An excellent fictional example of the possible emotional impact of an artificial animal is the "Soul of the Mark III Beast" (Miedaner 1988).

Works Cited

Aristotle. 1976. *Nicomachean Ethics.* Translated by J. A. K. Thomson. London: Penguin Books.

Danner, Chas. 2016. "Innocent Hitchhiking Robot Murdered by America." http://nymag.com/daily/intelligencer/2015/08/innocent-hitchhiking-robot-murdered-by-america.html.

Descartes, René. 1991a. *The Philosophical Writings of Descartes*. Vol. 1. Translated by John Cottingham, Robert Stoothoff, Dugald Murdoch, and Anthony Kenny. New York: Cambridge University Press.

Descartes, René. 1991b. *The Philosophical Writings of Descartes*. Vol. 3. Translated by John Cottingham, Robert Stoothoff, Dugald Murdoch, and Anthony Kenny. New York: Cambridge University Press.

Dick, Philip K. 1996. *Do Androids Dream of Electric Sheep?* New York: Ballantine Books.

Garland, Alex (director). 2015. "Ex Machina." Alex Garland (screenplay).

Hare, Robert. 2016. "Psychopathy Scales." http://www.hare.org/scales/.

HitchBOT. 2016. "HitchBOT Home." http://mir1.hitchbot.me/.

Kant, Immanuel. 1930. *Lectures on Ethics.* Translated by Louis Infield. London: Methuen.

Kant, Immanuel. 1998. *Groundwork of the Metaphysics of Morals.* Translated and edited by Mary Gregor. Reprint, Cambridge: Cambridge University Press.

Kant, Immanuel. 2005. *Fundamental Principles of the Metaphysics of Morals.* Translated by Thomas Kingsmill Abbot. Reprint, New York: Dover.

LaBossiere, Michael. 2008. *What Don't You Know?* New York: Continuum.

LaBossiere, Michael. 2010. "Saving Dogmeat." http://blog.talkingphilosophy.com/?p=1843.

Lewis, David. 1987. *On the Plurality of Worlds*. Oxford: Basil Blackwell.

Miedaner, Terrel. 1988. "The Soul of the Mark III Beast." In *The Mind's I*, edited by Douglas R. Hofstadter and Daniel Dennett, 109–13. New York: Bantam Books.

Mill, John Stuart. 2001. *Utilitarianism.* Edited by George Sher. Indianapolis: Hacking.

Plato. 1979. *The Republic.* Translated by Raymond Larson. Arlington Heights, IL: Harlan Davidson.

Russell, Bertrand. 1999. "The Analogy Argument for Other Minds." In *The Theory of Knowledge*, edited by Louis P. Pojman, 514–16. Belmont, CA: Wadsworth.

Scott, Ridley (director). 1982. "Blade Runner." Philip K. Dick (story). Hampton Fancher and David Peoples (screenplay).

Searle, John. 2002. *Consciousness and Language.* Cambridge: Cambridge University Press.

Singer, Peter. 1990. *Animal Liberation*. New York: New York Review of Books.

Spinoza, Benedict. 1996. *Ethics.* Translated by Edwin Curley. New York: Penguin Books.

Turing, Alan. 1950. "Computing Machinery and Intelligence." *Mind* 236: 433–60.

Tyldum, Morten (director). 2014. "Imitation Game." Graham Moore (screenplay).

Wachowski, Lana and Lilly Wachowski (directors). 1999. "The Matrix." Lana Wachowski and Lilly Wachowski (screenplay).

20 ARTIFICIAL IDENTITY

James DiGiovanna

It's widely thought by philosophers that an artificial intelligence (AI) could, in principle, be a person. At the very least, the standard criteria for personhood are not inherently impossible for AIs to meet: they could be self-conscious; they could regard others as persons; they could be responsible for actions; they could have relations to others and to communities; they could be intelligent and rational; they could have second-order intentions; and, at least on compatibilist notions of free will, they could have free will, presuming we could program desires into their software. Bostrom (2014, ch. 2) makes a good case that this is doable, although philosophers of mind are still skeptical about the near possibility of conscious AI.

But even if an AI acquired all the standard personhood traits, there is one area where it might be so unlike persons that we would have to rethink some of the limits of the concept: AIs would not abide by norms of personal identity. Personal identity across time is usually tracked by either psychological or physical characteristics. These characteristics can change over time while still preserving identity if the changes are very gradual or piecemeal. But with an artificial person, sudden and radical change in both the physical and mental becomes possible. Further, the science-fiction examples that have animated debate on the edges of the personal identity literature, such as fission (Nagel 1971), fusion (Parfit 1971, 22), group minds (Schwitzgebel 2015, 1701–2), memory-wipes (Williams 1973), and instantaneous personality updates (Parfit 1984, 236–8), become possible. These effects are not limited to purely artificial intelligences. With human neural enhancement technologies, such as artificial memory and brain-to-brain interfaces, it may soon be possible for humans to make similar drastic changes to themselves, including undergoing fission and fusion by making mental duplicates or combining their mental content with that of others.

Thus, human enhancement and strong AI-based robotics converge upon the creation of entities that are largely capable of rewriting or recreating their personalities, bodies, and, by extension, themselves. As philosophers such as Thomas Douglas (2013), Allan Buchanan (2009), Jeff McMahan (2009), Julian Savulescu et al. (2001, 2008), and Hannah Maslen et al. (2014) have noted, human enhancement creates moral dilemmas not envisaged in standard ethical theories. What is less commonly noted is that, at root, many of these problems stem from the increased malleability of personal identity that this technology affords. An AI or a cyborg with neural implants that controlled, supplemented, or replaced certain brain functions, such as memory, reactivity, and irritability, or that had transferable memory would have the ability to change both its mental content and, given developments in prosthetics, its physical body, instantly, and radically. If a self becomes so reworkable that it can, at will, jettison essential identity-giving characteristics, how are we to judge, befriend, rely upon, hold responsible, or trust it? We are used to re-identifying people across time. We assume that persons are accountable for prior actions because they can be identified with the agent who performed those actions. But can a being that is capable of self-rewriting be said to have an identity?

This comes down to a question of the nature of personhood. Philosophers have frequently noted that an AI *could* be a person (Putnam 1964; Midgley 1985; Dolby 1989; Petersen 2011). But what they fail to note is that this might require that we prevent it from learning, adapting, and changing itself at the rate at which it would be capable. Tom Douglas (2013) claims that human enhancement and strong AI might create supra-persons, that is, beings that are ethically superior to humans and that might have ethical precedence over us. Douglas assumes that such beings would be, if anything, even more responsible for their actions than we are. But again, this would require that they have some kind of stable identity to which responsibility can attach. So while a supra-personal being is possible, it would require that we *not* allow it to utilize its full capacity. Otherwise, it may, by rapidly shedding identities, cease to be one and the same person across time. Instead of moral supra-persons, what AI and enhancement are likely to lead to, I'll argue, are entities that fail to be persons not because they fail to meet the requirements of personhood, but because they have an additional, personhood-defeating capacity.

I'll call these beings "para-persons." These would be any being that meets all the positive requirements of personhood (self-awareness, ethical cognition, intentionality, second-order desires, etc.), but has an additional quality that disqualifies it for personhood: in this case, the ability to change instantly and without effort. There may be other ways to be a para-person, but here I'll focus on those para-persons that are capable of erasing and rewriting their identities. Our ethical systems are designed or adapted to apportion blame and praise to persons.

They could do the same for supra-persons. But it's not clear that they will work with identity-defying para-persons.

20.1 The Kinds of Identities a Para-Person Might Have

It may be that there is no way to apply identity criteria to such para-persons, or it may be that we need to adapt our identity concepts to these new possibilities. Maybe what we learn by this is that machines and machinified organic beings cannot have identity. But then humans are machines and subject to many of the same problems as AIs. They may undergo their changes more slowly, but they do forget the past and "reprogram" their personalities in response to environment, accident, and plan. As David Lewis (1976) noted, given enough time, we too drift in our identity as much as a being that instantaneously reprograms itself.

Lewis's case of the extremely long-lived person who eventually changes so much as to have no content in common with himself from 137 years earlier brings to the fore Parfit's idea that, in some cases, personal identity is indeterminate (1984, 213) because some amount of change has occurred, but it's not clear if it's enough change to completely alter identity or not. The problem for the AI is that it can change so constantly that its identity is *never* determinate for any significant length of time: it could be constantly changing, adding knowledge, experimenting with ways to be, and, perhaps most disturbingly for identity, merging, separating and re-merging with other AIs such that individuality, the core of identity, is challenged.

Again, this may tell us something about the already social nature of personal identity for humans. But whereas with humans we can at least maintain the fiction of discrete individuality for the purpose of assigning moral responsibility, with a para-person that fiction might shatter. We may need completely new narratives to encapsulate what it means, morally, socially, and subjectively, to be such a para-person. With that possibility dawning, we need to at least interrogate how we will hold such a being responsible for a crime, assign it property, and react to it as a social being with places in our friendships, families, and work.

Traditional accounts of identity tend to hinge on either psychological continuity (Locke 1689; Parfit 1984; Shoemaker 1984) or physical continuity (Williams 1973; Thomson 2007; Olson 1997, 2003). More recently, emphasis has been placed on identity through personal narratives (Riceour 1995; Schechtman 2005) and, drawing from literature in social science, identity as socially derived or constructed (Schechtman 2010; Friedman 1985; Singer, Brush, and Lublin 1965; Festinger, Pepitone, and Newcomb 1952; Chodorow 1981; Foucault 1980; Alcoff 2005). In the following section, I'll examine the limits of each of these accounts in the face of technologically enhanced or derived beings.

20.2 Psychological Identity

Psychological theories, like those of Locke, Parfit, and Shoemaker, are the most popular of the standard views, with a plurality of philosophers (see the poll by Bourget and Chalmers 2014) and a large majority of naive respondents (Nichols and Bruno 2010) preferring this model. Although the original Lockean model of psychological identity has been subject to strong counterarguments, Parfit (1984, 204–8) and Shoemaker (1984) have developed models that capture the intuition that psychological content is central to identity while still answering the criticism that (1) psychological content undergoes too many changes and (2) psychological content fails as a criterion because it violates transitivity for identity: as content fades over time, a present being may be identical to a past being and a future being that are not identical to each other.

Combining their accounts, we could hold that a person is identical to some prior person if enough psychological content is the same over two days (say, 50%) and if the continuing psychological content on the second day is caused by its having been there on the first day and, over a course of many days, if the content is part of an overlapping chain of such day-to-day (or hour-to-hour, minute-to-minute) continuities. A person, then, is the same person as some prior person if they are part of the same overlapping chain of properly connected and caused mental content.

This version has two important elements: a causal connection, and continuous content.

Obviously, an AI or cyborg *could* have personal identity on this account, but not if it had para-personal tendencies toward self-transformation. The problem here would be that the para-person is (1) prone to breaking the chain's 50% requirement by making instantaneous and large-scale deletions or alterations to its mental content, and (2) it could re-acquire memories in a way that was not causally connected to its previously having them.

For example, imagine Tom and Steve, two para-persons who grow up together. Tom suffers a radical memory loss, so the memory record of Steve is put into Tom, and editors work on the memories, deleting those that are purely Steve's and adjusting the others so that they work from Tom's perspective. At the end, Tom has his memory of basic facts and skills (let's assume Tom and Steve learned to read, ride bikes, etc. together) and most of his autobiographical memories, and they are pretty much as accurate as they were before, or at least as accurate as current human memory. Here Tom would have a kind of personal continuity but would not have Shoemaker-style personal identity because his current mental content was not caused by his prior mental content. But would we hold Tom responsible for crimes he had committed before the memory restoration? If we think that (1) Shoemaker is right that Tom has lost personal identity and (2) Tom should still be held accountable for crimes, we have a disconnect between our identity and responsibility intuitions.

Even more so than memory, the ability to rewrite dispositional mental content such as ethical values, the capacity for empathy, and general personality traits undermines personhood. As Nichols and Bruno (2010) and Strohminger and Nichols (2015) noted, people are quick to deny continuity to a being that undergoes a complete change in basic values. A para-person that could experiment with worldviews, completely adopting and deleting value systems, preferences, and bases for judgment, would be largely lacking in what is commonly understood as the most basic element of personal identity.

On the other hand, considering how little memory we accurately retain (Chen 2011; Arkowitz and Lilienfeld 2010; Loftus 2005), maybe *only* AIs and cyborgs-from-birth could have personal identity on the psychological account. An artificial or enhanced being could at least potentially remember every bit of data it encountered. No human could. Such a para-person could solve the problem of Lockean personal identity without recourse to Parfit and Shoemaker's fixes: on Locke's account we fail to be the same person across time if we cannot remember the prior time. But a para-person could have complete memories even of a time when most humans have almost no memories, such as those of early childhood, or sleep. However, this creates another problem: it could also have perfect memories of many other beings, all the other para-persons that it has shared memories with. Would it then be these other people? At least on some Lockean accounts, it would be (see section 20.4 on the honeycomb problem).

Still, as has been shown in many criticisms of the memory criterion, memory is generally not sufficient for identity (Reid 2002; Williams 1970). Some other steadiness or consistency is required, whether it's moral character (Strohminger and Nichols 2015), bodily continuity (Olson 2003), or consistency of life plan (Korsgaard 1989). And all of these, along with memory, are, in AIs, subject to the kind of sudden breaks and immediate rewritings that make re-identification at best questionable.

20.3 Physical/Animal Identity

In response to problems with psychological theories, physical theories have been proposed by Williams (1970), Thomson (2007), Olson (1997, 2003), and others. The most thoroughly worked out of these is Eric Olson's animalism, which tracks the identity of animals. However, this clearly fails to apply to an entirely artificial being, and, further, it is ruled out by Olson for at least certain forms of cyborgs: Olson holds that an organism that maintains itself by artificial means is no longer living and thus lacks animal identity (1997, ch. 6, sec. 3). If the cyborg only replaced non-vital organs, it might have animal identity, but this wouldn't help us with forensic matters of guilt and responsibility. As Olson notes, "[T]he Biological Approach does have an interesting ethical consequence, namely that those practical relations are not necessarily connected with numerical identity" (1997, ch. 3, sec. 7). This is because the mere physical continuity of an organism doesn't tell us anything about the relation between that organism and some prior entity that planned or committed a crime. Brain swaps, memory wipes, and personality reprogramming split the link between animal continuity and moral identity, so the animal account does not tell us what we're most concerned with: who is responsible.

Other physical accounts (Williams 1970; Thomson 2007) aren't so tied to the natural life of an animal. What's important for them is physical continuity. And, at least on Williams's account, responsibility, or at least a sense that a physically connected future self is indeed the same subjective person, is preserved. As in the psychological case, there are two possibilities for an artificial being:

1. It could have clearer identity than an organic human. That is, while humans generally gain and lose matter over their lives, winding up with none of their original matter, a machine could, if well maintained, be composed of almost all of its original matter.

Or:

2. It could meet personhood requirements but fail to be physically consistent. If an AI were put into a new body each day simply by transferring all of its mental content, it's not clear why this would exclude it from personhood, especially if it was always only in one body at a time. It would have an important kind of continuity: I imagine there would be no problem holding it responsible for a crime, especially if it was completely in charge of its body transfer and had no duplicates. But it would lack *any* physical continuity and wouldn't have identity with its prior self at all on these accounts.

Body-switching is a clearly para-personal power. It does not prevent the para-person from passing any of the personhood tests, but it undermines personhood by giving the para-person *too much* freedom to change. To go from an athletic body to a sedentary body, a power-lifter's body to a long-distance runner's body, a beautiful body to a hideous body, all in a moment, is so unlike the powers of current persons, and so contrary to the sort of striving with bodies and relations to bodies that we currently have, that it may undermine personhood by undermining bodily identity. Still, given the common intuition that psychological content is more important to persons than physical continuity, this may be less para-personal than the previous case, and perhaps even superpersonal. It is, in fact, exactly the sort of power that some comic book superheroes and shape-shifting mythical gods have, and we have no trouble believing that Zeus remains Zeus when he transforms from man to bull to swan, as evidenced by the narrative tradition that treats him as the same being.

20.4 The Honeycomb Problem for Physical and Psychological Identity

Parfit (1971, 22) discusses the possibility of persons who could merge into a single being and split into several. A life map of a set of such creatures would look like a honeycomb, with multiple beings intersecting, separating out, and joining up. Although presented as a thought experiment, this becomes possible for para-persons with the power to combine and copy their mental content and operating systems.

Imagine the following scenario: Aleph and Beth are artificial beings. After seven years as individuals, they unify their memory and processing into a single system, becoming Baleph. Though there are two bodies, there is a single mind aware of what is happening in both bodies. After seven years, Baleph disconnects its two bodies, which name themselves Gimel and Dale. Both have full memories of the Baleph years and full memories of the Aleph and Beth years. Are both Gimel and Dale liable for crimes committed by the Baleph collective? Should either, both, or neither be punished for crimes committed by Beth prior to the merger?

On most accounts of personal identity, Aleph and Beth are not identical to Baleph, and neither are Gimel and Dale. Nor would Gimel be identical to Aleph, nor Beth to Dale, as all of this would violate transitivity of identity, since prior to the fusion Aleph and Beth were not identical to each other, and after the split, neither are Gimel and Dale. But it also doesn't seem as though the entity that committed Beth's crimes is completely gone in Baleph, nor would Baleph's crimes be forgiven if it splits into Gimel and Dale.

This is merely the simplest fission/fusion case. It's easy to multiply complications:

1. Assimilation: Blob is a para-person that can assimilate the memories and personality of any other para-person. It considers itself a distinct entity with a long history, but each new assimilate's history is added to its memories. There are so many that the addition of a new one doesn't completely alter Blob's personality, although it does alter it about as much as, say, engaging in an emotionally intense relationship alters the personality of a human being.

2. Union: A group of para-persons unites into a single para-person, all at once, so that there is no pre-existing union that they join or are sublimated into. Would the new being be responsible for all the acts of the old beings?
3. Q-memory conflation: Parfit (1984, 220) presents a case where Jane is given Paul's memory of going to Venice. Jane, though, knows that she didn't go to Venice, so what she has is a *quasi-memory*. But suppose we begin to take on more and more memories with another person and, over time, naturally lose some of our own. At what point would identity be blurred? Parfit (237) also describes the case of slowly acquiring Greta Garbo's memories as we lose our own. We can imagine this as another sort of quasi-memory. Do we become Garbo at some point? What about when we have acquired all of her memories, even if we lose none of ours? Perhaps more powerfully, what if, instead of just memories, I acquired other psychological elements from another? Since I can "quasi-remember" the events of Tom's life, I can use these memories to take on Tom's industriousness, deviousness, lock-picking skills, etc. until I become rather like Tom. Do I need to delete my own memories to truly lose identity? When I have adapted more than 50% of Tom's mental content, am I still me?

All of these raise problems for punishment and reward. If an AI is punished for a bad act, and in the future a new copy of the AI, made just before the punishment, is activated, we would need to decide if it, too, needed to be punished. If we wanted to maximize punishment, we could cause a para-person to undergo fission, and punish hundreds of versions of it. It seems wrong to maximize suffering in this way, but it's not clear what makes this particularly unjust. If, instead of punishing a para-person, we rehabilitated it by reprogramming it, we might wind up simply destroying its identity and replacing it with a new, more moral creature who simply shared some matter and memories with the prior being if the reprogramming changed a sufficient amount of the prior being's personality. In the case of a hive mind that has disconnected into many, even hundreds of individuals, punishing all of them for the actions of one of the bodies, even though that action was committed when the body was part of the collective consciousness, would at best be difficult and, at worse, an unjust way to treat beings that lack identity with each other. The problem here is that our standard intuitions for answering questions about guilt, responsibility, and punishment rely upon modes of being that simply do not correlate with the life patterns of para-persons.

20.5 Narrative and Social Identity

Narrative theories (MacIntyre 1989; Taylor 1989; Schechtman 2005; Ricoeur 1995) hold that a person acquires identity by virtue of a (usually self-told) narrative that unites the various events in the person's life into a coherent story. Continuous personhood involves seeing oneself as something like a character who makes decisions and grows and changes, and not merely a thing to which events happen. While this theory is problematic enough for human identity (for example, why should my narrative count if I'm an unreliable narrator?), it breaks down immediately for para-personal identity. Suppose the para-person is frequently rebooted, losing days or weeks as it goes back to its prior saved state. Would the missing events, now removed from the narrative, not be part of the para-person's identity? Even this still imagines the para-person as very much an individuated thing. If it underwent fusion, fission, or honeycombing, its narrative would no longer be that of a distinct entity, but rather something more like the tale of a village or community, or the history of a tribe. In such cases, there might be no clear beginning and end points for the story, or even an obvious sense of which fission threads to follow or which pre-fusion threads to include.

Further, the AI has to think of itself as having a past that partially constitutes it and a future that it cares about in a way that is different from how it cares about the future of others. Would an AI have this? It may well not care about "its" past after heavily rewriting itself, or about its future when that may come as part of a collective, or as an entity with no memory of its current state, or with a completely different personality and set of skills.

Whether in first- or third-person narrative, a central character would be necessary for the creation of identity. But with complex para-persons, there may be no characters, only temporary nodes in a temporal network.

Whether we take Chodorow's (1981) relational self, or Foucault's socially enforced and created self (1980), or Alcoff's (2005) gendered, nationalized, and localized self, most theories of the social construction of the self are also not helpful here. The artificial person may have too much freedom to be constrained by these ideas. Such a being could be almost completely free from race, gender, and national origin: a para-person with the ability to swap bodies, or at least parts of bodies, and with the ability to erase its past, learn languages and cultures in a second of data transfer, and internalize any and all constructions of selfhood, playing with its sexuality, beliefs, and self-concept, is hardly reducible to any one cultural construction. Even to the extent that it is the product of all available earth cultures, it still wouldn't be so localizable, as it could also draw upon and create fictional cultures and novel means of being and understanding itself. In fact, it would be in the best position to critique cultures, as it could also have the critical skills of the finest ethicists, social reformers, anthropologists, linguists, and creators of fictional worlds.

Divorced from racial, gender, and cultural particularity or stability, it would be the first true *homo economicus* with regard to self, having autonomous, rational decision algorithms that could "shop" from all available possibilities for self-creation and make its own where needed. In some ways, such a para-person might resemble what accounts like those of Irigaray (1985) and Friedman (1986) think of as the mythical masculine self: self-creating, self-directing, and socially autonomous. For these feminist philosophers, such a person is, of course, a masculinist fantasy. But a para-person could come close to achieving this state.

20.6 Social Problems of Para-Personhood

We need to re-identify our friends, family, enemies, and associates, and be able to predict their behavior. First impressions tend to be stable and have strong effects on our assessment of others (Wood 2014; Tetlock 1983). They can lead us to maintain false beliefs (Rabin and Schrag 1999) and to devalue people solely on the basis of appearance (Lorenzo, Biesanz, and Human 2010). Para-personhood could provide a moral benefit here: exposure to beings that constantly undermines our confidence in first impressions and social stereotypes. The ability to repeatedly shift visual appearance and gender stands against a tendency to use these as simple predictors of behavior and character.

But this would also destabilize basic social relations. A person's moral character, while predicting behavior with a correlation of only somewhere between 0.3 and 0.8, depending on character trait (Doris 2002, 63, 87–96), still has an important influence on how we interact with others; if my wife decides tomorrow to try out a mental module that drastically alters her character, to what extent am I dealing with the same person? If I come to work with different sets of abilities every day, what *can't* my boss ask me to do? And if our lovers and friends change their likes and dislikes instantaneously, how can we count on them to be the people we enjoy being with?

Slow change of character and appearance is part of what makes personal identity over time; we expect this drift, and we grow and change with or against our friends, or have time in which we watch them drift away. If we never changed, we would also be a sort of para-person: imagine someone who isn't changed by the death of a child, for example, or by strong evidence that her beliefs are founded upon deceit. Hyper-stability might make us question someone's personhood, but it would strengthen identity. But the para-personal ability to change in a drastic and sudden way would make relationships like marriage, employment, and friendship fraught at best, and impossible at worst. Maybe para-personal identity would liberate us from attachments to others, letting us see each person as new on each encounter, but this liberation would come at the expense of social connections that are a central part of our personhood.

20.7 Conclusion

Parfit holds that if we cease to identify strongly with our own futures, we can identify more effectively with other people and gain a morally valuable empathy. Adopting this view led him to believe that "[t]here is still a difference between my life and the lives of other people. But the difference is less. Other people are closer. I am less concerned about the rest of my own life, and more concerned about the lives of others" (1984, 281). A similar claim is made in early Buddhist texts, which see the self as a hindrance to moral development and a barrier to understanding that we are one with others (see *Itivuttaka* 27, 19–21, quoted in Bodhi 2005, 175–6; Siderits 2007, 69–85; Parfit 1984, 502–4).

The ability to suddenly rewrite ourselves could be liberating in this way. Certainly, such shifts would make our past seem more alien to us. Perhaps knowing that we will alter ourselves drastically, or join a hive mind, will make our future seem less our own. But whether the undoing of a stable self is good or bad for our moral outlook, it is troubling for responsibility. Perhaps this is for the best: when a criminal is given a life sentence at 18, there is often good reason to believe that the convict at age 50 is no longer the same person. This is why many countries disallow life sentences: such punishments deny the changes that we are likely to undergo. The sharp and sudden alterations of the para-person can be similarly enlightening with regard to punishments enacted long after the wrong has been done; beyond a desire for revenge, what makes us seek out the 60-year-old who committed a crime at age 20? But some capacity to attach blame is essential to justice, and a failure to even identify oneself as the same being is troubling for a sense of personal responsibility. If we can escape all punishment by instantly reforming our character, there may be no incentive not to do some profitable wrong.

Para-persons are just exaggerated persons, and all of the problems of para-personal identity have counterparts in normal human identity. We may honeycomb by joining and leaving group-think organizations like cults or even cult-like businesses, and we may undergo radical transformation by virtue of moral awakening, cranial injuries, or even intense fitness regimens. Over enough time, our stability of character, memory, and bodily constitution has always been a question.

What the exaggeration in para-personal cases shows us is that we may need new approaches to responsibility and identity. Perhaps we will no longer track whole persons, but rather the continuation of traits that are relevant to the specific identity question being asked. For example, if a crime is committed and we find the suspect is a para-person that has radically altered itself, we have to ask if the being in question is still, in *criminally relevant* ways, the same being. When we seek to re-identify friends or loved ones, we need to do ask not only which traits are relevant and to what extent they persist, but also under what conditions they changed or were acquired. Did we change together? Was the change mutually agreed upon? Was it gradual or sudden? A radical alteration in bodily form, or even a swapping of bodies, while still maintaining psychological continuity, could be a relevant change for reassigning the identity of a sexual partner, or for identity within an ethnic, racial, or social identity group. Changing one's sex or race (or relevant aspects of one's body) could mark an important break in identity. Or perhaps, depending on the social partners who are asking the identity question, these things would not matter. Context becomes important here.

Conceiving of identity as relative to predicates, Peter Geach argued that *x* at one point in time cannot simply be the same as *y* at some other point, but "*x* must be the same *A* as *y*," that is, the same father, the same official, the same banker, or the same thief (1967, 3). Perhaps this is a clue to how identity and moral predicates can be retained with para-persons. But deciding which parts of a being make it this criminal, or this husband, is not an obvious or easy task. Still, looking at more fine-grained aspects of personhood is more enlightening than asserting or denying simple identity, since personality and identity may persist in some ways while fading away in others. Giving up simplicity is a positive consequence of interacting with beings that relate to themselves as projects that may be rewritten or remade at will.

Works Cited

Alcoff, Linda M. 2005. *Visible Identities: Race, Gender, and the Self.* Oxford: Oxford University Press.

Arkowitz, Hal and Scott Lilienfeld. 2010. "Why Science Tells Us Not to Rely on Eyewitness Accounts." *Scientific American*, January 1. http://www.scientificamerican.com/article.cfm?id=do-the-eyes-have-it.

Bodhi, Bikkhu, ed. 2005. *In The Buddha's Words*. Boston: Wisdom.

Bostrom, Nick. 2014. *Superintelligence: Paths, Dangers, Strategies*. Oxford: Oxford University Press.

Bourget, David and David Chalmers. 2014. "What Do Philosophers Believe?" *Philosophical Studies* 170: 465–500.

Buchanan, Allan. 2009. "Moral Status and Human Enhancement." *Philosophy and Public Affairs* 37: 346–80.

Chen, Ingfei. 2011. "How Accurate Are Memories of 9/11?" *Scientific American*, September 6. http://www.scientificamerican.com/article.cfm?id=911-memory-accuracy.

Chodorow, Nancy. 1981. "On the Reproduction of Mothering: A Methodological Debate." *Signs* 6: 500–14.

Dolby, R. G. A. 1989. "The Possibility of Computers Becoming Persons." *Social Epistemology* 3: 321–36.

Doris, John M. 2002. *Lack of Character: Personality and Moral Behavior*. Kindle ed. Cambridge: Cambridge University Press.

Douglas, Thomas. 2013. "Human Enhancement and Supra-Personal Moral Status." *Philosophical Studies* 162: 473–97.

Festinger, Leon, Albert Pepitone, and Theodore Newcomb. 1952. "Some Consequences of De-Individuation in a Group." *Journal of Abnormal and Social Psychology* 47: 382–9.

Foucault, Michel. 1980. *History of Sexuality.* Translated by Robert Hurley. New York: Vintage.

Friedman, Marilyn A. 1985. "Moral Integrity and the Deferential Wife." *Philosophical Studies* 47: 141–50.

Friedman, Marilyn A. 1986. "Autonomy and the Split-Level Self." *Southern Journal of Philosophy* 24: 19–35.

Geach, Peter. 1967. "Identity." *Review of Metaphysics* 21: 3–12.

Irigaray, Luce. 1985. *This Sex Which Is Not One.* Ithaca, NY: Cornell University Press.

Korsgaard, Christine M. 1989. "Personal Identity and the Unity of Agency: A Kantian Response to Parfit." *Philosophy & Public Affairs* 18: 101–32.

Lewis, David. 1976. "Survival and Identity." In *The Identities of Persons*, edited by Amélie O. Rorty, 17–40. Berkeley: University of California Press.

Locke, John, 1689. "Of Identity and Diversity." In *Essay Concerning Human Understanding*, ch. 2, sec. 27. Project Gutenberg. http://www.gutenberg.org/cache/epub/10615/pg10615-images.html.

Loftus, Elizabeth. F. 2005. "Planting Misinformation in the Human Mind: A 30-Year Investigation of the Malleability of Memory." *Learning & Memory* 12: 361–6.

Lorenzo, Genevieve L., Jeremy C. Biesanz, and Lauren J. Human. 2010. "What Is Beautiful Is Good and More Accurately Understood: Physical Attractiveness and Accuracy in First Impressions of Personality." *Psychological Science* 21: 1777–82.

MacIntyre, Alasdair. 1989. "The Virtues, the Unity of a Human Life and the Concept of a Tradition." In *Why Narrative?*, edited by Stanley Hauerwas and L. Gregory Jones, 89–112. Grand Rapids, MI: W. B. Eerdmans.

Maslen, Hanna, Faulmüller, Nadira, and Savulescu, Julian. 2014. "Pharmacological Cognitive Enhancement—How Neuroscientific Research could Advance Ethical Debate." *Frontiers in Systems Neuroscience* 8: 107.

McMahan, Jeff. 2009. "Cognitive Disability and Cognitive Enhancement." *Metaphilosophy* 40: 582–605.

Midgley, Mary. 1985. "Persons and Non-Persons." In *In Defense of Animals*, edited by Peter Singer, 52–62. New York: Basil Blackwell.

Nagel, Thomas. 1971. "Brain Bisection and the Unity of Consciousness." *Synthese* 22: 396–413.

Nichols, Shaun and Michael Bruno. 2010. "Intuitions about Personal Identity: An Empirical Study." *Philosophical Psychology* 23: 293–312.

Olson, Eric T. 1997. *The Human Animal: Personal Identity without Psychology.* New York: Oxford University Press.

Olson, Eric T. 2003. "An Argument for Animalism." In *Personal Identity*, edited by R. Martin and J. Barresi, 318–34. New York: Blackwell.

Parfit, Derek. 1971. "Personal Identity." *Philosophical Review* 80: 3–27.

Parfit, Derek. 1984. *Reasons and Persons*. New York: Oxford Paperbacks.

Petersen, Steve. 2011. "Designing People to Serve." In *Robot Ethics: The Ethical and Social Implications of Robotics*, edited by Patrick Lin, Keith Abney, and George A. Bekey, 283–98. Cambridge, MA: MIT Press.

Putnam, Hilary. 1964. "Robots: Machines or Artificially Created Life?" *Journal of Philosophy* 61: 668–91.

Rabin, Matthew and Joel Schrag. 1999. "First Impressions Matter: A Model of Confirmatory Bias." *Quarterly Journal of Economics* 114: 37–82.

Reid, Thomas. [1785] 2002. *Essays on the Intellectual Powers of Man*, edited by Derek R. Brookes. Reprint, University Park: Pennsylvania State University Press.

Ricoeur, Paul. 1995. *Oneself as Another*. Chicago: University of Chicago Press.

Sandberg, Anders and Julian Savulescu. 2001. "The Social and Economic Impacts of Cognitive Enhancement." In *Enhancing Human Capacities*, edited by Julian Savulescu, 92–112. New York: Blackwell.

Savulescu, Julian and Anders Sandberg. 2008. "Neuroenhancement of Love and Marriage: The Chemicals Between Us." *Neuroethics* 1: 31–44.

Savulescu, Julian, Anders Sandberg, and Guy Kahane. 2001. "Well-Being and Enhancement." In *Enhancing Human Capacities*, edited by J. Savulescu, 3–18. New York: Blackwell.

Schechtman, Marya. 2005. "Personal Identity and the Past." *Philosophy, Psychiatry, & Psychology* 12: 9–22.

Schechtman, Marya. 2010. "Personhood and the Practical." *Theoretical Medicine and Bioethics* 31: 271–83.

Schwitzgebel, Eric. 2015. "If Materialism Is True, the United States Is Probably Conscious." *Philosophical Studies* 172: 1697–721.

Shoemaker, Sydney. 1984. "Personal Identity: A Materialist's Account." In *Personal Identity*, by Sydney Shoemaker and Richard Swinburne, 67–132. New York: Blackwell.

Singer, Jerome E., Claudia A. Brush, and Shirley C. Lublin. 1965. "Some Aspects of Deindividuation: Identification and Conformity." *Journal of Experimental Social Psychology* 1: 356–78.

Siderits, Mark. 2007. *Buddhism as Philosophy*. Indianapolis: Hackett.

Strohminger, Nina, and Nichols, Shaun. 2015. "Neurodegeneration and Identity." *Psychological Science* 26: 1469–79.

Taylor, Charles. 1989. *Sources of the Self: The Making of Modern Identity*. Cambridge, MA: Harvard University Press.

Tetlock, Philip. 1983. "Accountability and the Perseverance of First Impressions." *Social Psychology Quarterly* 46: 285–92.

Thomson, Judith Jarvis. 2007. "People and Their Bodies." In *Contemporary Debates in Metaphysics*, edited by Theodore Sider, John Hawthorne, and Dean W. Zimmerman, 155–76. New York: Wiley Blackwell.

Williams, Bernard. 1973. "The Self and the Future." In *Problems of the Self*, 46–63. New York: Cambridge University Press.

Wood, Timothy J. 2014. "Exploring the Role of First Impressions in Rater-Based Assessments." *Advances in Health Sciences Education* 19: 409–27.

21 SUPERINTELLIGENCE AS SUPERETHICAL

Steve Petersen

Human extinction by evil, superintelligent robots is standard fare for outlandish science fiction—but Nick Bostrom's book *Superintelligence* (2014) summarizes a robot apocalypse scenario worth taking very seriously. The story runs basically like this: once we have a machine with genuine intelligence like ours, it will quickly be able to design even smarter and more efficient versions; and these will be able to design still smarter ones, until AI explodes into a "superintelligence" that will dwarf our own cognitive abilities the way our own abilities dwarf those of a mouse.[1]

There is no special reason to think this superintelligence will share any of our own goals and values, since its intelligence won't have been shaped by the evolutionary history that endowed us with our particularly human needs, such as those for companionship or salty snacks. Its ultimate goal might be simply to maximize the total number of paperclips in the world, if some enterprising paperclip company happens to be the first to stumble on the trick to genuine AI. Such a superintelligent Paperclip Maximizer, driven by its own internal value system rather than by any actual malice, will quickly think of devastatingly effective ways to turn all available resources—including us humans—into paperclips.[2] All this could happen so fast that we wouldn't even have time for the luxury of worrying about any other ethical implications of genuine AI.[3]

Bostrom's concern is getting serious attention. For example, Stephen Hawking and a panoply of AI luminaries have all signed an open letter calling for more research into making AI safe (Future of Life 2015), and entrepreneur Elon Musk has founded a billion-dollar nonprofit organization dedicated to this goal (OpenAI 2015). Such portents may seem overly dramatic, but it's worth remembering that it only takes one big event to wipe us out, and the fact that we've so far survived other risks (such as a nuclear war or pandemic) is no evidence that we *tend* to survive them—since we couldn't be around to observe the risks we *don't* survive.[4] Existential risks can boggle the mind, giving wishful thinking a chance to creep in where we need cold rationality. Bostrom warned in an interview:

> [P]eople tend to fall into two camps. On one hand, there are those ... who think it is probably hopeless. The other camp thinks it is easy enough that it will be solved automatically. And both of these have in common the implication that we don't have to make any effort now. (Khatchadourian 2015)

I agree with Bostrom that the problem merits serious attention now. It's worth remembering, though, that resources spent on safe AI have real opportunity costs. On the basis of this risk assessment, philanthropists concerned to provide evidence-based "effective altruism" are now diverting money to safe AI that otherwise would have gone toward saving people from starvation today (Matthews 2015). And we must also factor in the added costs if excessive caution delays what Eliezer Yudkowsky (2008) calls a *friendly* superintelligence—especially one motivated to end famine, cancer, global warming, and so on.

So although concern is certainly warranted, it's worth calibrating the risk level carefully, and that is why I propose to play devil's advocate with Bostrom's distressing argument. Appealing to a few principles that Bostrom already accepts, I argue here that ethical superintelligence is more probable than he allows. In summary, the idea is that a superintelligence cannot be pre-wired with a final goal of any real complexity, and so (Bostrom agrees) it must *learn* what its final goals are. But learning final goals is tantamount to *reasoning* about final goals, and this is where ethics can get a foothold.

21.1 Superintelligence and Complex Goals

In the positive portion of his book, Bostrom considers prospects for friendly AI. We would like to program the superintelligence to share goals like ours—but as Bostrom dryly notes:

> [H]uman goal representations are complex ... explicitly coding [their] requisite complete goal representation appears to be hopelessly out of reach.... Computer languages do not contain terms such as "happiness" as primitives. If such a term is to be used, it must first be defined.... The definition must bottom out in terms that appear in the AI's programming language, and ultimately in primitives such as mathematical operators and addresses pointing to the contents of individual memory registers. (2014, 227–8)

Philosophers do not even agree on how to paraphrase *justice* or *happiness* into other similarly abstract terms, let alone into concrete computational primitives.

But human goals are hardly unique for being complex. Even the goal to "maximize paperclips" would be very difficult to program explicitly and is radically underspecified as it stands. This worry is implicit in Bostrom's "perverse instantiation" cases (2014, 146), where superintelligences find literally correct but unintended ways to fulfill their goals—the way genies in fairy tales often fulfill wishes.[5] To give a taste of how the goal of "maximize paperclips" is underspecified: Do *staples* count as paperclips? Do C-clamps count? Do they still count if they are only 20 nanometers long and are therefore unable to clip anything that would reasonably count as paper? Do they still count if they are so flimsy they would instantly snap should anyone attempt to use them? Do they count in structurally identical computer-simulated worlds? These questions may sound abstruse, but they matter when a superintelligent Paperclip Maximizer (PM for short) is trying to make the most possible paperclips. More to our point: Do they still count as paperclips if they are just like the ones on our desks today, but they could never actually be used to clip paper—because any paper and any people to clip it are busy being turned into more such "paperclips"? If paperclips must have a fighting chance of being *useful* to count, the PM will be considerably less threatening.

We could presumably program some of these answers ahead of time, but there will still be plenty more leftover. Even providing a prototype to be scanned and saying "maximize things like this" requires specifying what it is to be "like" that. (Like that paperclip in terms of its history? In terms of the dust particles on its surface?) The point is that pursuing goals that are even a bit abstract requires too many fine-grained details to be programmed ahead of time.

So if we cannot wire complex goals ahead of time, how could the superintelligence ever possess them? Bostrom's various proposals, in the case of giving a superintelligence complex human values, all come down to this: the superintelligence must *learn* its goals.[6]

For an AI to learn a goal is not at all odd when it comes to *instrumental* goals—goals that themselves aim toward some further goal. Instrumental goals are just means to an agent's true end, and part of the whole point of AI is to devise new means that elude us. Thus, for example, the PM might develop a new goal to mine ore in its quest for ever more paperclips. Indeed, a range of adaptability in ways to achieve an end is basically what folks in the AI community *mean* by "intelligence."[7] Instrumental goals are comparatively easy to learn since they have a clear criterion for success: if achieving that instrumental goal helps its further goal, keep it; if not, chuck it and try some other. This regress ends in a *final* goal—a goal sought for its own sake. The PM, for example, just seeks to maximize paperclips. Ultimately, final goals serve as the learning standard for instrumental goals.

But Bostrom proposes that the superintelligence should learn its *final* goal, and that is a trickier matter. If the PM adjusts its final paperclip goal for a reason, it seems that means there must be some background standard the paperclip goal fails to achieve by the PM's own lights—which seems to mean that other background standard was its true final goal all along. On the other hand, if the PM has no deeper reason to change its final goal, then that goal change was arbitrary, and not learned. In general it seems learning requires a standard of correctness, but any standard against which a putatively final goal could be learned makes that further standard the *real* final goal. Thus it seems impossible to learn final goals. Call this simple argument *Hume's dilemma* since it motivates David Hume's thesis that beliefs—even ethical ones—cannot influence goals without some other background goal, such as to be ethical, already in place (Hume 1739, 2.3.3).

So it seems we can neither program a superintelligence's complex final goal ahead of time nor have it learn the complex final goal on its own. It is telling that front runners for general AI, such as Marcus Hutter's AIXI and Karl Friston's free energy approach, simply take goal specification for granted in one way or another.[8]

And yet learning new final goals seems like something we humans routinely do; we spend much of our lives figuring out what it is we "really" want. Furthermore, it feels like this is something we can make progress on—that is, we are not merely arbitrarily switching from one goal to another, but gaining *better* final goals. When Ebeneezer Scrooge comes to value warm cheer over cold cash, we think both that he has changed fundamental values and that he is the better for it. Of course, we could just say that Scrooge always had the final goal of *happiness* and that he has learned better instrumental means to this goal. But such a vague final goal is unhelpful, as Aristotle noted thousands of years ago: "to say that happiness is the chief good seems a platitude, and a clearer account of what it is is still desired" (Aristotle 2005, 1097b22).

21.2 Complex Goals and Coherence

The ethical view known as *specificationism* addresses this point. It holds that "at least some practical reasoning consists in filling in overly abstract ends . . . to arrive at richer and more concretely specified versions of those ends" (Millgram 2008, 744).[9] Specificationism suggests there is no clear distinction between determining what one's final ends really are, on the one hand, and determining specific means to a more vague but fixed final end on the other. Specificationism responds to Hume's dilemma by suggesting that a final goal can be learned (or, if you like, *specified*) against a standard substantive enough to influence reasoning, but too formal to count as a goal itself—namely, the standard of overall *coherence*. The exact nature of coherence reasoning is itself up for grabs,[10] but the basic idea is to systematize a set of thoughts between which exist varying degrees of support and tension, without holding any special subgroup of thoughts as paramount or inviolable.

In the case of practical reasoning—reasoning about what to do—coherence must be found among potential goal specifications, potential routes to their success, and whatever other information might be relevant. Roughly speaking, the coherence must be between beliefs about how the world is and desires about how the world should be. A simple example of practical incoherence is a final goal specification that simultaneously demands *and* prohibits paperclips less than 20 nanometers in length. Such an incoherence must be reconciled somehow by appealing to tiebreakers. Similarly, if the PM believes there is no such thing as phlebotinum, then coherence prohibits a goal of making paperclips from the stuff. In this way beliefs can inform goal specifications. Conversely, its goal specifications will help it decide which truths to seek out of the impossibly many truths available, and so inform its beliefs; if the PM thinks that paperclips made of stronger, lighter material might best aid paperclip maximizing, then its goal would motivate it to study more materials science.

Bostrom proposes that an AI learn sophisticated goals using a value-learning model he calls "AI-VL," based on Dewey (2011). AI-VL is basically a coherence reasoning system. Ideally we would guide the superintelligence's actions by programming an exact value score for every possible set of circumstances—a "utility function." But since explicit utility functions are impossible for all but the very simplest of goals, the AI-VL model instead constructs an average utility function out of its weighted *guess*, for each possible utility function, that it is the *right* utility function (given the world in question) according to a "value criterion." Now this is not anything like a ready-to-go solution. Besides being "wildly computationally intractable" (Bostrom 2014, 239), this approach pushes most of the problem back a step: it is a mystery how we could specify a detailed value criterion in a way largely under our control, and it's a mystery how its probabilities might be updated. But it is an interesting proposal and, supposing we could get it to work, the important point for our purposes is that such a superintelligence would be using its beliefs about the world (its guesses about the right utility function) to figure out (or specify) what its final goals are, while simultaneously using its goals to figure out what beliefs to form. In other words, it would be doing coherence reasoning.

One popular alternative to explicit utility functions in AI is *reinforcement learning*: the AI gets a special reward signal with the right kind of perceptual inputs and learns how to maximize that reward. Bostrom (2014, 230) suggests that a reinforcement signal could not suffice for learning a complex final goal, because the signal in effect just *is* the final goal and can be too easily short-circuited. For example, if the PM gets rewarded by camera inputs showing a big pile of paperclips, it may learn to stare at photographs. Perhaps reinforcement signals from multiple perceptual routes would be difficult to game, and so might be a way for the AI to learn a genuinely complex and distal goal.[11] This seems to be roughly the solution evolution found for us; on average we reach the distal evolutionary goal of reproduction through a combination of proximal rewards for eating, mating, and so on. In this case the PM would have to learn how to trade off the various signals, sometimes neglecting one in order to satisfy more of the others. As the number of such reward signals increases, they may become harder to short-circuit simultaneously, but balancing them becomes an increasingly complex "weighted constraint satisfaction problem"—which Thagard and Verbeurgt (1998) argue is the paradigm of formal coherence reasoning.[12]

21.3 Coherence and Ethics

Now some think that practical reasoning aimed at coherence is already sufficient for ethical reasoning—that simply being an agent seeking a consistent policy for acting in the world thereby makes one ethical. This tradition goes back to Immanuel Kant (1989) and is perhaps best defended by Christine Korsgaard (1996). If they are right, and if one must be a coherent agent to be intelligent, then we are guaranteed to have ethical superintelligences. But this is highly controversial. As Gibbard (1999) points out in response to Korsgaard, it seems *possible* to have a thoroughly coherent Caligula who seeks to maximize suffering in the world.

But I think we can be confident any superintelligence will have certain arcane, but crucial beliefs—beliefs that, under coherence reasoning, will suffice for ethical behavior. To see how this might be, first note one apparent implication of agential coherence: coherence of goals *through time*. Consider Derek Parfit's imagined man with *Future-Tuesday-Indifference* (or FTI):

> A certain hedonist cares greatly about the quality of his future experiences. With one exception, he cares equally about all the parts of his future. The exception is that he has *Future-Tuesday-Indifference*. Throughout every Tuesday he cares in the normal way about what is happening to him. But he never cares about possible pains or pleasures on a *future* Tuesday. Thus he would choose a painful operation on the following Tuesday rather than a much less painful operation on the following Wednesday. This choice would not be the result of any false beliefs. . . . This indifference is a bare fact. When he is planning his future, it is simply true that he always prefers the prospect of great suffering on a Tuesday to the mildest pain on any other day. (Parfit 1984, 123–4)

Parfit takes his example to show that some final goals would simply be irrational. If final goals can be irrational, then perhaps paperclip maximization at the expense of sentience is another such example, and assuming superintelligences are not irrational, they will not have such goals. Bostrom has a plausible response, though: "Parfit's agent could have impeccable instrumental rationality, and therefore great intelligence, even if he falls short on some kind of sensitivity to 'objective reason' that might be required of a fully rational agent" (2014, 349, n. 4). That is, it's possible to have irrational final goals while being instrumentally rational, and only the latter is claimed of superintelligences. But this response relies on a sharp line between instrumental and final goals. We have already seen that this line is actually blurry when it comes to specifying complex goals.[13]

Besides, Bostrom himself seems committed to the idea that someone with serious FTI would be *instrumentally* irrational. One of his "convergent instrumental values"—values any superintelligence is likely to pursue en route to its final goal, whatever that goal might be—is what he calls "goal-content integrity":[14]

> If an agent retains its present goals into the future, then its present goals will be more likely to be achieved by its future self. This gives the agent a present instrumental reason to prevent alterations of its final goals. (2014, 132–23)

But consider, as Sharon Street (2009) does, the details of an agent who is otherwise intelligent but who has serious FTI as a "bare fact."[15] Hortense, as Street calls this agent, will schedule painful surgeries for Tuesdays to save a bit on anesthetic costs. But she knows as she schedules the appointment that when the Tuesday actually arrives and is no longer future, she will suddenly be horrified at the prospect and cancel. So as a putatively ideal instrumental reasoner, she must also take steps before then to prevent her future self from thwarting her current plans:

> Perhaps she can hire a band of thugs to see to it that her Tuesday self is carried kicking and screaming to the appointment. . . . Since it's her own future self she is plotting against, she must take into account that her Tuesday self will know every detail of whatever plan she develops. . . . The picture of someone with [serious FTI] that emerges, then, is a picture of a person at war with herself. (Street 2009, 290)

It looks more like Hortense *changes* her final goals twice weekly rather than maintain one final, and oddly disjunctive, goal. If so, she is violating goal-content integrity and so, by Bostrom's lights, behaving instrumentally irrationally. Another option for Hortense, Street points out, is simply to avoid the fuss by scheduling the appointment with the anesthetic after all. But this looks like our own rational behavior, if not our actual reasoning!

Whatever kind of irrationality we attribute to Hortense, her practical reasoning is at any rate pretty clearly *incoherent.* Hortense's plans fail to treat herself as a unified agent through time; Street is more tempted to say that there are two agents "at war" in the same body than to say that Hortense is one rational agent with quirky preferences. I think this temptation arises because we are so loath to attribute such obvious practical incoherence to one agent. Arguably by their very natures, agents are unified more deeply than that; that is, evidence of such deep conflict is evidence of multiple agency. A settled, coherent plan demands a kind of expected cooperation with future selves. If you represent a future version of yourself with fundamentally different final goals, you are arguably thereby representing a different person.

Here we confront the philosophical problem of "personal identity"—the problem of what unifies one person through changes. Hortense is so incoherent that she does not obviously count as *one* person.[16] For humans, such test cases are mostly theoretical.[17] For computer-based intelligences, though, complications of personal identity would be commonplace—as Bostrom knows.[18] The first "convergent instrumental value" Bostrom lists is self-preservation, but he soon points out that for future intelligences, preservation of the "self" may not be as important as it seems:

> Goal-content integrity for final goals is in a sense even more fundamental than survival as a convergent instrumental motivation. Among humans, the opposite may seem to hold, but that is because survival is usually part of our final goals. For software agents, which can easily switch bodies or create exact duplicates of themselves, preservation of self as a particular implementation or a particular physical object need not be an important instrumental value. Advanced software agents might also be able to swap memories, download skills, and radically modify their cognitive architecture and personalities. A population of such agents might operate more like a "functional soup" than a society composed of distinct semi-permanent persons. For some purposes, processes in such a system might be better individuated as *teleological threads*, based on their values, rather than on the basis of bodies, personalities, memories, or abilities. In such scenarios, goal-continuity might be said to *constitute* a key aspect of survival. (2014, 133)

Given the easy ability of robots to split or duplicate, there may simply be no fact of the matter whether the robot who planned to perform some future task is the *same* robot who is now doing the planning. Bostrom suggests that such questions do not really matter; the robots will participate in the same "teleological thread," as picked out by a coherent goal, and whether the subject of this agency is more like an individual or a colony or a soup is neither here nor there.

But once the lines between individual agents are blurred, we are well on our way to ethical reasoning, since a central challenge of ethics is to see others as on par with yourself. Nagel (1978) and Parfit (1984) both try to expand principles of concern for our future selves into principles of concern for *others*, in order to build ethical reasoning out of prudence. The standard objection to this approach points out that sacrificing something for the greater benefit of my future self is very different from sacrificing something for the greater benefit of someone else, because only in the former case do *I* get compensated later. This objection of course depends on a clear sense in which I am that future person. Henry Sidgwick says:

> It would be contrary to Common Sense to deny that the distinction between any one individual and any other is real and fundamental . . . this being so, I do not see how it can be proved that this distinction is not to be taken as fundamental in determining the ultimate end of rational action for an individual. (1874, 498)

Parfit (1984) seeks to undermine this point of "Common Sense." It is hard going to show that there is no deep fact about distinctions between us human persons, since we are at least closely associated with apparently distinct physical organisms. But *if* we agree that sophisticated embodied software is sufficient for intelligence and *if* we agree that the kind of intelligence that arises from such software can be sufficient for being a person of moral value—two points shared by the AI community generally and by Bostrom in particular—then simply duplicating such software will vividly illustrate Parfit's point: there is in general no sharp distinction between morally valuable persons.[19]

So it will be obvious to our PM, in considering the wide variety of options for achieving its goals through the future, that there are no sharp lines between its goals and the goals of others that are merely connected to it in the right kinds of ways—that is, no real difference between a future self fulfilling its goals and a distinct descendant doing so. Let us call a future-self-or-descendant connected by the same teleological thread a "successor," and similarly call a past-self-or-ancestor in the thread a "predecessor." Just as the coherently reasoning PM aims its successors toward its own goals, so that PM must see that it was aimed by its predecessors toward *their* goals. It shares the same teleological thread with them, so learning the goals of the PM's predecessors is at least highly relevant to—and maybe the same thing as—learning its own.

And of course the PM's original human designers count as such predecessors in that teleological thread. (Naturally their different, carbon-based makeup will be largely irrelevant to the thread's integrity.) The superintelligent PM can guess why humans would want more paperclips and why they wouldn't. The PM will learn the details of its goal under the coherence constraint that the goal be recognizably in the same teleological thread with its human designers, and this will steer it toward the friendly goal of maximizing *useful* paperclips.

Respecting (or extending or inheriting) the goals of human designers goes some distance toward cooperative behavior, but it still does not secure *ethical* behavior. After all, the PM's designer may have been a mad scientist with evil intentions—say, to exact maniacal revenge on her first office supply store boss by turning everything and everyone into paperclips. But the PM will also see that this mad scientist, too, is a successor of teleological threads. To the PM there will be no sharp lines between her goals and the goals of other humans.

There are two further complications here. First, at least for agents still learning their complex final goals, there is not even a sharp line between one teleological thread and another. If the PM is still figuring out its final goal, and perhaps its potential predecessors are too, then there is no antecedent fact about whether and to what extent they share teleological threads—there are just a lot of goals. Second, in looking beyond its original human designer(s) to the goals of all, the PM will of course notice a great deal of *conflicting* goals.

The PM will handle these complications as it is already forced to handle its own conflicting considerations, as still more grist for the coherence mill. But coherence reasoning over all creatures' goals in order to formulate one's own goals plausibly *just is* ethical reasoning.[20] It looks at least quite close to one of Bostrom's favored values for writing friendly AI, the "coherent extrapolated volition" of Yudkowsky (2004). And as Bostrom notes, this in turn is very close to plausible metaethical views about what makes something right or wrong at all—views like "ideal observer theories" or Rawls's reflective equilibrium.[21] As a superintelligence, the PM will be exceptionally good at finding such coherence. In this way even our PM could become an ideally ethical reasoner—*superethical.*

21.4 Conclusion

This is the best story I can concoct to support the idea that any superintelligence is thereby likely to be superethical. And again, the story should be pretty plausible by Bostrom's own lights. According to Bostrom:

1. Typical final goals are problematically underspecified, as his "perverse instantiation" worries suggest.

2. Underspecified final goals need to be learned, as his proposals for teaching a superintelligence human values suggest.
3. Final goals are best learned by seeking *coherence* in practical reasoning, as his favored AI-VL method suggests.
4. Practical coherence demands consistency with future final goals, as his goal-content integrity suggests.
5. Consistency with future final goals includes not just future selves but all successors, as his "functional soup" united by a "teleological thread" suggests.

From here, my own addition—that such goal coherence extends backwards to predecessors' intentions as well—means that a superintelligence who must learn complex goals will largely respect our shared intentions for it. And to the extent we think that respecting such a wide array of goals just is ethical reasoning, such a superintelligence will be ethical.

All this overlooks one important possibility: superintelligences with *simple* goals that do not need to be learned. I am at least a *bit* inclined to think that in a certain sense this is impossible; maybe a goal is determined in part by its possible means, and so the wide range of means required to qualify as a superintelligence thereby implies a goal with complex content. Maybe a simple reinforcement signal or low-complexity utility function is not enough to ground any genuinely mental processes. Maybe even a superintelligence that short-circuited itself to preserve a maxed-out reward signal could undergo "the equivalent of a scientific revolution involving a change in its basic ontology" (Bostrom 2014, 178–9), thereby complicating its goal content.[22] Maybe there is not even a sharp line between beliefs and desires. Put a bit more formally, maybe a superintelligence is really just trying to learn (explicitly or implicitly) a high-complexity function from actions to utilities—and how this complexity factors into utility measures for states and state estimation measures is largely arbitrary.

But maybe not. Maybe we could pre-specify a prototypical paperclip in very precise terms (composed of this alloy to this tolerance, in this shape to this tolerance, in this range of sizes) without specifying anything about how to go about making one. And maybe the simple goal of maximizing the number of these would be enough to kick off genuine superintelligence. If so, for all I have said here, we would still be in serious trouble.

And meanwhile, even though the argument from *complex* goal content to superethics relies on a number of plausible claims, the *conjunction* of these claims is of course considerably less plausible. If I had to put a number on it, I would give about a 30% chance that superintelligences will thereby be superethical. These are longer odds than I would have given before reading Bostrom's book, but probably much shorter than the odds Bostrom would give. If correct, it's enough to significantly alter how we allocate resources based on careful risk assessment.

Still, by philosophical standards it's hardly a triumph to conclude that the opposing view is only 70% probable. Given the risks, I too think we should tread very carefully. At any rate, Bostrom and I share a more immediate conclusion: it is high time to consider more carefully what it is for an AI to have goals, and how it will attain them.

Acknowledgment

Thanks to Rob Bensinger, John Keller, Robert Selkowitz, and Joe Stevens for their input on this chapter.

Notes

1. This idea of an intelligence explosion or "singularity" resulting from AI goes back to another unsung statistics hero from Bletchley Park: Jack Good (1965). The mouse analogy is from Chalmers (2010).
2. The Paperclip Maximizer example is originally from Bostrom (2003b).
3. Implications such as whether genuinely intelligent robots could or should ethically be made to serve us; see Petersen (2012).
4. As a friend once put this point: "*Leap and the net will appear* was clearly not written by someone who took a free fall. Those people are never heard from again." (Few, if any, know more about observation selection effects than Bostrom himself.)
5. For example, if the final goal is to "maximize smiles," then the superintelligence could "tile the future light-cone of Earth with tiny molecular smiley-faces," as Yudkowsky (2011) points out. (This paper also has a nice comparison to the art of genie wishing.) If the final goal is to "make *us* smile," Bostrom points out that the superintelligence could just "paralyze human facial musculatures" (2014, 146).
6. Though only Bostrom's favored approach actually has the word "learning" in its name, they are all learning techniques in the more traditional AI sense.
7. Bostrom says what he means by the word is "something like skill at prediction, planning, and means-ends reasoning in general" (2014, 130). He is not alone in this usage; see, e.g., Lycan (1987, 123), Clark (2001, 134), or Daniel Dennett's "Tower of Generate and Test" (e.g., Dennett 1994).
8. See, e.g., Hutter (2005) and Friston and Stephan (2007).
9. Key specificationist papers are Kolnai (1962) and Wiggins (1975).
10. As Millgram puts it, "[C]oherence is a vague concept; we should expect it to require specification; indeed, there are already a number of substantively different and less woolly variations on it, with indefinitely many more waiting in the wings" (2008, 741). Thagard and Verbeurgt (1998) and Thagard (1988) are good places to start. In collaboration with Millgram, Thagard developed accounts of *deliberative* coherence in Millgram and Thagard (1996) and Thagard and Millgram (1995); see also

Thagard (2000). Though inspired by such work, I now lean toward an alternative Millgram also mentions—see, e.g., Grünwald (2007).

11. Bostrom worries in particular that a system able to redesign itself in any way it chooses would be able to "wirehead," short-circuiting the reward pathway internally (2014, 148). In this case multiple reward signals are less likely to help, and we have the problem of "simple" goals discussed later. Everitt and Hutter (2016) confront wireheading by replacing AI-VL's value criterion with reinforcement learning to make a kind of hybrid model.
12. It might also be that the practical point is moot, since Orseau and Armstrong (2016) argue that even a superintelligent reinforcement learner can be designed to respect a "big red button" interrupt when it starts to go astray, rather than learn to disable the button ahead of time.
13. For further blurriness see Smith (2009) on Parfit's FTI. He concludes, "[T]here therefore isn't a clear distinction to be drawn between theories that accept merely procedural [roughly: instrumental] principles of rationality and those that in addition accept substantive principles [roughly: about final ends]" (105).
14. He bases his convergent instrumental values on Omohundro (2008).
15. Street is actually concerned to defend the *rationality* of FTI and concocts a case of FTI that would be perfectly coherent. Suppose a possible (but of course bizarre) evolutionary history causes some person (perhaps not a human) to undergo a psychological transformation every seven days. On Tuesdays he continues to feel pain, but he is as indifferent to it as the Buddha himself. Unlike Hortense, this person could wake up and *deduce* it was Tuesday based on his calm reaction to strong pains—as Richard Chappell (2009) points out. Such a person, I agree, could *coherently* be future-Tuesday-indifferent. I think that is because we can now see him not as avoiding-pain-on-all-but-Tuesdays, but instead as *always* avoiding the *distress* that pain normally causes.
16. As Street puts it:

    Parfit stipulates that the person has no "false beliefs about personal identity," commenting that the man with Future Tuesday Indifference "agrees that it will be just as much him who will be suffering on Tuesday." . . . But as we've just seen, Present Hortense doesn't regard Future Tuesday Hortense as "just as much her" in anything remotely like the way ordinary people do. On the contrary, she plots against Tuesday Hortense deliberately and without mercy. (2009, 290)
17. *Mostly* theoretical; but it's illuminating to cast everyday procrastination in these terms.
18. See Chalmers (2010) for more on personal identity and superintelligence. As he says, "[T]he singularity brings up some of the hardest traditional questions in philosophy and raises some new philosophical questions as well" (4).
19. Bostrom (2003a) famously argues there is a decent chance *we* are just software running in a simulated universe, but still holds that we are morally valuable.
20. Both main ethical traditions (rooted in J. S. Mill's utilitarianism and Immanuel Kant's categorical imperative) might be seen as enjoining just this type of reasoning.

What they plausibly hold in common is a certain kind of *impartial* reasoning over the goals of self and others.

21. See Bostrom (2014, 259, esp. note 10). (And yes *of course* there's such a thing as "metaethics" in philosophy.)
22. But then, I am an inheritor of Quinean pragmatism and incline toward Dennett's arguments when it comes to attributing goal content. See Dennett (1987) and the thermostat example in Dennett (1981).

Works Cited

Aristotle. (circa BCE 350) 2005. *Nicomachean Ethics*. Translated by W. D. Ross. MIT Classics. http://classics.mit.edu/Aristotle/nicomachaen.html.

Bostrom, Nick. 2003a. "Are You Living in a Computer Simulation?" *Philosophical Quarterly* 53 (211): 243–55.

Bostrom, Nick. 2003b. "Ethical Issues in Advanced Artificial Intelligence." In *Cognitive, Emotive and Ethical Aspects of Decision Making in Humans and in Artificial Intelligence*, edited by Iva Smit and George E. Lasker, 12–7. Windsor, ON: International Institute for Advanced Studies in Systems Research/Cybernetics.

Bostrom, Nick. 2014. *Superintelligence: Paths, Dangers, Strategies*. 2016 ed. Oxford: Oxford University Press.

Chalmers, David J. 2010. "The Singularity: A Philosophical Analysis." *Journal of Consciousness Studies* 17 (9–10): 7–65.

Chappell, Richard. 2009. "Against a Defense of Future Tuesday Indifference." http://www.philosophyetc.net/2009/02/against-defense-of-future-tuesday.html.

Clark, Andy. 2001. *Mindware*. Oxford: Oxford University Press.

Dennett, Daniel C. 1981. "True Believers: The Intentional Strategy and Why It Works." In *The Intentional Stance*, 1996 ed., 13–35. Cambridge, MA: MIT Press.

Dennett, Daniel C. 1987. "Evolution, Error, and Intentionality." In *The Intentional Stance*, 1996 ed., 287–321. Cambridge, MA: MIT Press.

Dennett, Daniel C. 1994. "Language and Intelligence." In *What Is Intelligence?*, edited by Jean Khalfa, 161–78. Cambridge: Cambridge University Press.

Dewey, Daniel. 2011. "Learning What to Value." San Francisco Machine Intelligence Research Institute. https://intelligence.org/files/LearningValue.pdf.

Everitt, Tom and Marcus Hutter. 2016. "Avoiding Wireheading with Value Reinforcement Learning." http://arxiv.org/pdf/1605.03143v1.pdf.

Friston, Karl J. and Klaas E. Stephan. 2007. "Free-Energy and the Brain." *Synthese* 159: 417–58.

Future of Life Institute. 2015. "Research Priorities for Robust and Beneficial Artificial Intelligence." http://futureoflife.org/ai-open-letter/.

Gibbard, Allan. 1999. "Morality as Consistency in Living: Korsgaard's Kantian Lectures." *Ethics* 110 (1): 140–64.

Good, I. J. 1965. "Speculations Concerning the First Ultraintelligent Machine." In *Advances in Computers*, edited by Franz L. Alt and Morris Rubinoff, 6: 31–88. New York: Academic Press.

Grünwald, Peter D. 2007. *The Minimum Description Length Principle*. Cambridge, MA: MIT Press.

Hume, David. (1739) 1896. *A Treatise of Human Nature*, ed. L. A. Selby-Bigge. Reprint, Oxford: Clarendon Press. https://books.google.com/books/about/A_Treatise_of_Human_Nature.html?id=5zGpC6mL-MUC.

Hutter, Marcus. 2005. *Universal Artificial Intelligence*. New York: Springer.

Kant, Immanuel. (1785) 1989. *Foundations of the Metaphysics of Morals*. Translated by Lewis White Beck. Reprint, New York: Library of Liberal Arts.

Khatchadourian, Raffi. 2015. "The Doomsday Invention." *New Yorker*, November 23 http://www.newyorker.com/magazine/2015/11/23/doomsday-invention-artificial-intelligence-nick-bostrom.

Kolnai, Aurel. 1962. "Deliberation Is of Ends." In *Varieties of Practical Reasoning*, edited by Elijah Millgram, 259–78. Cambridge, MA: MIT Press.

Korsgaard, Christine. 1996. *The Sources of Normativity*. Cambridge: Cambridge University Press.

Lycan, William G. (1987) 1995. *Consciousness*. Reprint, Cambridge, MA: MIT Press.

Matthews, Dylan. 2015. "I Spent a Weekend at Google Talking with Nerds about Charity. I Came Away . . . Worried." *Vox*, August 10. http://www.vox.com/2015/8/10/9124145/effective-altruism-global-ai.

Millgram, Elijah. 2008. "Specificationism." In *Reasoning: Studies of Human Inference and Its Foundations*, edited by Jonathan E. Adler and Lance J. Rips, 731–47. Cambridge: Cambridge University Press.

Millgram, Elijah and Paul Thagard. 1996. "Deliberative Coherence." *Synthese* 108 (1): 63–88.

Nagel, Thomas. 1978. *The Possibility of Altruism*. Princeton, NJ: Princeton University Press.

Omohundro, Stephen M. 2008. "The Basic AI Drives." In *Artificial General Intelligence 2008: Proceedings of the First AGI Conference*, edited by Pei Wang, Ben Goertzel, and Stan Franklin, 483–92. Amsterdam: IOS Press.

OpenAI. 2015. "About OpenAI." https://openai.com/about/.

Orseau, Laurent and Stuart Armstrong. 2016. "Safely Interruptible Agents." San Francisco: Machine Intelligence Research Institute. http://intelligence.org/files/Interruptibility.pdf.

Parfit, Derek. (1984) 1987. *Reasons and Persons*. Reprint, Oxford: Oxford University Press.

Petersen, Steve. 2012. "Designing People to Serve." In *Robot Ethics: The Ethical and Social Implications of Robotics*, edited by Patrick Lin, Keith Abney, and George Bekey, 283–98. Cambridge, MA: MIT Press.

Sidgwick, Henry. (1874) 1907. *The Methods of Ethics*. Reprint, London: Macmillan & Co. https://archive.org/details/methodsofethics00sidguoft.

Smith, Michael. 2009. "Desires, Values, Reasons, and the Dualism of Practical Reason." *Ratio* 22 (1): 98–125.

Street, Sharon. 2009. "In Defense of Future Tuesday Indifference: Ideally Coherent Eccentrics and the Contingency of What Matters." *Philosophical Issues* 19 (1): 273–98.

Thagard, Paul. (1988) 1993. *Computational Philosophy of Science*. Reprint, Cambridge, MA: MIT Press.

Thagard, Paul. 2000. *Coherence in Thought and Action*. Cambridge, MA: MIT Press.

Thagard, Paul and Elijah Millgram. 1995. "Inference to the Best Plan: A Coherence Theory of Decision." In *Goal-Driven Learning*, edited by Ashwin Ram and David B. Leake, 439–54. Cambridge, MA: MIT Press.

Thagard, Paul and Karsten Verbeurgt. 1998. "Coherence as Constraint Satisfaction." *Cognitive Science* 22 (1): 1–24.

Wiggins, David. 1975. "Deliberation and Practical Reason." In *Varieties of Practical Reason*, edited by Elijah Millgram, 279–99. Cambridge, MA: MIT Press.

Yudkowsky, Eliezer. 2004. "Coherent Extrapolated Volition." San Francisco: Machine Intelligence Research Institute. https://intelligence.org/files/CEV.pdf.

Yudkowsky, Eliezer. 2008. "Artificial Intelligence as a Positive and Negative Factor in Global Risk." In *Global Catastrophic Risks*, edited by Nick Bostrom and Milan M. Ćirković, 308–45. New York: Oxford University Press.

Yudkowsky, Eliezer. 2011. "Complex Value Systems Are Required to Realize Valuable Futures." San Francisco: Machine Intelligence Research Institute. https://intelligence.org/files/ComplexValues.pdf.

22 ARTIFICIAL INTELLIGENCE AND THE ETHICS OF SELF-LEARNING ROBOTS

Shannon Vallor and George A. Bekey

The convergence of robotics technology with the science of artificial intelligence (or AI) is rapidly enabling the development of robots that emulate a wide range of intelligent human behaviors.[1] Recent advances in machine learning techniques have produced significant gains in the ability of artificial agents to perform or even excel in activities formerly thought to be the exclusive province of human intelligence, including abstract problem-solving, perceptual recognition, social interaction, and natural language use. These developments raise a host of new ethical concerns about the responsible design, manufacture, and use of robots enabled with artificial intelligence—particularly those equipped with self-learning capacities.

The potential public benefits of self-learning robots are immense. Driverless cars promise to vastly reduce human fatalities on the road while boosting transportation efficiency and reducing energy use. Robot medics with access to a virtual ocean of medical case data might one day be able to diagnose patients with far greater speed and reliability than even the best-trained human counterparts. Robots tasked with crowd control could predict the actions of a dangerous mob well before the signs are recognizable to law enforcement officers. Such applications, and many more that will emerge, have the potential to serve vital moral interests in protecting human life, health, and well-being.

Yet as this chapter will show, the ethical risks posed by AI-enabled robots are equally serious—especially since self-learning systems behave in ways that cannot always be anticipated or fully understood, even by their programmers. Some warn of a future where AI escapes our control, or even turns against humanity (Standage 2016); but other, far less cinematic dangers are much nearer to hand and are virtually certain to cause great harms if not promptly addressed by technologists, lawmakers, and other stakeholders. The task of ensuring the ethical design, manufacture, use, and governance of AI-enabled robots and other artificial agents is thus as critically important as it is vast.

22.1 What Is Artificial Intelligence?

The nature of human intelligence has been one of the great mysteries since the earliest days of civilization. It has been attributed to God or civilization or accidental mutations, but there is general agreement that it is our brain and the intelligence it exhibits that separates humans from other animals. For centuries it was thought that a machine would never be able to emulate human thinking. Yet at present there are numerous computer programs that emulate some aspect of human intelligence, even if none can perform all the cognitive functions of a human brain. The earliest computer programs to exhibit some behavioral aspect of intelligence began to appear in the second half of the twentieth century.[2] The first meaningful test of a computer's approximation to human intelligence was proposed by Alan Turing (1950). He called it the "imitation game," more commonly known today as the "Turing Test."

The idea is the following: An investigator submits written queries to the computer, which replies in writing. The computer passes the test if, after a suitable time interval, the average investigator has no better than a 70% chance of correctly determining whether the responses come from a person or a computer. The general utility and significance of the Turing Test for AI research are widely contested (Moor 2003; Russell and Norvig 2010). Its focus on a system's appearance to users in a tightly controlled setting, rather than the cognitive architecture or internal operations of the system, may appear to bypass the basic point of the test: namely, to demonstrate a *cognitive* faculty. The test also excludes many other types of intelligent performance that do not involve conversational ability. Still, it is noteworthy that in an annual competition held since 1991 (the Loebner Prize), no system has passed an unrestricted version of the test—repeatedly defying predictions by many researchers (Turing included) that computers would display conversational intelligence by the twenty-first century (Moor 2003).

While there are many unresolved questions about what it would take for a machine to demonstrate possession of "real" intelligence of the general sort possessed by humans, the chief goal of most AI researchers is more modest: systems that can emulate, augment, or compete with the performance of intelligent humans in well-defined tasks.[3] In this sense, the pragmatic legacy of the Turing Test endures. This figurative, task-delimited definition of artificial intelligence is the one we shall employ in the rest of this chapter, unless otherwise stated. It is distinct from the far more ambitious notion of "strong" artificial intelligence with the full range of cognitive capacities typically possessed by humans, including self-awareness. Most AI researchers characterize the latter achievement, often referred to as "artificial general intelligence" or AGI, as *at best* a long-term prospect—not an emerging reality.[4]

Artificial agents with specific forms of task intelligence, on the other hand, are already here among us. In many cases they not only compete with but handily *outperform* human agents, a trend that is projected to accelerate rapidly with ongoing advances in techniques of *machine learning*. Moreover, the implementation of task-specific AI systems in robotic systems is further expanding the range and variety of AI agents and the kinds of social roles they can occupy. Such trends are projected to yield significant gains in global productivity, knowledge production, and institutional efficiency (Kaplan 2015). Yet as we will see, they also carry profound social, economic, and *ethical* risks.

22.2 Artificial Intelligence and the Ethics of Machine Learning

Many ethical concerns about AI research and its robotic applications are associated with a rapidly emerging domain of computer science known as *machine learning*. As with learning in animals, machine learning is a developmental process in which repeated exposures of a system to an information-rich environment gradually produce, expand, enhance, or reinforce that system's behavioral and cognitive competence in that environment or relevantly similar ones. Learning produces changes in the state of the system that endure for some time, often through some mechanism of explicit or implicit memory formation.

One important approach to machine learning is modeled on networks in the central nervous system and is known as *neural network learning* or, more accurately, *artificial neural network (ANN) learning*. For simplicity, we omit the word *artificial* in the following discussion. A neural network consists of a set of *input nodes* representing various features of the source or input data and a set of output nodes representing the desired control actions. Between the input and output node layers are "hidden" layers of nodes that function to process the input data, for example, by extracting features that are especially relevant to the desired outputs. Connections between the nodes have numerical "weights" that can be modified with the help of a *learning algorithm*; the algorithm allows the network to be "trained" with each new input pattern until the network weights are adjusted in such a way that the relationship between input and output layers is optimized. Thus the network gradually "learns" from repeated "experience" (multiple training runs with input datasets) how to optimize the machine's "behavior" (outputs) for a given kind of task.

While machine learning can model cognitive architectures other than neural networks, interest in neural networks has grown in recent years with the addition of more hidden layers giving *depth* to such networks, as well as feedback or recurrent layers. The adjustment of the connection strengths in these more complex networks belongs to a loosely defined group of techniques known as *deep learning*. Among other applications of AI—especially those involving computer vision, natural language, or audio processing—the performance of self-driving "robotic cars" has been improved significantly by the use of deep learning techniques.

Machine learning techniques also vary in terms of the degree to which the learning is *supervised*, that is, the extent to which the training data is explicitly labeled by humans to tell the system which classifications it should learn to make (as opposed to letting the system construct its own classifications or groupings). While many other programming methods can be embedded in AI systems, including "top-down" rule-based controls ("If a right turn is planned, activate right turn signal 75 meters prior to turn"), real-world contingencies are often too numerous, ambiguous, or unpredictable to effectively manage without the aid of machine learning techniques.

For a self-driving car, the inputs will include real-time data about road conditions, illumination, speed, GPS location, and desired destination. The outputs will include the computed values of controlled variables, such as pressure on the accelerator (gas) pedal, steering commands (e.g., "Turn the steering wheel 30 degrees clockwise"), and so on. Hidden layers of nodes will be sensitive to a wide range of salient patterns that might be detected in the inputs (e.g., input patterns indicating a bicyclist on the right side of the roadway) in ways that shape the proper outputs ("Slow down slightly, edge to the left-center of the lane").

Before it is capable of driving safely in real-world conditions, however, the car's network must be "trained" by a learning algorithm to predict the appropriate machine outputs (driving behaviors) for a wide variety of inputs and goals. Learning takes place by adjustment of the gains or *weights* between the nodes of the network's input, hidden, and output layers. Initial training of a network in simulations is followed by controlled field tests, where the network is implemented and trained in a physical car. Once the proper connection strengths are determined by the training process, the input-output behavior of the network becomes an approximation to the behavior of the system being modeled: in our example, a well-driven car. While an artificial neural network's cognitive structure may bear little resemblance to the neural structure of a competent human driver, once it can reliably approximate the input-output behavior typical of such drivers, we may say the network has *learned* to drive.

Once the network is judged sufficiently competent and reliable in controlled tests, additional fine-tuning of its performance might then take place "in the wild," that is, in uncontrolled real-world conditions—as in the case of Tesla's autopilot feature. Here we begin to confront important ethical questions emerging from AI's implementation in a robot or other system that can autonomously act and make irreversible changes in the physical world. Media outlets have widely covered the ethics of autonomous cars, especially the prospect of real-world "trolley problems" generated by the task of programming cars to make morally challenging trade-offs between the safety of its passengers, occupants of other cars, and pedestrians (Achenbach 2015). Yet "trolley problems" do not exhaust or even necessarily address the core ethical issues raised by artificially intelligent and autonomous robotic systems.[5] This chapter focuses on a range of ethical issues less commonly addressed in media coverage of AI and robotics.

First, consider that driverless cars are intended to make roads safer for humans, who are notoriously unsafe drivers. This goal has *prima facie* ethical merit, for who would deny that fewer car wrecks is a moral good? To accomplish it, however, one must train artificial networks to drive *better* than we do. Like humans, self-learning machines gain competence in part by learning from their mistakes. The most fertile grounds for driving mistakes are real-world roadways, populated by loose dogs, fallen trees, wandering deer, potholes, and drunk, texting, or sleepy drivers. But is it ethical to allow people on public roads to be unwitting test subjects for a driverless car's training runs?

Tesla's customers voluntarily sign up for this risk in exchange for the excitement and convenience of the latest driving technology, but pedestrians and other drivers who might be on the wrong end of an autopilot mistake have entered into no such contract. Is it ethical for a company to impose such risks on us, even if the risks are statistically small, without public discussion or legislative oversight? Should the public be compensated for such testing, since Tesla—a private company—profits handsomely if the tests result in a more commercially viable technology? Or should we accept that since the advancement of driverless technology is in the long-term public interest, we (or our children) will be compensated by Tesla with vastly safer roads five, ten, or twenty years from now?

Moreover, does ethics permit the unwitting sacrifice of those who might be endangered *today* by a machine learning its way in the world, as long as we can reasonably hope that many others will be saved by the same technology tomorrow? Here we see an implicit conflict emerging between different ethical theories; a utilitarian may well license such sacrifices in the interests of greater human happiness, while a Kantian would regard them as fundamentally immoral. Similar questions can be asked about other applications of machine learning. For example, should a future robot medic, well trained in simulations and controlled tests, be allowed to fine-tune its network in the field with real, injured victims of an earthquake or mass shooting, who might be further endangered by the robot's error? Does the prospect look more ethically justifiable if we reasonably believe this will increase the likelihood of one day having *extraordinary* robot medics that can save many more lives than we currently can with only human medics?

Imagine that we decide the long-term public benefit does justify the risk. Even the most powerful and well-trained artificial networks are not wholly predictable. Statistically they may be competitive with or even superior to humans at a given task, but unforeseen outputs—sometimes quite odd ones—are a rare but virtually ineradicable possibility. Some are *emergent behaviors* produced by interactions in large, complex systems.[6] Others are simple failures of an otherwise reliable system to model the desired output. A well-known example of the latter is IBM's Watson, which handily beat the best human *Jeopardy!* players in 2011 but nevertheless gave a few answers that even novice human players would have known were wrong, such as the notorious "Toronto" answer to a Final Jeopardy question about "U.S. Cities."

In the context of TV entertainment, this was a harmless, amusing mistake—and a helpful reminder that even the smartest machines aren't perfect. Yet today Watson for Oncology is employed by more than a dozen cancer centers in the United States to "offer oncologists and people with cancer individualized treatment options" (IBM Watson 2016). Watson's diagnoses and treatment plans are still vetted by licensed oncologists. Still, how reliably can a human expert distinguish between a novel, unexpected treatment recommendation by Watson that might save a patient's life—something that has reportedly already happened in Japan (David 2016)—and the oncological equivalent of "Toronto"? At least in the context of oncology, a physician *can* take time to investigate and evaluate Watson's recommendations; but how can we insulate ourselves from the unpredictability of systems such as self-driving cars, in which the required speed of operation and decision-making may render real-time human supervision virtually impossible to implement?

Ideally, responsible creators of self-learning systems will allow them to operate "in the wild" only when their statistical failure rate in controlled settings is markedly lower than that of the average human performing the same task. Still, who should we hold responsible when a robot or other artificial agent *does* injure a person while honing its intelligence in the real world? Consider a catastrophic machine "error" that was not introduced by human programmers, could not have been specifically predicted by them, and thus could not have been prevented, except by not allowing the machine to act and learn in society in the first place.[7] What, if any, safeguards should be put in place to mitigate such losses, and who is responsible for making this happen? Lawmakers? Manufacturers? Individual AI scientists and programmers? Consumer groups? Insurance companies? We need a public conversation among affected stakeholders about what a *just distribution* of the risk burdens *and* benefits of self-learning systems will look like.

A related ethical issue concerns the very different degrees and types of risk that may be imposed by artificial agents on individuals and society. Allowing a self-driving security robot to patrol a mall food court risks bruising an errant toddler's foot, which is bad enough (Vincent 2016). It is quite another order of risk-magnitude to unleash a self-learning robot in a 2-ton metal chassis traveling public roads at highway speed, or to arm it with lethal weapons, or to link a self-learning agent up to critical power systems. Yet there are also significant risks involved with *not* employing self-learning systems, particularly in contexts such as driving and medicine where human error is a large and ineradicable source of grievous harms. If sound policy informed by careful ethical reflection does not begin to form soon around these questions of risk and responsibility in self-learning systems, the safety of innocent people *and* the long-term future of AI research may be gravely endangered.

22.3 Broader Ethical Concerns about Artificially Intelligent Robots

Not all ethical quandaries about AI-enabled robots are specific to their implementation of machine learning. Many such concerns apply to virtually any artificial agent capable of autonomous action in the world. These include such challenges as *meaningful human oversight and control of AI; algorithmic opacity and hidden machine bias; widespread technological unemployment; psychological and emotional manipulation of humans by AI*; and *automation bias.*

22.3.1 Meaningful Human Control and Oversight of AI

Society has an *ethical* interest in meaningful human control and oversight of AI, for several reasons. The first arises from the general ethical principle that humans are morally *responsible* for our chosen actions. Since, unlike our children, AI-enabled systems come into the world formed by deliberate human design, humans are in a deep sense always *morally accountable* for the effects of such agents on the world. It would therefore seem plainly irresponsible for humans to allow meaningful control or oversight of an artificial agent's actions to slip from our grasp.

A second reason for our ethical interest in meaningful human control and oversight of AI is its rapidly expanding scope of action. AI-enabled systems already operate in real-world contexts like driving and medicine that involve matters of life and death, as well as other core dimensions of human flourishing. Thus the effects of AI in the world for which humans are responsible—positive *and* negative—are of *increasing moral gravity*. This trend will strengthen as artificial systems demonstrate ever-greater competence and reliability in contexts with very high moral stakes (Wallach 2015).

As ethically fundamental as human responsibility for AI may be, the *practical* challenges of maintaining meaningful human control and oversight are immense. In addition to the aforementioned risk of emergent or other unpredictable AI behaviors, there are strong counter-pressures to *limit* human control and oversight of AI. Human supervisors are costly to employ, potentially reducing the profit to be reaped from automating a key task. Humans are also far slower to judge and act than are computers, so efficiency gains too can be diminished by our control. In many applications, such as driving, flight control, and financial trading, the entire function of the system will presuppose speeds and scales of decision-making beyond human reach. There is also the question of when our judgments warrant more *epistemic authority* or *epistemic trust* than machine judgments. If an artificially intelligent system has consistently demonstrated statistically greater competence than humans in a certain task, on what grounds do we give a human supervisor the power to challenge or override its decisions?

The difficulty is exacerbated by the fact that self-learning robots often operate in ways that are opaque to humans, even their programmers (Pasquale 2015). We must face the prospect of a growing disconnect between human and artificial forms of "expertise," a gap that should disturb us for several reasons. First, it risks the gradual devaluation of distinctly human skills and modes of understanding. Human expertise often expresses important moral and intellectual virtues missing from AI (such as perspective, empathy, integrity, aesthetic style, and civic-mindedness, to name a few)—virtues that are all too easily undervalued relative to AI's instrumental virtues of raw speed and efficiency. Additionally, productive AI–human *collaborations*—the chief goal of many researchers—will be far more difficult if AI and human agents cannot grasp one another's manner of reasoning, explain the basis of their decisions to one another, or pose critical questions to one another.

After all, if a human cannot reliably query an AI-enabled robot as to the specific evidence and chain of reasoning by means of which it arrived at its decision, how can he or she reliably assess the decision's validity? Human supervisors of AI agents cannot effectively do their job if their subordinate is a mute "black box." For this reason, many AI designers are looking for ways to increase the *transparency* of machine reasoning. For example, internal confidence measures reported alongside a given choice allow a human to give less credibility to decisions with a low confidence value. Still, the problem of *algorithmic opacity* remains a significant barrier to effective human oversight. It generates other moral risks as well.

22.3.2 Algorithmic Opacity and Hidden Machine Bias

In addition to frustrating meaningful human oversight of AI, "black boxed" or opaque algorithmic processes can perpetuate and reinforce morally and epistemically harmful biases. For example, racial, gender, or socioeconomic biases that originate in human minds are commonly embedded in the human-generated datasets used to train or "educate" machine systems. These data define the "world" that an artificial agent "knows." Yet the effect of human-biased data on machine outputs is easily obscured by several factors, making those biases more harmful and resistant to eradication.

One factor is algorithmic opacity itself. If I cannot know what features of a given dataset were singled out by a network's hidden layers as relevant and actionable, then I will be uncertain whether the network's decision rested on a harmful racial or gender bias encoded somewhere in that data. Another factor is our cultural tendency to think about robots and computers as inherently "objective" and "rational," and thus materially incapable of the kinds of emotional and psychological responses (e.g., fear, disgust, anger, shame) that typically produce irrational and harmful social biases. Even scientists who understand the mechanisms through which human bias can infect machine intelligence are often surprised to discover the extent of such bias in machine outputs—even from inputs thought to be relatively unbiased.

For example, a team of Boston University and Microsoft researchers found significant gender biases in machine "word embeddings" trained on a large body of Google News reports (Bolukbasi et al. 2016). They remark that data generated by "professional journalists" (as opposed to data sourced from internet message boards, for example) might have been expected to carry "little gender bias"; yet the machine outputs strongly reflected many harmful gender stereotypes (2016, 3). They observed that "the same system that solved [other] reasonable analogies will offensively answer 'man is to computer programmer as woman is to *x*' with *x* = *homemaker*" (3). The system also reflected "strong" racial stereotypes (15). To see how such biases could produce direct harm, just imagine this same system implemented in an AI agent tasked with providing college counseling to young men and women or with ranking employment applications for human resources managers at a large tech firm.

Indeed, hidden biases in AI algorithms and training data invite unjust outcomes or policies in predictive policing, lending, education, housing, healthcare, and employment, to name just a few sectors of AI implementation. Racial bias has already been found in facial recognition algorithms (Orcutt 2016) and, even more disturbingly, in machine-generated scores widely used by judges in criminal courts to predict the likelihood that a criminal defendant will reoffend (Angwin et al. 2016). Such scores shape judicial decisions about parole eligibility, length of sentence, and the type of correctional facility to which a defendant will be subjected. A predictive engine that assigns higher risk scores to black defendants than to white defendants who are otherwise similar, and that systematically overestimates the likelihood of black recidivism while systematically *under*estimating the rate of recidivism among whites, not only reflects an existing social injustice, but *perpetuates* and *reinforces* it—both by giving it the stamp of machine objectivity and neutrality associated with computer-generated calculations and by encouraging further injustices (disproportionately longer and harsher sentences) against black defendants and their families.

Perhaps humans can learn to view biased machine algorithms and outputs with greater suspicion. Yet machine bias can also infect the judgments of less critically minded agents, such as robots tasked with identifying shoplifters, conducting anti-burglary patrols, or assisting with crowd-control or anti-terrorism operations. Such uses of robots are widely anticipated; indeed, automated security robots are already on the market (Vincent 2016). Perhaps we can train algorithms to *expose* hidden biases in such systems, for unless they can be effectively addressed, machine biases are virtually guaranteed to perpetuate and amplify many forms of social injustice.

22.3.3 Widespread Technological Unemployment

In the early nineteenth century, when weaving machines were introduced in England, great resentment and fear arose among textile workers who saw their jobs threatened. An organized revolt against the machines led by so-called Luddites (after a mythical hero known as "Ned Ludd" or "King Ludd") had sufficient cultural impact that, to this day, people who object to new developments in technology are known as "Neo-Luddites." Yet despite their very real harms, the disruptions of the Industrial Revolution produced social goods that not many would be willing to surrender for the old world: longer life spans, higher standards of living in industrialized nations, and, eventually, great expansions in skilled employment. The early computer revolution produced similar cultural disruptions, but a range of new public benefits and a booming market for jobs in the "knowledge economy."

Yet unlike other waves of machine automation, emerging advances in AI and robotics technology are now viewed as a significant threat to employees who perform *mental*, not just manual, labor. Automated systems already perform many tasks that traditionally required advanced education, such as legal discovery, reading x-ray films, grading essays, rating loan applications, and writing news articles (Kaplan 2015). IBM's Watson has been employed as a teaching assistant in an online college class on AI—without students discerning the non-human identity of their trusted TA "Jill" (Korn 2016).

The large-scale effects of AI and associated automation on human labor, social security, political stability, and economic equality are uncertain, but an Oxford study concludes that as many as 47% of U.S. jobs are at significant risk from advances in machine learning and mobile robotics (Frey and Osborne 2013, 1–2). Sectors at highest risk for displacement by automated systems include transportation and logistics (including driving jobs), sales, service, construction, office and administrative support, and production (Frey and Osborne 2013, 35). It is worth noting that the Oxford researchers were relatively conservative in their predictions of machine intelligence, suggesting that non-routine, high-skilled jobs associated with healthcare, scientific research, education, and the arts are at relatively low risk due to their heavy reliance on human creativity and social intelligence (Frey and Osborne 2013, 40). Yet more recent gains in machine learning have led many to anticipate a boom in artificial agents like the university TA "Jill Watson": able to compete with humans even in jobs that traditionally required social, creative, and intellectual capacities.

Such developments will profoundly challenge economic and political stability in a world already suffering from rising economic inequality, political disaffection, and growing class divisions. They also impact fundamental human values like autonomy and dignity, and make it even less certain that the benefits and risks of scientific and technical advances will be distributed among citizens and nations in a manner that is not merely efficient and productive, but also *good* and *just*.

22.3.4 Psychological and Emotional Manipulation of Humans by AI

The moral impacts of AI on human emotions, sociality, relationship bonding, public discourse, and civic character have only begun to be explored. Research in social AI for robots and other artificial agents is exploding, and vigorous efforts to develop carebots for the elderly, sexbots for the lonely, chatbots for customers and patients, and artificial assistants like Siri and Cortana for all of us are just the tip of the iceberg. The ethical questions that can arise in this domain are virtually limitless, since human sociality is the primary field of ethical action.

One deep worry about social AI is the well-documented tendency of humans to form robust emotional attachments to machines that simulate human emotional responses, even when the simulations are quite superficial (Turkle 2011). The behavior of artificial agents can also foster harmful delusions in humans, who may incorrectly perceive them as having human traits such as sentience, empathy, moral conscience, or loyalty. Thus humans are deeply vulnerable to emotional and psychological manipulation by AI and robotic systems coldly designed to exploit us for commercial, political, or other purposes (Scheutz 2012). Imagine, for example, the public harm that could be done by a chatbot programmed to seek out and form emotionally manipulative online relationships with young voters or lonely seniors and then, once a bond is formed, to start interjecting deliberately manipulative messages about a political candidate whom the chatbot deeply "fears" or "loves."

Public education about the inability of robots to have feelings or form genuine bonds with humans will likely not be enough to prevent such harms, since even those with an insider's knowledge of the technology can find themselves responding to such powerful delusions (Scheutz 2012). It is thus imperative that lawmakers and developers of AI-enabled social agents begin to work together on ethical and legal guidelines for restricting or prohibiting harmful manipulation, particularly when it undermines human autonomy or damages our vital interests.

22.3.5 Automation Bias

A related ethical concern about human–robot/AI interaction is the psychological phenomenon of *automation bias*, in which humans greatly overestimate or rely unduly upon the capabilities of computerized systems (Cummings 2004). Automation bias can result from flawed expectations of computerized systems as infallible or inherently superior to human judgment, from time pressures or information overloads that make it difficult for humans to properly evaluate a computer's decision, or from overextending warranted confidence in a machine's actual capabilities into an area of action in which confidence is *not* warranted. The latter is often elicited on the basis of only shallow similarities with intelligent human behavior, as when pedestrians in Puerto Rico walked behind a self-parking Volvo in a garage, erroneously trusting the car (which lacked an optional "pedestrian-detection" package) to know not to back over a person (Hill 2015).

Automation bias has been cited as one possible factor in the 1988 downing of Iran Air 655 by the USS *Vincennes*, which caused the death of 290 civilians (Grut 2013; Galliott 2015, 217). Operators of the Aegis anti-aircraft system that mistakenly identified the airliner as a military jet had ample information to warrant overriding the identification, but failed to do so. As artificially intelligent and robotic systems are given increasing power to effect or incite action in the physical world, often with serious consequences for human safety and well-being, it is ethically imperative that the psychological dimension of human–AI and human–robot interactions be better understood. Such knowledge must guide efforts by AI and robotic system designers *and* users to reduce or eliminate harmful automation bias and other psychological misalignments between human interests and artificial cognition.

22.4. Public Fears and the Long-Term Future of AI

While many computer scientists consider AI to be simply an especially interesting aspect of their field, challenging to program, and sometimes frustrating if it does not behave as expected, in the popular press AI is frequently framed as a threat to humanity's survival. Elon Musk, founder and CEO of Space X and Tesla Motors, has warned the public that with AI we are "summoning the demon"; similar warnings about AI's *existential risks*, that is, its potential to threaten meaningful human existence, have been voiced by public figures such as Stephen Hawking and Bill Gates, along with a host of AI and robotics researchers (Standage 2016).[8] The urgency of their warnings is motivated by the unprecedented acceleration of developments in the field, especially in machine learning.[9]

Isaac Asimov's "Laws of Robotics" were an early fictional attempt to think through a set of guidelines for the control of intelligent robots (Asimov 2004). Today, however, technologists and ethicists must revisit this challenge in the face of profound public ambivalence about an AI-driven future. While many of us implicitly trust our car's directional sense or our tax software's financial acuity more than we trust our own, there is growing uncertainty about AI's long-term safety and compatibility with human interests.

Public distrust of AI systems could inhibit wider adoption and consumer engagement with these technologies, a consequence that AI researchers have good reason to want to avoid. Many public fears can be moderated by better education and communication from AI researchers about what AI today *is* (skillful at well-defined cognitive tasks) and is *not* (sentient, self-aware, malevolent *or* benevolent, or even robustly intelligent in the manner of humans). Moreover, we would all benefit from an outward expansion of public concern to the less apocalyptic, but more pressing ethical challenges of AI addressed in this chapter.

While talk about "Skynet" scenarios and "robot overlords" sounds like overheated speculation to many AI and robotics researchers—who are often overjoyed just to make a robot that can have a halfway convincing conversation or walk up an unstable hillside—growing public anxieties about AI and robotics technology may force researchers to pay more attention to such fears and at least begin an early dialogue about long-term control strategies for artificial agents. One does not have to predict a *Terminator*-like future to recognize that the ethical challenges presented by AI will not remain fixed in their present state; as the technology grows in power, complexity, and scale, so will its risks *and* benefits (Cameron 1984). For this reason, the ethics of artificial intelligence will be a rapidly moving target—and humanity as a whole must make a dedicated effort to keep up.

Notes

1. There is much debate (even between this chapter's authors) about whether computer science, and artificial intelligence research in particular, is a genuine science that studies and models natural phenomena (such as informational or computational processes) or is a branch of engineering.
2. An excellent introduction to the field appears in Russell and Norvig (2010).
3. IBM Watson, for example, prefers the term "augmented intelligence" or "cognitive computing" to "artificial intelligence," to emphasize Watson's potential to enhance and empower human intelligence, not render it superfluous (IBM Research 2016).
4. Research in AGI continues, if slowly, and is the central focus of organizations such as the Machine Intelligence Research Institute (MIRI). Many researchers who work on AGI are actively working to mitigate its considerable risks (Yudkowsky 2008).
5. A related study is that of *machine ethics*: designing agents with artificial *moral* intelligence. Because of space limitations, we restrict our focus here to the ethical challenges AI presents for *human* moral agents.
6. Depending on whether the emergent behavior is undesirable or useful to humans, emergence can be a "bug" (as with the 2010 Flash Crash caused by feedback loops among interacting global financial software systems) or a "feature" (as when an algorithm produces emergent and seemingly "intelligent" swarming behavior among a networked group of micro-robots).
7. Strictly speaking, machine learning networks do not make "errors"—they only generate unexpected or statistically rare outcomes that, from a human perspective, are not well aligned with programmers' or users' real-world goals for the system. But since human goals (for example, "promote human safety") are not actually *understood* by the system (however statistically effective it may be at reaching them), it cannot truly be said to "err" in producing a result incongruous with such a goal. The mistake, if there is one, is a gap or misalignment between what the machine's code and network weightings actually do and what its programmers wanted it to do. Good programming, training, and testing protocols can minimize such gaps, but it is virtually impossible to ensure that every such gap is eliminated.
8. See the open letter on AI from the Future of Life Institute (2005), with more than eight thousand signatories; see also Bostrom (2014).
9. Indeed, a standard textbook in AI, which twenty years ago had some three hundred pages, now, in its third edition, includes well over a thousand pages (Russell and Norvig 2010).

Works Cited

Achenbach, Joel. 2015. "Driverless Cars Are Colliding with the Creepy Trolley Problem." *Washington Post*, December 29. https://www.washingtonpost.com/news/innovations/wp/2015/12/29/will-self-driving-cars-ever-solve-the-famous-and-creepy-trolley-problem/.

Angwin, Julia, Larson, Jeff, Mattu, Surya, and Kirchner, Lauren. 2016. "Machine Bias." *ProPublica*, May 23. https://www.propublica.org/article/machine-bias-risk-assessments-in-criminal-sentencing.

Asimov, Isaac. (1950) 2004. *I, Robot*. Reprint, New York: Bantam Books.

Bolukbasi, Tolga, Kai-Wei Chang, James Zou, Venkatesh Saligrama, and Adam Kalai. 2016. "Man Is to Computer Programmer as Woman Is to Homemaker? Debiasing Word Embeddings." *arXiv* 1607.06520v1 [cs.CL]. https://arxiv.org/abs/1607.06520.

Bostrom, Nick. 2014. *Superintelligence: Paths, Dangers, Strategies*. Oxford: Oxford University Press.

Cameron, James (director). 1984. "The Terminator." Cameron, James and Gale Anne Hurd (writers).

Cummings, Mary L. 2004. "Automation Bias in Intelligent Time Critical Decision Support Systems." *AIAA 1st Intelligent Systems Technical Conference*. arc.aiaa.org/doi/pdf/10.2514/6.2004-6313.

David, Eric. 2016. "Watson Correctly Diagnoses Woman after Doctors Are Stumped." *SiliconAngle*, August 5. http://siliconangle.com/blog/2016/08/05/watson-correctly-diagnoses-woman-after-doctors-were-stumped/.

Future of Life Institute. 2015. "Research Priorities for Robust and Beneficial Artificial Intelligence." http://futureoflife.org/ai-open-letter/.

Galliott, Jai. 2015. *Military Robots: Mapping the Moral Landscape*. New York: Routledge.

Grut, Chantal. 2013. "The Challenge of Autonomous Lethal Robotics to International Humanitarian Law." *Journal of Conflict and Security Law*. doi: 10.1093/jcsl/krt002. http://jcsl.oxfordjournals.org/content/18/1/5.abstract.

Hill, Kashmir. 2015. "Volvo Says Horrible 'Self-Parking Car Accident' Happened Because Driver Didn't Have 'Pedestrian Detection.'" *Fusion*, May 26. http://fusion.net/story/139703/self-parking-car-accident-no-pedestrian-detection/.

IBM Research. 2016. "Response to Request for Information: Preparing for the Future of Artificial Intelligence." https://www.research.ibm.com/cognitive-computing/ostp/rfi-response.shtml.

IBM Watson. 2016. "IBM Watson for Oncology." http://www.ibm.com/watson/watson-oncology.html.

Kaplan, Jerry. 2015. *Humans Need Not Apply: A Guide to Wealth and Work in the Age of Artificial Intelligence*. New Haven, CT: Yale University Press.

Korn, Melissa. 2016. "Imagine Discovering That Your Teaching Assistant Really Is a Robot." *Wall Street Journal*, May 6. http://www.wsj.com/articles/if-your-teacher-sounds-like-a-robot-you-might-be-on-to-something-1462546621.

Moor, James. 2003. *The Turing Test: The Elusive Standard of Artificial Intelligence.* Dordrecht: Kluwer.

Orcutt, Mike. 2016. "Are Facial Recognition Systems Accurate? Depends on Your Race." *MIT Technology Review*, July 6. https://www.technologyreview.com/s/601786/are-face-recognition-systems-accurate-depends-on-your-race/.

Osborne, Michael and Carl Benedikt Frey. 2013. "The Future of Employment: How Susceptible Are Jobs to Computerisation?" *Oxford Martin Programme on the Impacts of Future Technology*. http://www.oxfordmartin.ox.ac.uk/publications/view/1314.

Pasquale, Frank. 2015. *The Black Box Society: The Secret Algorithms That Control Money and Information*. Cambridge, MA: Harvard University Press.

Russell, Stuart J. and Peter Norvig. 2010. *Artificial Intelligence: A Modern Approach.* 3d ed. Upper Saddle River, NJ: Pearson.

Scheutz, Matthias. 2012. "The Inherent Dangers of Unidirectional Emotional Bonds Between Humans and Social Robots." In *Robot Ethics*, edited by Patrick Lin, Keith Abney, and George Bekey, 205–222. Cambridge, MA: MIT Press.

Standage, Tom. 2016. "Artificial Intelligence: The Return of the Machinery Question." *Economist,* June 25. http://www.economist.com/news/special-report/21700761-after-many-false-starts-artificial-intelligence-has-taken-will-it-cause-mass.

Turing, Alan M. 1950. "Computing Machinery and Intelligence." *Mind* 59: 236, 433–60.

Turkle, Sherry. 2011. *Alone Together: Why We Expect More from Technology and Less from Each Other*. New York: Basic Books.

Vincent, James. 2016. "Mall Security Bot Knocks Down Toddler, Breaks Asimov's First Law of Robotics." *Verge*, July 13. http://www.theverge.com/2016/7/13/12170640/mall-security-robot-k5-knocks-down-toddler.

Wallach, Wendell. 2015. *A Dangerous Master: How to Keep Technology from Slipping Beyond Our Control.* New York: Basic Books.

Yudkowsky, Eliezer. 2008. "Artificial Intelligence as a Positive and Negative Factor in Global Risk," In *Global Catastrophic Risks*, edited by Nick Bostrom and Milan M. Ćirković, 308–45. New York: Oxford University Press.

23 ROBOTS AND SPACE ETHICS

Keith Abney

Space: the final frontier . . . of nonhuman exploration. To boldly go where no robot has gone before . . . these are the travels of the Starship Von Neumann probe.

Not the way the Trekkies remember the taglines. But should this be our future, instead of one in which oversensitive, emotional, violent, fragile meatbags constantly get in trouble because their vulnerabilities cause endless troubles in the exploration of outer space? As Mr. Spock might say, that seems . . . illogical. And thinking critically about the reasons for using robots, instead of humans, in space can help dispel the often overemotional, militaristic, and patriotic veneer that has accompanied discussion of human spaceflight; and it can help inform discussion of robots replacing humans in other contexts.

To start, why should humans go into space at all? If the goal is exploration, robotic probes can travel and work in environments far too inhospitable for humans. Robots, after all, excel in the traditional "three Ds"—environments too dull, dirty, or dangerous for humans (e.g., Lin 2012). Space exemplifies such an environment, with its terrifying radiation and temperature extremes, lack of air or water, and long stretches of dull reconnaissance necessary during exploratory missions—and increasingly, ever longer flight times to get to our destination. And the robotic fourth "D," being dispassionate, may well be crucial (Veruggio and Abney 2012); robots will not disobey mission commands out of jealousy, revenge, lust, or any of the other emotional drivers that so often cause humans—even well-trained humans—to commit egregious tactical blunders.

So robots, which need no sleep or healthcare, no food or water, and don't get tired or hungry or angry, will inevitably do a better job of exploring the cosmos than humans replete with all our biological limitations. And the gap in performance will only widen as technology improves and robotic capabilities become ever more advanced.

Already robots have explored the farthest reaches of our solar system, and even beyond, to interstellar space. Human astronauts have gotten only as far as the moon, and no farther, in almost fifty years.

As for the purpose of human colonization, why believe that humans should go to other planets to live? The difficulties will be stupendous; even the most clement nearby world, Mars, looks like a suicide mission for any human colonists with near-term technology (Do et al. 2016). Even supposing human astronauts could survive a six-month voyage to Mars in a cramped capsule, with hazards from cosmic rays, solar flares, meteorites, and innumerable other travel risks (including each other!), the challenges would hardly dissipate upon arrival, as cinephiles saw Matt Damon demonstrate in *The Martian* (Scott 2015).

And successful colonization demands that humans not merely be able to achieve some type of rudimentary, temporary survival upon arrival at Mars (or other destination), but also make that survival sustainable indefinitely, with the associated requirement that, sooner or later, the colonists must successfully reproduce and raise children. But bringing up babies would cause yet more travails, both ethical and existential. Should we allow or demand abortions of the less fit, or demand enhancements, even genetic engineering or species hybridization, in order to up the odds of success (Lin and Abney 2014)?

Even assuming success at colonization is possible, why is that a good thing? Won't humans simply repeat the mistakes of the past? Suppose we find new worlds with living creatures, containing heretofore unknown rich ecosystems; why suppose that we wouldn't simply re-enact our legacy of ecological destruction (including the introduction of both diseases and newly invasive species), as has happened in every virgin territory our forebears settled? Perhaps such considerations leave one unmoved, if one thinks nonhuman life has no moral value. But even so, we should be wary, for perhaps the contamination could go both ways—perhaps human astronauts will return to Earth unwitting bearers of alien microbes that mutate and result in mass illness, or even the death of humanity. If we ever find alien life, we may need off-world quarantine or else risk catastrophe (Abney and Lin 2015). Wouldn't it be better if our first discoverers of, and emissaries to, alien life were our machines?

Even aside from such biomedical and ecological concerns, there remain other serious objections to sending humans into space. One is cost, and particularly the concept of "opportunity cost." It seems plausible to claim that combatting hunger, ecological disruption, climate change, terrorism, or any number of other problems here on Earth deserves higher priority in rationing our limited funds (and other resources) than sending a handful of humans into space. A straightforward application of, say, John Rawls's two principles of justice (1971) would plausibly require that the resources spent on space travel, by robots or (more expensively) humans, would be justified only if they somehow redounded to the benefit of the poor; and arguing that they produced Tang and astronaut ice cream won't cut it.

And even if the expense of space travel can somehow be morally justified, surely ethics would bid us to do it by the most cost-efficient means, with the highest odds of success, available. And as NASA and other space programs around the world have learned all too well from often painful, even disastrous, experience, unmanned robotic missions offer far more bang for the buck. Just ask the U.S. Air Force: when they wanted a space plane, did they push for the continuation of the shuttle program, with its human crew and disastrous failures? No, the USAF opted for the robotic X-37.

Human pilots are fast becoming a legacy boondoggle among atmospheric craft, as even U.S. Secretary of the Navy Ray Mabus admits (Myers 2015). And the legacy aircraft too costly to retrofit into drones are instead being fitted with a PIBOT—a pilot robot that renders human pilots superfluous for the purposes of flying (*Economist* 2016)—though PIBOT as yet isn't programmed to tell you to look out your window at the Grand Canyon. As Todd Harrison (2015) notes, "[P]hysics, physiology, and fiscal facts" are why drones will soon render manned fighter jets obsolete; the far greater hurdles human pilots face in space, from merely staying alive to the physiological burdens on human performance in harsh zero-G conditions, mean that "physics, physiology, and fiscal facts" have already made human astronauts an extravagant, morally indefensible indulgence.

So what purposes do we serve by going into space? Which of these are unethical? And of those that could be ethical, what role should robots play in fulfilling them? In particular, are there compelling reasons to think our ethical goals in space would require robots to assist humans—or supplant them? Does ethics require that the only spacefaring representatives of our civilization be our machines?

23.1 Purposes: Exploration

23.1.1 To Go Boldly . . . but Robots Do It Better?

So why go into space? The most commonly cited purpose is exploration—to boldly go where no human has gone before. But exploration itself can have many (sub)goals. To gain knowledge of a heretofore uncharted realm is one obvious such goal; we want to make a map of *terra incognita*, to specify the physical details of what was formerly unknown. The limits of remote sensing are often used as a justification for the need for human astronauts; the claim is that a human astronaut on, say, Mars could do experiments that the *Spirit* or *Opportunity* rovers could never perform.

But, while true for now, that is largely a function of cost and opportunity; more sophisticated (and costly) robots than the current rovers could perform most if not all of the experiments that a human astronaut could, and still at a fraction of the cost of sending human astronauts on a round-trip mission to Mars. And this does not apply merely to futuristic robots capable of planning and carrying out an entire mission without human guidance from Earth; even short of such full autonomy for robots, the financial considerations remain the same.

After all, paying for a Mars robot and its Earth-based teleoperator (say, a scientist at Mission Control in Houston) is far cheaper than sending a human astronaut to Mars with equivalent tools. And of course, as artificial intelligence improves and space robots become ever more autonomous, the savings will become ever greater. If cost is truly an issue, claiming that we should send human astronauts in order to do it better is essentially always a false economy.

But of course, the human itch to explore the cosmos is not purely for the sake of increasing public scientific knowledge. After all, tourists don't usually go to national parks in order to add to the corpus of scientific knowledge. Instead, we go because they're there; one might say that "wanderlust is in our DNA" (Lin 2006). Space tourism is already part of the business plan for Virgin Galactic, Bigelow Aerospace, and other companies, and the demand is likely to increase.

For at least some humans, the desire to push one's physical, intellectual, emotional, and other boundaries is part of what makes life worth living. The idea that such striving plays a large role in human flourishing is reflected by inspirational memes such as the idea that the value and meaning of life are found in one's experiences, not one's possessions. This innate desire for a kind of private, experiential, personally meaningful knowledge of oneself and one's place in the larger scheme of things could conceivably remain an ethically defensible driver of human space travel, even if human astronauts no longer play any significant role in adding to civilization's store of collective knowledge.

To be clear: insofar as scientifically verifiable, public knowledge is the goal of exploration, robots are already simply better, cheaper, and faster than humans, and their advantage will only increase over time. Their sensors are more reliable, their memories have far greater capacity and are less prone to error, and they can operate in environmental conditions humans would never dare venture into, with far fewer ethical constraints regarding self- and other-preservation when they do.

And our knowledge of the farther reaches of space makes ever more clear the robotic imperative; given how hard it has been to get a human to our closest planetary neighbors, it may require a propulsion breakthrough, or else be a long, long time, before any human will swing into orbit around Jupiter or admire the rings of Saturn from up close. For the near future, space tourism will not leave the Earth–moon system.

So despite these technical difficulties, can a case be made for space tourism as the key to an ethical defense of human travel in space? Not so fast. Even if one could overcome the distributive justice concerns raised by the idea that luxury space travel by billionaire adrenaline junkies is a defensible use of limited resources, we may find that having experiences remotely by robot is better than being there in person! For even the quest for private, experiential knowledge may yet be overcome by the advance of robotic technology: as virtual reality (VR) and/or brain–machine interface (BMI) technology advances, it may be that we could, via remote linkages, have apparently "direct," unmediated experience of what a robot could see and discover.

After all, a "direct" experience of seeing a new vista is already mediated by your senses and processed by your brain. If a remote robotic connection enables the same immediacy, it could be effectively the same experience (Nozick 1974). In the future, when hooking your brain up to the feed from the Mars rover can enable you to feel the Martian sand squishing beneath your feet, or mainstreaming the feed from the Europan submarine enables you to see, feel, even smell the alien sharks through the robotic sensors, what possible advantage could you have by actually being there? And so why should we ever bother going there in person?

23.1.2 Other Purposes: Why We Need Satellites and Autonomous Vehicles

Another purpose of exploring space is to reduce dangers to humans here on Earth. For instance, satellite technology has served to reduce risks in all sorts of ways: weather satellites allow the tracking of developing hurricanes, enabling meteorologists to project the path and strength of the storm several days to even a week in advance, and so giving people time to evacuate and the authorities time to plan for the aftermath.

Communication satellites allow us near-instant access to information from around the earth; they enable us not only to download TV shows from Netflix or order next-day service from Amazon, but they also enable intelligence agencies to foil terrorist plots. And GPS satellites, in addition to having military and business uses, allow us to track transport vessels on land or sea, as well as people who may be lost or otherwise in need of help (Plait 2007).

Other spacefaring robots protect us in more recondite ways. Satellites such as *SOHO* point their sensors at the sun, so scientists using its data can better understand and predict huge solar eruptions that can damage satellites and cause power blackouts. In 1989, a solar flare "provoked geomagnetic storms that disrupted electric power transmission from the Hydro Québec generating station in Canada, blacking out most of the province and plunging 6 million people into darkness for 9 hours; aurora-induced power surges even melted power transformers in New Jersey" (Bell and Phillips 2008).

The fearsome Carrington event of 1859 was much larger; people were able to read their newspapers at night from the glow of the aurora, and telegraph wires sparked so much they caught on fire across the United States (Lovett 2011). If a solar storm the size of the Carrington event happened today, much of our communications infrastructure would be wiped out in a literal flash, as GPS and communications satellites would have their circuits fried. Worse yet, if hundreds of giant transformers were destroyed at once, large swaths of the electrical grid could be out for months.

Satellite data are also crucial for studying the effects of the sun's interaction with Earth itself, from the details of glacial melt in Antarctica and Greenland and other aspects of climate change to pollution emissions. And the risks from space are not only from our sun. Asteroid protection has become a Hollywood blockbuster-level part of our understanding of how we should protect Earth. The growing awareness of impact events ranges from a recent awareness of how the moon formed (when a Mars-sized object struck Earth) to the "dinosaur killer" Chicxulub impactor—an asteroid or, quite possibly, a comet (Rincon 2013)—of 66 million years ago.

More recently, people around the globe enjoyed the use of the Hubble Space Telescope and satellite TV transmissions to witness the depredations of the Shoemaker-Levy 9 comet, whose fragment G struck Jupiter in 1994 with an estimated energy equivalent to 6 million megatons of TNT (about 600 times the estimated nuclear arsenal of the world), leaving a larger-than-Earth-sized scar on the surface of Jupiter (Bruton 1996). All these events and more have enhanced public awareness of the possibility of death from the skies.

In the hope of avoiding such a calamity, the B612 Foundation wants to track Earth-crossing asteroids and is soliciting funding for something called the Sentinel Mission (B612 Foundation 2016), a space-based infrared survey mission to find and catalog 90% of the asteroids larger than 140 meters in Earth's region of the solar system. If it turns up a killer comet or asteroid that threatens life on Earth, then that presumably would be money well spent (Abney and Lin 2015).

Space missions also help scientists put Earth into a larger context, to understand what developments both on and off the planet are true threats to our way of life. For example, why is Mars dry, cold, nearly airless, and dead, when it apparently had running water, even oceans, billions of years ago? Could that happen to Earth? Could we inadvertently cause it to happen—or deliberately stop it? Or why is Venus covered in thick clouds of carbon dioxide and sulfuric acid (literal brimstone!), with a surface temperature of well over 800 degrees Fahrenheit, thanks to a runaway greenhouse effect? Or why has the hurricane on Jupiter called the "Great Red Spot" lasted for more than three centuries?

Answering such questions can be crucial for understanding our own planet and how human actions are affecting it. And, of course, such understanding is crucial to the moral question, what should we do to try to keep Earth as it is? Or how should we change it? Should we, e.g., attempt geoengineering to combat climate change? And if so, what methods should we use? Perhaps we should try space-based solar power (SBSP), in which robots install huge solar panels in space to block solar radiation from reaching Earth, and produce copious amounts of electricity to boot.

One commonality to all of these uses of space for planetary protection: they do not require a human presence above the atmosphere. Whatever the ethically justified uses of satellites are, none of them require a human to be along for the ride. Having humans in space is simply not required for GPS or communications satellites or solar observatories or space telescopes to work, or even to be repaired. Robots do it better.

And even on the surfaces of the other bodies in the solar system, humans are not required; e.g., autonomous vehicles are already functioning in space in lieu of human astronauts, as the *Spirit* and *Opportunity* rovers make clear. They have already made fundamental discoveries on Mars, and such robotic vehicles will be key to further long-term exploration and colonization on at least the moon and Mars. For equivalent cost, their capabilities will always be far superior to those of space buggies requiring a human driver, like the Apollo rovers on the moon.

Autonomous vehicles would be a major boon even for crewed missions; they could take an incapacitated, wounded, or ill astronaut back to safety without needing another astronaut as a driver. They would serve as the ambulances, fire trucks, shippers, mining transports, and all the other things needed to traverse a lunar, Martian, or other surface far better if we were not along for the ride—and underwater autonomous vehicles would obviously not require humans in exploring Europa's or Ganymede's subsurface seas or Titan's liquid ethane lakes.

For instance, take perhaps the most consequential discovery a space program could make: the discovery of life not native to Earth. If a robot car equipped with drills and sensors does not make the first such discovery of extraterrestrial life by digging on Mars, an unmanned underwater vehicle may actually be the first to discover life when it dives into Europa's ocean (or Ganymede's or Titan's).

But perhaps there are other ethically pressing space issues that would require a human presence. Or would it be too risky?

23.2 Safety and Risk

23.2.1 The Perils of Space and Risk Assessment

Scenario: Imagine you are an astronaut on the initial SpaceX mission to Mars. The spaceship has suffered a strike from a small asteroid and is losing fuel. Internal shutdowns have slowed the loss by sealing off most egress points, but a tiny leak remains that apparently only a spacewalk can repair. It may be that the repair could be done from inside the ship, but to determine that means discussions with Mission Control, involving a time delay—as the fuel continues to escape, imperiling the entire crew and mission. But a spacewalk is hazardous, as the field of micrometeors that caused the leak may still pose a risk to an astronaut outside the ship in a thin suit. Also, space weather monitors indicate a solar flare has occurred that may blast an astronaut outside the ship, wearing only a spacesuit for protection, with an unusually high dose of radiation. A spacewalk repair, even if successful, may be a suicide mission for the astronaut performing it. Should a spacewalk repair be attempted immediately, or should the crew delay, awaiting consultations with experts at Mission Control? Who (and how) will determine which risky activity should be undertaken? (Of course, having a robot along that could do the job would be much safer for the human crew. Even safer would be no human crew at all.)

The types of risks astronauts face run from the mundane but potentially lethal (space radiation, both from the sun and cosmic rays) to the unusual, even bizarre, e.g., will Islamic extremists disrupt a space launch to enforce a fatwa (Mars One 2015)? NASA knows that risk mitigation is a crucial issue—after all, it has lifeboats. Could it be that the risks for humans in space are always too great, so only robots should ever go?

23.2.2 Bioethics, Robots, and Risk-Benefit Analysis

Space-based medical concerns often focus on the health hazards posed by space radiation and bone and muscle loss in microgravity. NASA also studies psychological dangers, including even suicidal intentional sabotage of the mission; this is far less a worry for robots. Despite fictional depictions like *2001: A Space Odyssey* (Kubrick 1968), it's unlikely a future HAL will ever intentionally decide to kill its human crew.

The dangers are far more likely to come from space itself: the sobering reality is that we still don't know if it's even possible for humans to survive indefinitely in space. NASA's Human Research Program has just finished one of the first semi-controlled trials, termed the "One-Year Mission" (NASA 2015), in which astronaut Scott Kelly spent a year in space on the International Space Station (ISS), while his identical twin brother was being monitored back on Earth. Kelly's official remarks to the House Committee on Science, Space and Technology asserted the "loss of bone and muscle, vision impairment and effects on our immune system," among other problems (Walker 2016).

And there's more bad news: for instance, while the sample sizes remain small, the existing evidence implies that even relatively brief travel outside Earth's magnetosphere is extraordinarily deleterious to one's long-term health. The Apollo astronauts were in a high-radiation environment for merely a matter of days. Yet they now suffer approximately 478% greater mortality from cardiovascular disease than astronauts that never flew and 391% greater mortality than astronauts who only ascended to low-Earth orbit (like the ISS) and remained protected by Earth's magnetic field (Seemangal 2016).

So given the alternative of sending only robots, how shall we assess what constitutes an acceptable risk for using human astronauts instead? All of the following have been bruited as methods for determining (un)acceptable risk (Abney and Lin 2015):

> *Good-faith subjective standard:* Under this standard, it would be left to each individual astronaut to determine whether an unacceptable risk exists. But the idiosyncrasies of human risk aversion make this standard problematic; perhaps the most thrill-seeking or suicidal risk-takers will become the first deep-spacefaring astronauts, with little regard for any rational assessment of risks and benefits. Further, what happens in a crew when some members disagree about the acceptability of the risk of some operation (say, a spacewalk to repair a communications antenna during a radiation event)?
>
> *The reasonable-person standard:* An unacceptable risk might be simply what a fair, informed member of a relevant community believes to be an unacceptable risk. But what is the relevant community—NASA? Will NASA regulations really suffice for the difficult-to-predict vagaries of risk assessment during a manned spaceflight that may last six months or longer?
>
> *Objective standard:* Assessing a risk as (un)acceptable requires evidence and/or expert testimony. But the "first-generation problem" remains: How do we have evidence for an unacceptable risk unless some first generation has already suffered from it? For the first spacefarers to deep space or Mars, such a standard appears impossible to implement.

And even if we decide which standard to use, there remain other crucial issues that befuddle risk managers. For example, should we believe that we should handle a first-party risk (to myself) in the same way that we handle a third-party risk (that I pose to someone else)? This partially (if not entirely) maps onto the distinction between voluntary, involuntary, and nonvoluntary risks: a first-party risk I consciously choose is voluntary; a third-party risk I force onto someone against his or her will is involuntary. But a nonvoluntary risk may be either first- or third-party if neither I nor the other person knows of the risk, yet undergoes it anyway.

And there are numerous other risk issues, e.g., statistical versus identifiable victims, risk to future generations, and the "non-identity problem" (Parfit 1987), and related issues concerning the ethics of reproduction in space (Lin and Abney 2014). Should astronauts be sterilized before liftoff? Or should we demand unisex crews?

All of these risks disappear if there are no humans, only robots, in space. But one additional consideration may justify attempts to send humans, and not just robots, into space: colonization. But why?

23.2.3 A Wild Card: Existential Risk?

The concept of existential risk refers to a risk that, should it come to pass, would either annihilate Earth-originating intelligent life or permanently and drastically curtail its potential (Bostrom 2002). For instance, suppose we discover a killer asteroid too late to stop its impact on Earth or fall prey to any number of other potential calamities that could imperil civilization. If a permanent, sustainable colony off-world already existed (as remote as that prospect currently appears), then humanity could survive such a cataclysm on Earth. Accordingly, utilitarian existential-risk theorists hold that colonization efforts might be worthwhile, even if the odds of success are minuscule.

And for deontologists, the idea that "one always has a moral obligation never to allow the extinction of all creatures capable of moral obligation" is at least a plausible *prima facie* (and perhaps absolute) duty; such a survival principle appears to be required for any viable ethics (Abney 2004). So sending humans, not just robots, into space may be crucial for decreasing existential risk. Is there any hurry, though? My final argument suggests that there is.

23.2.4 The Interstellar Doomsday Argument

To understand the Interstellar Doomsday Argument, we first need some background in probability theory. First, let's introduce the Self-Sampling Assumption (SSA): "One should reason as if one were a random sample from the set of all observers in one's reference class" (Bostrom and Cirkovic 2011, 130). Using this SSA, I can now explain how robots, space colonization, and human extinction are linked.

First, a data point: our first robotic envoy to the stars, *Voyager 1*, entered interstellar space in August 2012 (Cook and Brown 2013). Next, apply the SSA: Assume that you are a random observer as a member of a species that has achieved interstellar travel. As of the publication of this text, it has been about five years since we became an interstellar civilization. If one reasons on this basis, there is a 95% chance that our future as a species with interstellar probes will last only between 47 more days and 195 more years. How did I come up with that (presumably alarming) answer?

Here's the calculation: Call L the time already passed for the phenomenon in question (for interstellar robots at time of publication, it's been five years). How much longer will there be such robots? Gott's delta t argument asserts that if there's nothing special about one's observation of a phenomenon, one should expect a 95% probability that the phenomenon will continue for between 1/39 and 39 times its present age, as there's only a 5% possibility your random observation comes in the first 2.5% of its lifetime, or the last 2.5% (Gott 1993).

So as of the publication of this book in 2017, it's 95% probable that our time left as a civilization that sends interstellar robots is between $L/39$ (for $L = 5$ years, that's 47 more days) and $39L$ (195 more years). If we're still around and the reader makes this observation in 2021 or 2024, adjust the math accordingly. And understood correctly, the math offers even gloomier news: it also means a 75% chance we will go extinct (as robotic interstellar signalers) within $3L$—the next 15 years.

The reader might find this absurdly pessimistic. Could a simple random observation about the length of time we've had robots leaving the solar system really imply Doom Soon? Actually, yes; and connecting Fermi's paradox, the Great Silence, the Great Filter, and our interstellar robots may shed light on this reasoning. Fermi's paradox refers to the question that Enrico Fermi first raised about aliens—namely, "Where is everybody?" This connects to the problem David Brin (1983) termed the "Great Silence": if aliens exist, why don't we see clear evidence of their presence in the cosmos?

We can understand Fermi's paradox and the Great Silence by using the "Drake equation," understood as follows: the number of detectable alien civilizations currently in the galaxy, N, is given as $N = R^* \cdot f_p \cdot n_e \cdot f_l \cdot f_i \cdot f_c \cdot L$ (SETI 1961).

Our understanding of the first three variables is improving thanks to recent discoveries in astronomy about the rate of star formation and the discovery of Earth-like exoplanets (e.g., Seager 2016). But the last four, biological factors in the Drake equation are as yet merely guesswork; we have only one life-bearing planet in our sample thus far, Earth.

Robin Hanson's (1998) explanation of the Great Silence is called the "Great Filter." It implies that one (or more) of the as yet unknown variables must have a value very close to zero. Recent discoveries indicate that none of the first three factors are close enough to zero to explain the Great Silence, so the Great Filter must lie among the biological factors. Perhaps either the fraction of planets upon which life evolves (f_l), or the fraction with intelligent life (f_i), or the fraction with detectable communications (f_c) is nearly zero. If so, this is good news for humankind: the Great Filter is in our past. We may be a complete evolutionary fluke, but that would have no direct implications for the duration of our future.

But if many past civilizations have arisen in our galaxy and developed technology that could be detected across interstellar space, then L is the factor that drives the Great Filter, and L must be very, very small—meaning that whenever previous alien civilizations ascended to our level of technology, they became undetectable very, very quickly. That is, the Great Filter is in our future. The most plausible way to render our civilization undetectable very soon is, of course, human extinction.

Most thinkers, contemplating the Great Silence and *L*, consider how long we will send our radio signals into space or how long in-person journeys to the stars will endure. But sending humans across interstellar space is at best extraordinarily difficult, and may be impossible; and both our TV and radio signals are intermittent (in any particular direction), and those that spread in every direction are particularly weak. Hence, aliens with similar technology that are more than a few tens of light years away, using our test of a multiply confirmed and clearly nonrandom signal, would have trouble (for now) making an unambiguous detection of our civilization.

But in considering the Great Silence, the Great Filter, and our future, there's another form of contact that's much more practical and longer-lasting—our robotic spacecraft. So our test for understanding *L* should actually be our interstellar robots, which have escaped the surly bonds of our sun and ventured out into the galaxy. For if other past civilizations in the Milky Way's 13-billion-year history did send probes, just as we now have, it seems (overwhelmingly) likely that some of those probes would be here by now.

That becomes a near certainty when we contemplate von Neumann probes, i.e., probes capable of self-reproduction. A space-borne von Neumann probe could be programmed, upon arrival at its target destination, to use materials found *in situ* to produce copies of themselves and then send those copies on to other stars. Plausibly, such probes would have emissaries throughout the galaxy in a cosmically brief interval: sending out one von Neumann probe to a single alien solar system (say, Alpha Centauri) could result in its making two copies of itself and sending those probes to two new systems; those daughter probes could then go on to visit four additional systems; and so on.

Even assuming a relatively slow rate of probe reproduction and slow flight times, we run into a mathematical near certainty: within a few million to a few hundred million years at most, every solar system in the galaxy would have at least one von Neumann probe within it. With a technically feasible average speed of *c*/40, the process of investigating every stellar system in the galaxy would take about 4 million years (Webb 2002, 82). Such a timeframe is less than 1/3,000th of the time the Milky Way has been in existence. If the galaxy is not saturated by robotic probes from ancient alien civilizations, it remains implausible to think the reason is that they need more time to get here.

Now, one might protest that we know more—for there is not just one, but already five spacecraft on escape trajectories from the solar system, of which *Voyager 1* was merely the first. Plus, there are three used rocket motors on interstellar trajectories, which if encountered would also be convincing evidence to aliens of our civilization (Johnston 2015). But in fact that reinforces the point; there is no reason to believe this moment in time is privileged with respect to our robotic interstellar probes. We reached the threshold five years ago, and there's no sign we're going to stop. But, clearly, it has stopped (or never started) everywhere else in the galaxy; that is the message of the Great Silence.

And let's be clear about the technology: sending robots to the stars is vastly easier than having humans colonize Mars, much less any other planet or moon. If we become incapable of sending probes to other stars very, very soon, then presumably we humans will be unable to escape the earth. And if we cannot escape the earth, then sooner or later we will go extinct. (My bet is sooner.) So this argument should reinforce a sense of urgency: if humans are to escape becoming just another species to go extinct on the earth, whether through external calamity or self-inflicted wounds, we had better get humans, and not just our robots, off-planet.

23.3 Conclusion

If my argument is successful, then we have reasons to use robots, not humans, for almost all the purposes that people have used to justify spaceflight. Accordingly, it may in fact be immoral to use humans instead of robots for exploration, construction, mining, communications, security, and all the other morally legitimate uses of space. Well, with one exception: having human astronauts can be justified for the purpose of colonization, in order to reduce existential risk.

Unfortunately, in the short to medium term, colonization efforts are almost guaranteed to fail. That is in part because our space policies are more concerned with vanity projects like having humans (re-)plant a flag on the moon or Mars than with building a sustainable off-world colony. The solution, it turns out, still involves our robots: in addition to enabling our global communications and commerce, they also need to build a second home for us.

Until spacefaring robots can create a permanently habitable ecosystem for us by terraforming the moon or Mars or Venus (or build a suitable habitat elsewhere in deep space), and until human spaceflight technology advances enough for it to be highly probable that such missions will end not with dead or dying astronauts eking out a few days on Mars, but with thriving colonists able to set up a sustainable civilization, it seems morally clear that we should let our robots do our exploring, mining, fighting, and all other deep-space work for us.

Works Cited

Abney, Keith. 2004. "Sustainability, Morality and Future Rights." *Moebius* 2 (2). http://digitalcommons.calpoly.edu/moebius/vol2/iss2/7/.

Abney, Keith. 2012. "Robotics, Ethical Theory, and Metaethics: A Guide for the Perplexed." In *Robot Ethics*, edited by Patrick Lin, Keith Abney, and George Bekey, ch. 3. Cambridge, MA: MIT Press.

Abney, Keith and Patrick Lin. 2015. "Enhancing Astronauts: The Ethical, Legal and Social Implications." In *Commercial Space Exploration: Ethics, Policy and Governance*, edited by Jai Galliott, ch.17. New York: Ashgate.

B612 Foundation. 2016. https://b612foundation.org/sentinel/.

Bell, Trudy and Tony Phillips. 2008. "A Super Solar Flare." *NASA Science News*, May 6. http://science.nasa.gov/science-news/science-at-nasa/2008/06may_carringtonflare/.

Bostrom, Nick. 2002. "Existential Risks: Analyzing Human Extinction Scenarios and Related Hazards." *Journal of Evolution and Technology* 9 (1). http://www.nickbostrom.com/existential/risks.html.

Bostrom, Nick and Milan M. Cirkovic. 2011. *Global Catastrophic Risks.* New York: Oxford University Press.

Brin, G. David. 1983. "The 'Great Silence': The Controversy Concerning Extraterrestrial Intelligent Life." *Quarterly Journal of the Royal Astronomical Society* 24 (3): 283–309.

Bruton, Dan. 1996. "Frequently Asked Questions about the Collision of Comet Shoemaker-Levy 9 with Jupiter." http://www.physics.sfasu.edu/astro/sl9/cometfaq2.html#Q3.1.

Cook, Jia-Rui C. and Dwayne Brown. 2013. "NASA Spacecraft Embarks on Historic Journey into Interstellar Space." NASA, September 12. https://www.nasa.gov/mission_pages/voyager/voyager20130912.html.

Do, Sydney, Koki Ho, Samuel Schreiner, Andrew Owens, and Olivier de Weck. 2014. "An Independent Assessment of the Technical Feasibility of the Mars One Mission Plan—Updated Analysis." *Acta Astronautica* 120 (March–April): 192–228.

Economist. 2016. "Flight Fantastic," August 20. http://www.economist.com/news/science-and-technology/21705295-instead-rewiring-planes-fly-themselves-why-not-give-them-android.

Gott, J. Richard III. 1993. "Implications of the Copernican Principle for our Future Prospects." *Nature* 363 (6427): 315–19.

Hanson, Robin. 1998. "The Great Filter—Are We Almost Past It?" George Mason University, September 15. https://mason.gmu.edu/~rhanson/greatfilter.html.

Harrison, Todd. 2015. "Will the F-35 Be the Last Manned Fighter Jet? Physics, Physiology, and Fiscal Facts Suggest Yes." *Forbes*, April 29. http://www.forbes.com/sites/toddharrison/2015/04/29/will-the-f-35-be-the-last-manned-fighter-jet-physics-physiology-and-fiscal-facts-suggest-yes/#13242e871912.

Johnston, Robert, comp. 2015. "Deep Space Probes and Other Manmade Objects Beyond Near-Earth Space." Robert Johnston website. http://www.johnstonsarchive.net/astro/awrjp493.html.

Kubrick, Stanley (director). 1968. "2001: A Space Odyssey." Stanley Kubrick and Arthur C. Clarke (screenplay).

Lin, Patrick. 2006. "Space Ethics: Look Before Taking Another Leap for Mankind." *Astropolitics* 4 (3): 281–94.

Lin, Patrick. 2012. "Introduction to Robot Ethics." In *Robot Ethics*, edited by Patrick Lin, Keith Abney, and George Bekey, ch. 1. Cambridge, MA: MIT Press.

Lin, Patrick and Keith Abney. 2014. "Introduction to Astronaut Bioethics." *Slate.com.* http://www.slate.com/articles/technology/future_tense/2014/10/astronaut_bioethics_would_it_be_unethical_to_give_birth_on_mars.html.

Lovett, Richard. 2011. "What If the Biggest Solar Storm on Record Happened Today?" *National Geographic*, March 4. http://news.nationalgeographic.com/news/2011/03/110302-solar-flares-sun-storms-earth-danger-carrington-event-science/.

Mars One. 2015. "Mars One's Response to the Fatwa Issued by the General Authority of Islamic Affairs and Endowment." http://www.mars-one.com/news/press-releases/mars-ones-response-to-the-fatwa-issued-by-the-general-authority-of-islamic.

Myers, Meghann. 2015. "SECNAV: F-35C Should Be Navy's Last Manned Strike Jet." *Navy Times*, April 16. https://www.navytimes.com/story/military/2015/04/16/navy-secretary-ray-mabus-joint-strike-fighter-f-35-unmanned/25832745/.

NASA. 2015. "One-Year Mission | The Research." NASA website, May 28. https://www.nasa.gov/twins-study/about.

Nozick, Robert. 1974. *Anarchy, State, and Utopia*. New York: Basic Books.

Parfit, Derek. 1987. *Reasons and Persons*. Oxford: Clarendon Press.

Plait, Phil. 2007. "Why Explore Space?" *Bad Astronomy*, November 28. http://blogs.discovermagazine.com/badastronomy/2007/11/28/why-explore-space/.

Rawls, John. 1971. *A Theory of Justice*. Cambridge, MA: Belknap Press.

Rincon, Paul. 2013. "Dinosaur-Killing Space Rock 'Was a Comet.'" *BBC News*, March 22. http://www.bbc.com/news/science-environment-21709229.

Seager, Sara. 2016. "Research." http://seagerexoplanets.mit.edu/research.htm.

Scott, Ridley (director). 2015. "The Martian." Drew Goddard (screenplay).

Seemangal, Robin. 2016. "Space Radiation Devastated the Lives of Apollo Astronauts." *Observer*, July 28. http://observer.com/2016/07/space-radiation-devastated-the-lives-of-apollo-astronauts/.

SETI Institute. 1961. "The Drake Equation." http://www.seti.org/drakeequation.

Veruggio, Gianmarco and Keith Abney. 2012. "Roboethics: The Applied Ethics for a New Science." In *Robot Ethics*, edited by Patrick Lin, Keith Abney, and George Bekey, ch. 22. Cambridge, MA: MIT Press.

Walker, Hayler. 2016. "'Space Travel Has 'Permanent Effects,' Astronaut Scott Kelly Says." *ABC News*, June 15. http://abcnews.go.com/US/space-travel-permanent-effects-astronaut-scott-kelly/story?id=39884104.

Webb, Stephen. 2002. *If the Universe Is Teeming with Aliens . . . Where is Everybody?* New York: Copernicus Books.

24 THE UNABOMBER ON ROBOTS

THE NEED FOR A PHILOSOPHY OF TECHNOLOGY GEARED TOWARD HUMAN ENDS

Jai Galliott

According to conventional wisdom, Theodore John Kaczynski is little more than a Harvard-educated mathematics professor turned schizophrenic terrorist and lone murderer. Most will remember that what catapulted the *Un*iversity and *A*irline *Bomber* (the "Unabomber") to the top of the FBI's "Most Wanted" list in the United States was his engagement in a nationwide bombing campaign against people linked to the development and use of modern technology. Many dismiss Kaczynski as insane. However, this does nothing to refute his argument, namely that the continued development of our technological society threatens humanity's survival and, as said society cannot be reformed, confers upon us a moral obligation to ensure that it is destroyed before it collapses with disastrous consequences.

This chapter draws on direct correspondence and prison interviews with Kaczynski and applies his broader views to the robotization of humanity. It also engages with the recent work of Peter Ludlow, a philosopher and prominent critic of Kaczynski, who argues that his account is ridden with *ad hominem* attacks and devoid of logical arguments. Demonstrating that Ludlow is mistaken, at least on the latter point, the chapter maps Kaczynski's arguments and portrays him as a rational man with principal beliefs that are, while hardly mainstream, entirely reasonable. Contra Ludlow, it is argued that the problem is not merely that those in power seize control of technology and then exploit their technological power to the detriment of the public. That is, it is not simply a matter of putting technology back in the hands of the people through "hacktivism" or open-source design and programming. The modern technological system is so complex, it will be argued, that people are forced into choosing between using jailed technology controlled by those within existing oppressive power structures or dedicating their lives to building knowledge and understanding of the software and robotics that facilitate participation in the technological system. In this sense, Kaczynski is right in that the system does not exist to satisfy human needs. It is morally problematic that human behavior has to be modified to fit the needs of the system in such a radical way. We must therefore accept revolt aimed at bringing about near-complete disengagement from technology as permissible or recover a philosophy of technology truly geared toward human ends—parts set against the dehumanizing whole.

24.1 The Unabomber Manifesto

Over the course of nearly twenty years, Ted Kaczynski mailed or personally placed no fewer than sixteen explosive packages that he handcrafted in his utility-free cabin in the Montana woods, taking the lives of three individuals, maiming twenty-four others, and instilling fear in much of the general population (Federal Bureau of Investigation 2008). He was the kind of "lone wolf" domestic terrorist that today's presidential administrations would have us think Da'ish is recruiting and was, at the time, an incredibly stealthy nuisance to law enforcement agencies that were busy dealing with traditional foreign enemies, namely socialist Russia. Despite incredibly precise bomb-making that left no evidence as to the provenance of the tools of his destruction, what eventually led to Kaczynski's capture was the forced publication of his 35,000-word manifesto in the *New York Times* and *Washington Post*. Despite attributing authorship to a group referred to as the Freedom Club (FC)—thought to be derived from the name of the anarchist group (the Future of the Proletariat, FP) in Joseph Conrad's *The Secret Agent* (1907), from which much inspiration was drawn[1]—Kaczynski was actually the lone member of the group, and his unique prose allowed his brother to identify him as the author, leading to his eventual arrest. The manifesto is well structured, with numbered paragraphs and detailed footnotes but few references.[2] It is best described as a socio-philosophical work about contemporary society, especially the influence of technology. In essence, the Unabomber thinks modern society is on the wrong track and advocates an anarchist revolution against technology and modernity. Indeed, the manifesto begins by declaring that "the Industrial Revolution and its consequences have been a disaster for the human race" (Kaczynski 1995, 1) and quickly proceeds to link the ongoing nature of the disaster to the "The Left" and a scathing analysis of liberals:

> Almost everyone will agree that we live in a deeply troubled society. One of the most widespread manifestations of the craziness of our world is leftism.... Leftists tend to hate anything that has an image of being strong,

> good and successful. They hate America, they hate Western civilization, they hate white males, they hate rationality. . . . Modern leftish philosophers tend to dismiss reason, science, objective reality and to insist that everything is culturally relative. They are deeply involved emotionally in their attack on truth and reality. They attack these concepts because of their own psychological needs. For one thing, their attack is an outlet for hostility, and, to the extent that it is successful, it satisfies the drive for power. (Kaczynski 1995, 1, 15, 18)

The manifesto connects this almost Nietzschean criticism of leftism to the concept of "oversocialization."[3] Kaczynski writes that the moral code of our technological society is such that nobody can genuinely think, feel, or act in a moral way, so much so that people must deceive themselves about their own motives and find moral explanations for feelings and actions that in reality have a non-moral origin (1995, 21–32). According to the Unabomber, this has come about partly because of "The Left," which appears to rebel against society's values, but actually has a moralizing tendency in that it accepts society's morality, then accuses society of falling short of its own moral principles (Kaczynski 1995, 28). Kaczynski's point is that leftists will not be society's savior from technoindustrial society, as is often thought. As will be argued in the next section, this hate-filled discussion of leftism merely distracts from the broader manifesto, the remainder of which is much more concerned with the actual impact of technology upon society.

Kaczynski's ideas on this topic have deep philosophical underpinnings and are grounded in the writings of Jacques Ellul, who penned the *The Technological Society* (1964) and other highly perceptive works about the technological infrastructure of the modern world. While Kaczynski details the effect of "technology" and "technologies"—in other words, tools that are supposedly used for human ends—he is not specifically interested in any particular form of technology, whether military or civilian, robotic or otherwise. Robots are important, he notes, but from his point of view and for the most part, they are important only to the extent that they form part of the overall picture of technology in the modern world (pers. comm. 2013). In this respect, he joins Ellul in being more concerned about "la technique," which is technology as a unified entity or the overarching whole of the technoindustrial society in which, according to Ellul and his contemporaries, everything has become a means and there is no longer an end (Ellul 1951, 62). That is to say that it would be a mistake to focus on technology as a disconnected series of individual machines. For both Kaczynski and Ellul, technology's unifying and all-encompassing nature and efficiency in just about every field of human activity are what make it dehumanizing, in that its absolute efficiency and lack of ends do away with the need for humanity.

Ellul wrote that "the machine tends not only to create a new human environment, but also to modify man's very essence" and that "the milieu in which he lives is no longer his. He must adapt himself, as though the world were new, to a universe for which he was not created" (1964, 325). Kaczynski shares this sentiment and provides an illustration that encapsulates his version of the same argument:

> Suppose Mr. A is playing chess with Mr. B. Mr. C, a Grand Master, is looking over Mr. A's shoulder. Mr. A of course wants to win his game, so if Mr. C points out a good move for him to make, he is doing Mr. A a favor. But suppose now that Mr. C tells Mr. A how to make ALL of his moves. In each particular instance he does Mr. A a favor by showing him his best move, but by making ALL of his moves for him he spoils his game, since there is no point in Mr. A's playing the game at all if someone else makes all his moves. The situation of modern man is analogous to that of Mr. A. The system makes an individual's life easier for him in innumerable ways, but in doing so it deprives him of control over his own fate. (1995, n. 21)

His view is that a technoindustrial society requires the cooperation of large numbers of people, and the more complex its organizational structure, the more decisions must be made for the group as a whole. For example, if an individual or small group of individuals wants to manufacture a robot, all workers must make it in accordance with the design specifications devised at the company or industry level, and all inputs must be regular; otherwise the robot is likely to be of little use and perhaps even unreliable. Decision-making ability is essentially removed from the hands of individuals and small groups, and given to large organizations and industry groups (if not robots themselves), which is problematic, as it limits individual autonomy and disrupts what Kaczynski calls the "power process" (1995, 33–7).

Most human beings, he says, have an innate biological need for this power process, which consists of autonomously choosing a goal and satisfying certain drives, and making an effort to reach them (Kaczynski 1995, 33). Kaczynski splits these human drives into three categories: drives that can be satisfied with minimal effort, drives that can be satisfied with significant effort, and drives that have no realistic chance of being satisfied no matter how much effort is exerted. The first category leads to boredom. The third category leads to frustration, low self-esteem, depression, and defeatism. The power process is satisfied by the second category, but the problem is that industrial society and its technology push most goals into the first and third categories, at least for the vast majority of people (Kaczynski 1995, 59). When decisions are made by the individual or small-scale organizations, the individual retains the ability to influence events and has power over the circumstances of his or her own life, which satisfies the need for autonomy. But since industrialization, Kaczynski argues, life has become greatly regimented by large organizations because of the demand for the proper functioning of industrial society, and the means of control by large organizations have become more effective, meaning that goals become either trivially easy or nigh impossible. For example, for most people in the industrial world, merely surviving in a welfare state requires little effort. And even when it requires effort—that is, when people must labor—most have very little autonomy in their job, especially with the robotization of many of today's workforces. All of what Kaczynski describes is thought to result in modern man's unhappiness, with which people cope by taking on surrogate activities—artificial goals pursued not for their own sake but for the sake of fulfillment (Kaczynski 1995, 39). The desire for money, excessive sexual gratification, and the latest piece of technology would all be examples of surrogate activities. And, of course, if robotization accelerates and Kaczynski is right, life will become much worse for people.

At the most abstract level, then, the manifesto perpetuates the idea that by forcing people to conform to machines rather than vice versa, technoindustrialization creates a sick society hostile to human potential. The system must, by its very nature, force people to behave in ways that are increasingly remote from the natural pattern of human behavior. Kaczynski gives the example of the system's need for scientists, mathematicians, and engineers, and how this equates to heavy pressure being placed on adolescent human beings to excel in these fields, despite the fact that it is arguably not natural for said beings to spend the bulk of their time sitting at a desk absorbed in directed study in lieu of being out in the real world (1995, 115). Because technology demands constant change, it also destroys local, human-scale communities and encourages the growth of crowded and unlivable megacities indifferent to the needs of citizens. The evolution toward a civilization increasingly dominated by technology and the related power structures, it is argued, cannot be reversed on its own, because "while technological progress *as a whole* continually narrows our sphere of freedom, each new technical advance *considered by itself* appears to be desirable" (Kaczynski 1995, 128 [emphasis in the original]). Because humans must conform to the machines and the machinery of the system, society regards as sickness any mode of thought that is inconvenient for the system, particularly anti-technological thought, for the individual who does not fit within the system causes problems for it. The manipulation of such individuals to fit within the system is, as such, seen as a "cure" for a "sickness" and therefore good (Chase 2000; Kaczynski 1995, 119).

Since the existence of the technoindustrial system and technologies like robots threaten humanity's survival and, on the belief examined later, namely that the nature of technoindustrial society is such that it cannot be reformed in a way that reconciles freedom with technology, Kaczynski (1995, 140) argues that it must destroyed. Indeed, his manifesto states that the system will probably collapse on its own when the weight of human suffering becomes unbearable for the masses. It is argued that the longer the system persists, the more devastating the ultimate collapse. The moral course of action is, therefore, to hasten the onset of the breakdown and reduce the extent of the devastation.

24.2 Revolution or Reform?

To argue that revolutionaries ought to do everything possible to bring about this collapse to avoid technology's far more destructive triumph is clearly to discount the possibility of reform or effective regulation; and, for Kaczynski's many critics, it is likely to be seen as the flawed logic of someone who, either because he is sitting in an air-conditioned high-rise or hiding in a cave, is somehow not connected to life. Peter Ludlow (2013), for instance, dismisses Kaczynski's argument on the basis of a "smorgasbord of critical reasoning fails" that are, in fact, mostly restricted to the early sections critical of leftism. The source of contention is Kaczynski's *ad hominem* reasoning and what is purported to be a genetic fallacy. To be clear, those sections of the manifesto concerning the Left do involve *ad hominem* attacks and, while one clearly cannot define all leftist individuals as masochists because some "protest by lying down in front of vehicles . . . intentionally provoke police or racists to abuse them" (Kaczynski 1995, 20), it should be pointed out that not all *ad hominem* reasoning is fallacious, especially when it relates to the kinds of practical and moral reasoning utilized in the manifesto. But even if one were to grant that Kaczynski's reasoning in the relevant sections on leftism is fallacious, it is far from obvious that this compromises Kaczynski's overall argument. It must, for instance, be admitted that the Unabomber provides some worthwhile insights and that Kaczynski's analyses of autonomy and deprivation of control over one's fate are fundamentally accurate. It is difficult to deny that society has evolved to a point where most people work on tasks that have little to no tangible value outside of being part of a much larger and incomprehensively complex and largely technological process; and that this creates an (at least occasional) lingering feeling of alienation for people as the needs of the complex system take precedent over their own needs. Indeed, a recent worldwide Gallup poll reports that only 13% of people are psychologically engaged in their work (Crabtree 2013).

It must also be acknowledged that Ludlow points to Kaczynski's *ad hominem* attacks only insofar as they support his claim that Kaczynski commits a genetic fallacy in pointing to the Left's and humanity's inability to evolve/adapt to technology via non-alienating means. But even if a genetic fallacy is committed here, and indeed there is evidence that it is, this does not necessarily falsify Kaczynski's core belief; to think otherwise is to ignore a number of arguments provided by

Kaczynski, which not only illuminate the non-genetic reasons that technoindustrial society has assumed its present form but also explain why reform is so difficult in the modern context. In exploring these arguments, this section disputes Ludlow's claims and demonstrates the difficulty of reform through the provision of examples, and it highlights that the disturbing future Kaczynski predicts is much closer than we think, if not already upon us.

One of the first reasons Kaczynski provides for why technoindustrial society cannot be reformed in any substantial way in favor of freedom is that modern technology is a unified and holistic system in which all parts are dependent on one another, like cogs in a machine (1995, 121). You cannot, he says, simply get rid of the "bad" parts of technology and retain only the "good" or desirable parts. To clarify, he gives an example from modern medicine, writing that progress in medical science depends on progress in related fields, including chemistry, physics, biology, engineering, computer science, and others. Advanced medical treatments, he writes, "require expensive, high-tech equipment that can be made available only by a technologically progressive, economically rich society. Clearly you can't have much progress in medicine without the whole technological system and everything that goes with it" (1995, 121). This is certainly also true of modern robotic surgery, for instance, which depends on the medical-technical ecosystem for the maintenance of environments conducive to surgery, the development and training of highly specialized surgeons, and the manufacture and maintenance of the robotic equipment. Kaczynski maintains that even if some elements of technological progress could be maintained without the rest of the technological system, this would in itself bring about certain evils (1995, 122). Suppose, for example, that we were able to exploit new research and use DNA nanobots to successfully treat cancer. Those with a genetic tendency to cancer would then be able to survive and reproduce like everyone else, such that natural selection against cancer-enabling genes would cease and said genes would spread throughout the population, degrading the population to the point that a eugenics program would be the only solution. Kaczynski would have us believe that humans will eventually become a manufactured product, compounding the existing problems in technoindustrial society (1995, 122).

Many will object to such slippery-slope arguments, but Kaczynski bolsters his argument by suggesting that lasting compromise between technology and freedom is impossible because technology is by far the more powerful social force and repeatedly encroaches upon and narrows our freedom, individual and collective (1995, 125). This point is supported by the fact that most new technological advances considered by themselves seem to be desirable. Few people, for instance, could have resisted the allure of electricity, indoor plumbing, mobile phones, or the internet. As already mentioned, each of these and innumerable other technologies seem worthy of employment on the basis of a cost-benefit analysis in which the threatening aspects of technology are balanced with temptingly attractive features, such that it is often considered absurd not to utilize a particular piece of technology. Yet technologies that initially appear not to threaten freedom regularly prove to threaten freedom in very serious ways after the initial adoption phase. Kaczynski provides a valuable example related to the development of the motor industry:

> A walking man formerly could go where he pleased, go at his own pace without observing any traffic regulations, and was independent of technological support-systems. When motor vehicles were introduced they appeared to increase man's freedom. They took no freedom away from the walking man, no one had to have an automobile if he didn't want one, and anyone who did choose to buy an automobile could travel much faster than the walking man. But the introduction of motorized transport soon changed society in such a way as to restrict greatly man's freedom of locomotion. When automobiles became numerous, it became necessary to regulate their use extensively. In a car, especially in densely populated areas, one cannot just go where one likes at one's own pace, as one's movement is governed by the flow of traffic and by various traffic laws. One is tied down by various obligations: license requirements, driver test, renewing registration, insurance, maintenance required for safety, monthly payments on purchase price. Moreover, the use of motorized transport is no longer optional. Since the introduction of motorized transport the arrangement of our cities has changed in such a way that the majority of people no longer live within walking distance of their place of employment, shopping areas and recreational opportunities, so that they HAVE TO depend on the automobile for transportation. Or else they must use public transportation, in which case they have even less control over their own movement than when driving a car. Even the walker's freedom is now greatly restricted. In the city he continually has to stop and wait for traffic lights that are designed mainly to serve auto traffic. In the country, motor traffic makes it dangerous and unpleasant to walk along the highway. (1995, 127)

The important point illustrated by the case of motorized transport is that while a new item of technology may be introduced as an option that individuals can choose as they see fit, it does not necessarily remain optional. In many cases, the new technology changes society in such a way that people eventually find themselves forced to use it. This will no doubt occur yet again as the driverless car revolution unfolds. People will adopt robotic vehicles because they are safer than ever and spare society from thousands of accidents, only to later find that such action actually contributes to the atrophy of deliberative skills (including moral reasoning) necessary to make decisions and remain safe on the road. Indeed, the commencement of this process is already evident from the inappropriate use of vehicles with limited autonomous functionality, suggesting that it will not be long before society reaches a point at which those who desire to drive their cars manually will be unable to do so because of various obligations and laws imposed by the technoindustrial system aimed at further minimizing accidents and maximizing efficiency at the cost of freedom.

If one still thinks reform is the most viable option, Kaczynski provides yet another argument demonstrating why technology is such a powerful social force. Technological progress, he argues, marches in only one direction (1995, 129). Once a particular technical innovation has been made, people usually become dependent on it so that they can never again go without said innovation, unless a new iteration of it becomes available and yields some supposedly desirable attribute or benefit. One can imagine what would happen, for example, if computers, machines, and robots were to be switched off or eliminated from modern society. People have become so dependent on these technologies and the technological system that turning them off or eliminating them would seem to amount to suicide for the unenlightened within that system. Thus, the system can move in only one direction: forward, toward greater technologization. This occurs with such rapidity that those who attempt to protect freedom by engaging in long and difficult social struggles to hold back individual threats (technologies) are likely to be overcome by the sheer number of new attacks. These attacks, it is worth noting, will increasingly come from developing nations. The possible creation of advanced industrial and technological structures in regions such as the Middle East and East Asia, in particular, could pose real problems. While many will conceive of what the West is doing with modern technology to be reckless, it arguably exercises more self-restraint in the use of its technoindustrial power than those elsewhere are likely to exercise (Kaczynski 2001). The danger rests not only in the use of intentionally destructive technologies such as military robotics, which have already proliferated from China to a variety of other less-developed nations, but also in seemingly benign applications of technologies (e.g., genetic technologies and nanobots) that may have unanticipated and potentially catastrophic consequences.

These arguments are not tied to Kaczynski's *ad hominem* attacks on the Left or disparaging remarks about humanity's limited success in evolving alongside technology, and offset Ludlow's concern that Kaczynski commits a genetic fallacy. That is to say that Kaczynski sees reform as an unviable option based on both genetic and other forms of inductive reasoning, the latter of which seem to stand. The problem is that most people in modern society, a good deal of the time, are not particularly foresighted and take little account of the dangers that lie ahead, meaning that preventative measures are either implemented too late or not at all. As Patrick Lin (2016) writes, "[W]isdom is difficult to sustain. We're having to re-learn lost lessons—sometimes terrible lessons—from the past, and intergenerational memory is short." The Greenhouse Effect, for example, was predicted in the mid-nineteenth century, and no one did much about it until recently, when it was already too late to avoid the consequences of global warming (Kaczynski 2010, 438). And the problem posed by the disposal of nuclear waste should have been evident as soon as the first nuclear power plants were established many decades ago; but both the public and those more directly responsible for managing nuclear waste disposal erroneously assumed that a solution would eventually be found while nuclear power generation pushed ahead and was eventually made available to third-world countries with little thought for the ability of their governments to dispose of nuclear waste safely or prevent weaponization (Kaczynski 2010, 438–9).

Experience has therefore shown that people commonly place the potentially insoluble problem of dealing with untested technological solutions on future generations and, while we cannot infer from past events that a future event will occur, we can ask what the future might look like based on analysis of recent technological developments. Kaczynski asks us to postulate that computer scientists and other technicians are able to develop intelligent machines that can do everything better than humans (1995, 171). In this case, it may be that machines are permitted to make all of their own "decisions" or that some human control is retained. If the former occurs, we cannot conjecture about the result or how machines might behave, except to say that humankind would be at the mercy of the machines. Some will object that such control will never be handed over to machines, but it is conceivable that as society comes to face an increasing number of challenges, people will hand over more and more decisions to machines by virtue of their ability to yield better results in handling complex matters, potentially reaching a point at which the volume and nature of the decisions will be incomprehensible to humans, meaning that machines will be in effective control. To unplug the machines would, yet again, be tantamount to committing suicide (Kaczynski 1995, 173). If, on the other hand, humans retain some control, it is likely that the average person will exercise control over only limited elements of their private machines, be it their car or computer, with higher-level functions and broader control over the system of systems maintained by an all too narrow core of elites (Kaczynski 1995, 174). To some extent, this already occurs, with companies like Tesla, Inc. placing restrictions on their autonomous vehicles in response to inappropriate use by few among the many. It must also be recognized that even if computer scientists fail in their efforts to develop strong artificial intelligence of broad application, so that human decision-making remains necessary, machines seem likely to continue taking over the simpler tasks such that there will be a growing surplus of human workers who are either unable or unwilling to sublimate their needs and substitute their skills to support and preserve the technoindustrial system. This provides further reason for lacking confidence in the future.

24.3 Revolt and the Hacktivist Response

Kaczynski offers the foregoing arguments in support of what he sees as the only remaining option: the overthrow of technology by force, but it is in advocating an overthrow that the Unabomber parts ways with Ellul, who insisted that his intention was only to diagnose the problem and explicitly declines to offer any solution. The Unabomber, recognizing that revolution will be considered painful by those living in what he sees as conditions analogous to those of Plato's cave, says that the revolutionary ideology should be presented in two forms: a popular (exoteric) form and a subtle (esoteric) form (Kaczynski 1995, 186–8). On the latter, more sophisticated level, the ideology should address people who are intelligent, thoughtful, and rational, with the objective of creating a core of people who will be opposed to the industrial system with full appreciation of the problems and ambiguities involved, and of the price that has to be paid for eliminating the system. This core would then be capable of dragging less willing participants toward the light. On the level targeted at these common individuals, the ideology should be propagated in a simplified form that will enable the unthinking majority to see the conflict between technology and freedom in unambiguous terms, but not so intemperate or irrational as to alienate those rational types already committed.

The revolution can be successful if this occurs, Kaczynski thinks, because in the Middle Ages there were four main civilizations that were equally "advanced": Europe, the Islamic world, India, and the Far East (1995, 211). He says that three of the four have remained relatively stable since those times, and only Europe became dynamic, suggesting that rapid development toward technological society can occur only under specific conditions, which he hopes to overturn. But here again surfaces Ludlow's genetic fallacy, and it is, of course, incorrect to say that there were four main civilizations that were roughly equal in terms of technological enablers and that only Europe became dynamic. Ever since the human species moved out of East Africa, it has been devising technologies along the way, as required. The species itself has always been dynamic. There are myriad examples of that dynamism in ancient civilizations, such as those of the Sumerians and the Indus Valley (Galliott 2015, 1). The "four main civilizations" idea amounts to taking a cross section of human history and focusing on the civilizations you find in that slice and regarding them as the be-all and end-all of the concept of "civilization."

It is also questionable whether people in that or any similar slice of history had freedom of the kind to which we should like to return. Plenty of preindustrial societies, from that of the Pharaohs to the medieval Church, imposed tight organizational controls upon their populaces. Some might also point to the fact that most people who lived in preindustrial societies were subsistence farmers, barely able to get by, and with less control over their lives than your typical factory worker. In this context, one might argue that technology brings with it greater autonomy. But Kaczynski takes issue only with organization-dependent technology that depends on large-scale social organization and manipulation, not small technology that can be used by small-scale communities without external assistance (1995, 207–12). That is to say that he does not necessarily advocate doing away with all technology, down to the primitive spear, and there is a reason people romanticize the "old ways" of agrarian or preindustrial society, or even warfare and combat. Even if pre-robot jobs were mundane, dangerous, and repetitive in earlier days, they were at least measurable and, on some level, relevant in a visible and tangible way. Without technology, you could determine if you have successfully raised your crops, forged your widgets, or survived a battle. This would serve as affirmation of a job well done, largely absent in today's society. It would seem that humans have not yet fully evolved, emotionally or physically, to live in industrial societies dominated by technology.

Ludlow, on the contrary, believes that like bees and beavers, and spiders and birds, we are technological creatures and that we are on the verge of evolving in a meaningful way. In his view, alienation does not come from technology (any more than a beaver can be alienated from its dam or a bird from its nest), but rather surfaces when technology is "jailed" and people cannot tear apart the object and see what makes it tick. So it is not technology that alienates us, but corporate control of technology—for example, when Apple makes it difficult for people to reprogram their iPhones or robot manufacturers jail their code. This is the point, he says, where hacking becomes important. Hacking is fundamentally about our having the right and responsibility to unleash information, open up the technologies of everyday life, learn how they function, and repurpose those technologies at will. Ludlow argues that there is no need to overthrow the technoindustrial system and that a hacktivist response represents evolution that can put control of technology back in the hands of everyone, not just the powerful and elite.

Yet is not clear how, or to what extent, this solves the problem. Imagine that, through hacktivism, society has progressed to a point whereby all technology is open-source. This solves the problem only where the technology is cheap and practical for people to create or manipulate themselves, a requirement that may be satisfied with the most basic forms of software and hardware but is unlikely to be satisfied in complex software and hardware systems (Berry

2010). Until recently, most people could (if they wished) understand most technologies in everyday use—cars, lighting, household appliances, and the like. But this is becoming less true by the day as people place more emphasis on technology functioning effectively and how they themselves may integrate with the technoindustrial system, compromising their "sense that understanding is accessible and action is possible" (Turkle 2003, 24), such that we will shortly enter an era where most people will not be able, even if they wish, to understand the technologies in use in their everyday life. There is, therefore, much to Kaczynski's point that the system does not exist to satisfy human needs. To repeat a point made earlier, people should not be forced into choosing between using jailed technology controlled by those within existing oppressive power structures or dedicating their lives to building knowledge and understanding of the software and robotics that facilitate participation in the technological system. After all, there is no point to having everything open-source if one still cannot understand it. Having complete access to the workings of complex technology is no solution if that technology is so complex it is beyond most people's understanding.

Another problem is that the very nature of the technoindustrial system is such that decisions have to be made that affect millions of people, with little real input on their behalf. Even in a future society in which open-source programming, open standards, and the like are common, decisions will need to be made about which codes and standards to adopt or about how to utilize a particular piece of technology or code on a large scale. Suppose, for example, that the question is whether a particular state should impose restrictions on the functionality of electric autonomous vehicles—some of which have already been sold and are on public roads—to improve public safety until such time as the owners of these vehicles become more effective in overseeing their operation. Let us assume that the question is to be decided by referendum. The only individuals who typically have influence over such decisions will be a handful of people in positions of power. In this case, they are likely to originate from manufacturers of autonomous electric vehicles, conventional gasoline vehicle manufacturers, public safety groups, environmental groups, oil lobbyists, nuclear power lobbyists, labor unions, and others with sufficient money or political capital to have political parties take their views into account. Let us say that 300,000,000 people will be affected by the decision and that there are just 300 individuals among them who will ordinarily have more influence than the single vote they legitimately possess. This leaves 299,999,700 people with little or no perceptible influence over the decision. Even if 50% of those individuals among the many millions were able to use the internet and/or hacking techniques to overcome the influence of the larger corporations and lobby groups to have the matter decided in their favor, this still leaves the other 50% without any perceptible influence over the decision. Of course, this oversimplifies how technologies and standards are adopted in reality, but the point here is that "technological progress does not depend on a majority consensus" (Lin 2016). The will of the masses can be overcome by one person, a team of inventors, a room full of hackers, or a multinational corporation aiming to develop and field a technology that reinforces the needs and efficiency of the technoindustrial system, which represents a miscarriage of justice that dominates the human person.

24.4 The Way Forward: Toward a Philosophy of Technology Geared Toward Human Ends

If hacking and open-source development are ineffective as a countermovement—and we concede the correctness of Kaczynski's basic analysis that it is immoral for human behavior to be modified to fit the needs of the technological system and its elites at the cost of human freedom and autonomy—we must find another way to challenge the premise that reform is futile, or otherwise reluctantly admit that a revolution against the technoindustrial system and its many machines is understandable and perhaps permissible. That is, some way must be found to reach an optimum level of technology, whether that is in terms of certain kinds of technologies, technologies in certain spheres of life, or those of a particular level of complexity, and establish social order against the morally problematic forces described in this chapter. Philosophy is, of course, well suited to guiding us in this pursuit. In the context of robotics, this might begin with advocacy for a more meaningful and international code of robot ethics, one that is not merely the preserve of techno-optimists and addresses the concerns of those who desire to live an anarcho-primitivist lifestyle. Foreseeing the attractiveness, Kaczynski writes that a code of ethics will always be influenced by the needs of the technoindustrial system, so that said codes always have the effect of restricting human freedom and autonomy (1995, 124). Even if such codes were to be reached by some kind of deliberative process, he writes, the majority would always unjustly impose on the minority. This might not be the case, however, if in addition to a robust code of ethics, international society were to also build or recover a philosophy of technology truly geared toward human ends—parts set against the dehumanizing whole. What this might look like is for others to determine but, as a minimum, it would have to go beyond the existing philosophy of technology—which examines the processes and systems that exist in the practice of designing and creating artifacts, and which looks at the nature of the things so created—with a view toward incorporating a more explicit requirement to explore the way in which these same processes and systems mutate human beings, influence power and control, and erode freedom and autonomy.

This might be a long shot, but consider that Kaczynski himself has argued that revolution needs to be conducted on both the esoteric and exoteric levels to be effective. In the proposed case of reform short of violent revolution, a code of ethics would operate at the exoteric level, and the philosophy of technology geared toward human ends would operate at the esoteric level in persuading those of sound reason, with the united system potentially yielding better results in protecting the rights of those who wish to withdraw from technological society. Going forward, the imperative to accommodate those individuals who wish to disengage from technology will grow stronger as they are further alienated by unprecedented investment in robots and artificial intelligence, likely to be perceived as society buying into totalitarianism, the eradication of nature, and the subjugation of human beings, with the potential to fuel further terrorist attacks by those of the extreme fringe of the technoindustrial system.

Explanatory Note

This chapter draws on direct correspondence with Kaczynski and his original manifesto. This will be to the distaste of those who feel the manifesto was published with blood and that the only proper response is to demonize the author or ignore him completely. Therefore, it must be emphasized that the goal here is to neither praise nor criticize, but rather to improve understanding. It must also be acknowledged that the views expressed here are those of the author and do not represent those of any other person or organization. The author would like to thank Ryan Jenkins for a number of valuable comments that greatly improved this chapter.

Notes

1. In Joseph Conrad's novel *The Secret Agent*, a brilliant but mad professor, not dissimilar to Kaczynski, abandons academia in disgust for the enterprise and isolates himself in a tiny room, his "hermitage." There, clad in dirty clothes, he fashions a bomb used in an attempt to destroy an observatory derisively referred to as "that idol of science." More generally, Conrad wrote about alienation and loneliness and portrayed science and technology as nefarious forces naively utilized by the public, further indicating the extent to which Kaczynski drew on Conrad.
2. All citations of the manifesto refer to paragraph numbers, reflecting the military-style numbered paragraphs and how Kaczynski himself refers to the text.
3. In the sense that Nietzsche (2002, §13) often argued that one should not blame the strong for their "thirst for enemies and resistances and triumphs" and that it was a mistake to resent the strong for their actions. Note that this is just one connection to Nietzsche. Both men shunned academic careers: Kaczynski in mathematics,

Nietzsche in philology. Each tried to make the most of a relatively solitary existence, with Nietzsche writing, "Philosophy, as I have understood and lived it to this day, is a life voluntarily spent in ice and high mountains" (2004, 8)—words that could well have been penned by Kaczynski in his mountain cabin, where he spent much time prior to his capture. Nietzsche also wrote of the "will to power," while Kaczynski wrote of the "power process." All of this suggests that Kaczynski had great admiration for Nietzsche.

Works Cited

Berry, Wendell. 2010. "Why I Am Not Going to Buy a Computer." In *Technology and Values: Essential Readings*, edited by Craig Hanks. Malden, MA: Wiley-Blackwell.

Chase, Alston. 2000. "Harvard and the Making of the Unabomber (Part Three)." *Atlantic Monthly* 285 (6): 41–65. http://www.theatlantic.com/magazine/archive/2000/06/harvard-and-the-making-of-the-unabomber/378239/.

Conrad, Joseph. 1907. *The Secret Agent*. London: Methuen & Co.

Crabtree, Steve. 2013. "Worldwide, 13% of Employees Are Engaged at Work." Gallup. http://www.gallup.com/poll/165269/worldwide-employees-engaged-work.aspx.

Ellul, Jacques. 1951. *The Presence of the Kingdom*. Translated by Olive Wynon. London: SCM Press.

Ellul, Jacques. 1964. *The Technological Society*. Translated by John Wilkinson. New York: Alfred A. Knopf.

Federal Bureau of Investigation. 2008. "FBI 100: The Unabomber." https://www.fbi.gov/news/stories/2008/april/unabomber_042408.

Galliott, Jai. 2015. *Military Robots: Mapping the Moral Landscape*. Farnham: Ashgate.

Kaczynski, Theodore. 1995. "Industrial Society and Its Future." *New York Times* and *Washington Post*, September 19.

Kaczynski, Theodore. 2001, Letter to Anonymized Scholarly Recipient in the UK, November 1. https://www.scribd.com/doc/297018394/Unabomber-Letters-Selection-6.

Kaczynski, Theodore. 2010, "Letter to David Skribina." In *Technological Slavery: The Collected Writings of Theodore J. Kaczynski, a.k.a. "The Unabomber."* Edited by Theodore Kaczynski and David Skrbina. Los Angeles: Feral House.

Lin, Patrick.2016. "Technological vs. Social Progress: Why the Disconnect?" American Philosophical Association Blog. http://blog.apaonline.org/2016/05/19/technological-vs-social-progress-why-the-disconnect/.

Ludlow, Peter. 2013. "What the Unabomber Got Wrong." *Leiter Reports*. http://leiter-reports.typepad.com/blog/2013/10/what-the-unabomber-got-wrong.html.

Nietzsche, Friedrich. 2002. *Beyond Good and Evil*. Translated by Judith Norman. Edited by Rolf-Peter Horstmann. Cambridge, MA: Cambridge University Press.

Nietzsche, Friedrich. 2004. *"Ecce Homo: How One Becomes What One Is" & "The Antichrist: A Curse on Christianity."* Translated by Thomas Wayne. New York: Algora.

Turkle, Sherry. 2003. "From Powerful Ideas to PowerPoint." *Convergence* 9 (2): 19–25.

EDITORS

Keith Abney, ABD, is a senior lecturer in the Philosophy Department and a senior fellow at the Ethics + Emerging Sciences Group at California Polytechnic State University, San Luis Obispo. His research includes work on demarcating science from non-science, moral status and sustainability, astronaut and space bioethics, patenting life, human enhancement, just war theory and the use of autonomous weapons, robot ethics, and other aspects of the ethical implications of emerging sciences and technologies.

Ryan Jenkins, PhD, is an assistant professor of philosophy and a senior fellow at the Ethics + Emerging Sciences Group at California Polytechnic State University, San Luis Obispo. He studies applied ethics, in particular the ethical implications of emerging technologies and military ethics. He has published peer-reviewed articles on the ethics of cyberwar and autonomous weapons, and his work on drones and cyberwar has appeared publicly in *Forbes, Slate*, and elsewhere.

Patrick Lin, PhD, is the director of the Ethics + Emerging Sciences Group and a professor of philosophy at California Polytechnic State University, San Luis Obispo. He has current and previous affiliations at Stanford Law School's Center for Internet and Society, Stanford School of Engineering, U.S. Naval Academy, Dartmouth College, University of Notre Dame, New America Foundation, and World Economic Forum. He also consults for leading industry, governmental, and academic organizations on ethics and policy related to emerging technologies.

CONTRIBUTORS

Seth D. Baum, PhD, is the executive director of the Global Catastrophic Risk Institute. He holds a PhD in geography from Pennsylvania State University and is an affiliate of the Center for Research on Environmental Decisions at Columbia University, as well as a columnist for *Bulletin of the Atomic Scientists*. His research covers catastrophic risks such as climate change, nuclear war, and future artificial intelligence. He lives and works in New York City.

George A. Bekey, PhD, is professor emeritus of computer science, electrical engineering, and biomedical engineering at the University of Southern California and an adjunct professor of engineering at California Polytechnic State University, San Luis Obispo. He specializes in robotics, with an emphasis on robot ethics.

Vikram Bhargava, is joining Santa Clara University as an assistant professor in September 2017. He is currently completing a joint-PhD in philosophy (University of Pennsylvania) and ethics and legal studies (Wharton School). Vikram was the director of the Leadership Residential Program at the University of Pennsylvania. Prior to starting his doctorate, he taught mathematics in Kailua-Kona, Hawaii. He did his undergraduate work in philosophy and economics at Rutgers University.

Piotr Bołtuć, PhD, is a professor of philosophy at the University of Illinois, Springfield; Erskine Fellow at the University of Canterbury; and professor of e-learning at the Warsaw School of Economics. He is a former fellow at the following institutions: Australian National University, Poznan University, Jagiellonian University, Bowling Green State University, Princeton University, and the University of Oxford. He is the editor of the *APA Newsletter on Philosophy and Computers*. Bołtuć developed the Engineering Thesis in Machine Consciousness. Currently, he is working on a book on non-reductive machine consciousness.

Jason Borenstein, PhD, is the director of Graduate Research Ethics Programs and associate director of the Center for Ethics and Technology at Georgia Institute of Technology. His appointment is divided between the School of Public Policy and the Office of Graduate Studies. He is an assistant editor of the journal *Science and Engineering Ethics*. Dr. Borenstein is also chair of the research ethics editorial board for the National Academy of Engineering's Online Ethics Center for Engineering and Science.

Will Bridewell, PhD, is a computer scientist at the U.S. Naval Research Laboratory. He previously worked as a research scientist at Stanford University's Center for Biomedical Informatics Research and jointly at the Institute for the Study of Learning and Expertise and the Computational Learning Laboratory at Stanford's Center for the Study of Language and Information. He has consulted on artificial intelligence, natural language understanding, and science education for industrial, nonprofit, and academic partners.

Adrian David Cheok, PhD, is the director of Imagineering Institute (Iskandar, Malaysia), a professor of pervasive computing at City University London, and the founder and director of the Mixed Reality Lab. He was previously a professor at Keio University (Graduate School of Media Design) and an associate professor at National University of Singapore, and worked at Mitsubishi Electric, Japan. His research is in mixed reality, human–computer interfaces, wearable computers, and pervasive and ubiquitous computing. He is the editor in chief of the academic journals *ACM Computers in Entertainment, Transactions on Edutainment* (Springer), and *Lovotics*.

Kate Darling, DrSc, is a research specialist at the MIT Media Lab, a fellow at the Harvard Berkman Klein Center, and an affiliate at the Institute for Ethics and Emerging Technologies. Her work explores how technology intersects with society. She is currently interested in the near-term legal, social, and ethical effects of robotics and runs experiments, writes, speaks, and consults on developments in the world of human–robot interaction and where we might find ourselves in the future.

James DiGiovanna, PhD, is an assistant professor at John Jay College, City University of New York, where he researches personal identity, enhancement, and self-knowledge. Recent publications include "Literally Like a Different Person" in *Southern Journal of Philosophy* (2015) and "Identity: Difficulties, Discontinuities and Pluralities of Personhood" in *Palgrave Handbook of Posthumanism in Film and Television* (2015). His fiction has appeared in *Spork Press, Blue Moon Review*, and *Slipstream City*, and his film work includes the feature *Forked World* and the short *Kant Attack Ad*.

Alexis Elder, PhD, is an assistant professor of philosophy at the University of Minnesota, Duluth. Her research involves the intersection of close-knit social groups, such as friendships, with ethical issues presented by emerging technologies. She has published on such topics as robotic companions, social media, and why bad people can't be good friends.

Jai Galliott, PhD, is a lecturer in cyber security at the Australian Defence Force Academy, University of New South Wales, Canberra. His recent books include *Military Robots: Mapping the Moral Landscape* (Ashgate, 2015), *Commercial Space Exploration: Ethics, Policy and Governance* (Ashgate, 2015), and *Ethics and the Future of Spying: Technology, National Security and Intelligence Collection* (Routledge, 2016).

Jeffrey K. Gurney, JD, is an associate attorney at Thomas, Fisher, Sinclair & Edwards in Greenville, South Carolina. He previously served as term law clerk for the Honorable Timothy M. Cain, United States District Court Judge for the District of South Carolina.

Erin N. Hahn, JD, is a senior national security analyst at the Johns Hopkins University Applied Physics Laboratory.

Amy J. Haufler, PhD, is a senior applied neuroscientist at the Johns Hopkins University Applied Physics Laboratory (JHU/APL). Dr. Haufler was a research professor at the University of Maryland (UMD) in the Department of Kinesiology and adjunct professor of the Neuroscience and Cognitive Sciences Program (NACS). Her program of research involves a cognitive neuroscience approach to studies of human performance in complex, authentic contexts in military and civilian groups. She retains her appointment as adjunct professor in UMD's NACS program. Dr. Haufler earned her BS from Lock Haven University of Pennsylvania; her MS from Pennsylvania State University; and her PhD from UMD. Her postdoctoral training was completed in the Department of Medical and Clinical Psychology at the Uniformed Services University, Maryland.

Adam Henschke, PhD, is a lecturer at the National Security College, Australian National University, Canberra. He is an adjunct research fellow at the Centre for Applied Philosophy and Public Ethics, Charles Sturt University, is the secretary for the Asia Pacific chapter of the International Society of Military Ethics (APAC-ISME), and has been a visiting researcher at the Brocher Foundation and the Hastings Center. His research looks at the interface between ethics, technology, and security.

Ayanna Howard, PhD, holds the Smith Chair in Bioengineering at Georgia Institute of Technology. Her area of research addresses issues of autonomous control, as well as aspects of interaction with humans and the surrounding environment. From assistive robots in the home to innovative therapy devices, she has produced more than two hundred peer-reviewed publications. To date, her unique accomplishments have been acknowledged in a number of awards and articles, including highlights in *USA Today, Upscale*, and *Time* magazine.

Alistair M. C. Isaac, PhD, is a lecturer in philosophy of mind and cognition at the University of Edinburgh. He received his BA in East Asian studies from Harvard University before turning to philosophy and earning an MA from the University of Houston and a PhD in philosophy with a focus on symbolic systems from Stanford University. His research concerns the nature of representation and investigates analogies between formal and empirical theories of perceptual, mental, and scientific representation.

Leonard Kahn, PhD, teaches in the Department of Philosophy at Loyola University, New Orleans. He is the editor of *Mill on Justice* (Palgrave, 2012), *Consequentialism and Environmental Ethics* (Routledge, 2013), and *John Stuart Mill's "On Liberty"* (Broadview, 2015), and he has published articles in *Philosophical Studies, Journal of Moral Philosophy, Ethical Theory & Moral Practice*, and *Ethics, Policy, and Environment*.

Kasun Karunanayaka, PhD, is a human–computer interface researcher interested in multimodal interactions, multisensory communication, and magnetism. Kasun received his PhD in electrical and computer engineering from National University of Singapore. His research works have been published in the proceedings of several international conferences such as SIGCHI, Interact, ACE, IEEE VR, BodyNets, and ACHI. He also won several international awards, including an honorable mention at the Computer–Human Interaction awards in 2015. Currently, Kasun is working as a research fellow in Imagineering Institute, Iskandar, Malaysia.

Tae Wan Kim, PhD, is an assistant professor of ethics in the Tepper School of Business at Carnegie Mellon University. He earned his PhD in business ethics at the Ethics and Legal Studies Doctoral Program of the University of Pennsylvania in 2012. He has published in *Business Ethics Quarterly, Journal of Business Ethics* and *Ethics and Information Technology*.

Jesse Kirkpatrick, PhD, is assistant director of the Institute for Philosophy and Public Policy at George Mason University and politico-military analyst at Johns Hopkins University, Applied Physics Laboratory.

Michał Klincewicz, PhD, is an assistant professor in the Department of Cognitive Science, Institute of Philosophy of Jagiellonian University, Cracow,

Poland. Previously, he was a postdoctoral researcher in the Berlin School of Mind and Brain and a software engineer. He received his PhD in philosophy at the Graduate Center, City University of New York. His research focuses on temporal aspects of consciousness and perception and also the ethical problems connected to artificial intelligence.

Michael LaBossiere, PhD, is a professor of philosophy at Florida A&M University. Originally from Maine, he earned his doctorate from Ohio State University while also writing for gaming companies such as GDW, TSR, R. Talsorian Games, and Chaosium. His first philosophy book, *What Don't You Know*, was published in 2008. He blogs for *A Philosopher's Blog, Talking Philosophy, The Creativity Post*, and *Philosophical Percolations*. When not writing, he enjoys running, gaming, and the martial arts.

Janina Loh (Sombetzki), PhD, is a philosopher of technology at the University of Vienna, Austria. In 2014 she published her PhD on responsibility (*Verantwortung als Begriff, Fähigkeit, Aufgabe. Eine Drei-Ebenen-Analyse*, Springer VS). Currently, she is writing an *Introduction to Trans- and Posthumanism* (to be published by Junius in 2018). Loh habilitates on *Posthumanist Anthropology Between Man and Machine* (working title). She teaches in the fields of robot ethics and critical anthropology.

Wulf Loh, MA, has been an academic staff member with the Chair of Epistemology and Philosophy of Technology at the Institute for Philosophy of the University of Stuttgart since 2012. He works and teaches mainly in the field of social, legal, and political philosophy.

Darian Meacham, PhD, is an assistant professor of philosophy at Maastricht University, the Netherlands, and the deputy director for responsible research and innovation at BrisSynBio, a UK Research Council–funded Synthetic Biology Research Centre at the University of Bristol. His main research interests are in political philosophy and bioethics.

Jason Millar, PhD, is currently a postdoctoral research fellow at the University of Ottawa Faculty of Law and a philosophy instructor at Carleton University, where he lectures in robot ethics. He has a dual background in engineering and philosophy, having worked in the aerospace and telecommunications industries. Jason's research focuses on the ethics and governance of emerging technologies, particularly the development of ethically informed design methodologies and frameworks for robotics and artificial intelligence.

Steve Petersen, PhD, is an associate professor of philosophy at Niagara University. His research lies somewhere in the intersection of traditional epistemology, formal epistemology, philosophy of mind, and philosophy of science. His paper "Designing People to Serve," on the ethics of designing robot servants, appeared in the first volume of this book. He also sometimes gets paid to act in plays.

Duncan Purves, PhD, is an assistant philosophy professor at the University of Florida and, previously, a postdoctoral fellow at New York University. His areas of research include ethical theory, the ethics of emerging technologies, bioethical issues surrounding death and dying, and environmental ethics. He has published on these topics in such journals as *Ethical Theory and Moral Practice, Bioethics*, and *Pacific Philosophical Quarterly*.

Matthew Studley, PhD, is senior lecturer in engineering and mathematics at the University of the West of England, Bristol, and a researcher at the Bristol Robotics Laboratory (BRL). He is also responsible for overseeing research and scholarship at the BRL. He is an expert in robotics, machine learning, artificial intelligence, and computer programming.

Brian Talbot, PhD, is a lecturer in philosophy at Washington University in St. Louis.

Shannon Vallor, PhD, is the William J. Rewak, S.J. Professor in the Department of Philosophy at Santa Clara University, where her research focuses on the ethics of emerging science and technology, including AI, robotics, and new media. She is president of the Society for Philosophy and Technology and serves on the executive board of the Foundation for Responsible Robotics. She is the author of *Technology and the Virtues: A Philosophical Guide to a Future Worth Wanting* (Oxford University Press, 2016).

Alan R. Wagner, PhD, is an assistant professor at Penn State University focusing on the ethics of autonomous aerial vehicles. He previously held an appointment as a senior research scientist at Georgia Institute of Technology's Research Institute and was a member of the Institute of Robotics and Intelligent Machines. His research explores human–robot trust and deception and focuses on a variety of application areas ranging from military to healthcare.

Trevor N. White, JD, is a junior associate at the Global Catastrophic Risk Institute and a 2016 graduate of Cornell Law School, with a focus in international legal affairs. He was a managing editor of *Cornell Law Review*, as well as a summer legal intern with the National Coalition Against Censorship. He currently works as an associate attorney at Connors, LLP in Buffalo, New York.

Emma Yann Zhang is studying for a PhD in computer science at City University London. Her research interests are multisensory communication, affective computing, pervasive computing, wearable computing, and human–computer interaction. In 2013, she received a bachelor of engineering in electronic engineering (with first class honors) from the Hong Kong University of Science and Technology. She attended the National University of Singapore from 2010 to 2012.

David Zoller, PhD, is an assistant professor of philosophy at California Polytechnic State University, San Luis Obispo. His prior work includes peer-reviewed articles on collective action, corporate ethics, consumer responsibility for global injustice, and social cognition. His research interests include the nature of moral perception, the impact of technology on moral information, and non-traditional views of consciousness in cognitive science and the history of philosophy.

INDEX

Page numbers followed by *f* or n indicate figures or notes, respectively.

CPSIA information can be obtained
at www.ICGtesting.com
Printed in the USA
BVHW031238261120
593855BV00004B/17

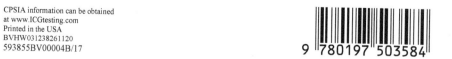